WHAT
LIES
BEYOND

WHAT
LIES
BEYOND

THE CYCLE OF GALAND, BOOK 6

EDWARD W. ROBERTSON

Mallon and Gask.

The Collen Basin and other lands.

EDWARD W. ROBERTSON

1

They set forth from the shining city with the determination of champions. The Realm of Nine Kings spread beneath them, verdant and unknown, waiting to be conquered. Dante felt as if he could reach down and grab it in his fist.

"So," Blays said. "Do you have any idea where we're going?"

Dante straightened the collar of his cloak. "Define 'idea.'"

"Oh good. For a moment there I was afraid we might actually have a chance of stopping the White Lich from annihilating our world."

"I don't quite know *where* we're going, but I know who we're going to see."

"Please tell me it's a mercenary we can pay to steal the Spear of Stars for us while we sit about in the shade with cold drinks."

"Not quite. We're going to find Arawn."

"You want to steal his part of the spear first? Why?"

"I want to see if he'll *give* us it. Or at least let us earn it, like Sabel did."

"And if he won't?"

Dante took a few steps down the well-kept cobbles before replying. "Then we'll borrow his piece."

"Without him knowing about it."

"Hopefully."

"Or consenting to it."

"If we have to."

"In other words, you're going to rob your own god."

"And then un-rob him once we're done putting down the son of a bitch who's menacing everything we hold dear."

"Just making sure you're not deluding yourself about what you're doing," Blays said, completely unconcerned. "So where is Arawn?"

"That's the part I don't know. But there looks to be a gate in the wall down there."

He pointed far, far down the switchbacking road. Half a mile below them, the slope at last settled into flat ground, quilted with farms. Past these, an old forest grew, but it was no more than three miles wide. A black wall had been built around the outer boundary of the woods, circumscribing the entirety of the spur of the mountain that hosted the shining town. The road ran down the center of this territory, beginning up the mountainside, through the city, down the slope, across the farms and forest, and coming at last to the wall. There, it was interrupted by what appeared to be a large gate, then carried on through the wilderness beyond the fortifications.

"Gates tend to have keepers," Dante went on. "I thought we'd ask them."

"We could do that. But we'd be better off finding some horses."

"To ask them for directions?"

"To borrow them."

"You mean steal them?"

"Acquire them against their owner's will. Consider it practice for the spear."

Dante reached the first turn of the switchback. The road steepened. Many of the stones were so smooth he could hardly see the seams between them, as if they'd been set by master nor-ren road-wrights. This made the footing slippery in places, downright treacherous, which the locals counteracted by scratching and scoring the paving-stones to allow for some traction. It made him wonder what kind of fool had decided to make such a steep incline so smooth in the first place, but after a minute he noticed the curb running along the cliffside edge of the road was neither smoothed nor scored. The builders hadn't polished the road: countless feet had, across countless years.

"I've committed theft enough times to understand the concept," Dante said. "I'm just surprised that you're leaping at the chance to steal some guy's horses rather than insisting we compensate him with a year of charmaidery to salve your conscience."

Blays nodded politely to a pair of women climbing up toward them, stepping to the side to let the pair pass. "The lich is about to devour everything, isn't he?"

"Yes," Dante said.

"And Taim and the other wise fellows who run this realm are about to let the Mists be destroyed, too."

"Also yes."

"Then it seems to me there is nothing more important than assembling the Spear of Stars *before* either of those dooms has the chance to calamatize us. Horses will make us faster, and faster is good. Thus horse-thieving, while *normally* the act of a total *scoundrel*, is in this case an act of great valor. You might even say we'd be heroes."

"When you put it in those terms, everything we do is justified. If it got us the spear, we could kill every person in the Realm and it would be an act of heroism."

"We won't *try* to kill everyone. But what's the good in having principles if you can't understand when it's time to violate them?"

The length of the decline gave them more than enough time to survey good candidates for horse theft. There wasn't a lot of traffic on the road, but Dante thought that had less to do with the trouble it took to hike up it—for a hardship was no longer a hardship once it became a routine—and more that all of the merchants, farmers, and worshippers had arrived at dawn for the opening of the gates.

He and Blays were obvious foreigners and just about everyone they passed gave them a good long assessment, rarely bothering to disguise their stares. The people's gazes lingered on their swords as much as their faces. While there was plenty of suspicion, Dante saw no outright hostility, and he and Blays came to the bottom of the switchback without being held up or questioned.

Down on the plain, it was several degrees warmer than it had been on the ridge that hosted the city. The wind was noticeably softer and the smell was different, too. Much greener. And, as they got closer to the farms, much more livestocky. The odors of which were being greatly heightened by the morning heat.

Short-legged dogs chased sheep around pastures that remained green despite the onset of late summer. Farmers and their families milled through the fields, hoeing weeds and digging up gophers, gathering unfamiliar orange berries from the shade of trellises. They were clearly simple and hard-working folk, and Dante might well have felt bad about having to rob them if he hadn't already decided to rob someone much wealthier.

That someone in question resided another two miles down the road, down a rutted and unpaved path and past an orchard of trees bearing fruit with pebbly green skin. There, Dante killed a pair of flies—and was tempted to kill hundreds more, the damn things were everywhere—and reanimated them.

He stayed behind the treeline while sending the flies to the closer of the two barns on the property. He'd had troubles with his undead scouts at the caverns of Talassa, but the flies were doing all right for now, and quickly ascertained that the barn held several horses in it.

"Got your stealing shoes on?" Dante said.

Blays glanced at his feet. "I never take them off."

"Then let's put them to use."

The peasants they'd seen in the other fields had been wearing a garment so loose and blousy it was practically a sack, cinched tight at the wrists, waist, and above the boots to allow them to work. Before leaving the cover of the orchard, Dante swaddled the two of them in an illusion of the garment. It wouldn't look right from up close, but if anyone got up close, the ruse wasn't going to survive anyway.

Blays held out his arms, assessing his new "clothes." "No one's ever going to believe this. It suits you well enough. But I'm afraid my bearing is just too regal."

Dante walked swiftly through the grass, which was studded with star-shaped blue flowers. It might have been his imagination, but some of them seemed to turn to watch him pass. He entered the barn. It smelled quite horsey and flies hummed about in the shade, landing on the animals' backs only to be scared off a moment later by the swish of the horses' tails.

Blays was more of a horseman and Dante let him pick two mounts from the multiple options available to them. Quick as a wink, they had the saddles on. Dante was in the act of stepping into the stirrup when a man appeared in the brightness of the barn door.

"Who are you?" His middle-aged face bent with outrage. "You're thieves!"

"We're far worse than thieves." Blays swung into the saddle. "Now stand aside before I decide to add barn arson to my lengthy list of crimes."

The man laughed and stepped into Blays' path. "You're a madman. Once I summon the King's Own Rangers, they'll be on you within minutes. You'll be swinging from the gallows by sunset!"

"I wouldn't do that," Dante said. "Not unless you want to watch the King's Own Rangers get executed in front of *you.*" To add some heft to his words, he brought the shadows to his hand, making them buzz and swirl like a storm of black bees. "Better yet, I'll save these Rangers the trip and kill you before you can call them."

He expected the man to back down. He *didn't* expect the fellow—who had been made strong by farm labor, and just a moment before had been quite forcefully threatening them—to collapse to his knees, bar his arms over his head, and begin to sob.

"Don't kill me! I don't want to die. You can't kill me!"

Dante stilled the swarming nether. "I don't want to, you crazy idiot. I just want to take your horses."

"Take them! *Please!*"

"We'd pay you if we could," Dante muttered. "As you've seen, I'm a sorcerer. If anyone in your household is sick, I can cure them. Or if they've been lamed in the field—"

"Take the horses!" The man lifted one hand from his head, which he'd been cradling this whole time, and waved at the doorway. His face was covered in tears and snot. "Just take them and be on your way, I beg you!"

"All right, we're going." Dante mounted the horse and prodded it forward. He kept his eye on the farmer in case it had all been an act to get them to let down their guard, but the man lay in the dirty straw, rocking back and forth on his side.

Dante rode from the barn at a trot, ready to kick into a gallop, but the only sounds coming from the barn were those of a grown man sobbing. He exchanged a look with Blays and headed back to the cobbled main road.

There, Blays twisted about to stare back in the direction of the farm. "What was *that* all about? He pissed himself!"

"You're one to throw stones?"

"Yes, but not because I was *scared*. I was *drunk*."

"And what about the time at Kandak?"

"Also drunk. Anyway, what just happened? Was he just a coward?"

"He didn't seem like it. Well, until he did."

"Maybe you were too cruel with him."

"This was *your* idea."

Blays put his hand to his heart. "It was my idea to relieve him of some of his yearly hay expenses. Not to frighten him until he wet his breeches."

Dante turned, ready to hit Gladdic with a jibe about how much he must have loved watching the farmer grovel and cower, but the words caught in his throat. For Gladdic wasn't with them. He was buried high on the mountain, above the doorway into this realm. The feeling Dante got from remembering this was unfamiliar, for he still wasn't certain they'd truly been friends.

But they *had* been companions. And after all the grueling battles they'd fought—first against each other, and then together—Gladdic had become, in his own way, as steadfast and loyal as Blays. That was a hard thing to find.

And a harder thing to lose.

They rode past the remaining farms and reached the forest, which protruded from the earth as abruptly as teeth from gums. The trees stood gnarled and tall, draped in moss like women in lace, almost all of them old and untouched, suggesting this was a king's wood, and untouchable. Then again, he and Blays had already incurred penalty of execution when they'd taken the horses, so he supposed there was no reason not to do a little poaching if the moment called for it.

The roadway sank until earthen banks rose above their heads on either side and the trees grew together above them like a woody tunnel. He'd seen such hollows before, but only where the roads were even older than any trees.

The light was dim and the air held the smell of moldering leaves, but the birds seemed cheery enough, and no animals or monsters raced out to attack them on the brief ride through to the open fields on the other side of the woods.

The road led onward, uninterrupted, yet Blays drew to a halt. "Where did the wall go?"

Ahead, the land was completely bereft of the territory-encircling wall they'd seen from the heights of the switchback. Dante turned in the saddle just to make sure they hadn't walked through a portal without knowing it. The towering ridge was right where they'd left it, topped by gleaming towers and churches, the mountains looming above the city like storm-clouds.

Dante pointed down the road. "The bridge is still right there. And where there is a bridge, there will be bridgemen. Bridgemen are usually reliable sources to ask about what's on the other side of their bridge."

They crossed the last mile to the bridge without seeing another living soul. Nearing the structure, two oddities became apparent: first, the wall had disappeared from sight because it wasn't a wall, but rather a massive moat dug around the entire territory. And second, the bridge, as was befitting a moat, was actually a drawbridge, far and away the largest and most mechanically complicated that Dante had ever seen—so complicated, in fact, that he couldn't tell quite how it functioned.

A stone guardhouse flanked it, housing both the control mechanism and a host of soldiers. As the two of them ambled to the base of the bridge, a lone soldier emerged. He was dressed in a yellow and black uniform and carried a pike in his hands and a short blade on his hip. He stood on the stone steps to the bridge, assessing them with a slight frown.

Blays motioned to the moat. "Nice pit. Just how deep is that thing?"

"Can you see to the bottom of it?" the guard said.

"No?"

"Well, it's even deeper than that."

"We're traveling to seek an audience with Arawn," Dante said, not quite believing that he was actually saying such a thing. "Do you know where his territory is from here?"

"Are you asking me directions?"

"Yes. We're foreigners."

The soldier hooted and stamped his pike. "You don't say!"

"Do you know how to get there or not?"

"Getting *near* it is easy enough. Follow the road east to the crossroads and take the southern fork until there's no more road to follow. But don't tell me you're so foreign you think you can simply enter the kingdom of Arawn!"

"That would be incredibly stupid of us," Blays said. "But just in case anyone that stupid is eavesdropping on us, why can't *they* get in?"

"It's forbidden to anyone but its subjects. Seeing as you didn't even know where it is, I'm guessing that excludes you."

Dante gestured to the moat. "What's keeping people out? Another moat?"

"He's got something a far cry better than that." The soldier sounded contemplative. "You won't even be able to see that it's there."

"As discouraging as that sounds, we have to try. So if you'll let down the bridge, we'll be on our way."

"But you've just confessed you're not from here. You have no right to order the bridge down."

"I may not have the right to give you orders," Dante said.

"But I do have the power."

The man chuckled, tilting his head. "One word from me and —"

"I'm going to throw him down the pit," Dante said to Blays. "You can figure out how deep it is by counting how many seconds it takes him to stop screaming."

The soldier shut his mouth with a click. "On the other hand, for the same reason you have no right to call down the bridge — being foreigners and all — I suppose there's no harm in evicting you from our land via the bridge." He cupped his hand to his mouth and lifted his head, about to call to the men in the guard-house, then peered at Dante in puzzlement. "But it's dozens of rowlands to the end of the road. You don't *really* mean to travel the Claimless Reach with just the two of you, do you?"

"Ah," Blays said. "Because of the giant bears?"

"No, he never comes down from the mountains. Well, *almost* never. But there are other things out there. Wilders and ramna. To say nothing of the beasts."

"If it's as dangerous as that, how does anyone get from place to place?"

"Caravans. Or by taking the safe routes, in those times when the barbarians are more settled, but there's no safety to be found on the southern road." The man had been looking at them with concern, but annoyance now stole across his features. "Then again, you're troublemaking outsiders, aren't you? So go die, if going and dying is what you're bent on doing. At the very least take your trouble away from our peaceful little holding."

He turned on his heel and shouted up to the guardhouse. Men stirred in the window. Metal squealed; a dull chunking sound boomed across the open ground. With a drumbeat of clanking chains, the bridge rolled forward, extending into the hundred-foot-wide gap. Once it was halfway across, it bumped to a stop. A wooden platform swung forth on its giant hinges, drawn by ropes connected to some unseen mechanism in the far cliff wall. The platform must have weighed several tons, but it unfolded as gracefully as a hawk on the wind, touching down on the far side.

"There, a bridge," the soldier said. "Now go on and use it."

Blays headed up the ramp. "You may have just helped save millions of lives."

The guard gave him a funny look. Dante followed after Blays, though the bridge was wide enough for them to ride alongside each other. The moat fell away beneath them. Dante reached down into it, trying to touch the nether within the earth at its bottom, but it lay beyond his range.

A cold draft seeped up from the depths, bearing the scent of pungent mold. The bridge rattled beneath their hooves as they reached the thinner secondary platform. It held perfectly firm, though, and they were soon back on solid ground.

Dante lifted his arm to give the bridgeman a wave, then continued east along the road. He'd only gotten a few steps forward when he was struck by sudden doubts about how hasty they were being. As long as they were right there, shouldn't they go back for more precise directions from the bridgeman? Or see if they could barter some supplies from the stocks in the guard tower?

But it was already too late: the soldier was calling to the tower. With a rattle of great chains, the bridge began to lift.

2

The road bore them east. Tall grass surrounded them on both sides. Dante watched it steadily for the rustling of predators, be they human or otherwise. Birds flew above the grass while mice ran around the stalks, but that was as threatening as their surroundings got. They came to the crossroads around two o'clock that afternoon. Crossroads often hosted a town grown around them. This one did not.

Instead, it hosted twelve-foot posts topped by person-sized platforms. The platforms were person-sized because each one of them bore a skeleton nailed to its surface.

Blays rubbed the back of his neck. "Looks friendly."

"No it doesn't."

"Well-ordered, at least. You know you're dealing with no-nonsense people when they nail their criminals to boards."

"Let's hope they *were* criminals."

"What else would they be?"

"Trespassers."

They turned south, or at any rate what the sun would have indicated was the south in their own world. Yet was that the case here? He glanced about the crossroads, but there were no sign posts or the like to indicate the cardinal directions, likely because the very thought of needing such a thing was ridiculous. So which way *was* south? Dante felt a moment of rising panic until remembering that the directions Elenna had given them to the doorway at Talassa had involved the same directional orientation he was used to.

Feeling much better, he turned right and headed what was almost certainly south. The bridgeman had told them the journey would be dozens of rowlands, which likely meant something between one and two hundred miles. Using the nether to keep their horses fresh, Dante hoped to cross the distance in three days.

The road had some cracks and gaps in the stones, but was still in fine shape. It unrolled across more prairie where green birds perched on the tips of tall, thick grass. Crickets sang to each other. Now and then weaselly creatures romped across the road.

Ten miles later, a forest swept across the landscape like gale-driven clouds. On entering it, it felt even older than the king's wood on the way to the bridge. Dante couldn't point to any one thing, but something about it felt wrong, and as the sun cut behind the western peaks, promising full darkness within another hour, he sighed, doubting they'd find their way out from it before they'd be forced to make camp.

They didn't. He would have liked to harvest a platform from high in a tree and pass the night there, but he was inconvenienced by the fact that horses couldn't climb trees, so he enclosed them within an eight-foot-high wall of earth instead. They ate some of the sausages and hard biscuits they still had from their earlier travels.

"We should start strategizing," Dante said.

"I thought we already had a strategy," Blays said around a mouthful of very dry biscuit. "Win what we can, and steal what we can't."

"Not for us. For the people back in our world. According to the *Book of What Lies Beyond*, it took Sabel months to acquire all of the parts of the spear. That's enough time for the White Lich to conquer the entire north."

"In that case, you'd better get the norren moving first. It could take months just to get all the different clans to agree that there's a war on the way."

"They won't all join us, but maybe we can at least convince the others to get out of the lich's path. The clans that do join us can look to organize raids to slow the enemy's advance."

"We can almost certainly count on Gallador to throw in with us, can't we? With the passes and the rift, that might even be the best place for Nak to make his big stand."

"Insisting on holding the battle in Gallador is about the only way we can guarantee they *won't* join us. We'll probably have to invite them to Narashtovik. The lich won't bother with their lands if they've already emptied them out."

Somewhere in the canopy, a bird hooted, the noise stark and loud in the darkness.

Blays glanced up into the dark boughs. "What was that?"

"The aerial hooting? I'm going to make the wild guess that it's an owl."

"Then it's the biggest owl I've ever heard."

"Unless you think it's an owl-griffin that's about to swoop down and snatch up the horses, I think we'll be fine. Now who else can we bring in on our side?"

"What about Gask?"

"Way too risky. If King Moddegan knows everything that's happening, he might try to sabotage us even with the White Lich on the rampage. At the very least, he'll work to rig any battle so that we get destroyed."

"Well if Moddegan's that much of a bastard, maybe we ought to convince the lich to go attack *him*."

"How do we do that?"

"By being brilliant and charismatic and irresistible to all women?" The owl hooted again. "I don't know *how* we're going to do it. I just know that we're going to, because it's our best chance to keep our people safe while we're over here."

"I'll get Nak to start thinking about it," Dante said. "Maybe we can—"

A dark shape swooped over their heads, so silent it might have been a living shadow. Blays ducked and reached for his sword. The two horses shuffled, stomping their hooves. Dante drew the nether to him, but the creature was already fading into the darkness.

Blays jumped to his feet. "That wasn't an owl."

"You barely got a look at it."

"Do you know a lot of owls with long dangly tails?"

Dante scowled and stilled himself, summoning a handful of ether. Its light glared up through the black branches. As he turned in a slow circle, the creature whisked over their heads. Its wings stretched nearly as wide as a man's armspan. But they bore no feathers. Instead, they were leathery. Its smooth chest was scaly. Rather than the mouse-like head of a bat, its head was clearly that of a lizard, and as it swerved toward one of the horses, it opened its jaws, revealing rows of slashing teeth.

Blays whipped out his sword, nether crackling down its steel, and flicked it at the creature. "Hyah!"

The flying lizard lurched upward and disappeared into the trees.

Blays sheathed his sword but kept his hand on its hilt. "If that thing really thinks it can carry off a horse, it's either much less dangerous than it looks, or a hell of a lot more."

It circled about for another pass. Dante shaped a needle of nether and fired it into the lizard's side. It wouldn't be enough to kill the thing, but he was hoping it would be enough to drive it off. It reacted with a trumpet of pain, flapping higher into the boughs.

"Some people say violence never solves anything," Blays said. "But that's just not been my experience at all."

Dante craned his neck up at the trees. The lizard honked again, more distantly. He eased his hold on the nether.

The air filled with the sound of stirring, featherless wings. Three lizards soared down from the trees. Then ten. Then dozens. Blays unsheathed both swords as Dante threw flechette-like blasts of nether at the sudden flock. The lizards at the front diverted from the assault, but many more swooped downward. The horses dashed around the earthen enclosure, shrieking as the lizards nipped at their flanks.

Blays threw himself to the side to avoid getting trampled. "Will you *do* something? I didn't go to the trouble of stealing those horses just to feed them to a flock of flying lizards!"

Dante shaped a new volley of nether. These bolts were large enough to kill, and when they struck their targets, the lizards trumpeted and veered away—or plopped dead to the ground. Yet the whirl of the flock was denser than ever, as if the brouha-ha was attracting even more of them from the depths of the night. He gathered a heaping mound of shadows to him, prepar-ing to blast the entire forest down if he had to, then thought bet-ter of it and sent it into the earth below them. Where he hit rock, he softened it and pulled it to the surface, flowing over the hard clay walls he'd originally raised to shelter them. The earth moved above their heads, sealing them beneath a roof of solid stone; alarmed at the unnatural motion, the lizards within the walls scattered upward before they could be trapped inside.

"Okay, so violence solves most problems," Blays said, breath-ing heavily and staring up at the rocky ceiling. "But magic is even better."

"Not necessarily true. We just didn't have enough violence at hand, forcing us to get creative."

Small claws scratched and dug at the outer surface. Dante shaped a few narrow holes into the enclosure to give them air. Snouts pressed themselves to the holes, snuffling hungrily. Yet for all its numbers, the flock made no progress in gaining entry to the bunker, and as Blays soothed the horses, the noise of the lizards diminished until the night was silent once more.

Blays rearranged his blankets. "Now I know why those bodies at the crossroad were offered to the sky like that."

"To be eaten alive? I hope they at least did something worse than stealing horses."

"Did those things look like dragons to you?"

"No, by virtue of the fact there is no such thing as dragons."

"But if there *were*, they'd look an awful lot like those things."

"Except much bigger."

"Well, maybe these are just their babies."

It was not a comforting thought that there might be so many dragons about that thousands of their babies were ready to enswarm them every night, but that possibility only helped Dante stay awake during his portion of the watch. The rest of the night passed without incident. Once the soft light of morning filtered through the breathing holes, Dante brought the nether to him, braced himself for assault, and swept open a horse-high hole through the side of the bunker. This revealed a perfectly normal morning.

A few of the dead lizards were lying about. Or their skeletons were, anyway; they'd been picked to the bone. Dante gave them a quick examination like he might a body brought to the carneterium.

He ran his fingernail down a score in one of the larger bones. "As an expert in gruesome matters, I'd say these animals were eaten."

Blays readied his horse. "Is that why none of their flesh is left? I'm just a simple person-stabber, and not a great sorcer-er-philosopher, but I'd suggest we get the hell out of here."

They did so, riding through the forest until it gave way around noon in favor of more grassland. Dante opened his loon connection with Nak and the two of them exchanged their plans and most recent intelligence. After Nak's defeat of the White Lich's overstretched Blighted in the forests of Mallon, the lich was doing his usual consolidation of forces, but there was no doubt he'd be back on the march shortly, likely looking to take the rest of Mallon before its people had time to react to the loss of Bressel. Nak's goal would be to get as many Mallish out of harm's way as he could, then harry, obstruct, and delay the lich to buy Dante and Blays as much time as possible—all without risking getting sucked into a head-on battle with the enemy.

Blays made an intrigued sound, pointing across his body. Miles away, a band of people were crossing the prairie, some mounted and others on foot. Nearly all of them seemed to be male and they were all armed with some combination of spears, bows, and axes.

"Better get a move on." Dante nudged his horse faster. "Before they decide we're somewhere we shouldn't be."

"What's the matter? Don't think we can handle a simple tribe of barbarians?"

"I *think* this place is very strange and we need to do our best not to get bogged down in any entanglements like always happens to us."

They detoured behind a low hill. When they emerged from it, the raiders were nowhere to be seen. The landscape shifted again, to a strange patchwork of small hills no bigger than a house mixed with broad, shallow divots filled with shrubs and standing water. The road did its best to stick to the high points, but stains on the rocky ground indicated the water sometimes rose high enough to flood it.

Blays squinted at one of the murky pools. "What happens if it starts raining?"

"We start cursing," Dante said. "And then we start floating."

He pushed onward, faster, alternating his horse's speed and refreshing it with nether to keep up the pace. The land was bleak, with no hints of human habitation. Something about it made him feel uneasy and he carried on after nightfall, lighting the way with his torchstone, until they passed from it and back into the prairie.

He built another bunker for them to spend the night in. Before sleeping, he paged through the *Book of What Lies Beyond the Land of Cal Avin*, searching for any places where Sabel might have approached Arawn's land and found a way past whatever made it inaccessible to outsiders. Nothing seemed relevant.

They moved on in the morning, stopping when they encountered wild vines bearing the orange berries they'd seen at the farms, which they could be reasonably sure wouldn't poison them. Several miles onward, giant stone columns lay shattered across the grass, hundreds of feet in length and scores of feet across. Their rough sides didn't appear to be shaped by human hands, but the end of one of the columns was largely unbroken. Its surface was flat—except where the foundations of houses had been carved from it.

Dante ran his hand over the worn stone. "They lived on top of these? What would drive them to do that?"

Blays shrugged. "They were probably trying to get away from all the ground-dragons."

Dante wanted to poke around the ruins for hints of who these people had been and what had had the power to destroy their pillar-towns. But he also wanted to save his own people from being annihilated by the Eiden Rane, and so he rode on, leaving the mystery behind him. Not long after, they spotted a lone figure walking down the road three miles behind them. For a while he seemed to be keeping up with them despite being on foot, but by the time Dante found a fly to kill and send back to spy on him, the figure had disappeared from the road.

Gusts of wind began to blow from the south, bearing dust and grit that caught in their eyes and teeth. The grass and shrubs turned from green to yellow. Soon after they became gray, then disappeared altogether, leaving the land empty, yellowed and desolate, the cracked, dry earth and coarse sand cemented together into one massive brick.

Then the road itself vanished. There was only the wasteland of the Claimless Reach and they continued into it but the land was all but featureless, lacking hills or even boulders to act as landmarks, and Dante had to reckon their direction by the sun itself, or by glancing behind him to confirm that at least the mountains were still there, although he could no longer see them directly to the east or the west. Dante reached into the nether to search for signs of hidden passages like the one Gladdic had found beneath the city of Barsil in the Mists, but saw nothing out of place.

Blays drifted to a halt, gazing behind him, then ahead. Sand rattled over the hardpan. "Are we sure we're getting anywhere?"

"The bridgeman said Arawn's territory was past the end of the road. Just keep your eyes sharp, the entrance is probably hidden from travelers."

"What I mean is I don't think we're moving forward any longer."

"That would seem to be contradicted by the fact our horses' legs are moving."

"But everything's staying the same. Look back there, where the last of the shrubs are. Have they gotten any further away?"

Dante was annoyed, but did so. The skeletons of the dead plants looked to be about two miles to their north. "Well, that's impossible. It's a good thing this is an unpopulated wasteland with no one around to laugh at you, because you're about to look like an idiot."

He nudged his horse into a walk. The sky was starting to grow hazy, likely with fine dust. Dante passed a rock that was just large enough and reddish enough to stand out a bit. He quite clearly moved past it, and when he turned around, it continued to recede behind him.

Yet when he looked back for it a second time, he couldn't pick it out from the landscape. And ten minutes of travel after Blays had made his ridiculous claim, the dead shrubs still looked to be right about two miles distant.

Blays shielded his eyes against a sudden gust of dust. "Now who looks like an idiot? It isn't me, and you're the only other one here."

"It's still impossible," Dante said. "It just so happens that it's actually happening, too."

"At least this means we won't have to go as far to retrace our steps on our way out of here."

"We're not going anywhere. Not until we've checked *this* where out."

"What exactly are we checking out? The dust? Or the other dust? It feels like we could keep walking forever and nothing would change."

"That just means there's less we'll have to investigate."

Dante reached for the nether, meaning to do some more searching for hidden passages or layers in the earth. He experienced a sensation something like walking through a dark room and dropping down a staircase you didn't know was there.

His mouth went dry. "The nether's gone."

"What do you mean the nether's gone?"

"I mean there's no nether!"

Blays tipped back his head and took a step forward, as if he was meaning to move into the shadows. Instead, he just took a step across the empty desert. "Oh. The nether's gone."

Dante tried a few more times, then cleared his thoughts and opened himself to the ether. It wasn't there, either. "We're either in the exact right place, or the exact wrong place. Do you see... uh, anything?"

"Not since the road ended. That's what I've been trying to tell you."

Dante kicked at the dirt, stirring a cloud of dust that didn't seem to know where to go. He turned in a slow circle. Behind him, the air glimmered, but it was so faint he could barely see it, so brief he wasn't sure if it was nether or ether. The potential threat made him summon the nether instinctually, but of course it still wasn't there. He gritted his teeth, hand on the grip of his sword, and watched the spot where the glimmer had been.

"What's that?" Blays said.

He was pointing south into the nothing. Except now there was a glimmer in the nothing, fading just as Dante caught sight of it. He tightened his grip on his sword. Then cocked his head.

For the nether around him in the world might have vanished —but he still carried his own within him.

He reached down into his trace, the nethereal piece of his soul, and withdrew a thread of shadows, sending it toward the air where the glimmer had been. As soon as it made contact, the black thread *unfolded*, erupting outward. Dante hopped back, drawing his sword.

Across from him, the nether stabilized. A tall arched door-way stood from the cracked earth, as thin as a sheet of parch-ment. Its interior was pure black with no hint of what might lie on the other side.

"Right," Dante said. "What do we do now?"

"Well, it's a doorway." Blays dismounted from his horse. "It's telling us just what to do."

Blays stepped through the darkness. And vanished from

sight.

3

Dante stood alone in the desert. After a moment of silence, he got down from his horse and followed Blays through.

There was no sensation of transfer or displacement. Yet the bright day of the desert became the calm of a starry night. Instead of blank hardpan, he found himself within a city of black buildings and shadowy towers. Silvery light glowed from lanterns on the corners of the streets. It appeared as though it could have been the middle of the night, but people strolled up and down the roads, coming and going from shops, public houses, and their friends' homes, as if it was the middle of the day.

Overhead, the stars burned like they were alive. Among them shined the full twelve constellations of the Celeset, which should not all have been visible at the same time. What's more, they were far, far bigger than he had ever seen them, bright enough to light the city better than the full moon, seemingly so close that if he stood on the roofs of the towers he might be able to reach up and touch them.

"This is it, isn't it?" Blays said. "Arawn's realm."

Dante could only nod.

Blays took a look down the street, perhaps to ensure they weren't about to be arrested or killed. "How exactly did we get here? And don't say 'through a magic doorway.'"

"I don't know." Dante turned around. Behind him, an arched

gate made of the same black stone as the buildings framed the gray desert they'd just entered from, where it was still daytime. "All I did was touch it with the nether. But there was no nether in the surrounding environment. Meaning you can only open the doorway if you know about the existence of traces."

"My next question would be where we go from here. But I think I've stumbled across the answer."

Blays nodded down the street. The center of the city was a raised plateau, as flat as one of the buttes of the Collen Basin. And on this platform stood an immense building that looked to be both cathedral and castle at the same time.

"If that's not the right place, they'll certainly know where the right place is." Dante started forward. "Now let's do our best not to spark any civil wars on the way there."

They headed down the street. Some of the residents had stopped to stare at them with a fair amount of wariness, which Dante presumed was because the doorway they'd come through didn't exactly get a lot of use. Or maybe it was the rather impressive swords they were carrying. He made eye contact with a few of the locals, nodding to them, but only one man nodded back.

They looked to be a different people than the ones they'd met in the town on the ridge, with sharper chins and almond-shaped gray eyes, taller, with something almost elfin about them. They wore robes fitted to their bodies like more sophisticated versions of the loose clothes the farmers outside the forest had worn and their garments, though mostly white or light gray, were adorned with complicated and colorful stitching and designs. Dante hadn't known what to expect from the people who lived in Arawn's own realm, but these people looked like they fit.

Once they got a few blocks away from the doorway, the stares grew less hostile, though they continued to draw their share of glances. It didn't seem likely that one of those wary glances would lead to a violent assault on their person, but just in case, Dante beckoned to the nether to make sure that he could.

He stopped so abruptly he skidded over the black and white mosaic of a tree on a hillside that was laid out across the street.

"The buildings," he said. *"They're made of nether."*

Blays furrowed his brow, taking a look for himself. "Er. Is such a thing...?"

"Possible? Not as far as I know. But neither is a literal end of the world that stops you from going any more south."

Around him, four-fifths of the buildings, and nearly every one of the towers and spires, was aglow with the dark light of the shadows. He moved into the nearest of them, a squarish block of mixed residences and shops. A few parts of it were made of typical, everyday stone, but most of it was solid nether, somehow fused fast.

This made no sense at all. You couldn't just fix nether in place, and even when you could capture it for some recurring use, like in the loons, these couldn't be used for the large majority of the day, or else the object would be destroyed within hours, if not minutes, as the nether depleted itself. Frowning, Dante sent his mind into a nonfunctional carving of a stylized wolf on the side of the building and attempted to draw its nether to him.

"Do *not* touch that."

Dante yanked his mind back and whirled. Three soldiers or guards stood across from him. To Dante's delight, they were dressed in black and silver just as the officials of Narashtovik were. Rather than the White Tree, however, their clothing was adorned with the icon of Duset, the two rivers, sign of Arawn. They carried swords on their hips, the guards gleaming with pure silver, the pommels adorned with searing blue sapphires.

The man who'd spoken looked Dante up and down, his brows as dark and thick as two smudges of charcoal. "How did you get here?"

Dante motioned in the direction of the doorway. "Through

the front gate. If you don't want people using it, you probably shouldn't have built it."

"But how did you *find* it?"

"Through the glimmer."

The man drew back his head, eyes skipping between Dante's. "Glimmer? What glimmer?"

"The one in the desert. When I touched it with the nether, the doorway appeared. If that's not supposed to happen, you probably want to look into it, and I'm happy to have brought the matter to your attention."

The official exchanged a look with the other two, quickly reaching a decision. "You will return with us to the doorway now, if you please."

The three guards moved closer, as if to bull them back toward the doorway.

Blays folded his arms. "This isn't a good idea."

"Neither was coming to our city without invitation. Be grateful I'm allowing you to leave peacefully."

"We can't leave," Dante said. "We're here to see Arawn."

The soldier huffed with laughter. "And I'm here to marry Lia's own daughter. This is the last time I ask you."

"I don't think you understand. I'm not some vagabond who tripped and fell through your gates. My name is Dante Galand, High Priest of Narashtovik. And I will have my audience."

"Fancy-sounding names. But if you think they mean anything to me, you're a fool of the first order."

"You don't know the names because they're not from your world. They're from mine. The world that lies on the other side of the Mists."

The soldier scowled, then laughed scornfully. "Are you claiming you're from the Fallen Land? I should cut you down for a spy here and now. Such a thing isn't possible."

"I keep thinking the same thing about *your* world. But do we look like we're from here? If we're to be judged as spies or not, let it be by Arawn."

The man drew back, brows beetled as he made his own judgment. He nodded sharply. "If you try to run from me, or do anything stupid, there won't be anything left of you but ash and memory."

He turned on the heel of his polished black boot and strode in the direction of the massive cathedral-fort. The other two guards followed at Dante and Blays' back. Everything about the city was darkly beautiful, the nethereal structures gleaming like they'd been conjured forth that very morning while the stone ones looked older than the ages.

The streets and spaces beneath the awnings were littered with human statues, too, so life-like it looked like if you smiled at one of them it might smile back. Blays, having similar thoughts, gave one of the younger female carvings a jaunty salute—and the statue turned her head away, blushing as she covered her smirk.

"Hang on a second." Blays spun around to walk backwards. "Why is that person pretending to be a statue? Or why is that statue pretending to be a person?"

"What else would she be doing? She's remembering."

"Remembering what?"

"Everything she doesn't want to forget."

Blays pressed the man to explain, but he said nothing that made any real sense. They moved quickly through the winding streets, hurrying past galleries, temples, and the most libraries Dante had ever seen in one place. He would have killed to be able to stay and explore them—in fact, he planned quite literally to kill the White Lich, and then return here to do just that—but for now he kept up with the guards, and was soon delivered before the palace.

There, despite the guards' insistence he not do so, he was

compelled to stop in his tracks. The spires of the palace climbed far higher than the spires of either the Cathedral of Ivars or the Odeleon of Bressel, which soared some four hundred feet into the sky. Before he'd even counted them, he knew there were twelve of them: one for each member of the Celeset, with Arawn's own the highest.

The logic of this design immediately bothered him, for it meant that if you needed to get from one tower to another, you'd have to climb down hundreds of feet of stairs, then ascend hundreds of feet more. Yet when he looked closer, he saw black, gossamer-fine platforms stretched between the towers. Walkways. They looked much too frail to support themselves, but they too were crafted from nether, and were likely stronger than stone.

Green and blue witchlights danced softly atop black posts, lighting the grounds. The front doors were thirty feet high, made of polished silver and carved with a language Dante had never seen before. They swung open, revealing a cavernous hall with a vaulted ceiling fifty feet high. A row of black pillars ran down both sides of the room. Guards stood along the walls, as still as the people Dante had mistaken for statues earlier. The floors were patterned with black and white stone so gorgeous it felt blasphemous to walk upon.

Dante tried to absorb all that he could as the guards hustled them out into a courtyard of graceful trees and riotously colored flowers. Despite the obvious care lavished upon the garden, a quarter of the plants were dying, and another quarter were dead, bare brown branches reaching like skeletal hands toward the brightness of the stars.

They entered the base of the tallest of the towers. Dante braced himself for a long climb. Yet once the five of them were all standing on the staircase, the steps *shifted*. Nether flowed beneath them, bearing them upwards along the spiraling stairs. Blays gave him a confused look. Dante could only shake his head.

They passed one landing after another. Narrow windows offered glimpses of the towers around them and the increasingly distant ground. Three full minutes later, they came to a stop. The guard nodded toward the chamber beyond, staying where he was as Dante and Blays entered a yawning room that spanned the entire top of the tower.

The walls were made of the purest glass Dante had ever seen, held up by thin runners of nether like the branches of a tree — or like blood vessels. The city lay dizzyingly far beneath them. It was no larger than Narashtovik, but it was far more beautiful.

It was another minute before a silhouette appeared in the door at the opposite end of the room from the staircase. The man was tall, almost supernaturally so, and well-built, and he walked forward with more natural grace than any king.

"You seek an audience with Arawn." The man's deep voice carried no threat at the moment, but had plenty of room for it. "I am here to grant it."

Dante's heart walloped against his ribs. A wave of chills ran down his skin, followed by a second. "You're..."

The man took another step forward, better entering the light.

"...not Arawn," Dante finished.

The man smiled thinly. He had a tightly-trimmed black beard and looked to be at least ten years older than Dante, although there was something about his age that was hard to place.

"You've met him before, then?"

"I might once have come close," Dante said, remembering, for just a flash, when the gateway had seemed to be opening beneath the boughs of the White Tree. "But if you were Arawn, I would feel it. I would know." He lifted his chin. "I asked for an audience with my god."

"Don't feel slighted. Be honored. For the gods grant an audience to no one—but yours has sent his highest servant to hear your words." His eyes shifted to Blays, considering him. "Is he important enough that you require him here?"

"Not really. But he'll make me repeat everything you say to me if you send him away, so I'd rather you didn't."

"My name is Draven," the man said. "I have been told who you are and where you come from. Speak what you have come to say."

Dante nodded, raking his thoughts together. "We are under threat by an ancient sorcerer known as the Eiden Rane—the White Lich. When I say we, I don't just mean myself, or even my people in Narashtovik. I mean that the lich intends to take the entire world. He has the power to do it, too. He's already conquered both Tanar Atain and Mallon, if you know them. Two powerful nations. But the combined army of all three realms wasn't enough to stop the lich. Unless my generals can delay him, I expect he'll take all of the north by the end of autumn. After that, it's only a matter of time until everything else falls to him, too.

"As grave as this is, it isn't only *our* world that's under threat. It's the Mists, too. Even now, they're being pulled apart by the lich's—"

Draven held up his palm. "Save your voice. We know of these things."

"Then you must understand why we've come here."

"We do. Arawn will not intervene on your behalf."

"I'm not asking him to fight our war for us. But in the course of our campaign against the White Lich, I became aware of the Spear of Stars. In the past, it's been used to destroy a lich just like this one. I'm here to ask for Arawn's portion of it."

"This cannot be done."

"What, because it has to be earned? Then give us a trial. Whatever you think fair."

41

Draven shook his head. "My meaning is lost on you because you don't wish to understand it. Arawn will not give you his part of the spear or allow you the chance to win it."

"Why in twelve hells not? Doesn't he understand what's happening?"

"He does. If you are truly his High Priest, you will understand why he will not interfere."

"He has no need for earthly affairs and never has. But this time is different."

Draven lifted an eyebrow. "How?"

"Everything is about to come to an end!"

The man moved toward the windows. "After the fall of his Mill, Arawn helped to construct your world so that it wouldn't need divine interventions. This meant that people would be born, they would grow old, and in time they would die. That is the natural order of the Fallen Land. Do you think your kingdoms, your civilization—even your world itself—should be exempt from this same cycle of nature?"

"Yes," Dante said. "Because I don't *want* my world to die!"

"And a person does not wish to die, either: but when their time comes, they must. That is the order your lord created for you, and that is the order that you will respect."

"There's a big difference between accepting your end when the time comes, and in rolling over and letting yourself die when there's still strength in you. You have to give us the chance to fight back."

Draven gazed down at him, the agent's eyes turning black as a rift into nothing. "You've had your chances, haven't you? One after the other, you've had them, and you've failed them. Until in your desperation, you have come here, seeking for answers in a world *beyond* your own. That means your cause has moved beyond hope. It is time. Time to let it pass."

"I don't have a choice, do I? If everything I know is about to be crushed, and even all memory of it destroyed, how can I not stand against our annihilation?"

"You *do* have a choice. Arawn knows of you. He knows of your exploits. You have brought much honor to his name. For your service, he will allow you to stay here and escape the coming doom."

Dante hesitated, then shook his head. "That is a very generous offer. But I can't walk away from my people and leave them to die."

"As part of his benevolence, your lord will allow you to bring three hundred others with you. They may be your kin, your friends, your wisest priests, even fast allies from other kingdoms. Whoever you find best suited to perpetuate your people in exile."

Dante glanced at Blays, but Blays was watching Draven. Dante turned, pacing toward the window. "This doesn't make any sense. If you're willing to preserve a piece of our world rather than letting it all succumb to the end of its cycle, why not lend me your piece of the spear to try to stop it altogether? Does Arawn *want* the lich to win?"

"Do you think this would be the first time that things have come to an end?"

"Yeah, we saw a vision of that one," Blays said. "I'm no all-knowing god, but when I saw the armies of demons killing and eating millions of people, I didn't side with the demons."

Draven shifted his gaze to Blays. "Did you think *that* was the first time?"

Draven lifted his hand. Images flashed through Dante's mind, almost too fast to process. Demons dashing across the cities, but different in shape from the ones they had seen in the Glimpse; a great wave of water arising from all the oceans at once, leaving nothing alive when at last they receded; a plague swirling from one land to the next, the afflicted vomiting blood until death, sparing no one.

Others came too quickly for him to catch. And he had the sense, somehow, that there were others yet beyond this. It might only have been a handful or it might have been hundreds; each one might have been real or no more than a vision.

He plunged into eternity.

He found himself kneeling on the rug. As if he'd fainted.

"Take up the offer," Draven said. "It will grant you more than you understand. To be here is to become deathless."

Dante furrowed his brow. "People die here just as they do in our world. Our friend fell here just a few days ago."

"People can die, yes. But they can also live for century on century."

"What *is* this place?"

"You mean you do not know?"

"I didn't know this *was* a place until a few days ago. Since then, I've spent almost all of my time dashing across the wilderness or trying not to get eaten by giant worms and hordes of lizards. That hasn't left a lot of time to delve into the local culture."

"That can come later. It is time to make your decision. Will you accept your lord's offer? Or will you ensure that no trace of the world you know escapes the scythe of the lich?"

"Let us take the spear. If that fails, then we'll take up your offer of exile."

Draven shook his head, eyes fading to black voids once more. "Now, or the offer is forfeit."

Dante clenched his teeth, taking in the splendor of the city below him. The calm glow of its ethereal lights. The peace of its streets. The beauty of its buildings.

And the hand of his god in all of it.

"Then it's forfeit," he said. "I won't stop fighting for my world. If it's doomed to die, then I'll die with it."

Draven waved his hand in dismissal, though he didn't look at all bothered by this decision. "Then the offer is no more. You won't get the spear, High Priest. And if you try, Taim will awaken in his wrath and come to snuff you out. Either path left to you, you have cursed yourself."

He nodded to the door. The audience was over. Numbly, Dante walked toward the staircase, Blays at his side.

Before he crossed through the door, he spun about, lifting his face toward the high ceiling. "I've crossed worlds to find you. Once I leave this place, I doubt that I'll ever see it again. I know you're listening. Show yourself to me! Just once, let me look on you!"

Draven raised an eyebrow. One moment passed, then another, the room as hushed as a funeral.

Then came the voice: "GOODBYE."

Hearing it, Dante knew. And tears sprung to his eyes.

4

"Well," Blays said. "At least this hasn't been a total loss."

Dante squinted at him. "Which part of it do you consider a win?"

"We've confirmed Arawn *does* have part of the spear."

"We almost already knew that. That's about as close to nothing as we can get without it actually being nothing."

They sat on the covered porch of a public house. They had arranged with Draven to be allowed to stay in the city, which was named Rovan, for one day, so that they might resupply for their journey onward. He had accused them of wanting to stay in order to scheme up a way to take the piece of the spear, but Blays had assured him they would never do any such thing.

Blays tapped his glass. "*Are* we going to steal the spear?"

"We have to get it somehow." Dante took a surreptitious look about the porch. He was almost certain they were being watched, but had no idea by who—or even if it was a who and not a what. "But now might not be the right time."

"When *is* the right time? Elenna warned us the owners of the pieces of the spear—which is to say, *the almighty gods themselves*—want to see the Mists destroyed by the lich, or at the very least don't want to get dragged into a fight about it. They don't care. If even Arawn won't give us his part of it, which one of them will?"

Dante sat back in his chair and had a drink of his black beer, which tasted as if it was the product of a masterful recipe honed over the course of hundreds of years of tradecraft. Which, he supposed, it probably was.

"Maybe we can try another kingdom. See if someone else will give us a chance. There's clearly *some* resistance to the destruction of the Mists out there. If we can get one of the gods to relent and let us challenge them for the spear, I have a feeling others may follow suit. It's just a matter of prodding one of them into being the first to step forward against Taim's wishes."

"I'm starting to think our efforts here are very optimistic." Blays lifted his mug. "On the other hand, they have delivered us to some of the best beer I've ever tasted, so maybe we're on the right path after all."

Dante grunted. He intended to have another two or three mugs to facilitate some serious brooding about what to do next, but something about the Realm of Nine Kings seemed overtly hostile to all of his plans. Their current situation was no exception, as he hadn't even ordered his next round when they were approached from out of the blue by a young woman. Her red hair was bound in a thick braid and she wore a long gray coat that bore the distinction of being quite weathered from travel yet also impressively clean.

Without asking permission, she seated herself at their table, scooted her chair closer, and leaned forward. "Are you two who I think you are?"

"That depends," Blays said. "Do you think I'm the most dashing man within five hundred miles?"

"It's clear that you're not from Rovan. But I don't think that you're from *any* of the realms." Her gray eyes slid between them. "You're the interlopers, aren't you?"

"If we were, I'd think we'd wonder what business you have with our loping."

"Is it true what I've heard? That you've come here to save the

Mists?"

"No." Dante watched her from over his drink. "But if some-one were intending to save what you call the Fallen Land, it might have the side effect of saving the Mists as well."

"And you're trying to gain the weapon to help you do that, right? But looking at you, you aren't showing the mood of men who are seeing a lot of success."

"I have to say I find your presence curious. There are only a handful of people in the entire realm who know anything about us. And only one of them in this city."

"Well that *is* curious. And who are the others?"

"Taim and a few of his followers. And then a third party which, if you're *not* with them, wouldn't really want me to name them to you."

She raised an eyebrow. "Oh, you mean Elenna?"

"If you're trying to get us to lay our cards on the table, you're going to have to show some of yours first."

"If I was your enemy, I wouldn't sit down to have a conver-sation with you. I'd just kill you. Or go find someone much scari-er to do the killing for me. It's not like you're lacking for poten-tial enemies."

Dante leaned closer. "*Are* you with Elenna?"

"Why would you trust me if I claimed I was? I don't have a silver token to prove it."

He exchanged a look with Blays, who gave a slight shrug, then turned back to the young woman. "What do you want?"

"I see that you're carrying swords. I sense that you've used them, and not sparingly. In life, there are two ways to get things done: the striking of swords, or the striking of deals. Swords are very nice things, I like them. They're both functional and pretty, which seems to me to be the highest class of objects of them all.

"But swords are also—excuse me for this—double-edged tools. You can kill your enemies with them, but a lot of the time, that has the curious consequence of creating even more enemies than you had to begin with. In contrast, deals *expand* your base of allies. That's why I prefer them. When possible, of course. You have to be a realist about these things."

"Let me guess," Dante said. "You're here to make a deal."

"You say that like it's a bad thing. What if I told you I know of someone who might lend you their shard of the spear?"

"Who? Gashen? Urt?"

She shook her head. "Carvahal."

"*Carvahal?*" Dante forced his voice back down; fortunately, none of the other patrons seemed to have heard him. "If I bought a dozen eggs from Carvahal, I'd expect to find that half of them were empty and the other half were filled with sand. And after I paid for them I'd count my change three times. He's the *last* person I'd go to for help."

The red-haired woman caught the eye of a rather melancholy-looking serving maid and beckoned for a beer, which the maid delivered at once. "Not remotely true. You're forgetting that when the gods kept the secret of fire for themselves, it was Carvahal who brought it down to man."

"In direct defiance of Taim."

"That's not the only time he's bucked Taim's rule. You should look to Carvahal *because* he's willing to rebel and betray."

"But how would we know he won't betray *us*?"

"You wouldn't, obviously. But with things the way they are for you, what would it even matter?"

"If I was convinced this was a good idea, can you get us to his realm?"

"That's what I'm offering, yes."

"Didn't you say you were interested in making a deal?" Blays said. "You're offering to bring us to Carvahal, but what do you get out of it?"

"Same thing Elenna wants. To prevent the collapse of the

Mists."

Dante set down his mug. "What's your name?"

"Neve," she said.

"Okay, Neve. Why don't you go inside for a minute so we can discuss your offer among ourselves?"

She swung to her feet, swooping up her mug. She tipped a quarter of it back as she ambled inside the pub.

"What's there to talk about?" Blays said. "She's right."

Dante frowned. "It's not so much her proposal as the circumstances surrounding it. Like why is she here in the first place?"

"It would hardly take a strategical genius for Elenna to guess that the High Priest of Arawn's first order of business might be to go see Arawn. She could have sent Neve to lend us a hand. Or maybe Neve was already here because Elenna's got her agents working across the whole Realm right now. There does seem to be a catastrophe in the making."

"Yes, or Neve knows who Elenna is because she's working *against* Elenna. Couldn't this be a trap?"

"Well yeah."

"How do we figure out if it is a trap?"

"We could try walking into it."

"What are our alternatives to blindly taking up her offer?"

"We could kill her."

"*Good* alternatives."

"Well be more specific next time." Blays swirled his drink. "One option is to continue on our own working on the assumption that we can steal nine different spear pieces from nine different gods without getting killed by any of them. Our other option is to give up on the Spear of Stars, go home, and pray that we stumble on some miraculous solution in the few weeks remaining to us before the White Lich completes his rampage. If we had any other hope, we wouldn't be here in the first place, would we?"

"Probably not."

"You were just talking about trying to win one of the pieces like Sabel did, through a legitimate test. How if we could get one of the gods to give us a chance, maybe it would break the dam for us. Why *not* Carvahal? Can you think of anyone else more likely to swim against the current?"

"No, but that's quite possibly because I don't know anything about this place. Then we'll trust her. For now. But if she winds up stabbing us in our sleep, I'm going to spend what little time the Mists have left by dunking you into the ocean so much you'll forget what land feels like."

The gate stood before them. The desert glared from the other side. The horses had wandered off, but Dante could see them a couple of miles away on the fringe of the wasteland. It was morning out there, but within Rovan it was still as dark as when they'd arrived. Even so, the eternal night of the city wasn't threatening but peaceful, and as Dante stepped through the doorway, he felt a tug of nostalgia and regret.

The sunlight was so bright he stood around blinking until his eyes adjusted. The doorway faded. He didn't see any glimmers about. If they somehow triumphed, and he returned here one day, would he be able to reenter the city? Or was it already lost to him?

Neve owned a horse of her own, and it was a good match for her, hale and pretty despite all the travel it had clearly endured. She helped round up their horses and they were soon on their way north toward the brittle gray shrubs at the boundary between the desert and the nothing of the Claimless Reach that surrounded the gateway to Rovan.

They'd hardly started out before Neve began to stare at them intensely, even expectantly. She stopped just before the desert and thumbed back her floppy hat. "Well?"

Blays swiveled his head at the dead tufts of grass. "Have we reached Carvahal's kingdom already? You must be worth your weight in the gold we don't have."

"Aren't you going to bother to check your waystone?"

"My what-stone?"

She eyed them, perplexed. "How exactly did you get down here?"

Blays patted the side of his mount. "By riding these two very much not stolen horses."

"But how did you avoid the ramna?"

"The little dragons? We just made ourselves dragon-proof houses at night."

"The nomads. The war bands. Those without kingdom."

"We didn't see many people along the road," Dante said. "We might have seen a war band once, but we hid from them."

Neve laughed, eyes gleaming. "Then you're lucky to be alive. *Very* lucky. The ramna always have eyes on the road. If they didn't come for you, they must have been distracted by something bigger."

"If travel is such a death sentence, how do you expect us to even be able to get to Carvahal's kingdom?

"With one of these." She opened her long coat and reached inside an inner pocket, withdrawing a dull red stone. She closed her hand around it. When she reopened her hand, the stone had brightened so much it looked to be glowing. White marbled strands slowly formed and dissolved within it. "Waystone."

Blays peered at it. "Well it's glowing, the universal sign that it's magical. So it can detect the presence of evil nomads?"

"How would it do that? By smelling them?" She waved her hand to the wide, wide valley ahead. "Out there, you've got hundreds of scouts. Rangers. Even a few bandits who don't mind earning some legit coin on the side. They watch for the ramna wherever they go. They carry waystones, too. Anyone who's been given a waystone can consult it to see what the rangers are reporting and whether there's bad news on the horizon."

"Travelers pay the guides to take them through the wilds, who in turn pay the rangers to tell them which paths are safe?"

"For the most part. Some of the rangers aren't getting paid. They're criminals who choose to work off their sentences in the outlands."

"And these criminals, whose crimes were so bad they get sentenced to work in a place that's trying to kill them all day and night: you trust them to always give you *good* information?"

"Yes. Because the only criminals chosen for this duty are the ones with families—ideally wives and children—back in their kingdom."

"Ah, the ol' 'We'll execute your family if you fail us' technique. Works every time."

"That still doesn't answer the question," Dante said.

Neve smiled at him. "They betray their duty rarely enough that it's much better to have them working out here than not. Anyway, we're clear. For now."

She led them onward and the wasteland soon fell behind. When they came to the end—or rather the start—of the road, Neve stopped to consult her waystone again. It was back to its former dull red color. After a few taps and shakes, which only produced a pair of brief-lived white lines, she carried on, placing the stone in a little holster on the pommel of her saddle where she could see it at all times.

The grass returned, short and yellowed at first, but growing tall and green by afternoon.

Neve pulled to a halt. Before her, the waystone had gone bright red, shot through with snow white threads.

"This way. This way *now*."

She broke to the left. She descended behind a short ridge, then broke into a hard gallop, her mount flinging turf from its hooves. Dante and Blays romped along behind her, the odor of their horses thickening as the animals began to sweat. Dante glanced behind him but saw nothing. He continued to see nothing for another mile, until they rode up the side of a hill and gained enough elevation for him to spot their pursuit some three miles to the east.

"I don't see more than ten of them," Dante said. "Unless those are the avenging angels of Taim, *they* should be afraid of catching up to *us*."

"It's not them I'm worried about," Neve said. "It's whoever's behind them."

They pushed their horses to the brink. Dante swept the exhaustion from the beasts' quivering muscles and Neve nodded in acknowledgement. Despite this effort, the riders kept up with them for another five miles until finally breaking chase.

Blays sat up in the saddle, looking behind them. "That's all these people do? Chase travelers around all day?"

"No," Neve said. "Most times, they catch the travelers and kill them."

They took a rest before moving on. Dante sent a few reanimated bugs up into the sky to supplement Neve's waystone. One soon died, eaten by a bird or something, but the others didn't see any more enemies. With the day wearing on, the three of them found themselves back in the grassland where the giant fallen pillars lay exposed to the rains and the winds.

Dante motioned to the ruins. "People used to live on these, right? What happened to them?"

Neve shrugged. "It didn't work out."

Dante asked her several more questions about the realm and its politics, but she was similarly tight-lipped. Then again, everyone they'd met in her organization seemed to be. With the sun behind the western peaks, and night on its way, they camped at the edge of the pot-holed wetlands.

As Blays tended to the horses, Dante kneeled, nicked his arm, and sank the nether into the earth, liquefying it and drawing it upwards into a circular set of walls.

Neve wandered up next to him. "What are you doing?"

Dante finished the walls and sent earth flowing up to close in the roof. "A perverse idiosyncrasy of mine. I have a strong aversion to getting devoured by swarms of lizards."

"The drakelets? I have blankets for that."

"Blankets! The drakelets won't stand a chance."

"We have a recipe. Rangers' secret. We preserve it in oil to make stadden oil. Dab some on your blankets, no drakelets."

"Well, I'm doing it my way. You're free to sleep outside if you want."

Neve snorted. "Who taught you how to manipulate the earth like this, anyway?"

"No one."

"So one day while the other kids were learning how to buckle their shoes, you up and discovered how to reshape the ground with your mind."

"Back in my home, there's a group called the People of the Pocket. They're all women, and they're all nethermancers. They're the only ones who know how to do this. They keep all knowledge of it a secret, but after I figured out that they *could* do it, I worked the skill out by myself."

"You just taught yourself?"

"It wasn't easy. But we would have died without it."

She watched him finish his task. "Interesting. Maybe it's not so hopeless this time after all."

As usual, she refused to explain anything more about what she meant.

Dante brought his insect scouts inside the earthen hut and ordered them to awaken him if Neve got up during the night. She didn't. Either she had no intention of betraying them, or she had all the time in the world to do so.

The next pair of days passed without incident. They traveled through woods and tall-grassed plains, veering northeast toward the middle of the valley, adjusting course whenever Neve's waystone began to glow.

The two ranges of mountains lining the valley on the east and west looked no more than a hundred miles apart, yet they never seemed to get much closer or further away, even after days of travel. Somehow, regions that were physically much *closer* than the mountains remained hazy, seeming to materialize from out of nowhere. It gave Dante the impression the Realm of Nine Kings was much larger than it appeared, but when he floated this theory to Neve, she only shrugged.

The ground ahead began to slope up into a low mountain range. The sides were lush green, but the tops were as vibrantly red as Neve's waystone. They got halfway up the forested heights by nightfall.

Neve had picked some knobby purple fruit which they ate along with some salted beef. She finished a fruit and flipped aside the fibrous core. "We should make it there tomorrow."

Dante looked up. "To Carvahal's kingdom?"

Neve nodded.

"Good news. And thank you for bringing us here." He squinted. "Although I'm still not entirely sure who you really are or why you're helping us."

She smiled coyly and jammed her thumbnail under the rind of another fruit. He expected her to brush him off like she always did, but she tossed the fruit to herself and leaned forward.

"You want to know why I'm helping you? To see what happens."

Dante blinked. "Not to save the Mists. Or the millions of people in our world."

"I could say that if you want me to say that. But I assumed

you were asking because you wanted the truth. The truth is I would find it very dull for extremely powerful people to set a plan in action and then for that plan to unfold without a hitch or any opposition to it at all. What is the point of life if there's no contest for it?"

"Now that's a high moral standard you've set for yourself," Blays said. "I might have to excuse myself for being too unholy to stand in your presence."

"You're just here to *survive*. To *save* people. I happen to think my reasons are a lot more interesting."

"Maybe so," Dante said. "But 'to see what happens' would also be a perfectly good justification to jump out and stab someone."

They went to bed. More rain came, hissing against the rocky roof of the shelter. Dante was awakened more than once by screeches and hoots. In the morning, the air was so misty it condensed on the leaves and fell from them like rain.

They crested the range at mid-morning. And saw, at last, what made it so bright red. That turned out to be the rocks at the top, which were so rain-battered and sharp that almost nothing could grow on them but red moss and lichen. The lack of undergrowth might have made for easy footing, but that possibility was undermined by the fact the ground was often broken up, too steep to climb, or entirely blocked by cliffs or rubble.

Blays gave it a bleak look. "Tell me you know the way through this mess."

"I don't know the way, because the way is always changing," Neve said. "But I've never not found *a* way forward. Some ways just take longer than others."

She gave her horse a pat and walked it into the blades of rock. It was slow going—very slow—but once they were a little ways in, it became clear that it wasn't half as impassible as it looked. Dante used his reanimated bugs to try to map a path for them. This helped them avoid the obvious dead ends, but the terrain was the main problem, and there was nothing to do about that besides push onward.

Besides, from the bugs' height, he could see a city in the distance.

They walked on, rocks clacking under the horses' hooves. Two-thirds of the way through, Neve's waystone began to burn scarlet red.

"That's impossible," Dante said. "My scouts don't see a thing."

"Mine do. And I trust mine a lot more than yours," Neve said. "Our only chance is to make the far slope. If they catch us in here, it's over."

Although the ground was a treacherous rubble of loose stones, Neve urged her horse faster. Dante could feel his mount's footing slipping beneath him.

"It'd be faster for us to go on foot," Blays said.

Neve shook her head, braid wagging. "They'd ride us down once we got to open ground. This is our only hope."

Dante's heart thumped. They squeezed through a crevice through the stone. The ground turned to rain-slick red clay and Neve's horse began to skid. Dante plunged his mind into the earth, solidifying it to flat, textured stone. The beast righted itself and ran faster.

The ground beyond was cracked and uneven and he smoothed this too. Ignoring his scouts, and trusting his horse to follow Neve without need for his guidance, Dante put all his attention into their footing, barely able to keep up with the horses' pace. He was so absorbed in his task that he flinched in surprise when they galloped free of the rocky labyrinth and into the grassy slopes of the far side of the mountains.

"There!" Blays pointed to the left.

A half mile away, dozens of mounted figures belched from

the cavern they'd been hiding in. At the same time, a second band emerged a little further to their right, as if from nowhere; they'd been hiding in a ravine overgrown with brush. Within moments, it became clear the ramna's horses were bred for chases, and would deliver the barbarians upon them within minutes.

"They'll cut us off long before we reach the city," Dante said. "We need to choose where to make our stand."

Neve shook her head again. "All we have to do is make it to the forest. They won't follow us there."

The woods lay beyond the base of the mountain. It would be close. For some time, there was little to do but ride and watch the ramna draw closer.

The left flank of riders outpaced the rest. Not trusting himself to cleanly cut himself at full gallop, Dante bit the inside of his lip. The nether swirled toward him before he even reached for it. He gathered it into six black darts and lobbed them back at the vanguard. He glanced behind himself as the darts were about to hit their marks—but were instead blasted apart by fast jabs of shadows.

"The barbarians have nethermancers?!"

Neve leaned forward in the saddle. "Why do you think I've been so keen to keep away from them?"

Blays loosened his swords in their sheaths. "Because they won't stop talking court politics at supper?"

Dante slung another volley behind them, but it was more a probe of strength than a meaningful attack. At least two nethermancers pitched in to defend the riders. Not a single bolt made it through.

"Good work," Blays said. "You've successfully provoked them."

An arrow fell behind them, followed by another closer and to the right. They were riding straight away from the enemy, making them easy targets, but if they veered to throw off the archers' aim, they'd lose ground, bringing even more archers closer. The forest was close but not close enough.

Blays juked to his right to avoid another arrow. "I'd offer to go back and distract them, but even if I shadowalked, they'd shoot my horse out from under me. Therefore I suggest *you* go distract them."

Dante swore and took in the scene. Archer-fodder if they stayed course. If they broke right, they'd run right into the spears and axes of the second group, which was closing on them from that side. He had a number of tricks to slow the enemy down. But he didn't want to plink away at them.

It was time to put some fear in them.

He reached ahead into the shadows, feeling them, then guided their three-person band toward a nondescript patch of ground. The slopes had borne little but grass but they'd just hit the flat stretch leading to the woods where some shrubs and small trees were scattered about. Dante angled past a line of them.

The pursuit grew closer. Arrows thunked into the ground at a steady pace, forcing them to weave back and forth. Dante drew in a great wave of nether. As the ramna barreled toward the line of vegetation, he thrust the shadows in front of them.

Half dived into the ground. The other half soaked into the brush. Where they touched the ground, the earth broke apart, yanking back from itself to form a jagged wound. Where they touched the brush, the plants crackled with life, harvesting tall and wide and thick. Hemming in both sides of the ravine.

The first line of riders had no time to react. They simply fell into the void. Some of those behind them tried to leap the rift. They failed. Others tried to stop; the horsemen behind them plowed into them, knocking them down and tangling the way. It couldn't have stopped them harder if they'd rammed into a castle wall.

The riders to their right wavered, yelling curses, but they were too far away to catch up even if they hadn't slowed at the sight of the chaos. Neve dashed into the forest. Dante watched through his scouts as the remaining riders carried forward, closer and closer to the treeline—and then yelled in anger and peeled away.

The comfort of their escape was short-lived.

The forest was so dense it made a worse labyrinth than the mountaintop, requiring them to dismount and lead their horses. It reminded Dante of the swamps of Tanar Atain, where lanes of water were crowded and blocked by trees. But at least those trees—or anyway, the ones outside the very deepest parts of the swamp—had been more or less normal.

These were anything but.

Vines hung from some, twitching slightly despite the absence of wind. Others bore bulbs that resembled the flammable candlefruit of the Plagued Islands—and exuded the same camphorous smell. Most disturbing of all were the ones that wielded thick, segmented limbs that ended in fat teardrop-shaped bulges, and were tipped with a long barb, as if they were scorpion tails. More subtly troubling were the berry-red flowers that seemed to turn to follow Dante as he passed them by.

Blays stepped carefully over a tangle of something short but extremely thorny. "Forgive me an insane question, Neve, but are these trees alive?"

She shrugged. "Are trees dead back where you come from?"

"But it's almost like they know we're here. And some of them appear to be...armed."

"Why do you think the riders didn't want to follow us in here?"

"It's Carvahal's version of a wall, isn't it?" Dante said. "Or his moat. Every place we've been in the Realm has had something to protect it from the wilds. Are the ramna barbarians that much of a threat?"

Neve glanced his way. "If they're not, the rulers of the kingdoms sure are wasting a lot of time and energy for no good reason, aren't they?" She led her horse down a fork in the trees. "Besides, out in the reaches, there are other things than barbarians."

As troubling as the forest looked, it did nothing to impede their passage. After a couple of miles of riding, they emerged into a wide stretch of farmlands and grassy fields. In the center stood the city: three enormously wide towers shooting hundreds of feet into the sky.

"Allamar," Neve said, her voice colored with fondness—perhaps even reverence. "The ancient city of Carvahal's realm."

On drawing closer, Dante saw that the towers weren't truly towers at all. Instead, they were massive pillars built on top of low hills, the tops of which were encrusted with buildings and spires. It wasn't unlike the columns they'd seen toppled in the prairie, though these were much broader and squatter. One of the pillars had a ramp spiraling up it to the platform's top.

They came to the base of the ramp, which was manned by a single guard in an orange and charcoal uniform. "Travelers? What's your business in Allamar?"

Neve met his gaze. "To see the sovereign."

The guard laughed. "The sovereign! By all means, milady."

He stepped aside, making a sweeping gesture as he did so. They proceeded up the ramp. The pillar was roughly 150 feet high and its first portion was made of earthen hill, but a third of the way up, the composition changed to packed chunks of stone, as if it were concrete made of giant grains. Yet there were squared-off patterns within it, too. Dante sank his mind into the stone, letting it roam.

"These pillars," he said. "They're old buildings filled in with rubble."

"That's right," Neve said.

"There's at least six layers of them. They built the city on top of itself as it grew. But that must have taken centuries."

Neve nodded indulgently, as if this observation was no more noteworthy than if he'd said "The sun sure is up today."

The ramp spiraled upward. At last, it brought them to the top of the platform. A second guard was posted there, but after taking a quick look at them, he waved them through.

In contrast to the serene peace of Rovan, the city of Allamar was as lively as a fair. People haggled in the streets and you could hardly walk a block without encountering an uproarious game of dice or cards. Portions of the outer rim of the column that supported this third of the city bristled with pulleys and cranes and most of the buildings had enormous squat barrels on their roofs which Dante suspected were there to catch rain.

The people wore brightly dyed clothes of a light material that could shield them from the summer sun but also provide cover against the winds that drove through the exposed platform. For a city, Allamar didn't bear many smells be they good or bad, likely due to those same winds, although Dante caught snatches of cinnamon bread and spiced wine.

Neve trotted across the living-platform to a bridge connecting it to the next one over. The bridge was extended, but looked to be able to be raised by the same mechanism the soldiers outside the shining city had used. This bridge was bracketed by guard houses, but none of the soldiers hailed them.

The structures on this platform were taller and more elegant, carved with foxes and sparrows and many other hallmarks of Carvahal, quite a few of which Dante had never seen before. The buildings stood wall-to-wall to conserve space, but many of the balconies had been packed with dirt and grew grass, flowers, herbs, and decorative trees. Despite the more upscale and even aristocratic flair of the place, it was almost as boisterous as the previous platform.

Their destination was apparent at once: a square palace four floors high with towers on each corner. The roof was tiled with blue clay and the walls were white granite that sparkled in the sun as if seeded with quartz. Past the arched entrances to the courtyard, a few score people were milling about sipping from glasses and playing games of strategy and chance.

Before the three of them could dismount, they were intercepted by a servant.

"We're here to see Majordomo Qualls," Neve said. The servant looked extremely skeptical, but as he opened his mouth to speak, Neve reached inside her coat and withdrew an ivory carving of a crow.

Without another word, the servant jogged off into the palace while a second man appeared to lead them into a sitting room off the courtyard. In almost no time at all, Palace Majordomo Qualls appeared, tall and grave-faced, the most serious-looking fellow Dante had seen since their arrival in the city.

After a glance at Neve, who nodded the okay, Dante briefly explained their purpose. The majordomo listened intently.

"Most interesting," Qualls said once he finished. "Some of this was known to us. Some of this was not. You will follow me."

He took them through airy halls lined with masterful paintings of derring-do and piracy. Tapestries were sewn with similar tales; Carvahal loved such stories, both proof of how brave humans could be, and how stupid.

Qualls halted inside a secluded hall, the ceiling vaulted above them. "Remain here."

His shoes barely made a whisper as he left.

"They're taking this more seriously than I expected," Neve said. "Good sign."

Blays inspected a painting of a boy and a soldier leaping off a waterfall, pursued by demons. "I like this place much better than

Arawn's boring, stuffy city. Hey Dante, you ever thought about switching worships?"

Dante scowled at such blasphemy. But before he could put Blays to the verbal sword, a side door opened to the chamber.

A man entered. A soft white glow surrounded his body, not unlike the blue-white light that emanated from the Eiden Rane, and at first it was hard to make out his features. The light faded; its absence revealed a face that was impossibly handsome, elegant rather than rugged, amusement glinting from the sharp green of his eyes.

"Hello," he said. "You may begin worshipping me as soon as you're ready."

A chill ran down Dante's spine. It was another moment before the understanding of his mind caught up to what his gut already knew.

They weren't being seen to by Carvahal's speaker or representative.

They were in the presence of Carvahal himself.

5

Dante fell to his knees. "Lord Carvahal."

To his left, Neve gasped, choking, and dropped so fast her knees hit the stone with a crack.

Blays looked at them, blinking, then considered the man across from them. "Are you really him?"

The god smirked. "Were you expecting thunderbolts?"

"It would have been a nice touch." Blays put his hand to his heart and lowered himself to one knee.

Carvahal watched them, nodding his approval, then waved his hand. "Stand. Unless you find it more comfortable down there."

Blays darted a look at Dante and opened his mouth to speak, eyes twinkling, but Dante jabbed him in the side.

"Do you already know the story we came to tell you?" Dante said. "If so, I won't waste your time with it."

A silver throne stood at the back of the room. Carvahal seated himself on its arm, resting one foot on its seat. "I expect that I know most of it. But once you grow old enough, there are few things better than a good story. Besides that: once you grow *really* old enough, you find that you can perfectly judge a man by *how* he tells his story."

Even if this was true, the statement felt as though it might be designed to wrongfoot Dante. Scratch that: Carvahal being Carvahal, it *had* been designed to throw him off. Which was surely a test in itself as well.

Regardless, Dante had an advantage: over the course of his life, there had been many times when he'd secretly imagined himself addressing a god, and thus wasn't altogether unprepared for the real thing. And as he got deeper into his story, he found himself more involved in it and less distracted by the presence of his divine audience.

"We've tried everything we can to stop the lich," he finished. "In fighting him, we've lost friends. Entire kingdoms. Now it's the world that stands on the brink. You're our last avenue. Our last hope."

"I see." Carvahal tapped the side of his jaw. "That's quite the interesting story, and just as interestingly told. Normally I'd assent to your request for that reason alone. But I'm afraid your tale of woe isn't about to stop being woeful."

Heat burned in Dante's heart. "You won't give us your part of the spear."

"Even if I did, the others still won't give you theirs."

"We can deal with that. We'll steal them if we have to."

"I'd love to watch you fail at that. I'd bet twelve pounds of gold that it would be the most entertaining thing I've seen in millennia. But I can't do that. You see, for you, the difference between one-ninth of a spear and no parts of a spear is nothing. For me, it's the difference between peace, and provoking war in this world. And I happen to be rather fond of the place."

"But you have always been the friend of man. Unless you help us, there won't *be* any more humans."

Carvahal lifted his head. "Whenever humans try to tell me what I can and cannot do, it makes me question why I ever thought them worth my help in the first place."

"You brought us the light of the fire when every other god— Arawn among them—kept it from us. It was this act that elevated us from savages to what we are today. Now we're about to die. All of us! And all of our dead with us! If that happens, then everything you've done for us—every risk you've taken for us— will be for nothing. Is that what you'd see happen? Are you too cowardly to stand up, just as you once did, and give us just enough aid to let us fight for our lives?"

"If you were the son of Arawn himself, I wouldn't let you insult me like this in my own hall."

Carvahal didn't move, yet he seemed to zoom forward until all Dante could see was his face—and then just his eyes, two black pits like holes punched through the sky, as bottomless and unsurvivable as his Glimpses into the deep deep past. In them lay the power to dash Dante into a million pieces.

And the will to do so.

Carvahal grinned crookedly, swaying back. "But it will be much funnier to watch you get killed by the others instead. Leave now. Before I throw you out. By which I mean over the side of my city."

Dante gritted his teeth until they squeaked. He felt the exact same frustration he had when facing Draven, aware that all of his words were achieving nothing, yet equally aware that he had no means to force a different outcome. In his own lands, this would have been but a minor setback, one he could solve through alternative, illegal, or violent means. Here in the Realm of Nine Kings? Here, he was helpless.

He lowered his head. "Thank you for seeing us. Forgive me my insults. We still remember what you've done for us."

With his arms folded, Carvahal waved one hand in dismissal. Dante turned to go. Beside him, Neve looked bitterly disappointed.

Blays didn't budge. "Now, my friend's had his say. As usual, he's cocked it up good. But I haven't had *my* say."

Carvahal disfavored him with a look. "Your words can't argue away my reality."

"Then it's a good thing I don't mean to use words. I mean to use swords. I challenge you to a duel."

The god barked with laughter. "A duel?"

"If I win, you'll hand over your part of the spear."

"You can't possibly hope to beat me in a duel."

"Then you have nothing to lose by accepting."

Carvahal took a pace to the side. "And if I win, you leave the realm. Not just my realm. *The* realm. On those terms, is this wager still what you want to stake your future to?"

"My alternative is to turn back, go home, fight a battle we can't win, watch everyone I know get turned into a shambling puppet, run away with my wife, and then get killed in front of her knowing my useless death will be the last thing she sees. So yes. Let's duel."

"Any one you like." Carvahal motioned to the racks of swords against the wall to the right of the throne. "What of the rules of the duel itself?"

Blays was already wandering among the racks. He unsheathed a slim sword. "First blood?"

"Nice try. Any fool can land a lucky strike and draw first blood. To the death."

Blays went still, staring into space as he considered it.

Dante stepped forward. "You can't!"

"But I have to. So it doesn't matter what I *can't*." Blays turned to Carvahal and nodded. "To the death. Very w—" He stopped and narrowed his eyes. "Wait a second. Can you even *be* killed?"

Carvahal shrugged. "Everything can be killed."

Blays pointed the slender sword at him. "Yes, but can you be killed by me, using this?"

The god laughed. "No, and clever of you to think to ask."

"Now that's just cheating."

"Just like you wanted to fight to first blood? Seeking advantage isn't cheating. So then?"

"To the mortal pose. Assuming you *could* be killed."

Carvahal considered this, then nodded. "Agreed."

"No sorcery, either?"

"Of course not. What are we, cowards?"

"I've only known you a short time, but it seems that in dealing with you, the terms of engagement need to be made very, very clear."

Carvahal grinned and went to select his weapon from the racks.

Neve edged next to Dante. "What's the mortal pose?"

Dante watched Carvahal closely. "The point at which it's clear you have put your opponent in a position where your next stroke would kill him."

"Carvahal's a master swordsman. What chance does Blays even have?"

"An ever so slightly better chance than we had of talking a god into something he doesn't want to do."

"You don't sound very hopeful."

"That means you have working ears."

Carvahal unsheathed his sword, hefting it a few times. "Traditionally we'd go do this in the dueling ring we keep around for just this sort of thing. But I'm not much for tradition. My own hall seems good enough." He snapped his fingers. A circle of pale ether inscribed itself across the floor, thirty feet in diameter.

Blays jerked his chin at it. "Purpose?"

"Forced out twice, and you lose." Carvahal stepped inside and raised an eyebrow at Blays. "Once you're ready."

Blays unbuckled the belts bearing his Odo Sein swords, cradling them as he lowered them to a table. He took up his dueling weapon, made a few practice cuts and thrusts, and entered the ring.

"Well," he said. "At least we're going to decide the future existence of my world like gentlemen."

Carvahal lifted his sword, pointing it at Dante. "If you make any attempt to interfere, I'll kill you."

Dante put his hand to his chest. "I wouldn't dream of it."

"You already were." The god extended his blade to Blays. "Good luck."

"I'd wish you the same," Blays said, "but I don't want you to win."

He held out his sword and they tapped the sides of their steel against each other. This done, they each took three long steps back.

And then fell into a guard.

Blays took a step forward. Carvahal stood up straight, lowering his sword until his arm was in a pose resembling a distracted mother holding the hand of her small child. Blays gave the king of tricks a skeptical, even disapproving look. He took a long step forward. Carvahal kept his guard down. Blays tightened his mouth, shuffled forward, and lunged.

Carvahal's sword flashed upward. Blays had been expecting as much and he rolled to his right, batting Carvahal's blade away with a flick of his wrist, then snapped a backhand attack at the god's neck. Carvahal ducked it, bending to his right and using his momentum to sweep his sword at Blays' middle. Blays leaped backward, jabbing his sword downward just in time to intercept the attack. He backpedaled two steps, grinning.

Carvahal snorted. "You're quicker than most."

"If you spend any time in the Mists, you'll find plenty of dead men who could vouch for that."

They watched each other a minute, doing a bit of circling and feinting with no real danger of a clash. Without a hint of what was coming—or one too subtle for Dante to see—they leaped upon each other, blades flashing, striking with a clang, followed by a string of blows, a brief pause, another flurry. Blays' eyebrows lifted high in concentration. Carvahal drove him two steps back toward the circle's edge, then three. As they neared the glowing line, Blays broke sharply to his right—and reversed course just as quickly.

His sword speared for Carvahal's exposed side. Carvahal whirled in time to deflect it, but when they broke apart, blood beaded from the god's arm.

Blays gave his blade a shake. "No wonder you didn't want to fight to first blood."

"Maybe I let you do that in order to make you overconfident."

"Or maybe I just did it."

Carvahal tipped his head to the side in a shrug.

They flew at each other again, blades moving between attack and counter as fast as silvery fish. This time, Blays began to beat Carvahal back toward the ethereal ring. Both combatants were sweating now. In Carvahal's case, this answered a longstanding theological question that was supposed to have been purely hypothetical.

Carvahal's back heel touched the edge of the ring. Blays came at him with a flurry of strikes, but couldn't get the god to relent another inch. For the first time, however, Carvahal looked worried. Blays rocked back, as if about to disengage, then lunged, correctly anticipating that Carvahal would attempt to slide to the left. Blays grinned and launched the attack that would bounce Carvahal from the ring.

It missed.

Dante didn't see *how* it happened, but he heard the metal scrape indicating Carvahal had somehow guided the jab past him. Carvahal's parry turned into a thrust. His sword took Blays in his extended forearm, only stopping once it hit bone.

Blays' face went white like sickly ether. Looking deadly serious, Carvahal slid his blade free and whipped it toward Blays' neck. Seeking the mortal pose.

Blays bent backward, cat-like, and tossed his sword from his wounded arm, catching it in mid-air with his left hand. Carvahal was already coming at him with another strike, but Blays turned it aside and skipped backward.

They both huffed for air. Carvahal eyed the blood flowing from the deep gash on Blays' arm. "Want to yield?"

"Because you cut my arm? That's why you gods gave us two of them."

Carvahal smirked and crossed the ring to reengage, pressing Blays mercilessly. But Blays was virtually as good with his left as with his right, and for a minute, Carvahal was mildly thrown by having to fight against his opposite hand.

But only for a minute. As soon as he adjusted, he pushed Blays back step by step. Blays was able to keep himself away from the very edge of the ring, but his face was a tight mask and he was both bleeding and sweating freely. He hadn't so much as scratched Carvahal since drawing first blood and couldn't seem to find the faintest crack in Carvahal's defenses.

Meanwhile, Carvahal stuck to him like the needle of a compass to a block of iron. Even to Dante's trained but non-expert eye, the strategy was clear: give Blays no rest, wear him down, keep up the assault until he made his mistake, and take victory.

Yet victory was so slow to show up it seemed to be sleeping off a bender. As the duel dragged on, Carvahal grew visibly annoyed. Then again, he wasn't known for his patience. Dante wondered if Blays could exploit that, but didn't ask so aloud: advising from beyond the ring typically earned you an official beating of some kind.

Carvahal pressed forth with another storm of attacks. Blays skipped away from them and emerged unscathed. Carvahal hacked at the air. With an audible growl, he charged.

As he began his lunge, his leading foot went out from underneath him. His eyes went wide as he hit the ground, his sword trapped beneath him.

Without hesitation, Blays pounced.

And Carvahal laughed.

He rolled to the side, his blade slashing upward toward Blays' left arm. He'd fallen on purpose: had *feigned* impatience, then set a trap, which Blays had just thrown himself into.

But this didn't make any sense. Because Blays was laughing, too.

In fact, he seemed to be *falling*. Right past Carvahal's sword. When the blur of motion came to a stop, Blays was in a crouch. Untouched. And Blays' sword was resting across Carvahal's throat.

The god began to laugh. Dante had no idea if it was in appreciation or in rage.

Neve grabbed Dante's sleeve, hissing, "What just happened?"

Carvahal cast his sword aside with a clang. "You bastard. You tricked me."

Blays lowered his blade to his side. "You were trying to trick *me*!"

"Yes, but mine was supposed to be the one that worked." Carvahal got to his feet, dusted off his exceedingly fine clothing, and collected his weapon.

"You could have beaten me," Blays said.

Carvahal inspected and sheathed his sword and returned it to its rack.

"If you'd just worn me down," Blays finished.

"Obviously."

"Then why take a gamble? To try to make me look like an ass?"

"There's nothing interesting about inevitability. About playing it *safe*. I chose to give you one last opening to see if you would notice it—and more important, if you could do anything about it."

He held out his hand. Blays passed him the dueling blade.

Carvahal replaced it, too, straightening it tidily. He turned and clapped his hands. "Now, the better question. Should I keep my word to you?"

Blays lifted his finger. "Don't make me teach you another lesson."

Dante's heart was thudding. Carvahal laughed. "Judging by the looks on your faces, I shouldn't keep my promise. Your wailing is something I'll remember for a long, long time." He tapped his chin. "Then again, the chaos you're likely to cause for my enemies will be a much greater show. Oh, very well."

He moved to an empty gap between the sword rack and one that held a number of exotic polearms. He muttered, as if confused, yet there was a chant-like rhythm to his words. He moved his hand in obscure patterns; glimmers of gray light trailed from his fingers.

The gap between the two racks began to glow. A new rack appeared, spectral, silver and white. A single weapon rested within it: or rather, a single *part* of a weapon.

Carvahal lifted it, careful not to touch its bladed edge. Held flat across his palms, he extended it to Blays. "I present to you my portion of the Spear of Stars."

6

Blays stared at the shining shard. He examined Carvahal's eyes, as if suspecting some final trick, then stepped forward and lifted the portion of the blade in his own hands.

"Is this really it?"

Carvahal nodded. "It isn't yours to *own*, mind you. Just to borrow. After all, on the vanishingly remote chance you put off your world's end to another age, there will come a day when someone *else* needs it."

In a state of awe, Dante cautiously sent his mind to the piece. "It looks like it's made of pure ether."

"Correct."

"If we can't win the other pieces, would we be able to kill the White Lich with this?"

Carvahal laughed. "I would not try that."

"That isn't a no."

"The whole is much greater than the parts. Even if you had the whole blade, and not just this third of it, it wouldn't be enough to do the job."

"Well, it's still rather nice." Blays found a grip on it and practiced a slow thrust. "Are there any poets around to immortalize this moment? In case you've all forgotten, I just *beat a god*."

Carvahal looked unimpressed. "What fun would there be in it if we didn't let you win once in a while?"

"Not to brush off such a triumph so quickly," Dante said. "But we still have eight more pieces to collect. How do we move forward from here?"

Blays tried out a chop. "We could demand they hand over their pieces or I'll spear the hell out of them."

"It seemed to us that some of the other gods were only holding rank because no one else had dared to break it," Dante said to Carvahal. "Now that you let us contest for your portion of the spear, will any of the others follow suit?"

Carvahal guffawed. "Not on your life."

"But I thought—"

"But nothing. Your plan relies on the assumption that the others will hear of my display of propriety and suddenly choose to recover their own. Well, they won't. Because they don't trust me. Because I'm *not* to be trusted." He gave them a moment to taste their disappointment, then smiled. "So it seems to me that you'd want to look for the one of us who's trusted by all the rest of us."

Dante began to run through the possibilities, but the answer emerged immediately. "Gashen? But aren't the two of you...?"

"Bitter enemies? That's hardly a secret. Nonetheless, thanks to his precious 'honor,' Gashen is respected by everyone. If he breaks rank to let you challenge him for his bit of the spear, I believe you'll find that most of the others will relent, too."

"Where is his realm? How can we find him?"

"Oh, it's not Gashen you want to find. It's his precious axe."

"It's missing?"

"Yes. Because I stole it."

"Now that's convenient," Blays said. "Can we have it?"

"Afraid not. It's missing, you see."

"But you just said—"

Carvahal waved his hand for silence. "I stole Gashen's axe because I thought it would be funny. And because I didn't want him to have it any longer. But then some wretched bastard went and stole it from *me*. Carried it off into the outlands."

Dante turned in the direction Carvahal had indicated. Not that there were any windows to see these outlands through. "So who has the axe now?"

"How should I know? My purpose was to keep it away from Gashen. It's more missing, and thus all the further from his hands, if I *don't* know where it is. Additionally, not knowing its location means that Gashen can't beat the answer out of me. What I can tell you is that the last I heard, it had been taken to the Red Valley."

Neve stiffened. "The Red Valley?"

Carvahal winked at her.

"And how long ago was that?" Dante said.

Carvahal puffed out his cheeks. "Three...no, four hundred years ago."

"Four hundred years?! It could be anywhere by now."

"So what? That can be said of anything that's been lost."

"This sounds like a wild goose chase. Or whatever your version of geese are."

"Sure, it could be a colossal waste of your time. But if you find the axe, it will chop down all sorts of doors for you."

"You're that sure of this? We find the axe, and Gashen will let us earn his part of the spear?"

Carvahal raised an eyebrow. "Are you kidding? He loves that axe more than he loves his own wife. Bring him the axe, and he'll lend you his part of the spear on the very spot."

Dante turned to Neve. "Can you take us to the Red Valley?"

"Of course she can. She's a ranger, isn't she?"

She stared nightmares at Carvahal. "This sounds like a death sentence."

"Then walk away," Carvahal said. "These two are the only ones who'll know about your shame. And they'll be dead shortly anyway, now won't they?"

She held his gaze. Then cursed, almost silently, and nodded at Dante. "I can take you there. But you might not like me for doing it."

Dante wanted to leave to find the axe right away. Carvahal insisted that it was tradition that, when a champion arrived and won a shard of the spear, he would be feasted for three days, and if they had expected him to follow tradition and allow them to vie for the spear, then they must follow tradition as well. Dante talked him down to one night.

The feast itself was largely indescribable, in that Dante had never eaten half of what was on the table and had little idea what it was. The rest of it was familiar enough—grouse, cherries, mead, beef, walnuts—but something about it was heightened, not only the flavor of it but also the *feel* of it, as if it wasn't filling him so much as it was intoxicating him. Although there *were* drinks as well, strong liquors he'd never tasted, and these seemed to heighten his mind even as they endrunkened him. Wanting to leave early in the morning, he was careful not to have too much.

Still, it loosened his tongue a bit. With the affair winding down, he turned to Carvahal. "Why is it so important for the Realm of Nine Kings to be kept a secret from the people of my world? To stop us from coming here? To test our faith?"

Carvahal gave him an amused look. "You still don't know what this place is?"

"Not in whatever way you seem to be hinting at. The solution to that is you could just tell me."

"You already know more about it than you think. It's right there in that book of yours."

"You mean the *Book of What Lies Beyond Cal Avin*?" Dante kept it on his person at all times and reached under his chair where he'd stowed it during the feast.

Carvahal gave it an uninterested look. "Sure."

"What about it?"

"As I told you, it's been right in front of you all this time. You just won't recognize what you're looking at."

Dante furrowed his brow, combing his memory of the book. Carvahal stood, excusing himself. After he'd walked out, Dante realized the god hadn't answered any of his questions.

In the morning, as Majordomo Qualls arranged their supplies, Dante studied the piece of the spear. First, to understand how it operated. And second, to see if he could understand how it had been *created*. For if he could do that, there was a chance he could forgo winning or stealing the other eight pieces and simply craft replacements for himself.

What he discovered was that the shard didn't really *do* anything. It was no more active or unusual than an everyday spearpoint, at least for now. As for how it had been made, well, it seemed to be forged of solid ether, just as the buildings in Rovan were built from pure nether. Dante had no idea how either of these things were possible, so his chances of duplicating the process were somewhere between glum and hysterical.

They started down the ramp from the platforms as the city's bells tolled ten o'clock in the morning. It was a quiet, sunny day, although not as hot as those conditions would seem to inflict, implying that the height of summer was now behind them.

"So we're going to the Red Valley," Blays said. "I have questions about this. Such as, what's the Red Valley? And once we get to the Red Valley, what do we plan to do, other than try not to wind up getting worn as a cloak by a barbarian?"

"Carvahal said he thought the axe was stolen by a ramna man named Sallen," Neve said. "It's possible Sallen will still be there."

"Er, you mean his clan?"

"I mean Sallen himself."

"Didn't Carvahal say this fellow stole the axe from him four hundred years ago?"

"So?"

"So unless we're traveling to whatever *your* version of the afterlife is, I'm not sure what good it will do to question his moldy skeleton."

"Have you seen a lot of old people here? Or children?"

"Now that you mention it, I've been wondering about that."

"People here don't grow old," Neve said. "Well, that's not quite right. They don't die from *being* old. And the older you get, the slower you age."

Dante blinked, absorbing this as they maneuvered past a mule-drawn wagon full of red tubers. "Are you saying everyone here is...immortal?"

Neve laughed. "Didn't Carvahal himself tell you that everything that lives can be killed? Including himself?"

"Yes, but I don't entirely trust that man. Call me narrow-minded if you like, but something about the 'Lord of Thieves and Treason' just doesn't sit right with me."

She pointed at the mule-driver, now uphill from them. "If you cut that man's throat—or put an arrow in his back—or shoved him off the ledge—he'd die like anyone else. Same's true of everyone in these lands. The regents don't invest so much gold in defenses to keep out the dangerous people just to impress each other."

Blays made a thoughtful noise. "Well, that explains why the farmer we stole—I mean, righteously requisitioned—our horses from was so afraid of us killing him."

"So you're not truly immortal," Dante said. "But you don't get old and die, either. How can that be?"

Neve shrugged, lifting one hand palm-up. "Maybe it's something in the air. Maybe it's living in the presence of the gods.

Maybe it's in our blood. Why can birds fly when we're condemned to the ground?"

"Because they have wings."

"And so do we, in our way. But you can't see these wings and I don't know what they are."

Dante proceeded to brood.

Blays motioned north, where they'd been told the Red Valley lay. "So even after all these years, there's a chance Sallen's still there, and still has the axe, and we can find him and bargain or wrest it away from him. Very good. Except I'm going to guess at least two of these conditions are going to screw us over somehow, if not all three. What then?"

"What do you think?" Neve said.

"If our past expeditions are any indication, we'll have to find a way to infiltrate the locals and attempt to navigate their local politics without kicking off any wars, rebellions, or collapses. We *might* be able to pull that part off. Either way, it's going to help to know what these barbarians are like."

"Unfriendly. To put it lightly. To put it heavily, they are likely to kill us. Though it might actually be to your favor that you're not from one of the Nine Kingdoms."

"Why's that?"

"Because they hate the Nine Kingdoms."

"Yes, I've gathered that much. But why do they hate the kingdoms?"

"For the same reason they hate the gods," Neve said simply. "The gods and their realms were supposed to protect these people. Instead, the ramna were thrown out. The gods fed them to the wilds. Worse, to the monsters that lurk in the wilds."

"The ramna must have done something dreadful to deserve a fate like that. Rebellion? Regicide? Stealing the last drink of the best red?"

"They were born."

"Ah...that's a crime here, is it?"

"It is if no one dies," Dante said. "As weird as your sense of distance feels here, the Realm isn't infinite. Keep having children, and sooner or later, it will fill up with people."

Blays rubbed his jaw. "So in their brilliance and mercy, the gods decided to throw their subjects' babies to the literal wolves? And the flocks of drakelets? And giant bears?"

"There was more logic to it than that," Neve said. "There *are* monsters beyond the walls. That's why they built the walls in the first place. So the rulers and their people came to an agreement. Male children, and all female children judged capable of bearing arms or handling logistics, were assigned into expeditionary legions. These would patrol the roads, root out nests of unwanted things, and otherwise fight the chaos always seeking to break through the kingdoms' barriers. Once the soldiers had fulfilled their service time, they could return to their homeland."

"Assuming any of them survived a years-long fight against everything the wilderness had to throw at them."

"Yes."

"Was that the point? To winnow them down until the population was small enough to integrate into the cities?"

"If that *was* their plan, do you really think they'd up and tell people as much? Anyway, whatever the intent, the system worked for a long time. The legionaries kept the wilds safe. A few of them earned their way back. Life went on. All according to design." She waited to pass a pair of travelers before continuing. "But nothing holds forever. No matter how well a king or god has shaped his design, sooner or later, all order breaks down.

"Ten years into his service beyond the walls, a legionary named Harald looked around himself and saw two things. First, that his brothers and sisters were dying and almost none of them would see any reward for their service to the kingdoms. And second, that the legionaries *already knew how to survive outside the walls*. He rallied his legion to walk away. To stop their patrols in service of the lords and go start their own life—one entirely for themselves.

"That was the beginning of the people who would become the ramna. Over the years, they grew powerful, forcing the gods to build higher walls and more fiendish defenses. The gods have tried to strike back countless times, but the ramna know the wilds so well that they're usually able to slip away or turn the land against its creators. Anyway, there are just too many of them. Now the two sides have been at war for longer than anyone's been alive but the gods."

Dante grunted. "If they still hate the gods that much, there isn't much chance Sallen's going to just hand over Gashen's axe. Not when we mean to return it to him."

"No," Neve said. "But after hearing the stories you told Carvahal, I doubt the owner's unwillingness to strike a deal will stop you from retrieving the weapon."

This might have been true, but it relied on the massive assumption that they were going to be able to find the axe in the first place. Right now, all they had was a name and a place. Opposing them stood centuries of confusion and entropy. It seemed very, very likely that they would hit a dead end almost immediately.

In fact, their mission seemed so loaded against them it made Dante suspicious that Carvahal was playing a trick on them, sending them off to hunt for something that couldn't be found, intending to waste their time or even get them killed in a manner he'd bear no direct responsibility for. Then again, it did seem more likely that Carvahal would be opposing Taim than secretly working for him.

On top of that, they now carried an actual piece of the Spear of Stars. The only weapon capable of felling the Eiden Rane. And if they'd gotten one piece, he was certain that they could get more.

They crossed north through the farmlands, entering the Guardian Trees ringing the kingdom. For the moment, Neve's waystone kept dim. She had warned them that once they reached the Red Valley, it would probably cease being of any use: the valley was ramna land, and there likely wouldn't be any rangers about to feed the locations of the barbarians to the way-stones.

They exited the forest. The way ahead was a mass of boulders, hills, broken rock, and tall, shuffling grass. Dante slew three bugs that looked like purple wasps and sent them up into the sky to watch for any surprises. This done, he activated his loon.

"Lord Dante." Nak sounded both tired and cheerful. "How can I be of service?"

Dante grinned. "We won a piece of the spear, Nak."

"*The* spear? Of Stars?"

"Unless Carvahal's deceiving us."

"So you made it to his kingdom?"

"You know how we were only able to speak to Arawn's messenger? This time, we met *Carvahal*. The Silver Thief himself!"

"You what!"

"It gets better. Blays beat him in a duel. That's how we won his part of the spear."

The loon went silent. Dante checked to make sure it hadn't malfunctioned, but Nak was simply dumbstruck.

"You met Carvahal," Nak said in slow wonder. "One of the twelve gods of the Celeset. If anyone but you was telling me this, I don't think I'd believe it."

"I can hardly believe it myself. It doesn't seem...real. But unless I actually died fighting the lich, and now I'm trapped in the Pastlands as the victim of an insane and endless illusion, this is where I am, and this is what is happening."

"Indeed. Still, the implications are..."

"Enough to drive you crazy? Fortunately for me, I've been too busy dealing with the madness directly in front of me to have time to consider the much greater madness of those implications."

He gave a quick explanation of their new task and its relation to their plan to assemble the rest of the spear.

"Gashen's axe," Nak said contemplatively. "If you're able to retrieve it, mightn't a weapon of that nature be able to hurt the lich as well? You might not even have to bother with the rest of the spear."

"During our celebratory feast, I asked Carvahal that very thing. He didn't think it would do the trick."

"At the risk of impugning one of the gods, couldn't he have been lying?"

"I considered it rude to ask him that. But if he's playing a game with us, it's one that's too perverse for me to hope to understand. Anyway, what's the news back in the mortal world?"

"Predictably grim," Nak said. "The lich has consolidated his army. He's taking it north. He's already sacked Whetton. We got most of the people out of harm's way, but there were some who didn't believe us, and others who *did* believe us but wouldn't leave town anyway. There are times when people make no sense to me."

"At those times, I've found it's usually best to get away from such people or to kill them."

"It gets worse. The lich isn't bothering to scoop up every little hamlet and village. He appears to be intent on continuing north."

"Toward Narashtovik?"

"One assumes he's grown tired of our meddling."

"He could be at the city gates within a month. It's taken us more than a week just to get one-ninth of the spear. You've got to do everything you can to slow him down. Make a stand in the Dundens. Continue rallying our allies."

"I'll do what I can. But..."

"He's the White Lich."

"I'm afraid so."

They left it at that.

Neve directed them through the craggy lands with the ease of someone who knew them well. With the image of the White Lich on the march with his army of Blighted fresh in Dante's mind, he insisted they ride onward, hoping to cut a three-day journey down to two. At last they called it quits and made camp in a half-ruined hilltop fortress Neve commonly used on her travels.

She claimed there were no drakelets in the area, and when they woke up their horses were still uneaten, so perhaps she was right. As with everywhere in the Realm, the landscape shifted with unnatural quickness as they went on, transitioning to steep-sided red hills with grassy swards on their crowns. Neve's way-stone glowed at four different occasions, but they detoured around the roving ramna each time.

As they rode, Dante pumped her for more information on the ramna, seeking anything that might help them find Sallen or the axe. He expected her to be as tight-lipped as on their trip to Allamar, but she spoke readily and at length—which he realized was because he was now asking about her profession. And like all professionals, there was little if anything she liked to talk about more.

The basic sweep of it was that nobody had really known what to do about the ramna—or perhaps more accurately had lacked the *will* to do something serious about them—until the raiders had already grown too big to be effectively dealt with. That truth was struck home when a charismatic fellow by name of Yotan had succeeded in uniting all the squabbling tribes, clans, and warrior-bands to his banner, and marched on the kingdom of Taim himself.

Taim won the siege, but the fighting was gruesome. In the aftermath, the gods coordinated their armies to sally forth and crush the ramna, but quickly discovered the difficulty in waging effective war against a mobile people with no permanent settlements or even real territory to defend. Battles were few. Futile chases of a faster opponent were many. On the rare occasions they could force a fight, their divine might inflicted significant carnage on the ramna, but the gods' soldiers were far more afraid to die than the ramna, who had grown up *expecting* to die in battle, and spent their lives believing there was no higher honor. The land and its creatures hampered the gods, too, as if these forces somehow resented the intrusion.

Eventually, the gods' coalition broke apart in frustration. They took their armies home. Since then, there had been occasional flareups and battles, but the overall situation had largely existed in stasis, with the gods in control of their kingdoms, and the ramna ruling the rest.

"And Yotan's coalition failed, too?" Dante said once Neve was done explaining. "The ramna are no longer united?"

Neve got a good laugh from this. "They're about as united as the rain."

"What about in the Red Valley? Is there more than one clan there?"

"The only time there isn't is when one band decides it's time to displace, absorb, or eradicate the others. Last I heard, there were six different bands in the valley."

"Judging by that bit about 'eradication,' they don't always like each other?"

"It's more often they don't than that they do."

"Without the help of *someone* in the valley, we'll never be able to find the axe. The easiest way to gain the help of one group will be to play it off against one of its rivals."

"We can do that if we need to," Neve said. "But before it comes to that, I'm going to ask my source if we can just talk to Sallen."

Her source was another ranger named Bert. The nature of the waystones made them capable of passing crude messages, and they met the man on a hillside just after dusk. When he lowered his hood, Dante nearly yelled out loud.

Bert was missing his right eye and his left ear. A patch of his scalp was warped with a burn scar; his nose had been broken so many times it seemed to point both ways at once; and his cheeks and brow were criss-crossed with scars, some of which had healed a lot better than others. It looked like he'd lived through nine different wars, which Dante realized was likely exactly what had happened: if you spent your days in a place where violence was the currency of the realm, you weren't forced to quit due to old age, and you survived for long enough, this was the natural result.

"Neve." His voice sounded as rough as he looked. "They are?"

"Foreigners," she said.

"Don't look like any foreigners I've ever seen."

"That's because you haven't. Still circling the Red Valley?"

"We're right next to it, aren't we?"

"Do you know of a ramna named Sallen?"

Bert's one eye glazed over as he thought. "Sallen. Prince with the Jessel Band."

Neve brightened. "He's still here?"

"Yeah. Right here in the ground."

"Damn it. What about the Jessel?"

"Still roaming. Last heard of them near the Larksbridge."

"Have you ever heard rumors that they might be carrying a weapon they weren't supposed to have?"

"The axe."

"So they have it?"

"That was the rumor."

"How long ago was this? Do they still have it?"

"Could be."

"Huh." Neve tucked her chin to her chest. "Are the Jessel open?"

Bert thought about this; whenever he paused, he seemed to become inanimate, as if he had to retreat so far into memory that his body was left abandoned. "No. But the Vastan are."

"And?"

"While back, the Jessel and Vastan made war on each other. Not pretty. Eventually made peace by marrying off their best young men and women to each other."

"So the Vastan are open. I go to them, use them to get to the Jessel."

"Waste of time. I already opened the Vastan. All you need is this." He reached into one of the seemingly infinite pockets of his long coat and withdrew an ivory rod carved with a script Dante had never seen.

"Bloodsigned?"

"Yeah."

"Perfect." Neve reached for it, but Bert didn't hand it over yet. She raised an eyebrow.

Bert made a small gesture. "What'll you give me in trade?"

"How's your supply of stadden oil?"

"Fine."

"Black salt?"

"Could be better."

They did some haggling, settling on the price and swapping salt for ivory. Neve turned the piece in her hand. "How will we know the Jessel when we see them?"

"Yellow flags on their spears. Like to clothe their horses'

heads to look like skulls."

"Men of culture and taste," Blays said. "I look forward to meeting them."

Neve ignored him. "How live is this news?"

The scarred ranger shrugged. "Few months."

"Thanks, Bert."

They nodded to each other, then Bert walked off, simple as that, mounted his horse, and rode into the twilight.

"Let me see if I've got this," Dante said. "Sallen's dead, but the band he was a part of — the Jessel — are still here. They may or may not have the axe. And you're going to use that…bone thing to convince them to speak to us?"

"Right," Neve said.

"What, is it sacred or something?"

"It's called a trasser. Have you seen the platforms they put up? With the bodies chained to them?"

"Thanks for the reminder," Blays said. "I'd almost managed to forget them."

"The ones you see out in the open are public. Any war band can use them. But each band keeps a private one just for itself. When one of their warriors acts like a coward, or betrays them, they bring him to their platform. They tie him to it. Spread out his guts. And wait for the drakelets to purify him."

"Enlightened," Dante said.

"The body's left there for at least a year and a day. Depending on how bad his crimes were and thus how much purification the corpse needs, it can take as long as thirteen years. Once the time is up, the band returns to collect his bones. The band's eldest sorcerer treats them, then turns them over to the bonewright, who carves them into trassers. These are sometimes given to someone who's done a good turn for the band as proof they can be trusted. There's no way to counterfeit them because, since each trasser came from the same body, they're all linked to each other. A sorcerer can take a look at the one you've got, compare it to the ones the band kept, and know immediately if it's real. They call that 'bloodsigned.'"

"I don't know whether to be repulsed or fascinated by all that. But what's to stop someone from killing a true friend of the band, looting their trasser, and using it to betray the band?"

"It's something the sorcerer does when they're treating the bones. They make it so the trassers are 'signed' by every owner they have. This includes a mark that indicates whether they gave it willingly to a trusted friend, or whether they just sold it or had it stolen from them."

"How on earth do they manage that?"

She tilted her head at him. "Do I look like a great sorcerer?"

This of course made Dante want to examine the trasser at once, but Neve wouldn't let him touch it, claiming that would corrupt it, and possibly even break its chain of ownership that proved it had always stayed in good hands. They were too close to the valley to risk traveling at dark, so they bedded down.

Feeling as though their task was now infinitely more tackleable, Dante started off in the morning in high spirits. The Red Valley became visible almost at once. While the stone and earth were red enough, it was actually comprised of several long depressions that seemed halfway between valleys and rifts, a blend of rocky ridges, woodlands, and open plains. Dante spotted a few sites that looked like ruins, but didn't see any settlements — although the smoke of camps rose from several of the little forests.

Neve swung around the region's nebulous borders, taking them to where they could reach the Larksbridge, where Bert had last seen the Jessel, while spending the least possible time within the valley proper. Dante's wasps ran steady patrols overhead.

Neve drew to a stop around ten in the morning. "The Larksbridge should be just a few miles due east of here. Can your scouts see it?"

Dante rerouted two of his wasps. They soon picked up the shimmer of a small river running north-south. He sent one scout upstream and one down. The southbound wasp soon came to a half-ruined stone bridge that had been patched over with wood pilings and planks.

"I've got the bridge," Dante said. "But I don't see any savages."

He ran a quick sweep of the land between them and the bridge. This was empty too.

"They might have moved on," Neve said. "We'll plant a flag."

Blays ran his fingers through his hair. "Are we conquering them?"

"Letting them know that if they're nearby, we'd like to talk." She guided her horse eastward into the thickening trees.

"And that's going to work? Aren't these people rampaging marauders? Burning villages, tying people to platforms to be eaten by flying lizards, and so forth? Why would they want to talk to us?"

"For the same reason the rangers do. Information. Which lands are safe and which are ripe for raiding."

Dante pushed a branch out of his way. "What happens if they reject our meeting?"

"We leave as peacefully as we can. But if peace is out of the question, do *not* kill any of them. Or else you'll also kill our chances of ever getting anywhere with them."

Hoofprints of both horses and cows were pressed into the forest floor, but these looked days old. With Dante's wasps circling overhead, they came to the western end of the bridge without seeing a hint of the Jessel.

Neve dismounted onto the mossy-smelling river bank. The waters were blue-green and clear enough to see the bottom except where it ran deepest in the middle. She took a long look around, then stalked over to the base of the oddly-mended bridge. She reached into her pack, did some rummaging, and emerged with a small green flag attached to a short stick as straight as an arrow, which she stuck into a notch in the stone footing. This done, she leaned down and spat on the rock next to the notch, which was worn both by age and by the runes someone had scraped into it long ago, and rubbed it in a circular motion.

She stood. "If the Jessel are nearby, they'll know someone wants to parley." She gestured into the trees. "And in case they'd rather let their arrows do the talking, I suggest we wait over there."

They relocated a few hundred yards back the way they'd come and waited. The forest was very quiet: a bit of a breeze, a few birds singing mysterious songs, a spangling of strange insects.

Dante jerked up his head. "I see movement in the trees. Riders. I can't see—" He swayed back, blinking. "Anything. My scouts just went dead."

"Er," Blays said. "Enemy sorcerer? Or the Golden Stream?"

"It didn't feel like either. Neve, is that the Jessel? How did they do that?"

She shrugged. "If the ramna couldn't stop the gods from spying on them, do you think they'd still be alive?"

"That doesn't answer the question," Dante muttered.

"Well," Blays said. "Should we run?"

"Not yet," Neve said. "But be ready to."

According to her, the protocol around such parleys was that the Jessel—or whichever band had replaced them in this region—would replace her flag in the bridge with one of their own: a white flag if they wished to talk, and a black flag if they didn't. The three of them would wait a while longer to give whoever was responding to their flag enough time to do so, then see which color had been left in the green flag's place.

Feeling rather blind without his flying sets of secondary eyes, Dante swiveled his head from side to side to keep watch the old fashioned way. It didn't do any good. One second, the forest was empty. The next, men on horseback appeared among the trees as if materializing out of thin air.

They bore spears adorned with long yellow pennants. Just as promised, the heads of their horses were decorated with paint and barding to make them look like fleshless skulls. The riders numbered twenty in all—or at least twenty of them had chosen to reveal themselves.

A large man with the bearing of a leader stomped his horse toward them. His face was painted to match his horse's and he had a build that might have made a norren hesitate to square off against him.

He looked them up and down, then snorted. "Godlanders."

"Not exactly." Neve didn't back away, but her voice sounded tight. "You're the Jessel?"

"If you came here to find us, you must be damn sure that you're a friend of us."

"We are." Keeping her eyes on the warrior, Neve reached into an outer pocket of her coat and took out the carved ivory trasser. "This is from the Vastan. It's bloodsigned. You can examine it yourself."

"I do not need to examine it to recognize the tokens of my enemy." His face twisted as if he'd been stabbed. "Kill them all!"

A score of sets of hooves charged toward them.

7

The ramna warriors screamed as they rushed in from all sides. Dante's eyes flew wide. Not expecting the encounter, he hadn't scratched himself, and had to bite the inside of his mouth. As soon as he tasted the cut-copper tang of blood, he sucked the nether to his hands.

As long as they didn't have a sorcerer hidden among them, it wouldn't have been any challenge to kill every one of the Jessel. But as Neve believed, with some reason, that killing the Jessel would also kill their chances of finding Gashen's axe, Dante would have to resort to less assured methods.

A pair of spears was already flying at his chest. He blasted them apart. This by itself would have caused any normal warriors to break and retreat, but the Jesselmen just grimaced at their poor fortune.

With a woody crackle, Dante harvested the trees in front of four of the riders, sending their horses crashing into a fence of green branches. Two others were drawing arrows, which made them look very stupid when he sent two small crescent-shaped blades of nether slicing through the strings of their bows just as the men tried to nock arrows to them.

Dant wheeled to follow Blays and Neve, who were tearing off to the north, then reached into the dirt behind him to rip open a pit in front of a pair of other riders, who obliged him by stumbling into it. The ramna were lining up behind them in pursuit and Dante was starting to feel pretty good about his chances of tripping or entangling them all when he had his horse shot out from under him.

His horse screamed. He might have too, but it was hard to say because the world seemed to be spinning around him. He came down in a pile of leaves and twigs. There seemed to be some extremely bright stars mixed in among them, too, but these faded a second or two later.

Dante got to his feet. His horse was struggling to do the same, but an arrow was wagging from its chest. He slapped his palm to the beast's front, ducking its jerking head and getting sprayed in the face with its froth, and sent the nether into it. The arrow popped from its chest like a pustule. Yet this only seemed to terrify the horse even more. It pushed itself to its feet and dashed away before he could grab the reins.

Hoofs pounded behind him. The ramna were charging him, spears lowered. Snarling their path wasn't going to do any good now that he couldn't outrun them. He brought a dust devil of shadows to him, not certain he'd have time to knock all the riders down before one of them got to him.

A horse flashed past him. Blays was hunched low in the saddle, both of his Odo Sein swords angled to the sides, their steel alight with excited nether. He gave a yell and raced straight into the enemy vanguard. A Jessel warrior went flying, neatly separated into two equal pieces.

Neve had turned around and was streaking toward Dante, motioning that he should jump up and get behind her in the saddle. But a new force of Jessel streamed from the woods to cut them off, launching a volley of arrows at Neve. She threw up her arm in surprise, coat flapping; by sheer luck or poor aim, none of the missiles hit her, but she had to veer away, leaving Dante alone.

Deprived of their target, this new wave of riders homed in on him instead, leveling spears and cocking back axes. He swore, deeply tempted to blast them into a horizontal red rain, but settled once more for locking them behind a dense wall of harvested branches. Horses screamed as they plowed into the new growth. Men yelled out and hacked at it with their axes.

Dante spun about. During his brief distraction, Blays had been dehorsed as well—the animal was nowhere to be seen—and was currently cutting a Jesselman down from his mount. The body hadn't even hit the ground before Blays charged forward at the pair of riders coming in behind the man he'd just killed.

Dante reached for the nether. Behind the front lines, the skull-painted leader watched, motionless. Something about the pleased smile on his face made Dante hesitate. Blays' crackling blades spun through the air, knocking another rider down to the dirt. The other warrior jabbed a spear toward Blays' back, but Blays juked to the side, as if he could feel the iron point coming for him, and leaped up the horse's flank, skewering the rider through the ribs.

Blays kicked off from the beast's flank and dashed toward the next batch of Jesselmen. They were looking much stonier-faced about their prospects than when the conflagration had begun.

"Stop!"

This came from the skull-faced commander. Blays paid it no heed, but the warriors halted their horses, straightening their spears to the sky and lowering their axes to their sides. Blays glanced side to side and pulled up short. Neve trotted back toward Dante and came to a stop. The grounds were completely still except for the dance of the nethereal lightning up and down the Odo Sein steel.

Blays raised his eyebrow at the commander. "Yes?"

The man was no longer smiling. Beneath the white paint on his face, he looked bemused. "What are you doing?"

"I'd say I'm kicking your asses."

"You'd fight us alone? With no horse?"

"You didn't bring enough men for me to need more."

The commander folded his arms, tapping his elbow with rough, scarred fingers. "My name is Dasya, and by that name I grant you two questions."

Dante furrowed his brow. "What is going—?"

Neve reached down from her saddle and slapped him across the face. "Shut it! He means what he says—two questions only, so make them count." She drew herself up, suddenly rigid. "They're not for you, anyway. They're for Blays."

"About time someone recognized my great wisdom." Blays eyed the other Jesselmen, then put away his swords. He met eyes with Dasya. "Do you know where the axe of Gashen is?"

The warrior narrowed his eyes, then shook his head. "No, godlander."

Blays lowered his chin, thinking over his one remaining question. "Do you know who might know where it is?"

"I know of no living man who knows that."

"Ah. Well, that's all we came here to ask. So it seems to me there's two things we can do from here. We can shake hands and go our separate still-alive ways. Or we can pick up where we left off. I have to warn you, though, we were doing our best *not* to kill you."

Dasya straightened in the saddle, holding his right arm at an angle from his side. He gazed across his men, considering what order to give them.

He turned back to Blays and grinned. "You have right spirit. You can leave. But you will not come back."

"But I'll miss your hospitality so much. Now where did my horse go?"

He kept one eye on the Jessel as he moved to fetch his mount. Dante moved to one of the men Blays had gored, who'd looked plenty dead a minute ago, but was now doing some twitching and half-conscious moaning. Dante drew a handful of nether, about to apply it to the man's gory chest wound.

Dasya jumped down from his horse. "Stop what you are doing!"

"I'm not going to hurt him," Dante said. "I'm trying to heal him."

"That is why I say do not touch him!"

Dante squinted. "Do you see all that blood there? You may not be a trained physician, but he needs that inside him."

"Then he will die. But if his spirit is strong, he will not. Why are you godlanders so afraid to pass into the afterlife your own masters created for you?"

"We're not 'godlanders.'"

Dasya snorted. "Well you're not one of us. What else is left?"

"That's what I tried to tell you earlier," Neve said. "These two aren't from any of the Realms. They're from the Fallen Land."

The warrior swung up his head. "What?"

"They're not your enemy. In fact, you have enemies in common."

"How is that so?"

"There's no point," Dante said. "We came here to find the axe. We have to keep searching for it within the valley, but you have my word we won't trouble you."

"Your word?" Dasya spoke this like it was holy, but then gave a hard shake of his head. "No. You came to *my* land. I will know why."

"Again, there's no —"

Blays waved a hand. "Oh, what's it matter what you tell him? Do you really think these skull-worshipping nomads are about to sell us out to Taim?"

Dante spent a moment determining what exactly he could divulge. "An ancient sorcerer has returned to our lands. He's wildly dangerous. He's already brought down two peoples and he intends to destroy all the others as well. As it is, we can't stop him. The only thing that *might* be able to stop him is the Spear of Stars. We came here to win it from the gods—but they're refusing to let us try. We have reason to believe that retrieving Gashen's axe will change that. That's what's brought us to your lands."

Dasya's eyes were nearly as pale as the White Lich's and as he listened to this they stayed as flat as a pond. "These are lies. God-tricks. You're a pawn of Gashen sent here to fetch his precious axe."

Dante nodded to Blays. "Show him the shard."

Blays shrugged off the pack he'd been carrying it in ever since acquiring it. He removed a cloth bundle and carefully unwrapped it—revealing the pearly purity of the third of the blade.

Dasya leaned over it, its celestial lights reflecting in his eyes. "How did you get this?"

Blays picked up the piece for a better look. "I beat Carvahal in a fight."

"You claim you battled Carvahal? And *won*?"

"Well, it was a duel. There were rules and things. Otherwise he probably would have had a better chance against me."

The warrior swung his head toward Neve. "Is this true?"

She tilted back her head and set her hand to the base of her throat. "Cut me dead if it isn't."

Dasya gazed at the ground, heavy brow wrinkled in thought. "I feel there is something wrong about you. Something that can best be cured by the blade of an axe." He grinned at his men. "But if you can cause this much trouble for the gods, then I will be happy to turn your wrongness against them instead."

Dasya and the Jesselmen led them deeper into the Red Valley.

After a few minutes, Dante leaned closer to Neve. "I get why Dasya agreed to help us: the gods have been rude to his people, so he and his people are inclined to be rude to the gods, and useful to anyone who means to do likewise. But why did he call his warriors off Blays?"

"You heard what Dasya said," she said. "Blays showed good spirit."

"By killing Dasya's countrymen. Typically, that's the sort of thing that makes you want to kill your enemy *more*."

"There's nothing more important to the ramna than right spirit. Along with their horses and cattle, that's all they have."

During the skirmish, there had looked to be no more than fifty Jessel riders. As it turned out, there were in fact several *hundred* of them concealed in the woods. As they rode on to their unknown destination—Dasya had refused to answer where they were going—some bled away from the main group, either to tend to temporary encampments of well-insulated tents, or just to roam about as they would. Nearly every one of them carried a bull's horn decorated with personalized glyphs.

"I feel like I've asked this a dozen times since entering the Realm," Blays said, "but it's a really good question, so I'm going to keep asking it."

Dante glanced toward Dasya. "Could this be a trap?"

"That's the one."

Neve waved off a fly that wouldn't quit dogging her. "Does it feel like one?"

"Not really," Blays said. "But a good trap never feels like one, either."

"In my experience, most aren't designed that way from the start. *Most* traps happen when you want something so bad that you'll ignore every sign of doubt or danger."

"Ah, so we're screwed then."

"In your experience," Dante said. "Just how old are you, anyway?"

Neve smiled. "Older than I look."

She wouldn't say more.

Dasya brought them along a ridge overlooking a small valley. Riders grazed their horses below. They were not Jessel. The two groups shouted insults and jibes at each other, and one of the Jessel went so far as to stand in the saddle and moon the second band. Dante drew the nether to him, but neither group seemed interested in an actual fight. If anything, the shouting seemed almost ritualized.

They left the valley behind and came to an open plateau. Dasya surveyed it, then led them across it at a quick trot.

Whatever danger he was expecting didn't manifest, however, and once they were a short ways into the woods on the other side, he ordered a short break. Just as Dante decided it was time to get some answers from the commander, Dasya shouted them onward again.

Dante trotted over to him anyway, ignoring the hard looks of the warriors at the commander's side, as the warriors appeared stern even when they were waving their naked asses at someone. Dasya glanced at him, but said nothing.

"Hello," Dante said. "Can I ask where we're going?"

"Why ask if you have permission to ask a thing? It's cowardly."

"Other people—less enlightened than yourselves, to be sure —sometimes consider it polite."

"These others are cowards. For you've now already asked the thing. Your words just make it pretend that you haven't."

Dante bit his tongue. "So where *are* we going?"

"To speak with Sallen. If I am able."

"Sallen? But he's dead."

Dasya's voice plummeted to a low growl. "Are you calling me a liar?"

"*You?* Not at all. On our way here, we spoke to another ranger. He claimed Sallen died years ago."

"But I already told your friend that I know no living man who knows where the axe might lie."

Feeling like the wrong word might provoke a sudden flurry of arrows and spears, Dante took a moment to think this through. "Sallen *is* dead. But you're going to speak to him despite his regrettable condition."

Dasya nodded, mollified. "If I am able."

"How are you going to do that?"

"It's none of your business, outlander."

"Can I—" Dante cut himself short. "How did Sallen come by Gashen's axe in the first place?"

"He stole it from the bastard Carvahal."

"That's what Carvahal said, although in slightly different terms. I was wondering about the specifics."

He didn't really expect an answer, at least not a useful one, but Dasya cleared his throat, uttered a few words under his breath, and launched into a story about how Sallen, Prince of the Jessel, came to learn that Carvahal had stolen the axe in secret from Gashen. Dasya's words sounded almost like poetry, or perhaps more like a chant: Dante was almost certain that, rather than retelling the gist of a story he'd heard elsewhere, Dasya was reciting a precise version of the tale he'd committed to memory.

According to this story, Sallen, being among the cleverest of their people to ever ride through the grass, immediately saw an opportunity to put this knowledge to use. He schemed to take the axe, prove that Carvahal was the thief, and therefore stir up trouble between the two gods. With the way Gashen loved his axe, Sallen hoped it would be enough to provoke him to declare war on Carvahal, a conflict that the Jessel and other ramna could exploit to raid or even invade the gods' kingdoms.

Sallen knew that Carvahal was too good at thieving to be stolen from himself. At least not within his own palace, which was where he was keeping the axe. So Sallen set in motion a plot to convince Carvahal that Gashen already knew that Carvahal had the axe, and was coming to get it back. Thinking himself clever, Carvahal had the axe sent away from his palace, ordering it be taken to a set of catacombs beneath an ancient monastery he assumed no one knew about.

Sallen knew all about it, though, and personally led a daring raid on the axe's handlers, slaying them and taking the axe back with him to the Red Valley. He was thus positioned to turn the gods against each other—but Carvahal was just as savvy as everyone said, and had placed an enchantment on the axe allowing him to see who had taken it from him. Before Gashen arrived, he came up with a way to blame the original theft on Sallen, which was rather easy to do now that the axe was in Sallen's hands.

But there was still no guarantee Gashen would buy it. Or he might decide they were both lying and in need of punishment. After a great deal of threats to Sallen, and with Gashen mere hours away, Carvahal offered to let Sallen keep the axe as long as Sallen quit using it to scheme against him. Sallen suspected an ulterior motive, but also recognized two things: first, he could use the axe to smite his foes. And second, it wasn't the best thing in the world to have a god for a personal enemy. He agreed to the deal.

"For once, Carvahal was good for his word," Dasya said. "The conflict was forgotten. Sallen kept the axe, and used it to raid and destroy other ramna. But one day, years later, it was lost."

"How?"

"That is what we go to find out."

They were soon blindfolded. Dante was tempted to cheat by trying to reanimate a new set of scouts, but resisted the urge, keeping his senses in the nether instead. This provided quite the distraction: the nether continued to feel more *intense* than it did in his own world, particularly when he looked at it closely. At the same time, whatever the differences, they were too subtle for him to tease out the details or causes.

He could tell when they entered another clearing by the shift in sound from the rustle of leaves to the hiss of grass, and also by the way the sun smelled on that grass. Then came shade, but not the kind cast by trees. Like that of city buildings, although he didn't think there *were* any buildings here, so more likely canyon walls. The Jessel traveled without the need for any words at all, like they weren't even human, but a stream of water following the natural contours of the land.

Again without the need for words, the band came to a stop. Hooves shuffled next to Dante; the blindfold was lifted from his eyes. He squinted against the sudden light, although it wasn't very bright at all.

"Please tell me you haven't taken us to yet another world," Blays said.

"We remain in the Red Valley," Dasya said. "But here is where the beyond comes closest to us."

Massive bones rose from the red dirt like curved pillars, bending together thirty feet above them. They ran a hundred feet or more from front to back and their high arches looked like nothing less than the ceiling of a cathedral. Dante's first instinct was that it was a thing like Barden, bones grown into a shape all unnatural for them—but other than their size, the anatomy of these bones *was* natural.

They stood inside the skeleton of the largest animal he had ever seen.

Neve turned in a circle, head tipped back at the "ceiling." "I don't like this place."

"This is what you asked for." Dasya got down from his horse.

Dante didn't know Dasya's official rank, but he was at the very least a soldier in possession of his own horse, and was likely a lieutenant or even a chieftain of some kind. In Narashtovik, Mallon, and nearly every other land Dante had ever seen, a groom or servant would have hurried up to lead the beast away and tend to it while its master conducted his lordly business. But there seemed to be none of that here; Dasya, despite his authority, was expected to take care of his horse by himself.

Could it be that no one was acting as his squire because *every* ramna man was a warrior? The thought seemed impossible: most men *weren't* born soldiers, and only some fraction more could be trained into it. Beyond that, if every man and even some of the women were warriors, how did they get anything else done?

Unless, of course, warring was all the ramna did.

Beyond the bones, canyon walls rose tight around them, with thick hedges and trees lining the upper ledges, casting the canyon in shadow. There was a sort of "cave" at the far end of the skeletal cathedral, which was of course the inside of the dead beast's skull. Its clenched teeth were as long as Dante's arm.

The floor of the skull was set with squat, low stone cylinders arranged in a circle. Dante could tell at a glance there were thirteen of them rather than the twelve used to represent the Celeset. They were carved with glyphs and scenes of battle. A wider stone was set in the center of the circle, its top shallowly concave.

Dasya turned and gazed across his men. "We need an eye."

Barely a blink of silence passed before one of the warriors stepped forward. There was gray at his temples and across most of his beard. "I will give it."

"Branya?"

"I'm growing old, aren't I? Too old for battle."

"You are far from too old. You could fight for centuries more."

The graying warrior shook his head. "It's not time that has made me too old. It's the wounds that come from time."

"Your hip. The blow you took last winter."

Branya nodded. "It never fully healed. And it is only one of many in my many years. I've done my best to hide my weakness, but in the forge of battle, all weakness is exposed. If I fight much longer, I'll get one of you killed — or much more than one. Let me make this last offering, then leave to tend to the cattle instead."

The corners of Dasya's eyes crinkled in pain, but he nodded. "Your arms weaken. But your wisdom strengthens. After this, you may retire. Not to become a shepherd of cattle — but to become a shepherd to my warriors, who will need your knowledge and your counsel."

There was a rumble of approval from across the band. Branya smiled, if grimly, and dropped to one knee beside the stone bowl. Dasya drew a short, thin knife, braced Branya's head with his other hand, and leveled the knife in front of the older man's left eye.

Dante's eyes widened. "What are you doing?"

Dasya didn't look his way. "What you requested of us."

"That's his eye!"

"The cost of speech is sight. This is the only way we can speak to the last of our people who saw Gashen's axe."

Of all the horrific injuries a person could suffer, total eyeball trauma was among Dante's most hated to witness, and he would have turned away if not for his certainty the Jessel would judge him for doing so. Dasya was quick, though, mercifully quick, and soon cast the goop upon the carved stones.

He turned back to Branya, setting his hand on the man's shoulder and touching their foreheads together. "Thank you, brother."

Branya nodded, but he was deathly pale and breathing so fast Dante suspected he was moments from passing out.

Dante gestured to the man's bloody face. "Can I at least heal him?"

Dasya straightened. "Pain is meant to be endured. But Branya offered his sacrifice believing there would be no salve to his pain. Therefore his will was true. You may heal him."

Branya held up a bloody hand as if to ward Dante off, but Dante ignored this. He summoned the nether and lifted his hand to the warrior's face. Shadows swooped and danced around the gruesome wound.

The bleeding slowed, then stopped. Fast as a striking snake, Branya grabbed Dante's wrist. "We've given blood for you. The bond is made. Dare to break it, and your own blood will be cursed."

Dante continued his work. "If you've turned your back on the gods, who do you expect to curse me?"

"Your adsal."

"My what?"

Branya stormed to his feet. "Your adsal!"

Dante cocked his head, utterly clueless as to why the warrior was so worked up and whether to pursue it.

Neve stepped in beside him. "Your adsal. Your soul-beyond-self."

"Ohh, my *adsal*."

After another moment's thought, he was actually quite curious if this was a reference to the trace and remnant, but Dasya was beginning a ritual of some kind, which he did not want to miss. To his surprise, nether was streaking toward the sacrificial eye in the stone bowl. Yet Dasya didn't appear to be summoning or shaping it in any way. At least not through any skill Dante was aware of. Instead he was chanting, a stream of words that rose and fell in pitch, rhythmic and mesmerizing, and though Dante had understood the language wherever he'd traveled within the Realm of Nine Kings, Dasya's words seemed to slip through Dante's mind like trout through a child's hands.

He was left with only vague impressions: a man alone at night on horseback, silent lightning flashing behind him. The same man dashing through a pounded-down wall with a torch in his hand, blood on his teeth as he grinned, a virgin city help-less before him. Then a river not unlike the one spanned by the Larksbridge, but untouched by any human life or structure, fish drifting in the perfect clarity of the waters.

A vertical line formed above the stone bowl, which was now empty; soon the line expanded horizontally as well. A doorway. Darkness behind it, the pinpricks of what looked like stars.

Before Dante could get a better look at what lay on the other side, a man stepped forth from beyond.

8

The man from beyond the doorway was dressed much like the other Jessel—hardened leathers, braced here and there with bone and iron—but his armor was trimmed with fur and decorated with claws and teeth. He was bearded and his eyes burned with inner authority. He looked almost corporeal, but portions of his body shimmered like oil in the sun, and an ethereal light seemed to come and go from beneath his skin.

Dasya kneeled. So did every other member of the Jessel. Dante did the same.

"Descendants," the man rumbled. "You have made yourselves many. This is pleasing."

"Longprince Sallen," Dasya said, still kneeling. "We have come to seek your knowledge. It's on a matter that has been lost to us. A matter that—"

"Waste no more words. You have brought me here for but a blink. My realm will bring me back within minutes."

Dasya stood, nodding. "What became of the axe of Gashen, ancestor?"

Sallen grunted, then laughed, sounding surprised by his own reaction, and grunted once more. "That blasted axe. It hasn't been of any use to anyone for many years. That's why you know nothing more of it."

"But it's of great importance to the outlanders we've brought to witness."

The half-spectral warrior gazed at Dante, Blays, and Neve. He did not look impressed. "Who are they to deserve the knowledge I died with?"

"The story is too long to be told. But take my word: they mean to cause much mischief for the deceitful heavens."

"I hear your word." Sallen inhaled deeply, exhaling throughout his nose. "It was after a battle in the Bluewood. We were drinking and I was boasting because it was my right to boast after what I had done in the battle. To the others, I told them my axe—Gashen's axe—could cut anything if I swung it hard enough. Urman, a chief of the Kranda, who were then our allies, denied that this was so. I insisted that it *was* so. He challenged me to cut down the Iron-Oak and made a wager of it: if I could cut the tree, I could choose eighty of his best cattle and any four of his horses besides the one he had rode that day. If I could not make my boast true, I would give him the axe.

"I feared nothing could fell the Iron-Oak. I also feared being made to look foolish and weak. Lost in my cups, I feared that latter weakness more. I agreed to Urman's wager. The next morning, we left the Bluewood and set out for the Iron-Oak. Though the axe never lost its edge, I spent most of the journey trying to sharpen it.

"We came to the Iron-Oak. I knocked on it with my fist and it rang in response. When Urman heard the sound, his laughter rang, too. But my anger at his mockery only strengthened my arms. I hefted Gashen's axe—*my* axe—and swung as hard as I could. The blow made the tree ring again—but it also made it crack.

"The axe had bitten into the trunk. Now it was my turn to laugh, and Urman's time to go silent, to dwell on the livestock he was about to lose to me. I swung again and I made my swing even harder than the first. Again I heard the ring and the crack as the axe took its bite. But when I tried to pull it loose, the axe stuck fast.

"Urman began to regain his color. 'It looks like the Iron-Oak has taken a bite from your axe!' Furious, I heaved on the haft. It would not budge, but I heaved anew and once more. With another ring — another crack — the axe sprung free.

"But the head fell in two parts to the ground. And a third part remained lodged in the tree. The Iron-Oak *had* taken its bite, and the axe was broken." Sallen laughed, shaking his head. "Urman declared victory. I gave him the two fallen pieces and told him the third stuck in the tree was his for the claiming. But he could no more dislodge the third piece from the Iron-Oak than I could cut the Iron-Oak down. So I left with nothing, and he left with trash. I do not know who got the better part of the deal. That is the story of the end of the axe of Gashen."

Dasya pressed his fist to his mouth, clearing his throat, then gave up and burst into laughter. "Why did you hide this story from us?"

Sallen glared at him. "My boastfulness and fear lost me Gashen's axe. I was ashamed."

"It is not a shameful story. It is a funny one!"

"It wasn't when it happened!" The dead warrior softened, if grudgingly. "But it is true that many of the stories that seem tragic when we first set them into song sound much funnier when time has caused their pains to fade."

"The chip in the axe that got stuck in the tree," Dante said. "Is it still there?"

Sallen shrugged; for an instant, his whole form flickered before regaining its mostly corporeal state. "The Iron-Oak couldn't even be cut with the axe of Gashen. How would anyone have gotten the chip out?"

"Then we have to find the tree."

"Why? Even if you find it, the axe is worthless."

"Maybe not to Gashen. And if I can find the chip, I can find the rest of the axe, too. So where is the Iron-Oak?"

Sallen flickered again, disappearing completely, just as a guttering candle would, before returning. "I have no time left. Dasya, do you recall the Saga of the Five Hands?"

"We don't need more stories," Dante said as fast as he could. "All we need to know is..."

But Sallen vanished. A wisp of nether rose from where he'd been, like smoke from a snuffed candle.

"Son of a bitch." Dante spun on Dasya. "Tell me you know where this Iron-Oak is."

"I don't." The warrior lifted his voice to his men. "Do any of you?"

He was met with silence and shaking heads.

Dante thumped his fist against his thigh. "Son of a son of a bitch! We were this close to finding the axe."

Blays folded his arms. "What if we use the stream? Try to catch a Glimpse of Sallen's chopping-contest and see where it took place?"

"We know so little about him and this valley, it would be a one-in-a-million chance to run down the exact moment that happened. Anyway, I haven't been able to access the stream since we got here."

"Yeah, me neither."

"Then why did you think I could?"

"Because you're not me. And thank the gods for that."

"You cry about everything," Dasya said, lightly contemptuous. "Sallen told us how to find the Iron-Oak."

Dante gritted his teeth. "You just told me you didn't know where it was."

"I don't. But the Saga of Five Hands does." He lowered his head, brow crinkling. The other warriors all turned to face him. Not quite singing, not quite chanting, Dasya recited:

The vale where the Needle of Heaven emerges,
And points to the north like the spear of a victor;
This guided the band to the Tunnel of Groaning
And into the gray of the forest beyond. To
The oak that repelled their axes like iron.

"That is the path the Band of Five Hands took to the Iron-Oak," Dasya concluded. "We will do the same."

Dante's heart lifted. "And you know where this Needle of Heaven is?"

"No. But I expect we will find it within a day."

Dante's heart sank beneath the lowly position it had occupied previously. But Dasya headed to his horse full of purpose and rode north like he knew exactly where he was going, which salvaged Dante's spirits somewhat.

As soon as he spotted more wasps, he struck them dead and reanimated them. But he'd hardly sent them into the sky before they dropped inert, his connection to them severed.

"Tell your sorcerer to stop that already," he told Dasya.

Dasya glanced over his shoulder. "Sorcerer? We have no sorcerer with us now."

Dante swore and slowed his horse to bring himself next to Neve. "Is there one of the...doorways near here? That lead to the Mists?"

"In the Red Valley? I don't think so," she said. "Then again, the constant occupation of the valley by the ramna means there's much about it that non-ramna know nothing about."

Dante found himself cut off from his undead scouts, but Dasya had plenty of living ones, and sent them ranging ahead. For all their effort, dusk came without them having found any hint of the Needle of Heaven. Dasya called for his warriors to make camp, which they did with disciplined speed. Tents seemed to pitch themselves; fires lit up from the ground. Men roasted meat on spits and in deep pans. It smelled like rabbit and venison, but Dante wasn't entirely sure that it was. Every military unit he'd witnessed had rationed out food based on rank, but all of the Jessel looked to be eating the same things and in the same quantities.

"Now," Dasya said once things were winding down. "You will tell us a story of yourself."

Dante swallowed a bite of the grainy and unknown root vegetable he'd been eating. "You already know the basics. There's a hyper-powerful sorcerer looking to exterminate everyone in the world and replace them with his own creations."

"I have no interest in that story. It isn't done yet and you will probably fail and be disgraced and the tale will be of no use but as a warning to others. I want to hear of a past triumph. A victory!"

"I suppose we've had a few of those. Why?"

Dasya threw the bone he'd been cleaning the meat from into the darkness beyond the fire. "If I don't know of your deeds and valor, how can I fully trust you? How can I be sure that you are even worth being helped?"

"That might have been worth figuring out *before* we started gallivanting around the forest talking to ghosts. Let me think."

He did so, then began to tell the tale of the time Cally had assigned him and Blays to investigate a series of killings in Narashtovik—killings which were rumored to be the work of a werewolf. Dante liked the story because it was both funny and sad, but Dasya looked confused, then visibly displeased.

"What is this?" the man interrupted after a minute. "Why are you telling it like that?"

"Well, you see, because that's how it happened."

"I mean how you *talk*. You talk like you are telling me how you woke up in the morning. Stories of spirit must be *voiced* with spirit. They should sound almost like a song. Like the part of the Saga of Five Hands I told to you."

"Like a poem? That's what you're expecting from me?"

"Yes."

"Are *you* a poet?"

"If you asked me what I am, I wouldn't say that I am a poet. But poetry is one of the skills I must command. I can tell by your face that this baffles you! How can you possibly rule if you are not a poet?"

"Because my kingdom isn't run on a legal system of rhyming verse."

"But how can you lead when you can't speak words that let your people understand who they are and what they do? That inspire them to achieve even more glories worthy of poem and song?"

"By being extremely good at everything else I do," Dante said.

"Lyle's balls." Blays wiped his mouth with the back of his hand and got to his feet. "Just don't think so much about it. Here, listen to this."

He launched into the telling of their first real journey together: when Cally had dispatched them to Narashtovik to assassinate Samarand. He left out a lot—including a lot of the parts Dante thought were most interesting—and the meter of his verse was far from perfect. But it was mostly right about on, astoundingly so given that he was making it up on the spot, and as Blays went on, Dante found himself less and less distracted by quibbles and more lost in the story.

"In days come after, I couldn't say if we'd been used for good or evil," Blays said as he brought the tale to a close. "But even if the act itself was fraught with malice, splendor grew from bleakest soil."

He bobbed his head and sat.

Dasya stared into the fire, frowning deeply. Without looking away from the flames, he said, "It is hard to condemn anyone deceived by the superiors they placed their faith in. That you survived such deceit when you were also so young shows high spirit. Especially when it was just the two of you, with no band of warriors to stand fast at your side. You make me wish to someday fight beside you, Blays Buckler."

"Don't get too hasty," Blays said. "The only thing more dangerous than fighting by our side is being a rat who's wandered in front of Dante."

The other warriors rumbled their approval. It felt as if they'd passed some kind of test, which Dante supposed was good. But he was mostly thinking about all the victories — or at least escapes — he and Blays had pulled off in the past. At the time, nearly all of them had felt unlikely, if not downright impossible. Yet they'd survived each one.

He supposed that should hearten him toward their quest to find the spear. But something about this time felt different. For they were much further from home — and far more alone — than even on that early day they had been sent to the north to murder a stranger.

"Just as the saga said." Dasya pointed ahead. "There! The Needle of Heaven."

As they approached it, the Needle looked like an ordinary spur of rock extending from the flank of a short mountain. As they swung around its northern face, however, the reason for its name became clear: when viewed head-on, its connection to the mountain was hidden, and the spur looked like a spindly natural tower reaching hundreds of feet into the sky.

Dante set his back to it. "Which means the Groaning Tunnel should be this way."

"And it will still be there in an hour," Dasya declared. "So we will rest now, and reflect on our achievement here."

Dante resented taking what seemed like a wholly unnecessary break, given that it wasn't yet the afternoon, but on the other hand, they'd reached the Needle just as Dasya had predicted, and without any trouble along the way. So he passed the hour-long rest swapping stories with Branya, who seemed eager to recount his life as a warrior now that he was about to retire from active fighting.

Branya didn't know exactly how long he'd been alive—apparently the ramna didn't really count years, per se, but "significant events," which nearly always involved fighting of some kind, be it raids of other bands over cattle, wives, honor, grazing land, and so forth; or even better, raids, skirmishes, battles, and outright war against the "godlanders." Dante got the impression Branya had been alive for at least two and possibly three centuries, which given all the aforementioned warring was quite long-lived for the ramna.

Branya's tales of constant roaming and fighting reminded Dante of the last two-plus years of his own life. He could hardly conceive of building an entire *culture* around such nonstop motion, unsettlement, and chaos. Yet despite their bitter enmity toward the gods that had forced such a way of life on them, the ramna, or at least the Jessel, seemed to love it.

Dasya called for the journey to resume. The land north of the Needle of Heaven was criss-crossed with streams and flooded with patches of standing water that made for slow going for the horses. Even so, there were two hours of daylight left when Dasya's scouts crowed that they'd located the Groaning Tunnel.

The scouts were rewarded with an extremely potent cider, which they drank in the saddle as the main body of riders converged on the Groaning Tunnel. This turned out to be a cavern in the base of a very rough block of bluish stone, a few hundred feet high and miles wide, that looked like it had fallen out of the sky and landed in the middle of the wetlands. As they neared the cavern, the sound of low, hollow moaning carried across the damp air.

Dante stopped his horse a stone's throw away from it. "Is it actually groaning?"

"Very confusing for these people to go and name a thing after what it does," Blays said.

"Well, it's probably just the wind."

"Or a monster so big its breath sounds like the wind. I vote Neve goes first. As our guide, it's only fair."

Neve gave him a look. "Are all Fallen Landers this chivalrous?"

"Maybe this whole rock is the beast and the tunnel is its mouth. It looks pretty out of place here, doesn't it?"

Dante knew this couldn't be true, but felt compelled to reach out into the stone and confirm that it was in fact stone and not flesh. "Dasya, is this passage dangerous?"

"That is likely so," Dasya said. "Most things in the Red Valley that weren't dangerous were killed long ago by those things that are."

So far Dante hadn't seen much in the valley of much danger other than the ramna bands themselves, yet something told him to be wary. "For all the roaming about you people do, you don't seem to know the land all that well."

"We know our land like you know your skin," Dasya said, clearly insulted. "And we know this land is bad. That is why we don't come to it."

Dante frowned at the entrance another moment, then conjured some ether and cast it inside the entry. It illuminated what appeared to be a perfectly normal cave. It smelled mildly dank but pretty clean by the standards of caverns, which tended to be fouled by bats and other unsavory things. Still, the impression of wrongness hit him as strongly as any smell of rot. But maybe that was just his memory of Talassa.

He thought about searching around for some mice to kill and send in first, but knowing the Jessel would scorn him for that, he drew a knife and scratched his arm. Dasya watched this with curiosity and approval. Dante sheathed his arms in nether and walked forward. Blays loosened his swords and followed at his side.

"Be careful," Neve said from behind them.

Dante turned. "What makes you say that?"

"Because you should be careful."

Blays and Dante entered the passage. Their footsteps echoed hollowly. Water dripped from somewhere ahead. The tunnel was still groaning, the sound rising and falling, but Dante didn't feel any wind on his face. Just as an experiment, he reached into the stone, attempted to manipulate it, and found that he could. *Not* like Talassa, then.

The groaning stopped.

So did Blays. "What did you just do?"

"Nothing."

"Yes you did. I felt you *fiddling around* with something."

"I was just testing if I could move the rock if I needed to. You know, like if it started collapsing or — "

A great clunk reverberated from the entrance, which seemed to have disappeared. The ground moved underfoot, sending Dante reeling; his stomach lurched downward like when his horse made a mighty leap.

"The ceiling's coming down on us!" Blays yelled over the grinding of rock.

"No it isn't. The floor's coming *up* on us."

"Well do something before we get chewed!" Blays threw himself flat.

Dante rolled onto his back, plunging his mind into the rock. "We're both wrong. The floor *and* the ceiling are coming together!"

They were already less than six feet apart and closing fast. No time to run. Dust and pebbles rained to the floor. Dante sank his mind into the stone above and below them. It resisted him like it was trying to spit him out or push him through a door. He yelled out loud, bulling past its efforts and tearing the earth away.

Ahead and behind them, the tunnel banged shut like the closing of a stone mouth. Leaving them trapped inside a hollow barely big enough to fit the both of them.

"Congratulations," Blays said, voice squeezed tight by the tiny space. "You've fitted us with a very nice coffin."

Dante sneezed stone dust, causing him to jerk his head upward and bonk his forehead against the ceiling. He muttered something unkind and returned his focus to the stone. It seemed to have gone still, momentarily stable, and so he dived as deep as he could into the resistance he'd felt when trying to manipulate it.

And his blood froze in his veins.

It was more than resistance. It was a *presence*. Certainly not human, and perhaps not even sentient, yet something far more alive than the simple nether he normally felt within the earth.

Dante rushed at it bearing a vision—almost more of a pure sense—of himself reaching deep into it on all sides, liquefying it, ripping it apart, shredding it into dust, and casting that dust to the wind.

The presence pushed against him. Felt his power to do exactly what he threatened. And withdrew.

With a whoosh of air, the tunnel retracted, ceiling and floor parting from each other. The passage began to groan again, though much more subdued. Dante got to one knee. Another few moments, and the tunnel was high enough for him to stand.

Blays craned his neck. "How'd you do that?"

"Just fiddled around with something."

With a soft jolt, the tunnel returned to its initial position. Dante reached out for the presence, but it had retreated too far into the rock for him to find it.

"I think we're all right for the moment," he said. "Now let's get through here before the tunnel changes its mind."

"Changes its mind? Tell me that's just a figure of speech."

"You really don't want to know."

They jogged back toward the entrance. Outside, Neve looked spooked; Dasya looked angry, even affronted.

"What happened?" he demanded. "The tunnel closed!"

"That's exactly what happened," Dante said.

"But you survived!"

"You might look like a wild barbarian," Blays said. "But your keen insight is matched only by your taste in face skulls."

Dasya glowered at him, then broke into laughter. "Then lead us through."

Dante hopped up on his horse, a move he was getting better at. "You're not afraid it's going to try to crush us again?"

"Why would I be afraid of the tunnel when you have already dominated it?"

That was a surprisingly convincing argument, and Dante led the way down the tunnel with a lightness in his heart he hadn't felt for some time. The tunnel was still droning on to itself and he kept his attention firmly placed within the stony walls. A couple minutes later, sunlight glowed ahead. Dante came to the exit and waited there like a sentry until all of the others were through.

"There!" Dasya gestured ahead of them. "I would say that the saga continues to lead us true."

They stood within a forest, though a startling one. Both leaves and bark were gray, the gray of ashes. The effect was disturbing to the eye, as if the entire forest had died to a fire and never recovered, or like it had somehow had its very soul sucked from it, as if by an immense vegetarian vampire. Yet it otherwise looked normal, with very average bees buzzing among the gray flowers, and very typical birds chirping from the gray branches.

Dasya retook the lead. As soon as the man was distracted with giving orders to his scouts, Dante rode up next to Neve. "You knew what was in there."

"I didn't *know*," she said hotly. "I just had a worry."

"A worry that there was a living presence in the stone itself that would try to crush us and possibly eat us? Is that a *common* worry in this place?"

"I wouldn't call it common."

"But it's real?"

"You were almost just killed by it, weren't you?"

"As a matter of fact, I was. Which raises the question of what I would have done if I *hadn't* been able to manipulate the earth?"

She shrugged. "If you couldn't pull off such feats, I doubt you'd have gotten to this place to begin with."

"This is all very interesting," Blays said. "But can we get back to the matter of *what the hell was that thing?*"

"'Presence' isn't a bad word for it. 'Spirit' works too."

Dante glanced back at the cavern exit, still visible between the gray trees. "Then it was alive?"

"Not like you or I am. For one thing, things like that are much *bigger*. You usually only find them out in places like this. Unclaimed and untamed places where humans are afraid to go."

"Apparently with good reason."

"Hey Neve," Blays said. "What's blue?"

She eyed him. "Tell me you foreigners know what blue is. Your *eyes* are blue."

"Not that. *That*." He pointed to her waystone. It was glowing brightly. Not the red they'd always seen it, but a sapphiric blue.

Neve blinked so hard she flinched. "One of the Nine Kingdoms has sent out a war party — and it's coming this way."

9

Dante took the news straight to Dasya. Dasya responded by reaching over from the saddle and gripping Dante by the throat. "A godlander war party? Did you bring this here? Did you betray us?"

Dante grabbed the man's wrist, but attempting to fight him off would be like trying to wrestle with a tree. "Yes, we're that special breed of traitor that warns you before our betrayal actually takes place. We have no idea what this is about, Dasya."

Dasya peered into his eyes. "You swear on your life? On your blood that will nourish or curse all your descendants?"

"If this war party is at all related to us, they've been sent as our enemies, not our friends."

The warrior let him go. "How dare these rat-men defile the Red Valley? I will find where they are, and the Jessel will aid in feeding their blood to the dirt."

He dispatched twenty riders to the southeast, the general direction the war party had been spotted. Neve had said they were "close," but apparently that could be fifty miles or more.

Dasya clearly relished the idea of getting to go kill "godlanders" on his home territory, which had the beneficial effect of causing him to push his scouts even harder to find the Iron-Oak so that he could be done with this task and ride off to slay his foes. As alien as the place looked, as they rode toward its heart,

Dante couldn't shake the feeling that he was somehow familiar with it. Obviously he'd never *seen* it before, but he'd somehow heard of it, or maybe had just seen it in a dream.

There was still plenty of daylight left when the scouts returned with the news they'd found the Iron-Oak. Dante expected this to turn out false, or for it to be the *wrong* Iron-Oak, but once he stood beneath its boughs, the grown-over wound in the base of its trunk let him know they'd come to the right place.

Instead of the ashen gray of the trees around it, the Iron-Oak was indeed the color of iron, with an oily blue shimmer to it. Though it was tall, it wasn't the tallest of the nearby trees, but it was the stoutest, and looked impossibly old.

Dasya grinned and ran his hand over the scarred wood. "So this is where Sallen made his sheva."

Dante touched the tree as well. It felt like bark, but it was cooler than wood, as if it *was* made of metal. "Sheva? What's that, an act of obvious foolishness?"

"How do you know that, outlander? Have you studied our ways?"

"Guessed from the way you and he discussed the event."

"You are only half right. Yes, a sheva is an act that is knowingly foolish. But it is also an act that must be done."

"Sallen *had* to lose the axe of Gashen over a drunken boast?"

"His honor thought so."

"You seem to be making a strong argument against the virtue of honor."

Dasya batted his hand at the air. "Honor sounds stupid until you watch how a people without it behaves. But the ways honor can be stupid is just what the sheva is. It is the worthy folly — the *noble* folly. The one acting knows their act is foolish, but their awareness only makes their actions more noble."

"Like, say, riding out alone to face down an enemy you don't think you can defeat."

"That is the most classic form of sheva. It is true that some shevas are more serious than others."

"I imagine Sallen's wasn't one of those."

Dasya laughed. "No. But the unseriousness of his folly is what makes it a good story. And it is also what has allowed us to find you your piece of the axe. Shevas have a way of echoing down through time long after other deeds are forgotten." The man stood, backing off a step and gesturing to the tree. "Now claim your part of the lost axe, and redeem Sallen's folly."

Dante made a small cut on the back of his arm. "Is there any taboo against, er…destroying the tree?"

"Why would you destroy it?"

"Because its flowers are looking at me funny. And because if this thing was strong enough to break the axe, if I want to get the axe back, I might have to break *it*."

"I wouldn't do that," Dasya said softly. "If Sallen had been able to cut down the Iron-Oak, it would not have been a noble folly, but a tragic one."

Dante nodded, placed his hand on the trunk, and sent his mind inside it. He had hoped the tree would be made of raw iron ore, which he'd be able to manipulate like any other lump of earth. But while there did seem to be some kind of metal laced within the tree, it was still a tree, which was to say that it was made of wood.

"Good news," he said. "We've come to the right place. I can feel the broken blade inside it."

Blays considered the trunk. "Judging from the fact you're not getting the blade out, I'm guessing there's bad news, too."

"The bad news is I don't know how to get it out."

"Have you tried fire? Fire solves all kinds of problems."

Dante squinted at the tree. Just in case, he moved into it as if it was earth and attempted to draw the trunk back from the chunk of blade buried within it, but the wood wouldn't budge.

Then again, the piece was only a few inches beneath the surface, and the trunk was many feet wide. Surely it could absorb that much damage without any severe consequences.

He shaped the nether into a chisel and gave the trunk a good hard tap. The chisel skidded off the surface while leaving only the faintest scratch. Dante frowned, drew back, and struck it harder. The shadowy chisel burst apart into nothing.

"This thing's as tough as the hide of a kapper," he grumbled. "Should have called it the Pain-in-the-Ass-Oak."

He attacked it a few more times, varying the strength and shape of the blows.

"That's not going to work," Neve said.

"How would *you* know?"

"Just trying to save you some time."

Dante formed a great axe of shadows and hurled it against the grown-over wound. The trunk boomed like an off-key bell. The nethereal axe shattered to pieces. The tree did nothing of the kind.

"I think," Dante said, "that this isn't going to work."

Blays rapped on the trunk, then shook his knuckles. "This is a *tree*, right?"

"By all indications."

"And didn't a certain islander teach you how to make trees do whatever you tell them to?"

Dante grunted and moved back into the Iron-Oak, taking up the nether to convince it to grow outward—and pull the wound open with it. The bark bulged out half an inch, then quivered and ceased growing.

"At least that did *something*." Dante sat back. The day wasn't particularly warm, but the combination of effort and frustration was making him sweat. He met eyes with Neve. "If there's something you know about this, now would be the time to spill your guts."

"I don't know anything about this tree." She gazed at the trunk. "I've just been out here long enough to know when something's going to work and when it's not."

Dante tried to harvest it a second time, but provoked even less growth than on his first attempt.

"It's a sad day when you're defeated by a tree," Blays admonished.

"It's not a real tree, or else I *wouldn't* be defeated by it."

Dante hadn't really meant anything by the words, but he swayed back half a step, then put his hand back on the tree. It wasn't really a tree, was it? Part-tree, or beyond-tree, but not anything he was used to. In fact, looking closely—

He moved down into the roots right under his feet. They were encased in a tough layer of minerals, perhaps to keep out rot and insects during the periods the tree didn't need sustenance, which he suspected were common. He swept the layer away, then sent the nether forth again to harvest.

Water and matter flowed up through the exposed roots. These were brought forth to the wound in the trunk. It bulged outward, crackling slightly. It was seamed like a scar and he grew one part up and one part down. The seam peeled apart. Metal gleamed from within. He continued harvesting the trunk-wound apart until the whole thing was revealed, then reached inside the bole and withdrew a long, thin triangle of perfect steel.

"Does that look like part of a god's axe to you?"

He'd been asking the question mostly of Blays, and also of Dasya, but Neve tipped back her head, peering at the broken steel. "Look at the red sheen it's got. That's Gashen's for sure."

"Excellent," Blays said. "Now we've got a piece of a spear *and* a chunk of an axe. A few more years of running around the countryside, and we might have enough to actually hurt someone with."

"I wasn't sure we'd even be able to find this much," Dante said. "If this piece leads us to the rest of it, that opens the door to acquiring the rest of the spear."

The *if* in his statement was larger than he wanted to admit. First off, it relied on there being nether within the broken axe, and there was no nether within the part of the Spear of Stars. Second, even if there was nether within the axe—and, glancing within it, he confirmed there was—there was no guarantee he could use it to track the other pieces. He suspected it *could* work, given that a god's own weapon ought to be potent and unique enough for there to be a strong connection within the nether, but the problem was the pieces had been broken and separated for a very long time. Long enough that the nethereal connection between them might have dissipated to nothing.

Offering a short, silent prayer to Arawn, he took hold of the nether within the axe and brought it into his own mind.

Pain tore through his brain; his hands jerked so hard he threw the broken axe blade into the dirt.

He clapped his hands to his forehead and collapsed to the ground. "Holy *shit* that hurts!"

"What's the matter?" Blays reached for his shoulder. "Did you catch a glimpse of your reflection in the blade?"

Dante sat up, rubbing the center of his brow. He recovered the piece of steel and reached back inside it as gingerly as if he was touching a steaming mug. He drew back his mind, fortifying it, and brought the nether inside himself again.

Despite his precautions, the connection was potent enough to send a throb of pain through his skull. "It isn't working. I'm getting a signal from it, but it's way, way too strong. It's almost like it's pointing to itself by mistake."

Blays squinted one eye. "How would *that* work?"

"It shouldn't. But it's the only thing that makes sense."

"And this thing that makes sense of yours, has it ever been

true in any other situation?"

"Not that I remember. Maybe the other pieces of the axe have been destroyed, so the only thing it can point to is itself."

"So the explanation that makes no sense and has never been true in the past could be the explanation to what's happening now. Or it could be that you're standing on top of the rest of the axe."

Dante stared at Blays. With a pang of excitement and embarrassment, he plunged into the nether within the ground, feeling outwards and down. There were all kinds of irregularities in the soil—rocks big and small, along with patches of buried leaves and logs—but one object stood out the instant he felt it.

He softened the dirt above it, lifting it upward until it broke the surface. The light gleamed from a piece of steel, still shiny and flawless despite its long years interred within the earth.

"Well," Dante said. "I suppose that explains why the signal was so potent. It makes no sense that Urman would just throw it away right after winning it, though."

"Really? If it turned out your 'winnings' were a pile of broken junk, what would *you* do with them?"

"Take them home with me for careful and methodical study, whether for the purpose of mending them back into a useful form, or to learn how to create new items like it for myself."

Blays motioned to the ramna riders. "Well these guys aren't as tedious as you. They'd just throw it away like a normal person."

"If that's true, then where's the rest of the axe?"

"Beats me. But you might use the parts you've got to find out."

Combined, the two pieces made up most of the axe's head. Dante took up the nether within the part he'd fished out of the Iron-Oak, then the one from the ground.

"I'm just getting one signal from each of them," he said. "And they're both pointing just west of south. We find the last piece, and we'll have the full axe."

They had just enough daylight left to return to the massive lump of blue stone, although they camped out of sight of the Groaning Tunnel. In the morning, the passage sounded almost grumpy, but the presence made no attempt to interfere with them.

Dante wasn't sure the connection to the last part of the axe operated on the same scale as it did when he tracked someone by blood, but it felt quite faint, as if it might be fifty miles away or more. After a bit of travel, he began to pay very close attention to the position of the sun.

"The signal," he told Blays and Dasya. "It's moving to the east."

"Sallen said nothing of the axe's haft having legs," Dasya said. "Someone must still carry it with them. Is this good?"

"I suppose that depends on who's carrying it."

Dasya veered further east than the signal was currently pointed at, hoping to shortcut the distance between them. Dante wasn't at all sure this was the right move, but Dasya's insistence was proven correct when the scouts returned to tell him that the kingdom's war party was now conducting active raids on the eastern fringe of the valley. The conflict would draw people of all kinds, including, quite possibly, whoever had hold of the rest of the axe.

Dasya dwelled on the scouts' news before calling the three outlanders to him. "I should be taking my people to fight the invaders, for glory and for vengeance. For now, I honor my commitment to you. But if we continue to be defiled by these men—weak men who only now dare step outside the safety of their walls and cities—know that I will leave you to pursue the axe on your own."

In the meantime, he dispatched another band of riders to rally the Jessel and prepare for war, leaving the hunting party with an escort of just twenty warriors. It was perhaps due to this lack of numbers that, on the following day's travels, a pack of wild dogs rushed from out of the woods to harry the horses. The beasts had flattened snouts and heavy forequarters and gave chase for several miles before breaking off to search for easier prey.

The signal continued to bear eastward, but either it was further away than Dante had thought, or the bearer of the axe-haft was traveling south as well, for it wasn't until the third day after leaving the Iron-Oak that the signal grew considerably stronger. Dante thought they'd catch up to it by day's end.

Around one in the afternoon, his loon throbbed. Nak had news from the front. The White Lich had rushed through Shay and the north reaches of Mallon. Nak had made a stand against him in the Woduns, looking to force the lich to detour, or at least to delay him. The lich had bowled right through them. It had cost him thousands of Blighted, but that hardly dented the enemy's army.

"Keep trying," Dante advised Nak, somewhat lamely. "That's all any of us can do now."

But he knew then that even if Nak had better luck in the next encounter, or the one after that, it wasn't going to buy Dante enough time to assemble the entire spear. Not before the lich reached Narashtovik. Maybe not in time to stop the enemy from destroying all of Gask. They'd already been in the Realm for two weeks and they'd only gotten their hands on a single part of the spear. Even if they could convince the other gods to let them earn the rest of the pieces, accomplishing their deers and quests would take months.

The intensity of the pressure in his head increased rapidly. Just when it was starting to get painful, a rider returned. He'd spotted another group of ramna some five miles ahead. And recognized them as the Kranda.

"The Kranda?" Dante said. "The band that Urman was with when he won the axe from Sallen?"

Dasya nodded. "The same. Urman died some time ago, but most of his children live on. If the Kranda have carried the axe all this time, one of his offspring will have it."

"Will the Kranda meet with us?"

"Probably. I don't think we've killed any of them lately."

Dasya said this lightly enough, but Dante didn't think it was a joke. They increased their pace to make sure they'd catch the Kranda before nightfall. Dasya sent messengers ahead. They returned within an hour. As Dasya had said, Urman was dead, but his son Addan was now leading the band, and had agreed to speak with them.

The meeting came about on the banks of another shallow, noisy river. The Kranda outnumbered the Jessel by at least ten to one and Dante was not at all happy about the fact the Kranda had made the Jessel ford the river to come speak to them: if anything went wrong, the Kranda could drive them against the shore. Knowing the ramna, they might decide to do so even if everything was fine.

Like the Jessel, the Kranda were all mounted on horseback, but beyond that, there were few similarities between them. The Kranda had more women among them, for one, and the men had red beards and black hair. Their faces were both ruddy and quite tan, resulting in an ocher complexion Dante had never seen before. They quite liked feathers, weaving them into their hair and sleeves and the tack of their horses.

"My head's about to explode," Dante told Dasya. "One of them has the last piece of the axe."

"Dasya!" A burly bearded man rode three steps forth. "Have you come here to shed the blood of the godlanders?"

"If I don't get to it soon, my right arm and my spear are likely to run away together and do it for me," Dasya said. "But there is one other thing I must do first."

"That is what brings you to me?"

"In normal times, I would share a drink and a story before charging into the matter of my business. But the more time I fritter away on friendliness, the longer I'm kept from skinning godlanders. We've come to bargain for your part of the axe."

Addan looked bemused. "The axe? You have none of your own?"

"Many, and I've just told you I want to see them embedded in the skulls of the worshippers, so stop playing games. *The* axe. Gashen's axe."

"And who says *we* have it?"

"Says me." Dante lifted his hand, shooting a beam of flame into the sky. "The wise and terrible sorcerer."

Addan's eyes seemed to recede. "Who is this? Dasya, have you partnered with *godlanders*?"

"He is no godlander!" Dasya laughed. "He hates them as we do."

"But he's no ramna, either. Is this foolishness supposed to be a riddle?"

"And it's one you seem to have no hope of solving, so I will cut to the chase. He is neither godlander nor ramna—for he is from the Fallen Land."

This provoked a stir among Addan's riders. Even Addan looked impressed. "Dasya, you vouch for this? You would bleed for the truth of this?"

"I would."

"This is why you seek the axe? To turn it against its former wielder?"

"In effect," Dante said. "The gods are leaving my world to die. I intend to thwart the disaster—and give the gods something to remember us by in the process."

Addan scratched his beard, looking thoughtful. He held out his right hand. "Veya! Bring me the axe."

A rather mean-looking woman rode up to a young man and withdrew a long-handled object from the supplies his extra mount was carrying. Chin tilted severely, she brought it to Addan, nodding to him.

Addan thrust it above his head. "Behold! The axe of Gashen."

"I can't help but notice," Blays said, "that this appears to be a shovel."

That was just what it was: a wide, square shovel head had been affixed to one end of it, with an extension of the shaft and a handle nailed to the other. These simple additions were quite at odds with the far more sophisticated craftsmanship of both the steel of the blade and the wood of the original handle.

"It was no good as an axe." Addan lowered the shovel to better contemplate it. "So I turned it into a shovel to scoop up the cow shit where the children want to play. I can't think of a better use for a god's most cherished possession."

"How about using it to get *revenge* on the gods?"

"That can't be done. It's broken beyond repair."

"I wouldn't be so sure of that."

"It is certain, you city-fed weakling. In my attempts to restore it, I took two of the pieces to Arawn's Mill itself."

Dante cocked his head. "Arawn's Mill? What's that?"

"It's the Mill of Arawn."

"And it...mills...things?"

Addan laughed gruffly. "Is the Fallen Land that backwards, or just you? Arawn's Mill is Arawn's Mill. The site where nether and ether are ground out into the world."

Dante's mouth went dry; his mind roared, momentarily obliterated. "And it can restore things that have been broken."

"The ether it grinds can. I took two parts of the broken axe to it. But the ether was of no use. After that, I brought the smaller part back to the Iron-Oak to bury it where my father had won it. And found my own use for the rest of it."

"I believe we can get a great deal of use out of it even if we can't restore it. Let us trade you for it."

Addan made a dismissive brushing gesture. "That can't be done. You have nothing to trade me."

"It's true that we don't have money. But I have many powers. I can heal your sick. Or build you a fortress against the godlanders."

"Heal the *sick*?" Addan parted his lips in revulsion, glaring at Dasya. "What kind of pervert have you brought to me?"

Dasya sighed. "I have told him that sickness is a blessing that improves us, but his mind is afflicted with the sickness of civilization. What can be done about such people?"

"The sickness of his mind must also explain why he offers me a fortress for me and my warriors to cower within. Like rabbits in the warren as the hounds bay outside."

"That seems like the best place for rabbits to hide from baying hounds." Dante ran a mental inventory of his goods that he might trade, but he barely had anything. After a moment's hesitation, he drew his sword. This in turn drew a ruckus from the Kranda, so Dante hastily held the weapon sideways, showing it to Addan. "Here. A weapon for a weapon."

Nether sparked along the blade, its bloodthirst obvious to any eye. Addan watched it, tempted, then clenched his jaw and shook his head. "This can't be done."

Dasya slapped his saddle. "At least let me wrestle you for it!"

"My father won this rightfully, spitting on Gashen himself in the process, and then passed it on to me. Some day, I will pass it on to *my* son. There is nothing you can trade me that would be more precious than this idol of my family."

Blays crossed his arms. "Your father hardly 'won' it. Didn't he mostly just stand there while Sallen made a fool of himself?"

Addan's ocher face flushed crimson. "What did you say?"

"That, er, your father was great. Everyone thinks so, really. And very handsome. And—"

"You know nothing. Leave my sight before I separate your body from your adsal."

Blays shut his mouth. Dasya lifted his hand to Addan. "War well, brother in struggle."

Dasya turned his mount and entered the river. His men followed. After a second, Dante did too.

Once they were on the other side, Blays glanced across the water, but the Kranda had already disappeared into the woods. "In hindsight, maybe I *shouldn't* have insulted his one and only father who he venerates more than anyone."

"You *think*?" Dante gestured broadly. "He'll never give the axe to us now!"

"That is true," Dasya said. "Does that mean you are giving up? If so, I'd like to go and kill some people."

"No, we're not giving up. Can't we just kill the Kranda and take the axe?"

Dasya laughed. "Yes, in normal times, we could kill them and take what we like and it would be good."

"But the gods are currently invading you, meaning times are far from normal."

"I can't damage the unity of our bands at the time we must be united against our common foe."

Blays stretched his arms behind his head. "I could just wander over and steal it."

"Shadowalking," Dante said.

"I know it has a lot working against it, like that it would be the easiest route for us, they'd never suspect it and could probably never even detect it, and that we could be done and on our way back to Carvahal in a matter of minutes. But I'd still like to give it a try."

Dante turned back to Dasya. "Did the Kranda have any sorcerers among them?"

"Not that I saw," Dasya said. "They were likely already sent to harry the war party."

"Then there's nothing to stop us."

"What you suggest is a lowly act. But as long as you are the ones doing the stealing, then you are the only ones whose adsals will be made low by it."

It was already late in the day, so they decided to wait to make their move until nightfall, as was traditional for lowly acts. The Kranda rode east for another ten miles before making their camp, at which point Dasya hurried to close the distance on them. He stopped a mile and a half away.

At midnight, with all the camp asleep except their sentries, Dante and Blays struck out on horseback. Neve had wanted to come with them, but Dante argued—gently at first, but with increasing annoyance as she continued to argue back—that they were less likely to get caught if fewer of them were involved, and that she had no special powers to protect herself if something went wrong. After much too much talk, she'd finally relented.

Small animals rustled around in the brush, going silent whenever the screech of an owl cut across the night. The air smelled cool; fall was coming. Dante typically liked this shift of seasons, as he'd never really cared for summer, but at that moment, the sight of the first red leaves just reminded him that time was slipping away.

He glanced behind them, as if they might have been followed. "Did you hear what Addan said about the axe?"

"The part where he said we could never have it?" Blays said. "Is *that* why we're about to steal it?"

"I mean the part where he took it to Arawn's Mill."

"It was chiseled into my memory. You looked like you were about to collapse into a pile of bony goo."

"Think about everything we've seen in the Realm. The people here don't age. Arawn's Mill is here—it's real—and it grinds *ether*. For the gods' sake, there are gods here!"

"Yes, we've established this place is strange. One might even call it 'foreign,' or 'literally a different world.'"

"It is, but it's also a world we know. Not just from the *Book of What Lies Beyond*. But from *The Cycle of Arawn*."

Their horses' hooves swished through the weeds. Blays' voice went quiet. "Only the *Cycle* wasn't quite right then, was it?"

"No. For the *Cycle* says the gods first built the world so that humans would live forever, sustained by the pure ether of the Mill. But as the world grew too heavy with human life, it toppled. The Mill fell and cracked. After that, it only ground nether, and the people were no longer immortal, but were born, grew old, and then died.

"But if this is the gods' original realm, then our world wasn't made *from* it. Ours was made *after*, separate from it. This place was first, and it still lives on."

10

"That," Blays said, "explains a lot about a lot. Like why this realm even exists to begin with."

"It also means our world isn't a *correction*. It's an *experiment*."

"Suppose that's why the gods don't seem terribly concerned if everyone in it dies?"

"If true, that isn't just because they see death and rebirth as our natural cycle, including, sometimes, the death and rebirth of our whole world. It's because they're not even sure *if those cycles are right*. They're just watching what happens. Seeing where it goes. And if the answer to that question turns out to be 'straight to hell,' they'll probably just create a new world and try again, just like they did with ours when *their* realm showed its big flaw."

"What if they made us to help test how to run things here?"

"That would make even more sense."

"So the gods used us to figure out how to make their own world work better. They're happy to look after and protect their own peoples. But if it all goes wrong for *us*, then we get thrown to the wolves. I'm beginning to see why the ramna aren't so fond of them."

"It might not be as simple as that," Dante said slowly. "They're still the gods. Their thinking might be incomprehensible to us."

"Or they could just be pricks. Well, you'd better hope you're not about to die chasing after some goofy axe. Otherwise you'll never be able to pass this revelation of theology along to Nak."

This statement hit Dante so starkly that he nearly pulsed Nak's loon then and there. But he knew that if he and Nak started talking now, they wouldn't stop until the loon was about to die, and he and Blays were almost to the Kranda camp. Anyway, deep theology would be the perfect thing to hash out *after* they were riding away from the scene of a crime.

They dismounted and tied up their horses. Dante drew a bit of blood and summoned the nether. They advanced in near silence, eluding one sentry along the way. The air smelled of horses two hundred yards before they caught sight of the dark camp.

"I won't have eyes on you," Dante said. "So if things start getting blown to hell, just yell out and tell me who to vaporize."

"The short answer to that is whoever's chasing me." Blays flipped a salute. "Now if you'll excuse me, I'm off to acquire a shovel."

Blays stepped forward and vanished into the nether. Dante could feel his presence as he ran toward the camp, but it diminished with every step, passing beyond his ability to sense.

After a bit of dithering about whether to crouch for better cover or stand to be able to react faster, he opted for the crouch. Leaves shuffled in the breeze. He was so used to relying on his reanimated servants that waiting alone in the dark made him feel half crazy, as if he'd actually gone blind. Then again, unless the Kranda had a sorcerer Dasya didn't know about, and they were awake, and knew what to look for, there would only be two or three total seconds when Blays would be vulnerable: the moment he stepped out of the shadows to pick up the axe.

Dante had just about convinced himself that everything would go off without a hitch when light speared up from the middle of the camp.

This was followed by a couple of confused voices, then several concerned ones, and then a hell of a lot of angry ones. Dante slipped toward the camp, clutching the shadows tight. A pair of torches flapped across the grounds, hastening to light others. Men and women shouted at each other, exchanging notions of "There he is!", "Get him!", and so forth.

Footsteps crashed toward Dante. He loped forward two steps.

Blays emerged from the gloom—and he was carrying the shovel. "Run, you jackass!"

Dante sprinted for the horses, which suddenly felt as far away as Narashtovik. Two men stomped through the undergrowth in pursuit. Dante threw a pair of black bolts behind him. Both men dropped dead.

Dante glanced over his shoulder. "I thought there weren't any sorcerers here!"

"Maybe there aren't," Blays said. "Maybe I accidentally conjured up that fountain of ether myself, then also accidentally kicked myself out of the shadows. Who knows?"

Dante let Blays lead, feeling behind them for any incoming attacks. Back at the Kranda's camp, horses snorted and gear clanked and jingled.

"They're coming," Dante said.

"It's a good thing we have your keen military mind to identify subtle things like a cavalry charge."

The Kranda rode out while Blays was still speaking. Dante might have killed a few to dissuade the others, but he doubted they'd be any more prone to intimidation than the Jessel had been. He blanked his mind the best he could, filling it with ether, then slung it to the right, keeping it dark until it was a hundred yards away, then bringing it to bloom. The riders at the fore yelled out happily, giving chase.

Dante led the light of the ether further and further in the

wrong direction, accelerating it as the riders neared it. The racket of pursuit dimmed. But they weren't quite back to their horses when the enthusiastic shouts curdled with dismay.

Dante and Blays exchanged a wordless look, running as hard as they could. Warriors shouted to each other through the trees. They reached their mounts. Blays vaulted into the saddle while Dante settled for sort of flinging himself bodily across his. Blays cut their tethers and they romped west toward Dasya and the others.

"What *happened*?" Dante said.

"Well there I was, minding my own business as I took away another man's most treasured possession, when some asshole came along and shoved me out of the shadows."

"Did you see who?"

"What are you going to do, go back and beat them up? I didn't even get a glimpse of them. It felt like they were way out on the fringe of the camp."

"How did you get away without the sorcerer blasting you to chunks?"

"Good question. Maybe once they saw me they couldn't stand destroying something of such beauty."

Their horses trampled through the woods. They'd built up a good lead and Dante thought they might just get away. Until he heard hoofbeats behind them.

A single rider dashed through the shadows. Before the man could call out for help, Dante formed a spike of nether and flung it behind him. His aim was unerring, yet as the missile screamed silently toward the man's chest, a bolt of light streaked past him and plowed into the attack, bashing it into harmless particles.

"I've found them!" the warrior bellowed. "The intruders!" He lifted his horn from his side and sounded a long, sharp blast.

Blays leaned forward in the saddle. "Shouldn't you be killing that guy?"

"I'm trying!" Dante threw three more spikes behind him, lending them all the speed that he could. Again, light flared from behind the rider, reducing the attacks to fading sparks.

Scowling, Dante fired his mind into the ground ahead of the rider, wrenching it apart with an earthy rumble. Ether glowed, blindingly bright; the rift clapped back together.

"I can't seem to get to him," Dante said.

"You can't fend off one sorcerer? Did the White Lich just portal in here?"

"We have to get back to Dasya. Take the escape route."

Dasya had scouted out a way to shake pursuit in case of a contingency like this, but it depended on Dante being able to block it with the earth, which now seemed quite vulnerable to the Kranda's elusive ethermancer. Then again, he wasn't sure what other option they had.

Dante ran the nether through their horses' blood, giving them a second wind. Even so, he began to catch glimpses of more Kranda warhorses among the trees behind them.

Blays pointed westward. "Trouble ahead!"

Dante gathered the shadows, ready to shred this new threat into smithereens. Then saw the ghostly white skulls adorning the incoming horses and some of their riders. Dasya, Neve, and the small band of Jessel bent course to match them westward.

"We heard the horns," Dasya said. "There weren't supposed to be any horns!"

"That's because there weren't supposed to be any sorcerers." Dante ducked a low-hanging branch. "There were."

"And you are too weak to overcome them?"

"Something funny's going on. Just lead us to the escape route, will you?"

Dasya barked orders, peeling to the south. The Kranda followed them, hundreds strong, though they were more spread out through the woods. Dante launched another barrage at the

rider who'd first found them. The unseen hand of the ethermancer knocked each bolt down. Dante had been expecting as
much, and ignored the results, hunting for the hidden enemy instead, but he still couldn't get a read on where the man was.

Some of the Jessel turned about in the saddle, firing arrows
behind them. Almost impossible to hit a mark, given the thick-
ness of the woods, the darkness of the night, and riding at full
gallop, but it hampered their harassers somewhat. Dante pitched
in by harvesting the shrubs in front of the nearest Kranda into
impassible jumbles, spilling several of them from the saddle and
snarling others.

Neve moved her horse next to Dante's. "This sorcerer with
the Kranda, what does he look like?"

"I wouldn't know," Dante said. "I haven't even seen him."

"What do you mean you haven't seen him?"

"I mean it's like he's invisible. Probably on account of the sorcery."

A dark cloud passed over her young face. "We have to get
out of here."

"Yes, I'd worked that one out for myself."

The ground began to run gently uphill. Dasya ordered Dante
up to the front.

"We must be careful," Dasya said. "For the way out I chose is
a—"

Dante's horse vaulted into the air. He yelled at it, then understood that it had made the right decision, as they had run right
off the edge of a cliff.

The ground lay forty feet beneath them. Feeling like his eyes
were as wide as wagon wheels, Dante shot his mind out into the
cliff and the ground below. With crude force, he liquefied the
earth and yanked it outward and upward into the shape of a
ramp.

His horse landed. He cringed, waiting for the snap of bone,

the stumble of its mass and momentum, but the animal hardly missed a step, galloping down the ramp.

Right behind him, Dasya bellowed with laughter. "You reacted so quickly I think you have done this before!"

"Generally speaking, it's considered polite to inform your traveling companions about any cliffs *before* they've fallen off them!"

Dante let Dasya retake the lead, watching behind them. As soon as the last of the Jessel was heading down the ramp, Dante tore it down, starting where it met the cliff. Soon they were all on level ground and the ramp was just a crumbled pile of dirt behind them.

The Kranda skidded to a stop at the top of the cliff, shouting in dismay and hurling insults, followed by plenty of arrows and three or four spears. As soon as they were out of range, Dasya and the Jessel turned around and stopped to hit back with boasts and insults of their own.

"Now isn't the time to be stopping." Neve's voice was taut to the point of snapping.

"Dasya, they still have the ethermancer with them," Dante said. "He might be able to create a route down from the cliff for them."

Dasya scowled, almost petulant. "But what is the point of winning if you don't get to laugh in your enemy's face?"

Blays shrugged. "Making sure you survive to beat him again in the future?"

Dasya cupped his hands to his mouth and yelled one last jibe, then wheeled his horse and dashed into the leafy forest. At first they traveled in silence, but after half an hour the men began to joke in low tones to each other. After another thirty minutes, Dasya sent three of them back to scout for Kranda, but they returned having seen nothing.

Some time later, the forest thinned; they walked their mounts into the ruins of a city, the first Dante had seen since entering the Red Valley. At last Dasya called for a rest.

They holed up in one of the better-preserved structures, a large round building with mostly intact walls. Nothing was left of the roof. Dasya insisted on seeing to his own horse and it was another twenty minutes before the warrior-captain joined the three foreigners.

He seated himself on a long flat stone encrusted with various colors of lichen. "That was a good chase!"

"We nearly died!" Dante said.

"That's what made it good!"

"Sorry for making a new enemy for you," Blays said. "I hope this doesn't impact your ability to kill the filthy invaders together."

Dasya made a chopping gesture. "The Kranda may forget it if we slay enough of the gods' soldiers. If that is not enough, perhaps whatever trouble you are about to cause the gods will convince Addan that it was worth sacrificing his treasure for."

"I hope to make his unwilling investment pay off sooner than he'd think," Dante said. "Taim's orchestrating an immense scheme. Not all of the other gods agree with him. If we can kick the legs out from underneath his plan, it could provoke open conflict between them."

Dasya's eyes glittered in the darkness. "Gods warring against gods?"

"I can't make any promises. But he's been relying on secrecy and silence to stop any dissent from cropping up while the troubles in my land play out on their own. If we thwart his plans for us, and he decides to take direct action to pursue them instead, his enemies might take direction action against *him*."

"When we first met, I didn't see why I should help you. But a voice inside my adsal told me that I should. I am glad I listened to that voice. Now, while I am sad that we are about to part ways, I look forward with great vigor to where our separate paths will lead us."

It was quite late, but Dante didn't feel particularly tired yet, and apparently neither did any of the others. They chatted on, discussing which route Neve might take to lead the three of them out of the Red Valley.

The light about them shifted. At first it looked like the moon was emerging from behind a cloud, but the moon was fairly dull, waning past the half, and there were no clouds nearby that could have been blocking it. Neve frowned. The light brightened another speck.

Something *shifted*.

A moment earlier, they'd been sitting among rubble as old as anything Dante had seen in the norren hills. Now, the wall beside them was pure and whole, the windows filled with fine glass, the floor a beautiful pattern of unknown pink stone, adorned with soft rugs woven with heroic figures. Though Dante knew he hadn't moved, it *felt* as though he had, though maybe that was just a trick of the eye.

For all the world, it looked like they'd been cast back into the past, before the city had been ruined. Yet just beyond them—within a stone's throw, if not spitting distance—the ruins were still there, weather-worn, lichen-scabbed, and the Jessel warriors outside the circle of light were still sitting among them, playing games of chance and telling tales of battle.

Inside the circle, it wasn't just the ruins that had changed. Blays looked a shade younger, but his hair was cut in a way he hadn't worn it in at least three years, if not four, and he was wearing a set of perfectly tailored clothes that had gotten destroyed nearly four years ago. Dasya looked mildly younger, too. But Branya looked *decades* younger, half his age, the white gone from his hair and beard, nearly all his scars erased. The only one who didn't look any different was Neve.

Dante had taken this all in over the span of two heartbeats. As he opened his mouth to ask what the hell was going on, Neve shot to her feet.

"Move," she said. "*Move now!*"

She sprinted for the ruins beyond the circle of light. Blays was first to follow. That seemed to be convincing enough for everyone else, who ran after them as fast as they could. As Neve neared the perimeter, she dived outside it, rolling as she hit the ground. As soon as Blays exited the light, his clothes and hair reverted to the way he'd looked all along.

Dante ran free of the circle, stumbling over a stone hidden in the grass. Dasya pulled Branya along. The two men exited the curious circle and got two steps away from it before it exploded.

The light was so bright Dante saw nothing after its first flash. But he could *feel* it, the same way he'd felt the heat of the burning lava in Kandak. Ether. A pure and murderous column of it driving down into the ruins.

Still blind, Dante lowered himself to the ground and rolled behind a stump of rock. Wind rushed over his face. He expected it to be hot, like the air driven forth by a forest fire, but it was cold, almost painfully so, stinging his nose and ears. The ether sputtered and died out, snuffing the wind with it.

Dante's sight was starting to come back, but he hastened the process by wiping the nether across his eyes, taking the dazzles with it. Everyone seemed to have cleared the circle of light in time. That was good. Because every piece of stone within its radius had been both melted and pulverized. Transformed into a dull, talcum white.

"Neve," Dante said flatly. "What the *fuck* was that?"

Her face had gone as pale as the pulverized circle. "They've found us. We have to get—"

The air around them brightened again; the ruins vanished, replaced by the illusion of the building that had once stood there; everyone's face reverted to a younger age. Neve bolted toward a broad gap in the wall. Dante ran after her. Yet as he neared the rim of the circle, *the circle moved with them*, tracking forward, walls and furniture springing into existence as it passed over the rubble.

Dante could feel it coming. Like the pause between drawing breath and beginning to scream. They weren't going to make it.

Wild-eyed, Neve spun around, punching her right palm into the sky. The beam of light—for that's what it was—wobbled, then began to drift away from her. Dante skipped outside its range. As the ether poured downward, he turned his face and squeezed his eyes shut.

The wind blew over him, frigid, staggering him. As soon as the light dimmed, he opened his eyes. Once more, a wide circle of ruins had been reduced to both slag and powder, uniformly white.

One of the Jessel warriors stood at its edge—or rather, half of him did. The other half had been blasted into chalky residue. The cut was perfectly smooth and Dante could see his exposed heart beating in his chest. The man blinked once, perplexed, then collapsed inside the white circle.

Neve darted toward the gap out of the building. "I'm not going to be able to keep doing that. You have to help me!"

Dante glanced around for the next manifestation of the eerie light. "How?!"

"It's ether. Just as it looks like. Find where it's weak and crack it!"

He chomped his inner lip, reeling in as much nether as he could hold. Half the Jessel men scattered in random directions while the other half stuck with Dasya. A new circle of light appeared around Dante, Blays, and Neve, tracking them smoothly. Dante drove his mind into it, feeling the ether whirling in unknowable patterns, and followed it upward toward its hidden source. Next to him, he felt Neve doing something similar.

The beam was already coming. He'd barely begun to explore its structure, let alone figure out where it might be weak. He shoved the shadows up at it blindly. They glanced off the ethereal column with a glassy scrape.

Neve sighed angrily. "Watch me, you imbecile."

She raised her hand as she'd done before. This time, however, cataracts of shadows gushed upward. Rather than attacking the pillar directly, they flowed around it, as if seeking entry — or parts that could be broken open. They found entry at one point, then a second, then a third, the nether racing upwards and branching out like blood in the veins of the column. Just as the light bloomed, preparing to annihilate them, Neve closed her outstretched hand into a fist.

The veins of shadow pulsed. With the ringing of a thousand shattered windows, the column of ether broke apart. Flickering shards of light rained down toward them. Dante flung his arms over his head, but when the shards struck him, they disintegrated into nothing. Like that, the light was gone.

Breathing hard, Neve gestured at the air. "Did you see?"

Dante goggled at her. "Did I see you summon up a huge gob of nether and somehow insert its threads into the structure of a killing beam the likes of which I've never seen before? Yes. Am I going to be able to do that myself, having seen it all of once? I hope you're not betting our lives on it!"

"Servants of Arawn are always such whiners." Neve grinned. Her eyes flicked up. "Are you ready?"

The circle of light showered down on them once more. A vision of manicured trees and a cobbled road materialized within it. Dante summoned the nether, then let it flow from him into the oncoming ether. It slid over the surface, finding no purchase or entrance.

"I can't find a way inside," Dante said. "It's ether. It's flawless."

Neve laughed. "No ether worked by human hands is *flawless*. If you can't find the seams, that just means you're more flawed than the person you're fighting."

Dante had changed his approach after her first sentence. Rather than attempting to saturate or overwhelm the column, he withdrew the shadows until the thinnest layer of them remained against the glassy light. Here and there, the nether began to seep into nooks and crannies he hadn't been able to see when the nether had been much denser.

The pulse was coming. Dante squeezed the shadows into the pillar of light, forming capillaries of blackness. Too slow. Neve growled and wrapped the ethereal cylinder in nether, which wended its way into every point of failure it could find. Dante felt the ether do its pause-between-breath-and-scream. Hurriedly, Neve closed her fist. Black cracks spiderwebbed across the column. It erupted into thousands of pieces.

Dante began to run, but Neve barred an arm across his chest. "No need. We've got this."

"If we're being attacked by Taim, the only thing we've 'got' is 'moments left to live'!"

"That's how you know it isn't Taim, don't you?"

"Who else would be flying around up there?" Blays said. "Don't tell me the dragonlets have learned how to do magic!"

Dante gathered fresh nether in his hands. His heart was beating hard, but Neve no longer looked as terrified as she had at the start of the assault. Long-dead trees and long-broken walls wavered into place around them. Another attack. Dante poured a layer of nether onto the column of light. As soon as it eased into the cracks, he pumped in more behind it, jetting veins of nether through the imperfections.

He wasn't sure that he needed to, but he clenched his fist. The nether surged through the pillar of light, shattering it while it was still in its harmless first phase.

Neve tilted back her head and called up at the sky. "This is pointless. Why don't you just tell us what you want?"

Blays gripped the hilts of his swords, but hadn't yet drawn them. "Who exactly are you talking to? Do you two know each other?"

Neve didn't answer. Some of the Jessel had arrows nocked to their bows and aimed at the night sky, but there was nothing for them to target.

"My name is Ka." The woman's voice rang from above. Her figure began to glow, but all details of her were blurred by a golden nimbus. "And I am the Angel of Taim."

11

Dante, Blays, and Dasya all asked the same question at once. "Angel of Taim?"

Dasya lifted his fist and shook it at the floating woman. "The gods have less honor than a starving dog. There is no righteousness in sending an angel to slay humans!"

"Do you consider that unfair?" Ka's voice was as smooth as a fresh layer of paint. "You have killed women and children, Dasya of the Jessel, and you would speak to *me* of fairness and honor?"

"That was only the ones who deserved it!"

The golden nimbus faded enough to see Ka smile. She hung forty feet above them as if standing on an invisible staircase. Her long hair was so blonde it looked gold — and, given that she was apparently an angel, and more than that an Angel of Taim, Dante supposed it might actually be so. It was impossible to say how old she looked except to say that she was beautiful, painfully so, each feature in proportion to one another, her skin as smooth as her voice. She was pale, but not in the way northerners were. If anything, her skin looked metallic, like warm silver or light rose: inhuman, or more likely, beyond it.

In one hand she carried a golden hammer and in the other a slender silver sword. She wore a white garment that seemed to be half robe and half dress. Her feet were bare.

She looked down on Neve. "You will tell me who you are."

"Just another ranger who's gotten in way over her head," Neve said.

"That's a lie, and not even a good one. You are like me, or close to it. Who do you belong to?"

"Maybe I serve myself."

"You are subtle. Do I sense Arawn?"

Neve scoffed. "Arawn's just a watcher. He doesn't get involved in these matters."

"Not true. He is just the only one who lies about doing so." Ka drifted a few feet lower.

"That's close enough."

Ka nodded, halting her descent. She turned her gaze on Dante and Blays. "I already know who you are and that you have been warned against what you now do. It was kind of you to deliver me the pieces of the axe. Once I return them to Gashen, you will have no way to tempt him toward your goals."

"There's one problem for you," Blays said. "You see, you *don't* have the axe."

She smiled pityingly. "You will fail, Fallen Lander. But we are not without mercy. You will forfeit the axe, then promise to depart this place and stir no more trouble. In exchange...your friend. The haunted old man. How long ago did he die? Three weeks?"

"Thereabout," Dante said.

"Do as I bid, and we will restore him to you."

"What do you mean, 'restore'?"

"I mean that his life will be returned to him, and thus he will be returned to you."

"Are you saying you can *resurrect* him? If you can do that, then why are the subjects of the gods so afraid of death?"

"For their lives cannot be restored once lost. The old man is not of this realm, and his death does not belong here either.

There is still time to reverse it, if only for a little longer."

Dante exchanged a look with Blays. "Even if you could bring Gladdic back to life, why would that tempt us? Without the Spear of Stars, he'll be killed again within a matter of weeks. Along with all the rest of us."

"That may or may not be what comes to pass, but it is clear that it is what you believe and there is no shaking you of that belief. Since you despair of victory, I will offer you a means to indulge your defeat. We have heard of Arawn's offer to you. You should have taken it: it would have saved you. But you were born stubborn, and so we will make that offer again."

"And I'll reject your offer for the same reason I rejected his."

"And I had such hope the inconstancy of mortals would for once work in our favor." Ka smiled again. "Then let our offer be richer than the miserly Arawn's. You will choose hundreds of your people, and you will bring them here. You will be allowed to live in peace within our walls. You will be allowed to study and train within whatever temples you choose. When your talents have been honed to cut like a razor, and power flows from your hands with the strength of a river, you will be allowed to leave the walls, claim your land from what is now unclaimed, and found your own kingdom upon it."

Dante licked his lips. "But I'm a mortal. Aren't your kingdoms each ruled by a god?"

"There are exceptions. It is also true that in the course of your scholarship and training, you will become much more than what you are as you stand before me now."

"No matter how much I learn and train, I can never become a god."

"That is not what I have promised. But you might become something much like the Eiden Rane—but rather than wielding his malice and conquest, you could wield kindness and enlightenment."

Dante lowered his head. "It sounds like you're bribing me to allow the rest of my world to be killed."

"You are the one that is consumed by such a conviction. You could choose to let it go."

"Not to mention the Mists. How can Taim rob the innocent dead of the afterlife he promised them?"

"The after he promised?" She raised a golden eyebrow. "What do you know of the purpose of the Mists?"

"If you people are to be believed, the Mists have strayed from their purpose. But the people there seem perfectly fine to me."

"That is because you know nothing of the deep history of their realm. What you call the Mists are far more fallen than your own realm—not just fallen, but diseased. How can you convince yourself that your cause is righteous when you are condemning every soul within the Mists to a subtle torture? Is it not better to cure the disease and lose what few are within the Mists at the moment than to let endless millions continue to be sickened?"

"I don't see any sickness there. Even if this wasn't what you intended the Mists to be, if people seem to be making it work for themselves, what's so wrong with that?"

Ka shook her head sharply. "You think you are being kind to them, but you are being cruel. Not just in some small measure, but in dimensions beyond your imagination's ability to comprehend. These are not the laws the dead were meant to live under."

"Yes, well, given that Father Taim is perfectly content to let two whole worlds die, I wonder if we really need to abide by your 'laws.'"

"We did not bestow our laws to confound or constrain you. Do you believe they are a punishment? They are the opposite. We crafted them with the intent of helping you to live in best alignment with the nature of both yourselves and the new world we made for you to exist within. When you choose to stray from them, it is like walking beyond the reach of the light and then blaming others when you stumble and suffer injury."

"But you also gave us the freedom to stray from the laws, right? What's even the point of that? To give us the free will to fail you? To suffer injury?"

"If you must. But there is another factor of greater importance. For just as each person is different from the next in character, so is each gathering of people different from the next. By granting you the freedom to explore, every people can find the nature of themselves and then find the compromise needed to reach their personal accord with the laws."

"If people can just change the laws to suit themselves, just how rigorous can those laws really be in the first place?"

"Some cannot be bent at all and must be taken in whole. But others are more important for their *spirit* and need not be so rigid: they are more like flesh than like bone, built upon the unyielding laws that form the skeleton. However, even the laws made of flesh are not wholly malleable. Any person or people who strays too far from the light of the law will find themselves growing colder, often for reasons they cannot explain; if they wander too far into the dark, they will either perish from the light's absence, or go mad and exterminate themselves."

"You make it sound like you've given us some great gift. But we've learned the truth of why you made the so-called 'Fallen Land.' We're nothing more than an experiment to help you learn how to rule *this* world."

"No!" Anguish creased her silvery features. "You are no mere experiment. You were brought forth to witness and take part in the beauty of your world. And to explore what remains a mystery even to us: what it means to know that your life is one of finite years, and that some day you will grow old and die. And lastly to know the joy of worship without being beholden as our slaves."

Dante stretched his neck, which was getting stiff from looking up at her. "It's one thing if you think the Mists has strayed too far from its laws and purpose and needs to be replaced. But how has *my* world strayed from the laws? There may be lots we don't know — which seems to be in large part because you try to keep it hidden from us — but on the whole I'd say we're doing pretty damn well."

Ka smiled. "Some have done so better than others. But yes, you have done well."

"Then why do we need to die?"

"It is not a matter of need."

"If we don't *need* to be destroyed by the White Lich, then why not give us a hand here? Step in and stop us from getting annihilated?"

"If a young man with his head in the clouds is about to step off a cliff, robbing him of the long years he might have expected, should one of the gods reach down to catch him as he falls?"

"That might not be a reasonable expectation. But if every single person on earth is about to tumble off that cliff, it might be nice to stop them — and warn them not to do it again."

"And when an innocent young child is out in the fields, and a bear ambles upon her and designs to eat her, should we reach down to stop that, too?"

"Er...yes?"

"No: you can have your freedom, or you can have our protection. The one eliminates the other. To take the role of your parent would define your role as children — far worse, children who can never grow up and come of age, and are trapped always in that helpless state. If this was what you would demand of us, then we would never have created you."

"You're talking hypotheticals. But I'm talking about something that's really happening. Nobody's asking for *constant* protection. Just this one — "

She held up her hand. A bang seemed to clap through the

air, although Dante wasn't sure if it existed outside his mind.

"I have indulged you with more than enough answers," Ka said. "The time has come for you to make the choice I have granted you."

"About whether to abandon our world. And relocate here instead."

"Just so."

Dante swallowed. "Neve, can we trust her?"

"The offer you've made them, Ka," Neve said. "Do you swear on the name and blood of Taim to uphold its terms?"

Ka nodded. "I so swear."

"And does Taim do the same?"

"Taim so swears."

Neve turned to Dante. "Yes. You can trust them."

"Well," Dante said to Blays. "What do you think?"

Blays nearly choked. "You're actually considering it?"

"We have to at least think about it. It's a guarantee of survival."

"Yeah, and so was the other one you rejected."

"That was before I knew we were being hunted by whatever the Angel of Taim is. Anyway, this one offers more than just a future where a few of us don't have to die. It gives us a future where we can thrive."

Blays lowered his brows until it looked like they might tumble off his face. "We've got the axe. There's a chance we can do this on our own terms."

"We have to be honest with ourselves. Even with the axe accounted for, what are the chances we can pry seven more parts of the spear away from hostile gods? Let me further remind you we're not perfectly sure the spear really can kill the lich. And we shouldn't be at all sure that even if it can, that we'll be able to kill him with it before he kills us. In the meantime, we still have to assemble the rest of the weapon before the lich finishes killing everyone in the world and renders the whole thing moot. What are the chances that all these different things work out in our favor? One in ten? One in a hundred? One in ten thousand?"

"We must have *some* chance, or else Taim wouldn't be making this offer to us in the first place."

"I'm not saying that it's hopeless. I'm saying that on the one hand, we have a chance to save something for a good and guaranteed future. On the other hand, there is a huge—possibly overwhelming—chance that we fail, and that *nothing* will be saved."

"No shit. And?"

Dante threw his arms wide. "And we *might* want to think about what our true goal is. Is it to kill the Eiden Rane? Or is it to save our world? At what point does the guarantee of saving part of our world start to look like a better option than gambling it all on an outcome with such a small chance of success?"

Blays lowered his head. "We've spent our whole lives weighing risks. Being practical. Making compromises in the name of politics and pragmatism and everything else that wears you away. We've bent every rule and law of the land, and I'm not sure if there's a single one of our personal morals we haven't broken as well. All in the pursuit of things that were good—though not so much for our poor enemies—but every time we pursued a good thing, the process of obtaining it made it...compromised. Dirty. Tainted."

He'd been speaking softly, gaining volume as he gained momentum, until his voice rang through the ruins. "If this good is the last good we get to chase, I don't want it to be like that. For once in my life, I want it to be pure. I would rather shoot for the chance for salvation—no matter how slight and stupid that chance might be—than flee here for safety, where we'll spend the countless gods damned years of our new immortality remembering how, when everyone needed us most, we turned our backs on them and ran away."

Dante tilted his head to the hovering Angel. "Your offer is most gracious. It is also most unacceptable."

"Then I have no more need to *be* gracious." Ka thrust her palm downward.

A single beam of ether shot toward them, crystalline white but shimmering with rainbow hues. Dante launched a barrage of nether at it and so did Neve. The forces collided with the sound of a shelf of glasses being dumped to the floor.

Ka extended her arms to the side, thin sword in one hand, golden hammer in the other. Dante brought forth more nether. Blays drew both Odo Sein swords. Neve lifted her hand. A sword seemed to grow from it, straight and such dark black it seemed more like a blade-shaped hole in the fabric of existence than a physical weapon.

Ka gazed down at them. She lowered her sword and her hammer. And vanished.

"You are very lucky to have your ally with you," Ka said from somewhere above. "The next time we meet, it will not be enough to save any of you."

Dante gazed upward, nether swirling around both hands. He tried to feel her presence in the nether, but even knowing she was there, he could only pick up a sensation so faint he wasn't even sure it was her.

"Don't worry." Neve opened her hand and the shadowy blade dissolved back into nothing. "She's leaving."

"Like that? Should we leave, too?"

"I doubt it will make any difference," Neve said. "But it will probably make you feel better."

Dasya's men rounded up their horses, a few of which had bolted during the fighting. They trotted south through the ruins, lighting the way with torches.

"An Angel of Taim," Dasya muttered angrily. "She knew all about the axe. How long has she been following you?"

"There's no way to know," Neve said.

"Since the moment you entered the Red Valley?"

"It doesn't matter now. What should concern *you* is whether the war party the gods sent in was just a feint to draw your men and any other nearby ramna away from us."

"I will see them dead either way. What is your plan from here?"

Neve raised an eyebrow at Dante.

He shrugged. "We came here to get the axe. Mission accomplished. The longer we stay at this point, the more we put Dasya and his people at risk."

Dasya straightened in the saddle. "Then I will escort you to the valley's edge."

Neve shook her head. "It's time for us to part ways. We'll draw less attention if the three of us travel alone. Besides, I wouldn't want to delay the appointment between your spears and the heads of the gods' soldiers."

"It's been good to travel with you. But before we ride our separate roads, I'll know one thing. Was it true what Ka said? That you are also a servant of the gods?"

"Would you hate me if I was?"

"A few days ago, I would have. Now I wouldn't know what to think."

"We don't *all* hate your kind, Dasya. It's been good to ride with you, too."

They exchanged hand-clasps and salutes. Dasya raised his fist, reared back his horse, and rode to the east, his small band of warriors strung out alongside him, vanishing into the dark. Neve took a moment to align herself, then struck out to the south.

"Well," Blays said. "I'm ready for this day to come to an end before it gets any more eventful."

"Neve," Dante said. "You lied to us."

She snorted. "You should be happy about that. If I was just another ranger, right now you'd be a pile of white ash."

"Not about that. What you told Ka. You're not really an Angel of Arawn."

She stared ahead into the half-forested field of broken stone. "I don't know what you mean."

"You're a servant of Carvahal. Although I doubt whether he's served by anything you could call an 'angel.'"

"Was it that transparent?"

"Arawn *wouldn't* get involved. But Carvahal certainly would. He'd do it just to annoy everyone else. Why would you lie to us?"

"You already know why," she said. "The more distance Carvahal can place between himself and an agent like me, the more room he has to accomplish his ends."

"Speaking of his ends, is he actually helping us for the reasons he claimed?"

"If you really knew Carvahal, I don't know why you'd expect me to tell you the truth—or that he'd even tell *me* the full truth. But yes, as far as I know—and as far as you can trust me—Carvahal wants to stop the destruction of the Mists."

"And our world?"

"Yes, I suppose that too."

Dante squinted into the gloom. "When we first met, you claimed you were working for Elenna. Is that even true?"

"In a sense."

"You didn't just accidentally bump into us in Rovan, did you? On the road to it, I thought I saw someone following us. That was you." He ran his thumb along his jaw. "The doorway to Arawn's realm didn't just start gleaming on its own, did it? That was you, too. Showing me the way."

"You appeared to be too stupid to locate it on your own."

"Is there anything *else* you're not telling us?"

She glanced at him. "Like what?"

"Like that you and Ka are estranged sisters, and her chasing us around is all part of a personal vendetta she's got against you? Or that you're not even human, or whatever you are, but three sentient dogs dressed up in a human-colored coat? How would I know what to know when I still barely know what this place is?"

"It seems to me that you're getting a decent handle on it. I can say two things. First, that if there is anything more I'm not telling you, I'm not going to tell you about it, at least not now. Second, however, Carvahal isn't intending to betray you. He does want you to attain the Spear of Stars and wield it against the lich."

"I don't know how much I trust this. On the other hand, you did just save us from getting melted by an avenging angel. So there's that."

"It's nice to have this all worked out," Blays said. "Now why don't we figure out what we're going to do with the axe?"

"You mean the one we're going to give to Carvahal so that he can give it to Gashen so that we can get the other pieces of the spear? That axe?"

"What about Gladdic?"

"I'm pretty sure he'll be fine right where we left him."

"Neve, Ka said that Taim could restore Gladdic back to life," Blays said. "Did she mean that literally? Or was that just some strange angel figure of speech?"

"Taim can bring him back," Neve said mildly. "But so can you."

Dante nearly fell out of the saddle. "What? How?"

"The same way Urman tried to restore the axe. By gathering the ether from Arawn's Mill."

"Why didn't you tell us this earlier?"

"You didn't ask, now did you?"

"It never occurred to you that we might be interested in undoing the death of someone who was both our friend and an extremely useful ally?"

"You heard what Ka said. There isn't much time left to save him. I assumed you were more interested in saving everyone else in your world."

"It still would have been nice to be able to decide for ourselves."

"Hang on there," Blays said. "Are you saying we're *not* going after him?"

"I'm saying the non-Gladdic portion of existence might deserve more of our attention than the Gladdic-sized part."

"But we can bring him back."

"And we could also go take a nice, relaxing fishing trip. It would be a lot more fun and better-tasting than what we're doing now. But as tempting as that sounds, world-saving should probably still be our priority."

"An hour ago, I might have agreed with you. But that was before we got ambushed by an angry angel. Under the circumstances, I wouldn't mind having Gladdic's ether at our side."

"You're serious? You really want to do this?"

"It's a good thing Gladdic's dead, or he'd be rather insulted that you don't."

"It's not a matter of what I want," Dante said slowly. "It's a matter of what has to be done. Neve, would this even be possible? How far away is Arawn's Mill from here?"

She looked up, calculating. "A week's ride, maybe. If you don't run into any trouble along the way."

"And what are the chances of that?"

"It's in the deep wilds. What are the chances of *anything* going to plan in the wilds?"

"More than a week to get there, then. You said there's a limited window of time that he can be brought back? How much time is left?"

"Good question."

"You don't know? Aren't you some kind of angel yourself?"

"Carvahal would get a good laugh out of that." Neve smiled, eyes flashing. "Do you know how rare it is for one of you people to cross over to this place? Let alone to die here, and then also have friends capable of bringing you back?" She brightened. "Ah! I've just remembered. After death, you have two cycles of the moon. After that, the soul passes beyond reach."

"Are your lunar cycles the same length as ours?"

"Yes, the same measures were granted to your world as ours."

"That leaves us nearly forty days to get to the Mill, collect its ether, and return to where we buried him. Is that all it takes, or are there other tasks we'd have to perform to get this done?"

"Gathering the ether will likely be harder than you imagine. And instilling it within the body requires a process of its own. But neither one is particularly time-consuming, if that's what you're asking."

"So it's possible, if in theory. The question is whether we *should*."

"Answer: yes," Blays said.

Dante rubbed his forehead. "But we could die trying."

"That's different from what we're currently doing how?"

"Because it's not strictly necessary. Even if we don't die in the attempt, we could just fail while wasting time we don't have to spare."

"But if we *don't* fail, we'll be a hell of a lot stronger than we are right now. Anyway, Taim's expecting us to come straight for the remaining pieces of the spear. Disappearing to chase after this is going to confuse him. A confused Taim makes us more likely to succeed."

"While also giving him more time to come up with ways to

screw us beyond repair. There's something bigger here, though. Even if everything goes off perfectly—we get to the Mill, restore Gladdic's life, then continue after the spear, unite all its pieces, and return to our world—we'll be granting the White Lich at least two extra weeks to conquer as far as he can. We might be able to save Gladdic. But we'll sacrifice hundreds of thousands of people to do it."

Blays was quiet for a moment. "That's true. But it doesn't change the fact that having Gladdic at our side would give us better odds of accomplishing everything else. If all you care about is comparing numbers and seeing which one is bigger, you still have to choose the path with the best chance of saving everyone."

"I see you've decided on throwing *all* compromise out the window," Dante muttered. "Why are you so adamant about this?"

"Because there's a sense in which Gladdic is a better person than any of us."

"Funny, *I* don't remember ever attempting to enslave the Plagued Islands. Or murdering thousands of Colleners with demons. Demons who were, now that I think of it, also his slaves."

"That's exactly the point. He did all of those things. *And then he came back from it.* He was trying to stop the Eiden Rane before we even knew what that was. He did a lot of terrible things to the world, but in the end, he still gave up his life fighting to save it. I don't think he was even looking for redemption—he was just doing it because he knew it had to be done. If we're not willing to fight for someone who came that far back—if we're not willing to redeem him—then I don't know if there's anything worth saving."

Dante pressed his lips together. The moon had fallen behind the western mountain range and it had become very dark, the shapes around them little more than the suggestion of trees.

"Neve, we've decided to do something immensely crazy," he said. "Would you be so kind as to show us the way to Arawn's Mill?"

12

They rode on through the night, pushing east as fast as they could, looking to be free of the Red Valley before any inconvenient wars could explode between the ramna and the gods' war party. With dawn nearing, Dante felt as dull-headed as a Blays, but it was well into morning before Neve declared that they'd put the valley behind them for safe grounds.

Relatively safe, anyway; they still had to set a watch. Between that and the limited hours they allocated themselves for sleep, Dante began the next measure of their trip in a foul mood that couldn't even be improved by the sight of the terrain, a mixture of flower-studded grass, groves of trees, and lazy streams that were as pretty as a Galladese lord's courtyard.

"It's time to make an important decision," Neve said. "Do you wish to take the faster way to the Mill? Or the safer way?"

"How much safer is the safer way?" Dante said.

"And how much faster is the faster way?" Blays said.

Rather than answering verbally, Neve snapped her fingers. A broad square shimmered in the air, hanging six feet in front of them even as their horses walked onward. The square coalesced into a map. A very detailed map. So detailed, in fact, Dante felt as if he could not only make out individual trees within the forests, but the leaves *on* the trees. The rivers appeared so realistic they almost seemed to glitter in the sunlight—which was, in fact, exactly what they were doing.

Dante jerked back his head. "Is this real?"

"The ground we're walking on is real," Neve said patiently. "What you're looking at is called a 'map.'"

"So what are our two routes?"

"Here's where we are right now." Neve motioned just to the east of what was marked as the Red Valley, which looked much larger than Dante had guessed it. Two orange lines imposed themselves on top of the map. They diverged as they ran north, but eventually came back together at their distant (and, compared to the rest of the map, oddly vague-looking) destination: Arawn's Mill.

"This is the fast way." The route to the left brightened while the more meandering line to the right dimmed. "Some of it has roads. It's more direct, too. Two problems. First, there will be more ramna that way. Second, it leads us right past Silidus' realm."

"Is she one of our enemies?"

"Your guess is as good as mine. She changes her goals as often as she changes her face. The other factor is we'll be more visible. When Ka comes looking for us—and I expect that will be sooner rather than later—she's more likely to search for us there."

"Regarding the threat of ramna along the way, aren't you the Angel of Carvahal? Are the ramna even a threat to you?"

"First off, I'm not *the* Angel. I'm *an* Angel. Second, if a thousand mounted warriors came for your head, do you think you'd be able to defeat them?"

"Yes. Maybe."

She chuckled. "Do you really believe that?"

"If they rode close enough together," Dante said. "And didn't shoot any arrows at me. And gave me the sporting chance to rest up if I ran out of nether."

"Power is always a nice thing for a person to command. But a large enough number of enemies can overwhelm the most powerful sorcery."

"All right, then what about the safer route?"

"It's safer because there isn't much there. Aside from the same routine horrors you'll find everywhere else. But the terrain's worse. Instead of four or five days, it'll be seven or eight."

"Whichever route we take, I'm sure we'll run into surprises, likely of the type where someone or something tries to make us dead. We're already spending time we don't have to chase after the Mill. We'll take the faster path."

Neve grinned. "Reckless in pursuit of goals. Unusual for one of Arawn's sworn faithful. Maybe the two of you have spent too much time around each other — or just enough."

Dante opened his mouth to ask her what the hell that meant, but she spurred her horse to the north.

And toward the Mill.

After that, Neve entered one of her laconic moods. Then her waystone began to shine and they spent the next three hours ducking ramna patrols, which were already more numerous than Neve had expected. Dante couldn't use his reanimated scouts to help avoid them, either: Neve warned him that if Ka was anywhere close, she'd follow the strands of his nether straight back to them. They hadn't been working too well for him recently anyway.

By the fourth time they had to detour or hide from the roving barbarians — or was it the fifth? — Dante was sorely tempted to just kill their way forward. After all, with the Angel of Taim hunting them, what were a few more enemies to deal with?

Before he could press this resolution into action, however, the terrain about them shifted from open pastoral surroundings to a marsh studded with a thousand little islands, impassable to anyone on horseback—unless, of course, one of your party could conjure up tiny bridges of solid stone. This (and the flies he was constantly swatting) occupied Dante for the rest of the day.

They traveled on after dark, very much not wanting to have to spend the night inside the marsh. One of the gods must have favored them, because they reached solid ground just before Dante's nether ran short. They encamped in a hollow between three huge boulders.

"The map you showed us earlier," Dante said after they'd eaten. "The land around the Mill looked almost blank. Don't you know what's there? Addan said *he'd* been to it when he was trying to restore Gashen's axe."

Neve grunted. "The ground leading to the Mill...changes. But whatever it turns out to be, you won't like it. It will test you."

"But I hate tests," Blays said. "Unless it's a test of how many pastries and spiced rums one man can endure." He glanced up at the shriek of a nocturnal bird. "Does Arawn still own the Mill? Or is it controlled by somebody who's going to give us a hard time about going to see it?"

"The Mill isn't controlled by anyone."

"That's a bit strange, isn't it? Here you've got an object with the ability to fix anything you could think to break, including the corpses of us Fallen Landers, and instead of killing all of their rivals for control of it, people just...leave it sitting there?"

"It's challenging to take possession of an object when most of the people who try to travel to it wind up turning back in terror," Neve said. "And when nearly everyone else dies in the attempt to reach it. It doesn't make sense to try to take it over. Which isn't to say that nobody's tried, because it won't be news to you that people are irrational. Note I don't say 'irrational' in condemnation. That's a fool's opinion. The wise person understands that irrationality can be a good thing. Every now and then, someone gripped in its throes goes out and does something that should have been impossible."

"Plus it just makes things more fun."

Neve nodded in agreement. "And that might be even more important. Still, for all the attempts, nobody's been able to permanently capture the Mill. The most famous effort was made by Midra, a captain and sorceress of Taim. She swore to capture the Mill for her lord. And she did, though it cost her half of the eight hundred troops and priests she brought to the mountain.

"For three months, they turned away anyone who tried to reach the Mill, and killed anyone who wouldn't turn back. Eventually, most people stopped trying to make the attempt at all, while others schemed to conquer the Mill away from Midra.

"But nothing they tried worked. It wasn't long before everyone just gave up trying. Some time later, though, a man named Gavan came to the mountain. Gavan was just an ordinary cobbler and never expected to leave the safety of his realm, let alone go on any great adventures, but one night he drank too much brandy while celebrating a compliment a lord had given his work, and he knocked down his wife's crystal cup.

"The cup broke, and badly. Most wives might scold or yell at their husband, or order him out of the house for a few days, but the cup had been passed down by the women in his wife's family for a dozen generations, and so she was madder than most. Even so, most would agree she overreacted when she ran from the house declaring their marriage was over.

"Gavan loved his wife and was heartbroken. He made countless attempts to apologize and offer to replace the cup. His wife accepted none of these. At last, Gavan understood she never would. Despairing, he set up a noose and was in the process of sticking his neck inside it when he had an idea: if he was going to die, he might as well do it attempting to pull off the one thing that could restore her cup.

"He gathered up the broken pieces and traveled toward the

Mill. Reaching it was not easy, but what's relevant to this story is that, five days after he began his ascent of Mount Arna, the peak that houses the Mill, he returned to the base of the mountain.

"He'd made it to the Mill. His proof? The cup was restored and intact. The same did not seem to be true of Gavan's mind. He claimed that nearly all of Midra's soldiers were now dead. During their occupation of the Mill, they'd gone mad. The officers had started executing their soldiers over trivial details, and then over utter nonsense. Priests accused others of heresy and impaled the so-called heretics on pikes, but then used the nether to heal them, keeping them alive and in endless agony. Some people mutilated themselves or committed suicide. By the end, they were chasing each other around in mobs. Gavan found hundreds dead. The only survivors were delirious, and on the brink of starving to death, though they admitted to having eaten their dead once they ran out of other food. They're the ones who told Gavan what had happened—and warned him to get away from the Mill as fast as he could.

"All of this was bad news for Midra, Midra's soldiers, and anyone else with an eye for conquering Arawn's Mill. But the good news for Gavan was that when he returned home to show his wife the unbroken cup, she took him back in.

"I take two lessons from this story: first, the Mill was made so it *couldn't* be controlled. And second, that the strange turns of fate can provide the most ordinary man the chance to become a hero, as long as he has the will to see his journey through to the end. For how many people can truly be said to have the courage and love of Gavan?"

That night was the first time Dante had felt cold since he and Blays had descended from the western mountains. The following day took them through a field of standing stones dusted with some silvery mineral that glittered even when the sky was overtaken by clouds. Swift, shallow streams criss-crossed the ground as well, so that everything around them was twinkling and sparkling, and nothing seemed rooted in place, but rather appeared to be in constant motion. It was very pretty, but the longer they spent within it, the more disorienting and unsettling it became.

"That's the road to Protus," Neve announced. "Kingdom of Silidus the Ever-Fluid. It's just on the other side of that hill."

It was normally a simple thing to spot a road by the traffic on it, but this being the wilds, there *wasn't* any traffic. With all the glittering, it took Dante a moment to see through the confusion and identify the road, which wasn't straight, but rather weaved between the streams, presumably to avoid the need for any bridges that would be difficult to maintain beyond the safety of Protus' walls.

They'd been traveling along a strip of dirt worn into the dense grass. As they neared the intersection with the road, Neve lifted her head, gazing east.

"Get off the path," she hissed. "Quickly now!"

She dashed into the grass, making for a stand of thick-trunked trees. No sooner had the three of them come to a halt beneath the boughs than the sound of hoofbeats rose from the east. Dozens of them, and nearly at a gallop.

Dante glanced at Neve's waystone, but it was dark. The vanguard trotted into view. Soldiers in shining armor. The banner they carried and the tabards they wore over their chest plates bore the same symbol: a white lion on a red field.

Three score more riders followed after the vanguard. Each one of them looked threatening and proud. Yet for all the fierceness of the others, one man stood out like an obelisk from the desert: astride a destrier that could have trampled a bull, helm shaped into the face of a snarling lion, his orange eyes blazing like fire.

The band of riders swept past them, the rumble of their horses dimming quickly.

Neve stared after them, eyes narrowed. "I assume you're pious enough to know those were Gashen's troops, but also ignorant enough of this place to not recognize the man leading them."

Blays swept back his hair. "A guy with a most excellent helmet?"

"His name is Odon Lars. And he's Gashen's high general."

"What would he be going to see Silidus about?" Dante said.

"I can only guess. But it might be worth our while to find out."

"How so? We've got a mission in front of us."

"Because politics of *some* kind is afoot. Possibly even the brewings of war. I imagine you'd find it useful to know if there's trouble among the gods." Neve shook her long orange braid loose from her shoulders. "It'd give you the opportunity to turn over the axe, too. Ka isn't likely to try to take it away from Odon Lars. That would turn Gashen against Taim for sure."

"There's no way the general's carrying Gashen's piece of the spear around with him. Would Gashen still honor the deal after we've given up all of our leverage?"

"Absolutely."

Dante gazed west down the road. "Ka will still be hunting for us whether or not we've rid ourselves of the axe. And we only have so many days until Gladdic passes beyond our ability to restore him. We can't spare any delays."

Neve nodded, but her lips were tightened, too. Dante kept his face neutral as he thought through the possible reasons for her apparent disappointment. Nothing had sprung to mind by the time she led them onward, crossing the main road and bringing them north at a trot.

"So I've got to ask," Blays said unprompted. "The gods almost never fully manifest themselves, right? Too afraid of getting killed or what have you. Doesn't that make people like you and Ka the *real* powers of the Realm?"

Neve snorted. "Does that make the swords you swing the real powers of *your* realm?"

"Well, no. But I'd get much less done if I didn't have my steel. Even worse, I wouldn't look nearly as great."

"We're the sharpest swords the gods own. But that doesn't make us rulers."

"If you're his favorite blade, it's rather interesting that Carvahal has thrust you out here in harm's way. Is there something more to his interest in us that you're not telling?"

She glanced at Blays. "You know he has a soft spot for humans. Thats a large part of it. But it's about balance, too."

"Balance? Between the gods and the ramna?"

"Balance between the gods themselves." Neve gestured at Dante. "You're the High Priest of your order, yes? How is the power of your order structured?"

"By our Council," Dante said. "The Council numbers twelve in all, selecting new members from our most talented and useful priests. The Council also chooses one of its own to rule itself and the city of Narashtovik."

"And what if there *was* no ruler?"

"Then everything would take much longer to get done. And I'd finally have the chance to get some rest."

"Do you think the Council would last?"

"Without my brilliant and inspired leadership? They'd be eating each other's flesh within days. But if they *hadn't* been spoiled by the glory of my genius, I don't see why they wouldn't last. They're good people. Our best, in fact."

"So it could last for a while on its own. But no matter how well it's maintained, it's inevitable that such a system will eventually bring in someone unworthy, selfish, or overly ambitious. That's when its flaws will be exposed. For without a singular ruler, the system will leak power. Eventually, one of your Council members will seek to take that power for themselves. And others will move to resist them, which can only be done by anointing *themselves* the leader.

"The results will be as obvious as they are natural. Your Council, once distributed in power, will either be consolidated under a single ruler, or split apart into competing groups—who will, having so much in common yet just enough difference to set themselves apart, likely become mortal enemies of each other."

"Right," Dante said. "Yet I can't help but notice that we have twelve seats on the Council *because there are twelve gods*. You guys aren't exactly united under a single king or high priest, are you? So why doesn't this unclaimed power make *your* system fall apart?"

Neve waved a hand. "Good fortune and careful intervention. You people still know the story of how Carvahal once tricked Arawn into getting locked up within his starry vault, right?"

"You mean the story that's central to our whole theology? Yes, it rings a bell."

"Well, it had to be done. Arawn was getting too big for his britches. Was about to upset the entire order of things. Besides, who do you think is the one that eventually let Arawn back out?"

Dante blinked; somehow it hadn't quite occurred to him that Arawn clearly *wasn't* still imprisoned, as most of his people believed true. "How long ago did that happen?"

"Long before your age. Long enough ago that *I* wasn't there for it. But my understanding is that Carvahal knew in advance he'd only keep Arawn locked up for a limited time, because someone—most likely Taim—would grow too large in influence while Arawn was away, which was exactly what happened."

"I see. And surely all of Carvahal's power-brokering and attempts to prevent one person from seizing the throne has nothing to do with the fact no one likes Carvahal and the new regent's first order of business would be to execute him."

"Carvahal has plenty of friends," Neve said indignantly. "When he wants them. But a person in his position doesn't always have the luxury of keeping his friends." Her face softened. "Anyway, if Taim succeeds in letting the Mists fall, and your world with them, he'll seize the opportunity to replace the Mists. Maybe start a replacement for your world, too.

"It doesn't take someone of Carvahal's foresight to see that this would lend Taim a great deal of momentum. From there, he'd likely make a push to exterminate the ramna. It's quite possible he'd succeed, but if he failed, he'd likely have exhausted himself so much that the ramna would destroy Taim and his allies instead. We don't want any of that to come to pass."

"Being such humanitarians as you are."

"No one among our people is putting on any airs about that. It's rather that a world with many poles of power is far more *interesting*. Rather than the total obedience that would be demanded by a single lord, a splintered world allows for real struggle. These struggles are often grim, to be sure. But they can bring out the best of people, too. Do you understand why you're fighting the White Lich?"

"Because as it turns out, I don't like being exterminated?"

"That's not it, is it?" Neve said. "If he offered to let you and your people live in exchange for your complete obedience, you'd still fight him to the death. Even though you've seen the future he means to build — and that it could well become a golden age. You fight him because that age would be a dull one. Gray. Flat. All differences erased. All power held tight in his hands. In such a place, what *spirit* is left for anyone?" She stared into the distance, jaw clenched, then smiled. "Carvahal doesn't want something similar to happen here. I'm inclined to agree with him."

The land before them grew more rugged, more littered with the glittering stones, with fewer patches of grass. By evening, they rode between scattered boulders, low but tooth-like ridges, and rocky, shattered hills. Dante thought there might have been ruins among them, but everything was too broken and worn to be sure.

The trail brought them to a depression that wasn't quite a canyon. Small caves pocked the rocky walls. The sun was almost down and they discussed passing the night in a cave, but the two entrances they approached smelled just bad enough to convince them to stay outside instead.

"Another two days, I'd say." Neve smoothed out her bedroll. "Then we find out whether seeking the Mill was a wise move after all."

Dante frowned, about to ask her what she meant despite being confident she wouldn't tell him, but a shadow swooped over him. He ducked reflexively. The creature swung upwards, then dived at Blays. It swerved at the last second, lost in the darkness.

Blays swatted at his hair. "What was that? A bat?"

"No." Neve's voice was stiff. "A drakelet."

"A drakelet? What are we doing sleeping in these oily blankets if they can't even keep the flying lizards away?"

The creature darted back toward Dante. Another followed on the spindly tail of the first. He reached for the nether, but they twisted past him. Neve scrambled to her feet. She snapped her fingers. The light of ether sprayed across the night.

Illuminating hundreds of drakelets, and thousands of needly fangs.

"Lyle's balls!" Blays said. "Did we camp on top of their nest?"

"This place is too exposed for a nest," Neve said. "They must have caught our scent and followed us here."

Ten of them broke from the tangled flock toward Dante. He barraged them with little bolts of shadows. Bodies thumped and scales fluttered to the ground. But more were already winging in from the edges of the ether's light. Blays yelped. A sting punched into Dante's calf. He kicked his leg, dislodging a winged lizard. He swung his fist at it, hammering it out of the air.

Blays drew his swords with a snap of nether, adding a purple glare to the white of the ether. Dante shaped the nether into a ball of whirling darts, its motion like a miniature mirror of the flock of drakelets, and launched it into the lizards. It cleaved a hole through their ever-shifting formation, dropping dozens of them to the bare earth. Yet more were arriving with each moment.

A horse shrieked. Dante grimaced, jolted by a vision of the flesh-hungry ziki oko attempting to strip his legs of their meat. "Into the cave!"

He swung into the saddle. Another drakelet bit him on the back of the neck and he retaliated by disintegrating it. The three of them galloped toward the nearest of the caves. A mass of drakelets swarmed behind them. The cave was just ahead; Dante moved into its walls, ready to yank them across the opening as soon as they were inside.

"Stop!" Neve thundered. "Do *not* go inside there!"

Dante shot a look at her, then sent a bloom of ether to the mouth of the cavern. The light gleamed on dampness. The interior of the cave seemed to tilt, as if Dante had yanked his ball of ether to the side. But the stone walls and floor stayed put—something inside the cavern was withdrawing into the depths.

Swallowing down his nausea, Dante wheeled about, galloping away from the flock and slaying the few that had gotten too close.

"We need a plan," Blays said.

"I know."

"One that isn't 'get swallowed by whatever that thing was.'"

"We can't outrun them forever," Dante said. "Fortunately, the gods saw fit to make stone stronger than lizards."

He glanced behind him, gauging how much distance they'd gained on the flock. Then reached ahead of him into the earth. Circular walls erupted from the soil. They jumped to a height of eight feet, then turned inward, shaping a slightly domed ceiling. Dante lit the way for the horses, then swept the wall shut behind them.

"Well," Blays said, voice echoing from the tight walls, "that was—augh!"

He shook his arm, which had a drakelet biting it. He cast it to the ground and put his sword through its head. Two others had gotten inside as well and Dante struck them down with nethereal bolts.

The horses shuffled about, spooked. Dante kneeled over one of the lizards. "This is the most aggressive I've seen them. What's gotten into...?" He leaned closer, then picked up the limp body, turning it in his hand. "They aren't alive."

Blays dabbed sweat from his brow. "Oh, is that what happens when you explode their heads?"

"They *weren't* alive, either—they were reanimated."

"Reanimated. Right. And...not by you?"

"For once."

"Ka." Neve's voice sounded like it was being scraped over the stone floor. "We have to get out of here before she finds us."

"That's a problem," Dante said. "Those things are practically filling the sky."

"Oh damn," Blays said. "I suppose we'll just have to go somewhere there isn't any sky."

Dante stared at him, then nodded. He sank the ground beneath them. The horses did not approve of this, but they didn't get a say in the matter. Once they were twelve feet down, he extended a tunnel horizontally and rode forward.

"This is bad," Neve said.

"You don't say," Dante muttered.

"There's virtually nothing north of here. She'll know we're headed toward the Mill."

"You're sure of this?"

"This might even be part of her plan. She told you it was possible to restore your friend's life to tempt you to travel to the Mill. That gives her all the more time to hunt us down. While getting *you* to waste time chasing something that isn't the Spear of Stars. We should have taken the safer route. We have no chance to reach the Mill now. She'll be sure to find us."

Dante pulled his horse to a stop and spun in the saddle. "If you knew this might happen, why didn't you *say* something?"

"Do I look like your commander? Your decisions are your own to make. I'm just here to help you see them through."

"Which you could do by giving us your advice *before* it's too late to make any difference!"

She stared back at him. "If you don't like my methods, I will be happy to remove myself from your presence."

"All I'm asking is for some basic guidance!"

"This is getting us nowhere." Blays' words hung on the damp, earthy air. "It would be idiotic to try to get to the Mill from here, right? So we don't do that. Instead, we go back to Silidus' realm."

Dante felt a headache coming on. "Why would we do that?"

"Ka won't expect it. We'll throw her off *and* give ourselves the chance to secure an agreement with General What's-His-Face for Gashen's portion of the spear. Once we've got that wrapped up, we'll put on a show of appearing to ride out to Gashen's kingdom to collect our reward, but once we're out of sight, we'll turn back for Arawn's Mill. The whole thing will only delay us by a day or two."

The thought of sacrificing time they dearly needed made

Dante's throat feel like it was throttling itself. But his haste had just cost them this delay.

"Then we'll make way for Protus," he said. "But if we spend more than two days there, I'm burning the whole place down before we can be tempted to spend a third."

He ran the tunnel to the west. They exited into a quiet night and he sealed the ground behind them. They put miles of distance between them and the drakelets before slowing down.

Protus wasn't as far away as he'd feared: they still had three hours of night left by the time they crested a hill and looked across at its walls and spires. It was surrounded by a marsh similar to the one they'd crossed earlier, but a causeway led straight to the city gates. Dante made way for it.

"I wouldn't do that," Neve said as he was about to direct his horse onto the cobbles.

"Use the only way to reach the city?"

"Do you want my advice or not?"

"So are you making our decisions for us after all?"

"This is Silidus' realm." Neve sounded irritated, but Dante didn't think it was aimed at him. "Don't trust anything you see."

She thrust out her fingers. A cloud of nether stretched across the causeway, blocking out the moonlight. The causeway seemed to collapse: parts of it were still there, strung out in bits and pieces, but more than half of it vanished. What remained wasn't steady, either, but rather slowly sank into the black water while other parts bubbled to the surface like hunks of mutton in a stew that was just about to simmer.

"I advise," Neve said, "that we wait until morning to cross."

"I've decided," Dante said, "that we'll wait until morning to cross."

They backed off, seeking shelter under a stand of trees. Dante harvested the branches and leaves tight to stop any wandering reanimated drakelets from finding them. He slept later than he meant to, and once he finally got up he rushed through the morning necessities as fast as he could.

Under the light of day, the illusion of the causeway had disappeared. A line of little islands stretched toward the distant city; some slowly sank beneath the surface while others rose from it. The air smelled like standing water with a whiff of sulfur.

Neve sniffed. "You'll want to be careful of the snakes."

Blays cranked his head around. "Please tell me they're illusions, too."

"Okay. They're illusions, too."

"Now why don't I believe you?"

Dante rolled his eyes. "The massive, crystal-toothed worms didn't phase you, but the possibility of snakes has you dancing around on your toes?"

"Well, massive worms aren't snakes, now are they?"

Dante nicked the back of his arm and drew the nether to him. He was concerned the earth wouldn't respond to him, as it had refused to do in Talassa, or that it would keep shifting in and out of the water despite his commands. Yet it obeyed his commands without wavering. A lane of solid dirt unrolled before them. Despite the sunlight, the water was almost as black as it had been during the night.

"What are those ripples?" Blays said.

Dante glanced away from his work. "At the risk of looking the fool, I'm going to predict that they're fish."

The marsh was a good half mile wide. In the interests of saving nether, he ran his path to as many existing islands as he could. When they were a third of the way across, Blays inhaled sharply.

"Snakes," Blays said flatly. "Snakes have arrived."

Dante looked back. Sure enough, three long green snakes

were wending their way up from the water toward the horses.

"Are they spitting nether at you?"

"No, but—"

"Then who cares?" With a wave of his hand, Dante blasted the snakes off the causeway, sending them cartwheeling into the water.

Blays clapped his hands. "I would never get tired of watching that."

Four more of them were already breaking the surface. Dante gave them a bop on their flattish heads and they vanished down into the black.

Neve made a noise that might have been a chuckle. "We've been spotted."

Riders had emerged from the gates. They made for the marsh, which yielded up a path for them. One that led directly toward the three intruders. Dante halted, keeping one eye on the water, but it was as though the Proteans had politely asked the serpents to stop.

The riders didn't tarry, but they weren't overly hasty, either. Their garments were somewhat loose and colored in the pure white of Silidus, making it difficult to make out their exact shape. Their blades—sheathed, at least for now—were as sinuously wavy as the snakes sewn on their chests.

They came to a stop twenty feet away, leaving a gap of open water between the two parties.

The woman at their fore bore strikingly dark skin. She lifted her chin in greeting. "We appreciate your interest in our city. Unfortunately, we are not seeing visitors at this time."

"Then it's a good thing we're not here to see your city," Blays said. "We're here to see High General Odon Lars."

"Unfortunately, General Lars is currently occupied."

"If you don't let us see him, the only thing he'll be occupied with is tossing you into your own marsh. We've brought something he very badly wants."

The woman smiled without any real warmth. "What is it you've brought that could be of more interest to him than Silidus herself?"

"His master's axe."

Her mouth made an O. After a glance at her fellows, she led the three outsiders across the marsh and to the city gates. These scintillated so brightly they were hard to look at—although on the side facing into the city they were quite dull.

The city was graced with airy towers and cathedrals, but much of it was impermanent: stalls, tents, carts; even many of the smaller houses were set on wheels, as if the residents couldn't stand the thought of always seeing the same thing through their windows. They were a tall people, and watched from the corners of their almond-shaped eyes as the three foreigners were delivered to the palace.

This was in the middle of a park, though it wasn't clearly delineated where the park ended and the palace began. Five white towers stood in a circle, each one topped by a moon at a different point in its phase. Two streams ran around and through the grounds, plashing noisily, along with several other channels that were currently dry but had the bleached look of places that had recently carried water.

The woman led them inside the tower crowned by the thinnest sliver of moon. She left two guards with them and glided away from the chamber.

"Be careful when you speak to the Proteans," Neve murmured once the two guards had wandered to the far end of the room. "They're subtle. They'll make you think they're agreeing with you when they mean no such thing."

"How can—?" Dante shut his mouth with a click; one of the guards was walking back in their direction.

Not a minute later, the door banged open; a wide-shouldered

man blundered inside. His face was as leonine as the icon on his chest. He was followed inside by four other men. Each varied in height and age, but they were obviously all soldiers, and good ones at that.

"Where is it?" General Lars stomped toward them, his withering gaze roving over their belts and weapons. "Give me the axe, or I will give you death."

Neve shrank back, though Dante now knew it was just part of her "I'm just an everyday ranger" act. He faced the general. "I wouldn't be so sure of your ability to do that. In which case I would be very cautious about making threats."

The general lumbered forward, placing his face within a foot of Dante's. "Whose realm are you from?"

"What does it matter?"

"I need to know whose city to raze to its ashes."

"If you're going to sow my fields with salt, then normally I'd tell you I'm the servant of Taim," Dante said. "But I've been promised that Gashen honors his bargains, so I'd rather tell you the truth."

Lars relaxed somewhat, though he seemed the type who only truly relaxed after a long day of slaughtering his foes in the street. "Then start with all that matters: do you have the axe?"

"It's been broken. But we have the pieces." Dante nodded to Blays. "Show him."

Blays unshouldered his pack and withdrew a long bundle. He set it on the ground and unrolled it. The faces of the five men brightened with wonder. They were silent for three full seconds. Then Lars kneeled and reached for the haft.

"Hang on now," Blays said. "We didn't go through three layers of hell to get this just to *give* it to you."

Lars looked up from beneath his brows. "Do you know how many people my lord would kill to get this back?"

"Until there are no more people?"

"That is right. Now make your offer."

"Normally I'd ask for Gashen's daughter's hand in marriage, but I'm already married. Plus I'm not sure how wise it would be to take on the god of war as my father-in-law." Blays bent back his thumb, cracking his knuckle. "Fortunately for you, we don't intend to ransom your kingdom. We just want to borrow Gashen's part of the Spear of Stars."

General Lars straightened, cocking his head. He laughed slowly. "You're the Fallen Landers."

"I'm afraid you've caught us."

"I heard you were supposed to be devils. That your skin was covered in scales and your eyes were like two holes down to hell." He looked them up and down. "You are a little ugly, but you are no devils."

"I'll forgive you for that, as Dante's ugliness must be so blinding you can't properly see my good looks. We were told that if we got Gashen's axe back, he'd happily give us his spear shard. Were we told right?"

"A man's word is not his bond until it is spoken out loud. And we had no agreement." Lars kneeled once more, reaching again for the haft. Dante's instinct was to block him from doing so, but he let the general take it up. Lars lifted it to the light, appraising it as if it was a glass of priceless wine. "The axe was stolen by a dirty thief. It is within my right to reclaim it in the name of the one it was stolen from."

"Ah," Blays said. "Yes, that's an interesting point. But we recovered it from the actual thieves, didn't we? Thus anyone who takes it from *us* would be a thief—including, say, the guy who might have owned it in the first place."

"No man in this world or yours has a claim to the axe of Gashen but Gashen himself." Lars stared Blays down, letting the haft dangle from his hand. Then he threw his head back and laughed.

"Are you joking? Because it appears that you're joking."

"The look on your face!" The general planted his free hand on his leg. His officers were laughing as well, slapping each other on the back. After a moment, Lars calmed somewhat. He twirled the axe haft in his hand, giving it another look. "You've done a good deed. I won't disgrace my lord by robbing you of the valor of your reward. By Gashen's word, you will have his ninth of the spear." Lars drew the axe back to his chest. "But there is one condition."

13

Dante cursed inwardly. "Name it."

"Tell me the story of how you found the axe."

"Then what?"

"Then our deal is struck."

"That's it? You just want me to tell you the story?"

"Much of the difference between a common item and a holy relic is the number of stories that can be told about it. The loss of the axe was a tragedy. When Gashen tells the axe's story to others, he'll want to be able to tell the triumph of its return as well."

Dante glanced at Neve, who gave a small shrug. Dante launched into the tale of how they'd sought Sallen of the Jessel within the Red Valley. Occasionally Blays took over. By implicit agreement, they glossed over Carvahal's involvement, along with the revelation of Neve's true nature when Ka had attacked them.

Still, everything else was true, and Lars was delighted to hear it, clapping his callused hands at each major turn of events.

"We saw you on the road yesterday, but we were in the midst of...another errand," Dante finished. "But when Ka's scouts found us last night, we decided we'd better come find you before she found us."

"The story is told and the deal is done," Lars said. "Will you swap blood with me to seal it?"

Before Dante could answer, the general drew a knife and cut his right palm, mouth twitching once in response to the pain. Dante raised an eyebrow but did the same. They clasped palms. When Lars withdrew his hand, Dante surreptitiously sent a bit of nether to his wound, purifying the blood of any disease that might have been lurking in the general's.

"That gives us one part of the spear in hand, and a second by promise," Dante said. "But I'm afraid our mission is about to stall out on us."

"I know of your troubles," Lars said, suddenly contemptuous. "The others refuse to let you sport for their portions of the spear. Well, we currently stand within the halls of Silidus. Why don't we go tell her she must allow you to contend for her shard, eh?"

He swung about and strode from the chamber. Everyone else followed after him, like he was the breaking of a dam and they were swept up in his current. He emerged into the daylight.

"Ithiana!" His voice echoed between the towers. "Ithiana, we will speak now!"

The same woman who'd met them on the causeway stepped into the half-forested courtyard, looking annoyed yet polite about it. She indicated that if they wished to see Ithiana, they should follow her into the tower topped by the full moon. Inside, she brought them into a hall of white marble with a domed ceiling and columns of carved women upholding its circumference.

"Her Lady Ithiana." The woman bowed her head and withdrew from the room.

Which appeared to be empty. Until a shadow passed over the white couch in one of its naves. When the shadow withdrew, a woman in a flowing white dress rose from the couch, a garland crowning her black hair.

"General Lars," she said. She looked as though she might be fifty, in as much as age could be trusted in this ageless place, yet her tanned-as-a-Parthian skin looked as youthful as Neve's. "I didn't expect the pleasure of your conversation until this evening."

"The axe of Taim," Lars crowed. "It's been returned to me!"

"What wonderful news. By these three? May I ask how you are acquainted?"

"By the last twenty minutes. It's time you knew them, too. These are the seekers of the Spear of Stars. For the axe, I have promised them Gashen's piece of it. It is now time for Silidus to let them earn *her* part of it, if they can."

Ithiana stepped forward with a whisper of silk. "You've promised them Gashen's spear-part? General Lars, are you drunk?"

"Of course I am! But my judgment is as unerring as Jorus' aim."

"Unless I'm gravely mistaken, you came here to discuss *not* allowing them to possess the spear."

"I was told they were goblins in the guise of humans. Instead, they come to me with a deed more glorious than any that I have ever achieved."

She puckered her face in reproach. "You go too far, General. Any one of your victories would — "

"Mean a hell of a lot less than this!" He shook the broken axe at her. "When someone is in the act of achieving glory, it is *ungodly* to stand in their way. I don't ask for Silidus to *give* them her part. Just to give them the opportunity to earn it, and see if they can win even higher valor than they have already attained."

"But what would the point be? Even if Silidus relented, would all seven others? Do you truly think Taim ever would?"

"That is up for Taim to decide! If each one of us chooses to let them earn or fail to earn the weapon — as we have always done in the past — then we can see how ready Taim is to stand alone, eh?"

Ithiana drew her thin brows together. "Does it matter how we addressed the spear in the past? It seems to me that if we never vary our ways, then we will never experience any variety to our lives. In which case we already know how each day will pass: and if that is so, what makes our lives worth living?"

Lars made a dismissive gesture. "If you had your way, we'd burn anything older than three seasons and never celebrate the same holy day twice. Our ways aren't our ways *just because*. Our ways have meaning and value within them. After the first time that a single mad sorcerer nearly drove all mortal life from the Fallen Land, it was decided to provide the people with a means of fighting back should such an encompassing threat ever rise again. Barrod forged the spear for that very purpose. But it wasn't to be a gift: those who'd fight back against impossible power would have to find their way to our land and then prove themselves worthy of it. It was a balanced and honorable solution. If we abandon it now, we declare ourselves unbalanced and dishonorable."

The woman appraised him. "That old axe has awakened something in you, hasn't it? You will forgive me—I had forgotten the long history of the spear. Even so, aren't you being far too hasty, dear general? Shouldn't we discuss this with the others? Perhaps even seek to hear from Taim?"

"What is *right* only needs to be put to discussion by those who are *wrong*. It's time for us all to remember our bond to these people."

"Perhaps you are right. But even if you are, General Lars, how can you be so certain that you know Gashen's mind on this matter? When he sent you here, he remained in agreement with Taim, did he not?"

"He did."

"Then how can you demand I commit to your new path when you yourself cannot say with full confidence that it is what your own lord wants?"

"I have known my lord for many centuries. How could I serve as his High General if I didn't know his thoughts as well as I know my own?"

"It is for that exact same reason I know Silidus could never agree to what you're asking while any uncertainty surrounds the matter. You're calling for an immense boon, General Lars. Can't you see that? If you would ask so much of us, won't you agree to return to your land and speak to Gashen? Is that so much to ask?"

Lars lowered his chin, releasing a slow sigh. "No, it isn't. And if it were you asking such a favor of me I would likely want the same certainty you do."

Ithiana smiled. "There are few things that comfort me more than knowing that even the lords of war also bear the sword of reason. Carry home, swiftly as you can, and return to me, and then we may reach our agreement."

The general nodded, putting his hand to his heart. "I will do just that."

He turned and made for the door, his officers forming a column behind him. Dante glanced at Neve, who shrugged. He made to follow the others.

"That was quite the feat of compromise," Blays said. "There's just one problem with it: we don't have time for it."

The stately woman looked on him with concern. "Sir, I am afraid the matter is too important to be hastened."

"Not true."

"Whatever do you mean? You have just heard all of my reasons that it is so."

"Yeah, but here's my reason you're wrong: we need your part of the spear right now."

"I have just explained that we are open to letting you vie for it. But this matter must be handled through proper channels."

Blays strolled toward her, resting his forearm on the hilt of one of his swords. "Wrong. You said the problem is uncertainty, right? Silidus doesn't want to oppose Taim's will and then get caught with her pants down. But it seems to me there's another way for her to be certain she's not making the wrong move. If you let us earn Silidus' part of the spear, and then it turns out Gashen doesn't want to oppose Taim after all, then I'll let you deliver my head straight to Taim. That'd calm him down a bit, don't you think?"

Ithiana's entire face went tight. "It is not your place to make demands of me—nor of the gods to whom you owe obedience."

"It seems like a very reasonable offer to me. If you do wind up needing to send Taim my head, you could even tell him that we tricked you into giving us the spear shard. Or that the whole agreement was just a devious trap concocted by Silidus to ensnare us and put an end to this whole mess."

"You do not understand our ways, mortal. There are protocols and channels that must be followed."

Blays squinted one eye. "The proposal I'm making is *better* for you than the protocol you insist on following. But you won't take it. That's the sort of thing that gets a fellow thinking. Specifically, it makes a fellow think that you don't really mean to let us earn the spear even if Gashen agrees to give us his piece."

"I have told you that you will make no demands!" She strolled forward, pointing her finger at him and then at the door. "What this shows me is that you are not a person who can be reasoned with or trusted. For that, there will be no deal of *any* kind. You will depart this city at once. And you will depart with him, Lars, for having such poor judgment to bring such a man to my hall!"

Lars gave an affronted grunt. "If that's the true measure of your hospitality, then I agree we have no place here! Come, you two gentlemen! We will go to see Gashen, and you will learn that there are still some among the gods who honor their bond with their creation."

Before Dante knew what was happening, they were all outside. It took an uncomfortable few minutes for the palace grooms to have Lars' steeds prepared and presented, but they were on their way soon enough, riding to the gate and then onto the causeway. They were escorted by the same riders who had allowed Dante, Blays, and Neve into the city, but the riders turned back for Protus as soon as they'd delivered their charges to the other side of the marsh.

"I am angered by Ithiana's treatment of you," Lars said as soon as the Silideans were gone. "But her insult will be undone ten times over by the celebration we will give you in our kingdom."

"I would love to see that," Dante said. "Unfortunately, we can't just yet. There's a different errand the three of us have to see to first."

The general frowned. "But didn't you come to me in order to obtain our ninth of the Spear of Stars?"

"Yes, and I trust your promise to me enough to know you'll honor it later. Whereas the thing we're going to do now can only be done now."

"Oh." The general sounded disappointed, if not outright wounded. "Then may fortune favor your travel."

"We'll come see you as soon as we're finished. It won't be more than a month."

"That will lend Gashen more than enough time to choose how to fete the ones who brought back his axe. Very well! We will meet again within a month's time."

"Before we go," Dante said. "Is there one more favor you could do us?"

"You aren't shy about asking for what you wish, eh? Make it plain."

"As you travel home, can you spread the word that we're traveling with you?"

"Ah—for you are still being hunted by Ka."

"That's the one."

"She's a greater pain in the ass than sitting on a pike. I don't like to lie. It's the behavior of the low. But I will do so for you."

They clasped hands and said their goodbyes. General Lars brought his people east while Neve reoriented them to the north, sticking for now to the thickest cover they could find.

"Well," Blays said. "That all went about as well as it possibly could have."

Dante smacked the heel of his palm to his forehead. "Talking a god *out* of giving us her spear is what you consider a major success? What do you plan to do for an encore, cut off our arms and legs?"

"You're only mad because you're being stupid. Ithiana didn't have any intention of giving us her spear part. That's why I had to push her into admitting it."

"You gave her a push right off the edge of a cliff. All we had to do was let Lars go speak to Gashen. We could have just spent the wait going to Arawn's Mill. You know, the thing we're doing right now anyway?"

"When exactly did Ithiana say she'd let us vie for the spear?"

"The several times she said exactly that!"

"She was very careful *not* to say that. You heard it because that's what you were looking to hear. Lars wanted to believe she was being honorable, too. But the only thing she promised was she might *consider* letting us earn Silidus' piece. It's a damn good thing we've got me around to save the day."

"He's right," Neve said. "She was trying to deceive us."

"Why would she do that?" Dante said.

"Maybe to buy herself time to figure out what to do, or maybe to get us out of the way while Silidus sold us out to Taim.

Silidus has reasons for everything she does, but woe to anyone who needs to figure out what those reasons might be."

Dante nodded, digesting all of this. "I suppose we've won Gashen to our side, which is more than we had yesterday. With any luck, he'll open some new doors for us. So what's the plan now?"

"We've successfully kicked up a ruckus," Blays said. "In my experience with ruckuses, the best thing to do in their aftermath is run away as fast as you can. We'll head for the Mill—and we'll bring back Gladdic."

They traveled into the wilds.

The road still carried into the north, but this time Neve took them off it, guiding them through reeking marshes, tangled woods, and fields of jagged rock. At all times, Dante kept his focus in the nether around them, seeking for more undead drakelets or any other sign of Ka's pursuit. For the time, though, they seemed alone.

It was slow going and the guilt of what they were doing lay on Dante's chest like a stone. For though he thought their mission to the Mill was for the best, back in their own world, Nak was doing all he could to stand in the way of the lich. But there was no stopping the enemy. As the threat approached them, the southern reaches of the Norren Territories emptied of their people, the clans slipping away in all directions: east to the Woduns, west toward the borders of Gask and Gallador, some even daring to circle south behind the waves of Blighted and seek sanctuary in the mountains of the Dundens.

Thus there was, for a moment, a respite from the carnage. But it would be a matter of mere days before the Eiden Rane drew within striking distance of real settlements, places like Arrolore and Tantonnen, or the norren towns that led toward Gask. Bloodshed was coming. And they weren't even to the Mill. The remainder of the spear felt a million miles away.

Two days after departing Protus, a mountain appeared from the wilderness.

"Is that it?" Dante said.

Neve nodded. "Mount Arna."

"Let me guess. The Mill is at the very top?"

"That's normally where they keep the best things," Blays said. "Either that or at the very bottom."

"What's the path like to the peak?"

"I can't tell you. Not because I don't want to, but because the truth is I don't know. It's unstable. My belief is the way upward alters to test whoever's daring to try to reach the Mill."

"It seems odd to go to all the trouble of making the Mill only to make sure sure no one can ever get to it," Blays said. "Did you guys even *think* to consult me when you were making this place?"

"There may be parts where it gets easy. But those are the parts when you should be most afraid. Because the mountain's lying to us. Trying to lull us."

"I wasn't aware mountains could do that."

She stared at the distant heights. Mount Arna climbed to a single immense peak and though it felt like early fall where they stood, the upper third of the mountain was layered with white snow.

"If we're separated," Neve said. "Or if tragedy strikes. Just make your way to the peak. There, stand beneath the Mill and gather the ether as it's made. Any vessel will do to carry it. But don't you dare stay in its presence for more than a few minutes. No matter how much you're tempted. Mortals aren't meant to be near it. Even when Midra tried to capture it, she kept her camp down the slope from it.

"Once you have the ether in hand, carry it to the body of your friend. Send it into his bones and heart. This may give you a...vision. But the way forward should be clear."

A shadow passed over her face. After a moment, she shook it off and moved on.

For the next day, the mountain didn't seem to get any closer, as if it was moving away from them as fast as they were riding toward it. Then all at once it seemed to dislodge from the horizon, as if it was gliding forward to meet them. The effect did nothing to quell the dread that had been building in Dante's heart ever since Neve had outlined, however briefly, the process of restoring Gladdic back to life.

Until then, it hadn't occurred to him that Neve might be going anywhere. She was an Angel of Carvahal, after all, and could probably kill them both with one snap of her fingers. Yet even she feared the heights of Mount Arna, and the Mill that labored at its peak.

It was in this mood that, when Blays drew to a halt without warning, Dante's heart spiked.

Blays tilted his head. "What's that sound?"

"The sound of you asking stupid questions?" Dante said. "I've grown so used to it I must not have noticed."

Blays shook his head and made a twirling gesture near his ear. "That right there. It's almost like...singing."

Neve glanced at him. "Singing?'

"Something *like* singing. Almost. It could just be a very talented wind."

Dante looked about; they were currently in a nondescript field of yellowing grass and occasional pine trees. "Well, I don't hear anything. Or see anything that could be making sounds that I can't hear."

"Blays is right." Neve smiled, but there was a look in her eyes that Dante couldn't read. "I hear it, too. Which means one thing: we've begun the ascent of Mount Arna."

14

Dante took a look about himself. Just as he suspected, they were still in a mostly open field of grass and pines. "Well, I hope the whole climb is this easy."

The main body of the mountain still looked miles away, but it must have been an odd trick of perspective, for they'd only continued toward it for another hour before its first heights unfolded before them like rocky pairs of wings. Neve examined the lay of the land, then headed for a ridge on the right-hand side of a deep valley. The vegetation thickened around them until Dante was afraid they'd have to dismount and hack their way forward, but a narrow trail revealed itself along the ridge.

"Now that's convenient," Dante said. "Do that many people travel here?"

"Hardly any," Neve said.

"Game trail? Animals live here?"

"Are you asking me if animals live in a wilderness?"

"I thought maybe the Mill drove them insane, too."

Blays touched the hilt of his sword. "Are there about to be things interested in maiming or poisoning us?"

"There are bears," Neve said. "And wolves. And at least two types of hunting cats. Snakes, too. Spiders as well. And other things I don't know about."

"So we should be fine as long as we avoid absolutely everything."

"That's probably for the best."

"What other things you don't know about?" Dante said. "Is this like the portals? Places like Talassa, where creatures—and guardians—just spring into existence?"

"Yes."

"Oh good."

The trail was tight enough they had to ride single-file, and Neve took the lead. She soon stopped to cut a branch to swipe all the spiderwebs out of the way. As annoying as these were for her, the presence of so many intact webs meant nobody—and no especially large animals—had been on the trail in at least a few days.

Ferns grew to both sides. In the sunlight, they smelled almost like licorice. When the trail ran close enough to the edge, they could see a cliff tumbling away beneath them. It was nearly vertical, yet it was coated in vines and shrubs nonetheless. A stream winked in the seam of the valley below and at least three waterfalls poured down the cliffs to feed it.

Dante edged his horse to the right. "Why are the prettiest places the ones most likely to kill you?"

"I often wonder the same thing about myself," Blays said.

The trail grew muddy as it fell into the shadows of a dense forest of hundred-foot pines with bark coarse enough to grind boulders into rubble. They made quick progress, ascending a good three hundred feet in the span of half an hour, and Dante grew heartened, wondering if they might even reach the heights by day's end.

This was proven stupid within minutes, as the towering pines seemed to run away in all directions, yielding the field to shrubs, vines, prickly grass, and all manner of undergrowth. More than once it choked the trail shut completely. Sometimes Dante was able to harvest it out of the way. Other times Blays needed to dismount and chop a path forward with an Odo Sein sword. Their progress was reduced to fits and starts. The air hung heavy with the smell of slashed greenery.

The only times it got better was when the path ran along the edge of the cliff. There, however, the ledge was eroded and crumbled, and Dante had to mend it one time after another.

All three of them were soon dirty, sweaty, scratched, and annoyed. Yet they pressed on the best they could. With the afternoon wearing on, the forest stole over the ridge once more, though the trees were much different, like birches but far taller and more squiggly up the trunk. With their appearance, the undergrowth was oppressed once more, clearing the way for them to ride forward at a speed Dante feared they were unlikely to see on the mountain again.

"Er," Blays said. "Who's that, then?"

Dante cranked his head to follow Blays' line of sight. Since beginning the climb, they hadn't seen a soul; in fact, they'd hardly seen any living creatures at all besides some flies, birds, and little things rustling around in the fallen leaves that Dante hoped were just mice. So even though the target was motionless, Dante's attention snapped straight to the anomaly of the man in the woods.

He was mounted on a healthy-looking horse, lurking in the shadows some three hundred feet away. He was dressed in mail and a sword hung from his left hip.

And he was watching them.

"Neve," Blays said. "Don't suppose you know him?"

Her brows knit together. "I don't recognize anything about him."

"He's looking at us like he knows *us*."

"None of us is wearing anything to identify us as belonging to any of the realms. If he recognizes us, you have to assume he knows exactly who you are."

"Like if he'd been sent by Ka," Dante said.

Blays rubbed his jaw. "Well, we could go kill him just to be sure."

The suggestion sounded flippant, but under the circumstances, it made enough sense that Dante was tempted to make good on it. As he weighed the matter in his mind, the man wheeled his mount and vanished into the woods like he was made of vapor.

"Keep an eye out," Dante said. "If he comes back, we *will* kill him."

Neve nodded and moved on. Dante glanced behind him. Something about the rider had been familiar. He couldn't say what, though, and the sense of it itched like dry grass beneath his shirt. Had he seen the man in Arawn's realm? This would make sense: after all, the Mill was Arawn's, too. Figuring this out suddenly seemed much more important, as Dante would really prefer not to murder one of his god's servants or lieutenants. Then again, he supposed if the man returned that he could just *ask* where he was from.

Leaves rustled off to their left. Dante bobbed his head, trying for a view through the branches, but saw nothing. The sound receded. Dante muttered to himself. Then a series of little thuds came at them at a rush. At last Dante saw it: a wolf, hackles raised, eyes like yellow gems.

"Good gods," Blays said. "I've seen smaller ponies."

Dante brought the nether to him. "Shoo! I said *shoo!*"

The animal padded parallel to them, tail held straight back from its body. It slunk a step closer. Dante fired a black bolt at it, slamming the nether into the ground in front of the wolf, spattering its face with dirt. It jumped back, shaking its head, then turned and ran.

"Well, that's it," Blays said. "We're sleeping in the trees tonight."

"And what should we do with the horses?" Dante said. "Advise them to run faster than that thing?"

"Do you think they'd take it to heart?"

The ground leveled out for a time, speeding them along. Clouds piled against the flanks of the mountain, but there was no rain yet. For the first time since setting foot on Mount Arna, the trail came to a fork.

"Any idea which way?" Dante said.

Blays rubbed his finger behind his ear. "The one that goes up?"

"I don't know which way," Neve said. "But that might."

She dropped from the saddle and headed toward a patch of ivy. She drew a knife and cut several strands free, revealing a waist-high post. It was made of black stone and inscribed with symbols foreign to Dante's eye.

"So the gods populated this mountain with huge carnivorous beasts, and if you spend too long here, your brains will simmer down to mush," Blays said. "But you think they left us *directions*?"

"The gods didn't put this here. These are ramna letters." Neve tugged loose another rope of ivy and leaned closer to the post. "It's a warning. Says we should choose to go back while we still have a life to make choices with."

"Is this the first time we've been threatened by a post?"

Dante pressed his lips together. "I'm not inclined to give the post's thoughts too much credence. We've *met* someone who's made it to the Mill, for the gods' sakes. I don't suppose the post bothers to explain *why* we're doomed if we make the futile decision to press on?"

"In fact, it's pretty explicit," Neve said. "It says that if we continue past this point, we'll be crushed by boulders, or spread across the mountain as bear scat. Or crushed by boulders and *then* spread across the mountain as—" She straightened. "Did you feel that?"

"Feel what?"

"It was like something *slipped*. Like it's—"

One moment, the ground beneath her was normal ground. The next moment, the ground was gone.

She had just enough time to widen her eyes before she fell.

"Neve!" Dante was thrown from his feet by the rumbling earth. Her horse galloped past him, shrieking, nearly trampling him.

He got to his feet and bit down on his lip, coppery blood washing over his mouth. He grabbed the shadows so hard he might strangle them. Running toward the pit, he cast his mind downward, deeper than Neve could have yet fallen, and jerked a layer of solid stone across the pit, sealing it. At the same time, he softened the walls around the seal, burying it in a deep pool of sloppy mud.

He ran to the rim of the pit. "Neve!" He'd kept his mind within the mud, awaiting her impact. None came. "*Neve!*"

He stilled his mind the best he could, filling himself with ether, which he sent down the hole as pure light. It ran some twelve feet in diameter with occasional pockets opening into the walls. He shined his light into these, hoping to see her holding tight within one, but saw nothing but blank stone.

Blays kneeled next to him, calling her name twice more. "Can you see her?"

"It's completely empty." Dante could barely get the words out. "I tried to make a pool for her to land in. But she must have already fallen past it."

Slowly, he drew away the mud and added it back to the walls. He kept expecting to see her body emerge from the muck, but soon he was down to the stone plug. And she still wasn't there. Abruptly certain he'd enveloped her with the plug at the exact moment she'd been dropping past it—entombing her—he withdrew this too, carefully so as not to drop her.

There was still nothing.

"It's too deep for me to feel the bottom," Dante said. "I'm going to go down and check with my own eyes."

Blays stared at him. "If it's too deep for you to feel where it ends, there's no way she survived that."

"We don't know that."

"Or we do, because we have a disturbing amount of experience with people being flung from towers and cliffs—experience we've acquired specifically because it's such an effective means of ending people."

"You and I have fallen from higher," Dante said. "So did Gladdic, when the White Lich was sieging us in Tanar Atain. Neve is an Angel of Carvahal. We don't know what she's capable of. Now keep watch for me."

To save time and shadows, Dante had a mind to sink his arm into the side of the pit and soften the stone beneath it, lowering himself as if by an invisible rope. But it occurred to him that if anything went wrong, he might find himself either stuck in the wall, or parted from his arm.

So he took the boring route instead, sending a staircase spiraling along the walls down into the darkness. His steps echoed softly. Once he was thirty feet down, he glanced up. The mouth of the pit was a small circle of light. Blays' face stared down from above. He already looked very far away.

Dante descended a hundred feet, then two hundred, then three, stopping now and then to call Neve's name, inspect his surroundings, or reach down to try to feel the bottom. The pit grew colder. Not much light left in the day. He stopped, resting an arm on the wall, then reached into it, withdrew a stone, and dropped it down the middle of the pit. He counted to thirty. Forty. A full minute. And still hadn't heard a sound.

He kept on for a while yet, but he'd left his hope somewhere back on the steps he'd built. Blays called to him to make sure he was still there. Dante continued down for another fifty feet, then kneeled on his stone platform and called Neve's name one last time. When all echo of his voice had faded, he rose and trudged his way back to the top.

"There's no sign of her," he said. "Nor of an end to the pit."

"What happened?" Blays said. "This was a booby trap? The post induces you to stop and read it, then a hole opens underneath your feet? Was it sorcery?"

"I don't think so. I didn't feel any movement in the nether."

"Then what was it?"

"She said the land here changes itself. I think it did this on its own."

"I would have thought she could...fly, or something. Like Ka." Blays looked away from the pit and up the mountain. "Should we try to get any further today?"

"You want to keep going?"

"Gladdic's still dead, isn't he? The only way to make him not dead is still up there. So there's where we have to go."

"But Neve's gone."

"What does that matter?"

"She was our guide. She knew how to get us to the peak."

"What does that *matter*? Has our goal changed?"

"No," Dante said. "Just our chances of achieving it. If we don't think we can do this without her, the only thing we can do is turn our back on the Mill and continue our pursuit of the spear."

"You'd do that?"

"Because I'd have to."

Blays' face grew pained. "We're already here."

"Some of the wisest moments in our very foolish lives were when we'd already taken a hundred steps toward our destination but realized that one more would ruin us."

"I've told you I'm done compromising."

"But it feels different now, doesn't it? If we knew we only had one chance in a hundred to reach the Mill at this point, would you still refuse to bend?"

"No. I wouldn't throw our lives away when I know we've got much more killing to do elsewhere." His fingers danced over the swamp dragon horn handle of his sword. "But I don't believe this is a one in a hundred chance. Because I believe in us. Because I've seen us pull off far more impossible and outlandish things than this. We *will* climb this mountain. And woe be it to the mountain if it tries to stand in our way."

"All right," Dante chuckled. "We'll climb the damn mountain. But we're done for today. It's almost dark. We'll camp here. See what happens."

"You don't really think she's going to show up sometime in the night."

"I know it's not likely."

"It's about as likely as convincing you to not dissect a new species you've just discovered."

"She's probably gone. But I'm not making assumptions about anything. Not in this place."

Dante took first watch. He sat near but not directly next to the pit, splitting his attention between listening for Neve, feeling the earth to make sure it wasn't about to try to swallow them too, and watching the forest around them. Some time after midnight, a faint voice rose from the pit.

"Neve?" Heart pounding, he got to his feet. "Is that you?"

But it wasn't. It was the not-quite-singing Blays had heard earlier that day. At last, Dante could hear it too.

She was still gone by morning. They never found her horse, either.

There remained the question of which path, if either, to take going forward. Intending to scout the terrain ahead, Dante killed a few horseflies, reanimated them, and sent them whirling into the air. With a flash like miniature lightning, they were all struck down.

"Well that's disturbing," Dante said.

"Divine intervention?" Blays looked up at the sky. "I always told you they didn't *really* approve of your necromancy."

Neither path was the obvious one, and in fact there was nothing to recommend either, which annoyed Dante greatly, as it meant the decision would be arbitrary. So he shifted the decision back onto the mountain's shoulders by finding a stone that was light gray on one side and dark gray on the other. He spoke his terms out loud and flipped the stone into the air. When it landed dark-gray-side up, he accepted the decision of the mountain — or possibly the gods — and took the right-hand path.

It was easy going for the first few hours, though a wolf (likely the same one as before) came at them again, and this time brought two friends. Dante hit them with the nether hard enough to make them yelp, vowing it would be the last mercy he'd show to them.

Recalling Neve's warning, the ease of the path made Dante uneasy. Then the undergrowth crowded the trail again, reducing them to a plodding walk, while at the same time the trail itself grew so rocky he had to smooth it in places for the horses. They were now traveling so slowly it felt as though their progress had to be against the mountain's will, though the downside of this was that they were making almost no progress at all.

The peak still hung so high above them they didn't seem to be any nearer to it at all. But the land to the south now spread before them like a king's table. Dante thought they might have made four thousand vertical feet since the start of their climb.

The trees grew taller. The shrubs grew shorter, then ceased altogether. The birds and bugs, whose songs and buzzes Dante didn't recognize at all, hushed like monks in an archive. A temple revealed itself before them.

Other than the ramna-written post, it was the first human-made artifact they'd seen on the mountain. It was a simple structure, two stories of gray stone topped by a rusted iron finial. The door, if there had ever been one, was long gone.

Above the entrance was carved the dual rivers of Duset, sign of Arawn. Next to the doorway, a plaque was set into the wall.

"'All those who seek to ascend higher will give to me an offering,'" Dante read.

"An offering?"

"I know you probably haven't stepped inside a temple since the day we had to try to kill Samarand while she was giving a sermon. But an 'offering' is a small gift or sacrifice to the gods."

"I think you know what I'm about to ask," Blays said.

"Is this a trap?"

"It does have a lot in common with the one that recently succeeded in killing one of us."

Dante probed his mind into the earth beneath the temple. "There's at least one major difference: there's no bottomless pit here."

"Maybe there wasn't a pit under the signpost, either. Right up until there was."

"Having caused my share of earthquakes, I think opening a shaft that massive would have produced a lot more than a little rumble. Anyway, I don't think Arawn would use his own temple to trick people to death. It would be wrong."

"Unless Arawn didn't put it here."

"If it wasn't him, he would have removed this slander to his name a long time ago. I have to place my faith in him."

He stepped through the doorway. Six feet inside, he stopped to let his eyes adjust—and to concentrate fully on the ground. Once he was reasonably assured it wasn't about to try to swallow him, he moved toward the altar at the far end of the single room.

Beams of sunlight pierced through chinks in the stonework. Moss grew on the ground in ovals larger than the narrow beams of light. A few benches faced the altar, but most of the room was empty. It smelled faintly musty, almost pleasantly so. Dante climbed the two steps to the altar. A platform against the wall held a shallow stone basin.

"So," Blays said. "What exactly do we need to offer?"

"That's obvious." Dante drew his antler-handled knife. "The same thing the nether always wants."

He cut the back of his arm, deeper than the scratches he typically used to feed the nether, making a fist so the drops would fall faster onto the basin. He gave it twelve drops, then stepped back and healed the wound with a smidge of shadows.

The blood sank away as if the stone was drinking it. As soon as the last drop was gone, soft light poured from the wall to the left of the platform holding the basin. A passage had been opened — or perhaps been revealed — to a hidden garden bearing a clear trail onwards.

They went back for the horses. The garden was blocked on the outside by trees. Rather than disturbing them, Dante coaxed his mount through the temple instead.

As they took to the trail, Blays stopped and cocked his head. "Is there anything else here? Specifically any other buildings?"

"What makes you ask?"

"Because it feels like there is."

"This is the only building. But there's a cellar of some kind underneath it."

"Then why aren't we going into it?"

"Because we don't particularly need any dust? Or rats? Or cellar spiders?"

"We should at least *look* at it. What if there's a shortcut to the

Mill?"

"And what if pigs fly?"

"Then I hope hope we've packed our pig saddles so they can fly us up to the peak."

Dante sighed. "All right. Just a look."

The cellar didn't seem to have a route down to it from the temple, and Dante thought he'd have to open a hole down to it. But as he inspected the earth, he found that such a hole was already there, covered by a wooden trap door hidden under the turf.

Blays pulled back the door and Dante moved to smite whatever horrors might emerge from it. But nothing came out except the smell of age. Dante lit the way forward and climbed down the ladder secured to the earthen wall.

"Congratulations." He stepped down to the floor. "You've successfully discovered a big pile of junk."

A number of tables cluttered the room, each of them further covered by objects so degraded by the passage of time it was hard to pick them out from the cobwebs, dirt, and general yellow-brown film that seemed to congeal out of the air in any place where the air had been trapped too long. There were a great deal of shelves, too, in similar disrepair. Blays tried to pick up a book, only for it to crumble all over his boots.

"Just as useless as every other book," he muttered. He looked from shelf to shelf, frowning vaguely, then eyed the far wall. "Wait here a second, will you?"

Blays slipped into the shadows. Dante felt him move toward the wall, then through it, into a space that Dante somehow hadn't noticed earlier. Dante readied the nether. Moments later, Blays returned.

"If I've learned anything from watching you," Blays said, "it's that people who spend their lives stealing relics know better than to put them out where someone *else* can steal them."

217

"I don't steal relics," Dante said. "Or anyway I *prefer* to make them for myself when possible. What've you got?"

Blays held up his hand. For a second Dante thought he'd caught a living drakelet that had gotten trapped in the cellar, but it was in fact a statue of marbled green stone, and the face and body of the dragon carved into that stone was quite a bit more fearsome than the local flying lizards.

"How did you know that was there?"

"Just a hunch." Blays gave the statue a waggle. "Jorus, right? Aren't his dragons associated with Arawn's Mill?"

"In some of the older texts. Let me see that." He took it from Blays, moving his mind inside the object's weight. Nether lurked in it, arranged in a pattern that Dante couldn't quite make out. "Be careful with that. It looks as though it might *do* something."

"Well, I didn't see any bodies in there with it. So its previous owner seems to have survived its powers."

They climbed free of the cellar and rode forth along the trail, which was in excellent shape for being so isolated. In an hour's time, they covered three miles, attaining five or six hundred feet of elevation, until the trail terminated in the shrubs on top of a flat vantage.

They took a brief rest. Motion caught Dante's eye: on a ridge hundreds of feet below them, a rider emerged from the trees. For a moment Dante thought it must be Neve, and he lifted his hands to his mouth to shout to her, but sunlight glittered on the rider's armor, and he was too big to be Neve anyway. Dante slowly lowered his hands. After another few minutes, he turned and carried on.

Without any trail at all, Dante was often reduced to harvesting a way clear or smoothing out a bit of bare earth. He also did a great deal of cursing the place for refusing him the use of his reanimated scouts to find a better way. Where it was feasible, Blays cut trail with his sword, nether sparking from the blade as branches and leaves whirled through the air as if caught up in a tiny tornado.

They were so engrossed in their business that they didn't see the rider until they were almost on top of him.

"Watch yourself," the man said softly. He wore chainmail and a black cloak and Dante was almost certain the man was the same one he'd seen on the lower ridge earlier that day. But there was no way the rider could have caught up to them so quickly, let alone passed them.

"That would seem to be good advice for all of us," Blays said. "Should we go our separate ways? Or is our meeting no accident, because you've been following us?"

The man swept his dark hair behind his ear. "Are you someone who deserves to be followed? Precisely who are you, then? To my eye you look strange."

"I am Sir None of Your Business, and this is my faithful if unhygienic squire Turn Aside and Be On Your Way, If You Please. And you are?"

"You will give me your true names. Or would you prefer I take them from you?"

"I *really* wouldn't do that." Dante swathed his right hand in shadows. "But if we're making threats —"

"Threats?" The man smiled. Nether coiled around his right hand as well. "Oh, I believe it's going to go a lot further than that."

15

Dante swore under his breath. He hadn't bothered with blood before, but he now unclenched his jaw and bit his lip. "I suspect you already know who we are. But if we've run into each other by chance, then I promise we're of no interest to you. Travelers, nothing more."

Wind ruffled the man's hair. He looked almost like a northerner, though Dante had no idea which realm that might correspond to here.

"I sense something...degraded within you," the man said. "The both of you. As if you carry pustules on your soul."

"Then you should probably get away from us in case we're infectious," Blays said.

"There is only one reason for anyone to come to this place. But I warn you, the peak cannot be attained by the impure."

Dante gave the man a second look. "Are you one of its guardians?"

"I already know what you would try to do to me if I said that I was."

"And what's that?"

"Murder me, here and on the spot." The man's gray eyes moved between the two of them. "For it would be far from the first time you've done such a thing, wouldn't it? Can you even put a number on your crimes? Just how many men have you killed on your journey?"

"What," Blays said, "today?"

"That many, then."

Dante tightened his hand, cracking the knuckle of his thumb. "You can see I know the nether. And that I'm not afraid to tell you to get out of my way. It's hardly a feat to guess I've used the nether to shed blood."

"Next you will tell me that all of your bloodshed was necessary. That it was justified. Perhaps even that you only killed to free the enslaved, and that you always saved more lives than you claimed."

"That's a good start, but you forgot all the times we were fighting in self-defense."

"And the times the other guys were just being pricks," Blays said.

The man sneered. "You can't give safe harbor to your crimes by hoisting above them a shield of wit. Not in this place. So I ask again: how many lives have you taken?"

Dante shook his head. "What does it matter?"

"How many wars have you started?"

"Have we *started*? None."

The rider laughed. "I fear you actually believe this."

"I've had others declare war on me, but I've never started one myself. I've seen its costs since I was a young man. War has always been my *last* resort."

"You define the word 'start' narrowly, to suit your own interests. How many wars have you been involved in that would not have happened without your involvement?"

"You'll have to ask whichever god you serve. I'm just a foolish mortal who doesn't understand the consequences of his own actions. But despite this fault, I know there are times when the only choice is to fight, to war — and, yes, to kill. Because the alternative is to be enslaved or destroyed."

"Who could question such a thing? It is as obvious as the stars above or the ground below. What matters is that in every case, you excuse away all culpability, letting the weight of your decisions slide free from your shoulders like a silk wrap."

"You talk like you know everything about us. Which is interesting, because you seem to be ignoring the fact that the war we're currently involved in is a fight to save our whole world."

The rider made a flicking motion. "Yet even then you are only 'saving' it from a blight you yourself unleashed on your world as a result of your ceaseless meddling. Thus the act of standing against that threat bears no more virtue than cleaning up after yourself after you've broken a cup."

"With the small difference that in this case, the 'cup' contains tens of millions of lives."

"Which only means you bear the greater fault for ever breaking it in the first place. Look back, now, on all your causes, all your wars, and see the pattern among them: each one was somehow an 'exception,' a special case that allowed you to undertake evil in the name of some so-called greater good. At the end of it all, what morals do you truly hold? Besides whatever exists in the moment to ensure your own survival, and to build your own power?"

"Everything we've done was because we thought it was the right thing to do."

"The same is true of the countless foes and 'villains' you've murdered. Do you not think that Gladdic himself, when he was slaughtering the civilians of Collen, did not also think to himself, 'This deed might upset others, but in the end, *it will help me to do what I think is right*'?"

Dante opened his mouth. The counter to this felt like it should be obvious, yet when he searched for it, it felt like reaching inside a jar and finding that it was empty.

"Of *course* he thought he was doing the right thing," Blays said. "As it turned out, though, he wasn't. So you can blow as many words as you like building clever lines of reason about how we're villains ourselves. And that when it comes down to it, we don't really have any principles or laws at all. Do you know what that means, though? It means *we're still here.* And we're the only ones standing between the White Lich and annihilation. So you can take all your hand-wringing and shove it up your pompous ass."

The mailed man shook his head. "In the end, then, might does make right. I had hoped for some higher revelation from you. Sadly, I have spoken the truth to you. And you will kill me for it."

"Enough of this," Dante spat. "You want to play the inquisitor? That only means something if I give a damn about you or your standards, and on that front I have some very bad news. Now get out of the damn way and let us get on with our business."

The man smiled ironically. "I knew it would come to this. With you, it always does."

Dante bit his lip. The taste of blood felt reviving; the breath in his lungs seemed ready to lift him from his feet. He brought the nether to him and hurled it at the other man.

But not to kill him. Rather to lock him, and his horse, to the ground.

The man pointed two fingers of his right hand at the earth. Shadows shot downward, severing the invisible bonds before Dante could wrap them around the horse's legs. Dante tried again, doubling his efforts, but the rider brushed them off like the spiderwebs Dante had spent the day blundering through.

"I tolerated your bullshit," Dante said. "I asked you nicely to stand aside. You refused, because you appear to be an asshole capable of taking on human form, so I tried to make you stand aside without hurting you. You don't get to whine about me killing you when you goad me into it!"

"We will see if you can do so," the man said soberly. "Or if, at last, your hubris has brought you to your end."

He thrust up his arm. A wave of shadows swooped toward Dante. He parried them, black sparks raining down upon him, and vaulted from the saddle. As he landed, he punched his fist into the ground.

The earth unzipped; a widening crack lanced toward the other man. The enemy made a backhand sweeping gesture, pouring nether into the soil. With a rumble and a jolt, the cracking stopped. The man motioned with his other hand, launching a second wave of nether at Dante. Yet halfway to him, the shadows vanished from both sight and feel. Dante's heart felt like it jumped three feet sideways. Acting on instinct, he filled himself with ether and dashed it before him.

It glimmered on the hidden bolts, revealing them once more. Dante struck them down moments before they reached him.

To his side, Blays dismounted and shifted into the shadows. Without even looking at him, the rider made a quick downward gesture, booting Blays from the netherworld so hard he fell on his ass.

Dante had hoped to do this quickly and efficiently; if he burned too much nether, they wouldn't be able to travel much further before taking a long rest. But their inquisitor was more dangerous than he'd expected. Nothing to trifle with. Instead, Dante hit at him with a barrage of bolts, followed immediately by a second wave and then a third. The air around the man grew so dark with dueling nether that for a moment he disappeared within a dim and expanding cloud.

At last the air cleared. The man remained.

"I have survived troubles much greater than you," he said to Dante. "You should have left this mountain when you had the chance."

Dante watched him, looking for an angle he hadn't tried. And felt something flying toward him. Fast as he could, he let the ether come to him, spraying it forward, illuminating the attack that was already on its way. He lashed out at the dozens of black darts, disintegrating nearly all of them.

But two made it through—thrown off course, partly, by Dante's defenses. Not quite enough. One grazed his side. The other pierced his shoulder.

He staggered, grunting, sending shadows to the wound. The pain went numb. At the same time, he fired back at the enemy, not hoping to bring him down, but to stop him from following up on his strike.

Blays had his swords drawn, but didn't dare take a run at the enemy. He shot a glance at Dante. "How many times do I have to tell you to stop messing around and do something?"

"How many times do I have to tell you that I'm trying?"

"Lyle's balls, do I have to do everything?"

Blays stooped and picked up a rock. He popped to his feet, wound back, and threw it at the rider, who was so distracted waging war on Dante that he didn't see the rock until it was only a blink away.

Rock hit skull with a thud. The man fell from the saddle, legs flying over his head. He thrust half-shaped nether in front of him, anticipating a strike from Dante, so instead Dante sent the shadows above him, forming a cloud—and poured down a pillar of red and white flames.

The man's horse bolted. The fire swept over his head, torso, and limbs, consuming him inside it. The flames faded slowly. When they were all but gone, the man lay prone, smoke curling from his cloak, chainmail scorched.

Blays edged closer, sword extended. "Is he...?"

The man groaned. Smoke wisped from his mouth. Despite all his wounds, he sat up, looked Dante in the eye, and smiled. "I knew you would find a way."

He was still smiling as his eyes fell back into his head. His skin blackened, peeling away from the skull, which was collapsing, crumbling into particles. All the rest of him was disintegrating, too. Until nothing remained but gray powder.

"Well." Blays made to nudge the smoking ashes with his toe. "Any idea what *that* was about?"

Dante released the nether from his hands. "Two options. First, he was another agent of Taim's sent to kill us. But after we turned Ka away, I don't see why Taim would send someone less-skilled and alone."

"Then what's the second option?"

"That it was one of the mountain's tests."

"Of what, exactly? Our ability to be scolded?"

"I could only guess. Did you really throw a rock at him?"

"It was the last thing he expected. Anyway, a good rock always gets things done."

They mounted up and headed out. For a time the way onward was so steep and rocky they would have had to turn back if Dante hadn't been able to carve steps into the worst of it. But eventually the ground leveled, and the forest returned, which felt like a blessing until it grew so gnarled and dense it formed a maze worse than any of the waterways in Tanar Atain.

Dante attacked this problem quite literally, blasting passages through the matted branches, at other times harvesting them apart. Blays hit on the idea of moving into the shadows to scout out routes through the maze. If they'd been ramna barbarians or common soldiers, navigating through the woods might have taken them a full day—even more, if they'd gotten lost and turned around—but they still had an hour of daylight left when they finally emerged onto a scree of broken rock.

The plains lay further below than ever. But there was still plenty of climb ahead of them when they broke for the night.

Dante drew a shelter together while they let the horses have at the grass.

Blays pointed to a wing of rock a few hundred feet above them. "That's snow up there."

Dante nodded. "We'll reach it by tomorrow."

"Assuming no more crazy people accost us in the middle of nowhere."

"Assuming that."

They brought the horses into the shelter. It was growing cold. It felt like Neve had been gone from them for weeks, but it had only been a single day.

They hiked upward. For the moment, the way wasn't treacherous, just steep and tiring. But it was a brisk morning and the sunshine felt good.

"Not again," Blays sighed.

Dante twisted in the saddle to follow Blays' gaze downhill. "Really?"

"Five of them. No, make it six."

"Maybe they're just seeking the Mill."

"We'd better hope so. If they're all as rough as the last fellow, I might not have enough rocks."

They watched a minute longer, then walked on up the mountain. It was soon clear the men below them weren't average pilgrims: every time they caught a glance of them, the group had gotten closer, as if they took the form of swift spirits whenever they were able to slip out of sight.

Dante watched the terrain closely, looking for a good place to make their stand. Uphill of the enemy, he thought: he could set off a landslide. Watch them try to dodge *that*. It didn't seem quite that cold yet, but they saw more and more hints of snow above them, nestled in shadowed crags where the sun rarely touched.

When it became clear their pursuers would soon catch them,

there was nothing for it but to find a ledge with some but not too much height to it, turn around, and wait.

There were indeed six of them, dressed in gray, though Dante saw no signs of hourglasses or hammers that would have marked them as servants of Taim. They climbed steadily, coming to a stop beneath Dante and Blays.

"Care to tell us who you are and what you want?" Blays said. "Or did you climb all this way just to get a better look at my statuesque features?"

"My name is Wode." This was spoken by a middle-aged man with black hair and salt-and-pepper beard. "We represent the law of the realm."

Blays took an exaggerated look around. "Is there a lot of law out here on the slopes of Mount Arna? Because we could have used you yesterday."

"Have you seen Basan of Vele?"

"Should I know who that is?"

"He would have been dressed in black. Armored. With eyes that never looked away from yours."

"Oh, the disagreeable gentleman who loved to talk? You can find him further back down the mountain. Just look for the big pile of ashes."

Wode's eyes deepened. "Then you killed him. I'm afraid you must hand yourself over to us to answer for Basan's murder."

"Ah, how so, exactly?"

"You will stand trial before a judge."

"I see. And then what?"

"Then, since you have just confessed to us, you will be hanged for the crime of murder."

Blays tapped his chin. "I have to tell you, it doesn't seem like there's much in this deal for us."

"That may be so," Wode said. "But it is the law. Step down and come with us."

Blays drew his sword, wagging it down at the lawmen. "I would love to go be executed by you. Unfortunately, my sword makes the decisions around here, and it seems to have other ideas."

Wode was well removed from the blade, yet he drew back, fear flashing over his dignified face. "Please sir, do no hurt to us. We're no more than soldiers. We don't have the strength to stand against you."

"Then it was a pretty curious decision to come accost us!"

"Yet that's the duty that the law commands of us. Now I ask again, won't you come with us, as is your own duty under the law?"

"No?"

"Do you hold yourself *above* the law?"

Blays put away his sword. "Well, that would seem to be the case, wouldn't it?"

"But no man is above the law."

"Wrong," Dante said. "The sovereign is."

Wode frowned in confusion. "Surely you don't consider yourself the sovereign of this land."

"If anything, I can't wait to get out of this place. But considering my friend and I are the only hope for our world—"

"Just dwell on how sad *that* is for a minute," Blays interrupted.

"—then we are, in a very real sense, the sovereigns of our world. This means I answer to the needs of *my* people. Not to your people, nor your laws, nor your gods."

"It could be that this is true," Wode said. "But it's only true for now. One day, you will be judged."

"I know," Dante said. "That's why when that day comes, I'd really like to have 'once saved his entire world' on the good side of the scale."

The lawman nodded. "We will see, in the end, if that is

enough."

He turned to go. Wordless, his men followed.

"Am I going crazy," Blays said, "or is it physically impossible for a band of watchmen to have caught up to us that fast?"

Dante clasped his hands together, withdrawing his mind from the earth he'd been waiting to drop on the lawmen. "I suppose it's possible they were following Basan of Vele and only chanced on us because of that."

"And if we were to bet on it?"

"I would take the side against what I just said."

"Then what were—"

"No gods damned idea."

Blays nudged his horse about. "Was there something familiar about them?"

"About the strange people I've never seen before?"

"Yes."

"No."

The mountain seemed to grant them a reprieve, offering natural switchbacks up its face. Fingers of snow reached down from above. There was much open ground, but the grass was patchy, the pines getting shorter. Dante had crossed enough mountains to know that summits were always further away than they looked, but he was certain they had advanced at least halfway toward the Mill, and were possibly much closer.

The sun felt wan, though it was still high in the sky. Two things changed, nearly at once: the snow now covered everything, and the way ahead rose in steep, rocky pillars.

Dante came to a stop. "Time to leave the horses behind."

"To do what? Get eaten by wolves?"

"If we take them up there, *they* won't have anything to eat. Anyway, wolves are the reason horses have hooves."

They dismounted, performing quick triage of their gear to leave anything they wouldn't need with the horses. Dante was about to say goodbye to them, then snorted in revelation. He cut his thumb, rubbing his blood on the animals' saddles and into the hair on their backs.

Blays made a face. "Leaving them a memento to remember you by?"

"Giving myself a way to track them down once we're back from the heights."

They'd barely gotten started on the rocky rises before the way forward grew impossible. Rather than trying to reshape a staircase all the way to the Mill, Dante only bothered to carve out occasional handholds; in the worst places, Blays would move into the shadows, where he had a much easier time climbing around than in the physical world, get to a stable spot, shift back into the physical world, and toss a rope down to Dante.

It was rough and athletic work. Dante tried not to look down. Three times, he had to wash the exhaustion from his muscles, the technique growing less effective each time. But faster than he would have thought possible, they scrambled up a final cliff (of that leg of things, at least), and stopped to rest. Dante thought he could make out the spot they'd camped the night before. It looked terribly far away.

The ground ahead was a manageable enough slope, a snowfield broken here and there by dark rocks and lone, rebellious pines. They'd just started up it before Dante rocked to a stop.

He shielded his eyes and gazed at the tallest point he could see. "That light there. That's the Mill, isn't it?"

"What else could it be?" Blays kicked at the pure snow. "I mean, it's not as if the entire mountain is covered in bright shiny stuff."

"But that's not snow. It looks like ether."

Convinced he was right, Dante strode up the field. The peak was closer than he had feared. Close enough to reach the next day.

The rest of that day was spent slogging through snowfields and heaving themselves up cliffs. It was only as night came on and they settled down to camp when he realize how cold it was. And how soaked his boots and the legs of his trousers were. Meanwhile, he could spark fire easily enough, but he had no fuel to keep it going.

He moved his mind into the rock. It seemed to resist him, hanging onto its solid form until he took hold of it through brute force. After a short struggle, he opened a cavity in a mound of rock that was just large enough for the two of them, then all but sealed it behind them, leaving a few small holes for the removal of stale air. He folded his cloak around himself, then swaddled himself inside his blanket, which smelled like horses.

"I was right," he said. "The horses would not have made it."

"Will we?" Blays said from somewhere inside the layers of his own blanket.

"I can probably find a way to use the nether to keep us warm. But I may have to stay up all night to do it."

"That's very thoughtful of you." Blays tossed on his side and snuggled into his covers.

Dante muttered something uncharitable and drew on the nether. He was almost certain he could convert it into warmth by using a more subtle version of the process of turning into fire, but unless he got real and sustained rest, his power wouldn't return to him. He'd used a lot on the day. Enough so that he wouldn't have enough to get them through tomorrow unless he got some sleep. But sleeping meant freezing to death. And staying up to prevent them from freezing to death meant he wouldn't have the strength to get them to the Mill come morning.

This was a problem.

Perhaps he could try to embed heat in the rock to keep them warm while he slept? Could he even do such a thing? More importantly, could he do it without accidentally cooking them to death? He sighed.

In the wan light of his ether, he couldn't see his breath.

He took his hands out of his cloak, turning them back and forth. "Have I gone crazy, or has it gotten warmer in here?"

"Did you do the thing you said you were going to do?" Blays mumbled. "Great news. Now let me sleep."

"That's just it. I haven't done anything yet."

Blays sat up. He shed his blanket, feeling the air with his hands the same way Dante had. He frowned, then crawled to his pack, which was resting against the wall of the chamber, and reached inside.

"Ah!" He yanked back his hands. Smiling, he wrapped them in his blanket, then extracted the statue of the dragon he'd taken from the cellar at the temple of Arawn.

It was glowing softly. Warmth rolled from it like music from a bell.

"Look at that," Blays said. "Is there any problem stealing can't fix?"

They stared at it a while, warming themselves. Outside, the wind whistled over the wastes. The mountain's song had grown loud enough to be heard whenever they weren't talking. Dante had never felt further from home.

Once he was sure it was safe, he settled into his blankets and slept.

The fields of snow reached to infinity.

They marched toward the peak. They seemed to be able to see the entire world, the valley of the Realm of Nine Kings stretching away to north and south, bounded on the east and west by walls of mountains. They were having some trouble catching their breath and they weren't advancing as fast as Dante liked. Still, bit by bit, the peak grew closer—and so did the dot of light at its summit.

Clouds massed below them, blocking out the lower reaches of the mountain and all sight of the valley except for the faraway mountain ranges. Now and then they had to scale a cliff. The rock was getting harder and harder to manipulate and Dante had to wrench his steps and handholds into place. Looking behind him a minute later, the stone he'd reshaped was in motion, flowing back to its original positions. He had never seen this before, but the explanation leaped into his mind: they were near enough to the Mill that its ether was reaching them, restoring all altered objects to their original forms.

Mostly it was a steady uphill trudge. Dante found his mind wandering. Old memories. Possibilities of the future. What awaited them at the Mill; if, once they had its ether, they could restore Gladdic from his purgatory; all of the pieces of the spear they had yet to obtain and how they might do so.

And scenes of the White Lich marching through Gask. Tens of thousands of Blighted charging before him, grabbing every man, woman, and child they could find. Nine-tenths of the captives cursed to become Blighted—and the last tenth fed to them. Towns and cities deserted. And every soldier and sorcerer who dared to try to stand against the onslaught, or to lead their people from harm's way, were ripped to pieces and scattered to the wind.

These visions were so vivid it shocked him whenever he emerged from them to find that he was still on the mountain. He'd glance around himself, then, and see that the landscape had changed, and that he had no memory of the last few minutes of travel.

"How are you doing?" Blays said.

Dante hit a soft spot in the snow, leg sinking past his knee. "Fine. Why?"

"My head's a bit...here and there."

"The air on high mountains has a different character than at normal heights. It has a way of intoxicating the mind. But we'll make it there soon. We just have to keep going."

They came to a set of cliffs set with streams of ice flowing down them just like a frozen waterfall. Negotiating this required his full attention. As they finished with the cliffs and came to the next field of snow, he resolved not to let his mind wander, but soon found himself back in the lands he'd help free from the Gaskan Empire, imagining—or watching?—the people there falling to the slaughter of the lich.

The sun dimmed. Clouds were coming to the upper heights, too. Flakes of snow twirled on the air. He told himself it was just the wind stirring up what was already there. Within minutes, flurries of snow spun about them, forcing him to lower his face.

"I can't see the eastern mountains anymore," Blays said. "The western range has gone missing, too."

"That's what happens when the air gets full of stuff."

"What happens if we lose sight of the summit?"

"Coming here was *your* idea!"

"I'm starting to think my idea might have had a few problems."

The snowstorm grew worse by the second. The wind couldn't decide which way it preferred to assault them from, so it took turns. The summit was getting hazy. Dante did his best to fix its orientation in his mind, but the unsteady wind was confusing him, and its roar—along with the mountain's song, which he could now hear at all times, even when he was speaking—made it hard for him to think straight.

He had to find a way to know where the peak was even if the storm obscured it. A light or sign in the sky wouldn't work, he wouldn't be able to see it from within a blizzard either, and would soon pass it anyway. And it had to be fixed in its orientation even if his own fell out of true. Hanging a nethereal arrow in front of his face wouldn't do any good if it didn't know how to keep itself pointed in the right direction.

While he was still searching for answers, another gust of snow blew over them. Taking sight of the summit away with it.

He walked onward, fighting to maintain his sense of where the peak was, shielding his eyes with both hands from the pummeling snow. One by one, all the landmarks before him were lost in the blizzard, until he could see nothing that was further away than Blays and his own two hands.

"Tell me you know where you're going!" Blays shouted against the roar of the storm and the song of the mountain.

"No better than you do."

"Followup question: are we about to die?"

Dante leaned into the wind, heaving himself another few steps forward. "The storm could blow itself out at any minute."

"Then maybe we should wait for that to happen within some kind of 'shelter.' You know, those things we use to stop nature from murdering us?"

This struck Dante as a very good idea. He bit his lip, getting a bit of blood going, then delved into the ground. The ground didn't budge. With a sinking feeling, he gave it a second shot. With his third attempt, he slammed into it with enough force to blast open a yawning crevice. The ground broke, and bits of it softened. He rushed to manipulate these bits into the base of a wall, but they were already reverting to rough, unbroken stone.

"I can't move the earth!" he yelled into the storm. "It's because of Arawn's Mill. If you alter something, the ether just restores it to its previous state!"

"I don't suppose anyone left a stray house around here?"

"If we try to hunker down, we'll be buried by the storm. We have to press on!"

Blays stared into the whiteout like his leg was caught in a trap and he was coming to the understanding that the only way to free himself was to cut off his own foot. He shook the snow from his cloak and slogged forward. Dante walked behind in the trail Blays drove through the snow. He sent his mind into the frigid earth ahead of them, feeling its contours to make sure they weren't about to walk off a cliff.

His mind drifted to scenes of war both remembered and imagined. An idea snapped him back in place.

He grabbed Blays' cloak. "Let me take the lead. I can't see a damn thing, but I can feel the ground—and I know when it's sloping up."

He moved to the fore, making a quick mental scan of the land ahead, sweeping his awareness back and forth as he advanced. Vague thoughts swam up from the corners of his mind. Faces, too. Many were recent, like Gladdic or Neve or Ara, but others were from long ago, like Lew or Larrimore.

Of those that had died, he wondered if they remained in the Mists. Of those who still lived, he wondered where they were now, and if they'd yet had to flee the advance of the lich.

A figure in gray appeared ahead of him in the snow. Dante gasped cold air, summoning nether, but the figure was already gone. He spun in a circle. Blays was looking at him in confusion. He wiped snow from his eyes and face and walked on.

"Look for any kind of shelter!" he called over his shoulder. "A cave, even a good boulder. We're not going to make it to the Mill in this."

"Did you hear that?"

"Hear what? The mountain trying to convert us into blocks of ice?"

"I thought I heard a voice!"

Dante cocked his head. "I don't hear anything."

"Right over there. She's calling us to shelter!"

Dante peered into the blinding snow, then turned on Blays in frustration. "I don't hear *or* see—"

His breath caught in his throat. Blays was no longer beside

him. Instead, he was dashing through the snow, already a vague figure—and then he was gone.

"Blays!" Dante cupped his hands to his mouth and screamed it. "*Blays!*"

Follow? Or stay put, so Blays could find his way back to him? There wasn't time to think. He took off running, following Blays' trail, but the blizzard was already filling it in, obscuring it. He called Blays' name again. The trail was getting tougher to follow; he was losing ground. He called on the ether, sifting it over the tracks to light them up so he could better follow them.

Light glared in his eyes from across the snow, blinding him worse than the blizzard. He whirled his head and shielded his eyes. *All* of the snow had lit up, not just the tracks, as if everything was so whipped up and disturbed by the storm that the ether saw everything as deeply altered.

It was a moment before the dazzle left his eyes enough for him to carry on. But he was no longer sure if he was following Blays' trail or a wind-blown disturbance in the snow. Yet there was nothing else he could do: so he ran on, stumbling and falling, calling Blays' name into the merciless wind.

He fell again. And was slow to get up. He should have roped them together to prevent them from getting separated. Or marked Blays with his blood, like he'd done with the horses. But he hadn't.

He trudged forward, uncertain what direction he was heading. His ears rang. Or maybe that was the mountain shrieking at him. He couldn't see anything but snow: no sky, no horizon, no features at all. It was blanker than even the unshaped fogs of the Mists. Was he dead? Had he frozen to death somewhere back there and everything since had been mere delusion? Had he stepped off a cliff? Been crushed under an avalanche?

His heart shuddered. At once, he was certain this was true— that *something* like it was true. It no longer felt all that cold and with nothing to orient himself to he couldn't even tell how much time was passing but he knew he needed to keep moving so that's what he did, one step after another, into a blizzard he now knew would never stop, toward a destination the mountain would never let him reach.

He could no longer even hear the wind. He squeezed his eyes shut, drifting to a halt. He couldn't *feel* the wind, either, as if every part of him was dissolving in the storm.

He opened his eyes. The snow was still falling, but it was no longer in maddening swirls. The wind had stopped. In the distance, he could see the vague outlines of rocky piles and spires.

"Blays?" He turned in a circle. "Where are you?"

His jaw dropped and he fell to his knees.

Before him, a white tree soared hundreds of feet into the sky. Its trunk grew from fused thighs; its branches spread like immense ribs; teeth and knuckles poked from its buds. It was an exact match for the White Tree. His head spun: the peak of Mount Arna was no longer there. Instead, mountains ridged the sky to his right. The unmistakable shape of the Woduns. To his left, a gray sea surged in a wintry storm.

It wasn't *like* Barden. It *was* Barden.

He was...home. In the wastelands north of Narashtovik.

An icy knife ran down his back. Dread building in his gut, he reached for the nether.

"Don't you touch that, you traitor."

He spun toward the source of the voice. An older woman revealed from the snow, her black hair pulled into a thick braid, her face both severe yet capable of much kindness. She was dressed in black and silver. And the chest of her doublet bore an image of the same tree she stood beneath.

Dante's tongue felt too thick to speak. "Samarand?"

"I know who sent you here," she said quietly. "And what they sent you to do."

Masses of shadows boiled from her hands. Dante pulled his defenses to him, but her attack shattered them like a pane of glass.

Darkness fell upon him.

16

"Wake up now, boy. Time for you to confess to your crimes. Time for you to be judged."

Dante inhaled with a start. He kicked his feet against the ground—stone, not snow—scrabbling away from the woman's voice. The scrape of his boots echoed from the close space. His backside scooted over straw. He was in a cell.

He was in a cell, and Samarand was standing over him, hands pure black with nether.

He jumped to his feet, summoning the shadows. Her lips tightened as she made a pulling motion. He found himself rooted in place, stiff as a stump, unable to break free.

"We've already been through this," Samarand said. "Draw the nether against me again, and I will cut off the hand that summoned it. Do you understand?"

Dante had been groggy a minute ago. He wasn't anymore. "Yes."

"Very good." She watched him a moment, then took a step toward the side of the cell, clasping her hands behind her back. "I've already learned some of your story, and can make guesses at the rest of it. But I'd like to hear it from you."

"My story?"

"The story of why you traveled nearly a thousand miles to kill me."

Blood thundered in Dante's ears. The room smelled familiar. Almost *comforting*. "Where are we?"

"The very place you weaseled your way into. Although I doubt it was your plan to end up in its dungeons."

Dante felt as if he'd tipped over a ledge. "We're in the Sealed Citadel."

"I kept you unconscious during the journey. For some reason, I didn't trust you to behave."

Dante felt behind him to confirm that the cell wall was real. It was cold, and stone, the slightest bit damp. He bit the inside of his lip. Not to fuel the nether, but to experience the pain. It felt just like pain normally did.

"This isn't real," he said.

"I assure you, you're wide awake. This isn't another dream."

"That may be, but it must be an illusion of a different kind."

She raised an eyebrow with the patient amusement he'd forgotten had been so much a part of her person. "And why is that?"

"Because you've been dead for sixteen years. I ought to know. I was right there when you died."

"This is supposed to have happened sixteen years ago? Are you even sixteen *now*?"

The remark was so strange Dante snorted, holding out his hands in helpless disbelief. His laughter died in his nose.

His left arm—the one he typically drew blood from—was smooth, almost entirely unscarred. And his right hand no longer had the dark stain of the netherburn he'd suffered during the great siege of Narashtovik.

He looked down at himself. He wasn't wearing his fine, if weather-battered, uniform of the High Priest of the Council of Narashtovik. Instead, he was wearing a rather plain doublet, one that had been mended many times. His trousers and boots were just as shabby.

"Ah," he said. Did his *voice* sound different? "I don't know what you're trying to do to me. Or what manner of illusion this is. But I remember my own life."

"I don't know what you've been dreaming," Samarand said. "Or what cruel sorcery Callimandicus has played on your mind. His thinking has always been...opaque." She tapped her fingers against the back of her other hand. "If I had to guess, I suspect you were wavering in your mission. Whatever he's done to your mind was a means of setting you back on your proper course."

"Uh huh. All right, if we're back in the Citadel, then where's Blays?"

"In our custody. He's unharmed. For now."

"If you so much as scratch the sole of his foot, I will see that —"

"You will *see* what I allow you to see, boy. And if you threaten me again, what you see will be nothing more than the four walls of this cell, from now until the end of your days." She stared down at him, then gave a small nod. "It's obvious you need some time to adjust before we speak further. Be warned: you are being watched. If you make any attempt to leave, you will be destroyed, and so will your friend."

She turned on her heel and strode from the cell. The door closed with a clank; a key turned, setting a thick bolt.

Dante stood in the middle of the room, head reeling. The cell looked exactly as the ones in the Citadel did. Same door, same lantern. It even *smelled* the same. Everything about the place felt real. More than that, it felt *right*. The same wasn't true of the illusions of the Pastlands: while that realm was more engrossing than any dream, it carried a dreamily gauzy sense of being just out of place.

Yet the story Samarand had told him could not be true. Because it meant the last sixteen years of his life hadn't happened. And, contrary to whatever they were trying to get him to believe, his memories of those years were...

His heart skipped a beat, then made up for it by trying to beat nine times per second. His memories of those years were much vaguer than he'd thought. As slippery as wriggling trout. He had impressions of the really big things, the wars and such, and he knew he'd just been on a high mountain, working to save his friends and the world. Which now seemed...really, the *world*? How could he have gone from a sixteen-year-old boy imprisoned beneath the Sealed Citadel to romping through the realm of the gods themselves on a quest to deliver everything he knew from annihilation? Was that really less crazy than the idea it had all been implanted in his head by Cally?

He clenched his teeth. Whatever the hell was happening, he wasn't going to play by its rules. Breaking through the door would call down Samarand's wrath, but he didn't have to be half as obvious as that.

He turned to the back wall and sent his mind into the stone, intending to tunnel out and find Blays. The wall didn't move. No matter how many times he tried. As if his ability to manipulate stone was as illusory as the rest of his memories.

Feeling like he might throw up, he took a seat. When this didn't help, he stretched out in the straw. He didn't mean to close his eyes, because that made his dizziness worse, but he was exhausted. He slept.

Few things woke a person faster than the opening of the lock to their cell door. As soon as the metal scraped, Dante's eyes popped open. He scrambled to his feet.

Samarand entered, looking as distinguished as ever. "How are you faring?"

"I'm not sure."

"It must be a lot to come to terms with. Under better circumstances, I'd give you more time to do so. Unfortunately, the circumstances are what they are. I need you to answer some questions. And I need you to answer them truthfully. Do you understand?"

"Yes."

"Why did you agree to assassinate me?"

"Because you were driving Narashtovik to war on Mallon."

"Did Cally at any time tell you who he truly was? That *he* used to lead the Council?"

"No."

"You swear on your blood that this is true?"

"I do."

Samarand considered him, softening just a little. "Then your betrayal could have been worse. You may have been a tool of a bitter old man, but at least you were an *unwitting* tool. Still, though, why would you agree to such a thing? You were practicing the nether at that time. In Mallon, they'd kill you for that. So why would you agree to murder the head of the faith that would have welcomed you in?"

"Because you were waging war on my homeland," Dante said. "I thought you were insane. That you had to be stopped."

"You understand he chose you because it's easier to manipulate a child. But I think he had further reasons for wanting to get his hooks in you while you were young."

"What do you mean?"

"He saw the potential of your power. Couldn't you feel it when you took up the true copy of the *Cycle*? What it unleashed within you? I would have bet my left hand that you could have become a member of my Council—and probably before you reached thirty years old. There's a real chance you could have become something even more special than that. In another world, you might have ascended to a nethermancer beyond all measure. Someone who, in his power, might even have been able to restore Arawn to his starry throne."

She began to pace, eyeing him in a way that was indecipherable but clearly not approving. "Why would you throw this away? Cast aside such a future to pursue a crazed old man's personal revenge?"

"I didn't want my people conquered. And if what you're saying is true, Cally manipulated me into it. He might have even used sorcery to do so. How would I have known better?"

"By thinking it through! You no longer followed the faith of Taim, did you? You hadn't since the day you picked up the *Cycle*. You should have been traveling here to join me. But you didn't think! You've taken everything your life could have been and thrown it away."

Dante lowered his head. Nothing made sense to him; he no longer knew what to believe. The only thing he knew was that he was here. "I didn't know. I *didn't* know."

Samarand looked ready to do some more yelling, then sighed instead. "There are no answers to be found from you. Only a sad story of waste. But maybe there's still an opportunity to salvage something from the wreck. I'm going to make you an offer. First, you can choose to die. Beheading, I think. Fast. Clean."

"You're going to execute me?"

She looked down her nose at him. "You came here to assassinate me. You're lucky your guts aren't being reeled from your body as we speak."

"What's my alternative?"

"Submission. Serve me, faithfully, for the rest of your life. You will begin your submission as something even lower than an acolyte, and it will take you years to work your way up from that before you can be trusted with more. I will need to be convinced that your penance is real, along with your loyalty to me, and your faith in Arawn.

"After that, after I'm *certain* of your reform, you may be allowed to rise among our ranks as you are able. But I will stress again that this won't be easy. You will be a servant. You will have no power and your training will be minimal. You will have responsibilities, but they won't be anything challenging—or, frankly, all that interesting. But what you will have is a chance, in time, to become a useful person once more."

She spoke all this like it would be a grueling punishment. Yet for some reason Dante felt...relieved by her terms. As if a giant weight was being lifted from his shoulders. Check that: lots and lots of weights. No one would be praising him for his deeds, but no one would be hunting him, either. Or demanding the impossible of him, because he was the only one who could even attempt it.

"If I accept," he said, "what about Blays?"

"Clean execution."

"Let him free. Let him free, and I'll submit."

"That's out of the question," she said simply.

"Why? Because he's no use to you?"

"*One* of you has to die. If I don't impose punishment on people who tried to *kill* me, then I'll look weak. If I look weak, someone else will come for me. Someone likely to be a lot less crazy than Cally." She glanced up at the wall, as if thinking there might be a window there. "It's getting late. I know this is a consequential decision, but I need an answer."

Dante's head thudded. He couldn't see a way out. The knowledge that Blays had been beheaded in his place would be too much for him to bear. Even if he offered himself up instead, she'd just have the both of them killed. He could try to attack her instead—strike her down, smash down the door, find Blays, and sneak upstairs and over the wall.

Delusional. She was the most powerful sorcerer in Narashtovik, and he was just an apprentice. There was no way out but submission. It couldn't be as bad as it seemed, could it? Blays had been a loyal companion, and they'd even become friends, but still, they'd only known each other a few months. Dante should forget him soon enough.

So why did he know that wouldn't be true? That it would stay with him forever? That it would hurt like losing the deepest friendship of his life?

When the understanding came, he almost laughed.

He lifted his gaze to meet hers. "I'd like to take your offer. There's just one problem. How can I submit to someone that isn't real?"

She sighed and rolled her eyes, gathering herself to argue with him some more. Then she saw the look on his face and her mouth twisted with a sneer.

"I'm far more real than you think. Allow me to show you."

Shadows flew from her hands, all but blocking out the light. Dante was ready. He pulled everything he could to him. Yet what came was much less than he knew he ought to be able to summon. No more than he'd been able to handle as a boy. Samarand's attack rampaged into his defenses, black and white cinders popping in all directions. A few weak blades made it through, cutting him on the face and arms, drawing blood but dealing no meaningful damage.

Samarand summoned a second round of nether. Dante reached for more of his own. The shadows refused to yield with him. A whirling wall of black blades streaked toward his body.

Everything *shuddered*; with a sound like ripping cloth, his full power came to him, a river of energy that extinguished Samarand's assault at its source.

Dante smiled. "Samarand was never this strong. What are you?"

She stared him down, the quirks of her expression such a perfect match for the dead woman that he had to wonder if it might be her after all.

"I am a future that could have been," she said. "One that ends with Dante Galand, the simple monk who spends his days lost in the books he loves, who many turn to when they need to know some piece of history or lore, but who rarely leaves the Citadel, and never leaves Narashtovik. A man who, when he dies, is all but forgotten within a year. Remember this future when you think to yourself that you might have the power to challenge the gods."

Samarand—if it was really her—struck at him a third time. But he turned it aside, striding across the prison cell, which was already disintegrating around him, and poured the shadows down upon her head. When the nether faded, she was gone, too.

He was surrounded by light, a light too bright for him to see anything else. It faded like sunset.

He stood once more on the heights of Mount Arna. The storm was over and the White Tree was gone. He was alone.

He called for Blays, his voice sounding thin and weak in the solitude. Something tickled his face; a drop fell to the snow, staining it crimson. He touched his face. Blood.

Wherever he'd been, whether what he'd faced had been Samarand or something else, the wounds it had given him were real enough. When he healed himself, he felt less nether stirring than he should have had at his command. His expenditure of it had been real, too.

He stood in the cold, but he had no way of understanding what had just happened. So he walked off to find Blays.

There was a chance Blays was gone, buried in a drift or fallen off a cliff. But Dante found him just a little while later, a few hundred feet downhill. He was standing perfectly still and the snow had collected on his head and shoulders and drifted around his legs up to the thigh.

Dante knew before he called Blays' name that he wouldn't respond to it. He walked in front of him, drew back, and slapped Blays across the face. That felt pretty good, so he did it a second time.

Blays blinked.

"Are you in there?" Dante said. "Please say no. I'm not done slapping you yet."

"What do you want?" Blays muttered.

"You're trapped in...well, I have no gods damn idea what you're trapped in. Except I think the mountain's trying to kill us with it. It's time to get out of it."

"But I'm with Lia."

"Oh." Dante turned to gaze across the blankness of the snow. "Well, it's time to come back."

"Just give me one last day."

"I can't do that. If you spend another day with her, you'll wind up spending the rest of eternity with her, because you'll have frozen to death and gone to the Mists. Although you'll probably wind up stuck with Gladdic wherever he is instead, which I don't think any of us wants. Now come on. Come back."

Blays' left eye twitched. So did the corner of his mouth. He trembled, as if from the cold, then swayed forward, catching himself before Dante could. His eyes were hollow with grief and yearning.

He blinked against the sunlight dazzling from the snow. And smiled. "Never seen a blizzard do that before. What do you say we get to the Mill and then get the hell out of here?"

More snow. More stupid, cold, slogging, miserable, gods damned snow. Sometimes the monotony of the snow was broken up by the agony of naked stone and they climbed instead of hiked. Dante could see the peak at almost all times now, along with the pure light gleaming from it.

They were getting closer. But Dante was getting tired. He

cleansed the exhaustion from their muscles. And walked on.

"We can't spend another night here," Dante said. "The mountain will kill us if we try. Even if we could find shelter from the next blizzard, we can't hide from whatever it's doing to our minds. We reach the Mill today, or we go insane and die."

Blays only nodded. Dante was vaguely aware that he was attempting to explain what they were up against to himself as well. They ascended another cliff, Blays shadowalking to the top and letting the rope down to Dante, but at the next bluff they faced, Blays' nether was spent, and they had to ascend it using nothing but their equipment and their muscles.

After, Dante had to flush the weariness from them again. Even with his healing, they needed a short rest before they were able to go on. The peak was a little larger now but every step felt like Dante's legs were about to go numb and collapse. They stopped speaking except for the simplest instructions. Dante couldn't seem to catch his breath even when they stopped to do just that.

Half a mile from the peak, as the crow flies, Dante's left leg buckled. He fell into the snow. And when he tried to get up, he couldn't.

He gave himself a moment, then braced himself and tried again. His legs would no longer support his weight. He washed the nether over himself, down his legs.

"Up you go." Blays leaned over, planting his hands on his knees. "Quit squirming around like a cave worm and let's get moving."

"I can't walk any more. I can't even stand up."

"Just a little further. We can do his."

"No," Dante said. "I can't."

"Oh, come on now. You're not really going to make me do this, are you?"

Blays dumped out most of his pack, keeping only the bare

equipment they'd need to continue, then did the same with Dante's, though he kept the *Book of What Lies Beyond Cal Avin*. The rest he piled on top of the snow. He'd been carrying one of the ropes around his waist. He uncoiled it, threaded it through a handle on Dante's pack, and tied a knot.

"You're going to owe me a lot for this one," Blays said. "I'm thinking a lordly title. Or maybe two of them in case I disgrace the first one."

He leaned forward. And trundled toward Arawn's Mill, dragging Dante over the snow behind him. Embarrassing as it was, Dante didn't have the strength to get loose even if he wanted to, and he let himself rest instead. His legs spasmed unsteadily. Blays' boots crumped in the snow while it scraped softly beneath him. Other than Blays' steady breathing, there was no other sound.

The sky was a perfect blue, darker than it seemed like it should be, given that it wasn't long after noon. Dante got so lost in it that he stopped thinking of anything at all.

He came to a stop. Something thumped into the snow.

Dante twisted around. "Blays?"

"Your legs seem to have passed their wasting illness over to mine." Blays was stretched on the snow lying on his stomach. "I just need a minute."

One minute passed. Then five.

"I might have been optimistic about the legs," Blays said at last. "Don't suppose you've got any final tricks up your sleeves?"

"My sleeves are frozen."

"Yes, I didn't think so. Well. Our legs may have abandoned us, but there is one last thing we could try."

"Crawl?"

"Crawl."

They crawled. The blizzard had set down a bed of loose snow and there were times they sank all the way beneath it.

They'd only been at it for a couple of minutes before Dante knew they wouldn't make it. Still, he kept going, and was proud of himself for doing so. It made it a little easier to accept it when his body gave out and he came to a stop in the snow and knew he wouldn't get any further.

"Thank goodness," Blays said. "I really didn't want to be the first one to quit."

"Outlasting me will be a great consolation when we're in the Mists for however many days they've got left before the lich's sorcery rips them apart."

Blays rolled on his side. "Should I get out the statue to keep us warm? Or should we let it happen quicker?"

Dante thought about it. "The statue, I think. If this place is going to kill us, we might as well make it work for it."

Blays fumbled with the cord of his pack, so exhausted he could barely operate his fingers. In time, he got out the statue of the dragon, which seemed to understand what was expected of it, for it started to emit warmth at once. Drops of water melted from the surface of the snow.

Dante lay on his back. The sky looked an even deeper blue than it had earlier. He tried to think of one last way to move forward, but his mind was as vacant as the firmament above.

Only the sky wasn't so empty anymore. Thin, curved clouds extended across his field of vision, white and branching. There was something funny about them that he couldn't put together until he could: they weren't actually clouds.

They were the limbs of the White Tree.

"Oh, gods damn it," he muttered. "Not this again!"

"Again? Just how many times have you been on the brink of death today?"

The voice wasn't Blays'. Yet it was, in its way, almost as familiar. Eyes stinging with sudden tears, Dante tried to sit up and found that he could; wherever he was, it was a place where he wasn't so exhausted.

He was back in the snowfield north of Narashtovik. An old man stood before him, long-haired and white-bearded, all of it more wild than it should have been for a man of his station. Mischief and merriment glinted in his green eyes — or were they blue today?

Dante's throat closed. "Cally?"

"So you remember me after all. That's good. There are times I feel like you've forgotten everything I ever tried to teach you."

"Are you real?

"Aha, so you've gone crazy. Yes, I feared this day would come."

"I'm not crazy," Dante said. "And if I am, it's the mountain's fault."

"Exactly what a sane man would say."

"That's what Mount Arna does to people. Don't you know of it?"

The old man waved an impatient hand in a gesture Dante remembered perfectly. "Never heard of it. Somehow in your still-young life you've managed to travel to places far more exotic than I ever did."

Dante got to his feet. "I've been…seeing things. It does that to you. Echoes of my past, when I was just a boy. The first things and people were just similar to memories of mine, but the last one was something more than an echo. I saw someone who claimed to be Samarand, who should be long dead, but I'm not sure it wasn't really her. So I'll ask again: *are you real?*"

Cally stamped his staff in the snow. "Why wouldn't I be real? Deceased, certainly, but I'm still present in the Mists, as I understand you've named the place. Very creative of you, what with all the mists there."

"If that's true, I couldn't be happier to hear it."

"Is that so? Then why haven't you come to see me?"

"It's hardly been a year since we even learned about the Mists. We've been more than a little busy since then."

Cally looked around himself. "Well it's certainly an interesting place, isn't it? I don't know what's funnier: how much we got wrong about it, or how much we got right."

"We're High Priests. We're supposed to get it *all* right."

Cally snorted, thumping his staff again. "I'm glad my death didn't stop you from not listening to a single word I ever said. I always told you that we don't know as much as we think we do, and hence it should come as no surprise when we're invariably proven wrong."

Dante nodded, examining the old man. Everything about him looked right, sounded right. Acted right. Then again, if Mount Arna was somehow drawing from his memories of Cally, its illusion *would* match right up.

"Why are you here?"

"You see, it seems as though you are about to die. That would be bad for you, obviously, but also for the world you'll leave behind. So I was…summoned, I suppose. Don't bother asking by who. I couldn't even quite tell you *what* it was."

"I don't see how you can help me. I'm too tired to go on. So unless you can step over to the mountain and carry me on your bony old back, this is the end."

"Glum, defeatist, and petulant, just as I remember. Ah, what a constant joy it was to be around you!"

Dante smiled. "And you're just as long-winded as I remember. Will you get to the point?"

Cally began to pace. Had Dante picked that habit up from him? Or had they just been alike in more ways than either of them would admit?

"It would seem, then, that the first measure of the heroic task settled upon my shoulders is to convince you not only that you *can* persist, but that you *must*. The logical tool to best achieve this end would be a great prophecy: I tell you that the disaster facing the world has been foretold all along, and that you are the chosen one ordained to avert apocalypse, indeed, *that you alone are the only one capable of doing so*, as revealed by one of our great mystics, or even by one of the gods.

"This doesn't leave you with a choice. When ancient prophecy — or the gods themselves — tell you that you must go and do something, you can't stand there and declare, 'Actually, with apologies to the gods, I can't.' No. Rather, you get up off your ass and go do it, no matter how fucking impossible it may seem from where you stand now. Further, a good prophecy lends you the confidence to endure no matter how absurd your present chances appear."

Dante crossed his arms. "That sounds effectively manipulative. But I'm guessing there's a problem with it?"

Cally flapped his arms. "The *problem* is that in your case it isn't true. Well, probably not, at least. I understand you fulfilled the Keeper's prophecy about becoming the avatar of Arawn, which makes the current situation quite interesting, given the nature of the various forces at play. Still, I don't feel like lying to you. Not anymore. Or at the very least not for now."

"How extremely considerate of you to finally start telling me the truth."

"If I thought you needed to be lied to, I would do it. But I don't. The truth is, I've long had a sort of prophecy of my own guiding my choices in life. Not that it was a prophecy in the sense of a divine revelation, mind you. Mine is borne out of two parts experience and observation, and three parts extrapolation.

"The troubles I saw weren't quite so extreme as what you're dealing with in the White Lich, but it was something *like* the events you're up against. Enough to cause me to understand that the world was much more fragile than it appeared — and that people like us were the ones who might endanger it. I also saw, in my travels, that you could be important in fighting the future I feared might one day impose itself on us. That is why I took you on as my apprentice."

"Funny, I always thought that was so you could use me as a tool to kill your rival so you could take Narashtovik over for yourself. When I spoke to her, Samarand had the same recollection."

"Well, that too." Cally cocked a thick brow at him. "But a clever man always has more than one plan in motion, as well as for the useful people and objects in front of him." He turned toward the soaring branches of Barden, scowling at them for some reason. "My vision, if you could call it that, stemmed from an event in my youth. One that took place when I was right around the same age as you were when we first met."

"So two days after the gods made the world? Or three?"

"Amusing. Now, as I've said, the event in question wasn't remotely as dangerous as the lich. But it did involve demons, ones that were quite hard to kill, even with the use of sorcery. When I looked at this event closely, it seemed to me that within it was the potential to destroy a nation—if not much more than that. And that the person wielding such powers might not even *intend* to unleash such devastation."

"Where was this, Narashtovik? You never told me anything about an event like that."

"Yes, that's *because* it was so dangerous. At the time we covered it up and spread misinformation—"

"You mean lies?"

"—*misinformation* about what had happened, so that no one could go and learn to do it again. We destroyed all the information around it, too. And it worked. The knowledge was lost. Purged. A man of lesser insight would have left it at that, but I thought it wise to discover, recruit, and train talents capable of stopping such events in the future."

"And I was part of that plan?" Dante said. "Apparently it was so critical you waited a hundred years to start it."

Cally made his dismissive brushing motion. "Of course you weren't the first. And of course other events intervened in the meantime. Like the rebellion down in Collen. And then Sama-rand's perfidy. Life's chaos has a way of pulling you away from your visions. That's why so little ever gets done.

"Still, despite all these distractions to deal with and fires to put out, I kept a hand on my plan. And I kept an eye on the world for signs of the threat I'd seen in my youth. Which turned out to be a very smart move. Because we may have purged the knowledge in question from our lands—but the world is a very big place, just immense really. And the same knowledge emerged in a place that had been hidden from my eyes."

"Tanar Atain."

"Just so. Though it took a different form than the one I knew."

"How do you know about what's happening now, anyway? Has it even impacted your part of the Mists yet?"

"You are aware that the White Lich has entered the north, yes? Where the lich goes, death follows. Those who've fallen have made their way here—to the Mists, I mean—and the upside of their untimely demise is they've brought information with them, which I've been absorbing with great interest."

Cally had been doing some pacing about, punctuated by the occasional "there you have it" gesture or stamping of his staff. Now, he turned on Dante, staring at him with burningly clear eyes.

"I found you so that if and when a day such as this raised it-self above us, we would have someone with the strength to do something about it. I passed on before I could train you as well as I wished—but you have progressed beyond anything I could have given you. Return. Deliver us, Dante. This has always been your destiny. Even if none of us knew it until it was upon us."

"I want to. More than anything." A pang of despair pierced Dante's heart. "But I can't go on. I can't even crawl. The mountain has beaten us."

Cally smiled craftily and reached inside a fold of his robe. "Yes, I thought you might need this. It won't return your strength, not truly, but it will help your body forget its weakness." He passed Dante a corked flask of black liquid. "You'll need to hurry. It won't last long. But I have the suspicion that once you're standing beneath the Mill, all will be made right."

Dante accepted the flask, which was the size of a large plum. "Even if you're not real — thank you, Cally. I wish we'd had more time together."

"Oh, we had enough of it to set things in the right direction. Now our time here is at an end, too. But if the world ever stops collapsing for long enough for you to take a breather, you *will* come see me, yes? I've heard quite a lot of what you've been up to in these last few years, but I'd still like to hear about it in your own words. You can even bring that wretched Blays along if you like." Cally's eyes glittered again. "Who knows! There may even be something left that *I* can teach *you*."

And then he was gone.

The branches of Barden softened back into a skein of indistinct clouds. Another few moments and these retreated from the deep blue of the sky. It was colder again, and the weight of Dante's exhaustion crushed him like a stone.

He held something in his hand. He propped himself into a stable position, then withdrew the cork with a squeak and a pop. The smell was like someone had raked together all the matter washed up on a beach, boiled it down to a thick concentration, and then, for some reason, leavened it with orange peel. It would be just like Cally to give him a supposed "healing elixir" that only made him vomit.

He held his nose and quaffed. It tasted as strong but not as bad as it smelled and the brackishness of it reminded him of shaden. Now that he thought to check, nether swirled slowly inside it.

His legs shook involuntarily, kicking his heels against the snow, then stopped with a shudder. Once the fit passed, he tried to move his legs on his own. They obeyed.

He grinned, drew himself up, and poked Blays in the side. "Never thought I'd need to encourage you to do *this*, but it's time to drink up."

With effort, Blays got up on his elbow. "You mean that appealing bottle of sludge?"

"I won't lie to you. It isn't good. But it will get us to the Mill."

"You had this thing that could save us all along and it didn't occur to you to use it earlier? Just saving it for when we're dying on an even taller, colder, more savage mountain?"

"I didn't have it until just now. When Cally gave it to me."

"I now suspect that it's a flask of insanity juice. It's got you looking better, though, so I guess I'll just go mad too." Blays took the bottle and drank, making a face. His legs spasmed out like Dante's had. "Well, would you look at that."

He rose. So did Dante. For what would be the last time — for now they either died on the slopes, or reached the Mill — they marched on.

Dante was certain the mountain would hurl one last spear at them. Another blizzard. Another vision. One of the deadly guardians that lurked in all the Realm's wildest places. Yet the light of the Mill grew brighter by the minute. It was too glaring to get a good look at what might be there, but he thought he saw it slowly spinning.

The approach to the peak formed a series of stone shelves. Some were short enough to climb without equipment. Others were a struggle. None would stop them.

He lost count of how many shelves they climbed. At least a score. They heaved themselves over one more, and then Dante saw something he hadn't seen since he'd first laid eyes on the mountain: there was nowhere higher to go.

They stood on the edge of a flat, circular plateau. Searing white light poured down from above the center of the peak. The song of the mountain swelled as if taken by a gust of wind, then dimmed, though it remained ever-present.

"Are we really here?" Blays said. "Because if it turns out we died down there and this is just the Pastlands showing us what we want to see, the gods better hope the Mists get ripped apart before I find a way to cross over and cut their throats."

"No," Dante said. "We're here."

He wanted to run to it. He forced himself to walk instead. The light burned from the snow, so potent he could hardly tell one object from another, until he was blinded altogether, reaching out in front of him, shuffling his feet through the snow so he wouldn't trip.

The light dimmed, still brighter than any sunlight, but bearable. He blinked the dazzles went away. Blays was gawking at the sky. Dante shielded his eyes and tipped back his head.

He looked on Arawn's Mill.

17

The Mill turned with a slow and terrible power.

It hung above them like a vast slate moon. There was no axle to hold it in place, yet it remained fixed in the sky just as it had since the beginning of time. It was cut from gray stone and its grinding surface was as smooth as glass. There was nothing for it to be grinding against—at least nothing visible—yet ether sifted down from it like the idea of snow, twinkling in the air, short-lived rainbows shimmering into existence, fading away, then reappearing elsewhere in the sky. Its rumble wasn't loud but it resonated within Dante's bones.

He would have fallen to his knees, but the presence of the thing was so awesome that he couldn't move at all.

"Okay, I admit it." Blays' voice was hushed. "That's a pretty impressive millstone."

"I never imagined I'd see it. I can almost *touch* it."

Grains of ether drifted around him. He was already feeling better, vigorous and restored. He stood there a little longer, letting it wash over him, then got out the now-empty bottle Cally had given him, uncorking it and holding it up to the air.

A minute later, and he'd captured three, or perhaps even four, grains of glowing dust.

"Er," Blays said. "How much of this stuff do we need again?"

"I was intending to fill the entire bottle."

"Then I hope you're also intending to build us a cozy little house to live in during the six months it'll take to fill that bottle up."

Dante visored his eyes, peering at the Mill. "The ether's pouring out of the axle hole. Which is an odd way for a mill to function, incidentally. But by the time it gets down here, it's too dispersed to gather."

"We need to get at least eighty feet closer. I *could* jump up and grab it, but I'd hate to embarrass your weakness like that. Can you build us some stairs?"

"I don't think it'll work. But I can give it a shot." Dante sank the nether into the ground, which he was alarmed to find was embedded with skeletons, presumably of past seekers of the Mill who'd been driven mad or directly attacked by the mountain. He attempted to lift a small pillar, but the ground would hardly budge, and reverted to its original form the moment he let go of it. "Not happening. Sometimes I hate being right all the time."

"Pretty rude of Neve not to warn us to bring a ladder. Okay, so rock won't work, but can you build us a platform of ice?"

"That's more of an ethereal thing. But maybe."

Dante uncluttered his mind. He'd seen Gladdic use the ether to shape the ice before and had a general understanding of how it worked, and after a bit of fiddling around, he was able to get some of the snow to fuse into a solid sheet.

"There's no way," he said, shaking his head. "It's not reverting half as fast as the earth, but it's still not stable. I wouldn't have nearly enough power to raise something tall enough to reach."

Blays put his hands on his hips. "I'd suggest we could pack the snow together by hand, but that'd take even longer than waiting for the bottle to fill. Right, have we failed, then?"

"This is bullshit. We didn't come all this way to get stuck right beneath the Mill!"

"Don't suppose you know a way to grow our legs eighty feet long?" Blays got a funny look on his face. "Or maybe it isn't us you need to grow." He opened his cloak and dug around an inner pocket, retrieving a small bundle of what turned out to be extremely well-gnawed apple cores. He extended this treasure to Dante. "Again, I really don't know what you'd do without me."

"Ah, your trash. How useful."

"Look a little closer and you'll see the apple seeds that are about to save your life."

"Apple seeds? Why are you carrying apple seeds up the side of the mountain?"

"So that you could grow us a tree in case we wound up somewhere weird where there wasn't any food."

"You want me to grow a tree to the Mill." Dante grinned at the massive revolving stone, then rubbed his face. "Even if I can get a seed to take root, the ether will probably just revert it like everything else."

"Well, you could quit whining and find out."

Dante gave him a look, then kneeled. The ground was frozen stiff, impossible to dig, so he swept open a small hole with the nether and dropped a seed inside. The earth flowed back into position on its own. Dante bent his head and sent the shadows into the seed. It held inert—and then unfurled.

But the frozen earth had it trapped fast. Heart racing, Dante softened the ground around it. Thread-like roots reached downward while a sprout nudged toward the surface. He blinked in surprise as some of the ether swirling around them diverted toward the tiny plant, turning the green shoot silver.

With the addition of the ether, and more entering it by the moment, the tree shot upward, forcing Dante to scramble back. Roots thickened and cracked through the rock-hard soil. The trunk climbed into the sky, extending boughs and leaves, all of it the same monochrome silver. Dante continued to guide its growth until its mighty crown loomed even with the Mill.

He stepped back and gestured to the tree. "Your turn."

Blays secured the bottle inside his cloak, rubbed his hands together, and started up the tree, pulling himself upward from branch to branch. Dante kept an eye on the tree's limbs to ensure they weren't about to snap under Blays' weight, but they showed no sign of strain. The Mill ground onwards, its revolution somehow both ponderous and breakneck.

Blays came to a stop close enough to the axle hole that he might have leaped inside it. He lifted the bottle to the stream of silver-white ether. The stream enveloped his arm to the elbow. He leaned closer to watch the progress of the bottle. Once he was finished, he lifted the bottle to the light, gave it a swirl, and corked it.

He made his way back down. When he reached the ground, he brushed some silver bark from his hands and clothes and handed Dante the flask.

Dante frowned at the glowing ether. "I've never tried to *bottle* the stuff before. I really hope it stays in there."

"You'd better make sure that it does. After this, I'm never stepping on another mountain again."

"If common cobblers and ramna barbarians have carried the ether out of here, it can't be *that* complicated."

Even so, he spent several minutes observing the bottle for signs of trouble. The brand-new ether seemed perfectly content to remain in its container.

He watched the Mill revolve a while longer. At last, with the day growing late, and having no intention of joining the skeletons heaped in the earth beneath it, they turned and started back down the mountain.

They passed the night in a crevice a little ways down from the summit. The statue of the dragon kept them perfectly warm, but Dante woke often to check on the flask of ether. When the dawn broke to the east, the light poured over the valley like a golden flood. The sun was far below them, dyeing the world in pink and orange and the palest blue-gray.

The weather remained nice, or at least calm, and they found their way down to the gear they'd left behind the day before. This in hand, Dante shaped the snow into a pair of shallow icy saucers two feet wide. They seated themselves and glided down the mountain.

Even with the occasional need to hop off their sleds and descend a cliff, they were back down among the trees in no time at all. Not holding out much hope, Dante activated his link to the blood he'd smeared on their horses. They found the animals in a small, snowy canyon, spooked and bleeding from a number of claw marks. Dante healed their wounds and waited for them to calm before mounting up.

They located the trail they'd broken during the ascent. It was so festooned with cobwebs Blays had to cut a leafy branch to sweep the way forward, yet they sped along it, shedding elevation by the minute. The air warmed around them; after their time in the heights, it felt thick enough to scoop up with a spoon.

The temple of Arawn was as quiet and deserted as when they'd found it. Blays got a troubled look; with a word about how others should have the same chance to find it that they did, he went to return the statue of the dragon to the cellar.

The day was almost extinguished as they reached the pit where they'd lost Neve. The pit was no longer there: the ground was restored, appearing completely innocuous. There was no sign that Neve or anyone else had been in the area in the last couple of days.

"Do you suppose she's really gone?" Blays said. "When one of the gods' angels hits a rough time, do they actually die? Or do they get reincarnated or what have you?"

"I don't know," Dante said. "But it's going to be much tougher without her."

He could already tell they wouldn't make it to the base of the trail before nightfall, but he pressed on anyway. At dusk, the wolves returned and he thwacked them away as he'd done before. The peak was now so far away it was hidden behind the clouds. Night fell. Dante kept it at bay with his torchstone, and when this gave out, by his own ether. Down one more ridge and the land became an easy reach of gentle hills.

Without warning, Blays stopped, furrowing his brow. "Do you hear that?"

"Hear what?"

"The singing."

Dante cocked his head. "Just the crickets."

"Exactly," Blays said. "The singing's stopped. We've left Mount Arna behind."

18

The peak wasn't yet a day behind them when they saw their first ramna.

Not just a few scouts or raiders, but a full-blown war party, three thousand strong, massing at a stream before crossing to the other side. Dante didn't see any of the Jessel's colors or insignias among them, and so watched from a distance behind the cover of a good deal of trees.

"We're a long way from the Red Valley," Dante said. "What do you suppose that's about?"

Blays shrugged. "Probably got riled up when some outsider suggested they might try taking a bath."

They waited for the band to ride clear from sight before continuing. Just two miles later, they halted again. The grass before them was trampled and torn. Hundreds of bodies were strewn across it. Soldiers dressed in navy blue and white, a longboat stitched onto the chests of their uniforms and on their muddied banners.

"Phannon's men," Dante said. "It appears there was a disagreement."

"Yeah, about whether Phannon's men should be allowed to continue to live."

"Just a one-off battle? Or did the attack the gods launched on the Red Valley kick the hornet's nest?"

There was no way to tell, and besides it didn't smell very good at all, so they didn't stay any longer. They rode through the wilderness, avoiding any roads or other signs of civilization. Dante didn't see any drakelets on the day, but he built them an earthen shelter anyway, then harvested a layer of grass over it to further conceal themselves.

Two days out from Mount Arna, the ether of the Mill was dimmer in its bottle. But Neve had promised them it would last long enough to bear it to Gladdic, and so Dante tried not to check in on it too often.

That afternoon, his loon pulsed. "Nak?"

"Hello, lord."

"Nak, I can barely believe I'm saying this—*I stood beneath Arawn's Mill.* Blays gathered the ether from it as it was being ground. I'm carrying it right now."

"Remarkable. Truly remarkable. I would assume that things are going well, then?"

"We lost Neve, our traveling companion and guide. And the mountain couldn't decide what it would rather try to do first: drive us crazy, or just kill us. But the tough part's behind us now."

"Those sound like famous last words." Nak paused. "My own news is rather less pleasant. The White Lich has burned Tantonnen."

"The city? Did the people make it out?"

"Yes, for the most part they were able to get away, but he didn't just burn the city. He burned *all* of it. The fields. The farms. There's nothing left."

"Razing fields? This seems like a new development."

"We've been retreating from him and evacuating any settlements before he can fall upon them. He's been advancing into new territory, then, but you couldn't say that he's making any tangible gains. Olivander believes the Eiden Rane is destroying our crops so that even if we keep running away from him, we'll have nothing to come back to, and will starve."

"I don't like this news at all. Have you figured out your next move?"

"We can't do much more to slow him down at this point. We have to do everything we can to stay ahead of him. We're retreating north."

"No," Dante said. "Go west."

He could almost hear Nak's eyebrow lift. "West?"

"There's nothing to be gained by retreating to Narashtovik. If you try to make a stand there, he'll slaughter you. If you abandon it to him, he'll burn everything we've got."

"So your idea is to induce him to burn Gask instead?"

"At this point it's not a matter of stopping the lich from burning things. It's a matter of deciding *where* is to be burned. Better Gask than us."

"Not that I think you're wrong, but it always impresses me how...ah...*readily* you make such moral calculations."

"Say the lich marches on Narashtovik. Rips down our walls. Smashes the Citadel. Even if you keep our people safe, and I return and kill him, what do you think King Moddegan of Gask is going to do when we're defenseless and there's no more lich for him to worry about?"

"Strategically reacquire us?"

"After the Chainbreakers' War, we'll be lucky if he leaves any of our citizens alive."

"You're right, of course. But if we go west, we'll bring the lich through a great deal of norren, too."

"I trust them to take care of themselves. After all, they've been doing that for as long as we've known about them."

They chatted a little longer, filling in less pressing details, then Dante closed the connection. He gazed across the bobbing grass of the lush prairie. "Did we make a mistake?"

Blays glanced over. "A mistake? No. By my count, we've made several thousand."

"The White Lich just put Tantonnen to the torch. We've been here for almost a month and we've barely started on the spear. He could roll across the entire north before we're even ready to fight back."

"It seems to me the lich was going to be a right asshole whether or not we detoured to the Mill."

"Then maybe the best thing to have done would be to minimize the time he could go on being an asshole."

Blays tapped his fingers on the horn of his saddle. "It seems to me that what's done is done. We've got the ether in hand. So we can either do some crying about the time it took to get it, or we can go bring back our friend — a friend, I'll add, who may be the only person I know who can give the gods a harder time than we can."

They had to elude two more ramna bands on the journey, but otherwise encountered no trouble as they reached the base of the western range and angled up its flank. Rain lashed the foothills, cold and harsh; while they'd been on the mountain, summer had gone.

For a while Dante traveled by dead reckoning, but soon spotted the shining city on the plateau, and used it to orient his way toward the bluff above the portal where they'd buried Gladdic. That night wasn't quite cold enough to snow, but if anything that would have been less miserable than the rain, which turned the hillsides to slop. Whenever Dante dismounted, his boots grew heavy with mud, leaving him irritable. There were few things he hated more than filthy boots.

In due time, they climbed high enough that tongues of snow lay in the shadows. The rain came to a blessed stop.

Blays ran his forearm across his brow, kicking at a patch of snow. "After the Mill, I never thought I'd be happy to see this stuff again. I'd consider myself quite the fool if I weren't given constant evidence that everyone else is even more foolish."

Dante hopped down to scrape what felt like nine pounds of clay from his boots. As he approached a rock, a white figure seemed to summon itself up from the snow. It was faceless and held a long, icy sword.

Blays drew his own blades. "Not these again."

Two more of the icy golems formed behind the first. Dante bit his lip, drawing the nether to him, quickly reminding himself how they'd dispatched the creatures—if they could be called that—when they'd first encountered them working with Adaine. Cutting them in half and ripping out their guts: yes, that normally did the trick.

The featureless guardians watched them eyelessly, as motionless as the boulders around them. Then all three sank back into the snows that had spawned them.

Dante lowered his hand, but kept the nether for now. "What do you suppose *that* was about?"

"Oh, they probably wanted to kill us. Then recognized who we were and did the smart thing instead."

Dante finished cleaning his boots, then saddled up. The clouds above them blackened, threatening a storm, and a bad one by the look of it. They climbed past the ravine that concealed the doorway to the Mists and the Split Crypt of Barsil. Dante wasn't certain he'd be able to remember the exact spot where he'd interred Gladdic, but recognized the long thumb of rock at once.

Even though he could feel the weight of the flask against his chest, he touched it to reassure himself it was still there. After a glance around for more icy warriors, giant bears, or whatever other surprises the wilds might have for them, he lifted his hand over the earth.

A rectangular pit opened in front of him, sinking steadily as first dirt and then rock flowed away. It soon revealed an eight-foot brick of limestone. He mounded earth under this, lifting it up to the surface. With a gesture, he began to dissolve it from the top down.

Both the cold weather and the stone entombment were very potent guardians against decay. Even so, Dante had expected *some* change to have overtaken the body. But Gladdic looked exactly the same as when Dante had sealed him inside the rock.

"He actually looks peaceful," Blays said. "I almost feel bad to bother him. Then again, he was enough of a bastard to deserve it."

"All right." Dante twisted the cork in the mouth of the bottle. "Uh, watch my back?"

"For what? Are you afraid you're going to accidentally turn him into a zombie?"

"I have no idea what kinds of things might go wrong. I've only resurrected somebody once before."

He hesitated, fearful of screwing something up and ruining their one and only chance. But he had no way to address that, did he? He pulled the cork.

The ether was much dimmer than when Blays had first collected it, but on exposure to the air, it pulsed, regaining some of its original brightness. Dante drew a breath and tipped the flask over Gladdic's body, attempting to pour it onto him.

But the ether, not being a liquid at all, began to drift in all directions, like dispersing smoke.

Dante yelped something that might have been a curse if his thoughts weren't scrambling too hard to form words. He erased all thought, merging his mind with the ether, guiding it down into the cold body. For a moment, the ether hung still in the air, then sifted downward.

Gladdic's skin took on a blue-white hue, glowing faintly.

Blays' voice was odd. "He almost looks like the White Lich."

The resemblance was non-trivial, but Dante didn't know what to make of it. He moved a portion of his attention into the nether within Gladdic's body, but while it seemed to be "breathing," as all nether did, it wasn't circulating in the way that nether within a living form did. Just in case, he mentally *willed* the ether to restore Gladdic's life, though in truth he couldn't say whether he was doing anything at all. Abruptly remembering that Neve had instructed him to send the substance into Gladdic's heart and bones, Dante guided the ether deeper, into the cores of the dead man's body.

Gladdic's skin gleamed brighter. But the ether in the bottle was almost gone, and Dante still saw no sign of life.

"I don't understand," he said. "Neve said it would be easy. That all we'd have to do is — "

"Er," Blays said. "What's that?"

Dante had already seen it, too. A golden spot on Gladdic's solar plexus. As small as a ladybug, it expanded wider, to the size of a fingertip, then a coin. It burst outward, filling Dante's vision, as if he were falling into it. And just when it felt like —

A gap. Like falling asleep in a carriage and waking up in a different place, but on every level of being.

Yet it was familiar, too.

A gray pond lay beneath the slate clouds. Snow rested on the naked boughs and carpeted the ground. A cabin stood back from the pond, a serpent of smoke wriggling from its chimney. An old man sat on the shore. He was fishing.

Dante laughed. "Gladdic?"

His voice carried across the flat and silent air, but the other figure gave no sign he'd heard. Dante crunched toward him through the snow. "Hey, old man!"

In the stillness, the pond was the color of mercury. The cork at the end of the old man's line floated motionless on the surface.

Dante came to a stop across from the man. It *was* Gladdic: his aged face not slackened by time, but made austere by it, as much the face of a cliff than of a man; his plain gray robe, completely unadorned.

Here, however—wherever "here" was—his right arm had been restored to him.

"You look in better health than ever," Dante said. "So don't try to pretend you've gone deaf."

Gladdic didn't turn his head. "Why have you come here?"

"Do you know where you are?"

"Yes. I am dead."

"Well as you know, I'm something of a physician. I'm here to treat your unfortunate condition."

"I know why you are here."

Dante blinked at the quiet homestead. "I feel like I'm not getting something."

"Your intelligence is enough that if you do not understand it is only because you do not wish to."

"The number of disasters I've accidentally kicked off has something else to say about your theory. But let's see. I'm here to bring you back. A normal dead person would be happy and excited by the prospect of going back to being a normal living person, but the idea seems to be making you even more irritated than you typically are. Because you don't *want* to go back?"

"You see? That was not so difficult after all."

"Yes, I can see why you're so bent on staying. You've got a pond *and* a cabin. You'd never get a deal like that back in the land of the living."

"It is not a matter of my comforts, which are few, though I am grateful for what I have."

"What, then? Screw the rest of us, you're done with it all?"

"Spite is always alluring to our nature, and I have more nature within me than most. But that is not it either."

"Considering your mind's as warped as a bent nail, I could spend all day trying to guess your problem and get nowhere close. Alternately, you could just tell me."

Gladdic pursed his lips, drawing in his fishing line hand over hand. He stood, less stiffly than before, checked his bait — a rather pale and drowned-looking worm — inspected his line to ensure it was free of tangles, and cast it back out into the wintry waters. It landed without so much as a ripple.

"There are few truly perfect things in life," he said at last. "My death was one of them."

"I'll grant that it was impressive, heroic even, but my definition of 'perfect' is the one where you *don't* die."

"Death is assured. That is the lesson of your own patient god. With the release of the Eiden Rane, my life took a turn. I did not seek vindication for what I had done earlier in life — but there can be no more perfect end than having found my vindication in mortal battle with the lich. My tale came to an end at its right and proper time."

"For you, maybe. The rest of us still exist in a time where we're about to get stomped into nonexistence. We're in deeper trouble than ever."

"It was no challenge for me to guess as much."

"At the same time, we're making progress, Gladdic. We've got one part of the spear in hand and a second promised to us. But we need your help to gather the rest."

"That is unfortunate."

Dante scowled at the floating bit of cork on the cold lake. "Do you ever even catch anything? What is this place, anyway? The Pastlands?"

"It does not feel like the Pastlands. My mind is more clear and more my own than it is in that place. Yet at the same time there are similarities and I suspect that easing the soul into the transition of death is the purpose of this place as well. Even so, there are differences: and that implies the gods saw some fault here which they sought to correct when they constructed the Pastlands for us."

"We've learned the people here don't age and die like we do. They seem to go on until death by misadventure. That makes them *more* afraid of death. More shocked by it." Dante waved his hand at the pond and the snow. "Maybe it turned out this place doesn't do enough to prepare these people for what lies beyond. So when the gods created our world, they assumed we'd need a stronger dose of medicine, something more dream-like, not knowing that our lives *as* mortals would make us more prepared for death."

Gladdic gazed at the pond. "That is interesting."

"We've been making all kinds of discoveries about the Realm. When we haven't been getting chased off by barbarians and angels, that is. You should come back and see it with us."

"I am sure there is great mystery to be found there. Yet in the end, what interest is the Realm to us? The gods shut us out of it. They did not mean for us to see it. If we believe in them, it follows that we should trust in their judgment."

"Their unquestionable judgment is about to get everyone in our world murdered. Anyway, did you know what else we discovered? That we had less than a month to find you here and bring you back. We barely made it."

Gladdic frowned. "I do not see the theological implications of this point."

"There aren't any. The point is that if you think you're going to get to just sit here freezing your ass off and not catching fish forever, I think you're wrong. You might only have a few more days."

"And why would I fear what comes next?"

"Because they might send you to the Mists. Which are about to be destroyed. Or they might send you *nowhere*. We're not supposed to visit the Realm, are we? That wasn't in the gods' design. It wasn't in their design for us to die here, either."

Gladdic drew his shoulders upward. "Why would you do this to me?"

"Offer you something that literally everyone who's ever died has wished for?"

"Return me to the nightmare. The living crawl of horror that is being."

"Come on, it isn't *that* bad. There are birds and things."

"You have seen enough to know that what is gruesome in life can far outweigh every one of its pleasantries. And I have seen even deeper than you."

"But that's what inspired you to turn against the lich in the first place, isn't it? To fight the horror. To drive it back so others don't have to endure it."

"And in so doing I have endured as much as anyone can be asked. Unto death itself. There is nothing left for me there. Nothing more to learn. No further virtue to achieve. If I had a purpose, surely it was fulfilled when the Eiden Rane struck me down: that was my fate and my meaning. And if instead there was no purpose or design, and my death was by bare happenstance? Then there is no purpose in life for any of us—and the delusion of our world is just as thick as that of the Pastlands.

"To die is only to pass free from an illusion. For the gods shaped a hereafter to comfort us. Not just one, but three: the soothing sleep of the Pastlands, the simple peace of the Mists, and the serene annihilation of the Worldsea. There is no reason for me to return to the illusion of physical being when this here is the design the gods spun for me."

"Yes, but there are still a hell of a lot of millions of people who *haven't* yet been relieved of their 'illusion of life.' And again, if the Mists are allowed to be ripped apart, then every part of your pretty little design is ripped apart with it."

Gladdic laughed, giving his fishing line a tug. "You refuse to face the truth before your very nose: the gods do not *want* us to prevail. If you claim to follow their will, it is now our place to die."

"There's a chance that even the gods can be wrong. Anyway, they're not united on that front. Carvahal and Gashen seem willing to give us a chance. If we try and wind up failing, so what? Then the gods were right after all. But even if they're right, our world is still worth fighting for."

"For you that may be so. For me it holds nothing. I have no legacy nor line to leave it. I have no children and knew that I never could. For if I had, it would have been tragedy, for it is almost certain that neither the power of ether nor nether would be among their talents: these skills are only rarely passed down from parent to child.

"But I am just as certain they would still inherit the will of their father. And so they would seek to impose their own will on the world, but lacking my powers, they would fail to do so firmly; and either they would suffer for it, or those they sought to control would suffer from their failure instead. Yes, I saw this long ago. Everything I did was done with the understanding that my line would end with me.

"The deeper truth revealed to me is that I am not alone in this state. For cannot the same condition be said to be true of all humanity? Our gods are our fathers and we are but pale shadows of them in terms of power—but *not* in terms of our will. In such a state, we wish to achieve within and impose upon our world, but we lack the might required to do so. Thus we are doomed to try to change what cannot be changed, to fight what cannot be fought, and to rule what cannot be ruled!"

"Maybe so," Dante said. "But in our world there are no gods. Not even the White Lich, or at least not yet. It's not as futile as you lament."

Gladdic turned on him, face wrenched with scorn. "Do you ever at any time apprehend the depths of your arrogance? First you believe you can stand against the Eiden Rane, and when that proves false, you follow it up with the belief you can stand against the gods! Do you know so little about the laws of nature that you do not see how your hubris tempts total destruction?"

"Total destruction? You mean like the kind that's going to happen if we *don't* try to stop it?"

"Have you considered that the lich might not be wrong to do what he attempts? If he is right, in attempting to stop him, you are making a monster of yourself!"

"I'm pretty sure his glorious plan to exterminate everyone and — "

Gladdic held up his restored right hand, eyes blazing with contempt. "Spare me the words you are about to waste. You cannot see our world with any clarity for you are both too immersed in it as well as a product of it. But in my absence from it I have dwelled upon it. There is far too little that is righteous and far too much that is ill. I know this as well as any man, for in my time I was a source of great illness — unless it is even worse than I perceive, and there *is* no side of the righteous, but only different forces of illness vying to see which one will be allowed to infect the people who scrape a living from the surface of the soil. There is no bottom to the blackness of the world of the flesh, Dante Galand. No, the lich is not righteous, as he believes. But he is no more than one more sickness among a legion of them."

"It's not that way for everyone. Even if the world is no longer for you, you can come save it for all those who still love it."

Gladdic said nothing for some time. He drew in his line, inspected his bait, and cast it forth again. "Perhaps there is virtue in letting them live on and be happy, as they do not have the vision to perceive what surrounds them. But even if I were to return to your aid, it would not be to your benefit in the end. For I see what I am as unblinkingly as I see the place that produced me. I no longer have the arrogance that so sustains you. Sooner or later, in my effort to stand against lich and gods, I would break, and everything that depends on me would fall with me."

A pang swept over Dante, as cold as the ends of Mount Arna. Whether Gladdic was right about everything, wrong about it all, or somewhere in the spectrum between, one thing was abundantly clear: he no longer belonged among the living. He had seen too much, done too much. Moved beyond it. Returning to such a place, be it the Realm of Nine Kings or the so-called Fallen Land, would only hurt him.

If Dante forced that hurt upon his friend, what kind of man did that make him?

Then again, he supposed it made him the same person he'd always been.

"You're wrong, Gladdic. You *don't* know yourself. Not as fully as you think. In your way, you've always been as isolated as the Plagued Islands. Now maybe you had the Eldor to give you orders, or various underlings for you to order around. At the heart of it, though, you were alone. A single beam holding up the roof. Whenever you cracked, the whole edifice came tumbling down with you.

"But I don't think you'll break now. Even if you do, the roof will hold. Because Blays and I will be there to hold it up with you."

Gladdic lowered his fishing pole until its tip hovered above the water. He closed his eyes.

"Damn you," he whispered.

Dante knew to say nothing.

Gladdic held the pose, then opened his eyes and fixed them on Dante. "There is one condition. Though perhaps it is better stated as a warning."

"Go ahead."

"Should I fall again—be it in the first hour of our trials, or in the last moment of our triumph—do not come back for me again. If you do, you will not find me."

Dante nodded.

Gladdic rose. He brought in his line, gazing down at the rod as if he might just throw it aside on the bank. Instead, he trudged to his cabin, entered, and put the tool away. He rejoined Dante.

A golden doorway stood where Dante had come into this slice of the afterworld. Gladdic led the way. At the door, he stopped and gestured toward it. "After you."

Dante eyed him. But if this was a trick, there was nothing he could do about it. He stepped through.

The gap, same as before. It almost felt good, like a far more profound sleep.

He was back on the mountainside. And he was lying down in a heap. Blays was seated over him, looking concerned. Seeing Dante's eyes open, he grinned.

"You collapsed like my old man after a long day of wine and not getting hired," Blays said. "What did—?"

His mouth fell open, gaze snapping to Gladdic. Whose eyes were open as well.

He wasn't moving. Or blinking. Just staring up at the cloudy sky. Dante couldn't tell if he was breathing.

"Gladdic?" Blays edged toward him through the snow. "You in there, old fellow?"

Gladdic still didn't stir. With a coldness stealing over his heart, Dante moved into the nether within him to check if it was circulating.

"Remove your presence from me."

Dante jumped, kicking back from Gladdic. The old man attempted to push himself up on his right arm, then snorted to find that it was no longer there. He drew himself to a seated position, taking in the snows and the pine trees of the cold slopes, and got to his feet.

"We thought you were dead!" Blays threw himself at Gladdic and embraced him. "Because you were!"

Gladdic grimaced, looking to Dante for help, then returned the hug, if somewhat stiffly. "I regret my return already."

"Even the peace of the afterlife can't make you any less bitter. The gods must have put you together from their leftover grape skins."

"Perhaps my mood is not the fault of my self, but of my present company."

"Where did you go, anyway? Was it like the Pastlands and the Mists? Or is it different here?"

Gladdic took a longer look around, scowling faintly. "The doorway Dante just opened is of a class that might have drawn attention of a type we do not want. I would move from this spot before allowing ourselves to bog down in conversation."

They only had two horses. Blays offered his up for use, but Gladdic refused, walking alongside them as they angled downward away from the tomb and the portal to the Mists. Gladdic's face remained unreadable. Dante felt some measure of euphoria, but what he felt most was a sense of surreality, as if Gladdic had never been gone at all, or as if this wasn't *real* at all, but rather he was still up in the icy wastes of Mount Arna, fallen in the snow, and he was freezing to death as the insidious mountain filled his mind with pleasant illusions of victory.

The thought spooked him, more so because he couldn't think of a way to disprove it. After a goodly descent, they called for a halt and made a camp.

Gladdic held his hand before the fire. "I will confess it is nice to have a fire. The fires where I was never felt quite right. As if I was always sitting just a little too far away from them to be warmed."

"We haven't had many at all lately," Dante said. "Too many people have been chasing us to risk it."

"You have created new enemies and fallen into pools of trouble? The two of *you*?"

This made for a good transition into the longer story of what they'd been up to since Gladdic had fallen, so Dante brought him up to speed, with Blays adding his own perspective and commentary. Gladdic said little, but the few questions he asked pierced like arrows.

"That's what brought us here," Dante said. "In short, we recently lost our best ally. But we've got potential support with Carvahal, Gashen, and the Jessel. And so far the only people we *know* want to kill us are Taim—"

"Is that all," Gladdic said.

"—and possibly Silidus. Our obvious move from here is to go see Gashen, not only to collect the second part of the spear, but to see if he can open up any new doors for us to barge through. After that, assuming he's not angry with us for the loss of Neve, Carvahal would be the safe bet."

"In our state of being, the safe bet is as selfish as it is foolish."

"So the safe bet is actually the worst bet. You really should put together a book of aphorisms, Gladdic."

"You value safety as your prime virtue when you should not. The wisest course is to immediately contest for Taim's part of the spear."

"That's your plan? Go take on the guy who least wants to help us and most wants us dead?"

"That is exactly why we should do so. Taim presents the greatest obstacle and the challenge most likely to send us to defeat. If we are fated to that defeat, it is best to learn this soonest, so that all who depend on us can soonest learn of it as well."

"But if we're their only hope, and we go out and get trounced by Taim, how does that help them beat the lich?"

Gladdic snorted. "Where did I imply that it would? The point is not that they might then be able to pursue an alternate victory. Rather it is to provide them with the greatest kindness that we can: the knowledge that all hope is lost, and that it is now time for them to play out the remainder of their lives without further illusions."

"Now that *is* kind," Blays said. "Really it's a shame the afterlife will collapse before all those people can find us and thank us for relieving them of the intolerable burden of having any hope."

"There is a certain logic to it." Dante squinted against a sudden change in wind that blew the fire's smoke into his eyes. "Although I wonder if you just want to settle this now so you can get back to being dead as soon as possible."

Gladdic jutted his jaw forward, smiling like a mountain lion. "Perhaps."

They lapsed into silence. But it was far from an uncomfortable kind. Gladdic already seemed less isolated than when Dante had found him beside the pond. If anything, he almost seemed happy, if only by his own extremely relative scale. It had been dark for an hour and it was late enough that they might have gone to sleep, but none of them seemed inclined to do so. Dante thought he knew why: they had only just been reunited and the wonder of it was still fresh. In the morning, after a night of sleep, that feeling would already have begun to fade. None of them wanted to let it go. Not just yet.

The fire brightened with another shift of the wind. Dante turned away, eyes passing over Gladdic. By some quirk of the light, all signs of age had vanished from the old man's face—his skin pulled tight, his features as severe as ever, but revitalized, as healthy and commanding as a hawk.

Sensing Dante's look, Gladdic turned toward him. This shifted the firelight on his face, casting half of it into shadow. Yet he still looked fifty years younger.

Dante's pulse tripled. He reached for the nether, afraid it was already too late.

19

"*Run!*"

Dante scrambled to his feet, thrusting a lance of nether up into the pillar of light that surrounded them. Blays sprinted from the illuminated circle, watching from over his shoulder.

Yet Gladdic remained in its center, unmoving as he stared up into the core of the light.

"Don't do that!" Dante hollered. "You're supposed to flee from it!"

His nether struck the source of the light, but it was a hasty blow; the beam dimmed and wobbled, then reasserted itself. Dante shaped a second strike, but it wouldn't be fast enough.

Gladdic raised his hand. Two powers shot up from it, one as rigid as a shining icicle, the other as tumultuous as a stretch of rapids, but as black as the inside of a body. With a peal of shattering glass, the pillar broke apart. Chunks of ether rained harmlessly around them, disintegrating as they fell.

Dante turned on his heel. "How'd you know how to do that?"

Gladdic continued to stare up into the sky. "Its form was revealed to me."

"Revealed? By who? The person about to smite you with it?"

Gladdic only shook his head. The sky glowed anew. Dante hoisted the nether like a javelin, ready to launch it at the heart of the high end of the pillar, but no pillar came. Instead, fist-sized spheres of ether hailed toward them.

But these were no harmless remnants of a shattered attack. They gleamed with killing purity. Expressionless, Gladdic hammered at them with both light and shadow, ripping apart all he could—which was a fair sight less than there were. Dante's mind darted from target to target, breaking one hailstone after another, but others were already slashing downward, slamming into the ground so hard that it shook, vomiting gobbets of hard turf, knocking wide craters into the earth.

Dante sprinted and danced away from them by feel, pelted by the debris of their impact. One landed a glancing blow on a boulder in front of him and he whirled to put his back to it. Hunks of rock pelted his back so hard he fell to his hands and knees.

Blays had run clear of the area almost as soon as the storm had begun. Now, though, a batch of ether-stones streaked toward him. Dante ran toward him pell-mell, swatting down one after another, oblivious to everything else. Blays swerved for the cover of a pair of boulders. An incoming fist of ether bent away from Dante's attack toward the same rock Blays was headed toward.

Dante was too focused on what he was doing to even call out for Blays to get down. The rogue ether-stone crashed into the boulder. Even though he was waiting for it, Dante flinched from the impact, covering his head with his arms.

Shards of stone hurled toward Blays. Enough to bash him into mush. Dante waved his hand and converted the debris into mush instead. He made the mud as soft as he could, but it was still enough to knock Blays head over heels.

Blays struggled on the ground, face coated in grime except for the whites of his eyes. "You did that on purpose!"

"Just good luck."

Dante turned back to the skies, ready for the next barrage.

Gladdic stood unharmed near the camp fire. Tossed-up dirt was still sifting through the pine needles and pattering the ground, but the night was abruptly quiet.

Gladdic chuckled raspily, voice carrying through the trees. "Are the servants of the gods that afraid to show themselves to the mortals their own lords created?"

A pale figure appeared sixty feet in the sky, just as she had the first time they'd seen her. Gladdic looked unmoved by the ethereal metallic beauty of her face and skin.

Ka gazed down on them, golden hammer in one hand, silver sword in the other. Cold though it was, her feet remained bare.

"It had been told to me that your little guardian had been destroyed." Her voice was as enthralling as it was haughty. Her eyes swiveled to Gladdic. "But I see she has already been replaced with a new one. Tell me, who has betrayed our edict against aiding you this time?"

"Guardian?" Gladdic scowled. "I am no one's guardian."

"Do you play word games with me? If so I speak of 'guardian' as a role and not a title. But from what I have just witnessed, I might even accuse you of being an angel. Who then do you serve?"

"I am no angel. If I was, I would serve no lord but grayness and nothing."

Ka laughed down at him. "Do you think you can deceive me? You even speak like one of our rank!"

"What of it?" Blays spoke with his hands on his hips, glaring up at her with happy contempt. "You guys with your big clever plans! Exactly how did you *expect* your allies were going to react after your little sally into the Red Valley kicked off a full-fledged ramna revolt that got masses of the gods' soldiers killed? Did you really think the other gods were going to see that and say to themselves, 'You know that Taim, his commands are really working out so well! We should keep following him without question!'"

"Do you speak of Phannon?"

Blays laughed merrily. "Wouldn't you like to know! The part that's *really* going to make your head spin is this: what if there's more than one defector?"

"If there are traitors, you will name them to me!"

"If there are traitors, it's because you and your boss have been bollocksing everything up. Everything you've done has only made them *more* willing to give us their parts of the Spear of Stars. If Taim had half a brain between his godly ears, he'd give us his part of it too, before there's a full-blown rebellion against him."

"You threaten rebellion?" Ka's eyes flashed with ether. "But how can there be rebellion when you are all dead?"

The air around her lit up with globes of ether. They sizzled downward in a second storm. There were too many for Dante and Gladdic to stop each one, but most of the strikes weren't close enough to harm them, leaving them able to focus on the portion that was. The globes they didn't deflect slammed into the earth, the impacts booming through the forest, dirt falling to the ground like rain.

Whenever Dante had the chance, he slung a bolt of nether up at Ka in return. She countered each one as easily as Blays would parry a thrust from a drunken old man. Gladdic only made a few attacks of his own, watching her for patterns or weakness.

The scene looked to be a stalemate, at least for the moment, but Ka appeared completely unconcerned. Because she knew she could wear them down? More and more convinced that this was the case, Dante varied his attacks on her, seeking to put her down before she could exhaust them.

"Someone please tell me that's *our* army," Blays said.

Dante glanced away from the hail of ether. Between the trees, men in scaled armor marched forward, armed with short-bladed swords. Much more intimidating, however, were their shields, tall rectangles that ran from their necks down to their shins, as silvery and reflective as mirrors. Their skin was metallic as well, though duller, more like polished iron.

Ka sounded amused. "Did you think I would return alone?"

Blays drew his swords and trotted forward, giving one of his weapons a twirl, trailing sparks of nether behind it. One of Ka's men—if they *were* men; Dante couldn't tell if they were humans or constructs—had gotten ahead of the others, and Blays lunged at him, whipping his sword in an overhand cut. The soldier lifted his shield. The Odo Sein blade bounced from it with a resonant clang.

"Well, that's no good," Blays said. "Good thing I can do this."

The soldier shuffled forward, stabbing at Blays from close quarters. But Blays vanished before the sword could strike him. The soldier rocked to a stop, hoisting his shield in confusion. The air rippled behind him. Blays emerged with his right-hand sword cocked back. He rammed it forward, skewering the soldier from behind.

"Hey Dante," he called.

Dante shielded his face from a spray of dirt from an ethereal globe striking down next to him. "Yes?"

"People normally have blood, right? Like a lot of it, especially if you cut them open? Because these things don't."

"Maybe you just need to stab them harder."

Blays was already fending off the attacks of an advancing shield wall. He ducked into the shadows once more. Without speaking, the soldiers broke ranks and began to put their backs to each other, but Blays was already among them, stabbing with both weapons, which clashed on the soldiers' scale but pierced it readily, unlike their mirrored shields. Three of them fell before they knew what was happening. Blays dodged back into the nether before the others could reach him.

Ka straightened her left arm. Dante felt a ripple within the shadows. Blays tumbled out of them with a curse and a grunt. The soldiers marched on him at once, unhurried and implacable. More of them emerged from the trees with each second.

Blays waved his sparking sword over his head. "Help?"

"He will be overwhelmed," Gladdic noted.

"And if one of us goes to help him, Ka will overwhelm the one who stays here," Dante said.

"Even so, you must hold her by yourself. I will be no more than a minute."

With no further discussion, Gladdic left the fight in a swirl of robes. Dante did some yelling at him as he strode off into the trees with his neck arched, peering at the ground. And then Dante couldn't see what he was doing, because Ka's bombardment was so intense that all he could do was hurl nether into the sky and dance across the increasingly broken ground to avoid being pulverized by blobs of ether big enough to smash him into something that could be spread across a piece of bread. Within seconds, the point at which he was able to deflect the glowing orbs grew lower and lower until it was practically close enough for him to jump up and touch them.

"Blays!" he called. "Back into the nether!"

Blays had to be skeptical this would do any good, but did so anyway, disappearing from sight. With another gesture, Ka knocked him back out of the shadows. But the momentary distraction was just enough for Dante to catch his breath, striking down globes higher above his head until he was destroying them halfway between himself and Ka.

At once, she began to overwhelm him again. Dante let the attacks drift a little nearer, then yelled Blays back into the nether, buying himself another few seconds as Ka turned to deal with Blays' tricks.

"Any day now, Gladdic!" Dante yelled. "Or else you're going

to have to make room in your cabin for two more!"

In response, a trumpeting shriek pierced the woods. The hair on Dante's arms stood up in terror. He laughed in surprise. Three glowing points appeared among the trees, hanging ten feet above the forest floor, rushing closer: the eyes and mouth of an Andrac. The demon galloped past Dante and bowled into the line of soldiers. They stood their ground with superhuman lack of fear, stabbing at the Star-Eater's legs and flanks, but it wasn't clear their weapons were doing any lasting damage.

The demon raked its claws at one of the soldiers, battering his shield from his hands. The next blow crushed him to the ground. The Andrac trumpeted again, carving into the enemy ranks.

Ether flared from the same spot the Andrac had come from, shooting upward to intercept Ka's bombardment from the side. Gladdic strode back toward Dante.

"About time!" Dante called.

Gladdic waved his hand. "You lived."

Together, they pushed back at Ka until she had no more time to deal with Blays, who seized the opportunity to zip in and out of the shadows, killing any soldier he could get behind. The Andrac was soon leaking nether—the soldiers' weapons must have had an ethereal component to them, though whatever it was didn't appear to be doing them much good. The ground grew heaped with their bloodless corpses, the bodies gleaming dully in the moonlight.

Face twisted with rage, Ka halted her bombardment, cutting at the Andrac with a flurry of ether. The demon staggered, the light of its eyes dimming, nether bleeding from it like smoke. Yet before she could send it to its end, Gladdic hammered at her with a volley of ethereal spears, obliging her to back off from her attack. The Star-Eater fell back from the soldiers, wounds slowly closing.

Gladdic smiled cruelly. "Perhaps it is good to be alive again after all."

"What," Dante said, "so you can kill things again?"

"It is not the killing that is the virtue, though there are many for whom it is just. No, it is the *struggle*."

"I'd like to do less struggling and more winning. Any ideas how to do that?"

"She is skillful. I do not think she will let herself fall to any frontal attack nor anything so obvious."

"Well, unless I can convince Blays to shadowalk up the trees and take a flying leap at her, I don't think..." Dante tilted his head to the side. "Those pines there. Think we can maneuver her close to them?"

"If she believes we are faltering, she will surely pursue us."

Picking up on the idea at once, Dante slowed his flow of nether, as if reaching the limits of his reserves. In any battle of sorcerers, a single moment of weakness was all that stood between victory and defeat, and as soon as Ka saw him back off, she pushed all the harder, raining ether down on their heads. Dante backed away through the trees. Gladdic grimaced and followed.

Ka soared after them, drifting lower.

"We must do something!" Gladdic roared, letting a note of panic enter his voice.

Dante shook his head hard, nether sputtering from his fingertips. Still backing away, his heel caught on a fallen branch and he fell. This wasn't supposed to be part of the act, but before his rear had even hit the dirt, Ka dived eight feet closer, spraying light at Gladdic to drive him away so she could land a killing blow on Dante.

Her latest maneuver had finally taken her below the tips of the trees. Dante took up the nether inside the pine that was closest to her and directed three of its branches to grow as violently as they could. He wasn't sure that it would work, but the branches sprouted outward so hard they shed their bark with a crackle.

One branch flew past Ka's side. The second gored her through the back of her shoulder and punched out the front. The third scraped along her neck, gouging a line through her white-blue skin.

She yelled out in pain. Dante sent his mind into the branch that had impaled her, willing it to sprout smaller branches inside her body and turn her inside-out, but Ka was already twisting about to hack it away with her silver sword, which passed through the wood like it was as soft as cork.

"Hit her now!" Dante yelled. "Everything you've got!"

But in the coldness of his mind, Gladdic had already grasped this, sending streams of black and white rushing toward Ka. With a scream, she pulled the branch free from herself and cast it aside. She drew on the ether, but it was too late to draw up the defenses to save her from what was coming.

She vanished.

Light and shadow flowed through the space she'd just occupied, soaring off into the sky.

"Where'd she go?" Dante spun in a circle. "That's cheating!"

Gladdic closed his eyes, lifting his hand over his head. "Do you feel that?"

Dante reached into the nether and felt nothing. And then realized Gladdic wasn't embedded in the nether, but the ether. With effort, Dante moved his mind into it instead. His sense of it wasn't remotely as fine as the shadows, but he felt a ripple. One that was receding rapidly. Gladdic grabbed at the presence, but it was already too far away.

Dante cursed. "What's she doing? Shadowalking, but through the light?"

"Either that or something much like it."

"Son of a bitch! We almost had her!"

"Yet we failed. So if you are to be angry, be angry with your-self."

Dante eyed him, ready to do some drubbing, then stopped. The forest had gone quiet. He could see Blays' swords glowing from a hundred yards away, but both lights went out as Blays sheathed them.

Dante jogged toward him. Bodies of soldiers were tossed all over the ground, but without any blood or viscera, the effect was much less grim than normal, less like the gruesome aftermath of a battle and more like the lord's armory had been struck by a storm that had scattered its contents across a field.

"Let her get away, did you?" Blays was sweaty, disheveled, and dirty, but didn't have any injuries deeper than some small cuts. "Well, I expect she's learned her lesson and that's the last we'll ever see of her."

"We almost had her," Dante said. "But she ether-walked, or something like it. Which explains how she's been sneaking up on us."

"So she can fly, ether-walk, and attack us in ways we've never seen before? This sounds horrible for us."

In contrast to Blays, the Andrac Gladdic had summoned was looking rather battered, with a dozen open wounds leaking little puffs of nether. It had shrunk in height and portions of its body had become translucent. Gladdic approached. The Andrac flexed its long black claws. Injured though it was, Dante could feel its yearning to be set free to seek and kill as it wished.

"You served well," Gladdic said softly. "But it is time for you to return."

He held out his hand to the demon. It lowered its head and nodded once. Gladdic touched its chest. It dissolved into a cloud of shadows that dissipated into the world around it.

They located the horses, packed up camp, and headed down-hill, the moon their only source of light.

"What was all that stuff you were saying to Ka?" Dante said. "Why would you tell her we've got all kinds of allies?"

"You mean why would I lie to our enemy?" Blays said.

"But what exactly were you trying to do?"

"Stir up chaos?"

"I mean to what *end*?"

"To, er, stir up chaos? How should I know how it will shake out? That's the entire point of chaos. It makes your enemies do stupid and crazy things. And when your enemy's all tied up doing something stupid and crazy, it's much easier to club them over the head."

"Unless the chaos you've kicked up is making *you* do stupid and crazy things as well."

"Then it's a good thing for us that I would never do anything stupid or crazy."

Dante had half a mind to make for the shining city on the plateau (which they'd pass by on their way down the mountain) to check in with Elenna and see if she had any information, resources, or advice for them. But it seemed best to lie low, or at least as low as they reasonably could, and so the first thing they did instead was return to the farmlands beneath the city and steal a horse for Gladdic.

For some reason this made Dante feel lower than any other crime to his name. Probably because the victim was innocent of everything but owning a horse when they were in need of one. But there was no way around it, fate of the world and all that, so he'd just have to live with his guilt.

He consulted the map he'd made in Elenna's courtyard what felt like a very long time ago. Gashen's realm was to the northeast. They rode for it as fast as they dared push their mounts.

Their first night on the valley floor, Gladdic found it amusing that Dante had to build them a shelter to protect them wild packs of flying carnivorous lizards. Beyond that display of mirth, however, Gladdic was distant, which was to say distant even by the standards of Gladdic, saying little that wasn't directly related to the terrain in front of them or their future plans, hardly responding to Blays' jabs. When he did, it was often after a delay, as if the quips had only just registered.

"I think I know what's the matter." Dante didn't mean to say it, but Blays had ridden ahead to scout the next hill and he and Gladdic were alone for the first time that day.

Gladdic said nothing.

"It's the same way I was when I was taken by the White Lich," Dante said. "I came back to myself, but my self wasn't the same."

Gladdic gazed across the plain as if he hadn't heard. "Yes."

"It's almost like this world isn't wholly real anymore. Like a…shadow's been lifted, or a veil's been dropped."

"It is more like the shadow has been cast where there had once been light."

"But things felt *more* clear to me."

"It is not a matter of clarity. It is one of darkness. Coldness."

"It gets better. Closer to how it was."

"Why do you assume that I would wish it to get 'better'?"

"Because staying worse is worse?"

"I have been granted sight into bleak places. Perhaps I would not have asked for this sight. Perhaps I have yet to adjust to it. Yet I will not give it up. For the ability to see into the depths is to be given a key that unlocks every door."

This was a bit off-putting, especially since Dante thought it was at least partially true. But Gladdic spoke the words with a spirit Dante hadn't felt in him since bringing him back. He thought the old man *would* adjust to it. After all, besides Blays, Gladdic was the only person he knew who had been through anywhere remotely as much as Dante himself had.

In the early going, they didn't see any ramna at all. Then all at once they seemed to be everywhere, both lone scouts and raiding bands of scores or even hundreds of riders. Dante and Gladdic did their best to hide the three of them with illusions, but they were caught in the open at least twice, and who knew how often by scouts hidden within cover. Yet the barbarians didn't seem to take any interest in them. Soon, Dante thought he knew why: it turned out the ramna were all going in the same direction. Up into the north.

"Tell me they're not headed to Gashen's kingdom, too," Blays said. "I'm going to be downright annoyed if they set fire to the place before we can pick up our part of the spear."

Dante squinted between his map and a band of two hundred men some three miles ahead of them. "It looks more like they're headed for the lakes."

"Phannon's realm?"

"Guess they're not done with her yet."

The day after, they crested a hill, all three of them stopping on the spot. Dante and Blays swore involuntarily. Ahead, ramna streamed across the landscape like an ant colony on the march. More than a war band. An army.

"I feel like someone has made a big mistake of some kind," Blays said. "Then again, as this is entirely to our benefit, I say mistake away."

Dante tapped his fingers on the horn of his saddle. "I wouldn't be so sure it's to our benefit."

"We *don't* want our enemies overrun by men who think it's charming to dress in the skulls of their foes?"

"What happens if they do manage to drive out one of the gods? Or even kill one? Will we still be able to get their ninth of the spear?"

"Hm. Maybe we should ride faster."

They could, if only marginally, and so they did. Soon, rivers and lakes gleamed to the west. So did the tips of the spears of an awful lot of heavily armed men. As they continued north, moving past Phannon's realm and approaching Gashen's, there were no more ramna to be seen.

A settlement appeared on the hills ahead: stone walls, houses packed together on the hilltops, smoke rising from chimneys. The domain of Gashen, which General Lars had said was named Denhild.

As they neared it, Dante got an update from Nak. He'd brought their forces away from Narashtovik and had intended to head toward Dollendun and the Gaskan interior, but the White Lich had cut him off, driving them into the slopes of Gallador Rift. Nak was afraid they were about to be forced into battle. One they'd have to fight before they'd be able to receive any reinforcements from Wending.

Dante swallowed and absorbed this with the same discomfort he would have with a lump of clay. "You can't let yourself get sucked into pitched battle. He'll crush you."

"We, ah, may not have a choice."

"Yes you do."

"You mean for me to send a rear guard to buy time for the rest of us."

"If that's what it takes."

"Yes," Nak said. "Then I will do what it takes."

Dante remained preoccupied with this as they traveled up the gently climbing road toward the walls, which were much cruder than the fortifications he was used to seeing around cities, and in fact appeared to be a giant pile of broken stones dumped on top of each other, though the sides were steep enough there must have been some amount of mortar sticking them together. Then again, maybe they were built like big rubbish heaps because they'd already been knocked down so many other times.

The gates through the walls were open. There wasn't just one set of them, but what looked to be at least six, constructed from various materials and designs: outer doors of solid steel; behind that an iron grille; another set of steel with little windows set into it; then iron-banded wood; and so on. The walls were thus sixty feet deep along with being twenty-five feet high.

Blays frowned at the size of them. "Do you suppose they don't care for visitors?"

"Being uncertain whether the gates being open is an invitation to enter, or an invitation to walk into a slaughterhouse, I'm going to err toward the not-slaughter option." Dante stopped before the outermost gate and tipped back his head. "Hello! A couple of weeks ago, we did a favor for General Odon Lars. He invited us to come see him as soon as we were done with our other business."

A soldier leaned over the wall, frowning at them, then asked for their names, which Dante gave. The man nodded. "You wait right there."

Other soldiers watched from above to ensure they obeyed, but they only had to do a brief amount of waiting before a second man appeared on the wall. He had a steel cap on the top of his head that only highlighted the extreme height of his forehead, the size of which might have been the reason he looked so angry.

"You claim you are Dante Galand and Blays Buckler?"

"That's us," Dante confirmed.

"And that you met with General Lars in the city of Protus?"

"Correct."

"Then I have one question: why are you lying to me?"

"I'm not?"

"General Lars told us such people would come. But you are not such people!"

"Er, then what such people *did* he say would be dropping by?"

"If you were they, then you would know!"

"I've got a simple solution to this dilemma," Blays offered. "How about you just go fetch General Lars so he can tell you whether we're his dear old friends or impostors who deserve the axe?"

The man crinkled the plane of his brow. "You are offering your lives if you are found to be lying?"

"Just so. Ah, unless Lars was a lot drunker when we met him than I thought he was."

The soldier glared down at them, then withdrew from the wall. Dante and Blays exchanged a look. Gladdic seemed completely unconcerned. Though they had a longer wait this time, it couldn't have been two minutes before a pair of figures appeared at the other end of the long gateway. One was the soldier they'd spoken to, and although he was built like a soldier, if on the lean side, the man next to him made him look boyish.

"These are the three," the soldier asided to General Lars, going so far as to blade his hand alongside his mouth as he spoke.

Lars strode forward until he was ten feet away, then tipped back his leonine face, his mouth slightly agape as he blinked at them. His brows lowered, then he broke into laughter and stalked toward them, arms spread wide, scooping Dante up and crushing him in an embrace, then turning the same greeting on Blays.

"My friends! I have been waiting for you!" Just as quickly as his joy had appeared, he turned on the soldier in anger. "What is wrong with you? I told you to be expecting them!"

The man pursed his lips, eyes doing some serious darting about. "My lord, you told me to be on the lookout for two men and a young woman."

Gladdic tilted his head to the side. "Have the last two weeks been that unkind to my looks?"

Lars laughed again. The soldier relaxed. Lars raised an eyebrow at him. "Don't think you're off that easy. Three days of rock-hauling duty. Well? Get to it!"

The man startled, then nodded and scampered back within the walls.

Lars made his introductions to Gladdic, then gestured them inside. "You have most auspicious timing, my friends. The gift preceded you here by a single day."

"The gift?" Dante said.

"You will see."

Lars switched the subject to how they'd been faring since their last meeting. They passed from the gates into the realm proper. The land surrounding the building-heavy central hills was largely flat farmland, though the main plots were surrounded by heavy stakes angled at just the right degree to pierce a charging horse. The farmland was also speckled with raised mounds, the bases of which were surrounded by stakes, and the tops of which were enclosed with fieldstone walls. These mounds were arranged close enough that the archers who would presumably take shelter in them during times of emergency could cover the entire field. Ditches criss-crossed the fields as well, both to carry water to crops and, presumably, make it hell for barbarian raiders to try to reach the city on the hills.

The city was composed of squat stone towers and wooden longhouses with sod-covered roofs. A small armory of axes and spears stood outside both the defensive towers and the everyday houses. Each one of the hills bore a wooden cathedral with a high spire. Men and women alike congregated in the grounds around the cathedrals, sparring with wooden swords, heaving stones around in semi-organized contests, shooting arrows into hay bales, climbing long ropes, and engaging in all sorts of physical feats—and singing unfamiliar hymns as they did so. They were the fittest people Dante had ever seen.

"Is every one of your people meant to be a soldier?" Gladdic asked.

"Of course." Lars looked nonplussed. "That is Gashen's design for us."

Most of the roads were rutted dirt, but a path of broad flagstones led them to the top of the central hill, the tallest of the lot. This hosted another longhouse, though it was clear at a glance that this one was the palace. The peaked roof was sixty feet high and its eaves, corners, and walls were all carved with curling figures of animals that seemed to be a system of glyphs. The trunks of whole trees had been shaved of their bark and set as posts outside the structure, spaced loosely from each other. These were covered in carvings from foot to tip: icons of soldiers battling, spears and swords, mounted and on foot, the dying and the victorious.

An armored honor guard flanked the front doors, dressed in Gashen's red, their helmets shaped like the heads of lions. They saluted Lars and swung open the doors. Lars headed down a golden carpet running down the middle of a great feasting-hall adorned with every conceivable class of weapon. Three steel locks barred the door at the far end. Lars opened them with three different keys—one copper, one bronze, and one iron—the door groaning as it heaved inward.

The space beyond was dark: a chapel, smelling of the dried herbs left on its wooden altars. A pair of hooded figures suddenly materialized from the gloom, causing Dante to inhale sharply through his nose. One of them carried a bundled object four feet in length. Lars nodded to them.

The two people in hoods fell in alongside the group as Lars continued to another door of dark iron, wrought with the same icons of fighting men that the poles outside had been. There was no visible handle for the door, but it opened to Lars' touch with a whoosh like the breath of some huge beast.

This chamber was even darker than the chapel. A handful of scattered candles cast off just enough light for Lars to make his way forward. With no sign of walls or ceiling, it was impossible to say how large the room was, but the sound of their footsteps and movements died in the air, suggesting...well, what it *suggested* was a space larger than should have been possible within the outside dimensions of the longhouse. Then again, given Dante's experiences to date within the Realm of Nine Kings, that was probably exactly what was happening.

The wooden flooring came to an end; they stepped onto raked sand. The candles looked to be floating chest-high. The air smelled like oil rubbed onto steel.

Lars drew to a halt. He threw his cape over his shoulder and lifted his chin. "Lord of war and host of battle," he intoned. "He who is all that remains when words fail. He who inspires men to commit their greatest deeds and their most gruesome ones as well. He who will always be with us, no matter how high we rise or how low we fall. I have brought my gift to you. And I have also brought to you the ones that let me make it."

He fell silent. Dante glanced around the darkness. A draft blew past his face, circling, then spinning upward.

The world tilted and split apart.

Just as fast, it crashed back together. A figure stood before them. A man, but far bigger, with muscles like a bear. His clothes were very old, very simple—a tunic with bronze buttons, a belt of strange leather, leggings, feet wrapped in cloth—yet they were regal beyond compare. A thick pointed beard grew from his chin like the prow of a ship. Everything about him looked solid, both in its bulk and in its ability to endure.

"Odon," he said to the general. "You have always done my work well."

His voice rang inside Dante's chest and flowed over his skin like water. It was deep with a hint of gruffness and he knew he very much never wanted to hear it turned on him in anger.

The figure turned on him with eyes the same green as the

patina on an ancient copper shield. And smiled. "You are the first Fallen Landers to look on me in an age. I am Gashen."

20

Dante's knees bent. The motion wasn't intentional and he was barely able to catch his hands against the sand. Beside him, Blays had succumbed to the same effect. But Gladdic remained upright. Bowing his head to the lord of war, the old man lowered himself to his knees.

Gashen waited for them to remain in this posture for five heartbeats. "You may rise."

Dante did, shakily, uncertain if that was his nerves or the result of some aura of the figure before them. "Lord Gashen. Forgive me. I know none of the protocols for standing before a god."

Gashen smiled disarmingly: "Your people were never intended to need to know that."

"Yes. Right." Dante wanted to elevate his language in respect for the occasion, but he could hardly string words together. "It's an honor. *Beyond* an honor."

"I understand you and your companions have done me a greater honor." His pale green eyes shifted to General Lars. "Though my faithful general hasn't bothered to tell me what that honor is."

Lars looked aggrieved. "I didn't want to brag of what might be done before I knew that it *could* be done."

"Has it?"

The general straightened his shoulders. "Findreg."

The hooded man bearing the long bundle extended it to Lars. With his face gripped by pure concentration, Lars accepted it, holding it out in one hand while ripping away the cloth with the other. He cast the cloth on the sand, revealing a golden axe.

"My lord." Lars kneeled, holding up the weapon across the flats of his palms.

It was the same pieces of axe Dante and Blays had recovered in the Red Valley. But it had become much more than that. Before, its head had looked like typical iron, and its handle like typical wood. But the head was now golden while the haft was red as bright as lacquer, though the grain of the wood was still starkly visible. Glimmers of heatless red flame rippled along its curved cutting edge, which was so sharp Dante bore an involuntary thought of how easily it would peel through his skin, muscle, and bone.

Gashen gazed down at it in disbelief. His eyes flicked to Lars', searching for signs of trickery, then he lunged forward and grabbed up the axe, as if to capture it before it could get up and run away from him again.

With the weapon firmly in hand, Gashen calmed his motions, holding it up in front of his eyes. He turned it back and forth, testing its edge against his thumbnail, examining the leather cords of the grip and the fearsome creatures carved along the shaft. For some time, he could do nothing but shake his head.

Eventually he lowered the weapon, though his eyes remained trained on it. His voice was ragged. "How is this possible?"

"It was broken," Lars said. "That was why we couldn't find it. Barrod was able to reforge the pieces. It is the finest work I've seen from him."

"But how were the *pieces* found?" Gashen's thick eyebrows bounced upward. "The Fallen Landers? How did you do this?"

"That would take some time to explain," Dante said.

"Time is the thing I have most of."

Uncertain how he'd refuse even if he wanted to, Dante launched into the story. He'd caught Gladdic up on the gist of it, but not in as much detail, and the old man listened almost as intently as Gashen.

Once he finished, Gashen shook his great head. "I noticed that you never explained *why* you sought to return my axe to me. Given who you are, I can guess. You sought the axe in the hope it would earn you my part of the Spear of Stars."

Lars lowered his head. "When they brought me the pieces of the axe in Protus, I promised that you would gladly accept such an exchange."

"You have no need for worry. Your promise is the same one I would have made." He eyed the three outlanders. "But I wonder how you came to know my axe was lost. And that it would guarantee you my part of the spear."

"Oh, you know," Blays said. "People talk."

"People?"

"Oh yes. People are *renowned* talkers."

Gashen smiled wryly. "I sense machinations. I don't like machinations. They're the sign you lack the strength to act outright against your enemies. But you have no lords or armies to command here, do you? That leaves you with few options besides machinations." He gave a slow swipe of the axe through the air. It made a whistling sound. "Do I sense the hand of Carvahal?"

"Maybe it's a cunning double-machination to make you *think* you sense Carvahal."

"The way you speak puts me of a mind that you're an agent of Carvahal pretending to be a Fallen Lander." The god held up his hand for silence. "Still your tongue, little mortal. It doesn't matter. But if you are indeed here at Carvahal's behest, you'll let him know he's not always as clever as he hopes. Now, wait here."

The seam in the fabric of being reopened behind him and though Gashen didn't move he somehow sank through it. Lars and the two robed attendants stood silent. Dante figured it was prudent to do the same.

In time, the seam returned and so did Gashen. A weapon rack came with him. A single object was held within it: a two-and-a-half foot section of shaft. It looked just as the portion of blade did, ether swirling within its outline like luminous clouds.

"Thank you for the return of my weapon," Gashen said. "In return, I lend you my part of this one."

Blays approached it and picked it up, giving it the kind of critical eye that was only possible from someone whose life revolved around being extremely fussy about weapons.

"Thank you, milord," he said with unusual gravity. "I'll treat it with the care it deserves—but I'm most anxious to put it to use."

"If we get there," Dante said. "We still have a long road toward getting the rest of the spear."

"You do, don't you?" Gashen nodded at his general. "Give them anything else they need."

Lars frowned. "Anything?"

"Short of direct military aid. Or anything that violates your discretion."

"Understood, lord."

"Once more, I thank you," he said to the mortals. "Your audience is complete."

The god faded from the darkened room. With his departure, everything felt dimmer, though the candles burned no less than before.

Lars nodded them to follow. He turned about, returning to the solid flooring at the entrance to the vast chamber, then exiting. In the chapel, the two hooded attendants departed.

"Now that was something," Blays said. "But one thing's got me confused. Why do the gods spend so little time in their own world?"

Dante glanced behind them. "Don't you remember? It's a danger to them. Even the gods aren't invincible."

"Gashen can't *really* think we pose a threat to him, can he? I might be a threat to steal his wife, sure, but not to *kill* him."

Lars looked puzzled. "It's true that our lords rarely venture outside their own realms for this reason. But there is much more to it than that. The figure you just saw was impressive, wasn't he?"

"Yeah, in about the same way you'd say a mountain has some rocks in it."

"But what you saw is only a small part of what he is. The only part that can manifest here. To manifest diminishes them in just the same way it would diminish you to try to squeeze yourself into a thimble. Their minds are very uncomfortable to be so limited. Especially when they know that dying here in their diminished form kills their full form as well."

"Fair enough. But it turns out I'm not terribly interested in trying to force myself down into a thimble. So why would the gods want to create a world for themselves that they can't even live in?"

"They didn't build these worlds for themselves!" Lars laughed. "They built them for us."

He showed them to their quarters and told them to prepare for a meal of celebration. They were packing a lot of grime from the road and it was going to take plenty of time to make themselves presentable.

Even so, the first thing Dante did when they got to their rooms was to hold the second piece of the spear for himself—and to silently wonder if they'd be capable of gaining the rest.

For the sake of politeness, Dante meant to restrain himself from beginning serious talks with Lars about what would come next until after their second cup of beer. But the evening's feast was so absurd that he found himself too occupied with food, drink, and the well-wishes of well-built men and women to even broach the subject with the general. As it turned out, the diet of the Denhild was very high in beef—though sometimes they branched out into a dish with beef broth or marrow—and spicy-tasting greens. It was only when the whole thing was over that Dante realized the only things he'd seen that even resembled bread had been the wrappers on the beef dumplings, and the multiple varieties of beer.

Rather than sequestering themselves in some private room, Lars eventually just ordered everyone else out. Glasses of something stronger were poured. At that point Dante didn't particularly need it, but after all the chasing about through the wilderness, he kind of did.

"If Gashen is serious about offering help," he said, "we're extremely ready to take it."

Lars leaned back in his chair. "For one thing, you need better horses. Yours look like you stole them from somebody's farm."

"I don't know what you mean. But I'm talking about more than provisions and such. The situation in our world is extremely tenuous. We have to accelerate our progress. We were told that if Gashen was convinced to let us borrow his spear piece, others would follow suit. Do you think this is true?"

"Certainly."

One of the many weights on Dante's shoulders dropped away. "Please tell me that *everyone* will?"

Lars and Gladdic both chuckled. The general swirled his cup. "Taim will remain unbent until the end. I have little to no hope for Silidus, either."

"I thought that if there was one thing you could count on

Silidus for, it's that you never know how she's going to decide."

"In most cases. But Silidus is nothing if not a survivor. She'll fear Taim's wrath. With the ramna on the march, she'll be even more wary of exposing herself. And Blays annoyed her badly enough that she won't forget it."

"Is there anyone else who we know can't be swayed?"

Lars counted off names on his fingers. "Now that one god has broken ranks, Carvahal will jump at the chance to spite Taim. Lia has never been happy that Taim would let an entire world of growth and life die, and even if she hesitates, you could use Simm to convince her to your side. Phannon's mind is less known to me, but she is always one to adhere to Taim's word. She could be a difficulty. Barrod carries enough honor that he will now let you quest for his piece. Arawn would prefer to stay beyond the politics, but the wider you open the door by winning the other pieces, the more he'll be convinced to follow the old agreement and let you try for his. And Urt? Well, Urt will always be Urt."

"Unknowable."

"That's one way to put it."

"This is not true," Gladdic said. "Urt will let us vie for his part."

Lars laughed, throwing his elbow over the back of his chair. "Did he crawl out of his barrel and tell you that himself?"

"Urt does not always keep himself hidden away. He emerges in cycles. The Eiden Rane is on the verge of ending one age and beginning another. Urt will wish to allow us to prove whether or not the age is due for such change."

The general nodded thoughtfully. "You're a scholar. But I can tell by the look of you that you're not afraid to wade into the thick of battle. These days, that's a rare thing."

Gladdic gave a small shrug.

Blays drained his cup and set it down with a clink loud

enough to attract a servant. "Maybe it's time to do as our scholar-warrior suggests and start working on the hard cases. We're not sure if Phannon will support us, and we know Silidus will never go for it. And both of their realms are nearby. If I didn't know better, I'd say the gods were giving us a sign."

"Of what?" Dante said. "Gashen and Silidus' kingdoms being right next to each other, which is why we met the good general in the first place?"

"For a High Priest, you're mighty skeptical. But I've got an easy way to find out who's right: we invade Silidus' realm and see if we win."

"Excellent plan. I'll just need a few centuries to domesticate the drakelets and breed them into giant war-dragons."

"Or we could just use the giant ramna army that's right over there."

"An army that's currently looking to reduce Phannon's territory to a pile of floating garbage."

"Unless we turn them against Silidus instead."

Dante squinted one eye. "Earning Phannon's favor in the process. And if Silidus is that jumpy about her survival, we can use the threat of invasion to ransom her spear part away from her."

Gladdic grunted. "If I had had you two as my lieutenants years ago, I would have conquered everything from Allingham to Dara Bode, and the Eiden Rane would never have grown the power to break from his prison."

"How in blazes do you mean to get the ramna to do your bidding?" Lars looked highly amused. "By *reasoning* with them?"

"Oh, we're old friends with the ramna," Blays said. "You've heard the story of how we got your axe back. Couldn't have done it without them."

"Even having heard the story, I hardly believe it. The ramna ally with no one!"

"Turns out they just really don't like you guys."

Dante rubbed his mouth. "We're not likely to find better conditions than this. If the plan works, we'll pick up two more shards in a handful of days."

"I doubt this will go as you hope," Lars said. "But I will hope to be proven wrong. What can the land of Denhild do to help?"

"It's better if we handle this leg of things by ourselves. No offense, but if the ramna catch so much as a whiff of divine interference, they'll offer us up on one of their funeral platforms."

The general chuckled. "If you think you can offend me by suggesting the ramna might not care for us, then you have no idea how many ramna I've killed."

"You may be able to help us in other arenas, though. Anything you can do to hasten our gathering of the other parts of the spear."

"Did you have anything specific in mind?"

"You'd know better than I do. Maybe you can convince those that are friendly to lend us their pieces without bothering to go through any trials. Or maybe you can convince those that are wavering to come over to our side." Dante leaned forward, hands spread on the table. "My people and my homeland are on the brink of being destroyed. After that, the lich will sweep through Gask, adding a million or more to his Blighted—and adding their souls to his individual strength. At that point, even with the spear, he may be too powerful to kill."

"I don't know how much we can do." Lars met his eye. "But it will be all that we can."

Their new horses were things of wonder: sleek and lean, yet with a look of tireless strength, a combination that reminded Dante of the dolphins that liked the coasts south of Bressel. The animals were so well-bred he instantly regretted not having stolen them at the very start of their venture.

They deserved saddles dazzling with jewels and silver, but that would have given away their origins, and so they disgraced the great beasts with plain saddles that wouldn't raise an eyebrow among the ramna.

Even as alternates, their old horses wouldn't be able to keep up, and Lars called for a groom to take them away.

"Be sure to keep them safe?" Dante said.

Lars patted the horse's flank. "Sentimental attachment?"

"Something like that."

Dante had allowed himself to sleep in late, and it was past nine in the morning before they were ready to be off. As they made ready to go, Lars approached him.

"You're resourceful types. I hope you'll have no cause to use this, and if you do that it's not used lightly. But if you find yourself in danger you see no way out of, shed a drop of blood on this and we will do what we can for you."

He handed Dante an iron disk with the profile of a lion raised on each side.

Dante flipped it over in its palm. "How will you know where we are?"

"This is the class of gift you don't get to ask questions about. Don't lose it, either."

"I'll try not to," Dante said. "Just so you know, if something goes terribly wrong and we provoke the ramna into coming to attack you instead, rest assured we didn't mean to."

Lars snorted and clapped him on the back. Dante mounted his horse and Blays led them through the six gates out of Denhild. They meant to stay off the road wherever possible, so Blays used the sun and the eastern mountains to orient them toward the waterways of Phannon's land.

"What happens if the Jessel aren't among the ramna?" Blays said once they were underway.

"Then we figure something else out."

"What happens if the Jessel are there, but they can't stop their buddies from sacking Phannon?"

"Then we figure a different else out for that if."

"I can't help but notice these aren't really answers."

"*I* can't help but notice that if your questions are so damn good, you should have asked them last night."

"If they wanted me to think good, they shouldn't have given me so much beer."

They spent a little time getting used to their horses at a trot, then spurred them to a canter that was possibly the fastest and smoothest Dante had ever seen. After slowing to a walk to let them rest, they broke into a full gallop. The horses all but hovered over the grass, charging along with a speed that made Dante's eyes water from the wind. They ran them all-out until they tired out—which Blays estimated took at least four miles, maybe even five.

"Now these are some horses," Blays said as they dropped back to a walk. "Suppose we can take them back through the Mists with us?"

"That is a good question," Dante said. "Although we'd better make sure they're a gift and not a loan first. I'd rather not give Gashen a reason to test his new axe on our necks."

Dante refreshed the horses with the shadows and increased his speed. Despite the lateness of their start, they still had plenty of daylight ahead of them when they caught their first glimpse of sunlight shimmering on the many rivers that surrounded and in some cases flowed through Phannon's realm of Crosswater. Dante hadn't been certain that they'd arrive in time to stop the sacking and was heartened by the lack of smoke that would suggest the city had been razed.

The ramna army cohered into view, the riders so numerous that they appeared to be a feature of the landscape, dark cataracts of horses and men. The barbarians advanced leisurely toward Crosswater, a distant and hazy urban blur protected by various moats and fortifications. The ramna wouldn't reach it by nightfall, but they could easily be upon it in the morning.

The three outlanders caught up close enough to start making out the banners and dress of individual war bands while staying far enough away to (hopefully) avoid provoking the ramna into coming over to stomp them. Dozens of individual bands had gathered together for the great raid to come, but there were untold numbers of different ramna peoples scattered across the Realm of Nine Kings and it was impossible to say what the odds were that the Jessel were among them.

Luck favored them, however—or else Dasya's aggression did—for Blays spotted yellow flags flying from long spears, and the white skulls on their horses and shields and helmets confirmed them as the Jessel. The nature of their plan, as well as the nature of the ramna, meant that they couldn't approach their old traveling companions directly, but after a bit of careful maneuvering through the brush, and some subtle manipulations of the nether to catch the eye of a wandering Jessel scout, they secured an audience with Dasya early that night.

He came alone. As before, his face was painted white, with thick black outlines around his eyes and mouth. "Friends to the Jessel! Have you come to help us smash Crosswater into dust?" He leaned forward, sniffing at them. "You smell like gods."

"Probably all the sweat," Blays said. "It's a common mistake."

"Who is this?" Dasya gestured to Gladdic. "Is he to be trusted?"

"He was once our worst enemy," Dante said. "But after a sequence of strange events, Blays is the only living person I trust more."

"Mortal foe won over to blood brother. I would much like to hear that story!"

"It isn't over yet. But once it is, if we can find our way back here, I'd be honored if one of the Jessel could craft it into an epic like the one you told us about Sallen."

Dasya lifted his eyebrows and nodded. "That could be an honor for the Jessel as well. And after tomorrow, we will have a new cycle to tell of ourselves!"

"That's what we're here about," Dante said carefully. "We're still making progress in our mission. In fact, I think we're about to make a major breakthrough. But if you attack Phannon tomorrow, it could destroy our hopes."

"How can that be? Are the gods not your enemies as well?"

"I'll be honest with you, Dasya—and I hope I'm not about to get punched for this—but we've made an alliance of sorts with Gashen. That's opened many doors for us. We believe Phannon will help us now, too."

"Which will be a lot harder for her to do if her head is on a pole," Blays put in.

The paint on Dasya's face sometimes made it harder to read him. At other times it exaggerated his expressions. Now, he was looking very confused, even angry, and it was hard to tell if it was just the paint.

"But don't worry," Blays added quickly. "There's plenty of *other* gods we can go mount on poles, or stretch out on platforms, or slap about the face until they start crying and then we threaten to tell their friends that they're little crying babies."

"You will tell me what you are proposing. In clear words."

Dante shifted in the saddle. "We need you to go after Silidus instead."

Dasya gazed at him. "Why would we do that when Phannon is the one who has been warring against us?"

"Because Phannon's only doing that on the orders of Taim, and she's about to start disobeying him. That means no more attacks on your people. Silidus is another matter. She'll hold the line. That's where the threat to you lies now."

"Threat? The ramna—and the Jessel—have always survived their 'threats.' For whenever they remember their spirit enough to stop huddling behind their walls and face us on the grass, we crush them."

"Then it seems like crushing Silidus would be just as effective to your ends as going after Phannon."

Dasya laughed. "Making them fear us is not why we ride out and fight. Phannon is the one who stole blood from us. Honor demands we reclaim it from her, not one of the others."

"You see, the problem with that strategy is it completely screws us over," Dante said. "So how about we team up to go ransom Silidus instead? We get the part of the weapon we're searching for, and you get...well, everything else in the city."

"That cannot be done. Even if you could convince me to march on Silidus, I would hold no hope of convincing the other bands to follow."

"Could you try anyway?"

The large man laughed lowly. "If I tried something so foolish, I would be mocked. My people would be disgraced by me."

"Then how about we try to convince them instead?"

This drew louder laughter. "You would have a better chance of winning a wrestling match with the Great Bear of the Western Slopes!"

"Sure, if we were to use something stupid like *words*," Blays said. "It'll be much more effective to raid them in their camp while pretending to have been sent by Silidus."

"Attacking under false colors? That is an unclean deed!"

"Yeah, well, dirty times call for unclean deeds."

Dasya looked between them. "I thought you were honorable men."

"I like to try," Blays said, quite serious all of a sudden. "But mostly, we're whatever we need to be."

"This is not a solution."

"Then what can we do for you to make it one?"

Dasya swung his head to the side, jaw tight. "You do not understand, Fallen Lander. We're here to turn Crosswater to ashes and Phannon's joy to grief. There is nothing you can offer us that is better than these things."

"My offer might not be better," Dante said. "But you're going to take it anyway."

"Do you make threats of me?"

"I will put this very simply. The lives of everyone in the Fallen Land hang in the balance. I will do whatever it takes to save them."

Dasya hadn't brought his spear, but he was carrying a side-sword, and his hand now drifted to its grip. "And how much will you be able to do for your people if I call my men to kill you where you stand?"

"You and all of the Jessel would die before a single one of us does," Gladdic said. "Once we finish with you and ride off at full speed, it is doubtful that any of the other bands could catch us."

"You think too highly of yourselves."

"I think of myself in precise accordance with the abilities that have allowed me to commit atrocities you could only dream of inflicting on the city before you."

Dante waited a moment to break the ensuing silence. "Dasya, the gods' own hubris has made them vulnerable. We're at a point where we may be able to rip their alliance apart. But if you go after Phannon right when she's ready to defect from Taim's grasp, it will only reunite them all against you. Even if you triumph here, it'll be the last victory you see."

Dasya clenched his jaw, glaring back at him. "If the justice of the heavens was real, it would strike you down right now. But there is no divine justice, is there? The history of my people proves that."

"So does what's happening to my people right now."

"It is dishonorable of you to ask for this and I think less of you for doing so." The warrior spat to the side and drew on his horse's reins. "But you have left me no choice. Make your false raid on the camp, and we will see if we can draw the ramna to Silidus instead."

21

"Well," Blays said. "Are we ready?"

Dante stared into the darkness ahead of them as if trying to read it. It was one in the morning and most of the camp's fires had drawn down, and though there were scouts and sentries about, the night was as quiet as nights got. Apparently even the barbarous ramna knew that a good night's sleep was the best way to ensure a smooth morning of slaughter and pillage.

He was getting a little tired himself. But they had to make their move that same night, or else, come daylight, there would be no move left to make.

"We're sure we've got the right ones?"

"Dasya said to look for the fellows with dead snakes tied around their heads, didn't he?" Blays sniffed. "Unless their dashing fashion has rightly caught on with others, I'd say we've found our match."

The group of sleeping warriors was known as the Atalls, and Dasya had named them as both enemies of the Jessel and as prideful cowards. In other words, the perfect target for a raid.

"You are delaying," Gladdic said. "Should I lead us forward in your stead?"

"I'm just making sure that everything's in place," Dante said, feeling himself getting testy. "It's not like we've had a lot of time to prepare."

"Yet we have done everything we can with what is before us. The rest relies on whether the Atalls swallow the bait—and how well Dasya helps to sell it."

He was right, of course, but that only made it more annoying. "Let's go."

Dante rode forward, the horse gathering its deadly momentum. He had already nicked the back of his arm and the nether ran to him with even greater speed than his mount. He pulled his hood up and used the shadows to make a few quick adjustments to their faces. The disguises wouldn't have looked believable under full daylight, but with no more than the moon to expose them, and what would hopefully be an awful lot of chaos to muddy the perceptual waters, he expected they'd be all right.

The Atalls' camp was on the ramna army's right flank. The army itself had set down on the eastern shore of a straight stretch of a river that ran as much as a hundred yards across but was rarely deeper than twelve feet, and included an easy ford in the middle of the Atall lines. Come morning, the ramna meant to use this as the staging point for their crossing, which would leave nothing but a few ponds and shallow streams between them and Phannon's city.

Which meant Dante was highly incentivized to destroy the ford.

Two bolts of nether zipped from Gladdic's hand, knocking dead a pair of sentries. Dante trampled past the bodies and sent his mind into the bank of the river. Lots of smallish rocks, along with soil that wasn't particularly firm, likely deposited there by a recent flood. Very easy to manipulate.

He loosened it into mud, letting the river do the work of sweeping most of it away while he sucked the harder clay beneath it deep into the earth. The entire bank collapsed. Sleeping men splashed into the water and immediately stopped sleeping and started screaming instead.

Dante hammered at the ford, sinking it by ten feet. Next to him, Gladdic hurled ether before him in sparkling gusts. Most of it was unusually poorly aimed, and in fact almost unerringly seemed to smash into trees and boulders instead, tossing up all kinds of debris and making a big loud mess...while doing very little damage to the Atalls themselves.

Warriors leaped from their bedrolls, grabbing up spears and swords and bows. Only a few of their horses were saddled, but that didn't deter them from hopping on to ride bareback.

"It's Phannon's sorcerers!" someone yelled. "Sent to stab us in the dark!"

Gladdic laughed in contempt. His voice boomed through the trees. "We are not sent by Phannon!"

"He lies! The river, it rises!"

"What if it does? The power of water is not Phannon's alone: for the moon can also lift the tide to wash away the filth!"

This only seemed to confuse them. Then again, they'd just been rudely plucked from sleep and thrust into battle, and their capacity for understanding probably wasn't at its sharpest. Dante had done about all the damage to the crossing that would make any difference, so he reached up his hand and cast a red illusion over the face of the moon.

"They are not of Phannon," a voice called out from the southern reaches of the Atall camp. "They are sent by Silidus!"

Blays responded with some malevolent laughter. Silidus' name rang out from several different warriors, passing deeper into the camps. The first horsemen were coming toward them, loosing arrows; Dante and Gladdic put down anyone who shot at them, ignoring the others for now.

Nether crackled from the camp. The ramna sorcerers had finally entered the fray. Under different circumstances, Dante would have been curious to hear how their theology worked—after all, their powers had been granted to them by the gods, who they'd string up by the ears if they had the chance—but it didn't seem the appropriate time for cultural exchange.

"I'd say we've kicked the nest," Blays said. "Is it fleeing time?"

"Absolutely," Dante said. "If we wait much longer, it's going to become 'dying to barbarians' time."

They curled away, ducking arrows and lobbing more ether and nether behind them. A swarm of Atalls followed. A horn blew, followed by several more, easing the tightness around Dante's heart. More and more of the war band camps were coming to life, lighting torches and bellowing about the treachery of the foul moon god. If Dasya was holding to his word, he'd be among them, insisting that this dishonorable and disgraceful attack must be met with iron and steel.

Either Dasya was an effective orator, or the others didn't need his encouragement. As Dante and the others ran from their immediate pursuit, more and more warriors beyond the Atall joined the chase. Gashen's horses could outrun all but the very swiftest of the ramna's animals, and the three of them eased back on their speed to entice the barbarians to keep following them.

The lead pursuit soon wore off their gallops and dropped back. Dante opened up a little more space, then slowed as well, flushing nether through the horses' muscles in case they needed to run again. But the chase then became a matter of endurance, with hundreds of torches and thousands of riders flowing after them.

Blays laughed. "Are they really switching targets over one little raid?"

"That was the plan, wasn't it?" Dante said.

"Yes, but I'm starting to get the crazy idea they just really like fighting."

"It's the sneakiness of it. And the fact it was unprovoked. For wildmen, the ramna seem to have a lot of ideas about how fights are supposed to be fought."

After a while, they were able to slow a little more, though the ramna kept sending well-rested horsemen to the front to replace those whose mounts were getting worn down. On the one hand this was good news, in that it proved the ramna's dedication, but it meant Dante and the others had to keep up a pace that would have exhausted lesser animals.

Blays glanced at Gladdic, then did a double-take. "What are you so happy about?"

"A plan conceived and executed smoothly," Gladdic said. "Did that not lift your heart?"

"Sure. But I didn't know you had one of those."

"If there exists a soul who feels no thrill at riding down his enemies in the dark, he is better off dead."

Dante didn't suppose the Atall were their enemies, per se, but he understood the sentiment. There *was* a verve to it, to any successful raid. Yet this one had something more to it: the sense that they had restored a fellowship that had recently looked lost for good. One that could challenge any obstacle that got in its path.

Around four in the morning, the ramna came to a stop and settled down, bringing an end to the pursuit. Dante, Blays, and Gladdic moved a mile away, then took turns sleeping while one kept watch. Dante was afraid the barbarians would decide the whole thing had been a lot of foolishness and go back to sacking Crosswater, but before he knew it Blays nudged him awake and told him the ramna were on the move.

And they were heading north. Toward Protus.

They shadowed the warriors from a distance. Despite the rough night, the ramna were in high spirits, chanting battle-poems to each other as they made their steady way north across a landscape of patchy fields of grass and bare stone sporting finger-like spires of basalt like trees stripped to nothing but their trunks. They'd covered a good deal of ground the night before and it wasn't long before the spires began to glitter and twinkle. Streams flowed here and there, adding to the visual confusion.

Protus cohered from the dazzle of the light. At this distance, its towers and spires looked insubstantial, more like wisps of steam than anything solid.

"Do you suppose she'll go for the ransom?" Blays said.

"There's no way she expected the war band to switch from Phannon to her overnight," Dante said. "She's already feeling antsy about the schism brewing between the gods. I don't see her opting to fight a pitched battle rather than hand over some treasure to get the barbarians to go away from her gates."

"You assume much," Gladdic said. "Even in times of peace, common people and their rulers alike cannot be counted on to act in ways that are wise."

"In any event, I suppose we'd better remind Dasya of the plan before any of the bands takes it on themselves to attempt something glorious."

Dante had dropped the illusions on their faces as soon as the chase had ended the night before, and they now changed cloaks as well, with him and Blays wearing the same things as when they'd first journeyed with the Jessel. Even so, it was a bit dicey to approach the ramna as a trio of horsemen, and they alerted the Jessel to their presence using a set of bird calls and subtle displays of nether they'd worked out with Dasya before the raid.

After some maneuvering through brush-choked gullies, they emerged into the middle of the Jessel, who didn't look remotely as tired as they should have. Dasya was in a mood to match his warriors, shoulders thrown back, smiling steadily at the approaching city.

"Well, that went off better than I could have hoped," Dante said on riding up next to him. "We did our best to limit the amount of actual damage. Just enough to get everyone very angry."

"I noticed," Dasya said. "I am sure you could have ripped every last Atall out by the roots if that was what you had wished."

"Which very much *wasn't* the plan. I'm sorry there had to be any losses at all, but I can promise you they'll be a lot fewer than if you'd attacked Phannon and—"

"You have no need to explain yourself to me. I know why what was done was done. Now we make for the gates of Protus, eh?"

"Right. The more threatening you make your approach, the better. We need Silidus afraid enough that she'll hand over her part of the spear without any fighting. We'd never be able to find it on our own."

"Perhaps it is better for things to have gone as they have. We will come away with the wealth of Silidus without sacrificing any of our might at the walls of the gods."

He nodded to them, then moved off to hold a rather intense discussion with several of his best warriors. The city drew closer, as did the marsh surrounding it; when the wind was right, Dante could smell its sulfur on the air. High-pitched horns piped from within Protus. A few citizens were out beyond the marsh on various errands, but only a few were able to retreat to the city, the others caught off guard, left with no choice but to flee into the wilderness and hope the ramna wouldn't bother with them.

The army came before the edge of the marsh.

Dante went to find Dasya and offer to extend a land bridge between the islands to the city gates, but a swarm of warriors was already dismounting and jogging to the waterline. Using picks and shovels, they heaped earth into the water, extending a path faster than seemed possible. Others followed behind them to tamp down the earth with their feet. Barbarian sorcerers were flicking at the work with both ether and nether, but Dante couldn't see exactly what their efforts were getting done.

The engineering team advanced with absurd speed. As they got further from shore, rendering it harder to acquire enough dirt, the nethermancers took the lead. Their sorcerers didn't have the ability to shape the earth in the sense the People of the Pocket did, but they *did* have the ability to just smash it out from the water and heap it into a pile, which the manual laborers flattened and extended. The walls of Protus bristled with defenders, but they made no effort to sortie.

With one last push, the ramna sorcerers heaped the final portion of their earthworks up to the broad semicircle of land outside the gates. The workers parted, allowing a single rider to advance.

During the work, the three outlanders had stayed at the edge of the marsh where they wouldn't draw any undue attention from the ramna. This also left them unable to hear what the ramna man was yelling to the people on the wall, or what they were saying back to him.

Whatever it was, it didn't take long. The ramna commander wheeled his horse to face his troops. He thrust up his fists and bellowed something. His men shook their spears at the sky, bellowing back, and charged toward the walls.

"Wait," Dante said. "What's happening?"

"Looks like negotiations broke down," Blays said. Nether darkened the gates, which then exploded. "Yes, I'd say they definitely broke down."

Ramna horsemen poured toward the mangled remnants of the gates. Dante galloped toward Dasya, who was beaming at the scene and waiting for the Jessel's turn to enter the causeway.

"What the hell is this?" Dante gestured to the invasion unfolding across the marsh. "You were supposed to ransom them, not ransack them!"

The captain grinned toothily. "Our lord of battle must have decided that peace was not an option. Who am I to question him?"

"Given that your lord and the Proteans spoke for four whole seconds, I'd almost think he made that decision before offering them the chance to pay the ransom!"

"You stopped us from taking blood back from Phannon. Did you really think we would not take it from Silidus instead?"

Motion at the causeway; the Jessel were riding forth. Dasya spun about and joined them, cheering as he went.

Smoke was already rising from Protus. Blays quirked his mouth. "Have we done a bad thing?"

Dante gripped the sides of his head. "This wasn't supposed to happen!"

"So, er, what do we do now?"

Gladdic watched the army pack itself inside the city. Screams lingered on the air. "Perhaps if we inquire politely, the savages will come to understand how much this inconveniences us, and bring their poor behavior to an end."

"It's beyond an inconvenience!" Dante gestured helplessly at the city. "What reason would Silidus have to give us her spear now?"

Blays cracked his knuckles. "Give?"

"How are we going to take it when we have no hope of finding it?"

"Something tells me it's going to be in the palace. Something *else* tells me our best chance to get to the palace is while the ramna are throwing everything into madness. We can figure out the rest on the way."

Dante felt the instinct to argue, but there was no part of it that could be argued. The ramna had their causeway completely clogged and it looked to be several minutes before the last of them would be through. Instead of waiting, Dante jabbed his arm to get some blood flowing, then lifted his hand and angrily conjured a bridge to the closest island, sending stagnant black

331

water splashing violently. He trotted across the bridge, extending another one to the next island. This drew a lot of attention from the ramna, but instead of shooting arrows at him, they just used it as a secondary route to get their people to the gates faster, following right behind Blays.

The series of bridges brought them to the gates, or rather to say the mangled wreckage of them. A lot of bodies had been thrown about, as many dressed in the silver and dark purple of Silidus as in the skins and leathers of the ramna. The air smelled like blood and broken stone. Stray arrows soared back and forth, but the barbarians had already pushed the fighting several blocks into the interior. And this despite concerted sorcery from the Protean defenders. Apparently it was very, very difficult to deal with entire armies on horseback, especially once they were past your defenses. Dante suddenly understood why the gods rarely ventured outside the fortifications of their kingdoms.

He oriented himself toward the gossamer spires of the palace. "It occurs to me that we might be headed for the most heavily defended part of the city."

"Are you kidding?" Blays said.

"Do I think that in times of invasion, the people might retreat to their palace?"

"Most of the palaces in the Realm haven't looked capable of defending themselves against a spring breeze. They're built to make you look at them and say 'Wow, these gods sure are worthy of being worshipped by us.' But for defense? Everyone who matters will be holed up in a place like that."

He pointed at a very stout tower overlooking a small lake.

Dante frowned. "And if we start rooting through Silidus' throne room and she decides to pop out and kick our heads around the room?"

"Do you really think she's going to stick her neck out in the middle of a war? Now quit fretting about everything and let's go steal."

Dante picked up the pace. Hordes of ramna were dashing all over the place, mostly split into individual bands, though some were grouping together to sack buildings that appeared like they might be full of valuable loot. There was plenty of resistance from Protean soldiers and sorcerers alike, but they were abandoning large portions of the city to concentrate their defenses in its strongholds.

Gladdic appraised this with a baleful eye. "If they cannot—or refuse to—defend their own people, it makes one question what these gods are truly worth."

Blays shrugged. "Presumably they're playing the long game."

On their first visit, large parts of the city had been impermanent markets, stalls, tents, caravans, and small wheel-mounted houses, but nearly all of these had been packed or rolled away in the few hours after the citizens had first seen the ramna approaching from afar, leaving empty fields and plazas everywhere, as if the city was the art of a mad painter who'd finished his work only to blot half of it out.

But some of these open spaces were much messier than others, suggesting their residents had had to act very quickly. As if they hadn't believed the ramna would really break through until it was happening. As Dante and the others penetrated deeper into the city, they entered a field where a group of locals fled with rolled-up bundles in hand. Something glimmered in the corner of Dante's eye; he just caught sight of the people disappearing into not-quite-thin air—escaping through the hint of a doorway, and down a set of stairs leading below the surface.

Dante swung around a corner and plowed right into the back of a melee, ramna horsemen exchanging spear-thrusts with a group of pikemen who were retaining admirably tight discipline. Dante could have blown the defenders apart with a few moments' work, but he swerved around them instead, detouring two blocks before returning course to the palace.

Its five white towers climbed into the sky. Dante slowed as he entered the parkland surrounding the spires. The noise of battle carried on elsewhere, but it was distant enough to hear the trickling of the streams through the gardens. It all felt very peaceful.

Right up until the moment that both arrows and nether poured out of the closest tower and from atop the stone bridge that ran above the entrance to the grounds.

Dante yelled out, swatting down sorcery and arrows alike. In silence, Gladdic cast a storm of sparks at the men on the bridge, doing them no harm but dazzling them enough to disrupt their aim. The three Fallen Landers turned about and dashed over the turf at full speed.

Dante ducked low in the saddle. "I thought you said the palace wouldn't be defended!"

"I said their *main* defense wouldn't be here," Blays said. "And it isn't. Or else we would have seen it before it started shooting at us."

"They've got hundreds of people holed up here. What are we supposed to do now?"

"I'd say we follow them inside."

Dante followed Blays' eyes to the right, taking in a completely empty street. But he could already hear the blunder of hoofbeats. Scores of barbarians entered the street and pounded down the smooth cobbles toward the palace. They drew back their bows and loosed a barrage at the defenders, who were right in the middle of attempting to shoot down on the riders. On both sides, people fell with arrows sticking from them. Screaming began, mostly from the Proteans, though the ramna had suffered more wounds.

Dante maneuvered through another full reversal of direction, chasing after the invaders. Sorcery flashed from both the tower and the riders, blowing up parts of each. A lone arm spun through the air still clutching its spear. The ramna chant-yelled death threats, boasts, and praise to their ancestors. A second band galloped into the park from the south.

Some of the ramna stayed on horseback to harry the defenders with arrows while others jumped down from the saddle, axes in hand, and rushed the door to the tower, which looked stout right up until the moment a ramna nethermancer exploded it inside the building. Axemen charged inside while the flinders were still falling. As Dante rode past the wounded ramna lying on the ground, he gave some thought to healing them, then remembered he'd only be disgracing them. A pair of barbarian sorcerers hung back, but they were ignoring the fallen in favor of healing injured horses.

Blays pointed toward the central tower. "Suppose the throne room's in the big one?"

"That's where I'd put it," Dante said. "Then again, knowing Silidus, she probably gets tired of it and moves it somewhere else three times a year."

Even if this was so, the tower was the obvious place to start. They rushed past it and into a stand of trees, where they tied up their horses, then ran back toward the tower doors. These were sealed with an ethereal ward of some kind and while Dante was inspecting it Gladdic simply ripped it apart and motioned for them to go inside.

Though it was the middle of the day, the interior smelled like dew on grass at night. A large foyer brought them to the sort of hall that was less about any specific functionality and more about getting newcomers to stop and gawk at the grandeur of its columns, tapestries, space, and ornamentation. Dante jogged forward, hunting for a staircase, and tripped over a servant girl he'd spooked from behind the cover of a purple chaise.

He got to his feet, extending a hand of warding. She trembled on the ground, barring her arms over his head.

"We're not going to hurt you," he said. "Where is the throne room?"

She glanced between the three of them. Face a panicked mask, she reached under her blouse and drew a long, thin knife.

Dante hopped back a step, wrapping his hand in shadows. "Don't you do it!"

The girl lifted the knife, then plunged it into her heart. Her head tipped back, mouth open in shock; the knife twitched with the beat of her heart, then went still. She toppled back.

Blays swore softly. "Apparently you need to warn young women before exposing your face to them."

Trying to scrub the image of her final expression from his mind, Dante reached the back of the hall, found a corridor, and at last a stairwell. This was empty of people, as was the next floor, which held moderately opulent private quarters. The third level was similar except the residences were both larger and more splendid. The palaces he was used to tended to have their main communal spaces on the ground floor, but the lords of the Realm seemed to have different ideas about architecture, and Dante wasn't surprised to find the throne room waiting on the fourth floor.

With its randomly scattered lanterns of white, purple, and blue, and the way everything seemed to be spun as much from dreams as from physical matter, he found the style of Silidus' realm the most enchanting of them all. But he had no time to admire the trappings of the throne room as he ran through it to the door at the rear. This was locked similarly to Gashen's inner chambers, but he forced it open, revealing a room that reminded him of a civilized, indoor version of the caverns of Talassa. The door at its rear boasted a more formidable lock, meaning that it took his and Gladdic's combined powers to break it.

"Hello," Blays said. "I'd say we found it."

In another echo of Gashen's palace, the room they found themselves in was questionably a room in the first place: too dark to see any walls or ceilings, and no echoes to suggest they existed. The air smelled of greenery and flowers, because that's what the room was filled with, particularly ferns, small trees, and creeping vines that sprouted flowers of every color. A pool gleamed ahead of them, reflecting the most arresting feature of the space: seven moons hanging in an arc across the ceiling/sky. The central moon, the highest of them all, was full. Descending along either side of the arc, each moon was a fraction less full than the one above it, until the pair at bottom right and left were no more than thin crescents.

Fairy-lights bobbed in the air, too. Yet despite these, the seven moons, and the reflection of their light in the pool, there still wasn't quite enough light to read by.

"Right," Blays said. "Now how do we find the spear?"

Dante tried to avoid stepping on any of the fragile plants and elaborate insects. "I don't know."

"Er, you don't?"

"That's kind of entirely why I wanted to make Silidus give it to us."

"Well, this sort of place is where all the other gods have kept their spears, right?"

"You mean the two whole other times we've even seen one of the parts? Times when the gods retrieved their parts from what might have been an entirely separate plane of existence?"

"Yeah. So it *could* be here."

"But we have no way of even knowing that. Or seeing it. Which is going to make it especially hard to take it."

"Not if you just find a way to find it."

Dante pressed his lips together in frustration. He looked to Gladdic for sympathy.

Gladdic took a measured step toward the pool, disturbing a

few tiny flies. "If we are uncertain that what we seek is in this room, then we must first become certain — or disabuse ourselves of falsehood. Even if we are unable to see the fraction of the spear, we may be able to sense it in other ways."

"What, like smelling it?" Blays closed his eyes and took a deep sniff. "I dunno, doesn't really smell like spear around here to me."

"Yet we do not seek a spear. We seek its *part*. Merely one of a greater whole. Just as the parts of a body and the blood within it may be used to locate its other parts, the same may be true of the weapon: for surely it was all forged of the same stuff." He held out his hand. "Give me one of the parts we already possess."

Blays cocked his head, then got out his pack and withdrew the shaft they'd been given by Gashen. "Here. Figure you prefer the non-sharp bit."

Gladdic took the glowing rod and scowled over it. Ether sparked from his fingers. He sent it into the length of the shaft, which pulsed, the ether that formed it swirling more quickly.

"The way I can track someone by their blood," Dante said. "You mean to see if you can track one part of the spear to the rest of it."

"I thought that I had made that perfectly clear."

"That's because you don't seem to have any idea what normal people are like."

"Says the man who favors the company of dead rats." Gladdic turned the ethereal shaft over, then kneeled and set it in the grass in front of him, moving his hand back and forth above it, brightening the light as he went. He sat back, brow furrowed and eyes narrowed. "Do I sense a thread?"

He gestured again with greater energy, fingers dancing like the legs of a spider spinning its web. He leaned forward, neck extended, and smiled.

And then immediate smacked his hand to his forehead, rictusing in pain. "It is here. Very close, yet veiled."

"Can you find its exact spot in the room?" Dante began to pace. "If so, we might be able to tear that part of the veil down."

Gladdic clamped the spear shaft under the stump of his right arm and stood, seeming to feel his way forward with his left hand, leaving traces of ether in the air as he went. He made a circuit around the quiet pool, then wandered to his left before returning to his original spot.

"No. The intensity of it is too much for me to sense it with any precision."

"I was afraid of that," Dante muttered. "Blays, you want to take a look in the nether?"

Blays nodded, rippled, and vanished. Dante had a vague sense of him moving about through space. While he was busy exploring the shadows, Gladdic sifted ether through the air, mumbling under his breath.

Blays returned with a shrug. "Don't see anything."

"You're sure?" Dante said.

"If a piece of the ethereal spear were in the shadows, it would stand out like a star in the night sky. A sky where all the other stars had gone dead. And it's yelling at you in a really big star voice."

Gladdic came to a halt, gazing up at nothing. "Do not search with such intensity for a piece of the spear that you look right past the seam or doorway behind which it might be hidden."

Dante could feel him making a very slow and methodical search of the ether for anything out of place. Dante's own sense of the light was infinitely clumsier, but he pitched in as well as he could.

"Hey Gladdic," Blays said.

"Do not interrupt me."

"You know I hate to do so. But please tell me you're doing that."

Blays was pointing up at the sky. There, all but the highest of the seven moons was moving upward. Watching for a moment longer, their apparent movement was an illusion caused by the lack of reference points. Instead, the crescents and half-moons were all becoming full, as if they were emerging from an eclipse.

As the two moons flanking the one in the center reached fullness, two black shapes slipped loose and fell to the ground.

Dante backed up a step, grabbing the nether with both hands. "Did you see that?"

Blays peered into the gloom, which hadn't lessened despite the extra brightness shed by the uncovered moons. "What am I supposed to be seeing?"

Gladdic waved his hand in a circle. Ether brightened the grotto. And outlined two things that made no sense to Dante's eye. They looked more like shapes than beings—black circles, flattened at the bottom—but long hands dangled from their sides, the fingers hardened into dagger-like claws. They drifted forward on unseen legs.

"What the *hell* is that?" Dante said.

Blays flicked out his swords. "Something we should kill."

Another pair of the constructs dropped down from two more now-full moons. Dante shaped the shadows into a curved blade and threw it at the closest of the things. Just as the nether was about to strike it, it blinked away, the blade sailing away into the distance. The construct blinked back into being the instant it was safe.

Gladdic was attacking the other member of the first pair with an ether-heavy strike mixed with a small portion of shadow. Just like its partner had done, the circle blinked out of being, the attack passing through the empty space where it had been, and then it returned.

"Nice trick," Blays said. "But let's see what tires out first: their tricks, or my arms."

He bobbed toward the one Dante had attacked. As he closed on it, a third pair dropped from the last of the seven moons, the ones that had appeared to be crescents earlier but now blazed like silver coins.

"They are demons," Gladdic said.

"You don't say?" Dante threw a trio of bolts at his target, staggering their placement, but the monster vanished until all three had gone past.

"Be fearful of their touch."

Gladdic assembled a sophisticated-feeling assault and drove it at the same one he'd attacked before. Dante didn't get to see how this played out, however, as Blays had closed on the other demon and was presently taking a good hack at it. The thing phased away, returned, then blinked again as Blays jabbed at it with his other sword. Looking smug, Blays flicked a lightning-swift backhand at it just as it rematerialized. The stroke cut through the demon's side, spraying shadows, but it lunged toward Blays, claws outstretched.

He jumped back, taking a wild slash at its strange, stubby arm. The Odo Sein steel bounced off the claws with a thud.

"I don't like this!" Blays backpedaled away from the demon, which pursued, flanked by the others.

Gladdic unleashed a swarm of darts, half light and half shadow, whipping them at the flank of the demon closing fastest on Blays. But it simply blinked away. Gladdic had anticipating this, swerving the swarm toward the next target, then back to the first. Again, they dodged. The darts began to frazzle beneath the constant redirection.

Blays fended off another lunge, falling back two steps in the process. "Is it time to run?"

"That's your answer to everything," Dante said.

"That's because it's such a good one."

The things marched forward like a shield wall. Without

warning, Blays pounced on them, driving two to wink away and clipping a small wound in the edge of a third, which stopped "bleeding" almost at once. Still, even that was more damage than Dante or Gladdic had been able to inflict on any of them.

As the faceless demons neared, Dante drew his sword with a snap of nether. "If we can't get rid of these things, it's only a matter of time before Silidus sends something even worse to finish us off. There has to be a way!"

One of the circular demons pounced at him. He had just enough wherewithal to jab forward and use its own momentum against it, aiming his sword for the upper spot where its face might have been. As expected, it vanished.

Dante blinked too. "Did you feel that?"

Blays ducked a claw swipe and counterattacked, brutally savaging an empty piece of air. "The advance of my impending death?"

"When it vanished. They're moving in and out of the nether!"

"Then let's see them escape from us both."

Blays shifted into the shadows. Dante jabbed at the demon as it came at him again, shooting a black dart at it for good measure. It blinked—and when it came back, nether roiled from a giant gash in its side, diffusing from the sword wound like blood dribbled into a puddle. Dante grabbed hold of it, wrapping the shadowy cords around his wrist, and *pulled*.

The circular demon shrieked from a mouth it didn't have. Thick strands of it piled in Dante's hands. He packed them into a wave of darts and launched them at a second creature as it bowled its way toward him. It vanished. Dante and Gladdic drew cataracts of nether from the wounded demon the same way Dante had once learned how to destroy the Andrac. The other four, alarmed or perhaps enraged at this, abandoned their steady advance in favor of a full-bore charge.

The disappeared demon shuddered back into view, leaking

shadows from four different cuts. Gladdic shifted to it before it could attempt to heal itself. Dante used his stolen shadows to launch dart after dart at the charging quartet. Yet rather than blinking out of being and risking the same fate as the other two, they lowered their circular bodies into the barrage. The darts knocked little puffs of shadows from them, but not enough to do serious harm.

With the sound of ripping cloth, Dante yanked the last of the nether from the dying demon. It wailed like a bent horn and dissipated into nothing. Dante flung another assault at the four constructs coming for him, then turned and ran, emptying his head. Ether dripped into it. He bent the light into a shining blade and whacked it into the nearest pursuer. The demon hissed as nether spurted from a deep wound.

It dropped back, letting the others take the lead. They skimmed over the ground with alarming speed. Purple light sparked behind them: Blays had jumped out of the nether and was sprinting toward the four demons from the rear. To Dante's right, Gladdic finished off the second demon that Blays had cut open and slashed its shadows into the sides of the others. This didn't so much as slow them down.

They were almost upon him. Dante stopped, hammering at the foremost demon with what bits of ether he could summon while jabbing at it with his sword. Smoke puffed from a half dozen minor wounds. The demon jumped toward him, the air growing cold as its presence neared. He batted aside its claws with his sword, but it pivoted impossibly fast, lashing at him with its other hand. The claws raked across his chest.

The pain was both fire and ice. Dante's eyes tunneled; he could feel himself drawing the nether for a strike, but it was like trying to swing a log. He stumbled. The purple of swords flashed as they rose and fell. Ether punched into the demons from the side.

Dante dropped from his feet. A hole seemed to open beneath him, swallowing him up, spitting him into another realm. He was no longer falling but he couldn't seem to feel any ground under his feet. He was surrounded by darkness, able to make out only the vaguest of shapes.

This way.

The voice spoke directly inside his head: he whirled, spying a small black creature with large eyes and rounded features that almost looked like a toy bear, albeit one with graceful wings spreading from its back.

No need to be afraid, it said. *You are welcome here!*

It turned, floating through the air. Half dazed, Dante followed after it. The air was warmer than it had been in—wherever he'd been before, he couldn't remember—and smelled like iron. A face loomed to his left, but when he turned for a better look, it was gone.

Just a little further now, the imp said, its voice kindly and charming. *You are very lucky to have found your way here. Very few are so privileged.*

Indistinct shapes shifted and bobbed around him. After a short walk, the imp turned, gave him a smile and a wink, then fluttered away.

Something drew Dante's eye to the right. A body lay on the ground. Half of one, anyway: it was a human man whose body had been severed at the waist, leaving tatters of flesh and organs strung out behind it. As Dante stared in dumb terror, the man lifted his head and met Dante's eyes.

"Help." The man raised his right hand. "You have to help me."

Dante stood frozen. The man should have been dead already. Even a great sorcerer would only have the scantest chance of saving someone wounded so badly. He reached for the nether. It refused to come.

One of the vague shapes cohered behind the wounded man. A huge hand, as black as pitch, casually reached for him, squeezing its great fingers around his armpits. The man's eyes bulged in panic as the hand dragged him backward. A giant mouth opened from the blackness and bit down halfway up the man's ribs. Crunched between its teeth, the man, somehow still alive even now, waved for Dante as the thing carried him off into the darkness.

The shapes surrounding Dante had grown larger. He turned in an unsteady circle, trying to keep track of them all. The darkness receded from around them like when the ocean had drained away beneath him in the Pastlands.

Out of that dark sea emerged a forest of horrors. The very smallest was the size of a man but most were far larger. A huge head, covered in eyes and sores, both eyes and sores leaking fluids. A gaping mouth, its hard lips ringed with needly teeth and writhing tongues. A lumpy sac of fluid, its skin transparent, revealing the human heads and limbs digesting within it. A thing of folded angles Dante's eyes couldn't make sense of. A heap of motile bones with thorn-covered tentacles slipping in and out of its cracks. A diseased phallus crawling along like a massive inchworm.

And scores more, each unique in appearance, but uniform in the revulsion they shoved into Dante's gut.

He ran as fast as he could. But the horrors stayed perfectly even with him, as if he wasn't moving at all. After another moment they began to drift closer. He screamed.

A circle of light opened above him. He was jerked up toward it so hard his head snapped back. He accelerated toward the light, terrifyingly fast, smashing through something like brittle glass—

He gasped, choking on thick mucous. He spat into the grass. An old man leaned over him, inspecting him with mild concern.

"You were poisoned," Gladdic said. "I managed to negate the venom."

"Nice work," Dante said.

"Indeed."

Dante closed his eyes, which was a terrible idea, as when he did he could still see the shapes of the horrors hanging in the darkness. They had looked like something from a hallucination, but a deep part of him suspected they'd been perfectly real.

Blays raised an eyebrow. "You look like you've seen a ghost."

"I wish." Dante got to his feet. He'd never realized how good it could feel to have solid ground underneath you. "Where did the demons go?"

"We killed three of them. Apparently that was enough for the others to decide it was time to go away."

"Away? Where?"

Blays waved at the dark surroundings. "Oh, you know, probably somewhere that they can leap out at us at the worst possible moment."

"Then the best way to avoid that is to get our hands on Silidus' spear before they regroup. I think we should be looking for a doorway of some kind."

"There is no need to search," Gladdic said. "For I have already seen the seam to the other side."

"Uh, have you?"

"During the battle, I saw it illuminated by our many energies." He strode toward the pool of black water, wading into its shallows. Fireflies danced around him. Hand aglow with ether, he lifted it over his head, tracing a line downward. And forming a seam. Gladdic completed the line and stepped back. "It is open. But the force I feel within it is…"

"Silidus?"

"I do not know. Only that it is beyond anything I have ever felt."

Gladdic had healed the claw-wounds Dante had suffered, so Dante drew his knife to feed the nether. "I'll go."

"No," Gladdic said. He drew back his shoulders. "I will not linger on the other side. No matter what sights might beguile me."

He stepped forward and was gone.

Blays had put away his swords, but he kept his hands on their hilts, gazing across the grotto. "If this place hadn't just tried to kill us, I'd say it feels downright peaceful."

Dante was tempted to investigate the seam, but kept his focus on his surroundings, including the nether. Overhead, all seven moons remained full. He felt no trace of the demons, either living or dead.

The seam rippled. Gladdic emerged from the other side like he was stepping through a waterfall. His face was gaunt and haunted, eyes darting in seemingly random directions.

"Did you make it through?" Dante said. "What did you see?"

"I will not speak of it." With visible effort, Gladdic took control of himself. "But I have done what was asked of me."

He held out his hand. He held a short rod glowing with ether. One end was rounded into a ball.

The cap to the butt of a spear.

22

Blays took the cap and bounced it in his hand. "Not bad work for a crazy old man."

"Now it seems as though each one of us has won a portion of the spear."

"There's no way you could have dealt with the moon-demons without me. Though I suppose you helped a *little*."

"By the way, those demons are still here somewhere," Dante said. "So I'm thinking we shouldn't be."

"Let's not be too hasty," Blays said. "Gladdic, was there any-thing else worth stealing on the other side?"

Gladdic shook his head with an involuntary jerk. "It is not a place that you or I should go."

"But that only makes me want to go more." Blays gave a dour look up at the moons. "You know that's where she hides all her precious god-gold. But if you guys aren't interested in priceless riches, I suppose we can go."

Dante hastened toward the doorway out of the grotto. A legion of fireflies buzzed after him, as if spying on him. He stepped through the door and the insects dispersed.

Leaving the inner sanctum, a wave of disorientation washed over him, as if he'd awakened from a long dream. He stumbled through the cave-like room beyond that might have been a chapel and then out into the throne room. Through the windows, he could still hear some fighting going on throughout the palace, but it sounded much more casual than before. More like a mop-up.

Downstairs, a few more bodies had joined that of the servant who'd committed suicide. They didn't see anyone living until they were outside and running toward their horses, which thankfully hadn't been harmed or stolen.

They mounted up and exited the palace grounds to the north, the closest exit, before breaking around to the south toward the smashed-down city gates. The air smelled like smoke and churned-up ground. The horses often had to jump over or swerve around a body or four, most of them Proteans, and most of them not in any uniform.

They exited a zig-zagging alley into one of the plazas that housed mobile, makeshift neighborhoods whenever there wasn't a war going on. This one was filled with ramna in various states of plundering. One group of warriors sat atop mounds of bodies swigging wine. Blood trickled along the mortar between the cobbles.

Blays slowed. "Have we done a bad thing?"

"*We* haven't killed anybody," Dante said. "That palace servant doesn't count, either."

"Without us, the ramna never would have come here. Should we do something to help?"

"Which side are we to aid?" Gladdic said. "The invaders who show no mercy to their foes but have never taken arms in anger against us? Or the people of the gods who want both our world and the one beyond it scrubbed out like a palimpsest?"

"You're right. On second thought, screw both of them."

They rode south at a speed intended to avoid attention from either the ramna or the Proteans. A group of horsemen stopped them at what remained at the gates, but after a bit of vouching about being friends of Dasya and the Jessel, the guards let them through, if grudgingly.

They crossed the causeway and stopped for a look back at the sacked city. It felt as if they deserved to celebrate—about obtaining another part of the spear, not as much about the slaughter—but for all their efforts, they still only held a third of the weapon.

They turned their backs on Protus and made way for Crosswater.

As it turned out, they never made it.

A day later and ten miles outside Phannon's city, with the road rolling alongside a fast stream, a longboat emerged from the trees ahead, followed by a second. Oarsmen pulled the boats toward shore with startling speed. Soldiers dashed through the shallows to seize the road, archers training arrows at the three outlanders—while six robed men and women drew light and shadow to their hands. They were all dressed in the navy and white of Phannon.

"We're not your enemies," Dante said. "We're—"

"Dante Galand and Blays Buckler." This came from a tall woman dressed more like an aristocrat than a soldier, though she did carry a graceful sword on her hip. "And a third man I don't reckon."

"Oh, that's because he was dead until a few days ago," Blays said. "What can we do for you?"

"You can start by staying six rowlands away from Crosswater."

"Why do I have the feeling you've heard about what happened at Protus?"

"Mayhap you possess a functioning faculty of reason."

"Then I hope your error is just a lack of correct information," Dante said, more hotly than he intended. "We're not here to wage war on you. We're the ones who bent the ramna *away* from

Crosswater."

The woman appeared to be a few years older than him and her eyes flickered with the wry amusement that seemed common among naval officers. "At the risk of insulting your intelligence, milord, that's the very reason you're barred from the realm."

"I'm sorry, I wasn't aware your defense strategy hinged on getting overrun and burned to the ground."

Gladdic scoffed. "That is not the meaning of her words. Rather the fear is that if we were allowed inside their city, we might conspire to destroy it as well."

"In that case, let me make our motives completely transparent. I suspect you might have heard we're trying to win the Spear of Stars. I know it's not quite the standard practice of obtaining them, but we thought diverting an enemy army from your doorstep would be a deed worthy of Phannon's part."

The woman looked between them, eyes narrowing. "Given your deeds elsewhere, I'm not sure I'd take your word on that. But it's a good thing for you that you didn't try to lie to me."

"At the risk of being an idiot," Blays said, "how do you know we're not?"

"Because it lines right up with what Gashen himself told my master when the lord of war vouched for you."

"He went out of his way to vouch for us? Has his wife ever come to terms with how much he loves that axe?"

"Are you mocking him?" The woman sounded aghast, though this was probably but not certainly mockery itself. "You should be thanking him. His love of that old axe is now responsible for you getting your hands on *two* parts of the Spear of Stars."

She unslung a bundle she'd been carrying over her shoulder and extended it to Dante. Blays took it instead, unwrapping it carefully, which turned out to be a smart move: for a second fragment of the blade lay within, ethereal and pure.

Dante laughed in surprise. "I was expecting to have to do a lot more arguing. Please let Phannon know how grateful we are."

The woman gave a nod. "My master said to take it with her blessings and her thanks."

"We're grateful to receive those as well." Dante fiddled with the reins. "At the risk of being rude, we should really be on our way. I'm sure you understand why."

"So soon? Then you don't want to hear about the conspiracy?"

"If he doesn't, I do," Blays said. "The only thing better than thwarting a conspiracy is being involved in one."

"Word of what happened to Protus has spread. Faster than you'd think. Its sacking wasn't met with high approval by the other lords of the realm."

Dante frowned. "There was nothing we could do to stop the ramna. All we could do was try to change who they were going to attack."

"Again, you're not getting me. What I'm saying is that among the other lords, the response to the attack on the city has been..." She tightened her eyes, rolling them up and to the side. "Well, you might say there's been a turn of the tide. Nobody is especially impressed by the way Taim has been steering the vessel. There's been a mutiny."

Blays jerked his chin at the longboat stitched onto her chest. "Are you obligated to speak only in nautical metaphors?"

She grinned at him. "Sometimes I like to see how long it takes for anyone to mention it. Back to the matter at hand. It's been decades since one of our cities was sacked as badly as Silidus'. Arguably centuries. It was one thing for Taim to betray the old traditions regarding the spear if doing so meant that the order of the Realm would be preserved. But if he's betraying our vows *and* kicking chaos into our faces with it—which is to say that we gave up our virtue *and* our order—then it's time to put a different hand on the tiller."

Blays glanced up at the sky. "Don't tell me there's about to be a revolution in heaven."

"Revolution? Hardly. More apt to call it a correction. First off, we're going to restore our vows. Not just for the sake of the vows, but to get you people the hell out of our hair."

"Such a correction would be in the interests of everyone involved," Gladdic said.

"Not quite *everyone*. But if it works, we can get back to business as usual, which is the way we prefer it. So." She clapped her hands, clasping them together. "Several of our masters wished to be done with this tomorrow. But when you do something as stupid as putting the matter to a vote, you wind up having to compromise.

"Here is what they came up with. Rather than making you contest for their parts of the spear, Barrod and Lia will just give them to you. If we're not mistaken, that leaves just Taim, Arawn, and Urt. Arawn won't make it as easy on you as Barrod and Lia. He's still sticking by the old ways, as in you have to earn his spear-ninth without favor or prejudice. Only he's got a clever wrinkle: his task for you is to finish *Urt's* task. You do that, and you get his and Urt's piece at once."

Dante scratched his jaw. "Why won't Urt—"

"If you think Urt's going to explain why he does what he does, you're not much of a priest."

"Yeah, all right. So this is all sounding extremely encouraging. Except I haven't heard any mention of Taim yet."

"Taim's mind is unchanged. There's no need for direct action just yet. But if you can earn eight of the spear-ninths, the other gods have made a pact to force Taim to give you the final shard."

"Do we need to make a formal agreement? If so: agreed."

"Barrod and Lia are making preparations to bring you their parts. Your next task is to go and see about Urt."

"So where's his realm?"

She drew back her head in rebuke. "Uh uh. Locating his realm for yourself is the first part of Urt's challenge. If and when you pull that off, he'll let you know your next test."

Dante nodded, absorbing all of this the best that he could. "Just how strong is this pact? Have the gods sworn oaths to it? Or is it liable to collapse if the ramna decide to pack up their axes and go home?"

"Once Gashen stood up for you, that shamed a lot of the lords and ladies who'd agreed to deny you the chance to unite the spear. When rumor started going around that even *Carvahal* had acted more honorably than them, well, that put a hair down their shirts. They'll back their word."

Dante took another stab at getting her to tell them how they might go about locating Urt's realm, but she'd have none of it. After a few more formalities and expressions of thanks, they ended the discussion, with Dante and the others riding east while she and her escort watched from the road to make sure they weren't about to try to sneak into Crosswater for some reason.

"One last feat wins us the full spear," Blays said. "And none of this would have happened if we hadn't turned the ramna on Protus. Guess there's something to be said for burning down your enemy's cities after all."

Gladdic smiled thinly. "I have made many similar arguments in the past."

"In any event, do we know where we're going now? Or is the plan to blunder around until we stumble into Urt's realm?"

"Denhild is just a short ride from here," Dante said. "We'll try there first. Gashen might allow us to research his archives for information on where to find Urt."

"Why don't you get hold of Lars on that thing he gave you?"

"I'd hardly call this an emergency. Anyway, we'll be at Denhild by tomorrow."

"Where there's no guarantee they'll give us a shred of help. Better to learn that sooner rather than later. Anyway, call me paranoid, but this feels like the most vulnerable part of our whole venture. Taim has to know we took part in the raid at Protus. Ka is probably out searching for us as we speak."

"This is true."

"There's also the possibility that Phannon is a double-agent and just fed us a huge line of bullshit to get us to expose ourselves to Taim. It would be nice to confirm her story with Gashen and Lars."

This was enough to make Dante reconsider. He got out the iron disk Lars had given him, running his finger over the raised lions as he dithered about whether the situation really called for it, then decided to hell with it, jabbed his knuckle, and dabbed blood onto the disk. It flushed bright red. The nether within it churned rhythmically.

He thought he knew the way to Denhild, but consulted his map anyway. He confirmed they were going in the right direction, then examined the map for hints of where Urt might be, whether direct ones—like, say, an X labeled "The Kingdom of Urt"—or indirect, like gaps in the landscape where a realm might be. But the landmarks weren't distributed at all evenly, and there was no telling where something deliberately unmarked might be located.

He was interrupted from his examination of the map by the pulsing of his loon. Nak reported that he'd maneuvered his forces as skillfully as he could to try to avoid direct warfare with the lich, but for all his efforts, he feared they were about to be outflanked. Barring some error on the lich's part, or an inspired escape on his own, he expected battle within the next day.

Dante told him to do all that he could. And that if it turned out not to be enough, that he understood.

They weren't quite halfway to Denhild when dust spiraled up from the road ahead: General Lars and his men. Dante and the other two hadn't been sparing their horses, so meeting at this distance between the two cities meant the general must have left within minutes of receiving Dante's message.

"Friends!" Lars scoured the horizons. "What danger threatens your life?"

"It's not quite here yet," Blays said. "Really, it's more of the looming kind. Or maybe the impending."

Lars gave them an angry look that was alarming despite being just a portion of what he was clearly capable of mustering. "Why was the signal raised when there is no disaster at hand?"

Dante and Blays explained quickly.

"Is the gods' offer true?" Dante said. "Or is this a way to destroy us?"

"Ah!" The general broke into a grin. "Rejoice, you persistent mortals. The offer is real."

"Incredible!" Blays punched his fist into his other palm. "But I don't see how we're expected to even be able to get to Urt's realm in the first place. How are we supposed to cross that desert?"

"The Desert of Yula? There are fearsome creatures within it, but the desert itself is not that wide."

"That's a relief, but that area beyond it—I don't even know how to describe it—"

The general crinkled his brow. "The Knifelands are not so imposing as their name implies. Especially for two sorcerers and a warrior of your caliber."

"Even so, it sounds like the sort of place you could get lost in for ages before finding your way to the doorway."

"The challenge you fear is not half as daunting as..." Lars

trailed off, mouth twitching at something he saw in Blays.

Dante had maintained a straight face this entire time. Although it must not have been quite as convincing as he thought, for when Lars glanced at him in suspicion, the general cursed and stomped his foot.

"You've been playing me! Plying me for information it wasn't mine to give! Is that the entire reason you summoned me?"

"Not the *entire* reason," Blays said. "We really did need to know if the gods' offer was legitimate. My friends here had no idea about the, er, other reason I was so insistent on speaking with you."

"I ought to gut you and leave you to the drakelets." Lars glowered at Blays, who was looking very innocent. The general swore again. "If this is what it means to be your friend, no wonder you are so much of a burr under the saddle of your enemies."

"You know, now that you've told us where Urt's realm is, you might as well tell us the best way to get there."

"You god-blind ruffians." Lars wasn't quite done being angry, but he was laughing now, too. "Figure the rest out for yourselves! Or you are not worthy of carrying the spear, even if your company remains welcome within our walls."

"Getting there should be easier than normal anyway," Dante said. "Given that most of the ramna who'd otherwise be crossing our path are currently in Silidus' wine cellars instead."

"You will have other challenges, but the ramna won't be one of them. They do not bother Urt."

"Are his mysteries that frightening to the savages?"

"Urt is the only one of the gods who has never harmed or betrayed them, though that is of course in *their* opinion. But he is also a seer. Sometimes the ramna come to him for visions or answers and sometimes he grants these requests." Lars leaned forward, dropping his voice so that the soldiers who'd come with him couldn't hear. "Though I have long suspected that some of the prophecies he gives out are not meant to *predict* the future so much as they are to *cause* it."

"That would be most clever," Gladdic said. "Position yourself beyond the politics and petty struggles of the realm while manipulating others to exert your will without understanding they are being so used."

"Then we'll take anything Urt says with a grain of salt. Assuming we've got any left by the time we get there." Dante tapped the horn of his saddle. "Why make such a big deal about not telling us where Urt's kingdom is? What if we'd just gone to a pub in Denhild and asked the locals where it is?"

Lars looked amused. "Then most would not have been able to answer, and the few who did would have given you false counsel."

"All right, then what if we'd asked the ramna? If they go to him for wisdom, I'm going to make the mad assumption they know *where* to go."

"That is only sometimes true. You assume that Urt's realm is just like any other. That is a foolish thing to do, considering that *Urt* is like no other! If you did not want people to know where your home was, how would you stop them from finding it?"

"Hide it?"

"No," Gladdic said. "I would hide it *and move it*. And move it again whenever word of its new position began to be known."

Lars nodded. "So Urt does with his kingdom. Congratulate yourselves for beguiling its current location from me. But if you do any dawdling along the way and then find that it is no longer where it once was, don't expect to find it again any time soon."

This was all the encouragement Dante needed to bring the conversation to an end. They parted on good terms—though the general made Dante promise not to use the disk again unless it was a real emergency—with Lars and his men heading east, back toward Denhild, while Dante and the others cut south-southeast, where his map indicated the Desert of Yula was located. The map's sense of scale was wanting, but given the endurance of their new horses, Dante thought it would take no more than five days to reach the desert, maybe as few as three.

For the time being the way was easy, open grassland with little threat of running into ramna bands. Despite the trouble-free path—or perhaps because it gave him nothing else to occupy his mind—Dante's nerves drew tighter and tighter as he waited to hear back from Nak regarding the results of the confrontation with the Eiden Rane.

The longer he went without hearing anything, the more convinced he became that Nak had fallen, with all the strength of Narashtovik perishing with him. Dante was compelled to loon him and check if that was so, but in case it wasn't, and Nak was still in the middle of the fight, then doing so would only distract Nak, perhaps ruinously. And so Dante bit his tongue, even as his worries threatened to drive him crazy.

At last the loon pulsed in his ear. Dante opened the line, half certain that it would be to the mocking laughter of the lich.

It was Nak. He sounded exhausted. Beyond exhausted. And the story he told made Dante's throat close so tightly he all but couldn't breathe.

Blays acted like he wasn't listening to the conversation, watching the wide-open prairie instead. But as soon as Dante shut down the line, Blays turned on him.

"Well? How'd they do?"

"They made their stand at Varradun Pass. A little south of Cling." Dante's head felt light and he squeezed his legs to his horse's flanks to stop himself from slipping. "The lich made his move. Marched his main force right up the pass at them—and in the meantime cleared a route for a secondary force to march on their right flank. There was nothing Nak could do."

"Oh." Blays' voice softened. "How many of them made it out?"

"You don't understand. Nak didn't get any reinforcements from Gallador. But he did get them from Pocket Cove."

"The People of the Pocket? How did they know to help?"

"You can probably answer that question better than any of us. But my impression is they don't keep themselves nearly as walled off from the rest of the world as they want us to believe. In any event, they turned the mountain against the lich. Brought landslides down on both Varradun Pass and the path the lich had built for his sneak attack. They killed thousands of Blighted before the lich knew what was happening. Still, the lich managed to stop them from crushing his entire army—and that's when the People of the Pocket dropped a cliff on him."

Blays went still. "Don't tell me..."

"He survived. Of *course* he survived, you'd have better luck trying to kill an ocean. But they did manage to wound him."

"Well, we've done *that* much ourselves. And it took them a whole army to match our feat."

Dante grinned, turning his face to the day. "They've bought us more time. Let's make the most of it."

23

They had grown used to traveling across the wilderness of the Realm of Nine Kings, and with the ramna pulled away to plunder the north, there was little to slow them down. The grassland gave way to undulating fields of boulders, then a pimpled land where muddy little volcanoes pushed themselves up from the earth, spewing loose and odiferous soil that Blays made any number of jokes about. In case Ka was on the hunt for them across the lands between them and Urt, they veered somewhat more easterly than Dante thought they needed to.

During the nights, Dante built their stone shelters, but disguised them to match whatever was around them—first the muddy volcanoes, then an all-but-sealed hollow in the side of the endless canyon they followed on the second day, then the turf-covered hillock in the forgotten reaches where wild horses played among the ruins of a city long dead.

On that same day, while watching the horses in silence as dusk stole across the reaches, they were attacked by three flying creatures with wingspans as wide as a king's road. Though the creatures were otherwise feathered, their long tails were scaled, and Blays swore he saw serpents' heads at their tips. They dispersed after Dante pelted them with a few darts of nether.

The following day, the fields remained verdant and flower-filled until they came to a wide river. The opposite bank was fringed with green, but beyond that, the land was all low, yellow hills.

Blays shielded his eyes from the sun. "Suppose that's our Desert of Yula?"

Dante gave it a once-over. "Unless the map I made in haste from a much larger one where I deliberately changed some of the signs and scale has made a mistake."

There weren't any bridges in sight, nor likely anywhere else on the entire run of the river, and Dante felt along its bed to confirm that it was much too deep to ford. But as he waded his horse into the shallows to raise up a land-bridge, the animal strode into the waters and began to swim. Blays shrugged and rode in after him. Dante dismounted into the water to swim next to the horse, pushing his saddlebag onto its back to keep the contents dry.

"Do not forget the lessons of the swamps." Gladdic illuminated the water around them. There were plenty of fish drifting about, but nothing like a school of ziki oko or anything longer than a man's arm, let alone the size of a swamp dragon, and they came to the other side without drawing interest from any animals.

A warm wind blew in from the south. They wrung out their clothes, Gladdic using some trick of the ether to hurry the process. Outside of some small game and a few grouse, they hadn't had much fresh meat on their recent travels, and Dante used the nether to spear several fish, which Blays said was cheating—although that didn't stop him from helping to eat them.

They entered the desert. The hills were gray dirt baked so hard that even the horses' hooves hardly scratched it. Sparse and dead grass rustled in the breeze. In less than a mile, the hills were replaced with dunes of coarse sand.

"Damn," Blays said. "It's *that* kind of desert."

Gladdic scowled at the ground. "In what cursed place was

the ground made of such shifting sands?"

"It's called Morrive. You aren't missing out."

"Even worse." Dante nodded to the east. "The horizons are getting blurry. Just like they did when we traveled to the Claimless Reach. We're not going to be able to tell what direction we're going."

Gladdic sounded amused. "Are you expecting the sun to be swallowed as well?"

"As it happens, that's exactly what happened last time."

"Then use a compass to guide your way."

"Those don't work down here. The iron just keeps spinning."

"I refer to an ethereal compass."

"A what now?"

Gladdic pressed his lips together. "You do not even know of the ethereal compass?"

"Have you ever seen him try to use the ether?" Blays said. "It's like watching a newborn deer trying to run. While playing chess. With its nose."

Gladdic muttered an exasperated appeal to the heavens, then lifted his finger and drew a glowing line in the air, aligning it parallel to the ground. "There. We have our compass."

"A line?"

"What is the needle of a compass if not a line? Look: I have set it north to south, and fixed it to the ether so it will not change direction when I do."

"At least draw an arrow on one end so we don't get turned around. What do you do when you're going to go to sleep and you have to shut down the ether? Draw a physical line in the dirt?"

"That is one way, yes. You are one who prefers complex solutions. Perhaps that is because you believe they display that you are clever. Yet the simpler the solution, the less likely it is to fail."

Dante presumed he should feel rebuked, but the insight didn't sting at all. As they walked south through the dunes, making their way toward the Knifelands, he kept one eye on the compass floating beside Gladdic. It seemed to be doing its job.

The dunes looked absolutely desolate, but there was life here, too. Birds with wings wider than a man's armspan glided across the sky, hardly ever having to flap, their long tails stretched out behind them. Lizards skittered through the sand, making strange trails as they went. Ants and colorful beetles scooped up anything left behind by the larger creatures.

There weren't any plants to be found, but small, gnarled rock formations broke the sand here and there, green and blue and orange, stuck together in round and knobby bulbs that reminded Dante of something you would see exposed at shore by a low tide. Some of the beetles, wasps, and small rodents took a particular interest in them, even trying to nibble pieces off of them. Rock-eating mice would have marked one of the oddest things he'd seen in the Realm until he came to understand the rocks weren't really rocks at all: in fact, they were tough, hard plants, or perhaps even a fungus.

The sand slowed their animals, and with a lack of any horizons to provide reference points, it seemed as though they weren't making any progress at all. Yet if Dante's map could be believed, they'd be out of the desert by the next day. Night neared, and the day's warmth fled; a sudden wind had them spitting sand and rubbing it from their eyes. Dante called a halt and hardened a shelter from the sand. They built a small fire and cooked the last of the fish they'd caught earlier that day, which Gladdic had preserved with the ether. Beady little eyes gleamed from the darkness, unseen paws swishing through the sand, but none of the animals approached close enough to the circle of firelight to see what they were.

The nights were growing longer and they were ready to begin again before the sun was up. Something about the light of the ether on the endless dunes felt threatening, or perhaps sacred, and they didn't speak to each other until the dawn flooded over the sands.

With the spell of silence broken, they passed the time recalling scriptures and stories about Urt in preparation for whatever he had in store for them. There wasn't much to be learned: Urt didn't come up often, and when he did, his motivations—even his role itself—were so opaque that scholars could spend a lifetime arguing the nuances of a single story.

"Yet there is one tale that could shed light," Gladdic said after a lull. "The Rebirth of Tulgen."

"Who died fighting the sea reavers." Dante had to think a moment to remember more. "When he fell, the ancient and far-away city of Tarmor was set to be conquered. Only Urt restored Tulgen to life. What significance are you seeing in this?"

"Many hold that Urt brought Tulgen back to the field to quench the fire of the reavers at Tarmor before it could spread across the interior. But it is my belief that he intervened to save the city of Tarmor itself: for it was the seat of the University of Nalgar, first of its kind to transmit knowledge of the nether in organized form. After Tulgen saved the city, its knowledge spread to many other lands, which arose from their dark ages to seed the soil for what came next: among them the two tribes of Rashen and Elsen in the north, that would become Narashtovik, and the tribes of Stotts and Helods in the south, that would become Bressel. If Tarmor and its university had fallen to the sea reavers, our world might remain in an era of darkness to this day."

"But why would Urt care about that? He's hardly a humanitarian. If anything he's destroyed more people than he's ever saved. He's not a huge proponent of knowledge, either. What about the time he flooded the Monastery of Alquibias?"

"His resurrection of Tulgen was not a matter of saving lives or lore. Rather it was to prevent a new cycle of civilization from being strangled in the cradle."

Dante waved a fly from his horse's neck. "That's pretty speculative. On the other hand, it would tie into what you told General Lars about Urt being the lord of cycles. After all, what is the cicada if not an insect that returns in…"

He lost the focus to complete his thought. Gladdic followed his eyes to the dune in front of them. There was no wind, and the ground beneath them was perfectly steady, but sand was spilling down the side of the dune, more and more of it with each second. A dimple sank into it, first a hand wide, then a foot, then a yard.

"What've we got," Blays said, "some kind of sand-mole?"

Reflexively, Dante drew his knife and scratched his arm, drawing on the nether. The first shadows touched his fingers as a domed shape six feet across broke free of the sand. A great worm extruded twenty feet into the air before bending forward on its thick body. It opened its mouth—four flaps making an X-shaped opening—and revealed a ring of huge, crystalline teeth.

Blays edged his horse back from the worm, reaching for his swords. "These things again? Did this one think Talassa was too gloomy and headed south for warmer weather?"

"Hit it down its throat," Dante said. "That's what hurt them worst."

"We could give it a fight, which seems to be what it wants from us. But why don't we just go around it?"

This seemed reasonable enough, so Dante angled his horse to the right. But the sand in front of him sucked downward. A second worm thrust its head into the sky, translucent teeth scraping against each other as it flung its jaws wide and then slammed them back together.

Blays unsheathed his swords, shaking his head. "Why does everything insist on making me kill it?"

Dante's horse was getting a little jumpy, but it responded to his command to get two steps closer to the second worm. The worm reared back, springing open its jaws again as it prepared to strike. Dante waited for it to snap its head toward him before launching his nether. Most of the shadows hit its teeth with a blood-curdling grate, but a few flew down its throat. The worm clacked its mouth shut, thrashing its head side to side.

Yet twenty feet to its right, the sand was sucking downward. A third one of the beasts emerged into the daylight, cutting off that much more of their angle of escape.

The first worm snapped at Blays, who backed just out of range. "Just how many of these things *are* there?"

Dante threw a bit of nether at the third worm to keep it occupied, then sank his mind down into the sands, seeking open tunnels or worm-sized gaps within the earth. When he found what he was looking for, he tried to swear, but the word stuck in his throat like a too-large bite of beef.

"There's just one of them," he managed.

"Just one more?" Blays swiped at his opponent as it extended further from the sand. "Well that's good news."

"No," Dante said. "It's not."

"But we dealt with much worse in the Cavern of —"

"Run! Run run run run!"

Dante yanked the sand away from beneath the worm that had been menacing him, half-burying it. He dashed past it, glancing back to ensure Gladdic and Blays were doing the same. His eyes went even wider.

The entire dune they'd been on was sinking, draining away like wine from a barrel with the bung pulled. More and more of the worms wriggled free from the loose sand. They were arranged in an orderly ring and for the moment none of them were giving chase.

The sand drained lower, revealing a hill of bare, tough rock.

In most un-hill-like fashion, the hill bobbed upward, the ring of worms that surrounded it rising with it.

"What the *hell* am I looking at?" Blays yelled.

Dante leaned forward in the saddle. "If you can still talk, you're not fleeing fast enough!"

Their horses struggled through the deep sand. Behind them, a worm the size of a river surged upward, a blizzard of sand falling away from its segmented body, the smaller worms — in truth, just tentacles — that ringed its mouth waving madly.

"By the souls of the gods," Gladdic said.

Blays' mouth hung open. "Why would they make something like that?!"

"I don't think they did," Dante said. "I think this world created it on its own."

The worm swayed in the air, as if getting its bearings. It didn't seem to have any eyes, yet it swung its enormous head straight toward them, then sprawled forward, landing so heavily the ground rattled, knocking sand down from the surrounding dunes. It squeezed more and more of itself out into the air, racing after them with horrible speed.

"Unless we go faster, it's going to eat us," Blays said.

Dante called down the nether. "I can see that."

"It's going to eat us, and its mouth is so big it won't even get to taste us."

Dante swept a lane of sand ahead of them, hardening it into solid ground. The horses clattered along it, tripling their speed. Which meant the monstrosity was only gaining on them at a modest rate rather than an insane one.

"Should we even bother to try to kill it?" Dante said to Gladdic.

Gladdic glanced over his shoulder. "That would seem slightly more likely to succeed than attempting to reason with it."

They lobbed a barrage of ether and nether behind them, but

while all of their attacks managed to strike the leviathan, Dante couldn't tell if they'd even scratched it. They fell into darkness: its shadow had caught up to them. It had at last fully emerged from the ground and was moving forward with a serpentine wriggle, although the contraction of its armored segments against the ground seemed to be propelling it as well. The hiss of its passage chased after them like a rainstorm heavy enough to dissolve the world.

The vast shadow raced ahead of them. The worm was rearing upward, preparing to smash down across the ground. Its body toppled toward them like a tower. Dante swept the weariness from the horses, allowing them a renewed burst of speed, and sent his mind into the sands just behind him. The worm's head swung toward them, the motion appearing ponderously slow despite its great speed.

The size of it gave Dante vertigo. He shook off the sensation. As the worm neared impact, he shaped the sand into a cone, the base twenty feet wide, the tip a sharp point.

The worm landed on the spike of rock in the fuzzy boundary between its head and its body. Rather than penetrating its skin, the rock burst apart.

The leviathan struck the ground. Dante had his hands pressed over his ears but the boom of the impact was so loud he almost passed out. The road Dante had been building for them shattered; the horses seemed to drop for a second, then to float. Dante's guts followed a similar process. Their mounts fought to maintain their footing on the shifting ground. Just as they steadied themselves, a cloud of dust and sand enveloped them from behind, blocking out all sight.

Dante rode blind, praying the worm wasn't already launching a second attack. The dust thinned; as soon as he could see the ground, he laid a new road beneath them, letting the horses race forward.

During the confusion, Blays had gotten ahead of him. Blays turned around in the saddle, face covered in dust from brow to chin. "Get us off the ground!"

"Unfortunately, we appear to be stuck to it."

"Off ground *level*!"

The worm had fallen back a little to collect itself after its attack, but was now shooting forward again, its shadow edging closer and closer. Dante pulled nether to him from all sides and pumped it into the ground. A squat column of stone rose beneath them, lifting them into the sky. Dante expanded its edges, building the base of the plateau bigger and stronger while keeping the top smaller and more compact so he could lift it higher.

The worm drove into the base of the plateau, rattling it. The blow did nothing to rattle the worm, however, as it drew back and slammed into the rock again, bashing free a hunk of stone.

"This will not save us," Gladdic said.

Dante wiped grit from his eyes. "Do you think your naysaying will?"

"We cannot outrun it. Nor can we elevate ourselves to safety."

The beast struck again, crumbling another piece of the platform. "Not helping!"

"Sure it is," Blays said. "We just have to do something that isn't one of those two things that won't work."

"I'm open to suggestion!"

"Well, you could ride off that way as a decoy to die helplessly while Gladdic and I ride off to glory. Or you could do something to stop the mini-worms from sensing us."

Dante braced himself as the leviathan pounded into the plateau again. "Mini-worms? The ones around its mouth?"

"They're the ones that found us, right? So just do something to stop that."

Dante gazed down at the beast as it drew back for another attack. There were dozens of the smaller worms and even if he could begin to disable or destroy them he imagined the giant one could destroy his platform much faster.

Then again, he didn't have to *destroy* them.

The worm swung its head at the plateau like a flail. Just as it was about to make contact, Dante softened the rock, pulling it over the worm's head like a sack. The beast made impact, but it was barely enough to shake the pillar. It drew back its neck in confusion and Dante hardened the rock coating its head, encasing it in yellow sandstone. The worm shook its head violently, which didn't help at all.

Blays laughed. "Like a dog with its head stuck in a bucket."

"I'm sure I'll find it a lot funnier once we're not in danger of being crushed into bloody human-parchment."

Rather than building a ramp down to the ground, Dante dissolved the plateau beneath them, which had the added benefit of guaranteeing the leviathan couldn't bash its head against it to knock the stone loose. They hit the sand. Dante's command was growing weak, but he extended a thin road beneath them, galloping south at full speed. The worm continued to thrash and squirm, falling further behind.

Only when the haze of the horizons swallowed it up completely was Dante comfortable enough to stop laying down road and let the horses slow.

Blays sleeved the sweat and dust from his forehead. "Please tell me that thing is too big for the desert to hold more than one of."

"I will tell you whatever makes your ears feel nice." Gladdic motioned to the empty sand before them. "Yet there is no way to know what lies ahead until we cross it."

They hadn't spent two full days in the desert, but when it came to an end, the relief Dante felt was as if they'd been lost in it for a year.

By name, the Knifelands promised something far worse. And maybe it might have been worse if they'd been ordinary travelers: for the land could hardly be more treacherous if it had been designed to be, which maybe it had. It was similar to the maze-like blades of rock they'd had to cross through on their way into Carvahal's kingdom, except far worse. There were tunnels, too, and pits to nowhere, and sudden cliffs, and little blind canyons, and some parts of the rock were treacherously smooth while other parts were ankle-breakingly jagged and uneven.

It would have been impossible to navigate on horseback, and only slightly easier on foot. Except that Dante could clear a path wherever it got too bad, and Blays could pop into the shadows to scout the best route like he'd done on Mount Arna. And though there were disorienting curves that often looped back on themselves, Gladdic's ethereal compass kept them pointed south no matter how much the landscape tried to turn them about.

All told, a passage that should have taken them at least a day to get through—assuming they didn't have to make too many detours, or get lost for more than a few minutes—only hampered them for three hours. Then they emerged from the knobs, pillars, defiles, and arches, and looked down on a new desert almost as stark as Yula had been.

At first, Dante took it to be a dried-out sea bed: a crusty gray mass stretching as far as the eye could see. A little closer, however, and features emerged. Dead trees. *Very* dead trees. Most of them didn't have more than a few branches left, and most of these were draped with old spiderwebs, or equally dead moss, or just general condensed filth. Likely all three. The ground looked to be coated in debris, but that debris was coated in turn by the same dry gunk the branches were.

Blays sighed. "We have to go into that?"

"Urt's realm is supposed to be just south of the Knifelands,"

Dante said, checking his map to make sure that was right even though he was absolutely positive that it was.

"Well, Urt's realm looks disgusting. No wonder he's always hiding away. I'd hide too if I was this much of a slob."

They crossed the dusty, unremarkable ground that formed a no man's land between the Knifelands and the dead forest. Dante reached into the nether and the earth to search for potential threats, but felt nothing.

They entered the forest, if you could call it that. Much of what appeared to be solid ground was in fact a spongy, desiccated layer of branches and leaves so time-worn they crumbled to dust beneath the horses' steps. Most of the tree trunks were broken off four to fifteen feet up. Some looked as spongy as the ground, but some looked to have been turned to stone.

On the ground, other objects lurked within and beneath the filth. Bones. Corroded objects that might have once been metal but were now just masses of green and red and orange knobs, not unlike the fungus in the desert. It smelled of an unpleasant variety of dust.

If anything the unsteadiness of the ground was growing worse. They dismounted to lead the horses on foot. Blays frowned at a skeleton leaned against one of the old trunks, its head tipped back and its jaw wide open. It wore the shreds of a robe that, whatever its original color, was now the same dull yellow-gray as everything else.

The skeleton leaned forward, its jaws coming together with a bony click. It stared eyelessly at Blays, then attempted to take a step toward him.

"So it's this kind of forest, is it?" Blays drew one of his blades and cocked back his arm.

"Cease!" Gladdic yelled, but Blays had already begun to swing. Gladdic, however, seemed to have anticipated this, blasting Blays aside with a blunt club of ether.

Blays made an involuntary dive into the clutter, disappearing under a cloud of dust and snapped debris. He thrashed about, stirring more of it. "What are you protecting that thing for? Are you half skeleton on your father's side?"

"Behold!" Gladdic extended his left arm, pointing to a shred of robe hanging from the skeleton's chest. Just visible beneath the grime was the faded stitching of a cicada with its wings folded behind it.

The skeleton swiveled its skull toward Gladdic.

"Who are you?" Gladdic said.

The undead stared at him, perfectly motionless. "I...do not remember."

"It can *talk*?" Dante said.

"And you may not," Gladdic snapped at him from the corner of his mouth. The old man tipped back his chin at the skeleton. "Are you a servant of Urt?"

"Yes," the skeleton said after a moment of thought. Its voice was the dry rasp of large stones dragged across each other from a distant room. "Yes, I was, once."

"We have been sent to find him. And once we do, to compete for his part of the Spear of Stars."

"Somehow I know this. How?" The man, or anyway his remnants, was gaining strength before their eyes. He tilted his head, and almost seemed to be trying to wrinkle his bony brow. "Well? What are you looking at?"

"Urt wishes to see us. As his servant, you are bound to direct us to him."

"I wouldn't say that he *wants* to see you. But if you want to see him, he's right in there." The skeleton swept its arm toward the depths of the forest.

"I don't mean to insult your beautiful woods," Blays said. "But it doesn't look like there's anything in there."

"But there is a path to Urt."

Blays narrowed his eyes. "Are *you* Urt?"

The skeleton laughed dryly. "If I was Urt, I would look much better than this."

"Well, the way you guys are, I figured I'd better ask."

"How do we find our way to Urt?" Dante said.

The undead swung its eyeless sockets toward him. "What are you here to do?"

"Like we said. Earn the Spear of Stars."

"Why is Urt allowing you the chance to do this?"

Dante thought for a moment. "To see if the time has come for the cycle to turn over into a new era—or if the people alive now should be allowed to live on for a little longer."

The dead man nodded gravely. "Seek the cycle. Find your way back to Urt."

"What do you mean, *back* to Urt?"

"I've served my purpose. Go seek him within the Great Wood, or turn away and leave me be."

He insisted they leave their horses behind, stating that it wasn't the place for them. The situation felt a little fishy, but there didn't seem to be anything else they could do. So they dismounted, leaving the horses with the servant, and made their way into the dead forest.

The skeleton stood motionless, diminishing behind them. Dante motioned to Gladdic's floating compass. "That thing still working?"

Gladdic turned in a circle. The ethereal compass stayed fixed in the air. "Just so."

A short way into the forest, the dead trees grew a little higher while the rubble on the ground thinned enough to walk through it without too much trouble. They still had to choose their footing carefully, however, as patches of it weren't solid at all, and they often found it crumbling beneath them with a brittle crackle as they sank to the ankle or even to the knee before hitting hard dirt.

Blays tried to break off a long stick to probe the ground ahead of him, but the first time he tapped it against the ground it disintegrated in his hand.

He sighed and threw aside the remnants. "Any clue what we're looking for?"

"Nope," Dante said. "But given that so far we've only seen nothing, when we see something, I think we'll know it."

It was early afternoon, but even the sunlight had gone wan, its beams barely able to creep past the dead, limbless trunks. Except for the occasional breeze stirring the dry, papery debris, there was no sound at all. Dante and Gladdic kept one eye on the ether and nether to hunt for hidden doorways. Every now and then they stopped to inspect something that looked slightly less worn-down than the total dullness of the surroundings, but none of their searches turned up a thing.

After the better part of an hour of walking, Blays came to a stop, frowning hard. "Haven't we been here before?"

Dante kicked at some garbage, which collapsed into powder. "I think I would remember if we'd ever been to a dreadful, mummified forest before."

"Not the forest. Right *here*. This spot."

"How can you tell? Everything looks the same. By which I mean horrifically ugly."

"That tree there that's fallen and leaned up against the other one. I swear I saw it earlier."

"But we've been traveling south the whole time. Haven't we, Gladdic?"

Gladdic turned an eye on his softly glowing arrow. "That is what the compass claims. Our question is whether we are able to trust it."

"Uh, do we have reason to believe we can't?"

"Yes."

"Which is?"

"That the entirety of this Realm does not always adhere to its rules—or more likely, we do not understand its rules—and that this place in specific might be exempt from some portions of natural law."

"So it could be screwing with us." Dante exhaled through his nose, then brought some nether to him. "I'll make us a landmark. If we stumble over it again, we'll know the truth."

He sank the shadows into the earth and lifted a tall slab of dark stone, shaping it into a door-like rectangle that couldn't be mistaken for a natural form. This done, they resumed their walk.

And in another half hour, found themselves standing beneath the rectangular slab.

"Gods damn it!" Dante smacked his palm against the slab. "How is this happening?"

"Because a god wants it to happen?" Blays said.

"Someone should tell him that it's very unsporting to mess with mortals like this."

"We are missing something." Gladdic gazed into the silent, motionless woods. "Either there is a way off the path that has eluded our sight, or there is something on the path itself that eludes us."

"Well that really whittles it down."

"And your whining provides clearer answers? We will try the path for a third time, searching it more closely as we go. If this turns up nothing, then we will try again, seeking a way *off* the path."

The idea was decent enough, so they started off again, more slowly this time, allowing Dante and Gladdic to search more thoroughly through the shadows and the light. This was encouragingly easy to do, because despite the abundance of death in the area, it had been dead for so long that most of the nether had been sapped away, leaving just a thin sheen within the ruins.

They were still within sight of the tall slab when Dante drew to a halt. "I might have something."

He walked to his left, stepping carefully through the crackly ground. A knot of shadows hid at the base of a tree. It wasn't much, but compared to the gossamer-thin background of nether, it stood out like a poke in the eye. Dante crouched over the matted-together mess of dried leaves and twigs. He gestured some of the other nether to him, then tentatively pulled up the dusty, crumbly matter above the pocket of nether.

"A sprout?" Blays peered down at the little green growth Dante had uncovered. "Track down two hundred more of those, and you'll have yourself a salad."

Dante probed the shadows within it. "It could mean something."

"Like what? That plants exist? If that's what Urt wants us to prove, I'm beginning to question his qualifications for membership in the Celeset."

"If you wanted me to tell you who's the sanest of the gods, Urt might take thirteenth out of twelve. But we've been looking for something out of place. Does this look like it's supposed to be here?"

"So what now? Wait for it to grow into a tree?"

"I'm not going to wait."

Dante reeled more nether to him, applying it delicately to the sprout, which didn't seem to be in great shape. It began to droop, its tiny head of leaves bending toward the ground. But rather than pulling back from it in alarm, Dante sent more shadows into it, pushing through its frailty. Its pale brown stem straightened and grew upwards, expanding into a foot-high sapling.

The world darkened. He registered the change in smell before he processed the change in sight: leaves and trees and grass. The dead forest was gone—replaced by one dense with life.

24

Dante stood. Trees grew on all sides, gnarled and tall, trunks painted with lichen, branches drooping with moss. High above, the canopy blotted out the sunlight, leaving them in shadows.

"Uh," Dante said. "What did I just do?"

Blays tipped back his head, taking in the web-like moss. "Are we in Urt's realm?"

"An extremely haunted-looking forest is exactly where Urt would live."

"Good job, then. I think. Shall we go and find Urt?"

"These trees look like they're about to strangle us," Dante muttered.

He reached for the nether and found it was abundant. The forest floor was carpeted with damp, moldering leaves. After the dry rot of the so-called Great Wood, it smelled strangely nice.

After a few minutes of quiet, Gladdic motioned to the woods. "Do you notice that?"

"Notice what?" Dante said.

"Just so. There is nothing."

"You don't see anything? Apparently your age is catching up to your eyes."

"There is a forest, yes. But there is nothing *in* that forest. No birds nor animals. I have not even seen a lowly beetle or fly."

Dante was about to reject this as impossible until he realized that it seemed to be true. He stirred some of the mulch, which should have been full of worms and beetles and other things he normally wouldn't want crawling around on his boots, but not a single vermin squirmed away from the disturbance.

Blays rubbed the back of his neck. "Maybe Urt hates bugs."

"The guy whose symbol is a cicada hates bugs?"

"Maybe he made his symbol the thing he likes killing most."

"When we find him, you should present him with this theory."

"Oh? You think he'll like it?"

"I think he'll take pity on you for having been kicked in the head by a donkey as a small child and give you his spear then and there."

Dante still wasn't seeing any wildlife, but the woods did look very spooky, and he carried the nether with him as they moved forward. There hadn't been any buildings at all in the Great Wood. Here, however, Blays stumbled quite literally over what turned out to be the ruins of something that, judging by the toppled and broken statues nearby, had once been a palace or temple of some kind.

Urt seemed just as if not more likely to keep himself in a ruined old temple as in an intact and functional one, so they spent some time poking around the toppled stones and creeping vines. Drawing on their last lesson, Gladdic and Dante spent time searching the nether as well. But it seemed to be a simple ruin, one that had been abandoned a long time ago. Gladdic sifted ether about the site, but turned up no footprints or other signs of recent visitors.

Dante had the feeling they were missing something, but there was also the possibility they were wasting time picking through a lot of old rocks, and they continued to the south, following an unpaved road worn so deep into the ground that it still hadn't been reclaimed by the forest. The daylight was thinning and though the woods had offered no overt threats—or, indeed, no overt anything—Dante didn't like the idea of staying there overnight.

Which gave him the troubling realization that they had no idea how to get out of it.

"You're not going to believe this," Blays said. "But we've been here before."

Dante groaned. "Don't tell me you mean what I think you mean."

"Then we are *not* walking in circles and *not* wasting our time."

"Again?" Dante cast about them. "How can you tell? Everything looks the same."

"I had a feeling something like this might happen. So before we started off, I made this." Blays motioned to a pair of sturdy sticks he'd planted in the ground and leaned against each other to form an X. "As the old saying goes, X marks the spot that means the sinister devil-forest is still playing tricks on you."

"So what does this mean? That we're not in Urt's realm after all? That we still have more progress to make?"

Blays crouched over his sticks, working his jaw around as he contemplated the forest. "What if we haven't traveled to a different place? What if we traveled to a different *time*?"

Gladdic grunted in thought. "You believe this is the same forest we were in before. Yet from a previous time, before it died."

"You can imagine it, right? The trees are about the same size. Just less broken. And decayed. And fallen apart into powder."

"Okay," Dante said, "but how is that even remotely possible?"

Blays shrugged. "Because these people are gods?"

"It seems a lot more likely this whole thing is an illusion. Like what we saw on Mount Arna."

"*Were* those illusions?"

"Whatever they were, they weren't entirely real. But an illusion makes way more sense than having flown back through time."

"The exact nature of what we find ourselves within is most likely irrelevant," Gladdic said. "What matters is that, by finding our way from the last wood to this one, we made progress. We ought look to repeat it."

"How did we make progress before? By growing a tree? I'd say this place is already way ahead of us."

"In this observation lies the answer. It was not the act of growing a tree that brought us here. It was the act of *restoring what had been lost.*"

"Now we're getting somewhere not entirely crazy." Dante began to pace across the forest floor. "What had been lost in the first forest was...well, everything. So what's been lost here?"

"Life?" Blays said. "Animals and such?"

"I have no way to do anything about that. I can't harvest a feather into a bird or a piece of fur into a dog."

"Well, then I guess we're trapped and screwed and we should just lie down and die."

Dante crossed his arms, tapping his elbow. "You know, the only people who know how to harvest at all are the Plagued Islanders and myself. It's a little convenient that's the talent that was necessary to let us take the first step here."

"If this is a test," Gladdic said, "then surely it is tailored to the abilities of those who come here. For after all, the ramna come to see Urt as well, and the ramna do not possess many of the powers that we do."

"If the ramna are involved, maybe the answer isn't to restore something, but to destroy everything." Dante jerked up his head. "Hang on a second. If the idea is to put things back how they were, the obvious place to start is the temple."

He almost turned back around before remembering that continuing forward would get them there too, and was probably a little faster. They soon returned to the temple grounds.

"Well." Blays nodded at what was left of the temple, which was strewn across hundreds of feet of ground, and was so thoroughly disassembled by time that it was impossible to know if it had been one building or several. "Good luck with that."

Dante brushed his hands together. "I didn't have to regrow the entire forest to get us here. Just a single tree. There's no way we're expected to put together the entire temple."

"Keep telling yourself that."

With spiteful enthusiasm, Dante scratched his arm and gathered the shadows. In most cases he'd have no idea which blocks belonged where, but there was a stretch of wall near him that had only recently fallen, as evidenced by the fact it had only broken into a few large pieces rather than having crumbled into its individual stones. He was just about to melt it down into mud and shift it up onto the stump of wall it had fallen from when it occurred to him that doing so wouldn't be *restoring* the wall, per se, but recreating it from something new.

He said as much. "There's only one option, then. Blays, lift up the wall and stack it on the base so I can mortar the seams back together."

Blays eyed the large chunks of wall. "Bad news. By the time I fashion enough rope and pulleys to lift one of these off the ground, you're going to starve to death."

"Nonsense. I'll be able to harvest all the fruit I want while I wait."

Gladdic strode toward the mossy stonework. "You fear that, by reducing the fallen portion into liquid rock, whatever you then build with it will not be the old wall, but a new one."

"That's what I said," Dante said.

"Besides a team of slaves, I know of no means to raise that section of wall as it exists. Yet I may be able to use the ether to retain an image of its former shape, which you could use as a map to reconstruct it as closely as possible."

Dante tapped the side of his leg in thought, then nodded. "Let's do it. Even if we mess this one up, there's plenty more rubble to try something else with."

Gladdic spread the fingers of his left hand, dusting the fallen parts of the wall with ether. His face grew increasingly furrowed as he concentrated on constructing, or possibly extracting, the "ideal form" of the stonework from this time-worn shadow of it.

"I am ready," he announced.

Dante dissolved the rock into liquid form, sending it flowing up the stump of wall that was still standing. Gladdic projected the ethereal map of the various pieces into the air above the wall, jiggling them about until he'd aligned their edges, fitting them together like the bits of a puzzle. He then settled the image onto the foundation.

Dante molded the rock to match the ghostly projection as best he could. He didn't attain the exact level of detail he was hoping to achieve, but by the time he was done, it was a very close match to Gladdic's projection.

He pursed his lips, looking about the forest. "I can't help but notice we haven't been transported to a new land."

"You mean sent back in time," Blays said.

"Try once more," Gladdic said. "It is conceivable that more work must be done to achieve the effect of restoration."

Dante and Gladdic went through the process a second time. Blays wandered off at once, tramping about the grass and nudging broken things with his toe. They got a second section of wall back up and in position, but this didn't accomplish anything beyond the act itself. With flagging enthusiasm, they gave it a third try.

"How's it going?" Blays said, returning from his stroll. "Still failing?"

"If you're not too busy wandering around, you might consider helping us at some point."

"And you could consider doing something that might actually work. Look what I found." He turned away, leading the other two to a toppled statue. It was weather-worn, and parts of it were broken away, but there was no mistaking the features of a crow, eight feet in height. "Why not try this?"

Dante leaned over it. "Why this?"

"Because it's a statue of a giant crow. Even if it doesn't work, it'll make the place look a lot better than a boring hunk of wall."

This struck Dante as more of an aesthetic argument than a logical one, but it was true that they hadn't been getting anywhere with the wall. He and Gladdic repeated their efforts with the statue. In under a minute, they had it back upright and attached to its pedestal. It loomed over them, one eye missing, the tip of its beak broken off, along with a few of its toes and most of its left wing.

"You're right," Dante said. "It is pretty great."

Blays rubbed his chin. "Except it doesn't really look like it did when it was built, did it?"

They exchanged a look.

"Neither did the walls I made," Dante said. "They just looked like shoddy old ruins. Gladdic, can you use the ether to see how this was supposed to look?"

"That is doubtful," the old man replied. "It is likely far too old for the ether to remember its original shape. But I will try."

And try he did, but he was right. The ether showed nothing of how it had once looked.

"It was a good thought," Dante said. "But these are too far lost to properly restore them."

Blays gave him a scornful look. "The hell they are. Most of the bits that are missing are parts of pairs. Just copy the part that's still intact."

"And the parts that have nothing to copy? Like the beak?"

"You're an almighty sorcerer. In your doings, you've had to conjure up ways to destroy whole armies, bring people back from the dead, and look thousands of years into the past, but you can't figure out what a crow's beak ought to look like? Just use your imagination!"

Dante muttered some unkind things, then sent his mind into the statue. Over the years, most of his work with the earth had involved very crudely practical measures, like boring tunnels through things or dropping cliffs on people. His experience with finer applications of the skill was minimal. For this reason he started with the broken toes, which seemed easiest to duplicate. After a couple of false starts, he drew out one toe, then another, growing in confidence as he learned more subtle manipulations of the stone.

Next he smoothed out a few chips and gouges from the bird's body. With the easier portions squared away, he moved on to its missing wing. This was large, and there was a lot of feather-work to do, but he was starting to enjoy the process. Midway through shaping the feathers, each one quite similar to the last but also unique to itself, he found himself so drawn into the act of creating that he nearly forgot what he was doing it for.

With nothing to copy it from, he saved the beak for last. But by then he was so comfortable with the process that he didn't hesitate. He drew out a long triangle, the underside flat and the top half thick and curved like an exotic dagger. He stepped closer, examining his work. Something was missing. He smiled to himself and added a divot to either side of the top of the beak, providing its nostrils.

A crow squawked. Dante let out a strangled yelp—had he brought the statue to life? The bird called again. From up in the trees. There, a murder of crows clung to the branches, shuffling their wings. Butterflies bounced up and down on the air. A squirrel clung to a moss-free tree trunk, head oriented to the ground, tail lashing violently.

Around him, the temple stood tall and sturdy. Though there were a few cracks in the walls, this only made it more beautiful.

"Well done," Gladdic said.

"Except I still don't see any people," Blays said. "We're still not there yet, are we? How many times are we going to have to do this?"

Dante gestured to the frolicking animals. "Well, at least we're one step closer. But we're dealing with a god whose greatest desire is to never be seen. Our real worry should be if we get to where we're supposed to be but have no idea that it's the right spot."

"We do not yet know that we are not in the right place," Gladdic said. "The temple is restored. It may have brought its master with it."

Blays eyed him. "An optimistic Gladdic? All right, I no longer think we're just moving back in time. This has to be a whole other universe."

They strolled about the temple grounds, which were a little wild but in reasonable repair. This all but insisted that people were around to tend the grounds, but while there was animal and insect life all around them, they neither saw nor heard any sign of human life. Until they attempted to walk inside the open front of the main temple and bumbled right into a man between late middle age and early old age.

"Visitors?" He gawked at them, then at the swords on Dante and Blays' hips. "But how did you get here?"

Gladdic laughed softly. "Do you not remember? For it was you who sent us here."

Blays blinked at him. "Apparently this is the universe where you were born without a functioning sense of sanity."

"Observe his robes. His bearing and his build. This is the same man we met at the edge of the dead woods."

The man's robes were the rich purple of Urt, decorated here and there with obscure symbols. The garment was just starting to get worn at the hems, but Dante could imagine it falling apart bit by bit until it became what they had seen the skeleton wearing. The man looked to be about the right height, and there was a similarity to the movements of this fellow and the undead's that was made uncanny by the fact that the latter had just been a bunch of bones.

"Lords above, I think you're right," Blays said. "We *did* meet earlier. Or much later, because you were, ah, just a little older. I don't think we caught your name."

"Tarlic." The man peered at them with eyes of a striking amber color. "I don't seem to remember this meeting. You will have to forgive me, I'm even older than I look and my memory isn't what it was. But I hope I was still in good health."

"For your age when we met you, you were extremely lively."

"I am glad to hear it. Yes, very glad."

"We've been sent to find Urt," Dante said. "Is he here?"

"He once was. But he's gone now, just like everyone else."

"What happened to him? And to his people?"

Tarlic thought, then gave a quick shake of his head. "I would say it was the war."

"They were killed in the fighting?"

"Only some of them. But the war brought a plague, and that killed many others. The two priests couldn't stop it, so they traveled into the forest for medicine. There, they were slain by great cats. Then we sent messengers to the south to beg for aid, but the messengers never returned. The plague mainly claimed the young and once it was finished there weren't enough strong laborers left to work the crops. More died of hunger that winter."

He paused to remember, his amber eyes shifting back and forth. "The hard times eased after that. But only a handful of our people were able to have children in the years afterward. It seemed as though all spirit had left us; several died of no visible cause, but we knew it was despair. Others took to the woods to forage. They didn't return. Maybe they were caught by beasts or maybe they just walked away to find somewhere that wasn't so cursed. Eventually there were only three left: myself, and a man and wife...their names slip my mind. We were starving and I warned them not to eat too much of the dila shrub root but they did so and that is what killed them. I buried them beneath the shrub that was their undoing. It is just north of here.

"When I was the only one left, my lord came to me and asked me to stand watch over this site. Then he left, too. I don't recall how long ago this must have been."

"I'm sorry to hear all this," Dante said, more than a little awkwardly. "We're trying to find our way back to Urt's realm as it once was. To do that, we need to find something broken or lost and return it to the way it used to be. Can you help us?"

Tarlic shook his head in a jerky back and forth. "No...no, if I once knew of what might help you, I don't remember now."

They asked him a few more questions, getting nowhere. Once it was clear they were wasting their time, they thanked him and walked into the woods. There was much less moss and mold on the trees and far more flowers and seeds growing from them.

Blays glanced over his shoulder. "Nice of his god to leave him here all by himself for eternity."

"We're not even sure this is really real," Dante said. "Anyway, part of serving the gods means obeying their commands. Even when they're terrible."

"Would you say you're doing a great job of obeying the gods' commands right now?"

"I don't see Arawn telling me to go home and let the lich kill me."

"When the forest was dead, our duty was to restore the forest," Gladdic said, ignoring everything they'd just said. "When the temple was crumbled, our duty was to restore the temple. From what we have learned so far, it is this place's people that now must be restored."

"If you mean to repopulate this wood, I have bad news for you," Blays said. "All three of us are male."

Dante swatted at a fly; it had been nice to be without them for a while. "We might not have to literally bring them back. It's probably enough to perform a symbolic revival."

"How do you propose to do that?"

"Tarlic said the last two people here died from eating poison. Maybe we can unpoison them."

"This sounds like something that's really not going to work."

"Considering it's all Tarlic could talk about, I think it's worth trying."

They headed north from the temple. Not knowing what a dila shrub was or looked like, the search might have taken them hours, which would have been unfortunate, given that it would be less than two before the sun was down, but Dante knew a grave when he saw one, and quickly located one at the foot of a shrub with glossy green leaves that were nearly circular in shape.

He moved into the earth beneath the patchy grass. "There are bodies here."

Blays stepped back. "Try to keep the excitement out of your voice."

Dante sank the earth from within the grave. There was no coffin—not surprising, given that they hadn't even had enough food to not die from eating poisonous roots—and the bodies lay three feet down, a respectable depth given Tarlic's age. Rather than being bare bones, the two corpses were wrapped in grimy but intact clothes. They still had most of their skin, too, though it had stretched and dried, mouths hanging open, making the bodies look like they were horrified to have been unearthed.

Dante had smelled much worse, but he hadn't been expecting any odor at all, and breathed shallowly through his teeth as he sent the shadows into the bodies. The poison was easy enough to spot, distributed through what little was left of their organs and long-congealed blood. As he neutralized it, it occurred to him to wonder whether this would have worked at all if they'd been bare skeletons like he'd been expecting.

He did away with the last bits of poison, then looked around himself. "Did it work?"

"It didn't." Blays gazed down at the bodies. "You seriously can't go one week without desecrating a corpse, can you?"

"Gladdic, take a look and see if I missed anything."

Gladdic stood over the bodies, investigating them, then touched them with a few dabs of ether. "They have been purified. Yet I see no shift in our surroundings."

Dante was pretty sure it was hopeless, but he'd already disinterred them, so he tried a few more tricks before conceding they'd been wrong and covering them back up with earth.

Gladdic rubbed his stump with his left hand. "How long do you believe they have been dead?"

"A lot of factors go into a calculation like that. What the winters are like, how voracious the bugs are—"

"Do not be tedious."

"No more than five years," Dante said. "Probably just one or two."

"Yet Tarlic made it sound as though they had been dead for far longer. Why would he mislead us?"

"Hang on. Are you saying *he* poisoned them?"

"It could be that what we are meant to restore is justice."

Dante stared to the south. "If he killed them, I don't see why he'd tell us where to find them."

"Sure," Blays said. "Unless he had the crazy idea that the first thing we did with such news *wouldn't* be to run off and dig up their bodies."

"He just doesn't strike me as a killer."

"Unless he is truly a piece of the workings of Urt," Gladdic said. "Where the truth is so obscured you can stare right at it without realizing what you are seeing."

On the possibility they were hunting in the entirely wrong direction, they walked on through the woods, eyes open for anything out of place or in need of revival. They looked for signs of other people, too. For Tarlic's memory didn't seem entirely trustworthy, and even if it was, Urt might be using him for purposes unknown to him. They found a few wooden houses and stone fences in modest disrepair, but didn't see any other people.

They weren't following any particular trail, nor even traveling in a single consistent direction, but they found themselves back at the temple grounds anyway. The sun was about to set and its weak yellow light fought to poke through the gaps in the branches. Tarlic was seated on a mat outside the main building, using the last of the daylight to read a thick folio spread across his lap.

"You are back?" He looked up, not closing the book. "Did you find what you're searching for?"

"No such luck," Dante said. "What are you reading?"

"It is a history. A history of our people. It helps me to remember what was."

"Can I see it?"

The man shook his head, almost shivering. "It was left to me. I am its guardian."

Dante moved toward him, holding out his hand. "But with more detail about what happened to the people that used to live here, we might be able to find our way back to them."

Tarlic stood, clutching the book to his chest. "Don't you come any closer."

"I'm not trying to take it from you. I just want—"

"No! I'm not to let the history pass out of my hands!"

"All right, all right." Dante held up his hands for peace. "Sorry I asked."

Tarlic stood in the wan last light, whiskered mouth hanging open, blinking at sudden tears. "I am...forgive me. I was entrusted. I can't recall enough on my own. If the book was damaged, or if it was taken, there would be nothing left of my people at all."

"Well, have you read anything in it that might help us?"

Tarlic licked his lips. "No. No, there is nothing that comes to mind."

Dante thanked him neutrally. They departed the temple, did a bit more discouraged wandering about, then returned to one of the abandoned houses to shelter through the night. It wasn't quite cool enough to require a fire, but there was plenty of wood stacked behind the house and no one around to use it, so they lit one anyway.

Smoke poofed through the house; the chimney was blocked. Dante used the nether to knock apart the bird's nest that was stuck near the top. Once the air cleared, he pulled up a chair a few feet from the blaze.

Blays pulled off his boots and socks, wriggling his toes in the heat. "We're not *really* going to not steal Tarlic's book, are we?"

Dante gave him a hard look. "I'm insulted you even have to ask."

"You speak of this like you are about to pinch a loaf of bread," Gladdic said, clearly disgusted. "Yet you intend to take away an old man's last connection to his people. Ones who have otherwise faded from this earth."

"And?" Blays said. "We can just give it back when we're done."

"So long as we ensure that no harm comes to the book."

"What do you think we're planning to do with it, burn it for warmth? Even if we tripped while carrying it and it fell in a puddle of mud that then caught fire and incinerated it, Tarlic won't even remember it a week later. He'll bounce back in no time." Blays then did a pitch-perfect exaggeration of both the old man's voice and the shivering way he shook his head. "'I seem to recall being sad about something, but I...ah, my memory...ah, look at that pretty bird over there!'"

"We're just going to borrow it," Dante said. "No harm will come to it."

"Plus we've forgotten all about the fact he might be a double murderer. If so, taking his book away is a pretty mild punishment."

Gladdic looked up from the fire and directed an intense look at Blays. "Make sport of him again."

"'Hi, I'm Dante,'" Blays said without missing a beat. "'I think I know everything. Would you like to hear all about it? Because I'm going to tell you anyway.'"

"Not him, you fool. Tarlic."

"'I should like to comply,'" Blays said, pairing the voice with another shake of his head. "'But making fun of a lonely old man is making me start to feel rather mean of spirit.'"

Gladdic laughed grimly. "Very good."

"You're a bit sick, do you know that?"

"I do not laugh at Tarlic. I laugh at our own blindness. Tarlic's memory is not poor because he is old, or because he is trying to recall events that happened in a much-distant past. His memory falters because he is stricken with the grayness."

Dante snapped his fingers. "The way his head moves. It's not as erratic as the cases I've seen, but he doesn't seem as bad as them in general, either."

"It further explains why he believes the poisoned man and wife have been dead for an age when their bodies indicate it has been no more than a year or two."

"The grayness?" Blays said. "Please tell me that's a disease the two of you can cure."

Gladdic rubbed his chin with his thumb. "Only in its most early stages can it be wholly reversed. However, we may be able to undo some of the damage."

"To restore him," Dante said.

"Perhaps more importantly, to restore his memory of his lost people."

It was dark out, not normally the hour that one went barging in on venerable holy men, but they'd just been talking about stealing the fellow's most meaningful possession, so an unwanted visit seemed almost heroic in comparison. Crickets sang from the grass. The moon was already up, and full, though its light didn't feel quite as welcome since their experience in Silidus' grotto. The eyes of what Dante hoped were raccoons glinted from the trees.

Tarlic was no longer outside the temple. A bit of smoke was unfurling from one of the chimneys. They passed between the columns holding up the building's front. Moonlight spilled across the floor from clever skylights.

Though there were plenty of larger rooms in the depths of the temple, they found the holy man in humble quarters. He didn't have a single candle and was using the light of his fire to read a little more of his book.

He got to his feet. "I am in no mood for visitors. If you have something you need of me, please come back tomorrow morning."

"Tarlic," Dante said. "My friend and I are physicians. We're afraid you have a condition known as the grayness. Have you heard of it?"

"Are you calling me *diseased*? I've asked you to go. Who are you to violate Urt's home like this?"

"Urt is no longer here." Gladdic loomed over the shorter man. "But we are."

"I have asked you to leave." Tarlic's eyes darted over his surroundings as if he might be searching for something to strike them with. "Get out. Get *out!*"

Dante glanced at Blays. Blays nodded and advanced on the older man. "Pardon me, sir. Would you hold this for a moment?"

With a deft swoop, he stepped behind Tarlic and snaked their arms together. Tarlic found himself ensnared. He wiggled and thrashed, but couldn't buy himself a half an inch of slack.

"Get your hands off of me! I have done nothing!" Tarlic's eyes brightened with tears. "You are attacking a servant of Urt!"

Dante ignored his pleas and drew on the shadows. Beside him, Gladdic did the same. They entered Tarlic's brain.

"It is there," Gladdic said.

"I see it." Dante sent a little more nether into the brain's wrinkles. The spots were very small, little bigger than pinpricks, a darker shade than the pink-gray matter around them. "The ether might be better at this."

"You do not trust yourself to treat it?"

"I'm saying the ether might be better at this."

Gladdic smiled. "Then we will see if your premise is correct."

Dante watched as Gladdic brought the light into Tarlic's brain and settled it over the pinpricks of darkness. This was chancy business. Despite being an organ whose importance might rival that of the heart—there was much argument among physicians on this point—and despite further being immensely rich in blood, the brain wasn't particularly dense in nether, making it difficult to navigate, as its folds and divisions made it the most complicated organ by far.

Gladdic's expression was so blank he might have been staring out to sea. In that moment, Dante was certain that even if Gladdic were to rupture Tarlic's brain, rendering him a moron, or even incapable of speaking and walking, Gladdic would feel no more than a momentary flash of guilt, which he would then discard as easily as the rind of an orange.

Then again, perhaps it was that very removal from human concerns that allowed Gladdic to go from one dark spot to the next and erase each one, leaving no sign of damage behind him.

Tarlic had been caught in Blays' hold this whole time, struggling his upper body while kicking and stomping at Blays with his legs. Now he went limp, sagging in Blays' arms.

"Are you guys done?" Blays said. "Or is he thinking he can fool me with the oldest trick in the book?"

"I am finished," Gladdic said. "But I do not know if my efforts succeeded."

Blays lowered the servant of Urt to the ground. The nether inside him was still circulating, so he wasn't dead. Although if Gladdic had just broken his brain, it might be easier if he *was* dead.

"Tarlic?" Blays said. "Tarlic, are you all right?"

The man's breathing was shallow, herky-jerky. Dante sent his mind into Tarlic's lungs and heart but saw no sign of what was causing his distress. With a shudder, he stopped breathing.

"Gladdic!" Dante sent the shadows into the man's brain.

Gladdic shook his head. "I see nothing."

"Me neither. But if we don't—"

Tarlic's amber eyes fell open. A film lay over them. The same film that Dante had seen on the eyes of countless dead, people and animals alike.

Then he blinked. The film slid away from his eyes—and all signs of age slid away from his face.

25

Tarlic inhaled with a jolt, flailing around in confusion. In physical appearance, he now looked to be in his early twenties. Knowing the way people aged in the Realm, he was probably centuries younger than he'd been a minute before.

He sat up, laughing apprehensively. "I'm sorry, I appear to've fallen down."

Blays extended his hand and hoisted Tarlic to his feet. "You all right there? How's your memory?"

"Oh my, did I hit my head when I fell?" Tarlic groped his scalp for a wound, inspecting his hand for blood. "I'm afraid I don't remember you at all."

"Don't worry, you're not *supposed* to be able to remember us. We're visitors. From a very, very long ways away. We've come to meet Urt. Can you bring us to him?"

"Oh, no."

"He asked us here. We're on a sort of quest for him."

"Even so, I don't have the authority for this. I'm just an apprentice! Please stay here while I fetch my master."

He asked for their names, then exited into the hall. They were in the same room as before—the quarters of a simple apprentice, ones that Tarlic had returned to as his memory had weakened—but it was now the middle of the morning, with lush daylight flooding in through the open shutters. Outside, a man and a woman spoke in low tones, then erupted in simultaneous laughter. An axe thocked methodically. Wheels creaked and a donkey brayed.

"Suppose we've done it?" Blays said.

"Unless we've overshot it." Dante leaned closer to the window. "Or unless we've been on the completely wrong track this entire time."

"Is that possible?"

"Laying a false trail for us to get lost down is among the most Urt-like things I can think of."

"If that's what's going on here, he's going to find a special deposit on this altar tomorrow morning."

It was a few minutes before the door reopened. Tarlic wasn't there; instead, he'd been replaced by a man with a clean-shaven head and a brick of a jaw. He was shirtless and shoeless, dressed in loose purple pants held fast by a drawstring. He looked the three of them up and down.

Dante introduced themselves, but the man gave no sign of hearing. Instead he folded his arms, giving every sign of being displeased with what was before him, then nodded and stepped out from the room. Dante wasn't sure if they were meant to follow, but thought it better to deprive the man of the option of leaving them behind, and stepped along behind him.

The man took them outside through various lawns and gardens, glancing back just once as they entered the forest, which was now as vibrant as any Dante had ever seen. Yet it felt familiar, too, like he might close his eyes and still be able to find his way along without any fear of tripping.

Then came something entirely new: a row of tall trees with trunks as straight as columns, spaced almost but not quite regularly enough to be mistaken for columns. The area beyond was quite dark, but despite the lack of sunlight to feed it, the ground was covered in a blueish turf. The shirtless man stopped a short ways into the grass, tucked his right hand behind his waist, and swept his left arm forward. Dante walked past him.

Once he'd reached the center of the space, he turned around to see if he was supposed to keep going. But the shirtless man was gone.

"Hello?" Dante called. "Helpful friend whose name I didn't catch?"

Blays craned his neck at the treetops. "This feels like the sort of place you'd be brought to be fed to a giant spider."

Dante didn't *really* think that was true, but on the pretext of making sure they weren't about to be ambushed by any more moon-demons or the like, he summoned the nether to him.

Gladdic grunted. Motion drew Dante's eye like a siren: long, spindly limbs unfolding behind one of the trees, much longer than a man's arm.

Blays reached for his sword. "Sometimes I hate being right all the time."

Dante shaped the shadows into the type of thing that would be well-suited for puncturing a hideously large exoskeleton. Yet the figure that detached from the tree wasn't scuttling over the turf on eight legs, but strolling forward on two: and rather than the bulbous abdomen of a spider, its body was much closer in dimension to that of a stick bug.

"Hello?" Blays said. "Should we be attacking you?"

The figure said nothing. It looked humanoid, if inhumanly tall and narrow, but its head protruded something like a flattened mushroom cap. It took Dante's eyes a moment to register this as a piece of clothing. Finally, the pieces fit together: it *was* a man, just a very tall and very thin one, the features of his face shadowed by the wide, circular brim of his hat.

He made no sound as he moved through the blue grass. He stopped across from the three outsiders, a stray bit of light catching his eyes as he examined them. "How long has it been since I saw Fallen Landers in the flesh?"

Blays let his hand drop from his hilt. "An age?"

"Good guess. Or was it a guess?"

"Are you Urt's viceroy?" Dante said. "Or one of his angels?"

The man lowered his head in thought, tilting his wide hat down over his face. "That's a question I have never had to ask myself. If I answered it too deeply, I might disturb myself."

"He *is* Urt." Gladdic lowered himself to his knee and bowed his head.

"Why do you do that?"

"Why do I honor a god? For that is what you made us to do. You honor us the more deeply by appearing before us as yourself."

"What if I was seeing whether you understood that?"

"Then you must not have much faith in the people you created."

"Would you?"

Gladdic smiled, disarmed. "Perhaps not. For at risk of blasphemy, from what I have witnessed, neither serves the other as well as we might deserve."

"Unless this was as it was meant to be."

Gladdic nodded, then planted his hand on his thigh and pushed himself to his feet. Dante and Blays stood as well.

Urt folded his hands behind his back. "Was your journey here a pleasant one?"

"I think we went the entire time without anything trying to kill us," Blays said, then frowned. "Well, except for the biggest thing that's ever tried to kill us."

"Was the path enlightening?"

Dante hooked a thumb into his belt. "What were we supposed to take from it?"

"What *did* you take from it?"

"I was trying so hard to work out each step of it that I haven't had time to look at the picture as a whole. Uh. We were working our way backwards, and at each step, we were restoring—reviving, even—something that had been lost."

Urt was silent a moment. "That description is tightly accurate."

"Thank you. On its own, I'm not sure I'd put any particular meaning into that process. But we understand that the reason you were willing to test us is to see whether it's time for the lich to usher our world into a new cycle—or if we should be allowed to fight for the chance for the current age to live on."

"You talk like your test is over."

"Is it?"

"Is a test ever over?"

Dante grappled for answers. "If you test your archers for skill, the test itself has a definite end. But I suppose there's a sense in which they're *always* being tested. Until the day comes when they finally fail, and are dismissed from their duties." He looked to Urt for signs of approval or disapproval, but the god gave none. "As for this one, I have no idea. It's your test."

"Hmm."

Dante waited until it was clear Urt wasn't going to say more. "Anyway, combining what we went through with what we knew already, it seems like we just played out the stages of a cycle—but one that didn't end with rebirth or renewal. Which means it *wasn't* a cycle. Just the end."

"That's logical, yes."

"There was no renewal at any stage, was there? That's why the forest died: there weren't any birds left to carry seeds around, or worms and beetles to ingest the dead matter and clear space for new life. But why did all *those* things die? Did it have to do with your people dying out? Or with something they did to the place before they passed on?"

Dante took a few steps around the grass, thinking this

through. "Restoring a tree restored the trees to the forest. Restoring a statue in the temple restored the animals to the forest. Therefore, through some unknown mechanism, the lives of the forest's creatures must have been connected to the temple. When it crumbled, the creatures died with it. Am I on the right track?"

Urt nodded. "That's good deduction."

"Lastly, restoring Tarlic's memory of the people that used to live here restored them. Which isn't to say that their continued existence relied on his being aware of them or something. We already know they died of various ill causes. Anyway, I haven't worked out every angle of it. But if what we went through wasn't a cycle, but a straight line—one with a definite end—what are we supposed to take from that? That we should *want* cycles to happen? Because the alternative is for everything to slowly die off and wither away. But isn't that already the entire premise our world is based on?"

Urt's face was so shadowed Dante could barely make out his frown. "Entire premise?"

"Unlike the people you created here, over in the Fallen Land, we were created to live, age, and die. To avoid issues like the ones your peers are always having with the ramna."

"That is why the others made it, yes."

"But that's not why you helped make it?"

Urt waved a hand. His fingers were long and bony, almost more like little branches than flesh. "So you are here to win the Spear of Stars and stop the entity you know as the Eiden Rane from destroying your people and lands. Do you think you've earned my part of the spear?"

"Can I answer 'yes'?"

"Why do you deserve the spear at all?"

"Because I don't think we deserve to die."

"Don't you? If the lich has the power to destroy you, doesn't that mean he deserves to be able to?"

"I would very much like to think not."

"Why?"

"Because I hold a deeply-held conviction against being destroyed."

Urt clasped his long fingers in front of his waist. "But it stands to reason that if you're here, then nothing and no one in your world has the power to hold off the Eiden Rane. He's eclipsed you. This is no more than the end of one era and the beginning of another. Such things happen."

"But that's the whole point. With the spear, we *can* stand against him."

"So you deserve the spear because without the spear you're too weak?"

Dante attempted to keep his frustration from appearing on his face. "If your main concern is the natural progression of cycles, then you need to know that the White Lich's will be the last one the Fallen Land sees. Either his grim utopia will work out like he plans, in which case it'll go on forever, or it will collapse —but I guarantee you that if that happens, he'll just murder all the new people he created for being failures. They'll be powerless to stop him. Our world will wind up looking like your forest after Tarlic left it. No people. No creation. No renewal. Just ruins and silence."

"How can you be so sure of this? Either of those futures is too far in the future to see."

"I know it's true because when we were fighting him in his homeland, he took me under his thrall. Made me one of his undead. That's when he showed me what the future will bring."

Urt made a quick, dismissive gesture. "Wouldn't he have shown you the future he wanted you to see? The one he wanted you to believe?"

"Even if he did, I just told you what he'll do if his plan to build a new order falls apart. He'd rather have a world where no one's left alive at all than one where the people he's created don't worship him—or worse yet, one where they try to rebel against him. I'm certain this is true. I saw his mind."

"Yes, I see." Urt reached above himself, his arms seeming to stretch further than should be possible. He grabbed a branch and pulled himself up to sit on it, legs dangling, shadowed face hidden even further by the leaves. "Even so, if that's your fate, then that's your fate. What of it? We can just let your world pass and build a new one. If we even decide it's important to do that much, and I'm not sure that we would. After all, if it turns out the inevitable outcome of a world without us gods overseeing it is to collapse into ruin, why bother making more?"

"But you *made* us. You're responsible for us."

Dante couldn't make out Urt's face, but he could somehow tell that the god had cocked his eyebrow. "All of the people *we* made died an extremely long time ago. Hundreds of generations have come and gone since then. It seems that responsibility over your existence passed into your own hands long ago."

Dante shook his head, searching for an answer.

"You know," Blays said, "for the lord of the obscure and the sublime, you sure do like reason."

Urt shrugged.

"No," Gladdic said slowly. "No, it is *we* who love reason."

Gladdic stared up into the tree, but Urt said nothing.

Dante folded his arms. "So what? Reason is how you figure things out. That's why it's called 'reason.'"

"He is not expressing his true beliefs. He is only mirroring the process that has guided our thoughts. This process has been nothing but cold reason."

"Are you making the rational argument that we need to be irrational?"

"I am arguing that we deserve the spear because of the very fact we are here."

Urt ducked his head for a better look at Gladdic. "What does that mean?"

"Deny that we deserve it!"

"Fine: I deny it."

Gladdic laughed scornfully. "We have thrown the Realm of Nine Kings into chaos. In so doing, we have broken the rule of Taim so mightily that he will soon yield his own ninth of the spear to us. Who are you to deny us your part?"

"I am Urt."

"You hide away from the world, placing yourself above its miserable politics and machinations. If you try that now, do you not see that we will pull you down from your perch just as we will soon do to Taim?"

Urt narrowed his eyes. "Are you saying I should kill you right now?"

"Yes. For if you mean to deny us, then we will make it our mission to bring you to sorrow."

"I will tell you that I find this conversation more interesting than the one we were having before it."

"Do you know the battles we have fought in struggle against the lich? The miles we have traveled—the very planes we have crossed—to stand here now?"

"Yes."

"Do you not see in this the pure reflection of the spark of the divine you seeded within us upon our creation?"

"And what is the Eiden Rane?"

"Disorder. One that would murder Order and wear its skin as a cloak."

"Doesn't he promise the ultimate order?"

"You would name a world of perfect slavery as 'order'?"

"I don't think that I would."

Gladdic had begun to stride across the blue turf, gesturing broadly with his left arm. At first Dante took it for an act, but in the face of Gladdic's mounting vigor, he was growing increasingly unsure.

"Aren't you glad we brought him back?" Blays said from the corner of his mouth.

Dante shot him a look, but Gladdic was too busy reaching for the next arrow in his verbal quiver to have heard.

"That tree you now sit in—" Gladdic swept his hand in an oval to indicate it. "If I were to cut it down, and then cut it into kindling and logs, and arrange these according to their size and use, would that be order? Yes: but of a kind that kills the tree. One that is *inferior to the order of the tree itself*. The order that emerges of its nature from a tiny seed into this stout trunk, these broad branches, these pretty leaves. A thing that anyone can look at and say, 'That is a tree.'"

"A little further," Urt said.

"Must it be so spelled out? The arrangement of peoples and lands that has grown across the Fallen Land sprung from many small seeds to form the natural order of not just a single tree, but an entire forest. It had no one architect nor designer. Yet the arrangement sought by the White Lich is one that cuts this forest down, sorts it into its neat piles, and congratulates itself for having reduced the forest into stacks so orderly they can never grow again."

Urt nodded slowly, the brim of his wide hat falling and rising. "Consider this point made."

"Then what point is left?"

Urt said nothing.

"Goodness, Gladdic," Blays said. "Has anyone ever told you that you ought to have been a priest?"

Urt beckoned at Blays. "Who are you?"

"Me? No one of consequence."

"I feel that isn't true."

"Who'd know better? Me? Or some god?"

"You cause things that maybe weren't meant to happen, don't you? Of course, in a sense this is true of everyone. But where most people cause ripples, you cause landslides."

"I'm just a fellow who'd like the world to stop ending so I can go home to my wife. Then maybe I'll sire a few kids I can bore with my war stories."

"No, there is more to it than that. Or else you wouldn't be here."

Blays shrugged. "Maybe I just like smiting bastards."

Still perched on the branch, Urt swung his legs like a child, albeit a very oddly proportioned one. "Yes, that feels true to me."

"Good. Now what sort of person are *you*? Or does nobody get to know that?"

"The more people know about you, the more they tend to treat you in ways meant to get something from you, or that will not trouble or offend you. I'm not very interested in that."

"Sounds kind of lonely, though."

Beneath his hat, Urt's teeth flashed—he was grinning. "I gather that you speak this freely to everyone. I'm surprised one of my peers hasn't killed you yet. You're wrong, though. It isn't lonely at all. If it was, I think I would have died a very long time ago."

"Well that's good. I'd like to think the people that can destroy us with a snap of their fingers aren't sad and angry all the time."

"Don't be mistaken, we have the same emotions you do. Plus a few more that we thought wouldn't really work for you. But I don't get lonely any more than anyone else does. How could I when I hear the voice of every person who prays to me?"

"You do?" Dante said. "Do all of you?"

"I don't know that it is good for your kind to know too much about us. That's a good reason to get you out of here as fast as possible, isn't it?"

"But why create us in the first place if we're not supposed to know you?"

"Quiet." Urt swept his arm downward, sleeve flapping. Light flared from in front of them, coalescing into a long, narrow triangle of moiling ether: a second part of the shaft of the spear. "For now, this is yours."

Dante looked up from the glowing shard. "Are you giving us this just to get rid of us?"

"I rarely do things for pragmatic reasons. That is boring."

"Then why?"

"I'm not going to tell you why." Up in the tree, Urt was harder to see than ever. "Take it. Take my blessing, too. I think that you will need it."

Blays moved to add the part of the shaft to the other pieces he was carrying.

Dante bowed his head. "Thank you, Lord Urt."

"I don't think that we'll see each other again," the god said. "But this has been interesting. I hope that you continue to be interesting."

Before Dante could reply, he was cut short by a startling whirr, one like the call of a hundred thousand cicadas. He flinched, blinking. When he opened his eyes, the forest had vanished.

Instead, up a short slope, the Knifelands carved at the sky. Urt was gone, and so was his realm.

26

They were back where they'd first entered the realm. Yet not everything was the same.

Most notably, the dead forest was no longer there. Neither was all of the debris that had been disintegrating within it. Instead, it had been replaced by a meadow, although quite a few saplings were springing up from nowhere, threatening to overtake the grass.

"My strange friends," croaked a man's voice.

A figure stood twenty feet away from them between a pair of waist-high saplings. The man was so old and bent it took Dante a moment to recognize him. "Tarlic?"

"That is so," Tarlic said. "I remember you now—and the things that you've done for me. Thank you for that."

"It wasn't entirely selfless." Dante inspected him. "Has something happened to you? I didn't know the people here could grow so old."

"It isn't typical. You see, I am to be replaced."

"Replaced?" Blays said. "I'm sorry to hear that."

Tarlic laughed hoarsely. "Don't be sorry! You can't be sad for me when I'm not sad for myself. A new spring is beginning. It needs someone younger to look after it."

"A new spring? You mean Urt's decided to start this place anew?"

"Just so. Now I believe you'll be wanting your horses. They're right over here."

He led them down a dip in the land. At the bottom, their horses were happily cropping grass, looking well-rested, a state of being they unfortunately weren't likely to see again for at least several days.

They mounted up, said their goodbyes to Tarlic, and rode up the acclivity to the Knifelands. Once they'd gained some elevation, Dante glanced back, curious if Urt or his people had built any new temples or the like, but the only things he saw were more grass and saplings.

"So Urt's starting a new cycle for himself?" Blays said. "That can't be coincidence, right?"

"What do you mean?" Dante said.

"As you might recall, this place was dead before. At least in this time. Or place. Or whatever the difference is between here and the other places we just saw and now my head is starting to hurt. Who knows how long it's been that way. And he only now decides to bring it back? Did we convince him to do that?"

"That is the only rational conclusion," Gladdic said. "Yet if you expect any of us to be able to understand *why* he was convinced, you will be left wanting."

They entered the Knifelands, following the trail they'd carved through it on the way to Urt's realm, at least when they could find that trail. When they couldn't, Dante smoothed a new one through the jagged labyrinth of rock. They quickly arrived at the desert, its yellow dunes stretching across the horizon.

Going further that day would require them to make camp in the desert overnight, which they mutually decided was a horrible idea. Instead, they settled into a cave at the fringe of the Knifelands, alternating between discussing Urt, deciding where they were going next (Denhild), and sleeping.

As soon as morning's first light turned the sands a ghostly

blue, they started off, traveling as fast as the horses could sustain. It was still so dark they were no more than silhouettes, but as soon as the sun itself broke from the east, they were starkly exposed against the naked dunes.

Dante kept his knife in hand so he'd be ready to draw his blood at the first hint of the return of the worm. Every shriek of a hawk made him jump. He kept his teeth clenched to stop himself from biting his tongue when he startled. After several hours of riding, what was left of the plateau he'd raised shimmered in the distance. Huge chunks of curved rock lay broken at its base. If a giant came by and fit them back together, they might have resembled the shell of a massive, round egg.

Blays gave him a look. "Couldn't you have made that thing too thick to escape from?"

"I could have tried. But the effort would have hit a snag when it took too long and I was bitten in half."

"You two may continue your argument as you please," Gladdic said. "I am getting the hell out of here."

Dante kept his head on a swivel for any shift in the sands. The wind picked up, sending the grains hissing across each other. The afternoon sun fell past the halfway mark between noon and sunset. They still hadn't seen any hint of the worm, but Dante had no idea how much desert remained, either. After some dithering about whether it would be safer to just ride through the night—and if the horses would be capable of doing so—he nicked his arm and paved the sand ahead of them into a thin strip of road, enabling the horses to travel much faster.

But the sun seemed committed to outspeeding them. Soon their shadows stretched long across the desert. The sun touched the horizon, a dull red blob, and fell away. The wind arrived to take its place. With twilight at hand, insects and reptiles squiggled from their burrows. In the very last of the daylight before they had to use ether to guide the way forward, they came to the black swath of the river that marked the desert's end.

Come morning, they forded the river and rode north for Denhild.

Hours later, Blays visored his eyes against the sunlight. "Is that a rider?"

Dante squinted. "Either that or a centaur."

"But I see a horse head and a human head. Definitely a rider."

"Maybe it's a mutant centaur."

"It appears," Gladdic said, "to be a ramna."

Blays glanced at him. "You're about nine hundred years old. How are your eyes better than mine?"

"You have been warned of the consequences of your habits."

The figure had caught sight of them and was now riding toward them. The spear he carried and the heavy furs he wore marked him as one of the barbarians.

"Suppose he's friendly?" Dante said.

Blays loosened his sword in its sheath. "Are any of them?"

No reinforcements appeared from the hills, but with typical ramna heedlessness, the rider came forward undaunted until he stood close enough that they'd barely need to raise their voices to speak, which was more than close enough for him to be obliterated by the nether.

"You are the outlanders." His skin was quite tan and while many ramna wore their hair long, his black hair was trimmed nearly to the scalp. "Did you succeed in what you were sent to do?"

Blays leaned forward in the saddle. "Would it be uncouth to ask why that's any of your business?"

"Did you succeed?"

"Yes," Gladdic said.

"Then come with me."

Dante sat a little higher. "Mind telling us where we're going?"

"To the foul city of Denhild."

"What if we were already headed there?"

"That was assumed. But you will not make it without me."

The rider turned and headed north without them. After a brief discussion, the three of them caught up to him. He was among the least talkative people Dante had ever met, but after much querying, they were able to pry two basic facts from him: first, that his name was Kavan. And second, that following the sack of Protus, the ramna bands had undergone a strange transformation, neither breaking up nor dispersing, but instead taking to the roads connecting the various kingdoms of the gods, looting every caravan and killing every soldier in sight, ripping up the roads themselves and toppling every outpost the gods had managed to maintain, a jeering orgy of destruction. Nobody —least of all the ramna themselves—could tell whether they were gearing up to go home, or to mount a new siege on another kingdom.

What it all added up to was the least safe conditions for travel in living memory. So while they didn't entirely trust Kavan, or even understand who had sent him to guide them, they went with him anyway.

His horse was almost as fleet as their own and while the first day was quiet the second brought them to the fringes of the ramna-occupied land. Bands rode leisurely through the forests and prairies, searching for any messengers, scouts, or military expeditions hapless enough to have been sent out into the madness. Kavan avoided most bands, hiding out in little vales or slipping away along stream beds, but now and then he recognized a group he was friendly with and negotiated passage.

The closer they came to Denhild, the greater the sense of dread grew in Dante's stomach, the sureness that something would lurch out to smash them before they could deliver the proof of having bested Urt's challenge that would earn them the other pieces of the spear, leaving Taim's as the last to be collected. Yet they hadn't so much as gotten into a skirmish with the ever-present ramna by the time they approached the realm of Gashen.

The god of war had maintained a few towers and forts outside the city itself. These were now smashed to their foundations. The soldiers who'd died in their defense had been heaped up and burned in a pyre, while a single large burial mound covered the bodies of the ramna, suggesting it was the barbarians who'd taken care of the dead—and suggesting further that Gashen was now entirely turtled up in his city.

The giant walls were still in good repair, however, though a team of men was lugging in stones and mortar to refill a section that had suffered the application of enemy sorcery. As they rode to the gates, Kavan wheeled about and galloped away into the wilderness without so much as a goodbye.

All of the gates were closed despite it being the middle of the day. But this time, the sentries were waiting for their arrival, and let them right through. The interior was amok with workers digging ditches, raising ramparts, and moving logs and stones around. Soldiers drilled more seriously and vigorously than during their first visit, though they seemed almost joyous about the strenuousness of it, as if being called to their purpose had elevated their souls.

They headed for the great wooden hall and were met halfway there by a very eager General Lars.

"We won Urt's part," Dante said, reading the question on his face. "Although someone might have thought to warn us about the giant sand worm. And the—"

Lars held up his hand. "Save your words. I will hear them at the same time you speak them to Lord Gashen." He brought them toward the hall, calling for pages to relieve them of their horses. "Did you meet your guide?"

"Who, Kavan?" Blays said. "Ramna fellow who acted like he'd taken three different vows of silence? How'd you get one of them to agree to help you in the first place?"

"Because we are ransoming his father," Lars laughed. "With the troubles in the wilds, we thought you might use help avoiding unnecessary adventure."

They ascended the hill to the great hall. The soldiers manning the entry saluted General Lars and pulled open the doors. Dante and the others soon found themselves back in the dark, seemingly unwalled space where they'd first met Gashen.

Blays picked up one foot, giving a disgusted look at the hard-packed sand on the ground. "After Yula, I was really hoping to never have to step on this stuff again."

The stout and towering figure of Gashen stepped forth from nowhere, arms crossed over the barrel of his chest. "Did you find Urt?"

"We did," Dante said. "And we won his spear."

They related the story, though Dante tried to stick to the facts and spend little time speculating about, say, what the precise meaning of their passage through the forest might have been. Gashen did a lot of chuckling once they got to the parts involving Urt himself.

"I do not get to speak with Urt often," Gashen said once they were through. "But every time I do, I either laugh more than I have ever laughed, or wind up wanting to punch his head in."

"What is he even about?" Blays said. "You've got your wars and such, Phannon rules over the waters, Arawn likes it when you die. But what's Urt's domain? That of doing nothing to help you when you can't figure something out on your own?"

"I'm not sure that I fully know. If I did fully know, I am almost sure that I wouldn't tell you. I have come to believe his realm is that of deep judgments. Ones made from places none of us can fully understand because we are not looking as deeply as he does. And none of us *can* look that deeply without *living* as he does."

"Alone, half insanely, and disappearing altogether for years on end?"

"That is only the half of it."

"We did what we were tasked with," Dante said after a brief pause. "Will the other gods give us their parts now?"

Gashen smiled knowingly. "I will see what I can do."

He stepped back, vanishing. They stood around in semi-awkward silence, unable to speculate or gossip about whether the other lords would actually do as they said with Lars right there, to say nothing of the fact Gashen could almost certainly hear everything they'd say as well.

The lord of war returned within a few snaps of his fingers. He bore three glowing objects. The last third of the haft. The last third of the blade. And a golden wrist cord.

Dante and Blays gawked at each other. Even Gladdic lifted an eyebrow.

"But how did you get them so fast?" Dante blurted, knowing it was probably a stupid question to ask of a god.

Gashen smiled avuncularly. "There was no need to wait for your return to gather them. That would only have delayed us for no good reason. The others trusted that if they were to leave them to me I would not gift them to you unless you had earned them."

Blays kneeled, untying and unrolling the tarp he carried the others in. He tried to fit the pieces of the haft together, but they didn't stick tight any more than three pieces of cut wood would. Still, Dante could see now exactly how the Spear of Stars would look when it was assembled, and the sight of the eight pieces gathered in Blays' grasp made his spirits soar.

"Then all that's left is the purestone," Dante said. "The gem that binds the spear's parts into a single piece."

Gladdic nodded. "Naturally that would be the portion that Taim keeps guardianship of for himself."

"Lord Gashen, do you still think you can get him to turn it over?"

"I do," Gashen said. "I will speak with him tomorrow to tell him that the contest is over."

"What if he still refuses?"

"He might do that. The crisis of the White Lich offered him the opportunity to deal with the degradation of the Mists, a problem that has vexed him for a great long time. Will he be pleased to give up his solution to this problem? About as pleased as I was to lose my axe!" Gashen got a good laugh out of this. "But look upon his position as if you were a general intent on sieging him. Most of his allies have abandoned him. The few that remain teeter on the verge of ruin.

"By contrast, you stand on the brink of victory, despite all opposition, and continued success makes that victory appear inevitable to those that are watching. Lastly, everyone involved is being menaced by a great horde of barbarians that were rallied to the field by Taim's own missteps. At the moment, we are incapable of coming together to put down this threat due to the very divisions and uncertainties I have described.

"Lord Taim will resist the inevitable. But only until he can come up with a solution that lets him lend you the last part while still saving face. If he cannot come up with one for himself, I will provide that solution for him. I don't think this process will take longer than three days. It may be finished by tomorrow. Does that satisfy you?"

He tilted his face forward, looking down at them from beneath the ramparts of his eyebrows.

"With fists as big as yours," Blays said, "does *anyone* ever tell you 'no'?"

"That's as much as we can ask of you," Dante said. "But feel free to hit Blays anyway."

Gashen clapped his hands. "Good! Then go and eat, and trade stories of your deeds with my soldiers, and forget your worries for your future until the morning."

They did just that. During their conversation in Gashen's inner chamber, soldiers had begun to fill up the great hall and were already hoisting tankards and eating meat-filled dumplings. The three of them were called over to a table of Lars' officers and those warriors who'd recently distinguished themselves in combat. Plates of food were brought out as they were prepared. Whenever a soldier finished his drink, he flipped his cup upside down on the table and a servant came by to refill it.

It wasn't the grandest feast they'd been treated to since entering the Realm—it wasn't even the grandest Gashen had thrown for them—but Dante had the feeling that would come later, and anyway it was very enjoyable nonetheless, especially once the sun went down and torchlight spilled across the laughing faces of men and women and the puddles of beer they'd spilled on their tables. Some of them were afraid that the ramna might invade Denhild as well, but unlike everyone else they'd met in the Realm other than the ramna, the people here didn't seem at all concerned with dying, at least as long as it was in honorable battle.

Eventually, knowing that if he stayed any longer his evening would stretch into about three too many drinks, Dante took his leave and retired to his quarters, taking the tarp of spear shards with him. Gladdic accompanied him while Blays waved him off, saying something about how he'd earned the right to celebrate and sleep in.

Their quarters were adjoined by a common room. Dante crossed through this to his room, set his candle on the table and the tarp by the foot of his bed, and looned Nak.

They were equally cheerful to hear from each other. Dante told Nak to go first.

"The bad news is the White Lich has recovered faster than we'd hoped," Nak said. "The very good news is that he seems hesitant to come after us in Gallador again. He's gone north instead, sweeping through all of the little towns there, although most have been abandoned. It looks as though his course is for Dollendun. We suspect he wants to replenish the Blighted he lost against us."

"Or to stop with all the detours and continue the general depopulation of the land," Dante said.

"Yes, or that. But this will force Gask to take to the field against him too, won't it? That ought to slow him down a little. Doesn't this give us some hope that you'll be able to assemble the spear before the lich comes for Narashtovik?"

"I don't know. Do you think tomorrow is soon enough?"

"*Tomorrow?* Just to make sure, they do use the same definition of the word in the Realm, don't they?"

"As we speak, I'm looking at eight of the nine pieces of the Spear of Stars. We think we can get the last piece within the next few days. I'm a little unsure of our timeline after that. If we have to use the same portal to get back to the Mists, that brings us to Barsil, meaning that we'll exit the Mists outside Bressel, and this is starting to make my head hurt just thinking about."

"But the point, if I am following you, is that you'll have a long ride ahead of you to the north."

"Right. Unless there happens to be a portal that would spit us out in the north, and we can use that one. Either way, we're close, Nak. All you have to do is hold on for a little longer."

They went through a few details, possibilities, and contingencies, then brought the conversation to an end. Dante felt as though he ought to be able to fall asleep right away, but it was stubbornly elusive, and seemed to take hours—wrapped in sheets that smelled like cut lumber, startled by sudden eruptions of hearty laughter from the hall somewhere downstairs—before at last he drifted off.

Light danced over his eyelids. Not daylight. No. Not even moonlight—close, but the color wasn't quite right, feel wasn't quite right, like waking up in a strange bed.

That thought woke him fully, and he indeed found himself in a strange bed. The light wasn't coming from the sun or the moon, or even through the window at all. Instead, it was coming from a female figure who was even now reaching for the bundle of spear shards Dante had set on the table across from the bed.

He chomped down on his lip, tasting copper. And brought a tidal wave of nether to him.

Five beams of ether leaped from Ka's fingers. Dante pulled together the shadows he had intended to beat her to death with and made a panicked attempt to save his life with them instead. The two forces struck like an unstoppable sword against an invincible shield. Dante couldn't have said exactly what happened when nether rammed into ether, but he found himself blasted against the wall, half trapped under a heap of smoldering sheets and the sharp flinders of what had very recently been his bed.

Dante struggled to free himself, broken boards rattling to the floor. A door banged open somewhere outside his room. Ka had taken the tarp up in her left hand, cradling it like a baby as she readied a second attack. Her fist disappeared within the blinding light of the ether. Dazed, half-wrapped in a smoking sheet, Dante drew forth the thickest wall of shadows he could command. It was just enough to turn aside the blazing ether, but he found himself right back in the middle of the bed-rubble.

The door flew open with a crack of wood; he'd locked it, but Gladdic ripped it down with an abstract axe of ether, which disintegrated into beautiful ashes.

His robe swirled about him as he planted his feet and turned a furious gaze on Ka. "Drop what you now hold!"

"It's Ka!" Dante yelled. "The Angel of Taim!"

He was about to start screaming for help, but soldiers were already barking the alarm from below. Ka hit at Gladdic with an ethereal whip. He deflected it into the wall, which dented and cracked, but the blow was enough to knock him back into the door frame. Gladdic grimaced as the wood and his back decided whether or not to break.

Dante stabbed at Ka's throat with a black blade. She broke it into a thousand pieces, baring her teeth. "It would have been sweet to kill you. But it will be even sweeter to know how you will despair for how close you came to your goal."

She blurred, flying toward the window. Dante and Gladdic rained hell at her, but she shaped a circle of light behind her that blocked each dart and sling. She exited the window. And vanished from sight. Dante tried to feel his way through the ether to find her, but he was clumsy while she was surgical. Within moments, she was gone altogether.

Gladdic gazed out the window. "We are lucky to have survived."

"Lucky?" Dante could barely spit out the word. "She took the spear. She took *all* of it. It's gone!"

"Yes."

"How can you be so gods damn calm?!"

"Because when I died, I came to believe that in the end, our world would not find a way to outlive me for much longer."

The outer door to the chambers banged against the wall. Blays rushed inside with both swords drawn, a troop of Gashen's soldiers at his heels.

"Dante?" Blays swung into the room, assessing it at a glance. "Who?"

"Ka." Dante's throat still felt like it was about to rip itself apart. "She took the spear."

"All of it?"

"Yes. But would it even matter if she'd only gotten half? Where were you, anyway? You've been the spear's guardian. You were supposed to be watching it, not downstairs drinking into the middle of the night!"

Blays cocked his head. "If I'd been asleep in my room with the spear parts, how could I have done anything to stop her? Seems to me she'd still have the spear and I'd just be dead."

Dante pressed his palms to his eyes, little lights dancing across his vision. Most of his mind was going uselessly insane, but he corralled what he could of it. "We have to speak to Gashen. He's the only one who can fix this."

Several of Gashen's soldiers stayed to keep the chambers secure, which was utterly useless at that point, but Dante restrained himself from saying as much. Down in the great hall, General Lars was just arriving from his own quarters, half drunk but quite alert. When Dante told him what had happened, the general went stone-faced. He swore once, then swore a great many times more, then composed himself and told them to follow him.

He made them wait outside the inner sanctum. A minute later, he returned, tight-jawed, and motioned them inside.

Gashen stood on the sand, awaiting them. "I am sorry to hear what has happened. It's a great loss."

"Not if we can undo it," Dante said. "Ka won't reach Taim's realm for many hours yet. Do you have any Angels of your own you can send after her?"

"I cannot do that."

"We may be able to ride her down, then. But we'll need help. How many sorcerers can you send with us?"

"You do not understand," Gashen said firmly. "I cannot help

you because your situation has changed. In losing the parts of the spear, you've lost your claim to them as well."

Blays sucked air through his teeth. "Before my friend does something crazy like, oh, say, insulting the god of war in his own sanctum, am I understanding you right? You won't help us recover what's been stolen from us because it's not really ours anymore?"

"Correct."

"This is bullshit!" Dante took a step forward. "We're in your city. You should have extended us your protection!"

Gashen gazed down at him. "If you were not confident in your ability to keep the pieces safe, you should have asked me to keep them safe for you. Ka would have found it a far greater challenge to take them from me." The god didn't move, but his presence loomed forward. "You did not do that. You proved you were unable to hold onto the spear."

"I'm not asking you to get it back for us yourself. Just to lend us a little more help."

"My aid to you has been generous enough to satisfy any warrior's sense of honor. You can remain in my city for as long as it pleases you; you still have my gratitude for the return of my axe. But as for the spear, you are now on your own."

He nodded to Lars, who escorted them out of the room and back to their chambers. The outer door was guarded by a pair of soldiers. Though they'd only been gone for a few minutes, the soldiers had employed military precision to remove the wrecked bed and replace it with a new one. Lars offered them different quarters altogether if they didn't feel safe where they were, but Dante informed the general that he strongly doubted Ka would return that night.

As soon as Lars was gone, Dante hammered his fist against the wall. "What kind of bullshit is this? An hour ago, we'd proven ourselves as worthy heroes. Then just because some crazy glowing woman flies in through the window, steals our stuff, and flies away, that suddenly means we're no good?"

"And yet we could not stop her," Gladdic said. "Nor can we recover the spear from her without Gashen's aid. Does that not proven Gashen's point?"

"No!"

"Yelling a thing does not make it so."

"We'll see about that!"

Blays half sat, half flung himself onto a sofa, legs sprawling. "When you think about it, we've been pretty lucky just to make it his far."

"Is that supposed to console me?"

"When we got here, it didn't seem like we'd be able to get our hands on a single piece of the spear. The ball only got rolling because Carvahal decided to be a bastard to his friends. Even then, we wouldn't have gotten any further than that if Neve hadn't helped us track down Gashen's axe. And then saved us from getting murdered by Ka, along with teaching us how to defend ourselves from her in the future. An awful lot of things had to go right before we could get to the point where you could be devastated by something finally going wrong."

Dante stared at him. "Bad things may happen, but good things happen too, so don't worry about it? You're choosing now to become a devotee to Lithic philosophy?"

"What I'm saying is you're being a fool. You've convinced yourself that Ka's done something bad."

"I'm going to kill you."

Blays waved his hand. "Has it even occurred to you that she might have done us a favor?"

"How's that? By annihilating the last dregs of our hope, clearing the way for us to commit shameful suicide?"

"Ka's carrying eight parts of the spear. As soon as she returns to Taim's realm, that will unite all nine in the same place. All we have to do is break in and rob the place—then we head home."

27

Dante considered this idea for a second, then shook his head with a jerk. "All we have to do is break into the fortress of the lord of the gods while he will absolutely be expecting us to try just that?"

"Yeah."

He lifted his hand. "Don't be alarmed when mud starts sliding out of your ears. I'm just using my powers to remove all the rocks from your brain."

"For one thing, I'm not convinced Taim *will* be expecting us to break in. He might be wary of it, yes, but the upside of it being an insane idea is he'll expect us to try something less crazy first. For a second thing, even if he is waiting for us, I still bet we can do it."

"Yeah, because if you lose that bet, we all die before you have to pay out on it. Anyway, I don't see how this is *better*. We were days away from having the whole thing."

"Assuming Taim could have been talked into giving us the last piece. But instead of giving it up, he might rather have tried something like, you know, sending his Angel to assassinate us."

Dante felt the urge to object to this and at least two other levels of this new plan, but the possibility of *having* a new plan had cleared his mind. This allowed him to accept the hard truths: the spear was gone. No one else was going to go wrest it away from

Taim for them.

So they would have to do it themselves.

"All right." He walked to the window. Outside, soldiers were patrolling about with lanterns. "We'll go speak to Gashen again. Tell him that we're not asking for direct military support. But that we do need his help figuring out how to get inside Taim's keep."

"Gashen has just told us that he will grant us no further aid," Gladdic said. "We cannot return to see him right now, or we will look as fools who give no weight to his words. Petitioning him in the morning will prove that we took the proper time to reach our new conclusion, and so he might also reconsider his denial."

Blays propped his foot on a table. "When did you learn to politick like that?"

"You forget that I spent decades maneuvering within the hierarchies of the Mallish priesthood."

Something about going back to sleep after tragically losing everything felt idiotic, but Dante went to bed anyway, and even got some sleep. He greeted the morning with the overwhelming urge to smash things. Not something like a glass or a plate, either. More like a neighborhood.

They made themselves presentable, requested to see General Lars, then went to eat what breakfast they could stomach, which for Blays turned out to be all of it. Lars sent for them while Dante was relentlessly chewing a hard-boiled egg that he couldn't seem to swallow. They met the general in his chambers. These were filled with weapon racks and paintings of people wielding weapons.

He gave them the sort of sympathetic smile often seen at funerals. "My friends. I am sorry to see it end like this. Have you figured out where you'll go next?"

"Yeah, we're going to rob Taim." Blays picked up one of the general's swords and examined the scabbard. "And you're going to help us."

"Gashen himself made it clear to you that we have nothing more we can offer you."

"So?"

"What my friend is saying," Dante said, stepping into the role as if they'd rehearsed it, "is that while we might have lost our claim to the spear, that doesn't change the fact that we're dead without it. We have no choice but to try to take it back. We're not asking Gashen to knock down Taim's walls for us. We just need some information on what we're getting into."

Blays took a practice swing with the still-sheathed sword. "And some quality equipment to do it with."

Lars looked between them, face growing less stern. "I understand why you think you must do this. But if I was planning such an action for my men, I would warn them to expect none of them to return. I don't see my lord supporting a venture that has no hope."

"Fine, then we'll head back to Carvahal, who will definitely help us out, and then when we succeed you'll be left out in the cold. Aren't you tired of him getting all the glory? If we're about to go out in a suicide run fit for a ramna poem, don't you want to be part of it?"

Lars looked away, scowling, made a kind of barking noise, then looked back at Blays. "I would have said no to any argument, whether it was fueled by emotion or by reason. But I cannot say no to good spirit! The venture itself will be yours to shoulder. But I will make sure that you are prepared to undertake it."

They reconvened in a rotunda above the great hall that owned a 360-degree view of Denhild below it; the walls were largely made of glass windows, not just one pane thick but two, which Dante had never seen before. To shut out the winter cold, sturdy shutters could be drawn across them from the outside while heavy curtains could be drawn across them from inside.

The largest portion of wall that wasn't filled with windows was faced with the cross-hatched shelving of what appeared to be a giant wine rack. This made no sense, as the room was just about the exact opposite of a cellar. Cylindrical objects rested in the X-shaped shelves. General Lars strolled toward them.

"What's going on?" Blays said. "Are we about to celebrate our new arrangement with a bottle or nine?"

Lars reached the shelves, walking parallel to them, apprising them. He stopped short, reached into a cubby, and withdrew a long, narrow cylinder.

"It's even better than wine," Dante said. "They're maps!"

Lars did a little more searching. There were many hundreds of map-cubbies, possibly well more than a thousand, and it took him a moment to pick his way through the assortment.

"Why don't I have one of these?" Dante reached his hand toward one of the rolled-up maps, but didn't touch it. "If we don't all die, the first thing I'm doing in Narashtovik is building myself a map room."

Lars took out a second scroll and brought his prizes to a wide, round table. He set the smaller scroll to the side and carefully unrolled the larger. Just as Dante thought, it was a map, enormous and incredibly detailed. Lars had brought a few servants with him, who placed metal weights along the edges of the map to keep it from rolling back up.

"Here is Denhild." Both the map and the table were too big to reach across, so Lars indicated the city's position with a slim wooden rod. The map appeared to be just a portion of the Realm; within the territories it covered, Denhild was located in the northwestern quadrant. Lars next tapped a city in the southeastern quadrant. "And here lies Chronus, the realm of Taim."

Dante leaned over the table. "How far is that from here?"

"Not quite fifty rowlands. Your horses might cross the road to it in two days."

"We can't take the road. It'll be watched."

"It will all be watched."

"But some parts will be watched much less than others. What kind of terrain can we expect in the wilds?"

"Who cares about the terrain?" Blays said. "What kind of *beasts* can we expect?"

Lars ran his wooden pointer across the area leading to Chronus. "Forests here and here. Neither one is too treacherous. This stretch is rough lands. Jagged rocks scoured by powerful winds and bitter cold, though the season is still favorable to cross it. It is awash with wolves, though you should be much more wary of the mammoths."

"Mammoths?"

"Do you know of elephants?"

"I've heard of them. Like a whale on land, right?"

"These are worse."

"We will need to travel in disguise," Gladdic said. "As ramna, or perhaps better as refugees displaced by the ramna."

Blays shook his head. "No way. We should travel as mammoths."

"Why would we wish to do that?"

"When will we ever get the chance to do it again?"

"Assume we make it through to Chronus," Dante said. "What's going to be standing between us and Taim's inner sanctum?"

Lars was leaned over the table, and looked up from under his eyebrows, chuckling wryly. "More than you want to hear."

His second scroll turned out to be several maps rolled into the same bundle. He spread them across the table, revealing several different perspectives of the same city. At first glance, it appeared to be three plateaus stacked on top of each other, with a giant tower rising from the highest plateau.

"First will be the Dauntless Wall." Lars tapped the bird's-eye map of the city. The wall was a semicircle, its ends connecting to what appeared to be mountains. "It surrounds all feasible approaches to the city. Behind Chronus, the mountains are a more effective wall than anything that could be built."

"Walls aren't much use against sorcerers," Dante said. "What are they made of?"

"The wall is plated with a foot of finest steel. Behind that stands thirty feet of the strongest stone known to us."

"Why'd there have to be steel? I can't tunnel through that. Blays can't shadowalk through it, either."

Gladdic made a dipping gesture. "But you could tunnel underneath it."

"If your wish is to draw the attention of the priests who watch the wall at all times," Lars said. "They will detect any effort to breach or subvert it."

Blays stretched his arms over his head. "Yeah, well no one said this was going to be easy. Pretend we've found a way past the wall. What's next?"

"The Stair of Landun." Lars switched to a drawing of the city in profile. Beyond the wall lay some farmland. He crossed it with his tapper and pointed out the switchback staircase that ran up the front of the massive stone plateau the first layer of the city was seated on. "Naturally, it is guarded along the way, with posts here, here, here, and here."

Dante rubbed his jaw. "This is the only way up? They don't have a ramp for carts and things? How do they get goods from the lower levels to the upper?"

"A large hoist."

"Aha!" Blays lifted a finger into the air. "So we disguise ourselves as sacks of grain and let them hoist us up to the top."

"It would not be to the top," Lars said. "It would be to the

Lower City. That is this section here."

The Lower City, the lowest of the plateaus, turned out to not be a solid plateau at all, but rather eight gigantic stone pillars. Six of these were arranged in a triangle, with the Stair of Landun running up the pillar that formed the vertex of the triangle that pointed toward the Dauntless Wall. The pillars were aligned closely to each other, but remained separated by narrow chasms, clearly for defensive purposes.

The other two pillars that weren't part of the triangle were set to either side of what Dante correctly guessed was called the Upper City. This layer was elevated significantly from the Lower City, with another staircase up to it, and was composed of three much larger pillars/platforms arranged in front of what was very obviously the Tower of Taim.

"On each layer, each platform is separated by a gap," Lars indicated. "These are crossed by bridges that are guarded on each side and can be retracted if one of the guards sounds his horn. As you can see, reaching the tower requires the crossing of no fewer than two staircases and six bridges."

"In other words, the frontal approach has a shitload of ways for things to go wrong." Dante planted his chin in his palm. "Then we don't use their approach. I build a staircase of my own up the far end of the tower. Bypass the whole thing."

"Do you think the tower is any less monitored by Taim's priests than the staircase?"

"Will you quit shooting down my ideas?"

"Would you prefer to be shot down by his archers?"

"Is there an option where neither one happens? Let's set aside the path to the tower for the moment. Tell us about the tower itself."

"The Tower of Taim is the oldest structure in the entire realm. It has never fallen. Never even been sacked."

"What're the ways in?" Blays said.

"Conventionally, there is only one: the front gate. No outsiders are allowed within it. Only those who serve the tower and live inside it may come and go."

"Well, easy solution to that one. We just kill three guys who live there and bluff our way in by wearing their skin."

"Chronus is set against the mountains," Gladdic said. "How close is the tower to the nearest peak?"

Lars didn't even have to check the maps. "If you're hoping to extend a rope or bridge down to the tower, the answer is much too far away."

"At this point it seems easier to just knock the tower down and sift through its rubble," Dante groused.

"Not possible. The tower is warded against just that form of sorcery."

"What do you mean, it's warded?"

"It is enclosed in wards, that protect it, so that people like you cannot do what you are suggesting you do to it."

Dante bent his mouth to the side. "I've never heard of anything like that. It almost sounds like propaganda meant to discourage sorcerers from trying to attack it."

"If you're skeptical, you are free to test them."

"We can't go over or under the wall. Even if we could, there's no chance we make it through all the stairs and bridges. We can't build ourselves a stair up to the tower or down to it from the mountains. Where does that leave us?"

Blays crossed his arms. "If I didn't know better, I'd think Taim built his city to intentionally keep his enemies out of it!"

"I should be taking notes. Chronus makes the Sealed Citadel look like a public square." Dante stared down at the maps in dismay, looking for anything he'd missed. "Remind me why none of us have ever learned to fly?"

"Don't suppose you guys know how to do that?" Blays said to Lars. "And would also teach us how?"

"No," the general said.

They spent a few minutes contemplating the maps and not getting anywhere. Dante got up and stalked to one of the big windows for a look at the green hills and fields of Denhild.

"Time to stop worrying about being wrong," he said. "Start dumping everything you've got."

Blays occupied a seat and, in deference to General Lars, slung his leg over its arm rather than propping his foot on the table. "What about your drakelet-taming idea? Can we find a giant flying beast, tame it, and have it fly us to the top of the tower?"

Dante eyed Lars. "Well?"

"There are such beasts," Lars said, visibly treating the idea with more seriousness than he obviously thought it deserved. "But you're unlikely to get close to them, and taming them would be impossible."

"Damn." Blays lowered his head in disappointment, then perked right back up. "Are any of these creatures intelligent? As in smart enough to talk to?"

Lars got a gleam in his eye. "You'd mean to bargain with them? There was once such a creature, the vardans, that had both wings and power of speech. But I have not heard of one being seen in more than three hundred years."

Blays snapped his fingers. "Thought we had it for a second there."

"Perhaps we should think in more conventional means," Gladdic said. "Others might not be able to navigate the mountains that surround the city, but Dante's powers would allow us to do so and so bypass the Dauntless Wall. Once we are inside the wall, we might scale the tower through ropes."

"That could work," Lars said. "But bear in mind you would be scaling a thousand feet of vertical rock, and if you at any time reach a point where you need to use your powers to ascend it, it will almost certainly be felt by the watchers."

Blays swung his leg back and forth. "I'm not sure Dante and I could pull off a thousand-foot vertical climb. And at the risk of being a dick, we've still got both our arms."

"It should not be rude to speak a simple truth," Gladdic said. "Especially among brothers."

Dante moved back to the table for a better look at the maps. "Even so, trying to scale the tower could be our plan B. Or maybe more like plan Q. Still, even if it's got a 99% chance of failure, that's a lot better than anything we've got so far."

"What if we throw the ramna at them?" Blays said. "Start another siege, then run in during the confusion?"

"I don't think we can pull that off a second time. Even if we hadn't burned our bridge with the Jessel, the ramna seem to have burned off their frenzy at Protus. They wouldn't be nearly as easy to dupe again."

Gladdic nodded. "To say nothing of the fact that bringing a war to Taim's doorstep will only lead him to heighten every dimension of his security."

They got stuck for a while. Every idea they produced was either too fantastical to have any hope, or practical enough, yet thwarted by some fiendish detail of the city's design. They stared glumly at the maps.

At last Dante brightened, having been struck by one of those rare ideas that comes from nowhere at all. "What if we're approaching this all wrong? If breaking into the Tower of Taim is so impossible, why don't we get Taim to bring the spear outside the city?"

"How would we get him to do that?" Blays said. "Tell him that his dear old grandmother is on her deathbed in Denhild, and her dying wish is to see the Spear of Stars one last time?"

"The obvious way is to make him think the tower is under threat."

"You mean like by menacing it with a ramna war band like

you just said we couldn't do?"

"And none of the other gods are likely to give us a hand threatening Taim, either. Okay, so we probably don't have the resources to pull that off. Just remember that there may be ways to regain the spear without breaking into the heart of the tower."

"Perhaps," Gladdic said. "Yet as long as Taim believes himself secure in his tower, he has no motive to leave it. He can simply wait us out as the Eiden Rane sweeps across our world and collapses the Mists."

Blays cracked his knuckles. "We may not be able to get the ramna to do anything fun for us. But what if we pose as refugees fleeing the ramna? Would they take us inside the city?"

"That might be enough to convince them to take you inside the Dauntless Wall." Lars only sounded a little intrigued. "But they would never allow you up into the city itself unless you could prove you were a citizen of it."

"Why not? Don't they allow merchants or travelers up there?"

"Yes, in normal times. But times when refugees are common are not normal, and in any event you would not be posing as a merchant or traveler."

"All right, what if we did that instead? Presumably they're a bit tighter right now on which merchants they're allowing inside, but could we bring them some goods so tantalizing they'll make an exception for us? They're halfway under siege right now, aren't they? Probably all it would take to get us through the gates is to sell them some not-rotten food. All we'd need is a few barrels."

General Lars got a funny look on his face. He called over one of his assistants, murmuring something into her ear. She nodded and left the rotunda. They spent a while exploring the merchant angle, with Lars occasionally objecting that they were probably too strange-looking to be accepted in as traders, and that even if they were, they would likely be constrained to the plains below the Stair of Landun.

The door opened and the assistant returned with a middle-aged woman. She wore one of the long, simple dresses of Denhild's laborers and had her hair in a practical bun.

Seeing General Lars, her eyes widened. She dropped into a deep curtsy. "My lord, I am honored!"

Lars gave her a nod of acknowledgment. "Your name is Issie, yes? Didn't you once live in the city of Chronus?"

"That is my name, sir, but if I might correct you, in just a minor way, those in Chronus proper wouldn't say I lived in the city. Rather, I lived on the Terraces of Heaven."

"And what are those?"

Issie looked down. "They're not nearly so lofty as their names, lord. Really they're just farms. But they *are* terraces. You see, the fields inside the wall aren't nearly enough to feed the city, so long ago Lord Taim ordered his people to go into the slopes of the mountains and cut the ground flat so that more crops could be grown there, up in the heights where his enemies would have a hard time either plundering or burning."

She blushed, as if fearing she'd gone on for too long. Lars gave her a reassuring smile. "If the terraces are designed to be so inaccessible, how does the food they produce ever get to Chronus?"

"Well, when the crops are harvested, they're packed into bins. The bins get floated down the mountain—the system is quite clever—but I won't bore you with it..." She briefly lost her way, but gestured with her hands until she conjured her line of thought back into being. "There's a river and some falls, you see, with full bins floated downward and empty bins hauled back up by the water-wheels they put on the river. Once the bins spill into the lake at the bottom of the heights, the bargemen gather them up and sail them to Pulley's Landing, where they're lashed to the cargo platforms and winched up to the top."

"The top being the Lower City?"

"No, lord. Most goods are brought into the Lower City, but the most valuable are delivered to the Upper City. This includes the bins of grain."

"Fascinating. And how are the crops distributed from there?"

"Why, they're taken to the granaries for storage."

"The granaries are one of the most vital organs of any city," Lars mused. "Does Taim keep them in the tower?"

"The granaries are not quite that well-protected, but they are kept in a sort of fort in the Upper City."

The general did some nodding, as if he was thinking all of this over. "It never occurred to me to pay attention to such a system, but now I am engrossed. I will have to go and observe this for myself some time. When are the harvests?"

Issie bit her lip. "Why, I would say the wheat is already done and over. But the corn will be cut any day now, sir, if it isn't already. After that, you would have to wait till late spring for the winter wheat to come at the scythe."

"Well, maybe things will have settled down enough by spring for me to go and see that. Thank you, Issie. This has been most interesting."

She bowed, backed up three steps, then turned and left, escorted by the same assistant as before.

Lars sat back in his chair. Throughout his questions and Issie's answers, Dante, Blays, and Gladdic had all maintained a politely interested silence. As soon as the door closed, they looked at each other and erupted into laughter.

Gladdic was first to recover. "You mean to disguise us as corn."

"No," Lars said, "I mean for you to disguise yourselves as corn. My hands will be kept clean of this."

"You realize I had this idea hours ago," Blays said.

"I'd forgotten about the bins until you made mention of barrels."

Dante did some pacing. "Unless they have a way of drying the seed out afterwards, the bins must be watertight. We'll have to find a way to breathe."

"There will be challenges to solve to make the tactic work. But if you do solve them, you will be delivered all the way to the Upper City."

"Leaving only the tower."

Blays tapped his nails on the table. "We don't dare head there right now, do we? Figure out the tower once it's in front of us?"

"No way. We've only got one shot at this. We can't take it until we've got a means to the top of the tower, too."

Dante had no doubt he was right. Even so, he bore the cold suspicion that finding that solution could take days—if it ever came at all.

By that afternoon, his suspicion was proving frustratingly accurate. They'd gone over any number of suggestions without finding anything Lars deemed remotely plausible. Eventually, Lars excused himself to tend to some of Denhild's business and get his people started on provisioning the three of them for their trip to Chronus so they could leave the instant they'd finalized their scheme.

Servants brought lunch, pacifying Dante somewhat. He was picking at the scraps when Lars returned.

"So." The general punctuated the words with a clap of his hands. "Have you found a way to get yourselves into the tower?"

"That depends," Blays said. "What's the biggest trebuchet you've got?"

"As you can see, we've got nothing," Dante said. "So let me switch to a different question that's been bothering me. Taim will probably take the spear to his tower. If he takes it to his tower, he will probably keep it in his inner sanctum. But."

"Probably is not the same as certainly," Lars said, "and if you count on this and turn out to be wrong, it will be the death of you."

"I don't suppose you have any way for us to know if we're in the vicinity of the spear? Or any way to track it?"

A neutral look crossed the general's face. "Nothing springs to mind."

"No, stop, hang on," Blays said. "I've thrown around enough bullshit in my time to know when it's being thrown at me. You *do* have a way to track it. You just don't want to give it to us."

The general was silent for a moment as he decided whether to bother to continue the ruse, then he sighed testily. "Do you even realize how uncouth it is to call your host a liar?"

"Just ten percent more uncouth than it is for the host to lie to his guests."

"I suppose that the sooner you complete your schemes, the sooner I can be rid of you." Lars' first words sounded bitter, but he was grinning by the end, if somewhat ruefully. "When Barrod forged the spear, he saved a bit of the ether from each piece. He shaped these bits into charms that would thus be linked to their piece and could be used to track that piece down if it ever went missing—or if a Fallen Lander earned the spear honestly, but then refused to yield it back once he was done with it."

Blays looked shocked. "What kind of degenerate would do something like that?"

"So to answer the question of 'Do we have a means to track the spear,' the answer is yes. But to the implied second question of whether you can have that means, how could we dare risk putting it in your hands when, if you fail at Chronus, the charm will be lost to us?"

"Because if we fail, then everyone in the Fallen Land is dead and none of us will ever come for the spear again. So who cares if the charm gets lost?"

Lars snorted. "Fair enough. But I will have to see if Gashen is as easily convinced."

He spun on the heel of his boot and left the rotunda. Dante went to the table and leaned over the maps of the city and the great tower, hunting for anything he'd overlooked. Blays wandered to one of the window seats and spread out with a book. Given the circumstances, this seemed like a complete waste of time, but it was so unusual to see Blays reading anything at all that Dante wasn't even mad.

Lars returned looking mildly amused. "My lord is growing exasperated with your cheek. But he would also like to see you deploy your transgressions against Taim, so he has agreed to let you take the charm."

He removed a black velvet bag from his pocket, loosened its drawstring, and tumbled a disk of ether into his palm. Its face was stamped with the sun of Barrod.

"You should take it," Dante said to Gladdic. "You'll be the one using it."

Gladdic accepted the bag. "Unless this is your clever effort to cast the blame on me if it is stolen from us as the spear was."

Dante motioned to the glowing charm. "Taim will have one of these too, won't he? That's connected to his piece of the spear?"

Lars inclined his head. "Just so. You will either want to steal it along with the spear, or make sure you run away from the crime with all possible speed."

"Where is he likely to be keeping it?"

"Why do you suppose I would have any idea?"

"If the charm is linked to its piece of the spear, then the piece is linked to the charm. Therefore we can use Taim's piece—the purestone—to find his charm."

"You are very optimistic about the length of time we will

have available to spend within Taim's holiest chamber," Gladdic said.

"We'll have to work *something* out. Or else Ka will track us right down and take back the spear. And this time, she'll be sure to take it somewhere we can't follow."

"You must by now understand that we do not really stand a chance. Our effort will achieve nothing more than to provide one last piece of sport for the gods."

Dante felt his face turn red. "Even if that's true, we have no choice but to act like it isn't."

"Everybody shut up and listen to me." Blays ejected himself from his seat, closing his book with a thump. "While you've been standing there moaning about the tragedy of our existence, I've been figuring out how to get us inside the tower. Turns out the answer was right under our noses all along."

Dante blinked, then noticed that the book Blays had been reading was the *Book of What Lies Beyond Cal Avin*. "Sabel got inside the tower when *he* was searching for the spear. And wrote down what he did." He drew back his head. "But Sabel didn't have to steal the purestone from Taim. He earned it by killing a dragon."

"You don't remember how his friend Gent was wounded in the fight? And Sabel had to gather all that stuff to heal him? That part was like half the stupid book!"

Dante rubbed his temples, going back over the tale. "Taim—I forget what Sabel called him, but it had to be Taim—wouldn't give Sabel one of the salts he needed for the tincture that would bring Gent out of his coma. Said it wasn't part of the deal. So Sabel broke into his tower and took the salt." He snapped his fingers. "The cloaca!"

Blays nodded. "The cloaca."

Gladdic gave them a disgusted look. "Why am I poisoned with the suspicion that I am about to wish that I was dead again?"

"It won't be as bad as it sounds. Probably. Anyway, you should be thanking me. I just got us inside the Tower of Taim."

28

The cask bobbed down the river, spinning slowly, tilting off-canter as it did so. Dante strained his eyes, but he couldn't make out any sight of the apparatus.

Gladdic couldn't cross his arms, so he'd developed the habit of resting his left hand on the knot of his rope belt. "Do you suppose it has fallen below the water?"

"I hadn't thought of that until just now. Uh. Can we make it go faster?"

"Increasing a river's speed is one of your talents, not mine. Although I recall your effort in Bressel requiring far more work than you could accomplish right now."

Suddenly troubled, Dante waded into the shallows, boots sliding over the mossy rocks. He was carrying a long pole with an iron hook on its end and found himself gripping it in both hands. A few of Lars' soldiers had volunteered to help, apparently just for the fun of it, and they waded out with him, ceasing their banter as they sensed the shift in mood.

They had positioned themselves at a bend in the river where the cask was sure to run aground in the shallows. Just in case it didn't, they had the poles with the hooks. As the cask bobbed closer, rather than being carried by its momentum to shore, a perverse current bent it away from those gathered to catch it.

Dante extended his pole, bending forward as far as he dared.

The cask was just moments away. "It's not going to be close enough!"

Gladdic shook his head. "Must I do everything?"

Gladdic lifted his hand, fingers spread wide. Ether zipped over the waters. Just to the right of the cask, the surface crackled with ice, shoving the container to the left, closer to shore. Dante and the soldiers stretched themselves to the limit, poles waving about like the feelers of an immense shrimp. One man landed a hook. The cask was large, the size of a coffin, and its weight threatened to drag the man out into the current.

Two of his fellow soldiers grabbed his jacket, stabilizing him. He drew the cask in that much closer. Dante snagged it as well, slogging backwards, three more soldiers getting their hooks in alongside him, securing it tightly.

They wrestled the container ashore. It was heavy enough it took four of the soldiers to drag and push it up onto dry land.

Something banged on the lid from within, causing several of the men to jump back. A second blow rattled the lid. The third shoved it open.

Blays sprung free, shedding a pile of dry corn kernels they'd included to make the experiment as authentic as possible. "I heard some shouting near the end there. Almost had me nervous. I'm fine."

"Big deal," Dante said. "What about the apparatus?"

Blays reached down into the cask, scooping away corn with both hands. "Worked like a charm."

Figuring out a way to hide in the grain bins without suffocating to death had had the potential to delay them for days. You couldn't just poke a bunch of holes in them. That would only lead to corn spilling out and/or water spilling in, which was likely to draw an inspection that would reveal not only were the bins full of holes, but also people. Anyway, packed within the corn, they might not be able to breathe no matter how many holes you knocked in the sides.

The solution seemed to require a breathing tube of some kind. Complicating things, it would need to be both flexible, yet rigid enough to prevent being collapsed by the corn. Putting these parameters together, Dante had stared at them with sick horror, convinced that there was no solution and they'd have to do something stupidly risky like clinging to the outside of the bins and disguising themselves with nether and hoping they didn't encounter any sorcerers along the way. This was dumb enough that he feared they'd have to ditch the whole thing and try to come up with another way into the city instead.

The answer had come to him as if Arawn himself—or possibly Carvahal—had whispered it into his ear: the worms they'd fought in Talassa. Their bodies were as flexible as they were strong. All he had to do was duplicate them, which he accomplished with a leather tube braced on the inside by metal rings. Lars' craftsmen put the first models together within an hour. After a few dry runs, and learning that they'd need to adhere the other end of the tube to the breathing hole with pine resin, Blays had been ready to squeeze into the cask and get chucked into the river.

"Well, that one's out of the way." Blays brushed some stray kernels from his doublet. "Shall we go see about the rest of it?"

Back in Denhild, Lars had requisitioned a number of metal rods, ranging from pitted old iron to shining steel, and had had a pair of laborers plant them in the ground like a strain of new crops—one that would be very hard on the teeth.

Blays drew his sword, nether snapping up and down the blade. With a casual flick, he cleaved one of the weak iron pieces in half. He moved to the next and repeated the motion. Again, a length of iron thumped to the ground.

Lars whistled, impressed. "Where can I get some of those?"

Blays advanced to the next bar. "In a fetid swamp on the

head of a colossal man-eating lizard. There may also be liches."

It wasn't until he reached the clean steel that he had to put any serious strength into his strikes. Rather than a full wind-up, he attacked the bars with the tightest, shortest chops he could manage. The kind he might have to resort to within a confined space. When he neared the end of the line, where the strongest steel stood against his blade, it took him multiple whacks to cut through, but even the last bar yielded in the end.

Blays inspected his blade, then put it away. "That cloaca doesn't stand a chance."

Gladdic bared his teeth. "Will you cease using that word?"

With the basics in place, Dante had the urge to ride for Chronus then and there. Reminding himself that they'd only have one chance at it, he convinced himself it was all right to spend another day or three to line themselves up, and used Lars' detailed drawing of the Tower of Taim to reconstruct the immediate approach to the inner sanctum, which was likely to be most patrolled. He did this outdoors, naturally, lifting walls up out of the turf so that he, Blays, and Gladdic could practice moving from room to room, familiarizing themselves with the layout until they knew exactly where they were going, along with all other entries and exits along the way.

All of this left one major element untouched: how they were going to get *out* of Chronus. They agreed this should be done as fast as possible while avoiding as many people and chokepoints as they could. To this end, Dante asked to speak with Lars' best woodsmen, who took him out past the wall and into the woods until they found an example of the type of vine he was looking for. He collected several.

By the time everything was in place, just two days had elapsed since Ka had stolen the eight pieces of the spear. Yet Dante feared it had already been too long.

For what might be the last time, they made their way into the wilds of the Realm of Nine Kings.

They were dressed like farmers, somewhat shabbier than yeomen. The horses Lars had given them were obviously too fine for such people, so the general had replaced them with ones whose lineage wasn't quite as physically apparent. When they tested the steeds' gallop, though, they found it hardly any less than the mounts they'd just given up.

Woods and crags waited in the distance, not a hint of human settlement within them. There would be animals ahead. Ramna, too. Possibly the soldiers of the gods, some friendly and some not. There would all but surely be other troubles they couldn't envision because nothing like them existed in their own world.

Yet Dante wasn't overly concerned. Having spent two months within the Realm, none of it was half as foreign as it had been when they'd first stumbled through the portal into the mountains.

They rode overland, sticking to as much cover as they could. They soon came under the boughs of a forest. It was early in the season and the leaves were just starting to turn, but the rain that came hissing down on them was like something from much later in the autumn. They raised the hoods of their rough farmers' cloaks and carried on.

They'd gotten a late start and sunset came while they were still crossing the first wood. The rode on by moonlight. Wolves had begun to howl the instant it got dark and their angry calls grew closer and closer until light glinted from their yellow eyes. Dante and Gladdic sent them yelping away with swats of nether.

"Does it feel like something's watching us?" Dante said.

"Yeah," Blays said. "A bunch of hungry wolves."

"Something else. A presence."

"Ka?" Gladdic said.

"Maybe. Keep ready."

They called it quits around ten that night. To avoid making their shelter too obvious, Dante sank it into the ground, then dumped some dirt over the stone roof. Dante was awakened in the middle of the night by some pawing and scratching, but nothing came of it. The daylight showed the tracks of both wolves and drakelets in the soil atop the roof.

To the east, the mountains loomed a little higher, but still looked further away than seemed right. After they'd gotten into the rhythm of the day's travel, Gladdic got out the ethereal charm Lars had given to them and prodded it with pins of light.

"The sensation remains different than when blood is used to track down the person it belonged to," Gladdic remarked. He'd familiarized himself with the charm before leaving Denhild and had claimed that it didn't give any indication of which direction its spear piece lay in. "However, it is undeniably stronger than before."

"Then presumably we're headed in the right direction," Dante said. "Keep checking in on it."

They crossed some broken-up ground and came to another forest. Just a mile inside it, they heard hoofbeats coming right at them. Wordless, they took cover within a hedge that Dante harvested shut behind them.

A minute later, a ramna scouting band of sixteen riders tromped past them, the warriors wearing red feathers and leather armor covered in snake skins. Two of them glanced at the hedge, but didn't notice the three figures lurking within it.

The sound of the riders faded to the west. Dante gave it another couple minutes just in case, then drew some nether to him and moved back into the open.

"I suppose it's a good thing to see ramna this close to Chronus," he said. "That mean's Taim's soldiers don't have control over their own—"

He bit his teeth together with a click, chomping painfully on his tongue. Appearing from out of nowhere, a dozen mounted soldiers stared back at them, dressed in the gray of Taim, the deep blue hourglass that was among his icons sewn across their chests.

"Did you see the savages?" the commander demanded.

Blays pointed past his shoulder. "That way. Careful, they outnumber you."

The commander drew closer for a better look at them. "Who are you and what is your business here?"

"Farmers and just trying to get away from the savages."

The man nodded as if satisfied, but his left eye twitched. Casually, he said, "Kill them."

Reacting as if the commander was giving orders *to* him rather than *about* him, Dante tamped the nether into bolts and fired them at the soldiers. Gladdic barely had time to get in on the action before Taim's men were all dead.

They dragged the bodies into a pile, then Dante lowered the earth beneath them and covered them up. The thought crossed his mind to dispose of the horses in similar fashion, but he didn't remotely have the heart for that, so they stripped the animals of their saddles and tack, smacked them on the rumps to send them west, then buried the gear next to the soldiers.

Blays swung into the saddle. "Any idea what tipped off the commander?"

"Nope," Dante said. "But that only reinforces the idea that once we're inside Chronus, we need to be seen by as few people as possible."

They traveled with even more alertness and caution than before, which turned out to be a good thing, because they had to dodge a much larger deployment of soldiers just a few miles later. It seemed that Taim was being rather proactive in making sure the ramna didn't get any ideas about doing to him what they'd done to Silidus.

Something was shuffling about in the leaves ahead. It didn't sound like it could be horsemen, but whatever it was, it sounded big. Blays pointed to a crack-riddled formation of rock and they quickly slipped inside. Dante filled his hand with shadows.

The shuffling drew nearer. Low thumps came with it. The sound stopped. Dante held his breath, listening.

A fat brown tentacle thrust its way inside the crack they'd taken refuge in. Dante swore in surprise, ready to hack at it with the nether, but it wasn't a worm. Rather, it was a groping, pre-hensile trunk—and it was attached to the ponderous, fuzzy head of a huge beast.

"Is that a mammoth?" Blays couldn't have been more incred-ulous if the animal had dropped to one knee and asked him to marry it. "It *is* a mammoth!"

"Now that is a smell you don't smell every day," Dante mut-tered.

Gladdic lifted his chin. "At last, a sight that may have been worth returning for."

Blays dismounted, then reached out, hesitantly, and touched the mammoth on the tip of its still-groping snout. The beast snorted fiercely, grabbing for his hand, which he pulled away.

"So that's how you want to play it, eh?" He jumped onto the rocky wall, scaling it like a lizard.

"What do you think you're doing?" Dante yelled after him.

"Something I've always wanted to do!"

Blays got to the top of the rock formation and jogged out to its end. He bobbed his head, calculating something, then jumped.

The mammoth jerked its trunk back and trumpeted.

Dante snuck to the edge of the crack. And began to sputter. "He's riding the damn thing!" He cupped his hands to his mouth. "You idiot! Get back here!"

The mammoth was trundling away from the rock formation

at high speed, rattling the ground as it went. Blays sat astride its back, gripping tight to its thick hair.

"Yah! Faster, mammoth!"

The animal obliged, plowing right over a small tree with no sign it had even felt it. It unleashed another deafening trumpet. Blays winced, but he was still grinning.

"Stop messing around!" Dante hollered. "They'll be able to hear that for miles!"

Next to him, Gladdic began to chuckle.

"Oh, you think that's funny?" Dante said.

"It is far more outrageous that you do not."

Dante scowled. This did nothing to damper Gladdic's amusement. And Blays was still clinging to the mammoth's hair, bumped and jostled by the violence of its rampage, yet undaunted. And away to the east, the mountains waited, the kingdom of Chronus within it, where if they failed, Dante doubted they would ever see a moment's levity again.

He began to laugh, too.

They dodged more ramna, more soldiers. The forest stopped and they rode among bashed-up rocks. There, they caught their first glimpse of the city. From a distance, it looked like a single titanic tower. Dante could just make out shelf-like structures in the mountains behind it that might have been the Terraces of Heaven, but they were too far away to be sure.

The night came and passed unremarkably. At nine in the morning, the mountains seemed to lurch toward them, the same way they'd appeared to do at other points in the Realm. They had veered to the north, putting them to the left of the city, and could see a few fields scattered around the heights now. Dante spent most of the ride trying to plot a course through the mountains that would bring them in right above one of the terraces.

Another forest swallowed them up. It was less than three

miles across, but when they emerged from the other side, the mountains had snuck up on them even more, like a towering wave of earth about to come crashing down on their heads. They came to a stop.

Blays gazed up at the peaks, the highest of which were dusted white. "What d'you suppose is on the other side?"

"I don't think there *is* another side. I think once you reach a certain point, it's like the desert outside Arawn's land. You can keep traveling forever and you won't actually get anywhere at all."

"Why would they make a place like that?"

Dante shrugged. "Maybe they hadn't worked up the imagination to put together a world as big as ours yet."

"Do you not see?" Gladdic said. "They did not build most of our world. Just the earth, the seas, and the stars. They left the rest to us."

They were quiet for a moment, unwilling to move on. Blays swept back his hair. "Gladdic, after the lich...the place you went wasn't so bad, was it?"

"In fact I preferred it."

"Well, that's good." Blays ran his arm over his mouth. "Okay. I'm ready."

They entered the foothills. They'd heard wolves both days, so when they came to a shallow valley after which the horses wouldn't be any more use, instead of tying them up, they left the animals to wander, though Dante blood-marked them the same way he had on Mount Arna.

Doing this brought the pang of the memory of Neve, along with a sense of guilt that their spate of recent troubles had caused him to all but forget their guide. Then again, she hadn't really just been a young woman making her way alone through the wilds, had she? She'd been an instrument of Carvahal, and had died in his service.

The mountains were hard work. Lots of hiking over broken, rocky terrain. Where it wasn't rocky, it was muddy from the rains. With no idea what was to come, Dante tried to use his abilities as little as possible, leaving them to rely on their arms and legs instead. The temperature dropped noticeably. A harsh and unsteady wind cast grit in their eyes.

Yet the path Dante had mapped out in his mind proved true. They passed through a winding cleft and came out just to the north of a terrace.

They were about two hundred feet above a plateau close to a mile in length and ranging from four to eight hundred feet wide. Most of it was covered in fields, and most of these had recently been harvested or were in the process of being harvested, with a wagon-driver rolling slowly along the stalks as fields of glove-wearing laborers went from plant to plant snapping off the ears and lobbing them into the wagon.

A stream ran down from the terrace, winding along the mountainside to the plains below. It then ran nearly straight across a fertile plain to the city of Chronus, which stood miles away and punched into the sky just like a spear. The platforms that composed both the Lower and Upper Cities were much larger than Dante had imagined. As was the Tower of Taim.

Barns and simple but warm-looking housing structured clustered near the center of the terrace, backed against the mountainside to protect them from the weather. This was fortunate, as it meant that, with a bit of maneuvering, Dante and the others were able to look down on the buildings from almost directly above them.

In one building, workers deftly shelled the dried corn and piled it up into wheelbarrows. Once one was full, another field-hand pushed it over to the adjoining barn—where it was then wheeled up a low ramp and dumped into a big fat bin. One more than large enough for a grown man to climb inside.

They lay flat behind the shrubs and grass and watched.

"Have to use bins that have already been filled," Blays said. "No chance of hiding in an empty one as they fill it. And if we tried to skip the corn and just take an empty one, we'd be bashed apart on our ride down the river."

At that moment, a wagon was approaching the edge of the terrace, where an artificial canal had been dug to meet the stream. A group of men accompanied the wagon and as it came to a stop next to the canal they worked with slow but steady precision to guide the bins down the wagon ramp and onto a set of logs that served as rollers, making it exceedingly easy to push the bins the rest of the way into the canal. All in all, they dumped six bins into the water, the containers evenly spaced as they flowed down the canal and into the stream, where they bobbed and spun in the current.

"What do you want to bet they always send six at once?" Dante said. "And that the workers at Pulley's Landing will notice if the count's wrong. That only leaves us with one real option. Get into the bins after they've been filled, then wait for the workers to send us downstream."

"And I'll bet *you* that they send each batch of bins down the mountain as soon as they've got six filled up. So how are we going to get into the bins in the first place?"

Dante didn't have an answer to that one. Unloaded, the wagon swung about and headed back for the barns, where there were already two filled containers waiting for it. Men heaved these up onto the vehicle's bed, then went to join the women shelling corn in the other building. Just as Blays had predicted, once the sixth bin was filled and loaded, the wagon made its way back to the canal, where the containers were shipped downstream.

"Look how they're sealed." Blays sounded dispirited. "Metal clasps, on the outside. Even if we find a way to get ourselves in, somebody's going to have to stay behind to seal the others in."

"I think I'd be able to nudge the clasps shut with the nether," Dante said. "It's just a matter of having enough time."

The day was drawing on, but it was harvest season, meaning everyone would keep working until the sunset sent them home. As dusk neared, they still hadn't spotted their window of opportunity. As the wagon got loaded up with bins, it wasn't directly monitored, but it was left just inside one of the barns, where anyone passing by could see it.

With the last of the light a few minutes away, a woman exited one of the bunkhouses, moving purposefully toward a small platform outside it. There, she vigorously rang the bell hanging from the scaffold over the platform. The various laborers spent a few minutes finished up their tasks, then trudged wearily but satisfied in from the fields and barns, leaving their work until the morrow.

Blays grinned. "See that?"

Dante felt giddy. "They didn't have time to run the last bins down to the canal."

"Now the only question is whether they bother to keep watch through the night."

Smoke poured from the chimneys of the bunk houses and the kitchen. The laborers sang harvest songs as they gorged themselves. Between the amount of work they'd done and the amount of food they were eating, it was no surprise when most of them took to bed within a half hour of finishing their meal. At that point the grounds were almost silent, just some murmuring and clinking of crockery as a few workers cleaned up after the meal. One by one, the lanterns were doused. In time, the only light left on the terrace was the clear cold shine of the moon, and the only sound left was the secretive rustle of the wind in the stalks.

Up in the mountains as they were, and at a simple farming

camp, Dante didn't expect much in the way of patrols. It soon became evident there weren't any at all.

"Only one question left," Dante said. "Do we bin ourselves now? Or wait until it's closer to morning?"

"We can't cut it *too* close," Blays said. "You know how dreadfully early these farming types start their day. It's enough to get the roosters complaining about them."

Still, it was hardly ten o'clock, and there didn't seem to be any rush. Lights gleamed from the spires and platforms of faraway Chronus, but up in the heights, all was still.

Blays was right about the waking habits of farm workers, though, especially at harvest, and they climbed free from cover before one in the morning, stealing down through the shrubs and short trees growing from the slope. Dante stepped onto the flat ground of the terrace certain that a lantern was about to flare to life as an alarm bell rang and rang. But the buildings were as silent as ever.

They passed into the deep shadows of the barn. It smelled earthy, like dried leaves and soil shaken free from roots. The laborers hadn't bothered to drag the filled bins up into the wagon and they were lined up as neatly on the ground as Dante could have asked for, five in all.

Gladdic moved to stand watch just inside the shadow of the entry. Easy as they could, Dante and Blays undid the latches on the rearmost container. The lid was bulky enough that it was practically a two-man job to lift it free, but Dante supposed he could handle the last one on his own.

The interior was filled nearly to the brim. Scooping the dry kernels onto the ground to make room for Blays would have made a lot of racket, so they found some burlap sacks, filled them up, and lugged them to a dusty corner of the barn.

Blays returned to the bin, climbed halfway in, then looked up. "When we're tumbling down the river, what happens if we get flipped upside down?"

"Ah," Dante said. "Well, in that case, Gladdic and I can break our way out."

"I can't help but notice this doesn't address the issue of me."

"If you get flipped, I suggest you do a lot of screaming to alert us to do something about it. Now shut up and get in the box."

Blays lowered himself, wriggling around to make space within the shifting kernels. Dante got one of the apparatuses from out of his pack and passed it to Blays. As Blays fitted the strap over his head, Dante shaped the shadows into a chisel and bored a hole through the side of the bin just beneath the lip where the lid fit on, where it seemed least likely to be seen. A water stain along the sides of the container indicated the hole should be well clear.

He attached the other end of the apparatus to the hole, sticking it tight with resin. Blays breathed through the tube for a while, getting used to the whole thing, then gave Dante a thumbs up. Blays stretched out in the bin and Dante covered him with corn. He gently wrestled the lid back into place, listening for any sounds of discomfort before he tightened the clasps, pulling the lid snug.

He sought out the nether inside Blays to make sure he was still doing important things like breathing and beating his heart. All good. Keeping this connection open and shifting it to the back of his mind, he motioned to Gladdic.

The old man helped him get the lid off the second bin, then Dante repeated the process he'd gone through with Blays. He was somewhat concerned that Gladdic's age would render him less able to handle what they were about to go through, but then again, the old man was as tough as a toenail.

Gladdic seemed to be having similar thoughts. "If I have survived all our past trials only to be smothered by a bin of corn, I will be consoled that the rest of all life will soon perish as well."

Once Gladdic was ready, Dante got the lid into place and snapped it down. Gladdic twiddled some shadows around the exit of the breathing apparatus, signaling that all was well.

Dante moved to the third bin. He opened it and excavated some of the corn from it, spending more time watching the entrance to the barn than what he was doing. If anyone walked in on him at that moment, he'd have no way to bluff his way out of it. He'd have to kill the intruder on the spot, cover them beneath the earth, and hope that come morning, the others would have too much work ahead of them to spend too much time worrying about where the missing person had run off to.

Yet the night remained as quiet as it had been while they'd been watching it from above. Dante then had to get the lid most of the way over the bin, climb down into the hollow he'd scooped out for himself, get his apparatus in place, drag the lid into position, and worm himself under a layer of kernels so nothing would look awry if the container were inspected, either here or when it was delivered to the granary. This process took so long and produced so much rustling and scraping around he began to feel nauseated.

At last, the lid slid into place. He wriggled downward, made sure he wasn't about to panic about being buried in corn while breathing through a tube, then turned his mind to the latches. After the preceding struggle, it turned out to be blessedly easy to use the nether to bump them closed.

After that, he had nothing to do. He was instantly glad they'd thought to relieve themselves before beginning their task. To make the most of his time, he ran through all the ways the next few hours could go wrong, and what he might do about it. Now and then he checked in on the nether in Blays' heart and lungs, which seemed fine.

Somehow he actually fell asleep. When he woke, his body

panicked, trying to thrash against the weight on top of him, but he was barely able to stir, and this only made it worse, cold sweat all but spraying from his pores, heart thundering—but even so, he was right where he was supposed to be. His mind calmed. His body hadn't quite got the picture yet but would catch up in a minute.

He had been awakened by noise outside his bin. Workers were shuffling around the barn. Scraping their tools about. Talking jocularly to each other in a way particular to a group of people who depend on each other to perform a vital task—and who know they'll get to do a lot of feasting and celebrating once the work is finished. Dante's right leg and left arm were so thoroughly asleep he was afraid he might develop gangrene, but with the laborers so close, he couldn't risk stirring the corn kernels with more than careful wiggles. Once he'd upgraded his limbs from totally numb to painfully tingling, he checked in on Blays and Gladdic's organs. As far as he could tell, they were perfectly all right.

Things got quiet for a while. Except for Dante's stomach, which was growling so loudly he thought it would give him away. Voices approached; hands scrabbled on the sides of the bin. It lurched, lurching him with it. Men did some good-natured swearing. The bottom of the container scraped over wood. Dante was shoved around some more, then left at rest.

Footsteps trudged off. More scraping and swearing. Then something large and solid bonked against his bin.

He was in the wagon. They were getting loaded up.

This seemed to take a lot longer than it should, although that was probably just because he had nothing else to do but wait for the next thing to happen. After four more bins were set in the wagon, it ground forward, the mules settling into a steady plod. Dante tried to work out how much distance they were traveling by using the rumble of the wheels and the swaying of the cart, but this was impossible — until he tried reaching into the earth, at which point he could tell precisely how much ground they were covering.

Soon, they were moving alongside a U-shaped depression in the ground: the canal. The wagon came to a stop. Yet more thumping and wrestling about. Then a low-pitched sploosh. The first of the containers had been dumped in the canal.

The laborers worked fast enough, but it was half a minute before they got the second one into the water. The current in the canal wasn't much, but once they hit the stream, they'd be racing down the mountain. Thirty seconds was going to put a lot of separation between himself and Blays. Probably too much to tell if anything bad was happening to Blays — like that he'd gotten flipped over, putting the exit-hole of his apparatus underwater.

He tried to think of a way around this. He still didn't have a solution by the time they slid him down a ramp, conveyed him across the log rollers, and deposited him into the water.

The bin bobbed up and down, tilting back and forth, spinning, moving along all three axes at once, and for a moment Dante panicked, unable to move his arm enough to reach his breathing tube and get it off his mouth before he was going to barf into it. But the bin's motion soon calmed, and so did he, along with his stomach. He reached his mind across the water, hunting for the nether of living bodies. He found one something like fifty yards ahead of him. Given the way the containers had been arranged, that ought to be Blays.

For a few minutes, they drifted along pleasantly. Then the bustle of hasty water sounded from ahead. As it peaked, Dante braced himself within the corn. At once, he was yanked forward, the box spinning again, though he was already somewhat acclimated to the motion, and was no longer at risk of chucking up what little if anything remained in his stomach.

This time, though, the bin never really settled down. Instead it swirled constantly, jostling and bobbing whenever the current picked up. None of this was enjoyable, but it was bearable, and at least he was making great progress downstream. Troublingly, though, he'd lost all sense of Blays.

Pressure grew in his ears and he yawned to pop them. Now and then he was pressed to the side as the container went around a bend. He did his best to keep his breathing steady, though it seemed louder than it should have been.

The warble and hiss of the water became a roar. Breathing harder, Dante braced himself once more. With a swoop, he was flying, and the corn and the box he was packed in were flying with him.

He struck the pool at the base of the falls. If there hadn't been any corn in the box, he would have been dashed against one of its sides. As it was, he suffered a heavy kick, squeezing a grunt of pain from his lungs. He felt himself tipping, tumbling; water splashed down the apparatus, bitingly cold. He drew the nether tight, preparing to bust the bin apart and swim free. With a final topple, he landed right-side up.

He cast ahead of himself, trying to find Blays and make sure he'd come out of it all right, too. But he couldn't feel anything. He kept trying anyway, praying to Arawn—and then, just in case, to Carvahal as well.

The current slowed. He quit rocking around. He was down from the mountain, being ferried across the plain toward the city.

Nothing of note happened for something like half an hour. This phase left him in such a state of sedation he nearly pissed himself when something scraped against the top of the bin. It sounded metal. More scraping ensued. He was hooked, possibly by multiple hooks, and dragged up onto something solid. He had reached Pulley's Landing.

After the constant motion of the water, it still felt like he was rolling around. Yet the wooden platform he was settled on wasn't moving at all. Until, quite suddenly, it was: it lifted free of the ground, swaying side to side as it was reeled steadily upwards.

This continued for a good two minutes. At last, he was pulled forward and lowered onto another platform, where he came to a brief stop. He was now high enough in the air that he'd surely have gotten vertigo if he'd been able to see anything. He was pushed or pulled up a short ramp, falling into place among other bins. Judging by the wooden clunk, he was inside another wagon.

He was already reaching for the nether to check if the others were there and alive when he remembered that, if he was where he thought he was, a priest could well be in the vicinity, too. He let the shadows go. With a call from the driver, the wagon rumbled forward over what was definitely stone paving.

The ground stayed flat all the way to their next destination. There, his bin was slid down yet another ramp, then dragged a short distance until it bumped up against something unyielding. Somebody did some scuffling around the edge of the box. Dante held his breath until it stopped. Several pairs of footsteps wandered away together.

After a few minutes of silence, he was sorely tempted to pop the latches and free himself. But for all he knew a horde of workers was milling around just out of his earshot. He waited on, listening so hard he thought his ears might burst.

After what felt like roughly half an hour, footsteps returned, and voices too, and rolling wheels, and then the scrapes and grunts of people shoving around big heavy wooden boxes. A second shipment of bins had arrived. The laborers set to storing them next to the first batch. They finished up with swift efficiency. The room went silent once more.

Dante counted up the seconds in his head until he hit three minutes. Drawing on the minimum amount of nether he thought it would take, he groped about with the shadows for the latch, nudging it.

It fell open with a metal rattle. Dante gave it another twenty seconds, then moved to the next latch. Refusing to hurry through the last few steps, he paused before both the third and fourth clasps. Then the lid was free to be moved. He hesitated. Why? What did he fear, that an army of soldiers had assembled to silently wait for whatever was inside the bin to emerge? He cursed under his breath and opened the lid.

He pulled off the apparatus. It felt amazingly sweet to taste air that didn't smell like his own breath. He was inside a large stone room that appeared to be dedicated to the arrival and storage of the bins. No one else looked to be in the room.

If things had been stored in orderly fashion, Blays and Gladdic would be in the two bins next to his. Keeping one eye on the large wooden sliding doors—currently open—he pulled open the latches on the next bin, revealing a whole lot of corn kernels.

"Blays?" he murmured. "Come on out."

The corn lay still. Dante repeated Blays' name, then reached down into the kernels, afraid of what he was about to find. He exposed half of Blays' face. Blays' eyes were closed, but as the corn stirred, they blinked open. He lifted his head, yawning.

"Were you *asleep*?" Dante said.

"What would I have gained from being awake? Now I'm refreshed and ready to steal."

While Blays walked off his stiffness, Dante moved to the next bin, popping open the lid. As soon as he spoke Gladdic's name, the old man broke his head free of the kernels, his bright eyes sweeping across the storage room and out the doors to the city beyond.

"Then it has worked." He sounded fairly surprised.

"Step one complete," Dante confirmed. "We're inside the city."

29

They cut the breathing apparatuses free from the bins—not that Dante expected to need them again, but he wanted to leave as little trace of themselves as possible—and got the lids sealed and clasped. After a quick look around, they left the granary.

Lars' maps had given them a sense of the scale and layout of the city. But it had done nothing to prepare them for its splendor. There were towers, of course, and the spires of grand cathedrals. As for its fountains and statues, Dante had seen plenty of those in every great city he'd traveled to, though perhaps not in such quantity or quality. The roads were exquisite, but he thought he'd seen better in humble norren towns.

The city's glory ran from something deeper, something Dante didn't pick up on for some time. First, most of the structures and ornaments weren't made from quarried stone that had been hauled up to the platforms to be shaped and fitted together. Instead, they'd been carved out of the platforms themselves, which in turn looked to have been carved out of a pre-existing mountain. Parts of the original carving process had been broken or worn down in the long, long, long years since the city's founding, but the differences between the original stone and their patchwork replacements only made the structures even more beautiful.

The second matter was harder yet to apprehend at first

glance, but once Dante saw it, he couldn't stop seeing it. Most cities were hodge-podges, allowed to grow and expand as they would. Occasionally, however, especially with holy sites, the buildings were arranged according to some central design, the structure of which was explicitly clear: a grid, say, or a hexagon, or some variation of the twelve houses of the Celeset.

Chronus didn't seem to have been left to grow naturally. Something about the curve of its streets and the contrasting heights of its buildings appeared ordered from above. But no matter how hard Dante examined his surroundings, he couldn't determine what exactly that order *was*.

Most of these insights came to him later. In the moment, he gave himself a few seconds to take in the city, then nodded to the others. They started down the street toward a block of digni-fied row houses. It was still just nine in the morning and plenty of people were on about their business. Both men and women wore long, light jackets that brushed the tops of their knees. The men donned shiny boots while the women wore narrower shoes that curled at the tips like the prows of little canoes. Something about the way the people walked and flowed about each other reminded Dante of the city itself, as if there was a hidden order to it, one his mind was too weak to make proper sense of.

Now that they were out of the granary, the next move was to get away from the crowds and assess their situation. Dante locat-ed an unpeopled alley to slip down. As soon as the coast was clear, Blays stopped, tore open his pants, and relieved himself against the side of a building. Under any other circumstances, Dante would have upbraided him, but he was about to die him-self, and had no choice but to do the same.

Dizzy with relief, he turned away from the building—and threw his hands above his head to protect himself. Yet it was only the Tower of Taim looming over him, punching into the sky like an act of nature. The lower sections bore many turrets, sub-towers, and so on, but as it climbed higher, it became an immense cylinder broken up by windows, balconies, and adornments that were too far away to make out with any clarity. It rose many hundreds of feet above the platforms of the Upper City, and was easily the tallest structure Dante had ever seen.

Blays swore. "We have to *climb* that thing?"

"By the end of this, we might be glad we lugged along enough food to last us several days," Dante said.

"Well, the bigger the tower, the more places there are for us to hide inside it. So. What now?"

"We make sure we're in the right place. Gladdic, can you feel the spear?"

Gladdic removed the charm from his robes, glanced about to make sure no one was watching, and touched it with a spark of ether.

He snapped his head back, then uttered something like an appreciative chuckle. "It is here. Unless I am grievously misreading the signal, it is within the tower."

"I suppose it was too much to ask for Taim to leave it lying in the street," Blays said. "I assume we're not moving on it until nightfall?"

"I'm not sure how much that matters," Dante said. "But better safe than sorry. We'll take a look at it and get a better idea of what's in front of us, then find somewhere to wait out the daylight."

They walked out of the alley and into a sprawling thoroughfare halfway roofed over by handsome trees. Two hundred yards away, the road terminated before a church, its mighty spire cradling the biggest clock Dante had ever seen. He would have liked to watch the activity for a while—they had plenty of time, after all—but they were drawing occasional glances from the cityfolk, implying it was best to keep moving.

The next street took them through the middle of what appeared to be an open-air monastery, with monks and laymen mingling together, mainly to play a figurine-based game that appeared similar to a much less complicated Nulladoon. Dante couldn't help himself from trying to pick up the mechanics of the game as they walked past.

A quiet, shaded street brought them to a plaza with a gleaming fountain. They moved about the perimeter, staying close to the buildings.

"Oh hell," Blays said.

Dante quashed his instinct to reach for the shadows. "What?"

"We have eyes on us."

He didn't seem to be looking at anything in particular, but he gave a subtle nod, pointing Dante to the thing he'd been avoiding looking at: a watchman or constable heading their way. The man wasn't particularly hurried, but there was an unmistakable purpose in the way he was watching the three of them.

He passed behind a cart selling little sweet cakes. Dante sensed motion beside him: Blays was gone. Dante glanced at the cart, trying to decide whether he had time to call out or run after Blays, but then Blays was standing next to him again, a perfectly nonchalant expression on his face.

Dante forced himself to appear to admire the fountain. After a time, however, it became unnatural to *not* acknowledge the constable, who was not only obviously approaching them, but was dressed in the uniform of his station—and was one of the very few people they'd seen in Chronus armed with a sword.

He took a stand across from them, feet spread at shoulder width. A narrow mustache was painted across his upper lip and intelligence gleamed in his eyes. "Good morning!"

"And to you," Blays said as cheerily as if they hadn't spent all night trapped in corn-coffins. "The view from up here is astounding!"

"Isn't it? You've picked a good time to visit. In another week or two, we'll see northern winds. Cold rain that won't stop until it turns into cold snow instead."

"Quite good, quite good."

"I must admit some puzzlement, however." The constable frowned. "For the city is not at this moment admitting visitors."

"Well, we're not *voluntary* visitors. I'm afraid that we're refugees."

"Ah, yes? From where?"

"Protus. The city was sacked so badly we didn't feel safe returning to it. The way things are out there, we didn't think we could make it past the barbarians even if we wanted to."

"So you traveled all the way here instead?"

Dante would have fallen for the trap, but Blays had a way of reading authority figures that couldn't be sharper unless he'd been raised in an abbey dedicated to their study. "No, sir, not exactly. Your men found us in the wilds."

"There must be some confusion. We're not taking in refugees at this time."

"Yes, I'd gotten that impression from the commander. But we have information on the ramna. Specifically the Jessel band, who seem to be one of the main groups driving the others to war. When we relayed this information, it was decided to bring us here to deliver as much knowledge as we could."

"I see!" The man raised an eyebrow, looking about himself significantly. "And what was the name of the man who delivered you here?"

Blays bit his lip, looking up at the sky. "I can't recall it. I don't have much memory for names. But I can tell you what he looked like."

He then rattled off a perfect description of the commander of the group of soldiers that had accosted them in the wild – the man Dante had killed and buried.

This, at last, seemed to satisfy the constable that they were telling the truth. "Captain Morlin."

"Yes, that sounds right."

"Where is he now?"

"Well, that's what *I'm* wondering, sir. He sent us here with a pair of his men to be kept safe until the captain—Captain Morlin—could return from the wilderness. They were bringing us to our quarters when a disturbance called them away. They told us to wait where we were, but it's been quite some time now and we were growing hungry."

"Unusual," the constable said. "But these are unusual times. I'll deliver you for safekeeping, then we'll see about finding your lost escorts. First, though, I need to ask you whether you're armed."

Dante's heart sank. Blays had just talked their way out of an execution. But as soon as the constable looked inside the pack he was carrying with their swords and gear, the plaza would explode with violence.

"I do have this, sir." Blays twisted, reaching for his waist. He drew a knife too small to even be called a dagger and gave the constable an inquiring eye. "In case the ramna came at us, you see."

The official gave him a look both sympathetic and pitying. "I'm afraid that wouldn't have done you much good against the horsemen."

"Oh, I know it," Blays laughed. "But if it came down to it, I just wanted to see if I could take one of them with me."

There was no sign of Blays' pack. Dante showed the man his own knife, which was even smaller than Blays'. Now in good spirits, the constable brought them several blocks south from the plaza to a four-story building that looked stout enough to serve as a fortress if the Upper City was ever besieged. As they entered, a church bell rang so sweetly it sounded like it was made of glass.

A competent young woman came forth to meet them. The constable explained the situation and that they were to be given quarters and breakfast. Before departing, he took the young woman aside for a brief word in private.

"We'll keep you here safe and sound," he said to them as he left. "I'll return once I find Captain Morlin's men."

The young woman brought them to a dining chamber. A pair of servants arrived bearing sausages, greens, and cornbread, which Dante assured himself could not possibly have been made from the same kernels they'd spent the last night sweating in. After, the woman delivered them to a sitting room with a small library and gave them a bell to ring if they needed anything more.

Fortunately, she closed the door on her way out, relieving them of the problem of incurring suspicion by doing so themselves. They sat in silence for half a minute.

"So," Blays said. "Do we make a break for it?"

"We do not," Gladdic said.

"A compelling argument. The argument *I'm* making is that I just told the constable nine hundred different lies, and as soon as he works that out, we're going to be tortured to death."

"Yet if we 'make a break for it' and he returns to find we have fled, he will sound the alarm, strangling what little chance we have to succeed."

"It's not a matter of *if* he figures out I lied to him. It's *when*. If we're not gone before that moment comes, we're dead."

Gladdic murmured to himself. "That is so. Yet accepting this means we must also accept that we are doomed unless we choose the correct moment to act. I believe we do not yet know enough to determine if that moment is now."

Blays raised an eyebrow at Dante. "What do you think?"

"I think we just got to this city and we're already in deep shit," Dante said. "But Gladdic's right. We're only going to have one chance. We can't blow it with an impulse dash."

They had little else to do but bide their time and think about what if anything they should do if their gamble failed and their lies were exposed. Dante opened a few of the books in the library. Under different circumstances, he would have found the histories and philosophy engrossing, but he could barely get himself to read the words.

The glassy bells tolled a new hour. Next came a longer melodic chime that had to be the announcement of noon. A little after the two o'clock bell, the door opened. The constable entered, looking thoughtful, with a hint of something else Dante hoped wasn't suspicion.

"I have been unable to locate the men who brought you here," he said. "They may have already left the city, which would be most frustrating. In the event they can't be located, Lady Tesse is most interested in hearing what you know of the ramna. Unfortunately, her schedule won't allow her to do so until tomorrow morning. You will be kept here until that time."

Dante thanked him for letting them know. The constable nodded, on the brink of saying more, then departed.

"Let's make the brash assumption he's not going to find the men who didn't bring us here," Dante said. "I'd say that gives us a pretty good idea of the right moment to act."

Blays leaned back in his chair. "You mean before tomorrow morning when we get interrogated by some lord, our story falls apart, and we're disemboweled in front of an angry mob?"

"Right. Knowing that, I'd say we're in better shape than we were a few hours ago."

"Arguable," Gladdic said. "This morning, we had days to achieve our ends, if necessary. Now, we have less than 24 hours."

In truth, 24 hours was generous. For one thing, it was closer to 18. For another, they burned up six of those hours just waiting for it to get good and dark.

They were served a plain but generous supper, then allowed some more time in the sitting room. As soon as the nine o'clock bell pealed, the young woman who'd been left in charge of their welfare arrived to suggest (in a way that made clear it wasn't a suggestion) they might want to retire for the evening. Their sleeping quarters were a single room with six simple beds. The woman assured them the constable would be by to collect them in the morning. She closed the door. This was followed by the distinct snick of a bolt being drawn shut.

"She locked the door." Blays sprawled in bed, hands behind his head. "That's good news."

"It's good news that they don't trust us?" Dante said.

"I took that part for granted. The part that's good news is that if she's locked the door, that's because there's no one out there watching it."

"Which means we can leave whenever we want."

"I suggest we leave sooner. We'll stand out less while there are still other people in the streets."

Dante had been expecting not to make a move until midnight. But Blays made a very compelling argument. And for all they knew there was a curfew on the streets, especially now, when being overrun by barbarians was a credible fear. As was, he supposed, being infiltrated by Fallen Landers who refused to take no for an answer.

Attempting to walk out through the front door felt like a bad idea. Dante hadn't seen any overt signs of sorcery among the people keeping watch over them, though, so they plumped up their bedding to make the beds look occupied, then Blays shadowalked out through the wall and returned to let them know the coast was clear. Dante opened a hole through the stone. Like that, they were out in an alley behind the building.

The mountain night was much colder than the day had been

and the air smelled like chimney smoke and dew on stone. Naturally it was quieter than when they'd last been on the streets, but voices chatted here and there, and plenty of candles and lanterns flickered in the windows.

They put a bit of distance between themselves and the structure they'd escaped from, then Blays called a halt. "You might have noticed I ditched our gear before it exposed us as bad men here to do bad things. Suppose I'd better go fetch it?"

"Right," Dante said. "The plaza isn't far to the north. After that, we head straight to the tower."

"The two of you are going to the tower right now. I'll pick up our stuff by myself."

"But—"

"But shove it. One person will draw a lot less attention than three, especially if the constable was paranoid enough to warn the watch to be suspicious of any outsiders traveling as a trio. Anyway, you know that if we're discovered, we have no chance of fighting our way out even if we stick together."

"He is right," Gladdic said.

"I know," Dante admitted. "North side of the tower. See you there."

Blays winked and headed down the street, losing himself in the shadows so well Dante would have sworn he'd stepped into the nether. Dante and Gladdic struck out to the northeast. Dante kept his eyes forward, as if he was out for a casual stroll, glancing at anyone approaching them to confirm they weren't wearing a uniform.

The tower hung above them, some of its windows lit and some of them dark. Dante made sure to keep several blocks of distance between himself and it as they came perpendicular to its front doors, which they glimpsed as they crossed the boulevard leading to them. A stout staircase led up to the metal doors. These looked to be twenty feet tall and were currently closed.

After a few more blocks, Dante began to curve to the east until they neared the edge of the giant platform that comprised this part of the Upper City. The rim was guarded by a short steel rail that didn't really seem sufficient, given that anyone who fell over it would find themselves dashed across the valley floor. Dante and Gladdic lingered there a minute, making sure there weren't any sentries before moving on.

Maybe the city had found it didn't need to run as many internal patrols when they'd made external access to it so difficult. Maybe there was less crime (and hence less need of watchmen) when arrest meant you could be thrown in a dungeon not just for years, but for centuries—and when execution meant the end of all your potential centuries. Or maybe he and Gladdic just ran into some good luck to counter the bad of having been made by the constable.

Whatever the case, they found themselves standing against the base of the tower, lost within the deepness of its shadow. After another look around, they moved further east along its curve, putting themselves out of view of the streets.

The bells tolled: ten o'clock. Within a minute, boots slapped from the front of the tower. Heading north. Toward them. Dante brought the shadows to hand. Two soldiers walked into sight, glancing right at Dante and Gladdic's position, but the darkness kept them safe.

The footsteps faded. Just as Dante began to relax, a new figure emerged, heading straight for them: but it was Blays, bearing the long sack that contained their swords and equipment.

"That got a bit dicey," he said. "Remind me to complain to you about it later."

They were already near the rim of the platform, but they now moved even closer to it. A buffeting wind came and went, gushing from below and up the face of the tower. They came to the railing at the edge of the platform. By leaning over it, Dante could see that the rear of the tower overhung the platform by as much as ten feet.

What he couldn't see was what they had come to find: the cloaca. This was a chute that ran up into the tower. Any non-usable waste was flung down it to fall to the plains far, far below. Its exit was hidden down where they couldn't see it, yet they knew right where it had to be, because Sabel had used it to break into the tower on his own visit to the Realm of Nine Kings—although Sabel's task of sneaking into the kitchen to steal one of its salts had been much, much simpler than the one before them.

Huddled against the side of the tower, Blays extricated their climbing gear from his bag. This had been loaned to them by General Lars, and involved pieces of a quality and sophistication that Dante had never seen before, including spring-loaded things that could be wedged into crevices and then sprung so that their metal claws would push against their surroundings so firmly they could support the full weight of multiple climbers at once.

Blays had gotten a bit of practice in with them before departing, and quickly found a nook in the side of the platform to insert the first. He threaded a rope through the loop attached to the clamp, knotted it, then tied the end to the railing. With his foundation in place, he lowered himself alongside the platform.

As Blays worked to extend the line, Dante moved his mind into the stone that made up the tower. And withdrew like he'd been stung. Ether lay embedded in the rock, arranged in strange lattices whose patterns were obscure to him, the same way the order of the city's layout was obscure. Wards? He'd never seen anything like them, but they had to be what Lars had referred to. Looking them over, he had the sense he could passively observe the stone. But if he tried to manipulate it, bad things would come to him.

Blays finished up and gave them a wave. He whispered, "We

must be in the right place. It smells awful."

Dante hooked a cable from his belt to the rope, then swung down and crawled along it. Gladdic did the same. A few feet down from the platform, the cantilevered bit of the tower angled back until it was flush with the smooth, sheer cliff. The wind brought Dante a whiff of what they'd experience during the next leg of their journey. It wasn't quite as bad as he'd feared, but he'd crawled through enough filth to know he was going to have to throw away his clothes after they were done.

The exit of the cloaca hung above them like...well, he supposed it was probably best not to make comparisons. Gladdic drew on a shard of ether and sent it into the stone tube, providing just enough light to see by.

Looking up, Dante wanted to vomit. And not because of the smell.

In Sabel's description, the exit had been barred with a simple iron grate. One that the Odo Sein swords could have cut through with ease. Instead they found themselves confronted with a block of iron that ran upward as far as the light permitted them to see. Foot-wide round holes had been bored through it to allow waste to fall through the plug.

Blays clung to the rope in confusion. "Well we can't chop through that, can we?"

"This can't be right," Dante said. "This isn't what Sabel wrote about at all."

Gladdic grunted with begrudging amusement. "That is because it is not what Sabel encountered. After the sorcerer cut his way through the grate to gain entrance, Taim saw fit that the act could not be repeated again."

"That's not really fair at all," Blays said. "Right, so my swords can't cut through it. But the nether can, right?"

Dante wanted to cut his rope and drop into oblivion. "Not without calling the wrath of Taim down on our heads. If he went to this much trouble to block it, he'll have set it up so his priests would be able to feel any attack against it. Otherwise this wouldn't stop a decent sorcerer any more than the original grate did."

He couldn't feel any wards within the iron (leading him to wonder if they could only be placed in stone), but he was certain he was right nonetheless.

Blays motioned above them. "The walls of the tower are just about flawless. There's no way to work even one of the clamps in, let alone enough to get us up to that window."

"That window" presumably being the one closest to them: a good fifty feet or more up the base of the tower.

"Then we need another entrance," Dante said.

"You can't just open a hole in the wall?"

"It's warded. Just like Lars said it would be."

Blays nodded absently. "We could do like we did with the corn. Find something that they're bringing inside the tower, and hide inside that thing."

"There's no way they'll be taking any deliveries before tomorrow morning."

"By which time our friendly constable will have discovered we're missing, and set the entire city out in search of us."

"Which means they'll be searching everything that goes into the tower, too."

"That sounds just like something those bastards would do." Blays leaned to the side, gazing at the ground many hundreds of feet beneath them. "We could always jump off and see if a friendly god will send a wind to blow us up to the top of the tower."

"There is an alternative," Gladdic said. "If all routes left before us lead to failure, we can withdraw from the city to seek a second attempt sometime in the future."

Dante steadied himself against a gust of wind. "Nak and our allies have finally blunted the lich's advance. But he's already back on the march. If we delay this, the entire north could be wiped out before we're even back in Mallon."

"Yes, that is possible. But though you will have lost those parts of the world you have fondness for, other parts will remain to be saved."

Dante nodded slowly, forcing himself to come to grips with the idea. "I thought we were done compromising. But there's no sense throwing away everything we've fought for. We'll regroup with our new information and come up with a new plan."

"Maybe if you build a staircase up from the ground to the top of the tower really, really slowly, they won't even notice until we're running off with the spear." Blays made a thoughtful and excited sound. "*Could* you do that?"

"Build a thousand-foot-high staircase without anyone noticing? I think we'd have a better chance praying for your godwind."

"Build the staircase *alongside* the tower. From here. Or would that trigger the wards?"

Dante rubbed his chin. "It would be tough to build enough support beneath it to hold up its weight."

"What if you forget the staircase and just stick some handholds to the wall?"

"That." Dante had no idea where he was about to go with the suggestion. "Is...something that could work. If it doesn't set off the wards. Or *look* like it's going to work only to collapse from under us and spill us to our deaths. Do we have any other ideas? Or should I give it a shot?"

With no one offering any alternatives, the matter was decided. At the moment, they were still dangling from the rope line, which would make it hard to flee if the attempt did trip the wards. They climbed back onto the solid ground of the platform.

Dante nicked his arm and gathered the shadows. He sent them into the side of the unwarded platform where nobody would notice a bit of missing stone and liquefied it. He didn't *think* the wards would react to it, but there was no point in risking that until he knew whether it would work in general, so rather than bringing the rock to the tower, he slid it along the wall of the platform, then molded it into a step, letting the liquid stone seep into every pore and crack and grab tight around every little protrusion. Once the fit was as seamless as he could make it, he turned the stone solid.

"Looks good," Blays said. "But since eyes are known liars, there's only one way to give it a proper test."

He clipped his rope to the railing and stepped over it onto the foothold Dante had built.

Dante sent his mind through the step and its connection to the wall. "I don't think it's sturdy enough. It's barely holding on."

"Then I'll shadowalk up them. I'm much lighter in the nether. Once I'm up to the window, I'll let down a rope for you poor sods that are stuck in this world."

Dante supposed that might do the trick. Heart racing, he dissolved the step and sent it up the side of the tower, watching the wards much more closely than his work. A few seconds later, and he'd glued a step to the wall, with no corresponding crackle of ethereal energy to announce he'd just betrayed them to the tower priests.

"One down," Dante said, mildly impressed to see Blays' suggestion working. "A whole bunch to go."

He drew more stone from the vertical face of the platform. Rather than trying to build an entire staircase, he spaced the steps out by several vertical feet, arranging them in a zipper pattern. He set the last one three feet below the dark window.

Blays undid his rope from the rail. "Well, wish me luck."

He blinked into the shadows. Dante could feel him moving up one step to the next, ascending them as quickly as he might run up a proper staircase. Just a minute later, he reappeared on the top step. He took a peek through the window, then climbed inside. After another few seconds, a rope tumbled down the wall of the tower, dangling right in front of them.

"You first," Dante said to Gladdic. "Take whatever time you need."

Gladdic curled his lip, tied the rope to his belt, and started up. Dante shifted his mind from step to step to follow Gladdic's progress. His ascent was stressing the steps' bond to the wall, especially when he first put his weight upon one, and in four cases the steps were loosened enough that he had to reseal them to the wall once Gladdic was up to the next one. Soon enough, however, Blays was helping pull Gladdic through the window, and Gladdic was casting the end of the rope down to Dante.

Dante secured the rope to himself and started up, easily heaving from one step to the next. He made himself slow down and ensure both the security of his footing and the integrity of the treads. A hard gust of wind tried to yank him from the wall and he waited for it to pass. Blays' face waited in the window above him.

When Dante was just ten feet away, the step crumbled beneath him.

By instinct, he grabbed tight to the rope, bonking against the side of the building. The step hit the one below it with a crack, knocking it loose. Before they could kick up a full pandemonium, Dante dissolved them into the loosest mud he could. This soon spattered itself out.

He hung against the wall, waiting for a reaction of some kind from within the tower. But the very lack of windows on the lower portion of the structure—intended, presumably, to make it harder to get in—meant that there was no one around to hear the noise. Dante wrapped the rope around his wrist and pulled himself up to the next step. It held. So did the rest, until hands were grabbing him, lugging him over the window sill.

"So this is the Tower of Taim," Blays said. "I'd say we're either about to have a very good night, or an extremely bad one."

30

Before doing anything else, Dante leaned back out to dissolve the steps in case someone happened to take a look at the rear of the building. For all he'd known the chamber they'd climbed up to was somebody's bedroom, but it turned out to be a study or the like.

"Well, good for us," Blays said softly. "But I've been doing some thinking. No outsiders are let inside the tower, right? Like, at all?"

"Right," Dante said. "Hence that dangerous sequence of events we just undertook."

"And meanwhile we're dressed like outsiders."

"Oh. Right. Hmm. That is a problem."

"Can I shadowalk around in here? Without drawing attention?"

"If you can't, we're probably in trouble. I mean, even worse trouble than we already are." Dante took a look around the shadows. "The wards are only on the outer walls of the tower. You can probably pass through the interior walls without setting anything off."

"Good. That should make it a lot easier for me to find us some proper clothes."

Blays vanished into the nether. Dante didn't dare do any exploring beyond the study, so he and Gladdic had nothing to do but twiddle their thumbs in near-total darkness until Blays came back, which luckily only took a couple of minutes. He was bearing three gray robes marked with white hourglasses.

They stripped off their travel gear and donned their latest disguises. Gladdic's was too short, showing off most of his bony shins. Dante and Blays belted their swords on underneath their robes.

Blays twisted from side to side, examining his fit. "Of course this doesn't solve the problem that everyone here likely knows each other by face, too."

"Easy fix," Dante said. "Just go and steal us three of their faces."

"They may even recognize everyone who belongs here by voice. So if I've got this right, all we have to do is avoid being seen or spoken to by absolutely everyone."

"That should be our goal in any case." Dante was grumbling, but that was in part because the true scope of what was in front of them was finally starting to sink in. Getting this far had taken a lot of planning and a lot of luck. Now that they were inside the tower, they'd run out of plan. He hoped the same wasn't true for their luck.

Blays had explored a bit of what lay beyond the study and guided them out the door and into a hallway with a high arched ceiling. The way was lit by unblinking balls of ether: torchstones. If every hall bore them, the tower must have thousands. The air smelled like baking bread, which was pleasant, but upsetting: that the bakers felt the need to start their work before midnight implied that the tower would be waking up early.

There were dozens of floors to the tower and this one didn't seem to be anything special, yet its walls were carved in exquisite reliefs. Some displayed battles, as was typical anywhere you went, but others showed the pious engaged in holy rituals, or just going about their simple, orderly days. After walking a ways, it seemed as if the reliefs were attempting to capture every sphere of human life, with special emphasis on representing the different stages a person experienced from earliest childhood to oldest age—though these experiences could be quite different in the quasi-ageless Realm than they were in the Fallen Land.

Blays brought them to a stout wooden door that looked to have been made from a single cut from an enormous tree. Its surface was arrayed with imposing sigils, few of which Dante recognized, but the door was unlocked and didn't try to incinerate them or the like as they stepped through.

This was a stairwell. An usually elegant and resplendent stairwell. The steps were made of black marble, the walls of an unknown white stone. The treads were too wide for a spiral, so they were arranged in landings instead.

And someone was walking down the one above them at that very second. They backed out the door, closing it quietly behind them, and waited for the low echo of the footsteps to pass them by.

"There is a great deal of distance between us and Taim's chambers," Gladdic said. "Perhaps we should plan for what we will do should we encounter others on our way there."

"Try to slip past them without drawing notice," Dante said. "If we're near a landing, we can exit the stairwell. Or I can hide us inside the wall. Those are the only things we can do."

"Incorrect. We could also kill them."

"Let's reserve that as a last resort."

They reentered the stairwell. It appeared to be empty, but they'd only advanced two landings before they heard more footsteps overhead. Blays ducked out the door into another hallway, conveniently empty. It looked the same as the others, but the reliefs were all different.

They waited for the person to pass by, then reentered the staircase. After ascending just a single floor, steps approached from above — and from below. Dante pulled a wisp of shadows to him and sent them into the stone wall. It opened like a mouth and he dived inside, pulling it shut just before either of the people approaching them came into view.

He left open a tiny peephole. Through this, he observed as both the person ascending and descending passed his line of sight. "Bad news. One of them's in uniform. All this traffic isn't just people coming and going. The stairs are patrolled."

"This should not surprise us," Gladdic said. "Even if all those who are within the tower belong here, they do not belong in every part of the tower."

"So far, we've made it what, three floors up?" Blays said. "With roughly a billion more to go? What are the chances we'll be able to dodge every patrol between here and the top?"

Dante pressed his palm to the cool stone. "About the same as your chances of ever finishing a book."

"Then it's worse than I thought."

Something snapped into place in Dante's head. "We've already solved the problem. Yes, it would be exceedingly difficult for three strange people to get all the way up the stairs. But what if we're not people?"

"I think Gladdic's already got that covered."

"I'm talking about *goods*. The tower can't possibly produce everything its residents need. They probably bring in a ton of goods every week. Probably *several* tons."

"Using porters to carry such a mass of goods up a stairway would be most inefficient," Gladdic mused. "You believe there is a lift system such as the one we used to gain entry to the city."

"I'm almost sure of it. We just need to find it."

He was afraid they'd have to go all the way to the ground floor to locate the lifting-station, but Blays pointed out a much better idea: stay right where they were while Dante groped around through the stone of the tower until he found something that felt right. Hardly a minute later, Dante located a vertical rectangular structure that was in the wrong location to be the cloaca and felt significantly too large to be a chimney or the like.

They slipped out of the wall and left the stairwell. Dante brought them to the vertical open structure, which was blocked off by a solid wall, but he simply opened a hole through it—exposing a pair of stout ropes.

Blays leaned his head in. "It's dark. But it goes up."

Dante extended a ledge for them to stand on, then closed the wall behind them. Gladdic lit a bit of ether, revealing that they were inside a space about twelve feet by eight. The shaft reached down to the base of the tower and as high up as Dante could feel.

After some strategizing, and a few exploratory tugs on the ropes, Blays tied himself to Gladdic, then swung out into open space. He wrapped his legs around the rope and secured himself to it with an ingenious little tool Lars had given them involving a loop of strong cord and a wheeled mechanism that could slide up or down a rope but could also be clamped tight; this would allow a climber to take short breaks during a long ascent.

Or, in this case, for Blays to lead the way upward while assisting a one-armed man to climb along behind him.

Dante waited for them to get their rhythm down, made sure his weight wouldn't make the rope do anything wonky, then started after the others. Their breathing echoed off the bare stone. Blays' climbing device made little clicks as he loosened it while moving upwards and tightened it to give Gladdic a hand up. After about thirty feet, they came to a proper landing with a pair of doors for goods to be offloaded. They stepped onto it to catch their breath.

Blays eyed Gladdic. "You're a lot heavier than you look."

"Then be glad for the chance to build up your strength."

They moved on as soon as they were able. It was tough going

and Dante was relieved to arrive at another loading platform fifty feet onward. It soon became a punishing endurance test, although one Dante could cheat at by cleansing their muscles with nether. He tried to count how many platforms they'd reached, but got confused after the fifth or sixth and gave up.

"Hello," Blays said. "We appear to have found the ceiling."

Flat stone hung above them, along with a number of pulleys and other machinery. Dante wanted to faint with relief. Blays and Gladdic swung from the rope to the final platform and Dante joined them.

The double doors were secured from the other side. Rather than breaking them open, Dante simply opened an exit through the stone wall. They entered a dusty-smelling room with a high ceiling. The space would have felt large, but it was filled with various crates, bags, barrels, and bottles, rendering it more cozy.

Dante felt upward into the ceiling, but had the foreboding sense he shouldn't explore too far. "There's still some more tower above us. But I don't think we have much further to go."

There was no light except for a lone torchstone in the middle of the ceiling and they made their way forward with care so as not to trip over anything. A rolling door led out of the storage room, currently open. They listened for any noise before exiting. And walked right into a man and a woman wearing work clothes and gloves.

The woman rocked back on her heels, eyes flicking over their robes. "Brothers. I must ask what you are doing here?"

"My master ran out of his favorite wine," Blays said without missing a beat. "Wasn't any in the usual places, so I thought we'd try here."

"But all access to the sundries is—"

Blays waved his hand and rolled his eyes. "Restricted, I know. Trust me, when he's in his cups, there's no reasoning with him."

Blays nodded as if the matter were finished and made to step past her. The man blocked his way.

"Who is your master?" the woman said.

"Why?" Blays said. "If this is going to get him into trouble—"

He flinched back; blood erupted from the foreheads of both workers. Gladdic lowered his hand as their bodies crumpled to the ground.

"Messy," Blays muttered.

Gladdic shrugged. "No choice."

"I know."

There was a lot of spatter. And bleeding. Before it could get any worse, Dante sank the bodies and their discharges into the stone floor. After he finished, Blays beckoned them into the room across from the storage room. This appeared to be a supplemental storage space, but it contained something the other one didn't: a window.

Dante leaned out his head. Judging by the stars, they were on the north face of the tower. From how small the Upper City looked, they were a long way up.

He bent his head upward to make sure. "We can't be more than a few floors below the inner sanctum. Gladdic, are we still headed in the right direction?"

Gladdic checked his charm. "Very close now."

After a bit of skulking around, they located another staircase. They were soon confronted with the sound of footsteps, but were expecting it this time, and ducked into the wall until the person passed. Three floors later, the staircase came to an end.

Dante gathered a handful of nether. He made sure his hood was low enough to conceal the upper half of his face, and opened the door.

At that moment, the bells rang out the hour. It was possible this saved their lives. For rather than stepping out into another hallway, they were entering an antechamber. Less than twenty feet away, a priest in officious gray robes stood before the opposite doorway. Due to the playing of the bells, the priest was glancing to his left, as if he might be able to see the spire of the cathedral the bells were sounding from.

This gave Blays the chance to slip to his own left, the opposite way the priest was paying attention to, and get behind a cyclopean pillar. Hurriedly, Dante dissolved the nether out of his hand.

Dante slowly moved forward, drifting subtly to his right. The priest snapped his head around to face them.

"Apologies," the man said. "The High Hall is closed for the evening."

"Yes, I was afraid that would be the case." Dante got a little closer. He lowered his head in imitation of thought. "Even so, you might still be able to help me."

"Unfortunately, I am in the midst of my duties."

"Yes, that's what it relates to. I have come to inform you that you've been relieved of those duties."

The priest made a scoffing sound. "If such an order had been given, it would have been given by—"

Whatever he was going to say next was cut off by the point of Blays' knife as it plunged into the side of the man's neck. Blays yanked the blade to the side, severing the priest's windpipe. Blood fanned down the front of his robe. Ether blinked in the man's hands, but before he could do anything with his powers, Blays snapped his neck.

Blays stepped back, letting the body do what it would. Dante confirmed the priest was dead and embedded him in the ground. Clenching the nether in his fist, he entered the doorway the man had been guarding.

The priest had called the room beyond the High Hall, which could have referred either to its elevation or the height of its ceiling—or, Dante supposed, to its status within the tower. The yawning space was all but completely dark, but the three of them had spent enough time practicing in Dante's mockup of the room that they practically could have made their way through it with their eyes closed. Pillars broke up the openness and they used these to cover their advance.

The back of the room was dominated by an altar adorned with all sorts of paraphernalia that Dante would have really liked to be able to see, as he was sure it was stunning. But the gloom was too much, and they had no time to linger.

The door behind the altar was hidden unless you knew where to look, so it was a good thing he did. As had been the case with the palaces of the other gods, the penultimate chamber before the inner sanctum was a chapel.

Taim's was as grand as any of them, lit by the moonlight pouring in through its shadowcut glass windows and down past its ribbed vaults. The floor was tiled in a pattern as inscrutable as the layout of the city and the statues of the angels and saints were so lifelike Dante nearly cried out in alarm. A sense of foreboding rolled from the place like cold fog. Dante's heart thumped. He took a silent step forward, then another, biting the inside of his lip until he tasted blood. He expected Ka to leap out and attack them right up until the moment they came to the final door.

This was locked, of course. Dante thought he'd be able to force it open if he had to, but Gladdic recognized that its mechanism was ethereal in nature, and only had too fool around with it for a minute before he had it sprung.

The three of them exchanged a significant look and entered the heart of the Tower of Taim.

Stars spun about them, drawn into constellations, some that Dante recognized, others that he didn't, more vivid and numerous than on the darkest night of winter, hypnotic in their beauty, revolving in cycles and epicycles that had been recurring since before anyone had been alive to see them and would continue for eternity after all witnesses were gone.

Between the stars, visions danced: people warring and singing and wedding and dying. Most were dressed in strange clothes and many were foreigners whose features and look Dante had never seen before. Somehow, he knew these were real people—both from this world and his own—and he was not only seeing across space, but across *time*, fleeting moments long forgotten, lost to everything but the kaleidoscope of Taim's chambers.

Just as he was about to look away, he froze. In the space before him, a giant of a man strolled across the ruins of a burning town, his skin alight with ether, his eyes glowing blue. Around him, throngs of pale, warped figures cascaded through the burning streets. Before the vision switched to another, Dante thought he recognized the bridges of Dollendun.

Between the cycling stars and the glimpses of exotic elsewheres, it was so much to take in that Dante only then noticed the Spear of Stars.

It was standing on its end, held up by nothing. Ether pulsed within it. Even more beautiful than the constellations behind it.

Gladdic was already staring at it. Blays saw it at the same time as Dante, his jaw falling open. He bulged his eyes and stepped toward it.

"Stop," Gladdic hissed. "Do not touch the spear!"

Blays glanced over his shoulder. "Now's not the time to get jealous. I'll let you see it once I'm done with it."

"That is not the spear. Whatever it is, should you touch it, you will forfeit our lives."

Dante was about to ask Gladdic what the hell he was talking about. Until he saw that Gladdic was holding the tracking charm in his hand, and that it was sparkling with ether.

31

Blays stared at Gladdic, puzzled to the point of anger. "What are you—"

Gladdic silenced him with a ferocious gesture. Then motioned to the door they'd come in through. Dante was first to exit. Blays hesitated, then joined him, shaking his head. Gladdic took them past the chapel and into an exceedingly dark corner of the High Hall.

"All right, we're out of there," Blays whispered. "Now will you tell me why the spear isn't the spear?"

"The object we were looking upon is only made to resemble the spear," Gladdic said. "When I tested it with the charm, the feeling was wrong."

"How do you know? Have you used it to find a lot of other Spears of Stars before this?"

"I am *right*." Gladdic was whispering, too, but spat this last word out hard enough for it to cut through the vaults of the hall. "That is not the true spear. I would stake my life upon it. I would stake the life of *everything* upon it."

Blays grimaced, pressing his palm to his brow and rubbing it in a circle. "You're saying the one in there is a decoy. To guarantee that even if we were crazy enough to try to do this, and good enough to get this far, Taim would still get to have the last laugh about killing us. Then what did he do with the real spear? Is it even in the tower?"

"Of that I am certain. It remains quite close to us."

"Then hopefully this tower isn't, say, hundreds of feet tall, and crammed with hundreds of people with orders to strike us dead—and oh yeah, probably an angel too, and also the lord of the gods."

"We can think this through," Dante said. "If the one in there is a decoy, then Taim guessed where we'd look for it. His sanctum. So where did he put it instead?"

"Literally anywhere else in the universe?"

"Somewhere that we cannot get to," Gladdic said.

"Ah. So a *different* universe."

Dante shook his head. "I don't think he can do something like that, or else he would have done it right at the very beginning. Besides, Gladdic says it's close. It's got to be in the tower somewhere."

"Then he'd put it in the equivalent of a different universe," Blays said. "Somewhere we couldn't get to. Somewhere we didn't even know was there."

Dante narrowed his eyes. "Give me a minute."

He sent his mind out into the stone of the building's structure, following it upward and downward, happy to travel wherever it would lead him. Working blind, it was hard to develop a full picture of what he was finding, and he was right about to start drawing it out so he could visualize it better when the matter became moot.

"He probably wouldn't just put it behind a locked door," Dante said. "He wouldn't even want us to know what we were looking at. The best place would be a room with no windows or doors at all. A place where there was no indication it even existed."

Blays pushed up his lower lip. "That's not a bad thought."

"I know. Because I just found it."

The space in question was two floors beneath them. Dante was feeling spooked enough that he didn't want to risk the stairs again—the more guards they disappeared, the sooner somebody was going to notice that something was seriously wrong inside the tower—so he moved back to the antechamber where they'd killed the priest, opened a hole in the floor, confirmed the room below was empty, and lowered them down into it. A little more sneaking around brought them directly above the space he'd identified.

He checked for wards and saw none. He moved inside the rock above the space and swept it aside. There was a chance he was completely wrong: that he couldn't feel inside the space because it was constructed out of wood instead of stone, or that it was just an architectural quirk. But as soon as he opened the room's ceiling and smelled the dustiness that arose from it, he knew he'd come to the right place even before their light spread across the objects stored within it.

He rearranged the stone from its ceiling into a crude staircase and took it down into the room. This was similar to the storage chamber they'd climbed the ropes into, although smaller, perhaps thirty feet to a side, and the items within it weren't ordered nearly as neatly, and in some cases looked to have just been dumped on the floor. A sconce held a torch at each end of the room, but the torches were unlit. Gladdic conjured forth light.

Dante closed the ceiling behind them just in case someone wandered across it. "Tell me if you start feeling lightheaded. I don't know how old the air is in here."

Blays peered about himself. "Not to say doom prematurely, but if it was down here, wouldn't we see it glowing?"

"It could be inside a container. Or it could be...blown out."

"Blown out?"

"You know. Like a candle."

"Hmm." Blays moved into the crush of objects. Gladdic produced a second gleam of ether to follow Blays around and light his way.

"What about the charm?" Dante said. "Does it say we're in the right place?"

Gladdic consulted it, scowling and flinching back as soon as the ether touched it. "I am not certain."

"It could tell you the other one *wasn't* the spear, but now you can't tell if we're on top of the real one?"

The old man waved his hand. "This art is more subtle than your crude blood-hunts. Now if you wish to find the spear, you might spend less time moving your mouth and more time using your eyes."

This wasn't really the answer Dante was looking for. As a matter of fact, it made him second-guess Gladdic's certainty that the spear in the sanctum had been a decoy. But they were already down here, and besides, the old man had a habit of being right when it mattered, so Dante began his search.

He made a quick initial pass to make sure it wasn't just hidden under a blanket or something, then began a methodical search, starting with the corner closest to him, which held a mix of scrap iron and leather-bound books. Dante couldn't help himself from taking a peek inside, but restrained himself to some brief skimming.

As if he had a nose for it, Blays located a case of wine, which of course he sampled, then cursed with contempt at whichever fool had allowed it to age into vinegar. Blays then found some old swords and hand axes, but nothing that resembled a spear, let alone a god-forged glowing one. Gladdic, meanwhile, was going from one container to the next, jimmying off the lids for a quick look inside.

Very, very faintly, the ringing of the bells filtered into the entryless room. Dante stood up from the junk he was sorting through to listen. It was after midnight. How long until a change of the guard revealed that someone had gone missing? Or until the entire tower began to wake up?

"What if we're wrong?" Dante said. "Or what if we're right that Taim hid the spear somewhere else, but wrong about the where?"

Blays looked up from the gardening tools he'd been going over. "Are there any other rooms like this where it might be?"

That was a good question, and as Blays and Gladdic continued to pick through the room, Dante explored the structure of the tower.

"I can only reach so far," he decided after several minutes of effort. "But I'm not seeing anything else like this place."

"We've just about searched everything here." Concern crawled into Blays' voice. "Maybe it's time to look somewhere else."

"But I don't *see* anywhere else."

"I tell you it is close." Gladdic was consulting the charm again, brow furrowed, mouth half open. "So close you might reach out and take it."

Just in case it was embedded in one of the walls, Dante felt them for gaps or irregularities. "If we're that close, then we have to be in the wrong spot. Because it isn't here. There are no other rooms like this, either. That means our whole theory is wrong."

"Or merely that it is incomplete." The tone in Gladdic's voice was one Dante had heard before. It was the same one that overtook philosophers and theologians when they had a dawning revelation. "If Taim's goal was to hide the spear, he would not simply toss it in the middle of a secret room and consider his work finished. He would render it so that even if an infiltrator were to somehow find the room, he could be looking right at the spear and not even know it."

"Check the shadows," Dante said to Blays. "Gladdic, you look into the ether the best you can."

Blays popped out of sight. Gladdic summoned straight rays of ether to him and scattered them across the room. Blays was back within a quarter of a minute.

"Not seeing anything," he said. "If there's any hint of it in the nether, it's as well-hidden as it is here."

Gladdic persisted for another minute, then let the light of his efforts fade. "For a moment I thought I sensed something. Yet when I reached for it, it was not there."

Dante exhaled in defeat. "There's no sense wasting more time here. We'll do some moving around while Gladdic monitors the charm. That way we can get a better sense of its exact location."

"Why do I have the feeling that's going to lead us right back here?" Blays said.

"Even if it does, at least we'll know for sure we're in the right place. Right now, we're just groping around in the dark."

Blays turned away, mollified. Then whipped his head back around. "Funny you should say that. Has it crossed your mind to ask why there are torches in here?"

"Because light helps us see?"

"But we haven't seen torches anywhere else. Just torch-stones." Blays' voice grew more certain as he went along. "Anyway, there's no ventilation in here. Light up a stinking torch and you'll choke yourself."

He was glancing between the two torches like a cat stalking an ignorant bird. Making some kind of calculation, he rocked forward, heading for the one furthest from him—which, now that Dante was thinking about it, showed no pitting or scorching, as if it had never been used.

Blays stood before the torch. He gripped it in one hand, tugging to disengage it from its sconce. It didn't budge. He took it in both hands, spread his feet apart, and pulled, rotating his upper body to add more torque.

With a glassy scrape, the shaft slid loose. Yet a great deal of it seemed to be embedded in the wall, for rather than pulling free of the stone, the shaft grew longer and longer as Blays drew it forth, until he had to take a step back to keep going, the pole now four feet long, then six. With a final heave, he drew the last of it free.

He goggled at what he had in hand. From end to end, the torch had to be ten feet long. Yet other than its absurd length, it was a perfectly ordinary torch.

"What the hell?" Blays said. "But it was such a good idea!"

"It must be ceremonial," Dante said. He made a pass of the nether within it. "Feels normal. Like typical iron."

"You know, for a second there, I really thought I had it. I guess sometimes, a torch is just a torch." He lowered the torch, rotating the shaft for a better look. "But what the hell is wrong with these people? Who makes a torch that's ten feet — "

The room exploded with light.

Something was exerting pressure on Dante's rear. It was the ground. He was sitting on it. He felt remarkably good, as if he'd just awakened from an enchanted sleep.

Ah. He'd fainted. That explained all the dazzles in his eyes. Gladdic was seated next to him, supporting himself with his arm, head nodding as he came back to his senses. Dante let his head clear a moment longer, then got to his feet, hanging onto a nearby crate for balance. He offered a hand to Gladdic, but Gladdic waved him off.

The room was exceedingly bright. Weird. If Gladdic had fainted, his ether should have winked out as well. Dante bladed his hand above his eyes and squinted into the glare.

The light was being cast by ether. There was no mistaking the clarity and the purity of it. But it was not being produced by Gladdic. Rather, it was coming from the head of the torch. And from Blays, who was still holding the torch, his skin glowing like the aura of the White Lich. He seemed taller, too, though Dante didn't think he actually was, but his *presence* loomed larger, as if he was more real than everything else around him.

Dante's eyes began to adjust. Enough that the torch no longer looked like a torch. His throat closed tight.

"We've done it." With the words, the reality sank in. He thrust his fists above his head. "We've taken the spear!"

"If only for the moment." Gladdic's voice was dour, but then a smile broke across his face. "Even so, this moment is not one that I expected to ever see. Perhaps fortune will stay with us a while yet."

Blays had been holding the head of the spear high. He lowered it and executed an exploratory thrust. The ether within the weapon tumbled like smoke in the wind. Blays made another pair of jabs, then twirled the spear's point in a tight circle, the way you'd knock an enemy's weapon out of the way. Then came another thrust, an upward slash—the spear's blade was as long as a short sword, and bore a keen cutting edge—followed by a horizontal bash of the butt, a hard and fast forehand cut, then a blur of subtle but vicious maneuvers that looked as though they would rip a hole through the front line of the heaviest infantry.

"I didn't know you were that good with spears," Dante said.

"I'm good with everything." Blays slid forward, twirling his feet, but twirling the spear much faster, such that streaks of its light trailed behind it. Yet he somehow avoiding striking any of the debris. "But not *that* good. The damn thing is leading me."

"Leading you?"

"This is a dangerous weapon. It wants to destroy things, and it knows how to do it."

"Well, be careful with it."

"Are you kidding? I can't wait to wreak hell with it."

"Then I suppose we'd better figure out how to get it out of here. It's, er, a little bright right now. Not to mention long. And spear-like. Don't suppose there's any way to get it back to look-ing like an ordinary torch?"

Blays hefted the spear. "Become a torch. Ready, go."

A part of Dante thought the weapon might actually heed Blays' command. It didn't. Blays cocked his head, focusing. The spear contracted at both ends, the light shrinking with it, until both the blade and the butt disappeared, and the shaft was no longer than Blays' forearm. Only the purestone remained un-changed in shape: a flawless gem the size of a green apple, perched at the top of the shaft like the rod of a king. Its light dwindled until there was no more than some extra sparkle to its facets.

"How'd you do that?" Dante said.

Blays shrugged. "I just wanted it to get smaller."

"What all can that thing do?"

"I almost hope they come at me and give me a chance to find out."

"Don't even say that."

Blays tucked the rod up his sleeve, fiddling about until it was secure. Gladdic called up some light to make up for the loss of the spear's. Dante had left his staircase in place and took it up to the ceiling. He motioned to Gladdic, who dimmed the light, and then he opened a hole into the room above.

He crouched there in the darkness, waiting for the others. With a moment to think, it surprised him the spear hadn't been somehow warded or watched over. Then again, doing so would have revealed that there *was* something to be warded or watched, making it less likely for any thieves to fall for the decoy —and far more likely to find the true spear instead.

Gladdic and Blays climbed up into the room. Dante covered the hole, leaving no trace of his work. They were currently with-in a wholly dark room with a bunch of soft chairs and a few ta-bles that suggested a space for casual socialization. He paused there to think through the choice ahead of them. On the one hand, they could return to the storage chamber, descend the rope to the platform Dante had built into the shaft, go back to the library, then rappel down the outside of the tower. But that would still leave them with the matter of getting down from the Upper City, and would involve a lot of scurrying around inside the tower in the meantime, so he decided to stick to the original plan instead.

A pair of people were out in the hallway murmuring to each other in the tone of an argument that was one wrong word away from turning hostile. As their conversation wore on, Dante supposed he could have murdered them—assuming, of course, they weren't about to murder each other. But finally they walked away, still hissing at each other, most likely to take the argument somewhere private.

While he'd waited, Dante had felt his way forward through the stone, mapping out the exact route to a room on the back side of the tower—one that contained a window. They made their way to it. After checking to make sure nobody was inside it, they closed the door behind them. It didn't have a lock, but rather than blocking it with furniture, Blays and Gladdic took up position to either side of it, the idea being that if anyone happened to step inside, they could kill the intruder before he could utter a peep.

With their security in place, Dante went to work.

He rifled through their bag of goods until he located his heavy, waterproof cloth, inside of which was a lightly dampened cloth, inside of which were the vines he'd collected in the woods outside of Denhild. One of them had died on their journey to Chronus, but more than enough remained.

He cut his knuckle and poured shadows into the vines, harvesting one end of each plant to wend through the room and wrap around anything solid. With these anchored firmly in place, he turned to the other tips of the vines, extending them a short way, then shaping the ends into loops. He stepped into one and pulled against the vine with all his might. It held without any sign of tearing. So did the other two.

He already knew the vines were absurdly strong, which was why he'd chosen them in the first place. But just to be sure, he secured a proper rope to himself, dangled one of the vine-loops out the window, then stepped into it, suspending himself on the outside of the tower.

After several long moments of testing it out, he climbed back into the room. "Ready?"

Blays came over from the door and stared down into the long, long drop to the bottom. "Are you absolutely sure you've got enough juice to get us all the way down?"

"More than enough to get us past the tower. After that, I can build us stairs, if we need to. Or handholds for us to work down with."

"Why do I have the bad feeling this is going to wind up with us stranded on the side of a cliff five hundred feet in the air praying that nobody happens to glance our way for however many hours of sleep you need to recover your strength?"

"Because you don't understand just how great I am." Dante slung one leg out the window. "Hard discipline until we're below the tower. Probably for a ways after that, too."

In silence, he got his foot in his loop and harvested his vine a few feet below the window, clearing room for the others to step outside and into their own loops. After both of them gave him the nod, Dante streamed the nether into each vine, lowering them alongside the tower.

The wind was cold and unsteady. From their angle on the tower, he could only see part of one of the platforms that comprised the Upper City. It looked unbelievably far away, two hundred yards at the absolute least. The Lower City was no less than another hundred yards beyond that, and the ground might have been another two hundred from there. At least a quarter mile. For three vines. He'd been very confident in himself just a minute ago, but now that the task was underway, he wasn't so sure. He wished very badly he had a single shaden.

He tried to block all of this out of his mind in favor of concentrating on getting them away from the god who would stick their heads on spikes if he caught them in his home. The vines reeled out one foot after another, dropping them past a darkened window, then another. The idea of dangling from a thousand-foot-long living rope that was only attached to the tower at a single point was clearly insane, so when they reached a decorative shelf running across the face of the tower, he grew the vines tight around the raised bits of it before continuing the descent.

A sudden gust rushed over him and he steadied himself against the wall with one hand. After a few seconds, the wind eased off, only to heighten again as soon as Dante resumed lowering them down the tower. He tried to wait it out, but it was soon clear that the winds weren't going anywhere, and unless he felt like clinging to the side of the building until they relented, in full view of the first insomniac to lean out a window for a breath of fresh air, they were just going to have to deal with the unfavorable change in weather.

He extended the vines steadily. The longer their living ropes got, the more play the wind had to sway or twist them around, and Dante secured them to an outcrop of short statues of falcons that served as both rain spouts and as a means of scaring off the pigeons who liked to make messes in hard-to-reach portions of the tower. They were almost a third of the way down the tower already and he spent some time examining the dark plain beneath the city, considering which way to flee. North would be the shortest route back to the horses, but if they needed cover, the mountains were closer to the east. The river that had delivered them to the tower was between them and the eastern mountains, though, so if they wanted to go that way, they'd have to cross it. Then again, that shouldn't be an issue, given that—

"Help," Blays blurted. "Help now fast."

Dante hurled his mind into Blays' vine. It was fraying around the falcon statues, which had sawed into it under the duress of the winds. Dante sent the nether racing upward to mend it, but it felt like it was about to snap at any instant, so by pure instinct he also reached into the stone just below Blays' feet, meaning to extend a shelf for him to stand on.

The stone didn't move an inch. But something else inside the wall stirred. All of Dante's guts seemed to drain out of him. He made himself stay focused, reaching the fray and harvesting it hard. Three new vine-branches shot out from beneath the fray as well, groping upward to find a hold among the rain spouts.

"There," Dante said. "That ought to do it."

Blays was staring at him. "Then why do you look like a boy who just cut off his own finger with his dad's wood axe after being warned not to touch it?"

"Because I should have been paying better attention to your vine. Now be quiet. We're almost to the next window."

As he unspooled more vine, Dante's entire body stayed rigid, like a mouse frozen by the screech of an owl. They came to another ledge of statue-spouts, which Dante secured them to. They were now halfway down the tower. Another few hundred feet, and everything was about to get a lot easier.

A bell tolled.

This was not the glassy, melodic ringing of the hour. Nor was it from one of the cathedrals. Instead, it came from overhead. And it was deep, and slow, and menacing. It sounded the way a thunderstorm might if it was a living thing—and if it was hungry.

Blays tipped back his head. "Why does it sound like the underworld just woke up and is very cross with whoever disturbed its sleep?"

Dante dumped shadows into the vines, sending them skimming along the face of the tower. "When you were about to fall, I reached into the stone. To put some ground under your feet."

"The *warded* stone?"

"I forgot about the wards. I thought you were about to die."

"Then maybe you were just predicting our immediate future."

"Hush!" Gladdic spat.

The bell was still ringing its belching tone. Dante was still feeding nether into the vines. Above and below them, heads poked from windows.

"We've been spotted," Blays said. "Next comes the part where we get shot full of arrows."

"Gladdic, make sure that doesn't happen," Dante said.

Shadows darkened around Gladdic. A good choice, as the light of ether would only have made them a better target. They passed another window; inside, men were arguing in loud confusion. Nether flew up from Gladdic's hand, striking a man forty feet above them. He slumped over the window sill. A bow tumbled from his hands.

An arrow whisked past them from below. Before Dante could react, Gladdic killed the archer dead. More and more soldiers popped from the windows like well-armed gophers, but they had a terrible angle of fire on the climbers, and their arrows flew wide. Gladdic neutralized them moments later.

The three of them were still eighty feet from the base of the tower when someone reached out a window and cut Dante's vine with a hatchet.

This wasn't just bad, it was double-bad. For they were climbing down the back end of the tower, where there were no platforms of the Upper City beneath them. Just the long, long fall to the plains.

Blays started shouting; his vine had been cut too. Gladdic's was in the act of being cut and there was nothing he could do to stop it, but that didn't rattle him enough to stop him from killing the man with the hatchet. Gladdic fell in silence, resigned to his fate, perhaps even looking forward to it.

Dante was rather less thrilled. The smooth stone of the tower wall flew past his face. He reached into the vines that were flapping around like they were in a panic and launched fresh growths from them, searching for any structure jutting from the tower.

Unfortunately, they were now soaring past the bottom fifty feet of the tower, which was completely featureless. Dante slapped their vines against the wall anyway, shooting out as many tendrils as he could make the plants produce.

His loop of vine jerked against his foot. He slowed to a stop as the dozens of tendrils hugged themselves to the rock, but they were already pulling loose from their tenuous hold. Dante and the others were now almost level with the base of the tower. Dante dived his mind into the unwarded rock underneath it and lifted a platform to meet him just as the plants ripped free.

He landed with a painful but non-bone-breaking thump. Blays and Gladdic plopped down beside him. Gladdic's face was excruciatingly neutral, but the ether he summoned and sent into his leg implied he'd been badly hurt, perhaps to the point of a fracture.

"Nice of them to give us a shortcut," Blays said. "What now? I assume we're done with the vines?"

"Very." Dante reached into the massive stone pillar that made up one of the three platforms of the Upper City. "We don't dare try to take the stairs, either. Good thing for us I brought something much better."

He drew out the wall, shaping it into a downward slope that

curved along the side of the pillar. He made sure its outer edge was rounded upward by a good eight inches.

Blays nodded his approval. "Ah, just like that time some asshole stopped me from killing King Moddegan."

Dante scooted across the level part of the platform and entered the slide, starting down it—a little too fast, in fact; he gentled its angle ahead of him, decreasing his speed to something less likely to fling him over the side. A glance back confirmed the others were following after him without issue.

They sliced along the face of the platform, spiraling downward. It was going to take a fair bit of masonry to deliver them all the way to the bottom, but in other days Dante had raised entire ramparts and rerouted rivers, and his shadows were still flowing freely. The doomy bell stopped ringing. Sometimes a shout cut through from high above, but for the most part all he could hear was the wind of his passage and the steady sough of his robe against the slide.

In less than a minute, they'd almost completed a full circle of the pillar, the Tower of Taim swinging back into view. As soon as it did, he felt the cold pulse of the ether above them, its light splashing over the dark pillar. But Dante felt the ether rising from Gladdic, too. Lights flashed overhead as the two powers collided.

"We face trouble," Gladdic said.

"Only until we circle out of view."

Gladdic grunted with the effort of holding off another assault. "That may prove to be too long."

Gladdic switched to a nether-heavy defense to better fend off what was now an all-out barrage. Most of Dante's efforts were locked firmly on creating more of the slide in front of them, but he drew forth some stray shadows and tossed them overhead to augment Gladdic's screen. They swung directly beneath the tower, where priests leaned out of windows and against the railings to either side of it, pouring heart-stopping quantities of light down at them.

Gladdic was just barely fending it off. Stray bolts stuck the cliffside, others disappearing into clouds of fading sparks. Dante ran the slide as far ahead of them as he could, then shifted his nether upward just before Gladdic's defense could collapse.

A star of ether smashed into the wall ahead of them, vomiting broken rock into the air and gouging a deep hole in the pillar —as well as obliterating a stretch of slide. Dante rerouted it and leveled it out to avoid the hole, slowing as he did so, which only exposed them to the barrage for longer.

"I cannot last!" Gladdic yelled.

A second globe of ether rammed into the wall. With a growl, Dante opened a passage into the pillar, diverted them into it, and closed the hole behind them.

"Forget the slide," he said. "We're taking the crane."

He swept the stone from beneath them, lowering them almost as fast as the slide would have. Ether thudded dully against the exterior of the column, but they were a good twenty feet inside and could barely hear it. Many years ago, Cally had taught Dante the means of making vacuums out of clever glass pieces, and it occurred to him that extending his originally quite small chamber into an extremely long one would probably reproduce that effect, and then they would suffocate and die. So once they were out of harm's way, he extended a horizontal shaft out to the side. Cold air rushed into the shaft in a gale, the influx calming down as the vacuum was undone.

They calmed themselves as well, catching their breath after the hectic clash at the end of the ride, their robes sifted with stone dust and rumpled by the winds. Gladdic's face was bleeding but he didn't bother to address it. Blays undid his pack, belted on his swords, and handed Dante his own weapon.

"I have the feeling you might need this. What's the plan

now?"

"With any luck, they won't figure out what I'm doing. Even if they do, we'll reach the bottom well before any of them can. We'll cut east across the river and get into the mountains as fast as possible, then circle around for the horses."

"I can't help but notice we didn't get our hands on Taim's charm."

"I know."

"He'll be able to track us."

"I know."

"He'll send Ka after us."

"I *know*."

"Please tell me you also know what we're going to do about that?"

"Kill her," Dante said. "Or die trying."

He lowered them steadily, keeping the chamber tight to minimize the amount of rock he had to manipulate. They were three-quarters of the way to the Lower City. They were set to emerge from the base of the pillar directly below the tower, but that would put them a good nine hundred vertical feet away from the nearest part of it, out of effective range of the enemy sorcerers.

He was just starting to feel good about their chances when they came to a sudden stop.

Blays glanced up, then at Dante. "Did you forget the people out there are trying to kill us?"

"It isn't me," Dante said. "They've discovered what we're up to—and they've stopped it. One of them knows how to work the stone, too."

"Then be better than them."

Dante shoved his mind into the rock underfoot, attempting the mental equivalent of stomping it down. It yielded another foot, then hardened against him. Dante struggled against it with everything he had.

Instead, the stone began to close in around them.

"There's a whole *team* of them!" He felt their minds in the rock, working their way toward him. "I can't push them back!"

Gladdic flung forth his arm with a flap of his robe. "If finesse has failed us, we must turn to force."

Ether seared from his hand and into the side of the chamber, slagging an exit toward freedom. The chamber warmed like a cook pot hung above a fire, growing hotter as the walls squeezed tighter, making Dante shuffle close to Blays. The stone pressed against his back. In moments, it would crush them like skinned tomatoes. Cold air punched into the tube: Gladdic had finished his doorway.

The closing of the chamber spat them out into nothing. Dante tried to rip forth a ledge beneath them, but Taim's priests kept the rock clamped firm. They fell.

They were, at first glance, eighty feet above the streets of the Lower City. Not good. Enough to splash them into a puddle beyond any healing of the nether. On second glance, however, there was a high triangular roof underneath them, reducing the distance to fifty feet. Much more survivable. Especially if he took the stone of the roof and softened it into mud to cushion…

Sending the nether into the roof, he swore. It wasn't stone. They were about to crash right into it, then bounce to the street. Either impact could kill any of them. Nothing to do but hold onto the shadows and get ready to heal as soon as they were done falling.

He tucked his chin to his chest and braced himself.

Two lines of purple light snapped into place beside him. Blays gave his swords an exploratory swing. The roof rose to meet them. Blays extended himself, slashing both weapons into the roof—it was thatch, and thick enough that normal steel would have gotten caught up in it. But not the steel of the Odo

Sein.

The thatch gave way with a fibrous rip, dumping them into a loft. A couple sat up in bed with a paired shriek.

Blays had already made his swords vanish. Now, he fluffed his robe, making sure the couple could see it was from the tower. "Fear not! Vile, handsome men have attacked our fair tower. But we're hot on their tails. Stay inside and don't say a word to anyone. We'll have the city safe again before you know it."

The woman nodded vigorously, a blanket held up to her face, covering everything beneath her eyes. Blays gave her his most winning smile, turned dramatically, and strode toward the ladder. They hurried downstairs, found the door, and exited as if they were chasing after the intruders.

They were now in the Lower City, the air two or three degrees warmer, the wind not quite as biting, the townhouses more homespun and motley than those above, though still quite venerable and elegant. A lot of hubbub was drifting down from the Upper City, but little of it had spread to this level. Several of the neighbors had thrown open their shutters to see what the commotion on the roof had been about.

Dante did his best to look officious. "Lock your doors! Keep away from your windows! The bells will tell you when the evil has been cleansed from the city."

He stiffened his posture as he walked away from the scene, gratified by the clap of shutters being swung shut. He turned north and put a block of buildings between themselves and the witnesses.

"What now?" Blays said. "I'm guessing any more fancy stonework is out of the question. What does that leave? The stairs? Or do we jump off the edge, spread our robes wide, and try our best flying squirrel impression?"

"The stairs would be suicide. We'd have to fight our way through every checkpoint," Dante said. "We're getting out of here the same way we came in. The cargo lift."

"Not as stylish as the flying squirrel route. Maybe next time, eh?"

They hustled to the north side of the city. The cargo lift that had brought them up in the bins went straight from the plains to the Upper City and Dante wasn't certain they'd be able to get to it from the Lower City without manipulating more stone, something the city's priests would be alert for, but they caught a break. The heavy ropes ran right past the edge of the Lower City platform, with an airborne dock allowing for goods to be moved on and off the pallets used to raise and lower those goods.

Even better, a pallet was waiting there for them. From their planning with General Lars, Dante knew it could be lowered automatically, but that didn't mean he knew how to do so, and they set to understanding the pulleys, levers, and gears that controlled it. Gladdic moved to the dock and probed into the nether.

"Got it." Dante stepped back from the controls and frowned at Gladdic. "What are you doing?"

"Covering our escape." Gladdic slapped his hand to the dock. Before him, a towering black shape seemed to conjure itself from within its own shadow. The Star-Eater grinned, the light of its throat flashing from behind its teeth, then shut its mouth tight, rendering it all but invisible within the darkness.

"Good thinking. But how did you know people would have died and left their traces here? They don't age. I doubt many invaders have ever gotten up here, either."

"It is a work site that uses large machinery. Deaths are guaranteed."

The Andrac took up position within the warehouse next to the dock. The three of them loaded themselves onto the pallet and Dante used the nether to nudge a single lever. The pallet lowered smoothly down the side of the gigantic column of rock. The river gleamed dully in the moonlight, encouragingly closer than the last time they'd seen it.

The sound of orders and questions being yelled back and forth stayed at roughly the same distance, implying the tower's priests and soldiers were making their way down the staircase from the Upper City to the Lower. The machinery controlling their descent made an occasional clicking sound, but nothing too loud. If everything held steady, they'd reach the plain and be on their way before their pursuit would even have time to search the Lower City for them.

Gladdic looked up. "Someone is approaching the dock. It is —"

The pallet rocked, then took a sharp drop. And kept dropping.

"They have severed the rope!" Gladdic yelled.

The pallet tilted, threatening to spill them; Blays scrambled to keep from being dumped over. "You don't say?"

Dante said nothing, as he was busy attempting to prevent their death. He'd been afraid of something like this and as soon as they'd gotten started he'd removed the vine from his robe, which he'd kept with him after getting cut down from the tower. A second rope ran parallel to the one that had been lowering their pallet. He threw one end of the vine at the other rope, harvesting it while also harvesting his end around the rope connected to their pallet.

They came to a sudden stop. This slammed the three of them flat. Gladdic skidded toward the edge. Blays grabbed his robe before he could fall off. Branches of the vine popped loose from the pallet.

"Grab the vine!" Dante grew two extensions of it toward Blays and Gladdic, wrapping one around Gladdic's waist and letting Blays take care of himself.

Just before the pallet ripped from the last of its ties, Dante stood and jumped toward the second rope, reaching for both it and the vine he'd snagged to it. He made contact with both. After taking a moment to let his mind stop exploding, he harvested the vines downward at a rapid clip.

"Gladdic," he said. "What happened to the person who cut the rope?"

Gladdic chuckled. "The Andrac consumed him."

"Oh good."

The pallet, still trailing its rope behind it, smashed onto the shore of the body of water at Pulley's Landing. To Dante, the noise seemed extraordinary loud. He hoped it was less loud up at the Lower City, which was now more than a hundred and fifty feet above them, and had grown increasingly noisy as Taim's soldiers and priests entered it and began questioning the residents and dealing out commands. It would be beyond naive to think they'd give up the search, no matter how long it took them. They'd find the cut rope and smashed pallet eventually.

But an extra hour's head start—or even just five minutes—might make all the difference in the world.

They touched down at Pulley's Landing. Dante had never been so glad to be standing in mud. He raised the nether to the top of the vine, cut it loose, stepped back to let it fall, then gathered it up and cast it into the water, which at this spot was almost more like a lake than a river, although there was still some current to it.

"We're heading east, right?" Blays said.

Dante called for more nether. "Right."

"Then I hope you're wearing your sneaking shoes. Or your killing gloves. Or both."

Dante was about to ask him what the hell he was talking about, then shut his mouth. Lanterns bobbed across the fields to the east. The patrolmen or farmers there had heard the foreboding bell. They were some ways away—difficult to tell in the night—but judging by the number of lanterns, there were scores of men, possibly hundreds.

"There's lights to the north, too." He gritted his teeth, running down their options. Every second mattered. "We'll go south. But not overland. We'll take the river."

He took off jogging.

"Interesting plan," Blays said, "except you seem to have hit your head during one of our falls. You're going north."

"They'll try to track us. We're leaving a false trail."

"Not bad. But if we head south, that leads us away from the horses."

"We'll see if we can come back for them later. If we can't, we'll head south. There's another portal not too far from here. We'll do our best to get to it before Taim's forces track us down."

"Great. More cave worms. Or worse. Say we cross through it and it spits us out on the other side of our world?"

"It doesn't matter if the portal sends us to the Mists on the moon. We'll wake up from the Mists in the same place we entered them: the forest outside Bressel."

He was almost certain this was true. He jogged on a little further, then messed with the ground some to give the impression they might have tunneled somewhere. With a trail nice and falsified, he backtracked to the river, got their pack from Blays, and took out the apparatuses.

"Gladdic, freeze a chunk of ice around the far ends. But be sure to leave the exits clear."

Gladdic dipped the flexible breathing tubes into the river, shaping a generous portion of ice around the ends opposite of the mouthpieces. They slipped the straps over their heads, pressed the mouthpieces tight, and waded into the water. It was early fall and it ought to have been decently warm, but it had spilled almost straight down from the mountains, with only a few miles of prairie to heat it up.

The loose ends of the apparatuses, encased in ice, would

float. Allowing them to stay underwater and thus out of sight indefinitely as the current carried them along, though they might need to gather some driftwood after a while to give their muscles a break.

Dante waded up to his waist. "If anything goes wrong, the signal will be 'Arrgh.'"

"That sounds like one I can remember." Blays gave a thumbs up and ducked under the water.

Dante followed, letting the current do its work as he got used to breathing through the tube again. It was incredibly dark, but using the ether to light the way would defeat the entire purpose of what they were doing, so they simply stayed very close together.

It worked every bit as well as Dante had hoped. The current was far gentler than the rapids that had delivered them in their bins to the plains, yet still had enough speed to it to sweep them away from Chronus. Dante tried to exert no more energy than was necessary to stop himself from sinking, but gradually swam away from the west bank and toward the east, straightening out once he was thirty feet from shore.

Dante used the nether to drive some of the chill from their bodies. After a while Gladdic added ice to the apparatus' melting floats. They still had several hours until dawn, and as well as things were going, Dante thought they'd let the river carry them until, say, five in the morning. At that point they'd emerge to see if there were any horses around to steal. If not, they could find a log, hide their apparatuses within it, and use it as camouflage to continue drifting downstream by daylight.

Something tickled his mind. He went still. It was so faint he wasn't sure it was real. If it was, it wasn't actively searching for them—or seemingly doing anything at all. After five minutes of waiting, he started to doubt he'd felt it in the first place.

They made a quick trip ashore for a bit of driftwood to help them stay neutral in the water, then carried on. The current was sending them along at a moderate walking pace. An hour after beginning their trip, Dante cautiously broke the surface. They'd put three miles between themselves and the towering city. The plains were spangled with lanterns and the harder glare of ether, but the searchers weren't putting any special attention on the south.

He got back under the water. Less than two minutes later, the river flooded with light, illuminating them. He turned around to scowl at Gladdic, but Gladdic had changed. Instead of the gnarled old man Dante knew, Gladdic now looked young and hale.

Ka had found them.

32

"Arrrrghh!" Dante yelled into the water, voice burbling crazily.

He bit his lip, tasting salty copper, and kicked to the surface. Shadows shot to him across the water. He launched them upward, not even sure where his target was yet. Gladdic broke the surface behind him, chasing Dante's nether with a surge of his own. Clearing the water from his eyes, Dante spotted the ether burning above and bent his sorcery toward it, hitting it just as it left Ka's hand.

He pulled a second bout to him, kicking for shore as hard as he could. Blays was already ahead of him, Gladdic lagging behind, in part because he was launching a counterstrike at Ka. Dante pitched in. Ka swatted their attacks away with ease, but at least it stopped her from assaulting them for a moment.

"Archers!" Blays lifted from the water and pointed ashore. "Incoming!"

Dante couldn't yet see the arrows, but he plunged his mind into the soil between Blays and the direction he was pointing and pulled it straight up. The river sloshed violently. He didn't bother to harden the dirt, trusting that two feet of solid earth would stop anything short of a ballista. A volley of arrows smacked into his wall.

Blays swam for the wall, reaching waters shallow enough to

stand in. He hunkered down behind the earth. Dante helped Gladdic disarm another one of Ka's beams of light and ran up behind Blays. Blays pointed ashore. A hundred feet away, scores of archers drew their bows.

The earthen wall barfed itself apart: Ka had clubbed it to pieces. The archers immediately loosed another volley. Dante threw himself flat while drawing forth a hasty replacement wall. A few arrows slashed into the water around them before the replacement wall caught the rest.

Ka flew above the archers, ether dancing around her hands. "Relinquish the spear and I swear to make your deaths fast."

In response, Dante hurled a barrage of black bolts at the lines of bowmen. Ka flicked her hands, neutralizing every last one of the darts.

"Do you think you can harm Taim's soldiers when I am their shepherd?" She sneered down at them. "Their arrows will claim your lives before you have claimed one drop of their blood!"

To punctuate her confidence, she lanced her light at Dante and Blays. Gladdic hit it from the side, spraying the air with sparks. The right-hand half of the archers fired at will, keeping Blays and Dante pinned while the left half jogged behind the others to become the new right flank, opening an angle of attack for themselves. Dante took another shot at them. Ka didn't let it get close.

"Ka's right," he said. "This is a classic tactic when sorcerers can't overpower each other. Just keep the enemy locked down and let your archers do the dirty work."

Ka chose that moment to batter the earthen wall again, requiring them to do some quick fixes and scrambling about to avoid being pin-cushioned by another volley.

Blays swabbed dirt from his face. "What can we do?"

"Hope we get a lucky shot at Ka. Otherwise, not much."

"To hell with that. After all the trouble we went through to get it, I'm not dying before I even get a chance to use this thing."

Blays reached up his sleeve, tugging loose the knots he'd tied within it. He dropped the collapsed rod of the spear into his left hand and transferred it smoothly to his right. He punched his hand forward.

A star burst into being.

The spear shot forth to its full length, dazzling and shimmering, blasting forth a sphere of white light that left Dante temporarily blind. The archers yelled out in fear: with any luck, they'd been blinded as well.

At that very moment, Ka delivered another attack of eye-watering beams. Gladdic hit back at them, but Dante could barely make them out, and lashed at them clumsily. Two of the beams diverted to Blays' high-held spear—and were absorbed with a flash.

"I have the feeling I'm going to love this thing." Blays grinned. "Cover my ass, will you?"

Before Dante could respond, Blays sprung from behind the wall, spear gripped in both hands. He sprinted toward the line of archers. Most were still rubbing at their eyes, but a few had recovered to loose arrows at him. Dante struck some down with nether, but the missiles were much too swift for him to catch them all.

Blays juked to the side of an arrow as if the archer had called out his shot. He ducked under another, the purestone glinting from below the head of the spear. A sergeant bawled out orders and the portion of the lines that had regained their sight drew back in preparation for a volley. Heart sinking, Dante flung a barrage of nether at them, hoping to intercept what fraction of their arrows that he could.

Running headlong, Blays extended the spear in front of him and jammed its butt into the ground. He jumped upward with all of his strength, using the spear to vault him higher, arrows swishing harmlessly beneath him. One struck the shaft of the spear and disintegrated with a sharp ping.

Blays arced high in the air, the spear pulling free of the ground. Yet he was still traveling upwards, higher than should have been possible; at last he peaked, dropping right at the enemy lines, wheeling the spear overhead and swinging it downward like an axe splitting wood.

High above them, Ka looked terrified.

A handful of archers loosed their arrows, but they were used to tracking human motions, and Blays was traveling much faster than that. His feet hit the ground. So did the head of the spear.

A white sphere erupted from the weapon. Something terrible happened to those caught in its initial radius. It expanded outward from there, booming like crystalline thunder, growing more translucent as it spread. A wave of archers tumbled into the air spraying blood behind them as if thrown by an angry drunk who, on discovering his wineskin has been punctured, hurls it away in a rage.

Before the sphere of destruction had spent itself, Blays leaped up from his knees, twirling the spear about himself. It reaped the enemy down wherever it went. Some men screamed, but others were silent, stunned by the light of the spear and the quickness of the one wielding it. A good deal of them turned and tried to run. Very few had the presence of mind to nock an arrow and take a shot at Blays. Sometimes Blays pivoted out of the way of those who did. Other times the spear darted forth to knock the arrow down mid-flight.

Ka tried to bring him down, but her ethereal lances that made it past Dante and Gladdic's first line of defense were sucked in by the spear—but not instantaneously, making Dante believe it could only handle so much at once. Blays ignored her, carving through the archers. Within a matter of seconds, every single one of them was either running away, injured beyond the ability to fight back, or dead on the ground.

Blays came to a stop, stamping the butt of the spear into the dirt and gazing up at Ka. "Got anything else?"

She hovered sixty feet above him, golden hammer in one hand, her wicked silver sword in the other. "I am not merciful, but my master is. He offers you one last chance to return the spear."

"And what? He'll spare our lives?"

"Yes."

"That offer's not terribly tempting when taking it up means the lich will just kill me a few weeks later. Besides, I don't think you can take it away from me."

He jabbed the spear in her direction. It was only a taunt, but a bolt of ether flew from the tip of the spear. Ka had to twist to get out of the way.

Blays shook the weapon in the air. "You're lucky I don't really know how to use this thing!"

"Are you denying my lord's offer?"

"You know, it's a tempting one. Why don't you come down here where we can discuss it better?"

"You reject the grace of Taim." Ka smiled in contempt. "It is better that way. I prefer to kill you."

Dante readied himself. He felt Gladdic do the same. Blays angled the spear across his body. Instead of coming toward them, Ka drifted backward. Lights bloomed a few hundred feet up the river bank. Dante sent his mind into the earth, ready to draw up a new wall, but the reinforcements weren't archers. Instead, infantry marched forward, swords and spears bristling.

But that wasn't what caught Dante's eye. "Priests. At least a score of them."

Blays glanced over his shoulder. "What do we do?"

"We have to find a way to kill Ka. As long as she's here, we'll never be able to run away."

"We haven't been able to kill her when we've had her by herself. How are we supposed to do it when she's got a small army with her?"

Ether glinted from the hands of several of the priests. As they drew closer, many of the men and women looked too young to be priests proper, monks at best, possibly just apprentices, as if they'd been summoned from a guard-post lower in the city. But more senior sorcerers walked among them as well. It seemed like more than enough to do the job yet not the full strength of what Chronus could bring to bear. Scrambling to get what they could to the field before the thieves found a means to slip away? Or did they fear something? An ambush?

Or the Spear of Stars?

The enemy slowed their advance, deploying into a standard formation for facing sorcerers who were unaccompanied by any armsmen, much looser than military lines tended to be. The common soldiers must have known they were unlikely to serve as more than a distraction, yet their faces were proud, dauntless.

Gladdic jogged toward Blays, robes tossing about his legs. He kneeled among the slaughtered archers and waved his hand back and forth. An Andrac popped into existence, ten feet tall if it was an inch, casting its arms wide and flexing its claws, provoking gasps of disgust and gestures of holiness from Taim's clergy.

Gladdic had just enough time to forge a second demon before the enemy's hands filled with the cruel geometry of ether.

Blays slashed his spear horizontally, sucking in the first beams of light that came for them. Gladdic's power was almost untapped on the day and he met the offensive with masses of light and dark. Dante backed them both, knocking down anything that threatened to get by.

Blays made a series of quick jabs. Ether pulsed forth from the point of the spear. His efforts were clumsy, and most of the light he produced soared away harmlessly or came at the enemy too slowly to be of real threat. Yet Taim's priests still had to contend with the wobbly bolts. At the same time, Gladdic sent his two Andrac dashing forward, the demons screaming with airy rasps that raised the hair on the back of Dante's neck.

He felt Ka readying an attack. But if he didn't strike now, while the line of ethermancers was back-footed, he might not see a second chance.

He dropped to one knee and punched his fist into the ground. The turf bounced upward in a line speeding toward the enemy. Stone cracked and rumbled; the ground broke apart, zigzagging toward the soldiers and priests like lightning. Dante's eyes widened. He held his breath, awaiting the sight of bodies tumbling into the yawning crevasse.

Armed men turned their backs and fled. Too late. The quake swallowed a dozen soldiers, reaching past them toward the robed monks and priests.

A woman sprinted from the lines, face hidden within a hood. She skidded on her knees over the grass with her palms pushed forward. Nether clouded her hands and sank into the earth.

The stone creaked like a sick old man. One branch of the crevasse jumped forward, dropping a pair of screaming monks into the depths. The other cracks shuddered. And came to a halt right beneath the knee of the woman who knew how to move the earth, who was now breathing hard, her hair spilling loose from her hood.

With the enemy driven in disarray before the earthquake, the Star-Eaters slashed into their lines, shredding armsmen to the ground, fighting toward those in robes. But with Dante's attack stopped in its tracks, the priests gathered themselves and pummeled the demons, tearing ribbons of nether loose from their alien bodies. Gladdic called the pair back to him before they could be destroyed altogether. Dante punched the earth, this time in frustration. Their best hope had failed them.

Led by Ka, who swooped in anticipation overhead, Taim's forces renewed their attack. Steady. Pounding. The three of them were just able to hold it off. Without the power of the spear, they would have been obliterated in moments. Dante fell back, the ash-like residue of neutralized nether dashing against his face. They couldn't make a break for it. Not when Ka could outrace them and slow them down enough for the priests to hit them from behind. Nor could Blays make a charge like he had at the archers. The ethermancers would vaporize him. If they'd had a single one of General Lars' prized horses, one of them could have galloped away with the spear to bear it back to their world. But they'd been caught. And they'd used up every trick they had.

"We're not getting out of this, are we?" Blays said, spear glowing with captured ether.

"Not unless you've got a brilliant idea."

"Fresh out. Shall we charge, then? End our cycle with one last act of glorious defiance?"

"In another couple of minutes, once my nether runs low. Then we'll give Taim something to remember us by."

They fought back a punishing barrage of ether, with so many sparks spitting toward his face he closed his eyes and flinched away. When he reopened his eyes, a stranger stood next to him. He yelled out in surprise and drew his sword, ready to cut her in half.

She gave him a reproachful look. "You weren't about to kill your savior, were you?"

Dante gawked. "*Neve?*"

Neve grinned and tossed her head, flipping her orange braid at him. "Why so surprised?"

"We thought you were dead!"

"Carvahal doesn't let those who serve him die easy. Speaking of dying easy, was that your plan here? Or would you like to help me kill these people?"

"They've got half an army. We can't even get off a counterattack."

She gave him a disappointed look. "Only because you haven't bothered to take care of Ka. She's already stolen the spear from you once. It didn't occur to you to make sure that couldn't happen again?"

He was about to object that there was a major difference between knowing that Ka was a problem and in being able to *do* anything about that problem, but Neve vaulted into the air, leaving him sputtering. The enemy priests were still hammering away at them, though, and he was too busy defending himself to do much arguing anyway, or even to absorb the full meaning of her arrival.

Bright, frightening-looking things began to happen in the sky. Weapons banged together and gold light flashed down on the faces of those fighting below. Dante risked a glance up and caught an image of Neve silhouetted within a glimmering silver aura. She dived toward Ka, who attempted to jump back, warding herself with both her sword and her hammer.

A narrow blade that looked forged of moonlight slashed across Ka's body. She tumbled back, gliding erratically toward the priests and their footmen, ether streaming from her wound.

Neve landed between Dante and Blays, breathing hard, her hair disheveled. "See, that wasn't so hard. Now how would the spear-bearer like to provoke terror in the foes?"

"The exact words I was waiting to hear." Blays clobbered down a lethal stream of ether. "If they won't let us run away, I suppose we'll just have to cut a path through them."

He jogged forward, spear gripped under his right arm. Gladdic and the Andrac flanked him on the left. Neve moved to his right, motioning Dante to complete the formation to her right.

Dante drew his sword, casting purple light before him. Neve carried her sword in one hand and the nether in the other, the shadows shifting in shape between straight swords, hand axes, curved or hooked blades, maces, and other weapons Dante had never seen.

The priests stood their ground, firing off even more ether than before, so much that it would have obliterated them if not for Neve, who threw the shadowy weapon in her hand at the largest beam of light, breaking it into bits, then immediately summoned a new black weapon and repeated the process. The soldiers threw some of the short javelins they'd carried to battle with them. But these were slower and larger and hence made much better targets than arrows did, and Dante and Gladdic shattered anything that threatened to strike them.

And then they made contact.

Blays swept his spear into the front line of soldiers. Men flew away from his blow like he'd punched them with a boulder. Beside him, Neve lunged forward so fast Dante would have sworn she'd teleported, her moon-silver sword cutting men into motionless pieces. Blays ducked a javelin, twirled his blade into a web of ether that had been on the brink of slicing him into cubes, then swung the spear over his head like a bolo, obliterating everyone around him and opening up an empty circle.

Neve smiled with perverse glee as she plunged through the line next to Blays. To her left, the soldiers held their ground until the Andrac's claws cut the first of the men down into diseased, gray-looking corpses. Everyone near the demons broke rank and fled.

Dante was used to leading the destruction, and even enjoyed taking that role, for he was quite good at it. But all it would take to cripple their counterattack would be a stray missile of ether striking Blays or Neve. So he took on the role of guardian instead, only lashing out with his sword when a soldier challenged him, and otherwise deflecting bolts and beams of light from the others. Gladdic caught on quickly, looking after Neve while Dante protected Blays.

Blays had already killed his way through the soldiers. He jumped forward, gutting a priest with a slash of the spear, then impaling a monk as she tried to heal the wounded man. Neve threw a nethereal axe at another priest's head, splitting it in half. Both of the Andrac were leaking shadows, one a little and one a lot, but with the armsmen driven before them, they fell upon the priests, too, their long claws soaked in blood.

A hooded figure jogged across the middle ranks of the ethermancers. Something in her movement caught Dante's eye. She dropped to her knees, skimming her palm over the ground. The earth stirred. Something raced through the ground toward Blays and Neve, yet it was a subtle thing right up until it wasn't, and Dante might have missed it if he hadn't already been watching for it. As it was, when the earth began to open up beneath the two warriors, he dashed the nether there from out of the woman's control, then launched a salvo of black bolts at her to give her something to think about.

One of the Andrac went transparent from its injuries, dissolving away into nothing. Neve was bleeding from the cheek and leg, but neither wound seemed serious, or at any rate did anything to slow her down as she gored another priest. The air was so frantic with bursts of ether and counters of nether it felt impossible for anything to remain alive within it. Yet one by one, the enemy priests responsible for the clamor were falling, the volume of their attacks decreasing with each death. Dante had been in more than enough battles to know they were about to hit a breaking point where Taim's sorcerers collapsed altogether. They'd dragged Ka to safety, but if Dante and the others routed the priests, they could find her and kill her — and then be free.

Taim's people seemed to realize this, too. They summoned a

wall of ether, pouring it down upon their foes so hard that Neve and Blays were forced to disengage and back up several steps. As soon as the ethermancers had extricated themselves from the melee, they turned and ran back in the direction of the city.

Blays hooted and stamped his spear, sending sparks jetting from its tip. "Are you running away? Don't you guys know that the back makes the best target?"

"Come on," Dante said. "We have to finish off Ka."

The five of them, including the surviving Andrac, started forward. They'd only taken two steps forward when an oval of space behind the priests began to glow with the purest light Dante had ever seen.

Neve flexed her fingers on her weapons. "Well, this is about to get interesting."

Blays leaned on his spear. "If what we were just doing *didn't* qualify as interesting, I don't think I like where this is going."

The retreating priests slowed, cohering into a more disciplined defensive formation with the shredded remnants of the soldiers. A silhouette appeared within the glowing oval. Tall. Immensely solid. The figure that stepped forward wore a cape and a garland and a kingly beard. Pearly shimmers crossed his skin. His shoulders were as squared as a brick and his face carried the authority of every lord who had ever lived. The silver of his eyes was more piercing than the Spear of Stars.

Dante's knees nearly gave out beneath him.

"Look upon me." The god's voice was a grasping hand of infinite strength. It rooted Dante's feet to the ground, but forced him to look up into Taim's silvery eyes. "You will lay down your weapons. You will surrender the spear. And you will kneel."

"That's the exact opposite of what these people have been doing the whole time they've been here," said Neve, who seemed to be the only one of them capable of movement or speech. "What makes you think they're going to do any different now?"

"For I have delivered my WORD."

"Your word doesn't mean what it used to. You soiled it when you refused to honor the compact of the spear. But it's not too late to admit your mistake."

"Even for an Angel of Carvahal, your haughtiness is profane." Taim stood even taller than the White Lich and between his size and his gravity it felt as though a mountain was staring down at her. "You will obey or you will be annihilated. Not simply your body. But your soul with it."

"With all due respect, my lord," Neve said, bowing deeply from the waist, "I suggest you back off before *you* are destroyed."

Without another word, Taim raised his hand. A circle of searing light formed on his palm. Heart galloping, Dante summoned as much nether to him as he could, Gladdic doing the same. The circle of ether was too bright for Dante to look at, but Neve gazed straight at it.

Power surged from Taim's hand. Dante and Gladdic both hit it with their all, but their all was only good enough to shave off a bare fraction of the ether. The beam struck Neve with a burst brighter than any lightning.

Even with his face averted, Dante was half dazzled by the flash. He blinked the light away from his eyes as it slowly faded from Neve. Somehow, she was still standing, but she tottered and fell to her hands and knees, flames burning along her clothes, her skin cracked and smoking.

The air smelled of burned wool and scorched flesh. Wisps of flame ran up and down her red hair. Her face sagged, peeling away; one of her cheeks slid loose and fell to the ground, landing with a sickening crinkle. Her chin followed, then her brow, plopping on dirt blackened and burned bare, and then the rest of it gave way, along with her scalp, dragged down by the weight of her still-flaming hair.

Head bowed, Neve began to laugh.

Taim's face creased with disgust. He raised his hand to deliver the killing blow.

"Taim, you idiot." Neve's voice croaked from the smoke. "Why can't you ever just listen?"

She began to get to her feet. Her face was indistinct, as if it had been drawn in oil paint and then smeared. As she straightened, her legs lengthened, as did her body. With a flip of her arm, she cast off her smoldering clothes.

She wore an entirely different set beneath them. And she was no longer a she. Rather she was a very tall and lean man, appearing somewhere in his middle forties, with a sharp nose and chin and a mocking mouth. Three faint scars ran down the left side of his face. His eyes were a bright green lit from within. He wore an exceedingly fine doublet, black trousers, boots as shiny as a beetle's back, and silver gloves.

Taim's entire affect changed to something less commanding and more familiar. "You *bastard*."

"There are times I suspect as much myself." The man brushed dust from his left shoulder. "Then again, it's very hard to know one way or the other, isn't it?"

"You will not defy me."

"Oh, but I will. I will defy you much worse than you fear. I warned you to relent already. You can try to tell me you dismissed the message because you didn't think the one delivering it had the authority to back it, but I think we both know you're not about to listen to me, either."

"Even you do not have the authority to make demands of me. You stand in the shadow of my tower. You stand in the shadow of *me*."

"You know I am nothing if not a realist. I know full well that if we come to blows, there's little chance I'll come out on top—although I do think I'd escape, to do something like this once more some other day. What *you* don't know is that if you choose to fight me, even if you win, you will lose."

"Now I know you're no imposter. You make as little sense as you ever do."

Carvahal—for that was the only person who it could be—crossed his wrists behind his back and began to pace in front of Taim. "Let me make myself perfectly clear to you. If you insist on continuing this little skirmish, yes, you'll likely win it. You'll kill the mortals, and I'll slip away at the last second, just as I always do. But we will kill many of your priests and wound you as well. You're going to find that very inconvenient when my army of ramna rides in and overruns you because you're too weakened to stop them."

Taim shook his head in contempt. "Your threats are as idle as the way you spend your days. You have no army of ramna."

"You know I never bluff."

This drew outright laughter from the lord of the gods. "You lie like clouds rain!"

Carvahal held up his palms. "Okay, you've got me there. But do you know how I really mess with your minds? Every now and then, I say something outrageous *that's also true.*"

"I am aware of your disgraceful tendencies. This is one of your worst lies yet, you scoundrel. If a single band of the barbarians had entered my land, my net of scouts would have told me so. An army could not come within sight of my borders without my knowing it."

Carvahal put his chin in his hand and looked thoughtful. "Unless some nasty pieces of work went and killed all your scouts. Someone like Ka might have noticed an act like that, but you kept her around to help keep watch on your tower, didn't you? Taim, my army's less than ten miles from here. If you take one more step forward, I'll have them tearing down your gates within an hour."

"If you are running your mouth in order to delay my

vengeance upon—"

Carvahal made a broad gesture to the west. "Why don't you ask your watchers in the tower what *they* see?"

A look as black as a cavern crossed Taim's face. But there was a hint of worry there, too. He straightened, gazing north toward the tower, then looked sharply to the west where the wilds lay.

"They light their flames to mock me." Taim's voice was almost a whisper, but as he turned on Carvahal, it roared back to life. "How dare you bring an army of the ramna to bear against one of the gods?"

"How dare *you* betray the compact between gods and our creation? You've even betrayed the order between us and the Fallen Landers' dead!"

"What foul lie or sickly bribe did you feed the cow-herders to convince them to come here?"

"I didn't have to bribe them." Carvahal folded his arms, speaking mildly. "I didn't even have to lie to them. All I had to do was tell them that if they followed me here, they might just get the chance to rip your palace to the ground."

"You wretched bastard."

"I believe we've already established that."

Flames rippled over Taim's face; Dante had no idea if they were illusory or real. The world seemed to lose its tethers as the god doubled in height, then tripled, then leaped taller than could be made sense of. Yet across from him, Carvahal did the same, the two figures titanic in size, standing over the flat plain like living towers of power and wrath.

Frightening shapes moiled across the gods' dark faces. Dante had a dead clear vision of them rushing each other, arms spread wide, shadows and light flowing to their command like unleashed seas, and then the two lords collided with a crash like two mountains uprooted and swung against each other. The thunder of the clash devoured all other sound and light: there was nothing but empty, black chaos.

The gods stood across from each other in the field, returned to their normal size. They were taking long, deep breaths, but otherwise showed no sign of what had—or had not—just happened.

"Go then." Taim's voice was that of pure command. He glared murder into Carvahal's eyes, then turned a look of burning fury at the three mortals. "You have the spear. But you carry it away against my will. I will come for you. I will claim the spear. I will claim your lives. I will claim your souls, and annihilate them down to the last spark of your being."

His eyes receded to black pits with no bottom, holes that reached beyond the stars. He put his back to the intruders, then kneeled and gathered up Ka, who was still lying on the ground, the glow of her skin dimmed and unsteady.

Taim left the field, and his army left with him.

33

The three humans stood beside the river. Darkness grew around them as the torches and torchstones of Taim's forces moved north toward their tower. Dante was afraid that if he said a single word, Taim might change his mind and come back to destroy them.

"Well." Carvahal clapped his hands; Dante jumped. The god motioned to the river. "Shall we?"

"Er, shall we what?" Blays said. "Go for a celebratory midnight swim in a cold river?"

"If you'd rather. But you'll have a hard time catching up."

Carvahal walked down the bank toward the water. Just as his next stride was about to dump him right into the river, mists rolled beneath his feet, revealing a wide-bottomed boat capable of bearing a half dozen passengers. Carvahal stepped into the prow. A lengthy but sturdy wooden rod appeared in his hands; Dante couldn't tell if it was a pole or an elongated paddle. Blays climbed aboard, followed by Gladdic and Dante.

Dante's butt was still three inches from the seat when Carvahal pushed off with a lurch. The boat slid smoothly from the shallows. Carvahal took it a third of the way out into the river, then concentrated on propelling them downstream with his paddle-pole. He didn't look to be working very hard, yet they were soon cruising along so fast that the bow of the boat lifted and a wake vee'd out behind them.

Blays was still carrying the spear, the beauty of its ether reflecting on the dark face of the river. He glanced at it like he'd just noticed it. "Is this really happening?"

"I'm afraid so," Carvahal answered cheerily.

"Do I want to know what there is to be afraid of?"

"You have the Spear of Stars. That means you now have to try to use it against the lich."

"Don't you think it will work?"

"I think he's probably going to kill you," Carvahal said. "And even if he doesn't, Taim certainly will."

"Oh." Blays concentrated on the spear, shrinking it down to the gem-tipped rod. "Were you Neve the entire time?"

Carvahal's teeth flashed white in the darkness. "Why would I tell you that? I've got to keep *some* tricks up my sleeve."

"Was it you when she—or you—fell into the pit at Mount Arna?"

"That sounds like a question you will enjoy considering for many years."

Blays did some thinking about this. "Either way, it's really you right now. I thought you gods didn't like to leave your holes. Wasn't coming here...?"

"Extremely dangerous? That's what made my plan work. And that's what made it so much fun, too."

"Is that why you helped us?" Dante said. "For fun?"

Carvahal continued stroking the long pole through the water. "I wouldn't have done it if it wasn't fun. But I didn't do it *because* it was fun. Instead, I had two reasons. The first is simple. If you're playing a game with someone, and the rotten dirty bastard keeps cheating you, what happens?"

"You run him through with your sword?" Blays said.

Dante shook his head. "You lose."

"Right. And I hate losing." Carvahal made an obscene gesture in the direction of the tower. "Once Taim started breaking the rules, there was no sense in me sticking to them, either."

"Then why make us infiltrate the tower and steal the spear? Couldn't you have done it much more easily?"

"And what, should I go kill your lich for you, too? You must *earn* the spear. That's the entire point. You prove yourself worthy. Or you prove that it's time for you to go home."

"And we proved our worth the moment we got the spear back in hand?"

"Not quite. In my eyes, your test was whether you could get the spear out of the city and down here on the ground. At that point, I was free to intervene."

"If I'd known we just needed to get it to the ground, I would have thrown it out the tower window as soon as we had it. So what was your second reason for stepping in?"

Carvahal tossed his head. "We'll get to that. Probably. But you've had an awfully long day, haven't you? Don't you think it's time for you to get some sleep?"

Dante didn't think so at all, and was about to say as much. But shadows rippled from Carvahal's hand, leaving Dante with no choice in the matter.

He woke slowly. It was morning and a mist was rising from the river; they were still barreling along, Carvahal standing tall in the prow, driving them forth at a speed on the water Dante had only seen matched by the *Sword of the South* at full sail. The mist was hugging the water and the sunlight was spearing cleanly through the trees overhanging the river, lighting up the insects dancing along the surface and the fish rising to meet them. It was a cold, clear, beautiful morning. Dante felt like he hadn't seen such a day in a very long time.

"No," Carvahal said without turning around.

"Huh?"

"It wasn't all just a dream. And no, no one is after us."

Dante frowned. "Did you just read my mind?"

"Once you have spent thousands of years dealing with humans, they become so predictable that anticipating how they're going to think becomes indistinguishable from reading their minds."

Gladdic was awake. Blays wasn't, but he stirred as Carvahal drove the boat aground on a gravelly beach to allow the three of them to do things Dante wasn't sure the gods needed to, like eat and relieve themselves. As soon as they were through, Carvahal shepherded them back onto the boat and carried on like he'd never need to rest.

"Where are we headed?" Dante asked.

"Home," Carvahal answered.

"Can Taim follow us along the river?"

"Not unless he wants the ramna to tear down Chronus stone by stone."

Dante lodged himself against a gunwale. "Last night, you said there were two reasons you helped us get away. What was the second?"

"I thought about it for a while and I decided not to tell you."

"What? But you—"

"Can break whatever promises I want," Carvahal said. "Which I had decided was more in my interests. But then I decided some things are too good to keep to myself. Though this might take so long to explain that you'll regret asking by the end.

"Let's begin with something that I gather has been on your minds a lot lately. The notion of *cycles*. Over time, everything that exists will change from the way it was when it first began to exist. Over a long enough time, everything that came to exist will *cease* to exist. Another way to put this is that everything is born, and will eventually die."

At that moment a gap opened in the trees on the eastern river bank, exposing the mountains beyond. Blays pointed to them. "I've found a problem with your theory. How can a *mountain* die?"

"Trust me, they die too. It just takes an extraordinarily long time. One way to think of it is that a mountain has an extraordinary amount of order within it. If you were to climb that peak today, and then return to it a hundred years later, it would more or less look exactly the same.

"This is *not* true of human societies. Particularly in your world, where the generations are always replacing one another. Compared to a mountain, a human society has a much lower degree of order and a much higher degree of chaos. But of course you don't want *too* much chaos, or else things turn into hell. At a certain point society ceases to exist altogether. So when it comes to mortals, there is a strong and unavoidable strain of chaos at work. This must be balanced by an equally strong strain of order. Wise rulership consists of understanding this and working to mold your laws and actions to it. By contrast, take this fellow who's giving you so much trouble."

"The Eiden Rane," Gladdic said.

"Right. Him. As I understand it, his vision is to subjugate all the world beneath his banner, yes? To kill all who now exist and convert them to his undead followers, from north to south and from sea to sea."

"Only at first," Dante said. "Eventually, he intends to create new living people to populate the world and worship him as one united society."

"Immensely stupid. His new order—for that's what it is, highly ordered, in its way—can't survive a world full of *people*. For one thing, they won't last as a single people for even a generation before they start splintering apart to pursue their own interests—and, more importantly, to pursue their own power. His order is doomed. Way too much chaos for it to last the way he thinks it will. The most stupid part about it is that he should know better. If *we* couldn't impose perfect order from above, how could he ever hope to?"

"That's what you tried to do when you made the Realm, isn't it? But it didn't work."

"Right. The ramna. The damned ramna. Although, for all the troubles they cause, there are those who nudge them every now and then into doing something extremely useful."

"Does anyone actually do that besides you?"

"Who, me? Taking advantage of unexpected chaos to alter the course of current events?"

"I apologize for making such an absurd accusation."

"Apology accepted. This time." Carvahal stopped propelling them forward with the pole and gazed up at the clear sky. "Let me clarify how balance works in practice. Think of it like this: a kingdom is ruled by a king. But he doesn't oversee every last detail of his realm. Instead he oversees the major issues, such as war and taxes, and also rules over his nobles, who in turn rule over their own portions of the realm, including the people within those portions, who in turn might rule over individual farms and plots, or live as laborers on the lords' land. This creates multiple layers of order to ameliorate the chaos you're going to find within any large human organization.

"But it is a big mistake to assume a structure like this always functions as intended. For instance, the kingdom might find itself ruled by a *bad* king, in which case the ostensible force of order actually becomes an agent of disorder. Then we reach an ironic state where proper order can only be restored through the judicious application of chaos. Like an assassination. Or a great big bloody civil war. In this way you bring things back to where they ought to be—or more realistically, somewhat closer to where they ought to be."

Blays stretched out on his bench. "When you put it like that, it seems like you could avoid the 'bad king' problem and cut out a lot of the middlemen by just letting the people rule themselves."

Carvahal got a good laugh out of that. "Do you really think people have never tried whipping up a mob, beheading the king, and ruling themselves? It always ends in tears."

"Are we still talking about why you came to Chronus?" Dante said.

"I'm getting there. You might be mortal, but you're not so short-lived that you don't have time to listen to a proper explanation." Carvahal resumed pushing them downriver. "So. When we designed your world, it was intended to function much differently than the one we created here. For one thing, there wouldn't be any gods directly ruling it who could prevent it from falling into misalignment.

"Thus we built your world to be layered in ways that would naturally maintain balance. One step was to make you mortal. The next was to make your world much bigger than this one. This was meant to make it impossible for any one person to take over the whole thing. Plenty of people would be able to create kingdoms, sure. Every now and then when someone was both extremely ambitious and incredibly competent, they might be able to seize a whole continent.

"But the world? No. Before such a ruler could get anywhere close to that, his mortal lifespan would run short. Then his heirs would struggle for power over his conquests, both with each other and with local nobles seeking to restore their own sovereignty, and eventually it would break apart, back into individual kingdoms, duchies, city-states, and so forth, each returning to its own layers, cycles, and epicycles of order and chaos—or, to put a new thought into your heads, of ether and nether.

"Such a system was intended to be self-perpetuating. Even though the people who lived within it would come and go, live and die, the world they lived within would be permanent. Except, well, we were wrong."

"For the Eiden Rane is the death of that system," Gladdic said.

"Not just him. Anything *like* him. Though yes, he is the most recent example of our miscalculation. It turns out your world isn't so balanced as it was meant to be. An overabundance of order or chaos can still destroy it after all. Hence why you're here. Now, a minute ago, I mentioned you could also think of order and chaos in terms of ether and nether. This should suggest one more way to think of it."

Dante cocked his head. "As Taim and Arawn."

Carvahal grinned. "Right. *With* the understanding that within *any* structure of order, there is also chaos: and within any structure of chaos, there is also order. Thus neither element should be thought of as perfectly pure nor as exact opposites of each other. Just elements that represent a wider trend toward one side or another.

"Got that? Good. What we're seeing in your world, then, is that the Eiden Rane is threatening all life with an overabundance of order. Therefore he's acting in the service of Taim. What, then, is the natural champion needed to oppose him?"

"Arawn," Dante said slowly. "Chaos."

"Correct. Though in this case it is that ironic form of chaos that exists to fix an order gone wrong, like in the earlier case of our bad king."

"Just to make things perfectly clear, that means we are the champions of Arawn?"

"Don't get ahead of me. Although even if you were Arawn's champions, note how even within your group there is a layer of order—that would be you, Gladdic—to balance the whole." Carvahal glanced back, looking amused and thoughtful. "Or does Gladdic represent *proper* order to be deployed against the lich, and it's you that's balancing his order with a layer of nethereal chaos? You see, when you start looking closely enough at any given detail, it's hard to be certain what's order and what's chaos. A clever fellow can usually find a way to argue either case."

"I'm not sure I—"

Carvahal waved a hand. "It doesn't matter. Not for our present purposes. Let us switch focus. Taim—the real Taim, not just the forces that are in general alignment with him—wishes for the White Lich to serve as a tool to usher in a new cycle. One that will allow him to replace the Mists, which no longer function as he intended them to, having fallen into a form of chaos, or at least a form of order he doesn't like. At the same time, since your world has reached a precipice as well, he's content to let it run its course and begin something new. This wouldn't be the first time."

"But you personally want to maintain balance between order and chaos. Like there was meant to be."

Carvahal laughed merrily. "Immensely wrong. I want to see what *happens*. For this time, the crisis is different than the others."

"How so? You just said it wasn't the first time. And I know you're right, because we've seen one of these crises—these cycles —ourselves, when demons overran our world and killed nearly every living soul. All civilization came to an end. It didn't return for a long, long time."

"Don't you see? There are forces of Taim at work here, embodied by the lich. And there are forces of Arawn as well, embodied by yourself."

"Hang on." Dante gripped tight to the gunwale. "The last time we fought him, the lich claimed he was the avatar of Taim. Before that, I unknowingly fulfilled a prophecy that supposedly marked me as the avatar of Arawn. Are you telling me the prophecy was *true*?"

Carvahal went silent. With how loquacious he'd been up to that moment, his hesitation was unnerving.

"That isn't something you need to know," he said at last. "Again, I have to maintain *some* mystery." A large fly buzzed around Carvahal's head. He gave it a dour look and pointed at it, annihilating it. "Two forces. Ether and nether. Taim and Arawn. That's been the way of every past cycle. But this time? This time, there is a third force at play."

"Carvahal," Blays said.

Carvahal shot a glance back at him, grinning in a way some might have called wicked. "You continue to not disappoint me."

"Do you ever thank whoever you gods pray to for how lucky you are?"

"I've always made my own luck. But perhaps I'll start."

They both laughed. A moment later, Gladdic snorted.

Dante waited until he couldn't stand it. "I'm about to pray to the god of sense to make you two start making any of it."

"The third force is Carvahal," Gladdic said. "And Blays, it seems, is his champion."

"A wrinkle we've never seen before," Carvahal confirmed. "Call me egotistical, if you like—and then find a way to escape the lightning I'll cast down on you for doing so—but I'd really like to see how this shakes out. Who knows, maybe Taim is right, and we are on the verge of a new cycle—but not the one he thought was coming. Instead, it will be something we've never seen before."

Dante did his best to take this in. "Well, that's a horrifying possibility. Now if Taim is order, and Arawn is chaos, what does this third force represent?"

"Beauty? Charm? Grace in the face of disaster? The yearning of that which *is* to bend itself to the charisma of what *might be*? Perhaps it's the shoe thrown into the works that spoils the plans of the machine. It could be the moment of inspiration when all hope is lost. Would you buy that? Not yet? Then maybe it's the turn of the last card that was needed to win the pot—or the pebble in the lane that makes the lead runner trip when it seemed the race was already decided."

Carvahal slashed at the water with his pole, driving them even faster. Perhaps it was the wind of their speed stinging Dante's eyes, but the trees and the river abruptly gleamed silver.

"Then again, maybe none of these things captures the full truth," Carvahal said, much more even in tone than a moment before. "Maybe it's something beyond the sterility of order or the mindlessness of chaos. Maybe it's a power that knows it's far more fragile than the mountain, yet is driven by a will that makes the mountain look like a molehill."

He shifted moods again, now mocking. "Or perhaps I flatter myself—and my reflection. We do that, you know. Gods and mortals alike."

At last he grew sober. "But that's more than enough of this. Even if I had the answer, giving it to you would spoil the question."

The three humans were silent for some time. Blays lounged on his bench, contented. Gladdic sat straight, stoic. Dante held his tongue for as long as he could, then cursed, though not out loud.

"Well, we own the spear," he said. "Does that mean we can defeat the White Lich?"

Carvahal gave another of his laughs. "How the hell should I know? Say that once upon a time, myself and my eleven peers were able to see the future with perfect clarity. Think how awful that would be. We'd be no more than puppets on a string! Why, if we'd ever had such an ability, we would have stripped it from ourselves long ago, if only to stop us from contemplating the horror of what it meant. So I barely know more than you do. Is it possible for you to find victory? Yes. Is it destined? No. Not at all."

"But when others before us have earned the spear, they've been able to—"

"Oh, do you ever get tired of hearing yourself speak? Even if I knew, I wouldn't tell you, because that would alter the future. Again, it's possible. But it's much later in the game than you should have ever allowed it to reach. That means you're counting on the turn of the only card that can save you from ruin. And even if fortune saves your hides from the lich? Well, your troubles with Taim are just beginning."

"What are you saying? That even if we stop the lich from destroying our world, Taim might do so anyway?"

Carvahal whirled, water whipping from his pole, his eyes alight with the divine. "I have said enough. *More* than enough, drunk on teasing those whose minds can't see as far into the possibilities as mine can. You have your weapon. From here, your fate is your own to make."

The river narrowed, squeezing the current faster, though the boat was already traveling fast enough that it hardly made any difference. The banks rose on each side. They were still primarily traveling south, but judging by the sun, the river had diverted some degrees to the east. The shores were crowded with trees, blocking out any glimpse of their surroundings. Maybe the rush of the river was drowning them out, but Dante rarely heard any birds calling to each other.

The river bent back to the south and a cliff appeared dead ahead. At first blush it looked like the current would smash them against the face of the rock, but an archway opened at the base, and they shot through it into a large tunnel of natural stone. The ceiling was riddled with gaps, about half of which were overgrown with trees. The open ones sent pillars of light shooting down onto the river.

Something broke the surface to their right. It sank back into the depths before Dante got a good look at it, but he saw enough to know that it was very large. "What is this place?"

"Aldax," Carvahal answered.

"Aldax? One of the portals back to the Mists?"

"We'll be to it in less than an hour."

"We're leaving? Right now?"

Carvahal glanced back, amused. "Have you grown so fond of us you can't bear to leave us?"

Dante had the instinct that they couldn't leave yet: they needed to say goodbye to General Lars and thank Gashen, and also to find Dasya, if they could, and try to patch things up with him. The sentimentality of this urge wasn't like him at all, and he knew at once what it really was: the fear of what they would face once they were back in their own world.

"To the portal," Dante said. "And back home."

They flicked in and out of the beams of sunlight cast by the holes in the roof. Half-seen creatures moved beneath the surface, sometimes breaking it with a fin or a claw. They were obviously drawn to the boat, and Dante had no doubt they would have attacked and capsized the vessel if not for Carvahal, whose presence drove the fish away with fearful flicks of their tails. For they were guardians, like the worms at Talassa.

A hissing sound grew ahead, more menacing than the typical rush of the water. A haze grew about them. All at once it was so thick Dante could no longer see the roof above them nor the way ahead. Carvahal steered them onward, making a number of course adjustments with his paddle-pole. The hiss was now a roar: a waterfall. They were racing blind toward oblivion.

Carvahal thrashed at the water, slowing them so much that Dante lurched forward. The bottom of the boat struck gravel, sliding to a rapid stop that tossed Dante down on his face.

Carvahal stepped from the boat onto a shore of shiny red

stones slick with mist. The wind from the falls stirred his light cloak. He led the way forward, the bead-like pebbles clacking underfoot.

"This isn't the doorway we entered through," Dante said. "Will it send us back to the same place?"

"To the same part of the Mists?" Carvahal said over the thunder of the falls. "No. But you'll wake from the Mists in the same part of your world that you entered them from."

"Is there any way to use the portals to travel across our world?"

"That would be a useful shortcut, now wouldn't it? Maybe you can work that out the next time you pay us a visit."

The winds heightened. The haze swirled and thinned, revealing that they were walking along a narrow strip of rocks suspended over open space. The river tumbled down a cliff behind them. A doorway stood at the end of the platform, shining fuzzily, its edges indistinct.

"And here we are." Carvahal came to a stop, inspecting them each. "Well. Good luck saving Rale."

"Saving what?" Dante said.

"Rale. Your world."

"I thought it was called the Fallen Land."

"Yes, that's the rude term for it. Rale is its true name. Have you people forgotten so much you don't even know the name of your own home?"

"Yeah, well over the years the ol' Fallen Land's had a tough time of it," Blays said. "But with any luck, we're about to put a stop to the latest apocalypse. Thanks again for the spear, by the way. I've got a feeling it's going to come in quite handy."

Dante did his best to avoid looking down the waterfall, which didn't seem to have a bottom. "One last thing. We would never have found the Realm of Nine Kings on our own. A woman named Isa pointed us to the doorway. After that, another woman named Elenna helped us find Adaine, the man who the White Lich was using to open doorways across our world—and rip the Mists apart in the process. They were working with you all along, weren't they?"

"No," Carvahal said.

"But we wouldn't be here without them. And at that time, you were the only one willing to work against Taim."

"But I wasn't working with them. I could only guess at their involvement. I do know they belong to the only kingdom in the Realm that doesn't belong to a god. They're out on their own, just as you are. Maybe that's why they feel more kinship for the people of Rale." He made a quick twirling gesture. "But I won't betray their confidence any further."

Dante turned to look across the misty river and the tumbling falls. "Now that we're about to leave here, I have so many questions. Almost all of our time was spent chasing the spear. It feels like we barely got to know the place."

"Really?" Blays said. "I got to know it much more than I wanted to."

Dante faced the portal. "Well."

"I wish you luck," Carvahal said. "Genuinely."

Gladdic wrinkled his brow. "Is that a blessing?"

"I'll be watching your progress with great interest. Here's my one piece of advice for you: if you die fighting the lich, you'll find yourselves in the Mists, yes? In that case, I would do your best to try to find your way back here before the Mists disintegrate along with everyone in them."

He gave them a cheery wave, spun about, and clashed away through the red pebbles, whistling as he went. Dante met eyes with Blays, then Gladdic, who both seemed to be waiting on him.

He stepped through the doorway.

Vertigo. The sense of his head being stretched far beyond his feet. A buzzing in his ears that tunneled down to the core of his brain. For a moment, he forgot who he was, or even *that* he was.

He was standing in a dim room, lit from behind by a doorway. Blays stood next to him, blinking unsteadily. Gladdic waited as blankly as a zombie awaiting its first command. Then he stirred, taking a sharp breath through his nostrils.

It was quite dark except for a small fire in the distance, intense but well-contained, suggesting a brazier. From the lack of stars, they were indoors, though the uncut stone ground suggested otherwise.

Blays stared at the distant brazier. "Does this look like the Mists to you? Don't tell me Carvahal duped us into sending ourselves to hell."

Gladdic closed his eyes. "The ether surrounds us. We stand within the Mists."

"Excellent. Then all we have to do is lie down and go to sleep."

"We can't yet," Dante said.

"Visitors here can fall asleep whenever they want. But if you don't think you're tired enough, I can help with that. Stick out your jaw."

"Not yet. I want to see what's outside."

"A bunch of cloudy stuff?"

Rather than wasting time arguing about it, Dante strode in the direction of the brazier. The others followed without further complaint. The brazier was closer than it looked, burning away by itself, shedding light on a wall of stone so black they might well have broken their noses against it. They were just able to make out a doorway through it.

This led into a labyrinth distressingly similar to the one they'd had to navigate in the Split Crypt in Barsil. And this time, they had no ethereal footprints to follow. The stone wouldn't listen to Dante's commands, either. After a great deal of bumbling around half at random, he was about ready to give up. Then again, if they got lost, all they had to do was go to sleep, so he gave it a few minutes more, and eventually wandered out of a gap and into an open field.

Grass swayed under the night sky. The wind carried the smell of something Dante was almost sure was flowers despite the tanginess of it. Behind them, the labyrinth resembled no more than a pile of jumbled rocks. Woods enclosed the grassy field and they crossed through the trees, swiping at spiderwebs.

The trees were just a narrow ring and within a minute they found themselves on the top of a short hill. At first glance they seemed to be looking down on a field of house-sized mushrooms. Fairly sinister ones, given that many of them were lit by red and green lights. It was the lanterns that made Dante realize the mushrooms *were* houses, two to four stories tall, their broad caps providing shelter for the balconies on the upper floors. Most of the structures were repaired or supported by materials foreign to the mushrooms, presumably to replace bits of them that had rotted or died, making it look like they'd donned patchwork armor.

Dante couldn't see any keeps or cathedrals or other landmark buildings that typically gave identity to a city, but the place was studded with small green hills that were themselves studded with windows, doorways, and balconies. It clicked into place: the hills *were* the keeps and cathedrals.

It was obviously a city. But if Dante hadn't been able to see a few people wandering within the subtly ominous green and red lights of the lanterns, he wouldn't have been all sure that it was a *human* city.

"Huh," Blays said. "Where the hell are we?"

"We already figured that out," Dante said. "The Mists."

"But the Mists are sort of split up, right? With each portion of them corresponding to a different portion of the world. So where in the world is *this*?"

"Any ideas, Gladdic?"

"None."

Blays put his hands in his pocket. "Carvahal wasn't kidding when he said the gods made our world much bigger than theirs. You could spend your whole life exploring Rale and still miss most of it."

That they were so close to an unknown part of it made it all the more painful that they couldn't go down into the streets, find a public house, and find out where they were—and what kind of drinks the locals served. But now wasn't the time. Dante consoled himself with the thought they probably wouldn't be able to understand each other's language anyway.

The hillside felt a bit exposed, so they returned to the trees, swept away the twigs and leaves, and settled down. Dante was about to ask who was going to take first watch when he realized that, for the first time in two months, they were in a place where such measures weren't necessary.

He closed his eyes. As always, sleep came much faster in the Mists. Dreams claimed his mind, one after another. They seemed to last for a long time.

He opened his eyes. He was still in a forest in the middle of the night. Yet something was different. He knew the chirp of the bugs. He knew the smell of the trees. He knew the feel of the season and the way the nether lurked within the dirt and the leaves.

He was home.

34

The others woke within moments of him. They gazed at each other in amazement, temporarily wordless, then laughed and got to their feet. The first thing Blays did was check up his sleeve to see if he was still carrying the Spear of Stars. It was there, reduced to its rod form. Dante reassured himself that he still had the *Book of What Lies Beyond*. He wasn't sure that its role against the lich was over.

Somehow it was night, which didn't make sense, as he'd thought the same hour was kept between the Realm and Rale. Either their trip to a strange part of the Mists had thrown that askew, or they'd slept for many hours before being brought back here, to the woods just north of Bressel.

A leaf crunched. Dante grabbed at the nether.

A woman stood frozen across from them. "You return."

"Winden!" Dante ran to her and embraced her, the first living mortal he'd seen since the White Lich had sacked Bressel. "It's so good to be back!"

She disentangled herself and looked him in the eyes. "Do you have it? Do you have the spear?"

With a grand gesture, Blays drew the rod from his sleeve. He held it horizontally before him and tilted back his head. The spear jumped forth from both ends, extending to its full length. The light of the purestone beamed into the night.

"It is beautiful." Winden gave a small bow of reverence. "This kills the lich?"

"If I know what I'm doing," Blays said. "Frightening thing for the fate of the world to depend on, eh?"

They exchanged more greetings, then told each other in brief about what had happened while they'd been separated. Winden didn't have so much to tell. After the lich had marched north from Bressel, some of the Blighted had trailed behind to seek survivors in the forest. After these had finally gone on their way, the refugees had emerged — but most of these were starving and fearful, and quickly turned bandit.

Winden, being a woman on her own, had made an appealing target. Right up until the bandits discovered she was a nether-mancer. Rumors spread of an evil witch haunting the woods. It had been more than a month since anyone had dared to bother her.

Dante let the conversation play on for a while, then broached what had been on his mind since before their return. "Our next step is to head north and confront the lich. But you should return to the Plagued Islands. Any of the ports to the west should be able to take you there, but Allingham might be safest."

Winden wrinkled her brow. "Sail to the islands? Why would I do this?"

"Because there's no need for you to stay. There's every chance we'll fail. If we do, it will be better for you to be with your people. You could have years before the lich finds his way to the islands."

"But I am here. I will go with you. What if the lich sends a second agent to the Mists? What if he tries to open another one of his portals?"

"Then we'd need to return to the Mists, too. In which case we'd really want to have you around." Dante smiled at her. "Welcome back aboard. But if our last minutes spent together involve us getting slaughtered by the lich, the Mists getting torn down around our ears, and our souls dissolving into nothing, don't say I didn't warn you."

Winden hadn't just spent her time in the forest twiddling her thumbs, dodging crazed undead and even more crazed refugees, and waiting for their return. She'd also been preparing. She had horses. Food. Supplies. They were thus able to ride north at once, veering east as they went, intending to intersect the Chanset and follow the road that ran alongside its bank.

Typically, Dante enjoyed traveling to new places. But he'd had enough traveling to new places in the Realm to last him a good thirty years, and was happy to be on the move in a familiar place. He slew and reanimated a few moths to keep eyes on the route ahead. After being without his scouts and spies for so long, he was immensely relieved to have them back.

Still, for as good as it felt to be home among normal things, it also felt duller in color. As if, despite being much younger than the Realm, it lacked the rawness and vitality of the godlands.

They made camp after a few hours, sleeping until late in the morning. It was past noon before Dante looned Nak. Nak received the news giddily, veering between laughter at their outrageous luck and grave concern for how Taim would choose to punish them for their crimes.

"Even so, it seems you had no other choice," Nak concluded. "How long do you suppose it will take you to reach here?"

"If we can find a second set of horses, I bet we can meet you in three weeks."

"Three weeks until the final battle. It's hard to believe it all draws so near." Nak let that hang in the air a moment. "You know, you should write down everything you went through in the Realm. If we do manage to prevent the White Lich from starting a terrible new cycle, then the next time the world comes to a crisis, your knowledge could be what saves it. Just like you couldn't have done this without the *Book of What Lies Beyond Cal Avin*."

"It will probably be thousands of years before anything like the White Lich ever emerges again. Nothing I write is going to last that long. That's what the Realm taught me above all else: how much of what we once knew has been lost. Much of that loss was caused by apocalypses like the one we're staring down right now. But most of it was caused by the slow chaos of time."

"Be that as it may," Nak said after a brief pause, "if anyone can figure out a way to preserve knowledge across thousands of years, it's you. In fact, such a mission sounds like the perfect way to keep yourself busy in the many boring years we're going to have once we've dealt with the White Lich."

This was quite optimistic. Then again, that was Nak's way. After some thought, Dante warmed to the idea. As just one possibility, he could write a tome, get his monks to make some copies, preserve them in ether, then embed *those* in blocks of stone carved with something to the effect of "Smash open in case of looming conquest by overpowering wizard."

As they traveled, he gathered the story in his mind, jotting down some notes when they took breaks or stopped for the night. Soon he was filling up pages of the blank book he carried with him. His work was hampered at times by cold and blustery rains, which spent the days alternating with calm, almost warm weather. They kept their eyes peeled for enemies—be they agents of the White Lich, or those of Taim, even Ka herself—but didn't see anything more threatening than a few handfuls of frightened, dirty people.

While he worked on his book, Blays worked with the spear. The first time he did so, its glorious light piercing through the black branches, Winden gawked in awe. Dante, meanwhile, cursed steadily, certain it would draw the attention of everyone for miles. As soon as he couldn't hold his tongue any longer, and said that if they weren't careful the lich's spies would learn they had the spear, Blays stopped to fiddle around with it. Within a minute, he'd somehow found a way to reduce its glow to nothing, allowing him to resume his jabs, sweeps, spins, and parries.

At times Gladdic joined Blays, lobbing ether and nether at him so he could practice deflecting, absorbing, and redirecting it. Blays had fought quite well with the weapon on the plain below Chronus, but each night he practiced, he seemed to get a little quicker, a little more precise, a little more adept at negating Gladdic's sorcery. Blays lamented his ability to spar—this wasn't really possible when the slightest misstep with the spear would blast his partner into stew meat—but from what Dante saw, he was doing just fine on his own.

After some days, they came to Whetton. Or what had once been Whetton. It now resembled a coastline after a tidal wave had struck it, receded, and allowed it to dry out.

"I've always disliked this place." Blays surveyed the sprawled chunks of lumber and stone. "But I didn't want *everyone* in it dead."

There were a few bodies, but much fewer than its population. Either they'd fled or been converted into the Blighted. Their fields had been ripped up, too. Before moving on, Dante harvested the roots of a tract of wheat into a ripe crop. He wasn't sure how any of the refugees haunting the woods would mill it, but he couldn't do everything for them.

They picked up five more horses there as well. Now able to alternate their mounts, they could ride faster and for longer durations. They continued to follow the Chanset to the north. Most of the fishing villages and little trading hubs had been obliterated. The few that remained were empty.

The Dundens rose ahead, deep blue, their peaks frosted with snow. They broke northwest along a tributary of the Chanset, which grew smaller and more turbulent as they entered the foothills. It was down to the size of a noisy creek as they came to the town of Shay.

This had been sacked, too, though not as badly as Whetton. But the monastery had been gutted, its windows smashed, its furniture hauled out and destroyed. It was as empty as the rest of the town. Though the Mallish priesthood drove people like him from their country, and enacted a new war or Scour against Arawn's faithful every generation or two, seeing the desecration of the Mallish monastery sank Dante's heart. He hoped that the monk Gabe had gotten himself to safety, and that he and his brothers had managed to take their art and relics with them. Gladdic said a blessing for the site before they left.

The town was the last one between them and the mountains. Nak had warned Dante that he and his nethermancers had fouled the pass to slow the advance of the lich, but Dante expected it would still be faster than detouring toward the Riverway. They were climbing steadily up the hard-packed road but still a long way from the pass when Dante heard from Nak.

The White Lich was still on the move. But instead of continuing to drive north and west, into Gask, he had turned northeast.

"Toward Narashtovik?" Dante said.

"Well, we don't really know that yet."

"What *else* is to his northeast?"

"Er, well. Perhaps he means to invade Houkkalli?"

"He's not going to march his army across an ocean to kill a few harmless wisemen when he's still got a half dozen major cities to convert into Blighted. He's heading for Narashtovik. Do you have a loon to anyone there?"

"Of course."

"Tell them to make preparations to evacuate. They need to be ready within two days."

"We made work in that direction as soon as the lich crossed

his army into the north. But there are many who refuse to leave no matter how much we warn them. You know how Narashtovik is. Its people have been sacked so many times they wouldn't leave their homes even if Taim himself came for the walls with his hammer in hand."

"Then order the military to *make* them leave. If they stay, they die. Worse than that: they get added to the lich's army. We have no reason to indulge them."

Nak allowed that he would take care of it. Dante hurried up the road, turning possibilities and contingencies over in his mind. But there was no avoiding the conclusion. If the lich was heading for Narashtovik, there was no way for Dante and the others to get there first.

The Eiden Rane would do with the city whatever he pleased.

Dante pushed them onward. The weather had been chilly the last few days and the temperature took another dive as they moved up the face of the mountain. They camped there overnight and pressed on in the morning, meaning to make it to the other side before nightfall. They entered the snows. A little above that, the way was clogged with boulders and broken trees, but the lich had already carved a generous route through it, leaving Dante with little to do but clear a path through the two landslides that had gummed it up since then. Where the snow ran deep, Blays brushed it aside with long sweeps of his spear that knocked the drifts into fluttering flakes on the wind.

The birds were all but gone now. The trees thinned, growing shorter. They neared the divide of the pass on schedule, stopping to gaze at the glaciers resting heavy on the mountains and the eerily green lake that was fed by them.

Blays folded his arms against the cold and grinned. "Do you remember the first time we came through here? With Robert Hobble?"

"How long ago was that?" Dante said. "Seventeen years

now?"

"Something like that. What I mean is that the first time we saw this, I thought it was one of the most incredible things in the world—and that only a crazy person would willingly travel through a hostile place."

"Whereas after crossing the Woduns, or climbing Mount Arna..."

"Right." Blays rocked on his heels. "Still pretty, though."

It was, and so they stayed a while longer, both for the sight itself and for the memories it evoked of their youth. In time, though, they moved on: they had no other choice.

"Norren," Blays said. "Suppose they're friendly?"

Dante peered through the rain. "Are they ever?"

"When they're building things. And sometimes right after they've just got done killing some of their enemies."

Dante nudged his horse forward. "Well, I doubt they'll try to trouble us."

"You're forgetting something. They're *letting* us see them."

"Oh hell. They've been following us, haven't they?"

"So we might as well see what they want and get it over with."

They'd had nothing but miserable weather for two days since descending the north side of the Dundens and Dante was in no mood to deal with the giants, who were oblique and difficult under the best of circumstances. But one of the few things you could do to them that was worse than disturbing them when they didn't want to be disturbed was to ignore them when they didn't want to be ignored, so he rode toward them at a walk. He scratched his arm as he drew near.

Rain bounced from the norren's oiled leather hoods. Many of them leaned on spears while others carried comically long bows, half hidden under their cloaks to protect their strings from the rain.

"Hello," Dante said. "Have you been following us?"

A man shrugged. Between the hood covering the upper part of his face and the beard covering the lower part of it, Dante couldn't make out his features at all.

"Would that bother you?" the norren said.

"As a matter of fact, it would. We mean you no trouble and we're just passing through. It's in both our best interests for you to leave us be."

"Is that any way to speak to your chieftain?"

"Your...?" Dante leaned forward in the saddle. "Hopp, is that you?!"

The man tugged back his hood enough to give them a look at his face. "We thought you looked like the two wayward members of our clan. And if you turned out to be you, we were going to offer you a meal. But if you don't want it—"

"Show us the way to camp, wise leader," Blays said.

Escorted by his warriors, Hopp brought them over the hills to a camp of norren yurts set up in a grove of trees and camouflaged with branches and moss. They were greeted cheerily and stuffed with roasted venison and fish stew, along with clay cups of norren beer, which in typical norren style was both extraordinarily strong and extraordinarily good.

After some joking and catching up, Dante grew sober, or at least as much as he was able, and gave Hopp the condensed version of world events.

"Do you really think we're so isolated that we don't already know of this?" Hopp said once Dante finished.

"It's not safe for you to stay here," Dante said. "You should take the Broken Herons south over the pass before it gets snowed in. Trust me, Mallon's in no shape to try to chase you out."

"Did you mean to ignore my question?"

"I'm not sure you understand just how serious this is."

"Do you think the lich marched an army of that size through our lands? And we didn't see it? And when we did see it, that we thought nothing of it?"

"Granted," Blays said. "But *you* have to grant that you guys are as stubborn as a mule's mother-in-law."

"Maybe this is one of those times." Hopp toyed with a straight little branch. Knowing him, he was thinking about whether it could be carved into a paintbrush that was up to his standards. "We are stubborn as often as we can afford to be, because when you *are* as stubborn as you can be, that lets you be even more stubborn, because people would rather throw up their hands and move on than wear themselves out fighting with you. But when you're that stubborn, you have to be very, very careful not to be so stubborn that you do something that gets everyone who depends on you killed."

Dante took a drink. "But that's exactly what I'm telling you is about to happen."

"Do you think I don't understand you? What you are telling me is that if you fail, then *everyone* dies. Can we hide from being part of everything?"

"If you hold on long enough, you never know what could happen."

"I know very well that if you can't stop him here, there will be no stopping him anywhere. That means we are to die. If we are to die, we will do that here. Under the skies of Josun Joh, where our ancestors lay as well."

There was no convincing him otherwise. Under any other circumstances, Dante probably would have persisted anyway, but he soon decided that if this was the last time he was going to see Hopp and the Broken Herons, he didn't want to spend it arguing in frustration with each other. So he relented in favor of trading stories about what they'd been up to since they'd last seen each other, and of course in drinking more beer, and he soon found himself having a very good time.

After the initial round of greetings, most of the clan's members had wandered off to pursue their own interests across the camp. Now, with full night upon them and an orange moon rising in the east, more and more norren returned to seat themselves around the fire where Hopp was speaking with the humans.

A quiet fell over the gathering. It felt like one of those natural lulls in a conversation that was soon replenished with chatter and laughter. Instead, an old norren man named Codd got to his feet with the aid of his staff and began to make a noise that it took Dante several seconds to recognize as singing.

His notes were very, very slow and equally deep. The kind of song a hill might sing. Others stood one by one, both men and women, some joining Codd's chant while others sang in more normal tones, though their tempo was slow as well. Dante couldn't understand the words—in fact, he wasn't certain that there *were* any words—but the mood of the song was that of a long-buried truth revealing itself, raising the hair on the back of his neck.

Dante leaned toward Hopp. "What's happening?"

"You don't know of the Farun Tarr?"

"Should I?"

"That was a joke, which you didn't get for the same reason you wouldn't know of the Farun Tarr. It's not a thing that humans see because it is only sung by a clan when that clan believes it is about to die. At that time we thank Josun Joh for the lives he gave us, the fields to hunt in, and the minds to pursue our works and so add what beauty we can to his world.

"It is not a song we sing often. None of our children born since the Chainbreakers' War would have heard it. It is not a song we sing in front of humans, either, because you follow your own ways and would not understand it. But for once, humans and norren share the same fate. It seems that if it's not yet our time to be called to Josun Joh, it will be because of the deeds you are about to deliver us. So we give you this, to remind you of all who depend on you."

"We are honored to bear witness," Gladdic said. "It will not be forgotten."

The song grew louder, the bass chants lifting goosebumps on Dante's skin and rattling his bones. The four humans listened in stillness as the singers gave thanks to their god in bittersweet tones both mourning and blessed. Did they have a beyond of their own? Listening to their song, Dante believed that they must. The gods would have granted them one the first time they heard the Farun Tarr.

In the same manner they'd joined the song, the norren dropped out one by one, seating themselves as they did so. Until only Codd continued to sing. He uttered one last note—it seemed to last a lifetime—then fell into silence.

The song was over. For now, the norren remained.

They rode north, and the lich marched toward Narashtovik.

There was little to the land but rolling hills, stands of pines, and rare ruins from times long ago. They saw a few norren but didn't speak with them. In the mornings they woke to frost on the grass. It should have been a time to celebrate the end of the harvest, with children rolling pumpkins through the yards while farmers gathered to drink each other's brews and dance and sing and tell tales. Yet as Dante and the others exited the Norren Territories and crossed into human lands, all of the villages were empty.

They were still four days out from reaching Nak when Dante got the loon he knew had been coming. The White Lich had arrived at Narashtovik. Facing no resistance of any kind, the enemy had claimed the city.

"Is he burning it?" Dante asked quietly.

"Not yet, at least," Nak said. "He appears to be holding it."

"He wants us to come for him. If we don't, he'll raze the city, move to the next one, and repeat until there's nothing left."

"But if he wants us to attack him there, how wise is it to take up his offer?"

"It might not be. We'll meet you in four days. We'll make our decision then."

He'd tried to prepare himself, but in the end, there was no preparing yourself for the news that a god-like malevolence had conquered your home. It hit him like a hammer to the heart. The weather matched his mood, slaty clouds that didn't allow so much as a crack of sunlight through, and often broke open to drench them in the biting cold rain of dying autumn.

Mountains emerged to the northwest. Narashtovik was now directly to their east, and they might have been able to reach it in a single day's hard ride, but they drove straight north toward the coast. And the fleet that waited them there.

The northern sea was an angry gray wrinkled with tin-colored waves. An army waited on its shores and an armada rose and fell on its swells. After nearly being outmaneuvered and destroyed in the eastern heights of Gallador, Olivander, their high general, had sent orders for Narashtovik to send every ship in its harbor to shadow the army's progress at sea. If the lich tried to use his army's superior stamina to force a fight, Olivander would load their people into the ships and slip away.

It was raining again and the soldiers looked ready to be washed away by it. They'd been on the march for the better part of three months since the fall of Bressel, and all of them had seen combat at least twice in that time, battles with no hope of victory —or, more accurately, where merely surviving the encounter qualified as victory. Now they waited in the cold and the wet while the very enemy who'd nearly exterminated them lorded it up in their holy city.

So Dante would have forgiven them if they'd met his arrival with sullen stares. Instead, they crowded about to greet the four riders with hollers, cheers, hails, whistles, and boisterous songs.

"I've been missing that," Blays said.

"Our people?"

"My rightfully adoring public."

Dante raised his hand to acknowledge their greetings. The crowd parted and Nak swished toward them, his Council robes heavy with rain. Dante dismounted to embrace him and thump him on the back.

"I'm so glad you're back," Nak said. "Now if things go wrong, my neck will be spared the blame."

"You acquitted yourself excellently. Every bit as well as I hoped you would."

"I did all right, didn't I?" Nak tugged at the front of his robe. "I'll admit to having some very good advisors."

"When it comes to ruling, the importance of collecting worthy people is one of those things you can't fully appreciate until you're the one depending on them."

The crowd pulled apart again, allowing forth a strikingly pretty woman of about thirty years old who moved with the authority of someone who knew secrets about the shadows few others did. Her eyes were locked on Blays. Seeing her, Blays flung himself from his horse as if it had just caught fire and crossed to her without seeming to touch the ground at all.

He hugged Minn tight, heaving her from her feet and drawing a loud huzzah from the observers. After a long squeeze, he set her down and they pulled apart, looking into each other's eyes before embracing again.

Dante stole a glance at Gladdic, who didn't seem to have the slightest interest in this reunion one way or the other. Then again, the old man must have long ago made his peace that he'd be traveling his path alone. Dante's thoughts turned to Ara, unable to leave the Silent Spires, and whether he'd see her again.

Nak brought their group—now six in number, including himself and Minn—down to the shore, where a large bay protected them from the worst of the tides. Even so, waves were surging far up the beach, leaving long lines of foam to congeal on the sand and quiver in the wind. The air smelled heavily of cold salt.

A figure awaited them, laughing deeply as they approached. "You have returned!"

"Naran!" Dante clasped the man's hand with both of his own. "It's incredible to see you!"

"You as well, my friend." Naran's face took on an entirely different shape as he turned to Gladdic. "You are...alive? But I heard you had perished in combat with the White Lich."

"I did," Gladdic confirmed. "Yet your friends risked their quest to restore me to this life. Does this displease you?"

Naran paused, an ambiguous light flickering in his deep brown eyes. "Then I trust their judgment. For surely we need every weapon we can muster for the last battle to come."

"We couldn't have gathered the spear without him," Dante said. "Anyway, what are you doing here?"

"Whatever I can to be of assistance, of course."

"But the last time we saw you, you were halfway up the Chanset."

"The last time you saw me, the leaves were still green and attached to the trees that grew them. We sailed upstream until there was no one left to warn about the advance of the lich, then heaved south and conspired to slip past the lich's army in the dead of night. But one of his underlings awaited us beneath the surface of the river. He set us aflame and punched a hole through our hull. We would have sank there and been drowned by the Blighted if not for the fact we were carrying priests from both Mallon and Narashtovik.

"The ethermancers restored the hull while the nethermancers fought off the lesser lich. We made our escape down the river, and from there out to sea. There, I put the question to my men if they would rather continue our business here, or sail away to safe waters to let others contend with the lich. Almost unanimously, they answered we must stay.

"So we made our way west, warning the Carlons and the Western Kingdoms of the threat that might soon find them, then made port in Voss to stuff our hold with all the food we could carry, knowing that if your soldiers made it all the way to the north, their stomachs would be wanting. We arrived only a few days before you. Our journey was not a tenth the glory of your own, but I am proud to have played what part we could."

Blays gave him a slap on the back. "Believe me, the land of the gods isn't what it's cracked up to be. Also Taim's probably going to come kill us anyway, so you'll get your chance to die helplessly soon enough."

Dante gazed out at the ships anchored in the bay. He wanted nothing more than to take his first proper bath since returning to Rale, then go eat some charred meat. From there, a nap sounded quite called for, the longer the better.

But though the crowds of soldiers, priests, and workers had given them space to speak to Naran, the people were still watching Dante and the others closely. They had spent many weeks delaying the lich to keep alive the slim hope that he could be defeated. The need to know their fight had not been in vain was etched into their weary faces.

They had performed their duty to Dante. He would perform his duty to them.

He reached into the ground beneath his feet, compressing the coarse sand into sandstone and lifting up a platform, elevating himself six feet in the air so that all of the thousands could see him.

"Countrymen and friends!" He laced his voice with the nether, amplifying it above the wind and the crash of the waves. "We have returned from our long journey—and we have brought a terrible weapon back with us."

He took a breath, ready to go on. But the crowd thrust up their fists and cheered. Hearing the power of their voices unified, Dante stood a little straighter.

"To obtain this weapon required the three of us to do great deeds. Now, we are *all* needed to achieve a much greater deed. Quite soon—likely within a matter of days—we will confront the White Lich. One way or another, this war will be brought to an end. Even with what we've brought back from the realm of the gods, it will be our most desperate day.

"But if, on that day, we stand together—if each one of us fights with every spark of our souls, inspired by the knowledge that everyone next to us is doing the same—we will have the chance to break the new cycle the lich means to end us with, and forge our names in the iron of history."

He bowed his head. The roar that came next was the loudest of them all, rising higher and higher, until Dante suspected the gods could hear it on the other side of the Mists.

35

"We are assembled today," Olivander said, "to bring about the death of the White Lich."

Olivander would admit he was past the prime fighting years that had helped elevate him to Narashtovik's captain of war. But though he was well into middle age, he looked no less formidable than when Dante had first met him when he was little older than Dante was now.

The *Sword of the South* pitched down a wave, causing several people to grab at the table. They'd managed to cram a veritable host of attendees into Naran's cabin. Dante, Blays, Gladdic, and Winden were there as well. So was Nak, who wasn't much of a strategician or a soldier, but who had ably guided the army in Dante's absence.

They were seated, but Somburr the master of spies had too much energy for that, the features of his brown face darting about like little birds, as if he could watch many different things at once. Hart the venerable norren was a pure contrast to the spymaster, sitting in his chair like a block of stone. Merria was almost as old as Hart, but the Councilwoman's gray eyes were as sharp as ever, and her tongue remained even sharper, not to mention infamously crude.

In peaceful times she spent most of her days strolling around Narashtovik's streets observing problems of all kinds, be it with the city's infrastructure, criminal elements, rat population, tax collection, traffic flow of pedestrians and carriages, shortages of goods in the markets that might be shored up by enterprising merchants, and all of the other various and sundry ways that something could go wrong in a large urban environment. She knew the whole of Narashtovik better than anyone else alive.

They'd brought numerous experts, aides, and servants with them, too, to the point where most of these were waiting out on the deck in case their name was called. They were currently getting rained on, but Naran had ordered his sailors to rig up some tarps to protect them from the storm that had hit the coast within minutes of the fleet weighing anchor and plowing east toward Narashtovik.

"There's no reason for the lich to abandon the city," Dante said. "Not when he can turn its defenses against us. We should assume he'll force us to try to fight our way in and root him out."

Olivander nodded. "Under any normal circumstances, I'd recommend a siege. Winter is near. To hasten the siege, you could round up as many rats as you could find. Kill them, reanimate them, and send them into the granaries to putrefy their supples."

"That sounds…effective," Dante said. "But I can already see the flaw."

Gladdic stirred. "That you ought to divert some of the rats to bring plague to the people instead?"

"That's a truly gruesome idea, but the problem is there are no people to be starved or plagued. There's just Blighted. You can't starve them. I doubt the cold will bother them, either."

"While the longer we wait, the colder and hungrier our troops become," Olivander continued. "Additionally, the White Lich destroyed a great deal of crops on his march north. There will be starvation this winter no matter what we do."

"Then conducting a siege would only hurt us. All right, I

want everyone's best ideas for how we're going to invade our own city."

"Just like this wouldn't be a typical siege, this won't be a typical invasion," Olivander said. "Firstly, the lich has no citizens he needs to defend. Nor will he care about saving the city from damage. This will free him to use the defenses as he pleases — and to abandon those defenses the moment they're no longer useful. The second significant difference lies in the *composition* of his army. It will outnumber us several times over. But it has no archers to hold fortified positions and take advantage of elevation, such as the upper floors of buildings. We will be fighting some sorcerers and a vast mass of infantry."

"And the White Lich himself."

"Well," Blays said. "At least we know the city's weaknesses."

Merria crossed her arms. "Of which there are a shitload. Just Dante's luck that his refusal to fix any of them might be the very thing that gets us inside."

"And you thought I was being cheap," Dante said. "Turns out my foresight is simply beyond mortal comprehension. Let's start with how we gain entry to the city. Is this best done through a conventional assault on the wall? Or should we land directly in the port and bypass the Pridegate altogether?"

"The port would be a significant risk," Olivander said. "We'll be more vulnerable on our ships. And the lich has shown significant ability to make tactical use of bodies of water. They're no obstacle to him. An amphibious landing might be *part* of our strategy, but I would only make such an attempt if the White Lich was distracted by a larger assault elsewhere."

After Bressel — to say nothing of the White Lich's long undersea march from Tanar Atain, as well as his use of the canals during the taking of Aris Osis — Dante couldn't argue with this. That left an attack on the walls as their primary option, and they spent some time discussing where would be best to attempt their breach, whether it might be best to attack multiple points at once, and so forth.

They soon concluded one of the chief impediments was going to be the sheer mass of Blighted. The lich could simply clog the streets with them, grinding their progress to a halt and opening them to be battered by the Eiden Rane and his lesser liches. There would be no chance of breaking the Blighteds' morale, either. Dante and Merria spent some time examining which routes and boulevards would be least cloggable while also providing them alternate routes in case the lich did something like drop a building in their path. They made such plans for several of the city's major defensive landmarks, but focused primarily on how to recapture the Sealed Citadel.

Dante leaned over the sketches they'd made. "The more we talk, the more clear it becomes that our chief strategy should be *speed*. We have to get to the Citadel as fast as possible. Otherwise the Blighted will bog us down. If they bog us down, they're in good position to halt us altogether. If we stop moving, I'm not sure we'll have the strength to fight free and continue toward the Citadel."

Blays made a flippant gesture at their maps. "Why are you so interested in capturing the Citadel?"

"Because it's the heart of the city?"

"So what? Why are you treating this like a game of Nulladoon?"

"I'm aware that Nulladoon isn't a perfect proxy for war. But there *are* a lot of conceptual similarities."

"But we're not playing Nulladoon. We're playing chess."

Dante stared at him a moment. "The goal isn't to recapture the Citadel. Or even the city. It's to kill the enemy's king."

"Well, that would have been a grievous oversight, wouldn't it?" Nak said. "The whole point of everything you fellows just went through was to retrieve the Spear of Stars, yes? For that's the only thing that can slay the lich. So our strategy is very simple: create a Blays Delivery System that lets the spear-carrier get at the lich."

The ship pitched down another wave. Outside the cabin windows, the sky was darkening, though hours remained until sunset. A drop of rain struck the window. Within moments, a downpour hammered the ship, but it eased off to a drizzle just as quickly.

Blays laced his fingers behind his head. "If the goal is to get me close to him, then we ought to make it look like we're exactly not doing that."

"You have a suggestion?" Olivander said.

"Sure. Hit the city with a full frontal assault."

"You mean exactly like we were just talking about."

"Well yes. But now it might actually get something done."

Olivander tapped his finger on the table. "If the goal is to deliver you to the lich, then we would increase our chances by creating more than one route of potential delivery. We will make an attack on the wall. But we will also invade through the port. A fifth of our forces will make landfall there a few minutes after the initial attack. If this draws the White Lich away from the wall, you might be able to strike at him as he's moving through the streets."

"What if we hit the wall at two places instead of one? Giving the lich another problem to worry about?"

"If we spread our forces between too many points, we risk one of those points being overrun. After that, the enemy will have little difficulty in turning aside any effort we make to push into the city with what we've got left. I would not attempt a third avenue."

They delved into the details of the plan to attack by land and sea, but Dante only paid it partial attention, even as they located a point on the Pridegate that would give the lich a clear lane to travel between there and the port—and, with any luck, would thus encourage him to do so.

"There is a third way to bring the spear to the lich," Dante said at last. "One that doesn't require a quarter of the army to make it work. The tunnel from the cemetery to the Citadel."

"That could put you upon him even as he's safe behind the Citadel walls," Nak said. "Do you suppose the lich knows about the passage?"

"The entry in the dungeon is sealed up. And he's only had a few days to get to know the city. Somburr, can you confirm he hasn't found the tunnel—without tipping him off that we're interested in it?"

"Consider how much more easily that is said than done," Somburr said. "But I can see what can be seen."

"Surely Blays won't travel through the tunnel alone," Olivander said. "If you're intending to escort him, you can't just walk away from the field of battle. The White Lich will smell a trap."

Dante pinched the bridge of his nose. "Does he even know I'm back? I could keep myself out of the battle altogether. Stay hidden. Then again, the tunnel's the backup plan. If we're going to catch the lich by breaking through the wall, we'll need to throw everything we've got at it."

Blays had slipped a small knife from his boot and was tossing it in the air to himself, something that seemed extremely reckless, given the swaying and rolling of the ship. Yet he hadn't missed a single catch.

"Pull a Lord Pendelles," he said. "Fake your own death."

"I'll fight at the wall with the main force. If it doesn't look like we can get at the lich there, I'll pretend to get badly wounded and retreat from the field. From there, we have the option to join the assault on the port, or make our way to the tunnel and ambush him at the Citadel."

Blays raised his eyebrow. "Do we have a plan?"

"I think we have a plan."

There were further refinements and contingencies to be added, but the genesis of the strategy was in place. Dante exited to the deck to take the air. A sheet of black clouds hung overhead. They weren't currently being rained on, but the gray curtain of a storm on the sea encircled them like a death shroud.

The wind grew stronger, the air colder. Rain lashed the deck in squalls. The war council resumed inside the cabin, brainstorming strategies against the Blighted based on their previous encounters. The ship pitched and rolled until they had to grab their chairs and brace their feet against the floor. Sailors yelled to each other outside.

The discussion switched to the possibility that all of their assaults would fail to penetrate the city, and if that came to pass, how they might lure the lich out from behind the ranks of his armies. Nobody had anything especially compelling.

Nak hadn't said anything for several minutes. After a particularly vicious drop of the boat, he clapped his hands to his mouth, kicked open the cabin door, and ran out onto the deck to pay a visit to the railing.

This seemed like a good indicator that the war council should take a brief hiatus. Most of the members took shelter belowdecks or in the couple of cabins they were all cramming into. Sailors grappled with the sails and rigging to prevent it from getting ripped apart by the mounting gale. Dante should have gone indoors, but he felt compelled to stand under the storm, to be reminded that, in its way, what they were sailing toward was nothing new, and that the world had been trying to kill those who walked it since the first day the gods had put them here. The ancestors of everyone who now lived had weathered countless storms to get here. Dante would see them through one more.

The wind drove the rain against the deck in a hard slant, though the angle varied greatly as the waves cast the *Sword of the*

South about with their terrible strength. The ship began what felt like a long roll only for some quirk of the sea to stop its momentum cold. High in the rigging, a boy screamed.

He plummeted from the mast, snatching at the ropes but missing each one. He struck the deck feet-first. For all the deafening bluster of the rain and the waves, the snap of his legs cut through the sound like a knife through a fish's belly.

The boy's left leg was bent backwards at the knee. His right thighbone pierced his trousers like a morbid sword. Even if he survived, his was the kind of injury that would leave him forever incapable of securing either employment or a wife, and the other sailors pressed their hands to their heads, groaning in sickened sympathy. The boy took one look down at his ruined legs and shrieked like a demon being banished.

Dante ran to the boy, slugged him on the head with the shadows to get him to stop screaming, then plumbed his bones with the nether. His right femur was shattered. Rather than attempting to locate every splinter and try to find its right place, Dante had to settle for packing the biggest pieces together, arranging them as best he could, then flooding the bone and its marrow with nether, encouraging it to fill in whatever was missing.

While it did its work, he turned to the boy's left leg. The tibia and fibula had simple fractures. The knee and its many tendons and ligaments was a mess. Dante successfully prevented himself from dwelling on just how *much* of a mess, focusing instead on reconnecting one ligament after another, then filling in the fractures with fresh bone. He turned back to the shattered femur. It was looking good. Not perfect, but good. More than good enough.

He sat back on his heels and brushed his sopping hair out of his eyes. He gave himself a moment to catch his breath, then sent another dab of nether into the young sailor's head. The boy's eyes popped open. He began to scream again.

"Oh, shut up," Dante said. "You're not even in pain anymore."

The boy quit shrieking, mouth hanging open. He glanced down at his legs, quickly, horrified at what he might see, then blinked and gave them a longer look, staring at them motionlessly, as if hypnotized. Finally, he lifted his left leg and moved it a few inches. Then his right. He looked up at Dante.

"You'll need several days of rest," Dante said. "But you'll be fine."

The boy shook his head back and forth, unable to respond. Dante stood. A group of sailors pounded across the deck, looking massively relieved, and picked the boy up from the ground, hustling him belowdecks to get him drunk, which was in one sense all wrong for him, but was in another sense probably exactly what he needed.

As if the storm had been sent by Phannon to try to claim a sacrifice for the sea, the wind gave one final frustrated blast, then died down to little whimpers. The rain receded to nothing. Dante tipped back his head. A single snowflake landed on his face.

Two days later, they made landfall outside Narashtovik.

They might have sailed right up to the city, but to avoid ambushes, and see if they might provoke the White Lich into marching out from the city, they disembarked six miles to the west. Snow fell slowly but steadily, just beginning to accrete on the sand and rocks above the tideline.

Thousands of soldiers had yet to reach shore in their longboats, giving Dante plenty of time to think about whether they were moving too quickly. There were other options. They could spend more time on strategy. Come up with a multi-step approach to draw the lich out from behind the city walls. Turn aside and seek reinforcements from Gallador, or even pursue an alliance with King Moddegan of Gask.

But they didn't have the food to keep their army encamped through the winter. And Taim might come for them at any day. Hadn't they already learned their lesson at Bressel? Trying to play it safe would only result in their ruin.

At last, the army was assembled. A fifth of the fleet remained embarked. They would wait with the unloaded ships until the army began its attack, then fly toward the city harbor.

Blays stood beside him, removing the thicker gloves he'd worn on the voyage and replacing them with thin ones suitable for the swinging of swords. "Still think this is a good idea?"

"I think it's our *best* idea," Dante said. "Although I'm starting to wonder if it was very stupid of us to turn down those offers to stay and live in the Realm."

He gave the signal to Olivander, who nodded to his officers, who ordered their flagmen to raise the flags indicating it was time to get on the march. The troops left the shore and entered the pine forest that began as soon as the soil was solid enough to bear the trees' roots. Scouts ranged ahead, both human and a small flock of reanimated flying insects. They would have had more of the latter, but there weren't many to be found in the current weather.

They'd encountered no sign of the enemy by the time they emerged from the forest into the open ground outside the city. Narashtovik was now just two miles away. Dante confirmed the spire of Ivars was still standing, along with the Sealed Citadel. Typically when winter fell on Narashtovik, smoke climbed from tens of thousands of chimneys to mingle in the sky. But on that day, despite the snows gathering on the ground and the rooftops, not a single hearth was lit.

They took a short rest before continuing across the stump-studded ground. Priests sent their undead insects ahead to try to scout the city, provoking the first combat of the day with the bugs the lesser liches had waiting for them.

The army came to the humble neighborhoods at the city's edge. Dante sent men to check the houses for survivors in hiding, but the buildings were as empty as the streets. Except for a scattering of Blighted sent out as spies, who flushed from cover like beasts and ran back toward the Pridegate. Dante had ordered all of his nethermancers to save their powers for the White Lich and his underlings, leaving the archers to attempt to take down the fleeing Blighted, but the undead ran erratically, and often required multiple arrows to fell. Half of them made it away to safety.

Dante found a moth dying in the premature cold, put it out of its misery, and sent it flying high toward the city. The falling snow made it hard to see much detail beyond a few miles, but only a full-blown blizzard could have hidden the motion of the Blighted in the streets. In some places, the streets seemed to *be* the Blighted, writhing like sickening rivers of maggots. An army larger than anything Dante had ever seen.

The moth's sight blanked out. Something had found it.

On the march toward the Pridegate, nearly all of the homes had broken doors or shutters—the result of the Blighted going house to house to drag out any citizens who'd chosen to remain —but only a fraction of the structures had been severely damaged or knocked down. It was much less destruction than Dante had feared the lich would inflict on the city. Then again, maybe the enemy simply hadn't bothered with things so unimportant they were kept outside the walls.

The Narashtovik of yore had been so crumbled and abandoned by one sack after another that its desolate streets had earned it the nickname of the Dead City. The moniker hadn't made much sense since its revitalization, first by Cally, and continued by Dante. Now, though, the name felt like prophecy.

The walls loomed ahead. Dante had once thought them imposing, but after the defenses and fortifications of the gods' kingdoms, the Pridegate looked wimpy enough to knock over with a good kick. As they drew near, pale, ghastly figures stood from the battlements. At first by the dozen. Then by the hundred.

Then by the thousand.

The advance slowed. Not due to the snow, though this now lay in a three-inch cover over the streets, but to watch for enemy attacks. But the lich made no attempts at ambushes or sorties, and in due time Dante stood in a square in easy bow shot of the gates they'd chosen to assault.

He turned his back to the enemy to look upon his people. He lowered the hood of his cloak, letting the snow swirl about his face. His soldiers stood silent, waiting with weapons ready, the priests and monks distributed among them so no section of the infantry would be without cover, anticipatory shadows wrapped around their hands.

There was no city noise to compete with, and the Blighted were quiet as well, with the snow muffling what little sounds the troops were making. Dante didn't need to amplify his voice at all.

"My friends," he began. "You know these walls we stand before. You know the streets outside them and the churches and temples within them. You know the riches of the markets of the Ingate. The glory of the spire of Ivars. The strength of the Sealed Citadel. You know the taste of the food grown on the farms that surround the city. You know the cold of these snows and that it will grow much colder—but due to that same cold, you know the relief of the first warm spring day when winter is behind us for another year.

"You know the people who live here, who you live and work and worship alongside; you know our long history, centuries of wars and struggle that date all the way back to the two tribes of the Rashen and Elsen. You know our culture of independence and perseverance. You know all of these things because this city is ours."

Dante closed his hands into fists. The gesture was not meant to be merely theatrical. Nor was the anger that now lifted his voice louder. "Though it is more true to say that it *was* ours. Now, it has been taken by a man whose mind is so warped he wants to exterminate every last person on earth. The ghouls you see there on the walls are the future he means to convert us to. Most of the dead are from other lands, but the White Lich killed everyone he found here and added them to his vile ranks. He'll use the shells of your own people to kill you.

"There is a part of me that's glad he took our city. For we aren't here to reconquer Narashtovik. No, we're here to kill every last one of them that we can. For even if we can't destroy the lich, we *can* murder his army. Even if we falter, and victory eludes us, every single Blighted we kill today gives those who come after us that much better of a chance to finish what we couldn't.

"It was a grave mistake for the White Lich to come here. For us, there *is* no defeat. Just vengeance. And we will fight all the more viciously to claim that vengeance in our own streets. You have fought the enemy before, and courageously, but it was without hope of anything more than survival. Today is different. Today, you fight for your souls—and the glory that comes from saving them. You fight for your city. You fight for—!"

"Still your tedious tongue."

The words cut short Dante's speech like the stroke of a sword. On a tower beside the gates, a lesser lich raised her hand, shadows dancing within it, her white dress flapping in the gusts of the storm.

"You speak like you're set and ready to invade!" Like the White Lich, her skin bore a blue-white glow, rendering her features difficult to make out. If her voice was anything to go by, they would look extremely arrogant. "Where is your sense of propriety?"

"You sack our home," Dante said levelly, "and speak to me of *propriety*?"

"Whenever there is a war, *someone's* home gets sacked. If the invaded later come to reclaim it, it is proper to hold a parley before the battle."

"At this point, what would the Eiden Rane and I possibly have to say to each other?"

"That can't be known until conversation begins."

"All right, then let me open the dialogue. Here are my terms. First of all, go fuck yourself. Second of all, I'm going to reach into your chest and rip out your wrinkled little heart. Thirdly, but no less important, when the White Lich finally shows his cowardly hide, I'm going to tie him by the ankles to the spire of the cathedral and—"

"Your words become very bold as long as you believe I am not there to hear them."

This came from a new voice—though Dante knew its source as deeply as he knew the feel of the ground beneath his feet. A massive head appeared from behind the wall, beardless, the man's eyes an ever-shifting but always-piercing blue. The White Lich took another step upward, revealing his massive shoulders and the cape draped from his shoulders. He carried his glaive. The blade at its end was big enough to gut a bull.

"Hello, little sorcerer." His eyes fell on Dante. "I thought perhaps that you feared to face me again. Where have you been hiding while your people fought in your stead?"

Dante hadn't prepared for this and feared he'd give it away by hesitating too long. Then he just thought about what Blays might say. "We thought we might hunt down the prime body and put an end to this thing. But then I thought that killing the shriveled little mummy you used to be wouldn't be very sporting."

The lich made a noise that might have been amusement. "You have so many funny ways to say that you have failed. Do you have a joke to make about your failure to protect the city I now stand within?"

"As a matter of fact, I do. I'll tell it to you right before I kill you."

"After so many losses, your bravado is forced, little sorcerer. This is a sad thing to see. I won't toy with you any longer." He turned his huge head to survey the army opposing him. "I come here to offer terms. For as you know, I am not quite the monster you make me out to be to your people. For you, little sorcerer, I have nothing to offer, for you have already turned your back upon the greatest gift I could give you.

"But I do have something to offer your people. The people of Narashtovik. I could scheme to lie to you, and promise that I will let you live if you lay down your arms and walk from these walls. But I have no need to lie. Instead I offer you this. I will not let you live *here* — and by 'here' I mean not just this city, but this world.

"But if I come to own this world, I will have no interest in the Mists. The life that comes after. You may live there as long as you like and I give you my promise that I will give you no trouble. Rather I vow to you to keep the Mists safe. No more damage will be done to them. You may live there in peace and without fear."

Dante laughed out loud. "What kind of an offer — "

"Silence. Did you not hear me when I said this offer is not for you?"

"Do you think we can't see right through you? You're making this offer because you're afraid of us."

The Eiden Rane laughed lowly. "You believe that I offer you this because I fear you? No. I offer you this because I pity you. In their hearts, these people know that you have nothing to offer them but annihilation."

"And you have nothing to offer them but lies."

"Why should I lie on this matter? My sole interest in the Mists is how they may be used to aid my conquest of these lands. You have seen my mind, little sorcerer. You know that I am not without honor."

"I also know that you will do anything to achieve your ends. Including betraying any promise you make."

"Yet I will swear on my blood that my offer is true."

"It may be that you would honor your words," Gladdic said. "Yet you make a promise you cannot keep. For even if you do nothing more to destroy the Mists, Taim will. Thus any man who takes your offer would sell his soul just to see it eradicated in the beyond."

"You know nothing of what will come to pass for the Mists should I choose to protect them. There is room for you there. You should take it, for there is no room left for you here."

"What a brilliant deal," Dante said. "All we have to do is forfeit our homeland, and in exchange we get to die. Did you really think that was going to work?"

"They have faced me before," the lich said gravely. "They understand that the end is only a matter of time. Yet they can choose to still have an after."

"An after." The disgust he'd felt since the lich had proposed his "offer" boiled up Dante's throat. "Are you so crazy that you think that's remotely appealing? Is it your age that's made you this insane? Or the amount of power you've gathered? Because this is *not* how people think."

"When no other choice is left to them, they will come to see reason."

"Do you know what the worst part of you is? None of this even has to be happening. Why didn't you just conquer Tanar

Atain and be happy with that? Even if you'd killed every last Tanarian, do you think anyone outside of the swamps would have cared about it? You could have ruled your land until the end of time. Done whatever you wanted with it. Turned it into your private paradise.

"But no. You had to try to take *everything*. As if the existence of people outside of your rule was an offense to you. Or worse, a *threat* to you. Combine this with your belief that all these people are living lives of crushing misery, and you're compelled to subjugate the whole world under your banner. You don't understand how our world works. There are supposed to be hundreds and hundreds of different kingdoms. That's the way it was meant to be."

"Meant to be? Why do you believe this fragmented world is superior than one that is united?"

Dante bit his tongue to prevent himself from saying "because a god told me, that's why." If he revealed they'd been palling around with the gods, it would only take a short leap for the lich to suspect they'd found the spear.

"All you have to do to figure that out is look at the world around you," Dante said instead. "Yes, neighbors go to war with each other. Sometimes they conquer each other. Sometimes the conquered rebel. There's plenty of strife. But there's nothing that threatens *everything*. Nothing except for you. Tanar Atain could have been your perfect vision made real — but it wasn't enough. For you, it never is."

"There are many men and women that is true of," the lich said. "But I am the only one with the power to make it so. Now the old ways will fall. And mine will replace them."

"That's why there can't be any deal. Why there was never any hope of peace. Because as long as you exist, it's either you or us." A cold understanding moved through him: he knew, finally, why the Mallish thought they had to exterminate nethermancers from their land. "And that's why our next task will be to learn how to find people like you before any of you can threaten us again. But I'm getting ahead of myself."

"In what way?"

"First, we have to destroy *you*." Dante turned away from the enemy and toward his people. "Now, we end this."

36

A volley of arrows flew from the archers. At the same time, a volley of nether flew from the priests.

And a roar of bloodlust flew from everyone.

Arrows bounced from the merlons of the wall. The Blighted were already retreating behind cover and few of the missiles found their mark. Yet the volley served its greater purpose: driving the lesser liches into cover as well, leaving them less able to defend against the flood of shadows streaming toward the wall.

The Eiden Rane made no move at all. Not even as the arrows struck him — most deflecting away or breaking, but two finding purchase, one in his chest and one in his neck. Even then, he didn't so much as flinch. Some unknown process pushed the arrows free from his skin. They dropped atop the wall without having shed a single drop of his glowing, pearlescent blood.

He bowed his arms to the side and lowered his head. Light exploded from his hands, a galaxy of ethereal stars that he sent crashing into the river of shadows. Scores of sorcerers had contributed to the attack against him. The lich neutralized it without the aid of a single one of his lessers.

He stared down at them in amused contempt. "You have rejected my offer of peace in the next world. You will soon see that it was generous beyond what you deserve."

He descended from the wall and disappeared from sight,

dashing any hopes that he might wade forward where Blays could get at him with the spear. Dante called to his priests and ordered a second volley. This time, though, the lesser liches co-ordinated their defense with their master. A few scant streaks of shadows made it past the deluge of light, but it wasn't enough to do more than gouge a few scrapes into the wall.

Dante ordered both archers and nethermancers to fire at will, hoping that in the full confusion of battle, the defenders would find it harder to focus on every single attack, allowing some portion to slip through. Archers shifted back and forth in search of better angles. Men brought ladders to help the bowmen up onto the roofs of houses. Even from higher vantages, they weren't able to strike many of the Blighted. Then again, stuck behind the wall, the Blighted weren't able to do any damage to the attackers at all.

The priests were having little better luck than the archers. So far they hadn't killed a single one of the lich's sorcerers, and had only put one meaningful crack in the wall.

"I don't think they even care about keeping us out," said Blays, who so far had had virtually nothing to do. "But it's a great way to get us to waste our supplies."

"Of arrows and nether," Dante agreed. "We could send a monk along the wall to a place that isn't guarded and breach it there. But if we can't force our way through here, I'm not sure how we're going to get the lich to expose himself anyway."

"Isn't that what the attack on the port is for? To split his attention?"

"That only works if it's a threat. Or the attack on the gate is. Right now, we're not."

"We only have to distract the lich for a second, right? That's all the time it will take to punch through the wall. So why not go tell him his mother is a lich-whore or something?"

"That just might work."

"Better yet, call his *dad* one."

Dante was already running away from the conversation and Blays had to make each word a little louder than the last. Not that Dante was actually running off to call the lich names. Rather he was heading toward Somburr, who was crouched beside an old home with a sod-covered roof and watching the action on the wall like he was considering kidnapping it.

"We're not making any progress," Dante said.

"I have seen that."

"But I've got an idea. I want you to throw an illusion at the lich. Something that will draw him away from the wall, if only for a second."

Somburr's brown eyes flicked between Dante's. "Illusion. Yes. Can he fall for one?"

"I suppose that depends on the illusion."

"Hmm. Go and get yourself ready."

Without another word—such as explaining what he was about to do—Somburr dashed away, heading for one of the ladders up to the rooftops. As Dante crouched among the shrubs and gathered the nether, one of his monks broke ranks and ran toward the wall, shadows streaming from his hands. The man meant to put his palms to the wall and blow it apart directly, with no chance of interception. A lesser lich pointed down at him and sent a flare of ether into the air. A rod of light arced from behind the wall and smashed the monk across the cobbles.

The monk's act had been an act of sheer bravery (perhaps overly so), and Dante said a short prayer for him. Just as he was finishing, a dark creature arose from the other side of the wall.

Dante hardly got a look at it: spiky, broad-shouldered, features that seemed ever-shifting, as if they were being seen through clear but rippling water. It didn't matter. Dante punched his fist through the paved stone street. A crack ripped toward the wall. Beyond it, ether speared through the air. But not toward the crack. Straight toward the "creature."

The ether hit the illusion and dashed it apart. The crack raced into the wall and dashed it apart, too. With a strange thrill—he was, after all, destroying his own city—Dante watched as the Pridegate tumbled to the ground.

"Into the breach!" he yelled over the crackle of stone. "Kill everything you can!"

He drew another batch of shadows to him and ran over the broken ground. Dust swirled over his face and coated his cloak. Stirred-up snow glimmered in the air, too, obscuring the faces of those assembling to try to block off the gap.

Fortunately, Dante knew they were all enemies. He lashed into them with everything he had, sending bodies flying into the air. The Blighteds' thick blood painted the snow. Others ran in behind Dante, nether sizzling from their hands. The rooftop archers unleashed a volley that cut down a score of Blighted just as they were massing to rush at Dante.

He crossed the ruins of the wall into the square beyond, shadows in one hand, Odo Sein sword in the other. Nether jabbed at him from a lesser lich, but someone behind him was already batting down the attack.

Dante killed another dozen Blighted, almost as an afterthought, then surveyed the dusty, snowy scene for the one thing that was missing: the Eiden Rane. His eyes leaped to movement near his right. Broken stones were sliding to the ground. A great white fist punched up from the rubble. The lich arose, dirtied by the collapse of the wall and bleeding from a few small scrapes, but looking generally untroubled.

For just a moment, Dante considered yelling at Blays to rush the lich with the spear. But the ancient sorcerer was already backing away from the breach as his Blighted—they seemed to be infinite in number—surged to halt the advance. As long as he kept hanging back, the lich still had far too much at his disposal for them to fight their way to him.

But they'd broken the wall. Maybe they could get him to stretch himself too thin in retreat. Failing that, they'd catch him by surprise from the depths of the Citadel.

Between now and that moment, then, the goal was to do exactly what Dante had been exhorting his people to do: slaughter as much of the lich's army as they could. He hurled a black lance at the White Lich's back. But it was a one-in-a-million shot, and Dante wasn't particularly disappointed when the lich knocked it down. He consoled himself by hacking through a throng of Blighted while shredding a second throng with a cone of nether.

Arrows flew steadily. Soldiers and sorcerers stormed through the wall. Maybe a rock had bounced off the lich's head and rattled him, because he wasn't doing much to stop them. Another minute and they'd be ready to start pushing the lich's army back into the city. If they pulled *that* off, there was a decent chance they'd have a shot at the lich himself.

Just as Dante had this thought, the Eiden Rane turned toward the break in the wall. He was smiling. Dante readied himself as the lich lifted his hands. White light gleamed from them, blinding and pure. But rather than hurling it at Dante or the monks fighting alongside him, he sent it high overhead—and down into the wall.

Stones groaned against each other. The dust picked itself up from the snow and flew toward the sliding and shifting rocks, which were piling upon each other, clicking into place and erasing the seams where they'd broken. All of this was happening almost as quickly as Dante had ripped them down. Another three heartbeats, and the work was done.

The lich had used the ether to restore the original shape of the wall, a fifteen-foot-high barrier of solid stone—and in doing so, had cut Dante and the others off from the rest of their army.

"You have made a mistake." The lich's blue eyes were fixed

on Dante despite the maelstrom of sorcery going on to all sides. "It will be your last one."

The lich strode toward him, glaive in hand, cape streaming behind him.

"Get back!" But it was Dante who backpedaled across the snowy ground. "You can't win. Not after all that we've done!"

"The moment is here. It is not the one you envisioned when you betrayed me, is it?"

Panic filling Dante's gullet, he gathered both nether and ether, hurling so much of it at the lich he thought his own hands would explode. The lich waved his hand through the air, dispersing the storm of power like so much smoke. The monks and priests who'd made it through the gap turned away from the Blighted they'd been savaging to cast their attacks at the lich instead. He was able to disperse most of them, but simply walked through the others. The attacks left nothing worse than little cuts. As shallow as the ones Dante used to feed the blood to the nether.

Dante plunged his mind into the earth, ready to tunnel away and close the route behind him. The lich reached down and arrested the dirt. Dante shaped a killing spike and drove it at the lich's forehead, preparing to dive through the ground if it managed to distract him. It didn't even get to him.

Soldiers hacked at the Blighted to hold back the hordes the best they could while the nethermancers of Narashtovik poured everything they could at the White Lich. The air blossomed with sparks and blasts and dying shadows. Still the lich came forward. Dante's back bumped against the wall.

"Now you die." The lich's voice rasped like a flurry of leaves over hard ground. "And I claim the world."

He stabbed forward with his long-bladed glaive. Dante twisted to the side, but it wasn't enough. He felt the horrid bite of metal piercing his chest. There was nothing else like it: the body knew at once that it was being destroyed. In terms of sheer terror, the initial sensation of that body-panic was worse than the pain that came after.

He tried to move free, to shatter the glaive with nether, to heal himself. Nothing worked. The edges of his vision closed in, becoming a tight tunnel.

The last thing he heard was Gladdic's voice. It felt very far away. He thought that he wouldn't hear it again.

37

He sat up. His heart was racing and his sheets were doused with sweat. He was in a small but cozy room—his bedroom—and though it was perfectly peaceful, with the shutters opened to the warming morning, he felt certain that something was terribly wrong.

For some reason he was afraid he wouldn't be able to open the door, but it swung wide without resisting him. He was bare-foot and the wood floor was still a little cold from the night. He was looking for someone, but somehow both the name and even the face wouldn't come to him; he must still be sleepy. But there were only two other rooms in the cabin to search, both empty, and he soon stepped out onto the front porch.

A white full moon hung alone in the pale blue of the morning sky. A small clearing surrounded the cabin, with woods beyond that. Bugs sang lazily.

A kindly man sat in a chair in the shade of the eaves, a mug resting on his knee. He was a monk. Seeing Dante's face, he lifted his eyebrows. "Is something wrong?"

"Yes." But Dante couldn't explain what. Not until he heard himself blurting it out. "I have to get back."

"Back? To what?"

"To where..." Dante gestured in a wide circle, as if trying to pluck the answers from out of the air. "I don't know. But my time. It isn't over. It *can't* be over."

The man stood, lowering his voice. "Slow down. You're frightening me. I can't understand what you're saying."

"But I'm saying that I have to go back."

He knew the monk wasn't his father, but the monk put a hand that felt fatherly on his shoulder. "Did you have a bad dream?"

"A dream?"

"You just woke up, didn't you? What else could it have been but a dream?"

Dante reached out his hand, but there was nothing but empty space before him. "But that doesn't feel right."

"Perhaps we can figure it out together. What do you remember about it?"

"That it was important. It felt like the most important thing I'd ever done. Something that I had to do, because no one else could." Saying this, he was able to remember a little more. "And I was grown up. And we were fighting a monster. Not just one from the stories, but a real one. But we didn't know if we could win."

"That *does* sound important. What kind of monster?"

"It was tall. And it glowed. And it could do magic. Really bad magic." Dante tried to recall more, but couldn't, and got frustrated, which only made it worse. "But that's all I remember."

"Well, that does sound frightening," the monk said. "But there are no monsters here."

"Yeah, but—"

"Here. Have some tea. You already feel better, don't you?" He passed Dante a cup that he'd had waiting. "Once you're done with that, we can take a walk. All the way down to the waterfall. Wouldn't you like that?"

"Yeah." Dante drank from the tea, which had cream in it and tasted very good. He wasn't feeling quite so hectic, but he was still troubled. *Had* it been a bad dream? It had to be, he'd woken up in his own bed, just like he had from any other nightmare he'd ever had. Nothing else made any kind of sense.

Even so, an essence remained in his gut. Not just the fear of the monster. But the fear his friends had been—were still—depending on him.

But maybe the walk would help him remember. He finished his tea and brought the cups inside like he was supposed to and the monk smiled and started down the path through the woods. It was a bright, cheerful morning, and there were plenty of birds and insects to look at, especially when they got to the stream, which Dante liked exploring. They made their way up it, and the monk didn't even seem to mind when Dante dawdled to turn over rocks or chase after the little orange frogs peeping from the banks.

Despite all his poking around, in time, the roar of the waterfall rose from the woods. It crashed down into a clear, deep pool, and the monk didn't let Dante swim it in when he was on his own, but the monk was there now to make sure nothing bad happened, and Dante stripped down to his smallclothes and waded into the cold, bracing water.

He swam beneath the falls, which was kind of scary but also exciting, and then he swam around the deep part, spooking himself with thoughts of what might be swimming around beneath him. When he got tired, he paddled back to the shallows to chase fish and find bugs.

It didn't seem like they'd spent that much time there, but the next thing he knew the light was growing long and buttery, and the monk said it was time to get home before darkness fell. Dante didn't want to go but he suddenly felt very tired. Twilight fell swiftly, painting the trees pink and purple. The cabin reappeared just as the last sunlight dimmed from the west and was replaced by the silvery moon hanging in the clear black sky.

Dante went to bed looking very much both to sleeping and to waking up in the morning. Just as he was drifting off, an image welled up from the deepest, blackest part of his brain: the cruel, hard face of a destroyer, his skin glowing silver, the eyes ever-shifting shades of blue, and far deeper than the pool beneath the falls. For a single instant, Dante remembered — and knew what a curse it was to remember.

The image faded, dissolving into some place hidden within him. He slept, and he dreamed of roaming through the forest, and when the sunrise woke him he remembered he wasn't here to worry about bad dreams. He was here to grow strong, wasn't he? Because his father was missing, and Dante was supposed to find him!

Outside, the monk sat in his chair and the moon hung in the sky. Dante ate his breakfast, then set out into the woods. At first he just walked, but soon found himself running across the trail, unencumbered, free, and more, simply *happy* to be in a place where nothing bad could —

A moment of blackness. Blackness like the gods must have seen before they created the worlds.

He could feel himself waking. But it took a long time, as if he was climbing a giant staircase, or swimming up from the bottom of the sea.

He smelled blood. Battle-sounds filled the frigid air. A face loomed over him, as round as the moon and just as pale — the man was terrified, the blood drained him his face until it matched the shade of the snow falling around them. Dante's chest was cold: his doublet had been torn open from collar to hem. He and Nak were surrounded by priests and gawkers, each one of whom looked just as scared as Nak.

"Lord Galand," Nak choked. "You're alive!"

News raced through the crowd like a fire. Some of the priests dropped to their knees to thank Arawn. Others bowed their heads to Dante, then turned and sprinted back toward the battle taking place somewhere beyond the wall, a hundred yards of which had been smashed down into rubble.

"Alive?" Dante took Nak's hand to help sit up. "Was I...? What happened?"

"The White Lich gored you with his blade. It didn't look... like you would make it. But Gladdic led an assault on the lich. It was enough for Blays to carry you here. It took everything we had to heal the wound. Even then, we thought..." Nak faltered, looking down, then smiled. "Well, we were wrong. And here you are."

"During the attack on the lich, did Blays reveal the spear?"

"What? *That*'s the first thing you ask about?"

"It's the only thing that matters."

"No. He didn't. But I did order the fleet to land at the port, in hopes it would distract the lich enough that he couldn't drive us back through the wall again. I'm pleased to report that my gambit worked. The lich had to dispatch some of his forces to the bay. As a result, he's presently in retreat, although it's an entirely controlled one."

Dante nodded his approval of this and got to his feet, dizzying himself. His vision cleared enough to make out someone dashing toward them through the ruins of the wall: Blays, who was absolutely covered in blood and Blighted ichor.

He skidded to a snowy stop in front of them, gave Nak a hug that lifted the stocky man from the ground, then looked Dante up and down. "The plan was for you to *pretend* to be wounded. You weren't supposed to throw yourself on the end of the lich's glaive."

"I thought it would be more convincing." Dante tugged at the scraps of his shirt. "Now will someone get me a new doublet?"

At his word, a pair of squires ran off through the snow. Blays motioned toward the city. "Are you up to speed on current events?"

"It's clear the lich didn't mean to truly defend the wall. At any rate, holding it wasn't vital to his plans. The Blighted can't get anything done from behind a wall. It was a trap to let some of us get past it and then cut us off from behind—and decapitate us."

"Which came damn close to working. But now he's switched to the next leg of his strategy."

"A measured retreat that exposes us to the Blighted horde at every step of the way."

"It's not a bad plan. He can wear us down with his expend-able bits while keeping himself and most of his sorcerers out of harm's reach. After all, he's got a lot of Gask left to conquer after this. Makes perfect sense to play it safe."

"Except that's the exact same mistake we made in the fight for Bressel."

"Hey, our strategy was perfectly brilliant right up until he started using those damn portals."

"Just like his will be perfectly brilliant right up until you ram the spear up his downward end."

"Which we're going to miss out on doing if we don't get into position quick. Shall we?"

At that moment, the servant returned with a new doublet. Dante shrugged out of his cloak, donned the doublet, then put on one of the nondescript cloaks that were to act as their disguis-es. He was about to send for Gladdic when he noticed the old man was already loping toward them from the breach through the wall. While sailing to Narashtovik, they'd had a lengthy dis-cussion of how many people should accompany Dante and Blays on their mission to the tunnel. In the end, Dante had argued that it was much more important for them to reach the tunnel with-out being seen, and that while adding more people might make them safer from attack, it would also compromise the entire endeavor. Besides, their army would be besieging the Citadel at the same time, and could do plenty to pitch in once the moment was right. Hence the mission would be undertaken by the same trio that had acquired the spear.

"Time for us to get moving," Dante said to Nak. "We'll stay in contact through the loon."

"But Lord Dante," Nak said, hands flitting about in front of him as if he was about to grab Dante's new shirt, "you just—"

"I'm fine. Even if I wasn't, it wouldn't matter. There's no one else who can do this. So quit fussing and wish us luck."

"Yes. Yes, indeed. Good luck then, milord. It's funny, I've known you'd be trouble since I first saw you when you were just a boy. But I had no idea just how much."

"Trust me, neither did I."

Nak chuckled, then grew sober. "If I don't see you again, it's been a hell of a lot of fun, hasn't it?"

"It has. And it's not done quite yet."

They moved east out of the square, keeping plenty of cover between themselves and any enemy eyes. It was only when they had put the noise of battle well behind them and were jogging steadily through the streets that Dante understood just how close he'd come to crossing a boundary there would have been no return from.

Around them, the streets held the eerie quiet of a snowy field. They were outside the Pridegate, circling counter-clockwise around the wall in order to reach the northern hill that bore the carneterium and the tunnel leading from it to the Citadel dungeons. After a few minutes, Nak looned Dante to update him that the lich continued to retreat and they continued to follow. It felt strange to be so far removed from the fighting, others dying for them as they walked the streets in peace.

Then again, if the three of them did their job, they'd be back in the thickest part of it soon enough.

The city had suffered minimal damage during the lich's initial occupation—largely because there had been almost zero resistance, although Dante suspected the lich had fully intended to use the city's defenses and so forth to his advantage—but all at once the buildings around them had been reduced to lumps of rubble strewn with patches of torn-up thatch and sod roofing. There were bodies now, too, most of the flesh chewed away by dogs or Blighted or both, their bones and hair and sinew half-hidden under the mounding snow.

A Blighted leaped out from behind a freestanding wall and charged at them like it had been waiting for them. Gladdic put a spike of ether between its eyes.

"Gods, I hate these things." Blays stepped around the body. "Please tell me that when we kill the lich, the rest of them will just drop dead."

Dante gestured at Gladdic. "Is that what happens?"

"I would not know," Gladdic said. "For in all the long history of Tanar Atain, he who commanded the Blighted—the Eiden Rane—was never killed. Only imprisoned."

"Oh. Right."

They got less than a block before a second Blighted emerged and ran at them with typical mindless hunger and fury. This time, Dante was ready for it, and parted its brains from its skull. It still hadn't stopped twitching when he heard the thud of feet from the northwest, partly muffled by the snow.

"I think we need to get out of here," Dante said. "Fast."

He ran northeast toward an intact neighborhood just a few blocks away. To his left, another Blighted charged to intercept them. Gladdic killed the thing as soon as they saw it, but another was right on its heels.

"Did we run into a nest?" Blays said. "Or are they bringing each other here now that one of them smelled fresh meat?"

Dante glanced over his shoulder. "Either way, the answer is

to do exactly what we're already doing."

As they ran, Gladdic waved his hand at the snow behind them, restoring it to its original form and erasing their tracks. Even so, they had to kill three more Blighted before they reached intact houses. Dante made sure nothing was watching them, then ducked inside an older three-story building. All of the shutters were already closed and locked, presumably during the evacuation, and Blays and Dante dragged a hefty table to block the front door.

This done, they retreated upstairs and eased open a shutter just enough to afford them a peek at the streets. They'd just gotten situated when the first of the Blighted came dashing down the street. More and more appeared with every second, until at least a few of them were in sight at all times, rushing back and forth until the snow was gray and churned.

Blays drew back from the window. "What are they doing? They're just running around like idiots."

"They *are* idiots."

"But they're normally a lot less obviously stupid."

"Maybe they've got different orders today."

"Like what?"

"Like stopping the advance of anyone they see moving around the city who isn't trying to flee it."

"If that's the case, the more of them we kill, the more we'll draw to us. Then what's the plan? Wait them out?"

Dante checked in quickly with Nak, then shut the loon. "We can try, but we can't wait long. The lich is retreating steadily toward the Citadel. I don't like the idea of making Nak besiege it for too long."

"Expecting a trick from the lich?"

"We'll be lucky if there's just one."

They waited several minutes. By then, the Blighted no longer seemed to be increasing in number, but nor were they thinning back out.

"Maybe we can just wait for them to tire themselves out," Blays said. "When does that happen with undead again? Oh, was it never?"

Dante rubbed his eyes. "There aren't any sewers or catacombs out here to sneak away through. I don't want to try tunneling, either. If all this running about has drawn a lesser lich to the area, and he feels us digging around below the surface, he's likely to warn the White Lich to watch for such things."

"What does that leave us?" Gladdic said.

Blays tapped the window sill. "A disguise. We could kill a few of them, walk their bodies inside, then skin them and wear the skins."

"That's ghoulish," Dante said.

"So are they. That's why it would work. Anyway, it's sort of like what we did that other time."

"I don't think that's going to work again. At least not here. But it does give me an idea."

Dante moved to the other side of the house, which had a view of the street where they'd killed the three Blighted. He waited until the still-living ones were running away from the bodies, then reanimated them. After a bit of practice, he had his zombies running around as well, if clumsily—though given the snow and the ramshackle way the others were patrolling the streets, it was hardly noticeable.

He sent all three of his corpses up the street, waving their arms in agitation. Two of the Blighted that were still under the lich's command ran after the trio, investigating what the fuss was about. It took them several seconds before they came to understand there *was* nothing to fuss about and returned to their own activities.

Dante moved the reanimated Blighted to the south side of the house and tried the trick again with similar results. "We'll have to move fast. They'll only buy us ten or fifteen seconds."

Blays cast an extremely skeptical look down at the street. "And what's going to buy us the other ten times as many seconds we'll need to get away?"

"I am. Just like usual."

Dante sent his Blighted running around at random as the three of them headed downstairs and lifted the table away from the door. He nicked the back of his arm and brought the nether to him from the cold corners of the room. He paused, allowing two Blighted to run out of sight to the south, then sent his three servants stomping north to draw off the last Blighted in immediate sight.

As soon as it had its back to them, he opened the door and ran to the east, angling toward an alley. The snow quieted his steps but slowed him down as well. The lich's Blighted was still chasing after his decoys, but it was already looking from side to side, its steps faltering. Just as it came to a stop and began to back toward the house, Dante and the others spilled into the alley. Dante drew an illusory wall to block the space behind them.

None of the Blighted gave chase. Dante directed the three under his control to scout the way forward, allowing the three humans to duck behind walls or inside doorways whenever one of the lich's Blighted came anywhere near. Soon the undead thinned until there were none left at all. Still, to avoid getting trapped again, Dante brought them all the way east into the pine forest that surrounded the farms that bordered the city.

The peace of the snowy forest was total, rendering the life-and-death struggle within Narashtovik all the more surreal. Dante sent his three Blighted along the fringe of the city to watch out for anything that might be coming for them. Nak reported that there had been another pitched battle at the Ingate, but once the forces that had landed in the port had broken through the wall from the other side, the lich had enacted another careful retreat. He was making for the Citadel.

This was very good, except that Dante (and more importantly Blays) had several miles between them and the tunnel. They
hoofed it onward. Theoretically there was no need for great
haste—if the lich sequestered himself within the Citadel, Nak
could just surround the walls without committing to an attack—
yet despite how well everything seemed to be going, the dread
Dante carried low in his chest grew steadily heavier.

Now and then he caught a flash of ether shooting from the
streets like a lightning bolt captured and dragged down to earth.
But mostly he saw and heard nothing.

They bent back toward the west as they circumnavigated the
Dead City. The snowfall had been steady but gentle, but as they
approached the north hill where Cally, Larrimore, and so many
others were buried, the snow fell faster and harder, until Dante
could no longer see the bay to the west.

The slope rose to meet them as they jogged among the tombs
and gravestones. Countless other times he'd come here, Dante
had felt contemplative and sad, wondering if he could ever find
a way to extend his life far beyond his natural years—or even
forever.

On that day, though, he prayed that if it meant the end of the
lich, he would happily add his life to all those who had spent
theirs in defense of the city, to rest here beside them for eternity
instead.

The snow squeaked beneath their boots as they crossed
around to the base of the hill and the cave-like entrance to the
carneterium.

Gladdic stopped at the threshold and lifted his chin. "Many
have died here."

"It wasn't *my* fault," Dante said. "We were trying to save
them."

"Then it is to our good fortune—or perhaps the stern hand of fate—that you lacked the skills to keep them alive. One moment."

The old man crouched down, whispering to himself as he probed into the deepest nooks of the nether. A towering Andrac popped into existence beside him, flexing its claws and gnashing its teeth with the relish common to the demons. A second soon followed. As he made work on a third, great gouts of ether flashed from around the distant Citadel—followed, after a brief delay, by human screams.

Dante pulsed his loon. Nak didn't answer. He waited ten very long seconds, but his own loon twinged just as he was about to try again.

Nak's voice was strained. "Where are you?"

"Just outside the tunnel. What's happening?"

"We surrounded the Citadel. Began to lay siege, though we weren't pressing too hard. Then the lich opened the pits."

"Pits?"

"Giant holes he'd dug into the ground—and filled with Blighted. They came at us from behind. Thousands of them. If we can't get free, we'll be crushed from both sides."

"Can you hold out ten minutes?"

"I'm not sure."

"Withdraw if you have to."

"I don't know if we—"

"Yes you can. Because if you can't find a way to hold out until we're inside the Citadel, then everything is lost."

Gladdic had already forged his third Star-Eater. Dante motioned them into the carneterium, Gladdic lighting the way. The recent events of Dante's life had kept him so busy elsewhere that he'd only spent a few weeks of the last two years in Narashtovik, but he had no trouble navigating the many tunnels beneath the hill until he came to the secret passage to the Citadel.

"Well." Blays gripped the Spear of Stars, presently in the

shape of the rod. "Let's hope we didn't invoke the wrath of the gods for nothing."

They sent two Andrac ahead in case any Blighted were lurking in the tunnel, then ran down it as fast as they could, their footsteps echoing from the bare stone walls. It was warmer than it had been out in the snows and the air was perfectly still. Dante began to sweat. He pulsed Nak for an update, but Nak didn't respond. Every minute felt like ten. Dante washed their muscles clean of fatigue. Ahead, the Andrac came to a stop. Gladdic's light glowed upon what appeared to be a dead end. But just two feet of stone stood between them and the Citadel basements.

Dante scratched his arm and reached into the wall. And yelled out in shock.

"Lyle's balls," Blays said, hunching over. "What'd you see, a scary pebble?"

"The walls," Dante said. "They're warded."

"Er...warded?"

"Like at the Tower of Taim. I don't know if I can get this open. Even if I can, it'll tip off the lich. He'll swamp us with so many Blighted we'll never get to him. Or just collapse the basement on us."

"Can we go around the wards? Or get in underneath them?"

"They stretch as far as I can see. They're woven into the floor, too."

"Is this as bad as it sounds?"

"It's worse. We can't get in."

"*You* can't get in," Blays said after a moment's thought. "But I bet I can still shadowalk through them."

"What about me and Gladdic?"

"Is this tunnel warded, too?"

Dante glanced up. "No. Not that I can see."

"Then back up far enough the lich won't see it and open a tunnel to the surface. You can join Nak in the siege."

"But if I do that, it might spit us out right in the middle of a horde of Blighted." Dante knew as soon as he said them that the words weren't what mattered. "We're not splitting up. We protect each other. That's what's gotten us this far. We'll all head back to the surface."

"What happens if we can't find a way over the Citadel wall?"

"The same thing that happens if any part of our plan goes wrong: we lose and we all die." Dante turned to go, already reaching up into the ceiling to attempt to find the outer wall.

"Stop," Gladdic said. He'd been staring at the wall the entire time the two of them had been talking. Now he moved toward it and placed his left palm upon it.

Ether sparked from his fingers, lighting up the lines woven into the wall. Patterns revealed themselves like the mysteries of a long-lost tome. Some were regular and obvious enough to be understood at first glance, but others, like so much of the city of Chronus itself, refused to easily yield their natures.

"Don't touch that," Dante said. "If you set them off—"

"Be silent," Gladdic said.

He sent more ether into the wall. The skein of lines and angles throbbed, dimmed, and brightened again to an angry crystal white that Dante had to shield his eyes against. Gladdic tensed his shoulders and bowed his head, muttering words that Dante couldn't make out. Ether crackled from the wall. Gladdic yanked back his hand, staring evilly at the wards, then slammed his palm back against them.

Dante flinched as light seared across the tunnel. With the sound of cracking crystal, the wards before them collapsed to the ground in a heap of threads, the ether fading away to nothing.

"There," Gladdic said. "A way forward."

Dante's jaw hung open. "How did you do that?"

"I have observed patterns similar to the wards within the Mists, as well as in the land like it that I have no name for.

Knowing the pattern, I was able to break it."

"And you couldn't have done that at the Tower of Taim?" Blays said.

"No, for the wards there were far more sophisticated. But I would not have been able to decipher these had I not seen those enclosing the tower, for the patterns there also held these ones within them."

"I've never seen the lich create anything like these before." Dante gazed into the rock to the left of the dead end, where the wards remained. "Suppose Taim somehow taught him to craft these?"

"If that is true, then they must have been in recent contact with each other."

"I don't like that idea much at all. But there's nothing to be done about it. Our people are dying up there."

Dante raised his hand and opened a passage through the wall, careful not to touch the wards beyond where Gladdic had dispelled them. A musty, sour smell breathed over them. It wasn't pleasant, but it was deeply familiar.

Dante stepped through the wall and into the occupied Sealed Citadel.

38

He emerged into a dungeon cell. Due to the presence of the tunnel, they hadn't kept anyone in that particular cell for years, but some very old and very stale straw was strewn around the floor to keep up appearances. Keeping the nether in hand, Dante opened the cell door.

Gladdic's light gleamed down the roomy passage running between the two banks of cells. Seemingly empty. The old man nodded to his Andrac, two of which moved to lurk ahead of them in perfect silence. In the dimness of the dungeon, they looked like little more than strange shadows shifting over the floor.

When they reached the stairwell, Dante motioned to the others to stop, then attempted to loon Nak again. This time, the Councilman answered.

"You're alive," Dante said. "Are you still at the Citadel?"

"Yes. For the moment."

"So are we. We'll be in position in just another minute."

"Try not to take any longer than that, please? It's a wonder we're still here at all."

Dante motioned the Andrac to continue upstairs. He followed. The steps felt good beneath his feet. He knew them so well he could have climbed them without any light at all.

There were still two levels of storage between them and the

surface, not to mention the walls of the keep, but he could already hear the pop of sorcery and the ring of steel. This grew louder with each step upward. By the time Dante emerged onto the ground floor, it was loud enough to cover their footsteps completely. In many ways, it sounded like every other war he'd been in. But in other ways, it was unique. There was something frightening to it. More desperate. The soldiers understood.

The light through the windows was wan and gray, yet practically dazzling after the dungeons and basements. Dante crossed to a window and pressed his face to the freezing glass; ice had climbed halfway up it. Outside, thousands of Blighted crammed the courtyard, faces lifted toward the walls, where more Blighted awaited any enemies who made the effort to climb in and numerous lesser liches held off the sorcerous assaults of the priests besieging them—with all of their efforts orchestrated and augmented by the Eiden Rane, who stood like a pillar in the center of the courtyard, arms stretched wide, fending off the attackers with great volleys of light.

Dante pulled back from the window and jogged in the direction of the grand foyer, passing in and out of the dim bands of light pushing through the curtains. A figure entered the hall between them and the Andrac: a woman in white robes who would have been pretty if not for her drawn and sunken features, prematurely withered hands, and deathly pale skin. In those ways she resembled the Blighted, except that she was clothed, and bore the spark of intelligence within her eyes.

"Invaders," she rasped.

Blays strolled toward her. "You're one to talk."

"Stay where you are, mortal. I said stay—!"

But Blays paid no heed to her words. She flexed her stiff fingers toward him, assaulting him with a tight helix of shadows. He broke into a sprint, swinging the rod forward. The spear sprung to its full length, casting the hall in the brightest moonlight, illuminating the fear-frozen face of the lesser lich.

The helix of nether was powerless to resist being bent toward the blade of the spear. The purestone blackened as it absorbed the shadows into itself. Blays drove forward, smoke-like tendrils of nether dissolving around him as he cocked his elbows and rammed the spear into the middle of the woman's chest.

Her spine arched in agony. White blood shot from her mouth, along with a steam-like essence that resembled nether but felt all wrong. Her eyes rolled in terror, darting between Blays and his weapon.

"You have..." She thrashed like a wounded centipede, trying and failing to free herself from the spear. "This was not supposed to be. I was supposed to..."

"Fuck off and die."

Blays slashed the spear at a downward diagonal. The blade cut through her body like she was parchment, emerging from her right hip. She lifted her hand—to heal herself, to strike at them, or both—but Blays was already reversing the weapon's course, backhanding its long blade at the lesser lich's neck.

It cut cleanly. Her eyes were still blinking as her body toppled backward and her head tumbled forward.

The room seemed to grow colder; her gnarled flesh fell in upon itself, boiling with decay for a horrid two seconds before crumbling into two piles of dry, gray dirt.

Blays kicked at the smaller pile, smearing the toe of his boot. He shook his foot. "Gross. Why did I just do that?"

"Because your brain isn't very good?" Dante said.

"Careful with that. You're not the most dangerous guy in the room anymore." Blays wagged the spear at Dante, then retracted it into its rod, stealing the excess light from the room.

Dante ran to the closest window. Outside, the battle raged on. He waited for some alarum or reaction from the White Lich, but the woman must have been too shocked to reach him as she died, and he was too busy at the center of the defense to feel that the cord between them had been severed.

The Andrac continued toward the front door of the keep. Dante activated his loon. "Nak, we're almost ready. We're going to need your help to keep him distracted up to the last second."

"It got a bit hairy for us there!" Nak sounded rattled but in the process of calming down. "But we've just about fought our way back. Give us just another minute."

The loon went blank. The front doors were open and a shallow drift of snow lay upon the floor in front of them. Dante crept up to the exit for a better view of the field. In the short time before he'd last looked on it, the tumult had gotten quite a bit worse—or, for their purposes, better—with regular explosions of shadows atop the walls that sent bits of Blighted tumbling through the sky. Arrows flew over the merlons and fell blind into the courtyard, though this was so filled with undead the missiles usually hit something. Dante could feel the priests battering the walls with sorcery as well, but the defenders were diverting a great deal of energy to protecting the barriers, and so far the priests hadn't been able to open a single breach.

"Right," Nak said in Dante's ear. "Just give us the word."

"The word." Dante closed down his loon and pointed to the lich, who stood some three hundred feet away in the midst of a heaving throng of Blighted. "Gladdic, send the Andrac out first in a wedge. We'll go in right behind them. The goal is to clear a path straight to the lich. Once we're there, our job is to do whatever it takes to keep Blays unharmed and unencumbered. No matter what happens to anyone else—or to us—that's all that matters."

"No pressure, then," Blays said. "Suppose I just...stab him? That's it?"

"I don't have any idea. But we're about to find out." Dante's scratch had stopped bleeding and he opened a new one.

"Ready?"

Blays lifted the rod. "To the breaking of the cycle."

At once, Dante had the unmistakable sensation that someone was watching them, though neither the lich nor any of his minions was paying them the slightest attention. He glanced up at the sky, but saw nothing.

He gathered himself. In a rush, it all came back to him: the rebellion in Tanar Atain that they'd aided, thinking they were doing a good deed, and in the process overthrowing the only people who'd known how to keep the lich imprisoned in the Riya Lase. The long struggle across the swamps, all in vain, that had provoked the Drakebane into executing the decades-long plot to subvert Mallon and take Bressel as a new homeland for his people. The scheme had somehow worked, except that it had simply drawn the lich to Bressel instead, and now the Drakebane was dead, and so were all but perhaps a few hundred of his people.

Somehow the search to kill the Eiden Rane had also led them to an understanding of the deep history of their world—of Rale—and the one beyond it, pushing them to acquire knowledge that had been lost for so long that no one knew that it *had* been lost. All of this now stood on the brink of being lost again, and this time forever.

It was a heavy thought to hold. Yet somehow it felt far graver to know that the city he'd built back from near ruins would become ruins again, lost first to the snows and then to the earth, along with all of his companions who had forged themselves into weapons strong enough to stand against the most potent enemy their age had ever seen.

"Well," Blays said. "Are we going to—"

"It's time," Dante said. "On my—"

"*SORCERER!*"

The hair stood up on Dante's arms and neck, pricking him

like they were made of iron filings. The copper-kettle voice of the White Lich hung in the cold air, so commanding that, for a moment, the entire battle came to a stop.

The White Lich glared at Dante with eyes that seemed to have been plucked out from a glacier. "You were supposed to be dead!"

With effort, Dante threw off his shock. "Afraid not. The gods must have been looking out for me."

"Do you believe you are mocking me? You should know better than anyone that there are few matters on which the gods are united. If there are those who favor you, then you must know there are those among them who favor me as well."

"What's he talking about?" Dante murmured.

"Taim," Gladdic answered. "They have been in contact. There can be no doubt."

Blays looked up into the snow. "Please tell me Taim isn't here now?"

"Do you believe you have caught me by surprise?" The White Lich laughed. "Come now and find out. It's time to bring this to an end."

"That sounds like an invitation," Blays said. "It would be rude to turn it down, wouldn't it lads?"

He drew his two swords, nether snapping along the blades and casting silver sparks into the falling snow, meaning to keep the spear concealed until he was upon the lich. Gladdic nodded to his Star-Eaters. They stretched their claws and rushed into the wall of Blighted.

Blays ran after them. With a surge of nerve, Dante did the same. The front row of Blighted fell to the Andrac, claw-wounds gaping from torsos and throats. The Blighteds' faces twisted with miserable fury: they seemed to understand that they couldn't hope to harm the demons, but that they had to throw themselves at the Andrac nonetheless. But the sheer weight of their numbers slowed the demons to a trudge.

Blays lashed out with his swords, sending limbs and heads flying hither and yon. Dante reached into the bodies with the nether and brought them back to their feet as his own undead. They stumbled into the Blighted, bashing at them with clumsy fists, freeing up Blays and the Andrac to slash their way forward. The air filled with the froggish smell of the undeads' cut flesh.

The lich watched their progress with bemusement and pity. "The three of you could not defeat me when we were alone in the cavern. What mad desperation makes you believe you can do so when my legions oppose you as well?"

Blays cut through two Blighted with one stroke. "If we told you that, it would ruin the surprise!"

Within the maelstrom of the undead throng, they were progressing toward the White Lich at a slow walking pace. So far he hadn't bothered to move or even to take any action against them. Now, though, he lifted his great hands. Lines of light strung between them as if on a loom.

"Gladdic!" Dante quit raising new zombies to gather the shadows instead. "Incoming!"

"I am not blind," Gladdic muttered, slaughtering a mass of Blighted as they attempted to leap on them from behind.

Dante closed one eye and squinted the other. A sun-like radiance of ether blared from the lich's hands. Aimed at the foremost Andrac. The demon snarled, still raking its claws back and forth among the Blighted as if harvesting wheat. Dante released every shadow he held. Gladdic matched him, a flock of nether dancing around a thinner spear of ether. Their combined forces ripped into the lich's beam, shredding layer after layer until it all dashed apart into harmless sparks.

In the brief time Dante had ceased lifting new zombies, a quarter of them had fallen. The Blighted pressed tighter on all sides; Blays fell to the rear to hold them off there, but without his blades, the Andrac were slowed even further. Bolts of nether flew at Blays from the right, the product of a lesser lich somewhere within the masses. Gladdic deflected most of them, the remainder pelting into a few zombies, dropping them.

And the White Lich had a new attack on the way. Their counters tore most of it apart, yet several shreds pierced the lead Andrac, tearing smoke-like tendrils of shadows from its body. It reared back with a reptilian shriek.

They were hardly moving forward at all. Dante ducked under the grasping fists of a Blighted and summoned another batch of zombies to their feet, but this barely relieved the pressure on them.

"I can't help notice we're not getting any closer." Blays carved up five Blighted with as many swings before he was forced to take cover behind a pair of zombies. "That's going to seriously hamper my ability to kill the lich."

Dante signaled his loon. "Nak, we're stuck in here. If you can't draw some of the heat off us, we'll never get near enough to the lich."

"We're doing our damnedest to break through the wall," Nak said. "But I'll see what we can do."

There had already been plenty of sorcery popping off around the wall, but at once it doubled in intensity. Dante and the others fended off another assault from the lich but the lead Star-Eater was now bleeding nether from ten different wounds that were slow to heal. Dead Blighted lay around them in such heaps that the others were having a harder time getting at them, but that didn't do anything at all to help their forward progress.

The lich's hands filled with another loom of light. Yet before he could strike them with it, the wall boomed, a crack sliding across its face, stone raining down to smash the Blighted gathered beneath it. The White Lich set his jaw and turned to the wall, sending his ether to it instead, restoring the crack just as he'd done to their first effort to break through the Pridegate.

It gave them enough of a breather for Dante to augment the ranks of his zombies and for Gladdic to heal the lead Andrac with shadows while using a scythe of light to butcher a 45-degree arc of Blighted. They bulled their way forward, scattering corpses in their wake. Many of the Blighted had once been Tanarian, but there were many Mallish among them as well, along with Gaskans, too. Dante had a sudden glimpse of how it would look, if they failed, to those on the other side of the world when the Eiden Rane came calling with an army of Blighted composed of hundreds of different peoples, nearly all of them unknown to those about to be swept out to death, made all the more alien by the ghastly warping of their undead features.

The lich prepared a new attack. Yet as soon as he turned his back to it, the wall broke anew, stone thundering, chunks of it flying straight into the air. Bony hands punched through the gap —no, not hands, but *branches*, growing madly from the expanding trunk of a tree. Winden had harvested it up from beneath the wall to demolish the structure, breaking it in a way the Eiden Rane couldn't simply undo with ether.

"Through the breach, lads!" A portly, balding, and berobed figure emerged beside the tree, waving his arm in a wide circle. "They won't last without us!"

He ran forward, carrying a staff in one hand. Dante laughed. He wasn't sure he'd ever seen Nak armed before. The Councilman took a two-handed swing at the head of a dazed Blighted, then fired a swarm of nether into a lesser lich trying to wriggle free from beneath a giant stone.

Soldiers and priests rushed in behind Nak, an expanding bubble of living humans within the jostling throng of the undead. Somburr appeared atop the wall as if from nowhere, materializing behind the back of one of the lich's sorcerers, driving a spike of nether through its chest and showering its innards on the Blighted in the courtyard below. The undead on the wall sprinted towards him. He killed the closest of them, then jumped down from the wall and vanished.

The lich lifted his hands and hammered the invaders with streams of light. Nether sprung forth from scores of hands until more shadows flitted through the air than flakes of still-falling snow. Some soldiers were dragged down by Blighted while at least one priest and one monk had died to the assaults of the White Lich and his lieutenants, yet the overwhelming majority of the sorcery was simply spent neutralizing the attacks of the other side, dissolving back into the weft of the world.

"Our people are throwing everything they've got at it," Dante said. "But they'll exhaust themselves within another minute. If we aren't on the lich by then, they'll all die—and we'll be next."

Inspired by Winden's breaking of the wall, he reached into the cobblestones beneath the trampled snow on both sides of their group and yanked the rock into a palisade of spikes, impaling the Blighted to right and left—and putting a barrier between themselves and the rest of the undead. As the Andrac pushed forward, Dante extended the palisades to match them, keeping most of the enemies off of the demons and allowing them to close ground on the White Lich as he bombarded the breach in the wall.

The bubble of troops inside the Citadel courtyard was still expanding, but the lich ceased his attacks on them and set his hands on his hips. With a smile, he turned back toward Dante and the others, barraging them with geometric lightning that ripped streaks of nether from the Star-Eaters.

"What's he doing?" Blays stepped over a pair of carcasses. "Isn't he supposed to be stopping the army from breaking into his fortress?"

"He has reached the same conclusion that we have," Gladdic

said. "He does not need to spare any worry for those at the wall, for the Blighted will stymie them until the priests' nether is all spent. They pose no threat to the lich at all. Only we do."

This thought sank like a stone in Dante's gut. They were still drawing nearer to the enemy, almost within a hundred feet. But it now became clear the White Lich had been fighting conservatively to that point. Holding back his strength in case they came at him with a surprise. He now fought without reservation, lines of ether spearing through the foremost Andrac far faster than Gladdic could heal them. Before Dante knew what was happening, the demon was flickering in and out—and then it was gone.

The two that had formed the trailing points of the wedge pulled together before a single Blighted could squeeze through the line, but Dante could feel at once that the loss of just one demon was the difference between the continued ability to advance and stalling where they stood. As soon as they stopped moving, the Blighted began to pile themselves alongside the stone palisades, allowing others to clamber over them and fling themselves at Dante and Gladdic—obliging them to fire dozens of black bolts into the slavering crowd.

Dante wheeled to parry a beam of light as thick as his body. He whittled it down, but portions of it pierced the Andrac on the left, punching gouts of nether from it. It howled an airy howl and flung its claws skyward. From afar, the lich reached into the demon's wounds and reeled forth the shadows that comprised its body. Gladdic grappled with the enemy for control of the Andrac's life-stuff, requiring Dante to turn to the business of cutting down the Blighted threatening to overwhelm them from right and left.

And with both of them so distracted, both were a half a step too late to nullify the attack that came after.

A chevron of ether swooped into the ground before them. Cobbles cracked and burst into the air. The Andrac were knocked back, slamming into Dante and Gladdic; though their nethereal bodies seemed to weigh much less than was natural for their size, Dante was crushed into the broken and heaving ground. His stone spikes disintegrated. Like water flooding into a crater, the Blighted flung themselves upon them, their sheer numbers blanking out the sky.

Dante's sword had been knocked from his hand, its nether fizzling out as soon as it was removed from the connection to his trace. A mass of bodies squeezed the air from his lungs. Claws groped at his clothes and dug into his skin. Half-panicked, he pulled the nether to him, punching it into anything he could be sure was a Blighted, their sickly cool blood leaking over him. But as soon as he killed one it was dragged away by the others and replaced with another.

Something shifted in front of him: an Andrac shoving its way to its feet, slashing the horde down around it. A streak of ether pulsed toward them. Dante felt it pound into the demon and rip the Andrac apart.

Clammy flesh pushed down on Dante's mouth. He snapped his head back and forth, struggling to breathe, but other Blighted were piling onto the one smothering him. He pulled his jaw open and bit down as hard as he could, teeth sinking into its soft tissue, and retched as cold, salty fluid spilled into his mouth. The Blighted didn't even try to pull back. Dante groped with his mind, located its head, and pounded a thick nail of nether through it. The body went limp, but countless others were still crushing down on it—and him.

He tried to scream, but the flesh was pressed so tight to his mouth he couldn't force any air out. Head spinning, eyes dazzling with spots, he clawed at the nether, not yet certain what—if anything—he could do with it.

The crushing weight on him suddenly became a lot less crushing. He shoved his face to the side, hunting for a pocket of air. Glass rung; with a crunching sound that almost had him retching again, the weight lessened further, enough for him to wrestle his shoulders loose from the dead Blighted, then his head. He drew a sharp breath of freezing wintry air, then hacked out a mouthful of stuff he did not want to think about. He felt air moving about his head, snowflakes stinging his cheeks. He climbed free and swayed to his feet.

He found himself standing among a mound of Blighted, all dead or hideously wounded. To his left, Gladdic wormed free of the corpses. His hair and robe couldn't have been more disheveled than if he'd spent the morning tumbling down the side of a mountain.

There were still thousands of Blighted in the courtyard, but none of them were rushing toward Dante. Instead, they had formed a wide-open ring. Blays stood in their middle.

Heavenly light glowed upon his face. In his right hand he held the Spear of Stars, its butt planted in the churned-up snow, its blade and gem shining like the light that guides the traveler home. The wind rippled his cloak behind him.

"You know what this is, don't you?" Blays called. All of the field had fallen silent. "You know that I hold your death in my hands."

The lich watched him like everyone and everything else had ceased to exist. There was no mistaking the look in his eyes: not surprise, but recognition. He had ferreted out the knowledge of what was coming for him. Or been informed of it from beyond. No wonder he'd taken such pains not to put himself at risk since they'd come to the city.

But there was something else in his blue eyes, too.

Fear.

The White Lich stirred from his momentary trance. "There was once a time when the weapon could have saved you. But I have ascended beyond even the reach of the Asdar Yula. All of your efforts have been to waste."

Blays tilted the spear, leaning on it. "Let's find out, shall we?"

Relaxed just an instant before, he leaped forward, already at full speed by his second step, boots finding traction despite the stomped-down slick snow underfoot. The Eiden Rane gestured with a single finger. The Blighted, who had retreated for the first time Dante could recall seeing, gushed forward to cut him off.

"We follow him," Dante said. "Or we're dead."

He bolted forward, sprinting to catch up with Blays before the Blighted could cut them off from each other. Gladdic loped along just behind him, accompanied by the lone Star-Eater that still survived. Blays laughed as the first lines of Blighted neared. He lowered the point of his spear until it was parallel to the ground, lashed it to the right, then back to the left.

The spear swatted the undead away like they were no more substantial than the snowflakes skirling around its blade. The bodies plummeted into the rows of enemies behind them, knocking scores of others from their feet. Blays didn't even have to slow down. A few of the Blighted closed in on Dante and Gladdic, but they killed them without resistance, the bodies skidding through the snow.

Dead ahead from Blays, the White Lich took a step back. He brought lines of ether to his hand, wrapping them around his forearm, and propelled them toward Blays. Dante had already filled his hands with nether. He threw it forward, afraid the distance was too far to close in time.

A few Blighted stood between Blays and the lich. The ether obliterated them without so much as slowing down. As the lines of light closed on him, Blays hopped forward, bent his knees, and vaulted into the air, flipping forward. He whipped the spear along beneath him, slashing its point through the ether. The shining lines bent and drained upwards into the spear.

He landed and swung the weapon in an overhead stroke

straight at the lich. Light beamed from the point of the blade. The lich dropped back another step, gathering more ether to him, hastily arranging it into a simple pattern and sending it at the beam. The beam sliced it in half, scattering the pattern like dandelion seeds. The lich gritted his teeth and turned his left shoulder. The beam struck him square, sending him stumbling backward. Ghostly white blood steamed into the snow.

"Would you like to discuss the terms of your surrender?" Blays strolled forward, spear held across his body at a downward angle. "Mine are just two words long, and end in 'you.'"

The lich clasped his hand to his wound, blood leaking between his fingers. "Your hope is false. You are no more than a man."

"Are you sure about that? Once upon a time, that's all *you* were, too."

Blays had slowed enough that Dante had almost caught up. He dashed forward once again, spinning in a circle to bat away the crush of undead that were throwing themselves between him and the White Lich. Cheers hailed from the break in the wall, where the fighting had resumed with a vengeance. Due either to a boost in their morale, a decline in the Blighteds', or the execution of a favorable tactic, Nak and Olivander's army was shoving themselves steadily into the courtyard. It seemed to be all the lesser liches could do to stop them from plowing a path toward the lich.

The lich was backing up now, gripping his glaive in one hand while slinging another attack at Blays. Blays drew back his elbows, thrust the spear forward, and twirled the tip at the ether, as if to roll it up like a plate of noodles. The lich crooked his finger at the ether. It swerved downward, dodging the spear's blade and skimming along the ground toward Blays.

Blays snapped his wrists, flicking the spear into the ground, the ether pinned on its point. The light sank into the purestone.

Blays lashed it back at the lich. The lich was expecting it this time, and turned most of it aside with a dirk of ether. But rather than fizzling into sparks, the attack broke into shards that scored deep cuts in the lich's arm.

The lich flexed his fist, squeezing out the shards like they were bits of glass. He leveled his glaive at Blays. "Dare to stand before me, and it will be the last thing that you do."

"The last thing I do in my life will be to order one of my many great-grandsons to bring me another mug of rum," Blays said. "But that will be a long time from now. I suppose that means I have to deal with you first."

He dropped into a half-crouch and ran forward. Dante chopped down a pair of Blighted as they lunged toward him, raising them as zombies to throw in the path of the others. Glad-dic used his Andrac to keep the undead at bay while he killed one after another. The White Lich watched Blays close on him, channeling the ether to him, but not yet using it. Not against the spear-holder.

As Blays closed on him, the lich flung forth a blinding globe of light. Blays raised the spear, but the lich's attack was no more than a feint to cover his true assault: the glaive thrusting toward Blays' chest.

Blays had turned his head away to avoid being dazzled by the ether, yet still saw the incoming jab—or perhaps it was the spear that saw it. He seemed to skim over the snow as he juked out of the way, thrusting the shaft of the spear over the top of the glaive's long haft to keep the lich from adjusting mid-attack. He jerked his right elbow, swinging the spear across the lich's chest.

The lich stepped back and looked down. A glowing white line was etched across his chest, leaking his strange ethereal blood down the front of his tabard.

Among the bulge of troops within the wall, the soldiers cheered like a new king had just been crowned.

"Don't start cheering just yet," Blays muttered. "A scratch is a long ways from a kill."

He ducked a whistling swipe of the glaive and jabbed at the lich's leg. The lich pivoted his hips to draw his leg out of harm's way, using his momentum to backhand his glaive at Blays. Blays planted his spear and vaulted over the strike, wheeling the weapon in a tight circle and slashing down at the lich's head. The lich ducked to the side, taking it on the spaulder strapped to his shoulder.

The banded armor was crafted of flawless steel and strengthened with the ether. But under the spear's blade, it cracked in half, one piece clanging to a bare patch of ground while the other dangled from the lich's shoulder.

"Give up now," Blays said. "Or the next time it'll be your cod-piece."

The lich grunted and made a series of swift jabs at Blays, driving him back a couple of steps. With the two of them squared off against each other, the Blighted attempted to rush Blays from behind. Blays swept the Spear of Stars through them, whirled to face the lich, and ducked beneath the arc of the glaive, its glowing point slashing through Blays' cloak and sending a long ribbon of black fabric fluttering to the snow.

Another wave of Blighted was already rushing toward him. Dante unleashed a barrage of nethereal bolts, dropping them all, then waved his hand through the air, summoning them back to their feet. Gladdic and the Star-Eater moved to Dante's right, holding off the Blighted on Blays' flank. Dante shifted to cover his other side. Dante had hoped to be able to assault the lich alongside Blays, but the crush of Blighted was too constant and intense for him to do anything but hold them back so that Blays was free to duel.

He and the White Lich moved back and forth, Blays skidding over the snow and flinging himself through the air, whirling and then darting back, the lich thundering forward to strike and bending away to dodge with impossible grace for his size, swinging his glaive with awesome strength yet keeping such total control of the weapon that he never fell off balance.

Blays hit the lich on his exposed shoulder, drawing blood, then grooved his side. They exchanged strikes and parries with no change in outcome, then Blays rolled under a jab and popped to his feet with a thrust of his own, sinking the point of the Spear of Stars two inches into the lich's stomach.

The lich fell back and Blays pursued, striking him several times. None of the wounds were particularly deep, certainly not enough to be mortal. Yet each one bled, and Dante didn't think any of them were healing. Either he was imagining it, or the lich was slowing down. It would only take a single well-placed blow for the White Lich to strike Blays dead—but even so, with enough time, Blays might simply wear his opponent down.

Unfortunately, they didn't have that kind of time. Over at the wall, the advance had stalled. The nether that had once been bursting through the air everywhere he looked had decreased to irregular flashes. His people would soon exhaust their strength. Once that happened, the lich could retreat into the throng of Blighted, using their sheer numbers to overwhelm Dante, Gladdic, and Blays.

Even as he had this understanding, the White Lich stumbled back from an exchange of blows, another wound dribbling blood down his chest. His face and body were laced with cuts and gouges. There had always been a blue-white aura to his skin, but it now radiated from somewhere deeper within to shine out from the cuts, casting bluish light on the snowflakes that scattered in the wake of the spear and the glaive.

"Now's the time," Dante called to Blays. "Finish him off!"

"Is *that* what I'm supposed to be doing here?" Blays hollered back. "Why didn't anyone tell me?"

"You have to bring him down! Another minute and—"

"I know, I know. It's the doom of everyone and everything."

Blays feinted, fell back, then propelled himself into the air, stabbing down at the lich with a blow that might have pierced the enemy's throat. The lich slid his glaive along the blade of the spear, guiding the strike to the side. Once it was safely past him, he swung the butt of his weapon at Blays' head. Blays dropped, tucking his chin to the chest. The butt of the glaive glanced off his shoulder. Oblique though the blow was, it was enough to send Blays rolling through the snow. The lich closed on him in two long steps, ready to gore Blays through the heart, but Blays popped to his feet with the spear in a guard.

"Not bad for a thousand-year-old-man," Blays said. "But you must be getting tired. Don't worry, I'm about to give you a very long rest."

He launched a flurry of attacks, the spear lashing out like it was a part of him, or like it was alive. The lich countered most of them, absorbing a few more scratches and pokes in the process, but almost never struck back. Dante assumed at first this was because Blays' offensive was too potent for the lich to find a moment to do so.

Except there was no need for the lich to take the risk of a counterattack when all he needed to win was to last until the city's nethermancers exhausted their powers. Had he picked this up on his own? Or only made the realization after Dante had blurted it out loud?

Blays launched another offensive, but there were hints of desperation in his attacks, allowing the lich to parry them adroitly. Dante felt down into the ground. He summoned another heap of shadows to him—his control was starting to get sloppy; the priests within the wall weren't the only ones who weren't going to be able to keep their hold on the nether for much longer— and used it to massacre every Blighted that was close to him. He promptly reanimated as many of them as he could in one go. They tore into their former brethren.

He turned away from the Blighted-on-Blighted melee, temporarily relieved of the need to combat them himself.

"Blays!" he yelled. "Watch your left!"

Blays didn't seem to hear him, launching a four-blow combination at the lich that ended with the spear slicing across the enemy's shin. Dante sucked in cold air to yell at him again—had he forgotten their old signs?—but before he could do so, and possibly give up the game, Blays slid in the snow, falling on his rear. The lich shuffled toward him, jabbing at him, but not in a way that would leave himself exposed to a ruse. Blays scrabbled back, kicking snow at the lich's face. He popped to his feet and retreated several steps, righting his spear and lifting it back into a guard. The lich followed, taking another exploratory jab at him.

And dropped his front foot right into the muddy hole Dante had softened beneath the snow.

The lich tripped, fighting to keep himself from toppling forward. Dante shot his mind into the mud and hardened it into solid stone. The lich spat curses in an ancient foreign tongue. He reached for the ether, meaning to break the stone away from his leg.

Blays had already vaulted high overhead. He peaked and began to fall. The lich shattered the ground and stepped free of the hole. Blays rammed the spear downward. The blade pierced the lich's back—and thrust out the front of his chest.

The Eiden Rane gaped at the ethereal blade. Glowing white blood spilled from his mouth. He groped outward with both hands as if blind.

Blays pulled on the spear, but it wouldn't come loose. "Where do you suppose *you* go when you die?"

He gave another hard tug. With the spear stuck, he gave it a twist instead. The lich gasped and spewed more blood.

"The reason I ask is that you keep saying you're not a mortal. That you're something more." Blays clenched his teeth and pulled again, then tried shoving the spear forward. "But the Mists aren't made for immortals. They're made for normal people who are born and live and die." He twisted the shaft again. "See, I don't think you'll go anywhere. I think you'll become nothing. Lost like smoke on the wind."

The light that had been shining from the lich's many wounds was dimming. So was the blue of his eyes. But Dante felt something stirring within him.

"Take him down!" he yelled. "Don't let him get back to his feet!"

He fired an immense stream of nether at the lich, who had fallen to his knees, massacred the Blighted who were starting to break past his already-dwindling zombies, and launched a second salvo at the lich. The first was just hitting him, shredding into his flesh, though even now, battered and impaled, the lich remained so potent that the shadows could only dig a short distance into his skin before dispersing.

Blays twisted the spear once more. Blood spurted from the lich's chest. "Will you let go of this so I can put you out of your misery?"

Gladdic was too occupied fending off the hordes to lend any ether to the attack, but with a jerk of his chin, he sent the Andrac running toward the lich. The demon drew back its right arm, spreading its fingers wide as it prepared to slash its knife-like claws across the throat of the slumping lich.

The lich jerked up his head — and shot out his arm.

His iron-like fingers gripped the Andrac by the neck. He got his feet under him and stood, lifting the demon clear of the ground even as it clawed at his arm. His eyes smoldered like the blue flame at the heart of a forge. Shadows poured out of the Andrac and into the lich.

The wounds on his face and arms sealed shut. Blays gave a mighty yank on the spear. At last it slid free. Blays stumbled backwards, fighting to keep his footing in the snow. The lich moved his free hand down the front of his chest. As the last of the Star-Eater dissolved into his body, the hole in his chest closed over as if it had never been there.

The Eiden Rane tossed his head and laughed. "You came closer than anyone has in a very long time. But I fear that won't console you, will it?"

He lunged at Blays, swinging the glaive down at him along the diagonal. Blays raised the spear to intercept, stepping to the side at the same time, but the lich swung so hard that Blays was knocked from his feet and into the snow. The lich stalked toward him.

A loud clear horn sounded from the wall. Even before he looked, Dante knew it as Olivander's. The general charged into the courtyard on horseback—flanked by Somburr and Merria, with a troop of mounted soldiers and priests alongside them. They carved into the Blighted, Olivander's expression as hard and determined as the steel of the saber he swung, Merria aflame with fury, Somburr as wild as lightning. Blighted fell before them on all sides.

The lich paused at this, giving Blays just enough time to flip to his feet and take up his defense. The lich slung a wave of ether toward the cavalry, then spun about to take a vicious hack at Blays. Blays backpedaled. Dante cut down a trio of Blighted as they made way for Blays, flesh flying from his Odo Sein sword, then pulled up a palisade of rock spears, goring a line of the undead.

But his wall was only of use for a few moments: the lich pressed forward, jabbing and slashed at Blays like he'd been completely reinvigorated by the nether of the Andrac. It was all

Gladdic and Dante could do to keep the Blighted at bay.

"You are growing slower," the lich said to Blays with disapproval. "Have you lost your will so soon? Or is the weapon you thought would provide your salvation proving to be of less worth than you had hoped?"

Blays glared at the lich and punched the spear's blade at his chest, following this with a blur of strikes. Yet the lich fended them all off and resumed pushing Blays back toward the keep. Was it Dante's imagination, or *was* Blays a little slower? Not much—just a hair—and still quick enough to have dominated any other foe. Was the spear simply wearing down?

And if there was, was there a way to reverse that?

"Gladdic," Dante called. "Feed the ether to the—"

Behind him, Gladdic grunted in pain, falling back from the attacks of a lesser lich that had stripped himself naked and infiltrated the Blighted. While Gladdic fended off the next blows, Dante sent the nether to him, healing him. By the time they smashed the lesser lich dead and drove the Blighted back enough to earn a little breathing room, the light coming from Gladdic's hands was shaky. Dante feared it was about to start sputtering.

In desperation, he softened the ground in front of the lich, meaning to pull off the same trick that had nearly killed him before. Feeling his efforts, the lich snorted and stepped over the hidden mud. The next thrust of his glaive cut through Blays' cloak and gouged his side. Blays' eyes widened, but he fought on, blood pattering the snow as he fell back.

Over at the wall, the cavalry charge had penetrated halfway to the lich, but was already stalling. As Dante watched, Olivander was dragged down by the Blighted. He disappeared from sight. Merria roared, slaying one after the other with her nether, but they were surrounding her too, her horse rearing back.

Gladdic gasped. Blighted threw themselves on him with

wild abandon. Dante smashed them off; as the old man pushed himself to his feet, something slammed into Dante from behind and tackled him to the ground. Fingers scrabbled at him. He blew the brains out of the Blighted and those sprinting in behind it. A blue-white barrier thrust into the air not two feet in front of him—Gladdic was doing something with the snow, compacting it into an icy wall to block out the undead. For all the good it would do. Dante could already hear them thumping about on the other side, piling themselves into an inhuman ramp for the others to climb.

Blays retreated so fast he nearly tripped over Dante. The White Lich strode after him, eyes as shiny as blue mirrors, and jabbed forward. Before their weapons made contact, the lich rolled his right wrist, swinging his glaive upward—and then straight down at Blays' head.

Blays blocked the blow, his arms bouncing downward from the strength of the lich. Dante tossed a few shadows at the enemy, hoping to at least distract him, but the lich absorbed them with no more than a few scrapes, jerking the glaive upward and hammering it at Blays a second time. Blays dodged out of the way, but was off-balance in the snow as the lich made a third downward stroke, and had no choice but to block it straight on again.

The force ripped the spear from his left hand; if not for the cord looped around his right wrist, he would have dropped it altogether. The lich snapped the glaive's blade down at Blays' head. Blays jumped forward and was struck by the shaft instead.

He sprawled to the ground and didn't move. Blood leaked from his skull. The spear fell from his grasp, still looped to his wrist, but dimming the moment it left contact with his hands. With the weapon disarmed, the lich gazed down on Dante with the coldest eyes he'd ever seen.

He had just enough time to raise a shield of nether before the

White Lich struck him with a massive beam of light.

He found himself lying on the ground with his back pressed against Gladdic's wall of ice. The keep hung above him, as if judging his failure. A second beam of ether pounded Gladdic to the ground. The lich made a quick assessment of the ruin before him, then bent down and pulled the spear away from Blays.

Dante supposed he could have attacked the lich. But what was the point? Instead he sent the nether into Blays' head. Blays was alive but bleeding badly. Dante's own head was ringing, but he mended Blays' with all the skill he'd accumulated since first learning the nether more than half his life ago. He wasn't sure why he was bothering with this, either. But better to spend his last act healing his friend than to make a fruitless attack against the lich.

Snow fell on his face. He hardly felt it. Hands as white as the snow groped for the top of the ice walls and slid back down. Blays groaned, his right hand twitching, swatting violently at nothing. Dante hoped the spasm was the result of the healing and not the damage. There wasn't much noise coming from the Citadel wall any longer. He couldn't see it due to the ice, but he presumed the people there had been killed or driven back outside.

The lich stood. He gripped the Spear of Stars in one hand and raised it high in the air to better inspect it. "I should thank you for putting in so much effort to deliver the gods' weapon to my hand. My vision is now inevitable." In his hands, the spear's purestone glimmered a frosty blue. He stood over Dante but didn't yet lift the weapon. "It is over. Would you like to beg to join me after all?"

"I'll only beg you for one thing." Dante sat slumped against the ice wall. Melted snow seeped through the seat of his pants. "Write down what we did. Keep the record safe and put it somewhere it can last for an age. So that when your sick order crum-

bles—even if it takes ten thousand years—the people who reclaim this world will know that we fought you to the very end."

The lich smiled and raised the spear. The stone glowed like
the light of the north star. Gazing up at it, Dante felt something
moving in the nether high above. Ka? Sent to gloat over their defeat? Carvahal, turning away in disappointment?

Or an agent of Arawn, watching impassively as his other
agent died?

The spear swung downward. Dante had thought there
would be some glory in his final moment of defiance, but the last
thing he knew was the stabbing awareness that he had not been
good enough.

39

It had been, to put it frankly, a hellish journey.

Had started easily enough. Lots of riding. Through places that only the most country of bumpkins could ever care about. Upside to that was there was almost no one around to bother them. And once they got to the mountains, there'd been no one at all. The mountains had been pretty, but they were a little *too* empty, and she'd been glad to be done with them.

Next came all the hills and plains. And all the giants wandering around them. Avoiding them had taken work. She could have kept clear of them better if she'd been on her own—would have been faster, too—but she'd made her decision on the road outside Bressel. She'd stick to it.

Coming north, the energy in the hamlets had been strange. Everyone was begging them for news. Third time it happened, she pretended she didn't know anything, and made him pretend he didn't, either.

At last the city congealed between the forest and the sea. She felt something relax in her, as if she'd been gripping something tight in her own gut for all that time. Bressel had been bigger and grander, but as soon as they stepped into it, it felt right. It *smelled* right. They'd arrived at dusk, which was a bad idea: the touch of the night made her want to run off and find her crew and forget everything else she had to do. After all, they'd created this mess. Let them deal with it.

That had always been her way. Only she didn't think she could do that this time. She had the feeling that if she tried, there was nowhere to run to that would be safe when it all came crashing down.

That's when they ran into a problem. The worst problem they could be hit by.

The piece wasn't where she'd left it.

Staring into the broken-open wall, she'd felt the big chill. The one that only pierced you when it dawned on you that something you'd thought had been good had been screwed all along. For all her precautions, someone had been watching her. Following her. Might have meant to kill her. Probably would have, if she'd stayed.

She went out and had a drink. Then a few more. The kid had the sense not to say much. Once she'd calmed down, she started making the rounds. Asking questions. Not always about the piece itself—the last thing she wanted to do was alert the thief that she was back, and she was looking for it—but about the kinds of things that could only be done by the person who was carrying it.

Days later, all she had was dead ends.

That's when the kid suggested they try his way. So they'd geared up and traveled north. Nothing but mountains to the east, a cold sea to the west, and wastelands in front. Just days of that. More than enough time to make her question their decision to leave the city. And then at the end, a vision out of a nightmare: a bone tree, hundreds of feet high, Barden itself.

The kid needed a piece of it. She thought it was a very bad idea to try, but as he poked and scraped at the fused bones of the trunk, no god opened a hatch in the sky to strike them down. Still, the damned tree seemed impervious. Took him three days just to pry off a little chip of it. When he tried it out, he got this

heartbreaking look on his face and said he couldn't feel anything.

Come on, she'd said. Maybe it will work once we're closer.

She'd doubted. Hard. Was secretly angry at him for wasting
so much of their time while the trail was growing even colder.
But two days out from the city, when he tried again, he laughed
and slapped his forehead. He had it. It was dead ahead.

Coming back to the city, she hadn't felt the same feeling
she'd had the first time. Something felt off. Dark. Should have
listened. Her instincts were never wrong. It had gotten colder
while they'd been away, almost wintry, but there were a lot of
people on the streets carrying heavy bags or pushing wheelbarrows of goods. There was talk of invasion. They were getting out
before talk became reality.

The kid brought them through the streets, closing on the target until he was squinting from the pain in his forehead. She
wasn't at all surprised when they wound up outside a tenement
on the border of the Sharps.

It was afternoon and she hated operating in daylight so they
posted up in an abandoned room on the third floor across the
street. Fifteen minutes after sunset, a robed figure approached
the tenement. Gaunt like a skeleton. The figure went inside.

Her instincts told her something was wrong. This time, she
listened.

They hustled into the street, into the tenement, up its stairs.
Found the room. And the piece. The thief was dead. The skeletal
man in the robe had killed him—and the killer was still there in
the room. The kid tried to talk to him. She went for her knife.
The man turned on them, face drawn, eyes sunken. She knew at
once what it was. It was smart enough to go for her first. Blade
of shadows. Her counter was too slow.

The kid wasn't. He threw himself in the way. She went for
the thing's throat. When it was over, the thing was dead. And so

was her partner.

The stupid kid had been right. And it had cost them every-thing.

She took up the piece. But she no longer believed in the mis-sion. The enemy's agents were already inside the city. Rest of the army on its way. The entire trip had been a waste and now he was dead. She checked herself for any cuts—couldn't afford to leave any blood on the scene, they'd use it to track her down—and walked out.

Should have left right then. She chose payback against the High Priest instead. Headed for the Citadel. The place was emp-ty. Evacuated. She ran up the stairs of the keep, meaning to loot everything she could. Take it, sell it, get as far east as she could manage, maybe an island somewhere, see if it could be waited out, and if not, enjoy herself and her wealth until the day it came for her, too.

That's when she ran into her next problem. The lesser lich in the tenement hadn't been the only one of them to infiltrate the city. She was up on the top floor when they came for the Citadel. She did what she knew: she hid.

She was right about to make a break for it when they put up the wards.

Divine punishment? In response to her greed? Her betrayal? Then to hell with the gods: she'd wait it out and head east as soon as the lich was done with the city.

The walls filled with undead. The White Lich came and went. She stayed put. After a few days, it felt like he might be there for an extended stay. She made one trip downstairs to scrounge food and hunt for a break in the wards. Found the for-mer but not the latter. She returned to her bolthole on the upper floors. The next day, they marched out from the Citadel. The wards stayed up, but if their army stayed gone, she wouldn't have to worry about setting them off. She'd leave that night.

Once again, she'd misjudged. They weren't leaving. They were meeting the enemy. Soon enough, they returned to the Citadel to make their defense. Galand's men followed. They weren't nearly enough. The wave of Blighted hidden beneath the streets beyond the walls nearly overran them. Would have, if not for the disturbance below.

She watched the fight between the White Lich and the three men with dry fatalism. Only when Buckler shoved his spear through the enemy's chest did she begin to hope.

But that hope turned out to be as false as all the rest.

Below, the soldiers and priests began to die. She started thinking about how she was going to get out. The three men had gotten *in*, right? From the keep. Meaning somewhere *below* the keep. Hidden passage? Gap in the wards? Either way, even if the lich stayed here after he won, she had her way out.

She would have taken it. Was all ready. Except she looked back down and there was Galand knocked in the snow saying something to the lich. They were too far away for her to make out any of the words, but she could see his face, and maybe it was just the distance between them, or the distortion caused by the falling snow, but she would have sworn it wasn't Galand, but the kid.

Something stuck in her throat. She grabbed the window sill and whispered, I promised you.

She'd meant to break that promise. Would have done it days ago if she'd had the chance. But no one had to know that now, did they? No one but herself.

She picked up the piece. She grinned. And she jumped.

If there was a servant of the gods watching him from above in the nether, it certainly wasn't hovering there. If anything, it was…plummeting.

The White Lich stabbed the spear at Dante's chest. He rolled to the side. The blade pierced his cloak and the cobbles beneath it, pinning him to the ground. Dante shaped the nether into a spike and drove it at the lich's face, but it swerved toward the spear, absorbing into the weapon.

With a scrape of glass on stone, the lich pulled the spear's blade free from the ground and lifted it up for another jab. Something appeared in the air above him, resolving from the snowstorm like a ship from the mist.

A woman.

She was falling toward the lich, her ponytail and light cloak flapping behind her. This was quite remarkable, but Dante fought to allow no hint of it to alter his expression. Not even when she cocked her elbows and drew back a curved white sword.

She swung downward. So did the lich. At the last moment, he felt her presence, jerking to his right. Due to his movement, rather than stabbing Dante through the heart, the spear stuck him through his side. And rather than the sword cleaving through the top of the lich's head, it cut him between his neck and shoulder.

It sank deep. As deep as anything besides when Blays had rammed the Spear of Stars through his chest. For the woman was Raxa, and the weapon she bore was the bone sword Dante had once taken from the White Tree.

The lich faltered to the side, luminescent blood shooting from the wound. The spear fell away from him. The sword splintered in Raxa's hand; somehow, she landed on her feet. She dived into the nether, but the lich knocked her free of the shadows with a wave of his hand and hit her as hard as he could with his fist. She flew into the ice wall and struck it with a crunch. She dropped to the ground.

The White Lich swiveled to face Dante. Shards of the bone sword jutted from his upper chest. He put one hand to the wound, flooding it with ether, but the flesh didn't want to mend. Face pulling back into a rictus of rage, he lifted his other hand over Dante.

"You and your vermin have troubled me for much too long," the lich said wetly, a dollop of his strange blood trickling from his mouth. The ether sparked in his hand, ready to be unleashed. "Now you—"

"Die." Blays had picked up the Spear of Stars from where the lich had dropped it. He now rammed it through the lich's heart.

The lich pulled back, taking the spear with him. The ethereal shaft twitched with each beat of his heart. He grabbed the shaft as if to wrench it loose. Arms shaking, he lowered his head.

"I would have brought you peace." The metallic echo of his voice was now just a dull scrape. "Instead you will return to your chaos and wars. Your strife and your misery and your pain without end."

"Sure, none of us really likes that stuff," Blays said. "But at least they're *ours*."

He bared his teeth, bore down with all his strength, and twisted the spear. The lich raised a quivering hand, then let it fall. His eyes blazed so bright they looked ready to burn forth from his skull.

They faded to dimness instead.

His skin cracked, the light of the ether shining from within. He began to shrink—no, to *collapse*, his shoulders tumbling down into his chest, his thighs buckling, his neck falling into itself, his head tilting back in response, mouth hanging open in horror, the dull pits of his eyes searching the sky for deliverance.

His skin began to flake away, swirling on the winds, indistinguishable from the snow. So did his cape and his armor and his flesh, exposing bones that looked forged from the same pure ether as the Spear of Stars. What little didn't soar on the winds fell into a pile of white dust.

Dante tried to heal the wound in his side, but he could barely move the nether. "Is it over?"

"Yeah," Blays said. "It's done."

Blays rested the butt of the spear against the ground. Dante closed his eyes. Snow fell upon his face. He felt like he was sinking, down into the ground, and there was nothing he could do to stop it, but it didn't matter.

40

He woke feeling better than he had in a long time. At peace. Soft sunlight seeped through the shutters of his cozy room. The floorboards were cool beneath his feet. He hurried through the main room to the front porch. Outside, a pale full moon hung in the washed-out blue of the morning sky.

"Hello," the monk said from his chair. "You're looking better. Did you finally get some rest?"

"Yes," Dante said. "Has it been that long?"

"Oh yes. You got lost in the forest, don't you remember? You went through nine hells—pardon my language—trying to find your way back here. But you did, and now that's behind you, and you can rest as long as you like." The man smiled. "But don't rest *too* long. You have your studies to get back to, you know."

Dante took a deep breath. There was a yard past the cabin and a forest beyond that and the air smelled like that time of spring when the trees had grown confident that winter was defeated for another year. It was good to be back. Yes, good to be back, wasn't it? He couldn't quite remember being lost in the forest (he must still be shaking off his long sleep), but he could remember feeling afraid, like it might never end, that he might never find his way back here. Here to the cabin in the woods, where he waited for the day his father would return.

Dante looked up. His father was dead. He'd died in the

Plagued Islands years ago. And Dante had killed the man who'd killed him.

Cold sweat moistened Dante's back. This place wasn't real. It was the Pastlands. He was in the Pastlands, and that meant he was —

He sat up in bed covered in sweat. He clutched his side, but the wound was gone, replaced by the pink of newly-healed skin. The bed felt familiar. It was *his* bed. After being gone from it for so long, he was back in his own room.

"I'm alive?"

"And a good thing," Blays said from the corner, startling him. "The way they're acting, if you hadn't made it, they would have tried to make *me* High Priest."

"Was I that close?"

"Hardly. You've been way deader before."

"I wasn't really there, then. I was just dreaming." He wrenched his head around at Blays. "We won, right? That part wasn't a dream?"

Blays patted the rod of the condensed spear hanging from his belt. "We won. Somehow."

Dante rubbed his eyes. "Thank the gods. Whether they like it or not."

"This isn't their world anyway. I don't see why they get a say in it."

Dante was about to agree, but he was overtaken by a rush of emotion. They'd done it. The lich was dead. And so was his sick vision. He lay back in bed, feeling like he was floating and also like a giant hand was pressing him down into the mattress. The air in his lungs tasted sweeter than any fruit. They'd *done* it.

A minute later, he was interrupted from his daze when Blays reached down to the floor, picked up a jug that was larger than his head, and took a deep swig.

"Are you drinking?" Dante glanced out the window. "It's

nine in the morning!"

Blays took another swallow, then set down the jug with a solid clink of pottery. "We just slew the White Lich. The Eiden Rane. The fellow who destroyed two nations, nearly made ours the third, and would have burned down the rest of Rale once he was done with us. The same guy who nearly killed us a dozen times, and who *did* kill Gladdic—though don't worry, he's fine too. So yes, I'm drinking. And I intend to keep drinking until I feel properly celebrated out."

Dante frowned at him, then the jug. "Give me that."

Blays nodded in approval and passed him the jug.

"Dante!" Nak stood from his table, papers fluttering away from him. He looked tired but healthy enough. "Or should I say *Lord* Dante, the Lich-Killer!"

"That was mostly Blays," Dante said. "And Raxa."

"Yes, but Sir Dante the Blighted-Wrangler doesn't have quite the same ring to it. How are you feeling?"

"Good." Dante strolled forward and found a chair. "It's only been a day, right?"

"That's right." Nak tilted his head, peering into Dante's eyes. "Are you...?"

"Blays came by. He brought his jug."

"Ah, the jug. I might make its acquaintance later myself. I'd say we've earned a celebration or ten!"

"We'll celebrate soon enough. Right now I need to know exactly where we stand."

"You think we're not out of the fire yet? Regarding Moddegan? Or Taim?"

"Or both."

Nak nodded, seating himself and glancing over his papers. "Where to start. Well. Within the Council, Olivander is...well, he's dead. Killed in the field."

"I was afraid of that. What about the others who rode with him?"

"Merria was wounded. Quite badly. The priests are still tending to her. But they believe she'll live, though perhaps not at her former health. As for Somburr, he's gone."

"Taken by the Blighted?"

"No, I mean he's *gone*. Vanished. It's possible the Blighted killed him, but we haven't found any trace of him."

"If he wasn't killed, why would he just run off?"

Nak shrugged his round shoulders. "I wouldn't presume to try to explain anything Somburr does. In my heart, I feel like we'll see him again soon enough. But I wouldn't be that surprised if we don't."

"I know what you mean. What about beyond the Council?"

Nak consulted some of his papers and began to read out the names of priests and monks. This took some time. When he came to the soldiers, he spoke mostly in numbers, though he named a great many officers as well. Dante was a little troubled that he didn't know all of the names. A few years ago, he would have recognized each one. He supposed a lot had happened in the last few years.

Once Nak finished, Dante leaned his elbows on the table, wishing for another consultation with the jug. "That's more than half our fighting force. We've been gutted."

"It hasn't looked pretty since the defeat at Bressel," Nak said softly. "Then again, compared to Bressel, we got off lightly."

"Everything I've built since joining the Council has been wiped out."

"Not everything, has it? Most of our leadership remains. As do the institutions you've wrought and strengthened. It will take time to find and train good people—be they soldiers or sorcerers—but we know this can be done, don't we? For you've already done it."

"Yeah. I have. But it feels like fifteen years of my life have just been taken from me. It's going to take even longer than that to do it again. The people we lost were special. You don't find people of their talents just running around the streets."

"Except in your case," Nak said dryly. "And quite a few others I could name."

"The point remains." With a jarring scrape of his chair, Dante stood, crossing to the window. They were next to the Council chambers high in the Citadel and he had a full view of the courtyard below. There had been a bit of sunshine when he'd woken up, but it was cloudy once more and small flakes of snow had just started to fall. "You did say it's only been a day, right? Where are the rest of the bodies?"

"Er, other than the piles of thousands?"

"But where are the rest of the Blighted? There had to be three times that many just inside the walls. You can't have cleaned them up already."

"Well, no. But they didn't all just drop dead when the lich fell."

"They didn't?!"

"Not at all." Nak joined him at the window. "Though they didn't much seem to like it when their master died. Most of them went mad. Madder than before, I mean. Ripping at themselves or whoever was next to them. Others stampeded out from the breach and ran through the streets in a panic. We didn't have nearly enough people left to stop them."

"Where are they now?"

"Some are still out in the streets. According to the scouts, most of them are roaming around in the woods."

"We can't have thousands of Blighted out in the woods. We're going to need to organize teams to hunt them down. Primarily nethermancers, ideally with a shield wall for support. We don't want to fight them all at once. The goal should be to hit any group that splits off from the main lump. In fact, forget the shield wall. Put them all on horseback." Dante ran his fingernail down the ice that had formed inside the window pane. "We'll need a second team. Wagoneers. To bring back the bodies and store them here."

"Bodies?" Nak frowned. "*Store* them?"

"We just got done talking about how many people we've lost. Moddegan probably won't march on us now that the first snows are on the ground. But if and when he comes, we'll need every body we can throw at him."

"Which you mean quite literally. Well, that's a tad gruesome. But thank goodness you're so...ah...far-thinking." Nak blinked. "Speaking of bodies, when the lich died, he left this behind."

He reached into his robe and withdrew a fold of black silk, unwrapping it to expose a white gemstone the size of a fist. Ether shifted slowly within it just as it did within the Spear of Stars.

Dante stared at it. "This came from his body?"

"We believe so. Besides some ash, it was the only physical trace he left behind."

Dante stole it from Nak's hand, dropped it to the ground, stepped back, and smashed it with a hammer of shadows. The nether broke apart into a cloud of nothing, revealing the gem was completely unscratched. He spiked it with black bolts, but these had no effect either.

Dante waved away the fading black vapor of his failures, then crouched to examine the gem. "Any idea what it is?"

"None whatsoever," Nak answered.

"Do you suppose it can bring him back?"

"We didn't want to explore it much before you awakened. So far it seems inert. But I don't know if there's anything left of him within it. Did Sabel mention anything like this in the *Book of What Lies Beyond*?"

"Nothing I can remember. What am I supposed to do with it?"

"I will trust that decision entirely to you."

Dante reached out for the stone, hesitated, then picked it up. "I'll keep it with me. That way, if it...does anything...I'll know." He pocketed it.

"That transcendent judgment is precisely why you were elevated to your current position." Nak folded his hands together. "Lord Dante?"

"Yes, Nak?"

"Well done. You saved us. Although it was much more than that, wasn't it? You saved the *world*."

He got to his feet, casting another look at the piles of bodies in the courtyard and the snow that was covering them up. "We all played our part."

He spent the rest of the morning preparing them to weather the next few days and weeks. First thing was to assign a team of monks to send dead mice and whatever flies they could find into the forest to keep eyes on the Blighted. After a bit of consideration, he sent a moth of his own as well: he wanted to see how the undead were acting firsthand.

Next was grappling with the provisions report. It was not good. As part of his ongoing strategy to render the places he invaded incapable of mounting an ongoing resistance, the White Lich had emptied out the granaries. There was no food in the city beyond what little had been left in the abandoned shops and what Dante's army had brought with it. This wouldn't be enough for them to last out the rest of the year, let alone make it till spring. On top of that, the first of the evacuees were already returning to the city to flee the Blighted they'd seen roaming through the woods. More mouths were arriving by the hour.

Dante sent out rationing orders, but with their current stocks, he predicted people would begin starving within three weeks. The thought of having survived the lich only to die of mundane hunger grated against his sense of justice.

They couldn't send hunters to the woods until the Blighted were dealt with. But they could send fishermen along the coast, along with laborers to gather mussels. He met with Winden to plant their fields and experiment with harvesting wheat and potatoes amid the snow. Last, he dispatched riders to Wending and Tantonnen to negotiate for whatever they could spare. But given that the White Lich had raided and besieged those lands as well, he wasn't counting on much.

He was sitting in his chambers dwelling on these matters and wondering if it might be better to march his people south to Mallon for the winter when he got word that Raxa had woken up.

He hurried to her room. They'd healed her broken bones and internal bleeding, but she still looked ragged, dark circles around her eyes, a thinness to her body that hadn't been there the last time he'd seen her, when he dispatched her to retrieve the bone sword. She watched him arrive without saying anything.

"We'd all be dead right now if it wasn't for you," he said.

She shrugged.

"I know, we all played our part. I've said so myself. Even so, we owe you a great debt."

"Great. A debt from a priest. Why couldn't you be a banker instead?"

He let a moment pass. "We haven't seen Sorrowen. Is he...?"

"Dead."

"How?"

Raxa stared past his shoulder, drawing a deep breath through her nose. "When we got here, the piece—the sword—wasn't where I'd stashed it. Someone had stolen it."

"*Stolen* it? Who?"

"We'll get to that. I hit the streets, asking questions. Couldn't come up with any leads. It felt gone for good. Then Sorrowen had an idea. The piece was part of the White Tree, right? So maybe if we went and got another part of the tree, he could use it to track the sword. That's what we did. It worked."

Dante laughed. "That's brilliant. But I'm surprised he was able to break anything loose from the tree."

"Wasn't easy. But he did it. And followed the trail back to the city. Thief was holed up in a rathole next to the Sharps. But when we went up to kill him, we found someone had just beaten us to it. Or more like some*thing*. A lesser lich."

"A lesser lich? But how would it know about the sword? Or where it was?" He waited, but she just stared at him. He furrowed his brow. "Because the thief was trying to sell it to the Eiden Rane. But the lich figured it was a lot cheaper to just take it."

"Could be. Or the lich *sent* the thief to find where I'd hidden the sword. Then betrayed him and took it. Haven't figured that out yet. I'm about to start searching for answers. If I find anyone else connected to it, I'm going to kill them—and you're going to look the other way."

"All right."

She watched him to make sure he was serious, then nodded. "All right."

"So you killed the lesser lich?"

"Would have died except for Sorrowen. He sacrificed himself for me. Gods know why. But if you want to thank someone, thank him. If not for him, I wouldn't be here."

Something ironic glinted in her eye, but Dante didn't know what it might mean. "We'll honor him. As he deserves. Then how did you wind up inside the Citadel? How'd you even get inside?"

Raxa stared at him for several seconds. "Luck, mostly. Or

maybe the gods had a plan for me. I didn't go there meaning to fight the lich. But things have a way of working out. Don't they?"

"Sometimes. Most often in conjunction with working absurdly hard to make them work out." He tapped the side of his leg. "I'm going to be very busy for a while. We all are. But I haven't forgotten our deal. I'll resume your training as soon as I can."

She shook her head. "Forget it."

"I'll find time. You've more than earned it."

"I don't want it. Or more like I don't want to be part of this machine any longer. That's for people like you. Me, I want to go back to what I was."

"Running an organized crime syndicate?"

Raxa smiled. "Don't worry. I'll leave your city alone. You've got enough on your plate. But once I finish tracking down anyone tied to the man who stole the sword, I'm walking back into the night. It's who I always was."

"Where will you go?"

"Dollendun, maybe. Feel like there's lots of trouble to be had with the norren."

"You're not wrong."

"But if some blue blood's jewels go missing in the meantime, consider that part of my payment. After all, you never said I had to return the sword to you in one piece."

He snorted. "Thank you. For everything. And know that there's still time for you to change your mind."

"Maybe."

She was humoring him. He knew it. He smiled anyway. "If you're lucky, some day I'll introduce you to Carvahal. I think he'd like you."

It was her turn to snort. "Don't you have a city to govern?"

For just a moment, he envied the freedom she had to just walk away, the freedom she was choosing to preserve. Then he walked outside and went to the window and looked down at the city he had once rebuilt and would now rebuild anew, the city of which he was the keeper, the city that depended on him and he on it, and he remembered that freedom was but one of the joys the gods had granted to their creations.

The snows ceased. But the cold stayed. Too cold, and too soon.

Two days later, and three days after the fall of the lich, he called a service at the Cathedral of Ivars. Walking up to it, he saw the facade was barely scratched. Even the Citadel was in decent shape. Dante was grateful for that much. They had enough to restore as it was.

He was early, but the cathedral was already near full, the crowd parting to allow him to ascend the dais. A second crowd soon gathered outside in the square. It was mid-morning, but the clouds strangled out the sun's light, leaving little to pass through the tall windows of the church. Yet there was just enough for Dante to recognize Raxa as she slipped inside and found a spot against the back wall.

"The snows are early this year," Dante began. "But they don't feel like much of a burden compared to the far worse winter we've just endured. One so harsh that even our victory feels closer to tragedy. One where half the people who entered the season didn't survive to see its end. One that's left this city more silent than it's been since I first came here."

When he had the opportunity, he typically wrote out his speeches and sermons from beginning to end. This time, he hadn't felt the need to do so. For he'd been thinking about what he might say if this day came ever since the loss at Bressel. At that time, imagining such a speech had allowed him to hope that this day might ever come to pass. He'd been turning bits of it over in his head all across their travels through the wilds of the Realm, and then again as they rode north to enact the siege of their own city, all the while keeping that weak flame alive, insisting to himself that he could, in the end, deliver it home.

So he spoke of the Tanarians' belief in the Body of their people, each limb and organ contributing to a greater whole, and how the people of Narashtovik had done the same to achieve the impossible: the destruction of the lich. He spoke of the Mallish belief in the perfect order of Taim, and how easily it degraded or was torn apart, how even the hereafter could be afflicted in this way, and how that core belief stood against the White Lich's desire to replace Taim's order with an order that *looked* better but was nothing more than chaos in disguise.

He spoke of the people who had died along the way. What they'd been like, what they'd stood for, what they'd sacrificed in the war against the enemy. And he spoke of Narashtovik: the virtues of its foresight, of its daring, its love of knowledge, and most of all its enduring resilience.

"I haven't spoken much of my own journey," he said. "My own part in the fight. But I expect you've heard the rumors. That, with the aid of my friends, I traveled to the realm of the gods. It's time to put an end to those rumors. Because they're true."

This drew a buzz of shock and wonder. He waited for it to calm. "I'll have more to tell you of these travels once I've begun to understand them for myself. For now, I can assure you that the gods are real—and that they're not always united in their desires. We've long known this much. It's in both the *Cycle of Arawn* and the *Ban Naden* of Taim.

"What we *didn't* know, and what I've since learned, is that while they built this world for us, it was built a long, long time ago. The view they take toward us is much longer than anything we can conceive of. If we wish to endure, it will always be through our own effort and our own will. In the war with the lich, we stood on the brink of the end of our world and the beginning of one where our only role was to feed the worms. Three days ago, we put an end to the bleak future of the Eiden Rane."

This drew a cheer, one that bounced from one wall of the cathedral to the other, and might well have lasted for some time. But Dante held up his hands. The hall fell under a hush.

"The threat of the lich is gone—but some of those who wanted him to succeed may still mean to bring about great changes to our world. If they try, I believe we can save our age and preserve it for many years to come. As long as we persist. As long as we endure. And as long as we hold fast to the will that has just let us do the impossible."

After just a little more, he was done. He scanned the back wall, searching for Raxa, but she was already gone.

They buried Olivander in a tomb on the hill. Sorrowen, too. Many people spoke for Olivander. Far fewer for Sorrowen, who hadn't let many people get to know him, but Dante was among them. It was snowing once more, clusters of flakes floating gently to the ground.

"He needs a statue," Blays nodded to Olivander's tomb once the ceremony was done. "On top of a rampaging warhorse. Beheading a foe. Make it *two* foes. In fact, how many foes can you fit in a single statue?"

"He'll get his statue," Dante said. "The question is what kind of a monument do we put up for Sorrowen."

"One that can't quite look you in the eye? He was young, though. And he still did enough to get us the sword. I wonder how much further he might have gone."

"He still has his time in the Mists. Thanks to what he did, so does everyone else."

"But it isn't quite the same, is it? That's why we decided to stand against the lich even before we knew about the damage he was causing to the Mists."

"Yes. It's not the same as living in Rale. But despite that—and despite the fact Taim wants to destroy it—the people there must enjoy their lives. Otherwise they'd cross over to the Worldsea."

Even as he said the words, he wasn't sure they were true: it was possible, after all, that people only stayed in the Mists because they *feared* the Worldsea. Typically, this was the sort of flaw in reasoning Gladdic would have seized on. But either Gladdic was distracted or felt it didn't matter, for he let it pass with a simple nod.

"What is next for us?" the old man said instead.

"Us?" Blays said. "You mean to stick around?"

"Would I not?"

"Bressel's in a bit of a shambles. I thought you might be off to help try to restore the place. After all, the only reason we began this strange alliance was to thwart the lich. Considering Dante's carrying his corpse around in his pocket, I'd say the lich has been quite thwarted."

"This is not wrong," Gladdic said. "However, the service I once dedicated my life to is no longer a path I feel anything for. Yet I will leave here, if that is your wish."

"Eh? You don't have to go anywhere. I have the creeping feeling the world isn't done with us yet. Besides, who else has the chance to die *twice* for their cause?"

"With logic so strong, I am compelled to stay."

Dante watched a group of mourners walk off through the snow. "Anyway, our next steps are to make sure the lich is gone for good, and try to stop Taim from revenging himself on us. Regarding the first, I want to learn more about the gem the lich left behind. We'll get in touch with the Tanarians and see what they know. We'll also send someone to the lore-keepers on Houkkalli Island. We may even hire someone like Naran to try to make it to Cal Avin and see if any other knowledge has been handed down since the time of Sabel. Even if the White Lich is truly dead and gone, we should make it our responsibility to stop anyone else from ever becoming like him again."

"Okay," Blays said. "But that sounds like work." He motioned to Dante's pocket. "You know what the gem looks like to me?"

"An extremely valuable rock?"

"The purestone."

Dante shut his mouth with a click. "It does. Well, I don't know what to make of that. Which is all the more reason to find out."

"Did you have a plan to deal with the lord of the gods who wants us dead?"

"As a matter of fact, I do. We're going to return to the Realm and see if we can broker a truce."

"Does Taim seem like the trucing type?"

"The lich is gone. The Mists are repairing themselves. He has no reason to come after us now."

"Except spite. And vengeance. And all those other reasons people do mean things more or less constantly."

"We still have to try. And before we travel to the Realm, we're going to pay a quick visit to the Mists."

"To make sure they're all right?"

"Yes—and to find Cally."

Blays' mouth fell open. "Right. He died here. Do you think he'll still be in the Mists?"

"He's the type who'd spend centuries there before he learned everything he wanted to know. That's just how he is—and that's why I've always felt like he knew much more about Rale than he ever taught me. He may have advice for us. About all of it."

"Cally," Blays said contemplatively. "Considering how cranky he was when he was alive, I'm not sure I want to know what he's like when he's dead."

The thought might have been troubling, except Dante believed he already knew. For Mount Arna had shown him: and reminded him that some of what had been lost was not as far gone as he had once thought.

The next few days were sunny and bright, but still bitterly cold. Icicles gleamed from the eaves like the blade of the Spear of Stars. Ice crusted the top of the snow, crunching loudly with each step.

There were times when none of it felt real. They'd been under the shadow of the lich for so long and so deeply that he couldn't fully believe the lich was dead. Yet at the same time, it felt like *none* of it had ever happened, that it had all been some awful fever dream.

Then he remembered how Tanar Atain had been butchered. How Bressel had been conquered. How his friends had died. And he thought that perhaps the reason he couldn't believe it was that it had been *too* real.

Unlike the lich, who had disintegrated upon death, the bone sword had merely broken into a bunch of pieces. Dante asked Gladdic to see if they could use either the ether or their combined skills to put it back together. After a full day's struggle, he concluded the weapon was broken beyond any repair.

He picked up one of the shards, careful to avoid its edge. "Just my luck. The first time I've seen my sword in over a year, and it got broken the very first time we tried to use it."

Gladdic raised an eyebrow. "You believe this was *poor* luck?"

"When the most powerful weapon I've ever seen besides the spear itself broke into a hundred pieces? I wouldn't call that the most fortunate moment of my life."

"For you have not considered the full meaning of the moment. The sword was not enough to end the lich. That required the spear as well. If you had had the sword any earlier, you may have been able to wound the Eiden Rane. But you must believe that it would have broken just as it did here, leaving you without it when you finally had true need for it. Therefore it was only brought to bear at the only point in time when it could fulfill its purpose."

Dante stared at him. "No. No no no no."

"Yes?" Gladdic frowned.

"You are *not* saying that Raxa wasn't actually Raxa, but was an agent of Carvahal sent to make sure things turned out the way he wished. That this was all planned in advance."

"I must entertain such a claim, for it is not beyond reason. Yet you are correct: I do not believe she was acting as the hand of Carvahal, any more than I believe that you are the hand of Arawn, or that the lich was the hand of Taim. But perhaps there was...an echo."

"An echo?"

"Or perhaps Carvahal woke one night from a dream he could not quite remember—then went to his window and whispered its essence into the wind. And perhaps Raxa woke in the night—be it that same night or one many years later—with a dream of her own."

Dante bulged his lower lip with his tongue. He had his doubts about this theory.

But after everything they'd seen, it didn't feel like the right time to be a skeptic.

Though the sword was destroyed, he kept its pieces. He meant to study them when he had the time. He also thought one of them might be fashioned into a dagger, if they could find a way to grind the damned thing. He locked most of the pieces in a chest in his room and the others in a chest in his lab.

But on a whim, one that was admittedly half mad, he took one long splinter to the graveyard on the hill. There, he excavated a hole in the soil and planted the piece of bone. He tried to harvest it larger, but this didn't work, likely because although it was part of the White Tree, the White Tree wasn't really a tree at all.

He sat back. It was snowing again. Little flakes for now, but he knew the weather well enough to know the roofs and streets would be thick with it by the next morning. He glanced about himself to make sure he was alone, then drew his knife, cut the meat of his left arm, and watered the bone with his blood.

He didn't know if the cutting would grow. Or, for that matter, what in the world he might do with it if it did. But he knew that Barden was powerful, one of the few pieces of Rale that seemed transplanted from the Realm of the gods. He regretted not asking about it when he'd walked among them. He supposed he might still have the chance.

With that in mind, he went to see Winden and check in on her progress with the dreamflowers.

"The flowers, they are not good." She shook her head at the sickly yellow petals. "See the color, it's very wrong."

Dante bent closer for a better look. "They're mottled, too. Do you know what's causing this?"

"The weather, it could be too cold. Or it's too far north. Or the earth here is bad. Or the flowers miss the islands."

"Well, we really need them. Suppose we could try them anyway?"

Winden shook her head vigorously. "Do not. It could poison you. Or send you somewhere wrong."

"Somewhere wrong? Where else is there to go?"

"I can't say."

"Are you hiding something from me?"

"A rumor I will not repeat. But the flowers, they're bad. We can't dare use them."

Dante folded his arms. "We've kept them indoors, so I doubt it's the cold. If it's the soil, we could send for some from Gallador Rift. Everything grows there. In the meantime, keep trying. If we can't get back to the Realm—"

"I know," Winden said. "Then it is only some time before the

Realm comes for us."

Dante crouched over the pale green shoots, willing them to grow taller. And get less pale. And otherwise do what they normally did when he harvested grains of wheat into adult plants. It wasn't that he couldn't grow them at all. Rather it was that it was much harder than it normally was. Part of that was due to the ground, which was frozen, requiring him to soften it and shake it loose enough for the roots to expand.

This helped a little. But it still took a frustrating amount of nether to grow the plants tall enough to seed. Gladdic, who Dante had forgotten had also picked up the skill, was hardly doing any better. For lack of anything better to do, Blays was hanging around them; he'd wanted to go out and kill Blighted, but Dante wanted to keep the Spear of Stars close at all times. Close enough that if the lich's gem tried to manifest something, Blays could stab it to death before it could attempt anything foul.

"This weather isn't doing us any favors," Dante muttered. "But there's something else going on here. It's like the lich was a hooded snake who bit us before we could cut his head off. He might be dead, but his venom's still working its way through our veins."

Blays packed a snowball and threw it into Gladdic's back. "You think he cursed us?"

"I don't know what he did. Or if he did anything. All I know is we're not growing nearly enough grain. This was supposed to be our staple. We've got plenty of boats in the water, but the north is already too stormy for them to fish in. They'll only bring back fewer and fewer fish as winter deepens."

"The hunters?"

"A few deer. Some pheasants. Better than nothing, but not nearly enough."

"The citizens are starting to return home, too. There'll be

thousands more by year's end. What's it add up to?"

"It adds up to the fact that most of us won't make it through the winter."

This brought a temporary stop to the conversation, the same way it might stop if it had been punched in the nose. Dante couldn't tell if it was snowing yet again or if the wind was just stirring up the powder. He'd wanted to harvest the wheat in the grounds around the hill that bore the cemetery and the carneterium, but some people had found the idea of growing their food around all those bodies "disturbing," so they'd moved to a field on the south side of the city outside the Pridegate that was used as a communal farm by the homes that surrounded it.

It was far enough out that they could see the empty fields of grass beyond Narashtovik and the pine forest beyond that. Dante kept one eye on the wilderness. Most of the Blighted had gathered in a single blob and were currently miles to the east, but without the lich to give them orders, a steady trickle of undead had been breaking away from the mass to pursue whatever it was that drove them now that they had no master.

"I'd say that 'most of us' would like us to try to do something about that," Blays said. "Is there any way to squeeze some more food out of this place?"

"Cut the rations further. Get the soldiers to start checking every empty home for preserves. Set up foraging parties."

"This time of year, they won't bring back much. Maybe it would be best if we just accept we won't have enough food for everyone."

"And start deciding who won't make it to spring?"

Blays gave him a disgusted look. "You *could* just tell them to leave and fend for themselves. Alternately, if getting enough food is impossible here, we could go somewhere that isn't here."

"I sent a rider to Gallador to bring back some of their dirt to try to grow more dreamflowers in. On the same principle, we could relocate there. I doubt Wending has anything to spare, but the weather's milder and the soil's better. We might be able to harvest enough to see us through to the growing season."

"Plenty of fish in the lakes, too."

Absently, Dante sifted some nether onto his wheat, coaxing it a few inches higher. "We'd need to leave as soon as possible. Every day we're here, we're burning through supplies. And the way we're having to ration, if we wait too much longer, the people might not even be able to handle the march."

"How long? A week?"

"Something like that."

"Then we start preparing now. If we haven't thought of anything better within a week's time, we make for Gallador Rift."

Dante nodded, hating the idea of abandoning the city so quickly after they'd reclaimed it. They'd be vulnerable, too, both along the march and in Gallador. There was also the chance they wouldn't find themselves any better off within the Rift than they were here. If he took the gamble and something went wrong, he'd never forgive himself.

But if he let his fear of failure stop him from acting when to stay was to watch his people die, he no longer deserved to lead.

"One week, then," he said. "But we're going to spend every hour that we're not preparing working to find a way to stay here."

"Food may no longer be our first worry," Gladdic said.

Blays scuffed at the snow. "Oh no? If you've just figured out a way to transcend our mortal bodies, you're probably in line for a prize of some kind."

"It is not that the danger of our starvation has been solved. But rather that it has been eclipsed." He stretched out his arm and pointed south.

Dante inspected the treeline for Blighted, but Gladdic was pointing higher than that. With all the snow fluttering about, it took him a moment to home in on the movement in the sky. It might have been an eagle, but he didn't know many eagles that traveled north for the winter. Nor that flew so perfectly straight. Nor that had the silhouette of a human woman.

"Is that Ka?" Blays said.

Dante froze where he stood. Deep in his bones, he'd feared this had been coming. In the course of securing the spear, they'd chosen to set the torch to another person's plans, turning them into a mortal enemy. It was hardly the first time they'd done so. One way or another, they'd either outmaneuvered or outrun all such enemies, or sent them to a grave.

This time, though, they'd crossed a god. One of the beings who'd created their very world. There was no running from that.

They'd preserved Rale from the White Lich. But it may have been no more than a reprieve.

AUTHOR'S NOTE

If you're getting a kick out of these characters, you can read about their younger exploits in *The Cycle of Arawn* trilogy.

ABOUT THE AUTHOR

Along with *The Cycle of Arawn*, Ed is the author of the post-apocalyptic *Breakers* series. Born in the deserts of Eastern Washington, he's since lived in New York, Idaho, L.A., and Maui, all of which have been thoroughly destroyed in *Breakers*.

He lives with his wife and spends most of his time writing on the couch and overseeing the uneasy truce between two dogs and three cats.

He blogs at http://www.edwardwrobertson.com